The World's Greatest
Horror Stories

The World's Greatest Horror Stories

Edited by
Stephen Jones & Dave Carson

BARNES
&NOBLE
BOOKS
NEW YORK

Contents

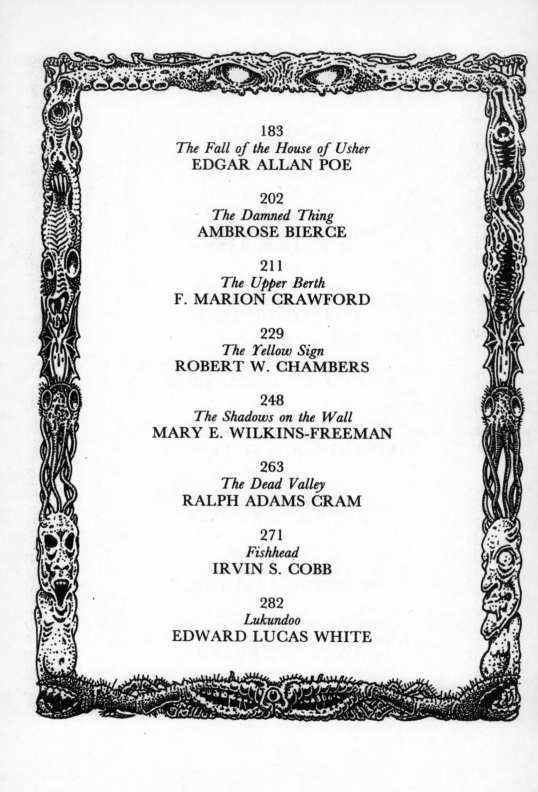

Acknowledgements

SPECIAL THANKS TO Linda Krawecke, Ramsey Campbell and Robert Weinberg for all their help and support.

'Supernatural Horror in Literature' by H. P. Lovecraft. Copyright © 1939, 1945 by August Derleth and Donald Wandrei. Originally published in *The Recluse* (1927) and *The Fantasy Fan* (1933–35). Reprinted by permission of the agent for the author's Estate.

'The Signalman' by Charles Dickens. Originally published as 'No.1 Branch Line: The Signalman' (1866).

'The House and the Brain' by Edward Bulwer-Lytton. Originally published as 'The Haunters and the Haunted: or, The House and the Brain' in *Blackwood's Magazine* (1859).

'The Body Snatcher' by Robert Louis Stevenson. Originally published as 'The Body-Snatchers' in *Pall Mall Gazette* (1884).

'The Spider' by Hanns Heinz Ewers. Published in *Creeps By Night* (1931).

'The Foot of the Mummy' by Théophile Gautier. Originally published as 'The Mummy's Foot' (1863).

'The Horla' by Guy de Maupassant (1887).

'The Fall of the House of Usher' by Edgar Allan Poe. Originally published in *Burton's Gentleman's Magazine* (1839).

'The Damned Thing' by Ambrose Bierce. Originally published in *In the Midst of Life* (1898).

'The Upper Berth' by F. Marion Crawford. Originally published in *Wandering Ghosts* (1911).

'The Yellow Sign' by Robert W. Chambers. Originally published in *The King in Yellow* (1895).

'The Shadows on the Wall' by Mary E. Wilkins-Freeman. Originally published in *The Wind in the Rose-Bush and Other Stories of the Supernatural* (1903).

'The Dead Valley' by Ralph Adams Cram. Originally published in *Black Spirits and White* (1895).

'Fishhead' by Irvin S. Cobb. Copyright © 1913 by The Frank A. Munsey Company. Copyright renewed © 1941 and assigned to Argosy Communications, Inc. Originally published in *The Cavalier*, January 1913. 'Fishhead' is a trademark of Argosy Communications, Inc. All rights reserved. Reprinted by arrangement with Argosy Communications, Inc.

'Lukundoo' by Edward Lucas White. Originally published in *Lukundoo and Other Stories* (1927).

'The Double Shadow' by Clark Ashton Smith. Originally published in *The Double Shadow and Other Fantasies* (1933). Copyright © 1939 by The Popular Fiction Publishing Company. Published in *Weird Tales*, February 1939. Reprinted by permission of the agent for the author's Estate.

'The Mark of the Beast' by Rudyard Kipling. Originally published in *Life's Handicap* (1891).

'Negotium Perambulans' by E. F. Benson. Originally published in *Visible and Invisible* (1923).

'Mrs. Lunt' by Hugh Walpole. Originally published in *The Ghost Book* (1927).

'The Hog' by William Hope Hodgson. Originally published in *Carnacki, the Ghost-Finder* (1947).

'The Great God Pan' by Arthur Machen. Copyright © 1948 by Alfred A. Knopf Inc. Originally published in *The Great God Pan and The Inmost Light* (1894). Reprinted by permission of the agent for the author's Estate.

'Count Magnus' by M. R. James. Originally published in *Ghost Stories of an Antiquary* (1904).

'Afterword: Lovecraft and the "Literature of Cosmic Fear" ' Copyright © 1993 by Stephen Jones.

SUPERNATURAL HORROR IN LITERATURE

H. P. Lovecraft

[1890–1937]

'*The oldest and strongest emotion of mankind is fear.*'

– H.P. Lovecraft

1. Introduction

THE OLDEST AND STRONGEST EMOTION of mankind is fear, and the oldest and strongest kind of fear is fear of the unknown. These facts few psychologists will dispute, and their admitted truth must establish for all time the genuineness and dignity of the weirdly horrible tale as a literary form. Against it are discharged all the shafts of a materialistic sophistication which clings to frequently felt emotions and external events, and of a naively insipid idealism which deprecates the aesthetic motive and calls for a didactic literature to 'uplift' the reader toward a suitable degree of smirking optimism. But in spite of all this opposition the weird tale has survived, developed, and attained remarkable heights of perfection; founded as it is on a profound and elementary principle whose appeal, if not always universal, must necessarily be poignant and permanent to minds of the requisite sensitiveness.

The appeal of the spectrally macabre is generally narrow because it demands from the reader a certain degree of imagination and a capacity for detachment from everyday life. Relatively few are free enough from the spell of the daily routine to respond to rappings from outside, and tales of ordinary feelings and events, or of common sentimental distortions of such feelings and events, will always take first place in the taste of the majority; rightly, perhaps, since of course these ordinary matters make up the greater part of human experience. But the sensitive are always with us, and sometimes a curious streak of fancy invades an obscure corner of the very hardest head; so that no amount of rationalisation, reform, or Freudian analysis can quite annul the thrill of the chimney-corner whisper or the lonely wood. There is here involved a psychological pattern or tradition as real and as deeply grounded in mental experience as any other pattern or tradition of mankind; coeval with the religious feeling and closely related to many aspects of it, and too much a part of our innermost biological heritage to lose keen potency over a very important, though not numerically great, minority of our species.

Man's first instincts and emotions formed his reponse to the environment in which he found himself. Definite feelings based on pleasure and pain grew up around the phenomena whose causes and effects he understood, whilst around those which he did not understand – and the universe teemed with them in the early days – were naturally woven such personifications, marvellous interpretations, and sensations of awe and fear as would be hit upon by a race having few and simple ideas and limited experience. The unknown, being likewise the unpredictable, became for our primitive forefathers a terrible and omnipotent source of boons and calamities visited upon mankind for cryptic and wholly extra-terrestrial reasons, and thus clearly belonging to spheres of existence whereof we know nothing and wherein we have no part. The phenomenon of dreaming likewise helped to build up the notion of an unreal or spiritual world; and in general, all the conditions of savage dawn-life so strongly conduced toward a feeling of the supernatural, that we need not wonder at the thoroughness with which man's very hereditary essence has become saturated with religion and superstition. That saturation must, as a matter of plain scientific fact, be regarded as virtually permanent so far as the subconscious mind and inner instincts are concerned; for though the area of the unknown has been steadily contracting for thousands of years, an infinite reservoir of mystery still engulfs most of the outer cosmos, whilst a vast residuum of powerful inherited associations clings round all the objects and processes that were once mysterious; however well they may now be explained. And more than this, there is an actual physiological fixation of the old instincts in our nervous tissue, which would make them obscurely operative even were the conscious mind to be purged of all sources of wonder.

Because we remember pain and the menace of death more vividly than pleasure, and because our feelings toward the beneficent aspects of the unknown have from the first been captured and formalised by conventional religious rituals, it has fallen to the lot of the darker and more maleficent side of cosmic mystery to figure chiefly in our popular supernatural folklore. This tendency, too, is naturally enhanced by the fact that uncertainty and danger are always closely allied; thus making any kind of an unknown world a world of peril and evil possibilities. When to this sense of fear and evil the inevitable fascination of wonder and curiosity is superadded, there is born a composite body of keen emotion and imaginative provocation whose vitality must of necessity endure as long as the human race itself. Children will always be afraid of the dark, and men with minds sensitive to hereditary impulse will always tremble at the thought of the hidden and fathomless worlds of strange life which may pulsate in the gulfs beyond the stars, or press hideously upon our own globe in unholy dimensions which only the dead and the moon-struck can glimpse.

With this foundation, no one need wonder at the existence of a literature of cosmic fear. It has always existed, and always will exist; and no better evidence of its tenacious vigour can be cited than the impulse which now and then drives writers of totally opposite leanings to try their hands at it in isolated tales, as if to discharge from their minds certain phantasmal shapes which would otherwise haunt them. Thus Dickens wrote several eerie narratives; Browning, the hideous poem *Childe Roland*; Henry James, *The Turn of the Screw*; Dr. Holmes, the subtle novel *Elsie Venner*; F. Marion Crawford, *The Upper Berth* and a number of other examples; Mrs. Charlotte Perkins Gilman, social worker, *The Yellow Wall Paper*; whilst the humorist, W. W. Jacobs, produced that able melodramatic bit called *The Monkey's Paw*.

This type of fear-literature must not be confounded with a type externally similar but psychologically widely different; the literature of mere physical fear and the mundanely gruesome. Such writing, to be sure, has its place, as has the conventional or even whimsical or humorous ghost story where formalism or the author's knowing wink removes the true sense of the morbidly unnatural; but these things are not the literature of cosmic fear in its purest sense. The true weird tale has something more than secret murder, bloody bones, or a sheeted form clanking chains according to rule. A certain atmosphere of breathless and unexplainable dread of outer, unknown forces must be present; and there must be a hint, expressed with a seriousness and portentousness becoming its subject, of that most terrible conception of the human brain – a malign and particular suspension or defeat of those fixed laws of Nature which are our only safeguard against the assaults of chaos and the daemons of unplumbed space.

Naturally we cannot expect all weird tales to conform absolutely to any theoretical model. Creative minds are uneven, and the best of fabrics have their dull spots. Moreover, much of the choicest weird work is unconscious; appearing in memorable fragments scattered through material whose massed effect may be of a very different cast. Atmosphere is the all-important thing, for the final criterion of authenticity is not the dovetailing of a plot but the creation of a given sensation. We may say, as a general thing, that a weird story whose intent is to teach or produce a social effect, or one in which the horrors are finally explained away by natural means, is not a genuine tale of cosmic fear; but it remains a fact that such narratives often possess, in isolated sections, atmospheric touches which fulfil every condition of true supernatural horror-literature. Therefore we must judge a weird tale not by the author's intent, or by the mere mechanics of the plot; but by the emotional level which it attains at its least mundane point. If the proper sensations are excited, such a 'high spot' must be admitted on its own merits as weird literature, no matter how prosaically it is later dragged down. The one test of the really weird is simply this – whether or not there be excited in the reader a profound sense of dread, and of contact with unknown spheres and powers; a subtle attitude of awed listening, as if for the beating of black wings or the scratching of outside shapes and entities on the known universe's utmost rim. And of course, the more completely and unifiedly a story conveys this atmosphere, the better it is as a work of art in the given medium.

2. The Dawn of the Horror Tale

As may naturally be expected of a form so closely connected with primal emotion, the horror-tale is as old as human thought and speech themselves.

Cosmic terror appears as an ingredient of the earliest folklore of all races, and is crystallised in the most archaic ballads, chronicles, and sacred writings. It was, indeed, a prominent feature of the elaborate ceremonial magic, with its rituals for the evocation of daemons and spectres, which flourished from prehistoric times, and which reached its highest development in Egypt and the Semitic nations. Fragments like the Book of Enoch and the Claviculae of Solomon well illustrate the power of the weird over the ancient Eastern mind, and upon such things were based enduring systems and traditions whose echoes extend obscurely even to the present time. Touches of this transcendental fear are seen in classic literature, and there is evidence of its still greater emphasis in a ballad literature which paralleled the classic stream but vanished for lack of a written medium. The Middle Ages, steeped in fanciful darkness, gave it an enormous impulse toward expression; and East and West alike were busy preserving and amplifying the dark heritage, both of random folklore and of academically formulated magic and cabalism, which had descended to them. Witch, werewolf, vampire, and ghoul brooded ominously on the lips of bard and grandam, and needed but little encouragement to take the final step across the boundary that divides the chanted tale or song from the formal literary composition. In the Orient, the weird tale tended to assume a gorgeous colouring and sprightliness which almost transmuted it into sheer phantasy. In the West, where the mystical Teuton had come down from his black boreal forests and the Celt remembered strange sacrifices in Druidic groves, it assumed a terrible intensity and convincing seriousness of atmosphere which doubled the force of its half-told, half-hinted horrors.

Much of the power of Western horror-lore was undoubtedly due to the hidden but often suspected presence of a hideous cult of nocturnal worshippers whose strange customs – descended from pre-Aryan and pre-agricultural times when a squat race of Mongoloids roved over Europe with their flocks and herds – were rooted in the most revolting fertility-rites of immemorial antiquity. This secret religion, stealthily handed down amongst peasants for thousands of years despite the outward reign of the Druidic, Graeco-Roman, and Christian faiths in the regions involved, was marked by wild 'Witches' Sabbaths' in lonely woods and atop distant hills on Walpurgis-Night and Hallowe'en, the traditional breeding-seasons of the goats and sheep and cattle; and became the source of vast riches of sorcery-legend, besides provoking extensive witchcraft-prosecutions of which the Salem affair forms the chief American example. Akin to it in essence, and perhaps connected with it in fact, was the frightful secret system of inverted theology or Satan-worship which produced such horrors as the famous 'Black Mass'; whilst operating toward the same end we may note the activities of those whose aims were somewhat more scientific or philosophical – the astrologers, cabalists, and alchemists of the Albertus Magnus or Raymond Lully type, with whom such rude ages invariably abound. The prevalence and depth of the mediaeval horror-spirit in Europe, intensified by the dark despair which waves of pestilence brought, may be fairly gauged by the grotesque carvings slyly introduced into much of the finest later Gothic ecclesiastical work of the time; the daemoniac gargoyles of Notre Dame and Mont St. Michel being among the most famous specimens. And throughout the period, it must be remembered, there existed amongst educated and uneducated alike a most unquestioning faith in every form of the supernatural; from the gentlest doctrines of Christianity to the most monstrous morbidities of witchcraft and black magic. It was from no empty background that the Renaissance magicians and alchemists – Nostradamus, Trithemius, Dr. John Dee, Robert Fludd, and the like – were born.

In this fertile soil were nourished types and characters of sombre myth and legend which persist in weird literature to this day, more or less disguised or altered by modern technique. Many of them were taken from the earliest oral sources, and form part of mankind's permanent heritage. The shade which appears and demands the burial of its bones, the daemon lover who comes to bear away his still living bride, the death-fiend or psychopomp riding the night-wind, the man-wolf, the sealed chamber, the deathless sorcerer – all these may be found in that curious body of mediaeval lore which the late Mr. Baring-Gould so effectively assembled in book form. Wherever the mystic Northern blood was strongest, the atmosphere of the popular tales became most intense; for in the Latin races there is a touch of basic rationality which denies to even their strangest superstitions many of the overtones of glamour so characteristic of our own forest-born and ice-fostered whisperings.

Just as all fiction first found extensive embodiment in poetry, so is it in poetry that we first encounter the permanent entry of the weird into standard literature. Most of the ancient instances, curiously enough, are in prose; as the werewolf incident in Petronius, the gruesome passages in Apuleius, the brief but celebrated letter of Pliny the Younger to Sura, and the odd compilation *On Wonderful Events* by the Emperor Hadrian's Greek freedman, Phlegon. It is in Phlegon that we first find that hideous tale of the corpse-bride, *Philinnion and Machates*, later related by Proclus and in modern times forming the inspiration of Goethe's *Bride of Corinth* and Washington Irving's *German Student*. But by the time the old Northern myths take literary form, and in that later time when the weird appears as a steady element in the literature of the day, we find it mostly in metrical dress; as indeed we find the greater part of the strictly imaginative writing of the Middle Ages and Renaissance. The Scandinavian Eddas and Sagas thunder with cosmic horror, and shake with the stark fear of Ymir and his shapeless spawn; whilst our own Anglo-Saxon *Beowulf* and the later Continental Nibelung tales are full of eldritch weirdness. Dante is a pioneer in the classic capture of macabre atmosphere, and in Spenser's stately stanzas will be seen more than a few touches of fantastic terror in landscape, incident, and character. Prose literature gives us Malory's *Morte d'Arthur*, in which are presented many ghastly situations taken from early ballad sources – the theft of the sword and silk from the corpse in Chapel Perilous by Sir Galahad – whilst other and cruder specimens were doubtless set forth in the cheap and sensational 'chapbooks' vulgarly hawked about and devoured by the ignorant. In Elizabethan drama, with its *Dr. Faustus*, the witches in *Macbeth*, the ghost in *Hamlet*, and the horrible gruesomeness of Webster we may easily discern the strong hold of the daemoniac on the public mind; a hold intensified by the very real fear of living witchcraft, whose terrors, wildest at first on the Continent, begin to echo loudly in English ears as the witch-hunting crusades of James the First gain headway. To the lurking mystical prose of the ages is added a long line of treatises on witchcraft and daemonology which aid in exciting the imagination of the reading world.

Through the seventeenth and into the eighteenth century we behold a growing mass of fugitive legendry and balladry of darksome cast; still, however, held down beneath the surface of polite and accepted literature. Chapbooks of horror and weirdness multiplied, and we glimpse the eager interest of the people through fragments like Defoe's *Apparition of Mrs. Veal*, a homely tale of a dead woman's spectral visit to a distant friend, written to advertise covertly a badly

selling theological disquisition on death. The upper orders of society
were now losing faith in the supernatural, and indulging in a period of
classic rationalism. Then, beginning with the translations of Eastern
tales in Queen Anne's reign and taking definite form toward the
middle of the century, comes the revival of romantic feeling – the era
of new joy in nature, and in the radiance of past times, strange scenes,
bold deeds, and incredible marvels. We feel it first in the poets, whose
utterances take on new qualities of wonder, strangeness, and shuddering. And finally, after the timid appearance of a few weird scenes
in the novels of the day – such as Smollett's *Adventures of Ferdinand,
Count Fathom* – the release instinct precipitates itself in the birth of a
new school of writing; the 'Gothic' school of horrible and fantastic
prose fiction, long and short, whose literary posterity is destined to
become so numerous, and in many cases so resplendent in artistic
merit. It is, when one reflects upon it, genuinely remarkable that
weird narration as a fixed and academically recognized literary form
should have been so late of final birth. The impulse and atmosphere
are as old as man, but the typical weird tale of standard literature is a
child of the eighteenth century.

3. The Early Gothic Novel

The shadow-haunted landscapes of Ossian, the chaotic visions of
William Blake, the grotesque witch dances in Burns's *Tam O'Shanter*,
the sinister daemonism of Coleridge's *Christobel* and *Ancient Mariner*,
the ghostly charm of James Hogg's *Kilmeny*, and the more restrained
approaches to cosmic horror in *Lamia* and many of Keats's other
poems, are typical British illustrations of the advent of the weird to
formal literature. Our Teutonic cousins of the Continent were equally
receptive to the rising flood, and Burger's *Wild Huntsman* and the even
more famous daemon-bridegroom ballad of *Lenore* – both imitated in
English by Scott, whose respect for the supernatural was always great
– are only a taste of the eerie wealth which German song had
commenced to provide. Thomas Moore adapted from such sources
the legend of the ghoulish statue-bride (later used by Prosper
Mérimée in *The Venus of Ille*, and traceable back to great antiquity) which echoes so shiveringly in his ballad of *The Ring*; whilst
Goethe's deathless masterpiece *Faust*, crossing from mere balladry
into the classic, cosmic tragedy of the ages, may be held as the
ultimate height to which this German poetic impulse arose.

But it remained for a very sprightly and worldly Englishman – none other than Horace Walpole himself – to give the growing impulse definite shape and become the actual founder of the literary horror-story as a permanent form. Fond of mediaeval romance and mystery as a dilettante's diversion, and with a quaintly imitated Gothic castle as his abode at Strawberry Hill, Walpole in 1764 published *The Castle of Otranto*; a tale of the supernatural which, though thoroughly unconvincing and mediocre in itself, was destined to exert an almost unparalleled influence on the literature of the weird. First venturing it only as a 'translation' by one 'William Marshal, Gent.' from the Italian of a mythical 'Onuphrio Muralto,' the author later acknowledged his connection with the book and took pleasure in its wide and instantaneous popularity – a popularity which extended to many editions, early dramatization, and wholesale imitation both in England and in Germany.

The story – tedious, artificial, and melodramatic – is further impaired by a brisk and prosaic style whose urbane sprightliness nowhere permits the creation of a truly weird atmosphere. It tells of Manfred, an unscrupulous and usurping prince determined to found a line, who after the mysterious sudden death of his only son Conrad on the latter's bridal morn, attempts to put away his wife Hippolita and wed the lady destined for the unfortunate youth – the lad, by the way, having been crushed by the preternatural fall of a gigantic helmet in the castle courtyard. Isabella, the widowed bride, flees from his design; and encounters in subterranean crypts beneath the castle a noble young preserver, Theodore, who seems to be a peasant yet strangely resembles the old lord Alfonso who ruled the domain before Manfred's time. Shortly thereafter supernatural phenomena assail the castle in diverse ways; fragments of gigantic armour being discovered here and there, a portrait walking out of its frame, a thunderclap destroying the edifice, and a colossal armoured spectre of Alfonso rising out of the ruins to ascend through parting clouds to the bosom of St. Nicholas. Theodore, having wooed Manfred's daughter Matilda and lost her through death – for she is slain by her father by mistake – is discovered to be the son of Alfonso and rightful heir to the estate. He concludes the tale by wedding Isabella and preparing to live happily ever after, whilst Manfred – whose usurpation was the cause of his son's supernatural death and his own supernatural harassings – retires to a monastery for penitence; his saddened wife seeking asylum in a neighbouring convent.

Such is the tale; flat, stilted, and altogether devoid of the true cosmic

horror which makes weird literature. Yet such was the thirst of the age
for those touches of strangeness and spectral antiquity which it reflects,
that it was seriously received by the soundest readers and raised in spite
of its intrinsic ineptness to a pedestal of lofty importance in literary
history. What it did above all else was to create a novel type of scene,
puppet-characters, and incidents; which, handled to better advantage
by writers more naturally adapted to weird creation, stimulated the
growth of an imitative Gothic school which in turn inspired the real
weavers of cosmic terror – the line of actual artists beginning with Poe.
This novel dramatic paraphernalia consisted first of all of the Gothic
castle, with its awesome antiquity, vast distances and ramblings,
deserted or ruined wings, damp corridors, unwholesome hidden
catacombs, and galaxy of ghosts and appalling legends, as a nucleus
of suspense and daemoniac fright. In addition, it included the
tyrannical and malevolent nobleman as villain; the saintly, long-
persecuted, and generally insipid heroine who undergoes the major
terrors and serves as a point of view and focus for the reader's
sympathies; the valorous and immaculate hero, always of high birth
but often in humble disguise; the convention of high-sounding foreign
names, mostly Italian, for the characters; and the infinite array of stage
properties which includes strange lights, damp trap-doors, extinguished lamps, mouldy hidden manuscripts, creaking hinges, shaking
arras, and the like. All this paraphernalia reappears with amusing
sameness, yet sometimes with tremendous effect, throughout the
history of the Gothic novel; and is by no means extinct even today,
though subtler technique now forces it to assume a less naive and
obvious form. An harmonious milieu for a new school had been found,
and the writing world was not slow to grasp the opportunity.

German romance at once responded to the Walpole influence, and
soon became a byword for the weird and ghastly. In England one of
the first imitators was the celebrated Mrs. Barbauld, then Miss Aikin,
who in 1773 published an unfinished fragment called *Sir Bertrand*, in
which the strings of genuine terror were truly touched with no clumsy
hand. A nobleman on a dark and lonely moor, attracted by a tolling
bell and distant light, enters a strange and ancient turreted castle
whose doors open and close and whose bluish will-o'-the-wisps lead
up mysterious staircases toward dead hands and animated black
statues. A coffin with a dead lady, whom Sir Bertrand kisses, is finally
reached; and upon the kiss the scene dissolves to give place to a
splendid apartment where the lady, restored to life, holds a banquet
in honour of her rescuer. Walpole admired this tale, though he

accorded less respect to an even more prominent offspring of his *Otranto* – *The Old English Baron*, by Clara Reeve, published in 1777. Truly enough, this tale lacks the real vibration to the note of outer darkness and mystery which distinguishes Mrs. Barbauld's fragment; and though less crude than Walpole's novel, and more artistically economical of horror in its possession of only one spectral figure, it is nevertheless too definitely insipid for greatness. Here again we have the virtuous heir to the castle disguised as a peasant and restored to his heritage through the ghost of his father; and here again we have a case of wide popularity leading to many editions, dramatization, and ultimate translation into French. Miss Reeve wrote another weird novel, unfortunately unpublished and lost.

The Gothic novel was now settled as a literary form, and instances multiply bewilderingly as the eighteenth century draws toward its close. *The Recess*, written in 1785 by Mrs. Sophia Lee, has the historic element, revolving round the twin daughters of Mary, Queen of Scots; and though devoid of the supernatural, employs the Walpole scenery and mechanism with great dexterity. Five years later and all existing lamps are paled by the rising of a fresh luminary order – Mrs. Ann Radcliffe (1764–1823), whose famous novels made terror and suspense a fashion, and who set new and higher standards in the domain of macabre and fear-inspiring atmosphere despite a provoking custom of destroying her own phantoms at the last through laboured mechanical explanations. To the familiar Gothic trappings of her predecessors Mrs. Radcliffe added a genuine sense of the unearthly in scene and incident which closely approached genius; every touch of setting and action contributing artistically to the impression of illimitable frightfulness which she wished to convey. A few sinister details like a track of blood on castle stairs, a groan from a distant vault, or a weird song in a nocturnal forest can with her conjure up the most powerful images of imminent horror; surpassing by far the extravagant and toilsome elaborations of others. Nor are these images in themselves any the less potent because they are explained away before the end of the novel. Mrs. Radcliffe's visual imagination was very strong, and appears as much in her delightful landscape touches – always in broad, glamorously pictorial outline, and never in close detail – as in her weird phantasies. Her prime weaknesses, aside from the habit of prosaic disillusionment, are a tendency toward erroneous geography and history and a fatal predilection for bestrewing her novels with insipid little poems, attributed to one or another of the characters.

Mrs. Radcliffe wrote six novels; *The Castles of Athlin and Dunbayne* (1789), *A Sicilian Romance* (1790), *The Romance of the Forest* (1792), *The Mysteries of Udolpho* (1794), *The Italian* (1797), and *Gaston de Blondeville*, composed in 1802 but first published posthumously in 1826. Of these *Udolpho* is by far the most famous, and may be taken as a type of the early Gothic tale at its best. It is the chronicle of Emily, a young Frenchwoman transplanted to an ancient and portentous castle in the Apennines through the death of her parents and the marriage of her aunt to the lord of the castle – the scheming nobleman, Montoni. Mysterious sounds, opened doors, frightful legends, and a nameless horror in a niche behind a black veil all operate in quick succession to unnerve the heroine and her faithful attendant, Annette; but finally, after the death of her aunt, she escapes with the aid of a fellow-prisoner whom she has discovered. On the way home she stops at a chateau filled with fresh horrors – the abandoned wing where the departed chatelaine dwelt, and the bed of death with the black pall – but is finally restored to security and happiness with her lover Valancourt, after the clearing-up of a secret which seemed for a time to involve her birth in mystery. Clearly, this is only familiar material re-worked; but it is so well re-worked that *Udolpho* will always be a classic. Mrs. Radcliffe's characters are puppets, but they are less markedly so than those of her forerunners. And in atmospheric creation she stands pre-eminent among those of her time.

Of Mrs. Radcliffe's countless imitators, the American novelist Charles Brockden Brown stands the closest in spirit and method. Like her, he injured his creations by natural explanations; but also like her, he had an uncanny atmospheric power which gives his horrors a frightful vitality as long as they remain unexplained. He differed from her in contemptuously discarding the external Gothic paraphernalia and properties and choosing modern American scenes for his mysteries; but this repudiation did not extend to the Gothic spirit and type of incident. Brown's novels involve some memorably frightful scenes, and excel even Mrs. Radcliffe's in describing the operations of the perturbed mind. *Edgar Huntly* starts with a sleepwalker digging a grave, but is later impaired by touches of Godwinian didacticism. *Ormond* involves a member of a sinister secret brotherhood. That and *Arthur Mervyn* both describe the plague of yellow fever, which the author had witnessed in Philadelphia and New York. But Brown's most famous book is *Wieland; or, the Transformation* (1798), in which a Pennsylvania German, engulfed by a wave of religious fanaticism, hears 'voices' and slays his wife and children as a sacrifice. His sister Clara, who tells the story, narrowly escapes. The scene, laid at the woodland estate of Mittingen on the Schuylkill's remote reaches, is drawn with extreme vividness; and the terrors of Clara, beset by spectral tones, gathering fears, and the sound of strange footsteps in the lonely house, are all shaped with truly artistic force. In the end a lame ventriloquial explanation is offered, but the atmosphere is genuine while it lasts. Carwin, the malign ventriloquist, is a typical villain of the Manfred or Montoni type.

4. The Apex of Gothic Romance

Horror in literature attains a new malignity in the work of Matthew Gregory Lewis (1773–1818), whose novel *The Monk* (1796) achieved marvellous popularity and earned him the nickname 'Monk' Lewis. This young author, educated in Germany and saturated with a body of wild Teuton lore unknown to Mrs. Radcliffe, turned to terror in forms more violent than his gentle predecessor had ever dared to think of; and produced as a result a masterpiece of active nightmare whose general Gothic cast is spiced with added stores of ghoulishness. The story is one of a Spanish monk, Ambrosio, who from a state of over-proud virtue is tempted to the very nadir of evil by a fiend in the guise of the maiden Matilda; and who is finally, when awaiting death at the Inquisition's hands, induced to purchase escape at the price of his soul from the Devil, because he deems both body and soul already lost. Forthwith the mocking Fiend snatches him to a lonely place, tells him he has sold his soul in vain since both pardon and a chance for salvation were approaching at the moment of his hideous bargain, and completes the sardonic betrayal by rebuking him for his un-natural crimes, and casting his body down a precipice whilst his soul is borne off for ever to perdition. The novel contains some appalling descriptions such as the incantation in the vaults beneath the convent cemetery, the burning of the convent, and the final end of the wretched abbot. In the sub-plot where the Marquis de las Cisternas meets the spectre of his erring ancestress, The Bleeding Nun, there are many enormously potent strokes; notably the visit of the animated corpse to the Marquis's bedside, and the cabalistic ritual whereby the Wandering Jew helps him to fathom and banish his dead tormentor. Nevertheless *The Monk* drags sadly when read as a whole. It is too long and too diffuse, and much of its potency is marred by flippancy and by an awkwardly excessive reaction against those canons of decorum which Lewis at first despised as prudish. One great thing may be said of the author; that he never ruined his ghostly visions with a natural explanation. He succeeded in breaking up the Radcliffian tradition and expanding the field of the Gothic novel. Lewis wrote much more than *The Monk*. His drama, *The Castle Spectre*, was produced in 1798, and he later found time to pen other fictions in ballad form – *Tales of Terror* (1799), *The Tales of Wonder* (1801), and a succession of translations from the German.

Gothic romances, both English and German, now appeared in multitudinous and mediocre profusion. Most of them were merely ridiculous in the light of mature taste, and Miss Austen's famous satire *Northanger Abbey* was by no means an unmerited rebuke to a school which had sunk far toward absurdity. This particular school was petering out, but before its final subordination there arose its last and greatest figure in the person of Charles Robert Maturin (1782–1824), an obscure and eccentric Irish clergyman. Out of an ample body of miscellaneous writing which includes one confused Radcliffian imitation called *The Fatal Revenge; or, the Family of Montorio* (1807), Maturin at length evolved the vivid horror-masterpiece of *Melmoth, the Wanderer* (1820), in which the Gothic tale climbed to altitudes of sheer spiritual fright which it had never known before.

Melmoth is the tale of an Irish Gentleman who, in the seventeenth century, obtained a preternaturally extended life from the Devil at the price of his soul. If he can persuade another to take the bargain off his hands, and assume his existing state, he can be saved; but this he can never manage to effect, no matter how assiduously he haunts those whom despair has made reckless and frantic. The framework of the story is very clumsy; involving tedious length, digressive episodes, narratives within narratives, and laboured dovetailing and coincidence; but at various points in the endless rambling there is felt a pulse of power undiscoverable in any previous work of this kind – a kinship to the essential truth of human nature, an understanding of the profoundest sources of actual cosmic fear, and a white heat of sympathetic passion on the writer's part which makes the book a true document of aesthetic self-expression rather than a mere clever compound of artifice. No unbiased reader can doubt that with *Melmoth* an enormous stride in the evolution of the horror-tale is represented. Fear is taken out of the realm of the conventional and exalted into a hideous cloud over mankind's very destiny. Maturin's shudders, the work of one capable of shuddering himself, are of the sort that convince. Mrs. Radcliffe and Lewis are fair game for the parodist, but it would be difficult to find a false note in the feverishly intensified action and high atmospheric tension of the Irishman whose less sophisticated emotions and strain of Celtic mysticism gave him the finest possible natural equipment for his task. Without a doubt Maturin is a man of authentic genius, and he was so recognized by Balzac, who grouped *Melmoth* with Molière's *Don Juan*, Goëthe's *Faust*, and Byron's *Manfred* as the supreme allegorical figures of modern European literature, and wrote a whimsical piece called *Melmoth Reconciled*, in which the Wanderer succeeds in passing his infernal bargain on to a Parisian bank defaulter, who in turn hands it along a chain of victims until a revelling gambler dies with it in his possession, and by his damnation ends the curse. Scott, Rossetti, Thackeray and Baudelaire are the other titans who gave Maturin their unqualified admiration, and there is much significance in the fact that Oscar Wilde, after his disgrace and exile, chose for his last days in Paris the assumed name of 'Sebastian Melmoth.'

Melmoth contains scenes which even now have not lost their power to evoke dread. It begins with a deathbed – an old miser is dying of sheer fright because of something he has seen, coupled with a manuscript he has read and a family portrait which hangs in an obscure closet of his centuried home in County Wicklow. He sends to Trinity College, Dublin, for his nephew John; and the latter upon arriving notes many uncanny things. The eyes of the portrait in the closet glow horribly, and twice a figure strangely resembling the portrait appears momentarily at the door. Dread hangs over that house of the Melmoths, one of whose ancestors, 'J. Melmoth, 1646,' the portrait represents. The dying miser declares that this man – at a date slightly before 1800 – is alive. Finally the miser dies, and the nephew is told in the will to destroy both the portrait and a manuscript to be found in a certain drawer. Reading the manuscript, which was written late in the seventeenth century by an Englishman named Stanton, young John learns of a terrible incident in Spain in 1677, when the writer met a horrible fellow-countryman and was told of how he had stared to death a priest who tried to denounce him as one filled with fearsome evil. Later, after meeting the man again in London, Stanton is cast into a madhouse and visited by the stranger, whose approach is heralded by spectral music and whose eyes have a more than mortal glare. Melmoth the Wanderer – for such is the malign visitor – offers the captive freedom if he will take over his bargain with the Devil; but like all others whom Melmoth has approached, Stanton is proof against temptation. Melmoth's description of the horrors of a life in a madhouse, used to tempt Stanton, is one of the most potent passages of the book. Stanton is at length liberated, and spends the rest of his life tracking down Melmoth, whose family and ancestral abode he discovers. With the family he leaves the manuscript, which by young John's time is badly ruinous and fragmentary. John destroys both portrait and manuscript, but in sleep is visited by his horrible ancestor, who leaves a black and blue mark on his wrist.

Young John soon afterward receives as a visitor a shipwrecked Spaniard, Alonzo de Moncada, who has escaped from compulsory monasticism and from the perils of the Inquisition. He has suffered horribly – and the descriptions of his experiences under torment and in the vaults through which he once essays escape are classic – but had the strength to resist Melmoth the Wanderer when approached at his darkest hour in prison. At the house of a Jew who sheltered him after his escape he discovers a wealth of manuscript relating other exploits of Melmoth, including his wooing of an Indian island maiden, Immalee, who later comes into her birthright in Spain and is known as Donna Isidora; and of his horrible marriage to her by the corpse of a dead anchorite at midnight in the ruined chapel of a shunned and abhorred monastery. Moncada's narrative to young John takes up the bulk of Maturin's four-volume book; this disproportion being considered one of the chief technical faults of the composition.

At last the colloquies of John and Moncada are interrupted by the entrance of Melmoth the Wanderer himself, his piercing eyes now fading, and decrepitude swiftly overtaking him. The term of his bargain has approached its end, and he has come home after a century and a half to meet his fate. Warning all others from the room, no matter what sounds they may hear in the night, he awaits the end alone. Young John and Moncada hear frightful ululations, but do not intrude till silence comes toward morning. They then find the room empty. Clayey footprints lead out a rear door to a cliff overlooking the sea, and near the edge of the precipice is a track indicating the forcible dragging of some heavy body. The Wanderer's scarf is found on a crag some distance below the brink, but nothing further is ever seen or heard of him.

Such is the story, and none can fail to notice the difference between this modulated, suggestive, and artistically moulded horror and – to use the words of Professor George Saintsbury – 'the artful but rather jejune rationalism of Mrs. Radcliffe, and the too often puerile extravagance, the bad taste, and the sometimes slipshod style of

Lewis.' Maturin's style in itself deserves particular praise, for its forcible directness and vitality lift it altogether above the pompous artificialities of which his predecessors are guilty. Professor Edith Birkhead, in her history of the Gothic novel, justly observes that 'with all his faults Maturin was the greatest as well as the last of the Goths.' *Melmoth* was widely read and eventually dramatized, but its late date in the evolution of the Gothic tale deprived it of the tumultuous popularity of *Udolpho* and *The Monk*.

5. The Aftermath of Gothic Fiction

Meanwhile other hands had not been idle, so that above the dreary plethora of trash like Marquis von Grosse's *Horrid Mysteries* (1796), Mrs. Roche's *Children of the Abbey* (1798), Mrs. Dacre's *Zolfloya; or, the Moor* (1806), and the poet Shelley's schoolboy effusions *Zastrozzi* (1810) and *St. Irvine* (1811) (both imitations of *Zofloya*) there arose many memorable weird works both in English and German. Classic in merit, and markedly different from its fellows because of its foundation in the Oriental tale rather than the Walpolesque Gothic novel, is the celebrated *History of the Caliph Vathek* by the wealthy dilettante William Beckford, first written in the French language but published in an English translation before the appearance of the original. Eastern tales, introduced to European literature early in the eighteenth century through Galland's French translation of the inexhaustibly opulent *Arabian Nights*, had become a reigning fashion; being used both for allegory and for amusement. The sly humour which only the Eastern mind knows how to mix with weirdness had captivated a sophisticated generation, till Bagdad and Damascus names became as freely strewn through popular literature as dashing Italian and Spanish ones were soon to be. Beckford, well read in Eastern romance, caught the atmosphere with unusual receptivity; and in his fantastic volume reflected very potently the haughty luxury, sly disillusion, bland cruelty, urbane treachery, and shadowy spectral horror of the Saracen spirit. His seasoning of the ridiculous seldom mars the force of his sinister theme, and the tale marches onward with a phantasmagoric pomp in which the laughter is that of skeletons feasting under arabesque domes. *Vathek* is a tale of the grandson of the Caliph Haroun, who, tormented by that ambition for superterrestrial power, pleasure and learning which animates the average Gothic villain or Byronic hero (essentially cognate types), is

lured by an evil genius to seek the subterranean throne of the mighty
and fabulous pre-Adamite sultans in the fiery halls of Eblis, the
Mahometan Devil. The descriptions of Vathek's palaces and diver-
sions, of his scheming sorceress-mother Carathis and her witch-tower
with the fifty one-eyed negresses, of his pilgrimage to the haunted
ruins of Istakhar (Persepolis) and of the impish bride Nouronihar
whom he treacherously acquired on the way, of Istakhar's primordial
towers and terraces in the burning moonlight of the waste, and of the
terrible Cyclopean halls of Eblis, where, lured by glittering promises,
each victim is compelled to wander in anguish for ever, his right hand
upon his blazingly ignited and eternally burning heart, are triumphs
of weird colouring which raise the book to a permanent place in
English letters. No less notable are the three *Episodes of Vathek*,
intended for insertion in the tale as narratives of Vathek's fellow-
victims in Eblis' infernal halls, which remained unpublished throughout the author's lifetime and were discovered as recently as 1909 by
the scholar Lewis Melville whilst collecting material for his *Life and
Letters of William Beckford*. Beckford, however, lacks the essential
mysticism which marks the acutest form of the weird; so that his
tales have a certain knowing Latin hardness and clearness preclusive
of sheer panic fright.

But Beckford remained alone in his devotion to the Orient. Other
writers, closer to the Gothic tradition and to European life in general,
were content to follow more faithfully in the lead of Walpole. Among
the countless producers of terror-literature in these times may be
mentioned the Utopian economic theorist William Godwin, who
followed his famous but non-supernatural *Caleb Williams* (1794) with
the intendedly weird *St. Leon* (1799), in which the theme of the elixir of
life, as developed by the imaginary secret order of 'Rosicrucians,' is
handled with ingeniousness if not with atmospheric convincingness.
This element of Rosicrucianism, fostered by a wave of popular magical
interest exemplified in the vogue of the charlatan Cagliostro and the
publication of Francis Barrett's *The Magus* (1801), a curious and
compendious treatise on occult principles and ceremonies, of which a
reprint was made as lately as 1896, figures in Bulwer-Lytton and in
many late Gothic novels, especially that remote and enfeebled posterity which straggled far down into the nineteenth century and was
represented by George W. M. Reynold's *Faust and the Demon* and
Wagner the Wehr-Wolf. Caleb Williams, though non-supernatural, has
many authentic touches of terror. It is the tale of a servant persecuted
by a master whom he has found guilty of murder, and displays an

invention and skill which have kept it alive in a fashion to this day. It was dramatized as *The Iron Chest*, and in that form was almost equally celebrated. Godwin, however, was too much the conscious teacher and prosaic man of thought to create a genuine weird masterpiece.

His daughter, the wife of Shelley, was much more successful; and her inimitable *Frankenstein; or, the Modern Prometheus* (1817) is one of the horror-classics of all time. Composed in competition with her husband, Lord Byron, and Dr. John William Polidori in an effort to prove supremacy in horror-making, Mrs. Shelley's *Frankenstein* was the only one of the rival narratives to be brought to an elaborate completion; and criticism has failed to prove that the best parts are due to Shelley rather than to her. The novel, somewhat tinged but scarcely marred by moral didactism, tells of the artificial human being moulded from charnel fragments by Victor Frankenstein, a young Swiss medical student. Created by its designer 'in the mad pride of intellectuality,' the monster possesses full intelligence but owns a hideously loathsome form. It is rejected by mankind, becomes embittered, and at length begins the successive murder of all whom Frankenstein loves best, friends and family. It demands that Frankenstein create a wife for it; and when the student finally refuses in horror lest the world be populated with such monsters, it departs with a hideous threat 'to be with him on his wedding night.' Upon that night the bride is strangled, and from that time on Frankenstein hunts down the monster, even into the wastes of the Arctic. In the end, whilst seeking shelter on the ship of the man who tells the story, Frankenstein himself is killed by the shocking object of his search and creation of his presumptuous pride. Some of the scenes in *Frankenstein* are unforgettable, as when the newly animated monster enters its creator's room, parts the curtains of his bed, and gazes at him in the yellow moonlight with watery eyes – 'if eyes they may be called.' Mrs. Shelley wrote other novels, including the fairly notable *Last Man*; but never duplicated the success of her first effort. It has the true touch of cosmic fear, no matter how much the movement may lag in places. Dr. Polidori developed his competing idea as a long short story, *The Vampyre*; in which we behold a suave villain of the true Gothic or Byronic type, and encounter some excellent passages of stark fright, including a terrible nocturnal experience in a shunned Grecian wood.

In this same period Sir Walter Scott frequently concerned himself with the weird, weaving it into many of his novels and poems, and sometimes producing such independent bits of narration as *The Tapestried Chamber* or *Wandering Willie's Tale* in *Redgauntlet*, in the latter of which the force of the spectral and the diabolic is enhanced by a grotesque homeliness of speech and atmosphere. In 1830 Scott published his *Letters on Demonology and Witchcraft*, which still forms one of our best compendia of European witch-lore. Washington Irving is another famous figure not unconnected with the weird; for though most of his ghosts are too whimsical and humorous to form genuinely spectral literature, a distinct inclination in this direction is to be noted in many of his productions. *The German Student* in *Tales of a Traveler* (1824) is a slyly concise and effective presentation of the old legend of the dead bride, whilst woven into the cosmic tissue of *The Money Diggers* in the same volume is more than one hint of piratical apparitions in the realms which Captain Kidd once roamed. Thomas Moore also joined the ranks of the macabre artists in the poem *Alciphron*, which he later elaborated into the prose novel of *The Epicurean* (1827). Though merely relating the adventures of a young Athenian duped by the artifice of cunning Egyptian priests, Moore manages to infuse much genuine horror into his account of subterranean frights and wonders beneath the primordial temples of Memphis. De Quincey more than once revels in grotesque and arabesque terrors, though with a desultoriness and learned pomp which deny him the rank of specialist.

This era likewise saw the rise of William Harrison Ainsworth, whose romantic novels teem with the eerie and the gruesome. Capt. Marryat, besides writing such short tales as *The Werewolf*, made a memorable contribution in *The Phantom Ship* (1839), founded on the legend of the Flying Dutchman, whose spectral and accursed vessel sails for ever near the Cape of Good Hope. Dickens now rises with occasional weird bits like *The Signalman*, a tale of ghastly warning conforming to a very common pattern and touched with a verisimilitude which allied it as much with the coming psychological school as with the dying Gothic school. At this time a wave of interest in spiritualistic charlatanry, mediumism, Hindoo theosophy, and such matters, much like that of the present day, was flourishing; so that the number of weird tales with a 'psychic' or pseudoscientific basis became very considerable. For a number of these the prolific and popular Edward Bulwer-Lytton was responsible; and despite the large doses of turgid rhetoric and empty romanticism in his products, his success in the weaving of a certain kind of bizarre charm cannot be denied.

The House and the Brain, which hints of Rosicrucianism and at a malign and deathless figure perhaps suggested by Louis XV's mysterious courtier St. Germain, yet survives as one of the best short haunted-house tales ever written. The novel *Zanoni* (1842) contains similar elements more elaborately handled, and introduces a vast unknown sphere of being pressing on our own world and guarded by a horrible 'Dweller of the Threshold' who haunts those who try to enter and fail. Here we have a benign brotherhood kept alive from age to age till finally reduced to a single member, and as a hero an ancient Chaldaean sorcerer surviving in the pristine bloom of youth to perish on the guillotine of the French Revolution. Though full of the conventional spirit of romance, marred by a ponderous network of symbolic and didactic meanings, and left unconvincing through lack of perfect atmospheric realization of the situations hinging on the spectral world, *Zanoni* is really an excellent performance as a romantic novel; and can be read with genuine interest by the not too sophisticated reader. It is amusing to note that in describing an attempted initiation into the ancient brotherhood the author cannot escape using the stock Gothic castle of Walpolian lineage.

In *A Strange Story* (1862) Bulwer-Lytton shows a marked improvement in the creation of weird images and moods. The novel, despite enormous length, a highly artificial plot bolstered up by opportune coincidences, and an atmosphere of homiletic pseudoscience designed to please the matter-of-fact and purposeful Victorian reader, is exceedingly effective as a narrative; evoking instantaneous and unflagging interest, and furnishing many potent – if somewhat melodramatic – tableaux and climaxes. Again we have the mysterious user of life's elixir in the person of the soulless magician Margrave, whose dark exploits stand out with dramatic vividness against the modern background of a quiet English town and of the Australian bush; and again we have shadowy intimations of a vast spectral world of the unknown in the very air about us – this time handled with much greater power and vitality than in *Zanoni*. One of the two great incantation passages, where the hero is driven by a luminous evil spirit to rise at night in his sleep, take a strange Egyptian wand, and evoke nameless presences in the haunted and mausoleum-facing pavilion of a famous Renaissance alchemist, truly stands among the major terror scenes of literature. Just enough is suggested, and just little enough is told. Unknown words are twice dictated to the sleep-walker, and as he repeats them the ground trembles, and all the dogs of the countryside begin to bay at half-seen amorphous shadows that stalk athwart the moonlight. When a third set of unknown words is prompted, the sleep-walker's spirit suddenly rebels at uttering them, as if the soul could recognize ultimate abysmal horrors concealed from the mind; and at last an apparition of an absent sweetheart and good angel breaks the malign spell. This fragment well illustrates how far Lord Lytton was capable of progressing beyond his usual pomp and stock romance toward that crystalline essence of artistic fear which belongs to the domain of poetry. In describing certain details of incantations, Lytton was greatly indebted to his amusingly serious occult studies, in the course of which he came in touch with that odd French scholar and cabalist Alphonse Louis Constant ('Eliphas Levy'), who claimed to possess the secrets of ancient magic, and to have evoked the spectre of the old Grecian wizard Apollonius of Tyana, who lived in Nero's times.

The romantic, semi-Gothic, quasi-moral tradition here represented was carried far down the nineteenth century by such authors as Joseph Sheridan LeFanu, Wilkie Collins, the late Sir H. Rider Haggard (whose *She* is really remarkably good), Sir A. Conan Doyle, H. G. Wells, and Robert Louis Stevenson – the latter of whom, despite an atrocious tendency toward jaunty mannerisms, created permanent classics in *Markheim*, *The Body Snatcher*, and *Dr. Jekyll and Mr. Hyde*. Indeed, we may say that this school still survives; for to it clearly belong such of our contemporary horror-tales as specialise in events rather than atmospheric details, address the intellect rather than a malign tensity or psychological verisimilitude, and take a definite stand in sympathy with mankind and its welfare. It has its undeniable strength, and because of its 'human element' commands a wider audience than does the sheer artistic nightmare. If not quite so potent as the latter, it is because a diluted product can never achieve the intensity of a concentrated essence.

Quite alone both as a novel and as a piece of terror-literature stands the famous *Wuthering Heights* (1847) by Emily Brontë, with its mad vistas of bleak, windswept Yorkshire moors and the violent, distorted lives they foster. Though primarily a tale of life, and of human passions in agony and conflict, its epically cosmic setting affords room for horror of the most spiritual sort. Heathcliff, the modified Byronic villain-hero, is a strange dark waif found in the streets as a small child and speaking only a strange gibberish till adopted by the family he ultimately ruins. That he is in truth a diabolic spirit rather than a human being is more than once suggested, and the unreal is further approached in the experience of the visitor who encounters a plaintive child-ghost at a bough-brushed upper window. Between Heathcliff and Catherine Earnshaw is a tie deeper and more terrible than human love. After her death he twice disturbs her grave, and is haunted by an impalpable presence which can be nothing less than her spirit. The spirit enters his life more and more, and at last he becomes confident of some imminent mystical reunion. He says he feels a strange change approaching, and ceases to take nourishment. At night he either walks abroad or opens the casement by his bed. When he dies the casement is still swinging open to the pouring rain, and a queer smile pervades the stiffened face. They bury him in a grave beside the mound he has haunted for eighteen years, and small shepherd boys say that he yet walks with his Catherine in the churchyard and on the moor when it rains. Their faces, too, are sometimes seen on rainy nights behind that upper casement at Wuthering Heights. Miss Brontë's eerie terror is no mere Gothic echo, but a tense expression of man's shuddering reaction to the unknown. In this respect, *Wuthering Heights* becomes the symbol of a literary transition, and marks the growth of a new and sounder school.

6. Spectral Literature on the Continent

On the continent literary horror fared well. The celebrated short tales and novels of Ernst Theodor Wilhelm Hoffmann (1776–1822) are a byword for mellowness of background and maturity of form, though they incline to levity and extravagance, and lack the exalted moments of stark, breathless terror which a less sophisticated writer might have achieved. Generally they convey the grotesque rather than the terrible. Most artistic of all the continental weird tales is the German classic *Undine* (1814), by Friedrich Heinrich Karl, Baron de la Motte Fouque. In this story of a water-spirit who married a mortal and gained a human soul there is a delicate fineness of craftsmanship which makes it notable in any department of literature, and an easy naturalness which places it close to the genuine folk-myth. It is, in fact, derived from a tale told by the Renaissance physician and alchemist Paracelsus in his *Treatise on Elemental Sprites*.

Undine, daughter of a powerful water-prince, was exchanged by her father as a small child for a fisherman's daughter, in order that she might acquire a soul by wedding a human being. Meeting the noble youth Huldbrand at the cottage of her fosterfather by the sea at the edge of a haunted wood, she soon marries him, and accompanies him to his ancestral castle of Ringstetten. Huldbrand, however, eventually wearies of his wife's supernatural affiliations, and especially of the appearances of her uncle, the malicious woodland waterfall-spirit

Kuhleborn; a weariness increased by his growing affection for Bert-alda, who turns out to be the fisherman's child for whom Undine was changed. At length, on a voyage down the Danube, he is provoked by some innocent act of his devoted wife to utter the angry words which consigns her back to her supernatural element; from which she can, by the laws of her species, return only once – to kill him, whether she will or no, if ever he prove unfaithful to her memory. Later, when Huldbrand is about to be married to Bertalda, Undine returns for her sad duty, and bears his life away in tears. When he is buried among his fathers in the village churchyard a veiled, snow-white female figure appears among the mourners, but after the prayer is seen no more. In her place is seen a little silver spring, which murmurs its way almost completely around the new grave, and empties into a neighbouring lake. The villagers show it to this day, and say that Undine and her Huldbrand are thus united in death. Many passages and atmospheric touches in this tale reveal Fouque as an accomplished artist in the field of the macabre; expecially the descriptions of the haunted wood with its gigantic snow-white man and various unnamed terrors, which occur early in the narrative.

Not so well known as *Undine*, but remarkable for its convincing realism and freedom from Gothic stock devices, is the *Amber Witch* of Wilhelm Meinhold, another product of the German fantastic genius of the earlier nineteenth century. This tale, which is laid in the time of the Thirty Years' War, purports to be a clergyman's manuscript found in an old church at Coserow, and centres round the writer's daughter, Maria Schweidler, who is wrongly accused of witchcraft. She has found a deposit of amber which she keeps secret for various reasons, and the unexplained wealth obtained from this lends colour to the accusation; an accusation instigated by the malice of the wolf-hunting nobleman Wittich Appelmann, who has vainly pursued her with ignoble designs. The deeds of a real witch, who afterward comes to a horrible super-natural end in prison, are glibly imputed to the hapless Maria; and after a typical witchcraft trial with forced confessions under torture she is about to be burned at the stake when saved just in time by her lover, a noble youth from a neighbouring district. Meinhold's great strength is in his air of casual and realistic verisimilitude, which intensifies our suspense and sense of the unseen by half persuading us that the menacing events must somehow be either the truth or very close to the truth. Indeed, so thorough is this realism that a popular magazine once published the main points of *The Amber Witch* as an actual occurrence of the seventeenth century!

In the present generation German horror-fiction is most notably represented by Hanns Heinz Ewers, who brings to bear on his dark conceptions an effective knowledge of modern psychology. Novels like *The Sorcerer's Apprentice* and *Alrune*, and short stories like *The Spider*, contain distinctive qualities which raise them to a classic level.

But France as well as Germany has been active in the realm of weirdness. Victor Hugo, in such tales as *Hans of Iceland*, and Balzac, in *The Wild Ass's Skin*, *Seraphita*, and *Louis Lambert*, both employ super-naturalism to a greater or less extent; though generally only as a means to some more human end, and without the sincere and daemonic intensity which characterizes the born artist in shadows. It is in Théophile Gautier that we first seem to find an authentic French sense of the unreal world, and here there appears a spectral mystery which, though not continuously used, is recognizable at once as something alike genuine and profound. Short tales like *Avatar*, *The Foot of the Mummy*, and *Clarimonde* display glimpses of forbidden vistas that allure, tantalize and sometimes horrify; whilst the Egyptian visions evoked in *One of Cleopatra's Nights* are of the keenest and most expressive potency. Gautier captured the inmost soul of aeon-weighted Egypt, with its cryptic life and Cyclopean architecture, and uttered once and for all the eternal horror of its nether world of catacombs, where to the end of time millions of stiff, spiced corpses will stare up in the blackness with glassy eyes, awaiting some awesome and unrelatable summons. Gustave Flaubert ably continued the tradition of Gautier in orgies of poetic phantasy like *The Temptation of St. Anthony*, and but for a strong realistic bias might have been an arch-weaver of tapestried terrors. Later on we see the stream divide, producing strange poets and fantaisistes of the symbolic and decadent schools whose dark interests really centre more in abnormalities of human thought and instinct than in the actual supernatural, and subtle story-tellers whose thrills are quite directly derived from the night-black wells of cosmic unreality. Of the former class of 'artists in sin' the illustrious poet Baudelaire, influenced vastly by Poe, is the supreme type; whilst the psychological novelist Joris-Karl Huysmans, a true child of the eighteen-nineties, is at once the summation and finale. The latter and purely narrative class is continued by Prosper Mérimée, whose *Venus of Ille* presents in terse and convincing prose the same ancient statue-bride theme which Thomas Moore cast in ballad form in *The Ring*.

The horror-tales of the powerful and cynical Guy de Maupassant, written as his final madness gradually overtook him, present individualities of their own; being rather the morbid outpourings of a realistic mind in a pathological state than the healthy imaginative products of a vision naturally disposed toward phantasy and sensitive to the normal illusions of the unseen. Nevertheless they are of the keenest interest and poignancy; suggesting with marvellous force the imminence of nameless terrors, and the relentless dogging of an ill-starred individual by hideous and menacing representatives of the outer blackness. Of these stories *The Horla* is generally regarded as the masterpiece. Relating the advent to France of an invisible being who lives on water and milk, sways the minds of others, and seems to be the vanguard of a horde of extra-terrestrial organisms arrived on earth to subjugate and overwhelm mankind, this tense narrative is perhaps without a peer in its particular department; notwithstanding its indebtedness to a tale by the American Fitz-James O'Brien for details in describing the actual presence of the unseen monster. Other potently dark creations of de Maupassant are *Who Knows?*, *The Spectre*, *He*, *The Diary of a Madman*, *The White Wolf*, *On the River*, and the grisly verses entitled *Horror*.

The collaborators Erckmann-Chatrian enriched French literature with many spectral fancies like *The Man-Wolf*, in which a transmitted curse works toward its end in a traditional Gothic-castle setting. Their power of creating a shuddering midnight atmosphere was tremendous despite a tendency toward natural explanations and scientific wonders; and few short tales contain greater horror than *The Invisible Eye*, where a malignant old hag weaves nocturnal hypnotic spells which induce the successive occupants of a certain inn chamber to hang themselves on a cross-beam. *The Owl's Ear* and *The Waters of Death* are full of engulfing darkness and mystery, the latter embodying the familiar over-grown-spider theme so frequently employed by weird fictionists. Villiers de l'Isle Adam likewise followed the macabre school; his *Torture by Hope*, the tale of a stake-condemned prisoner permitted to escape in order to feel the pangs of recapture, being held by some to constitute the most harrowing short story in literature. This type, however, is less a part of the weird tradition than a class peculiar to itself – the so-called *conte cruel*, in which the wrenching of the emotions is accomplished through dramatic tantalizations, frustrations, and gruesome physical horrors. Almost wholly devoted to this form is the living writer Maurice Level, whose very brief episodes have lent themselves so readily to theatrical adaptation in the 'thrillers' of the Grand Guignol. As a matter of fact, the French genius is more naturally suited to this dark realism than to the suggestion of the unseen; since the latter process requires, for its best and most sympathetic development on a large scale, the inherent mysticism of the Northern mind.

A very flourishing, though till recently quite hidden, branch of weird literature is that of the Jews, kept alive and nourished in obscurity by the sombre heritage of early Eastern magic, apocalyptic literature, and cabalism. The Semitic mind, like the Celtic and Teutonic, seems to possess marked mystical inclinations; and the wealth of underground horror-lore surviving in ghettoes and synagogues must be much more considerable than is generally imagined. Cabalism itself, so prominent during the Middle Ages, is a system of philosophy explaining the universe as emanations of the Deity, and involving the existence of strange spiritual realms and beings apart from the visible world of which dark glimpses may be obtained through certain secret incantations. Its ritual is bound up with mystical interpretations of the Old Testament, and attributes an esoteric significance to each letter of the Hebrew alphabet – a circumstance which has imparted to Hebrew letters a sort of spectral glamour and potency in the popular literature of magic. Jewish Folklore has preserved much of the terror and mystery of the past, and when more thoroughly studied is likely to exert considerable influence on weird fiction. The best examples of its literary use so far are the German novel *The Golem*, by Gustave Meyrink, and the drama *The Dybbuk*, by the Jewish writer using the pseudonym 'Ansky.' The former, with its haunting shadowy suggestions of marvels and horrors just beyond reach, is laid in Prague, and describes with singular mastery that city's ancient ghetto with its spectral, peaked gables. The name is derived from a fabulous artificial giant supposed to be made and animated by mediaeval rabbis according to a certain cryptic formula. *The Dybbuk*, translated and produced in America in 1925, and more recently produced as an opera, describes with singular power the possession of a living body by the evil soul of a dead man. Both golems and dybbuks are fixed types, and serve as frequent ingredients of later Jewish tradition.

7. Edgar Allan Poe

In the eighteen-thirties occurred a literary dawn directly affecting not only the history of the weird tale, but that of short fiction as a whole; and indirectly moulding the trends and fortunes of a great European aesthetic school. It is our good fortune as Americans to be able to claim that dawn as our own, for it came in the person of our most illustrious and unfortunate fellow-countryman Edgar Allan Poe. Poe's fame has been subject to curious undulations, and it is now a fashion amongst the 'advanced intelligentsia' to minimize his importance both as an artist and as an influence; but it would be hard for any mature and reflective critic to deny the tremendous value of his work and the persuasive potency of his mind as an opener of artistic vistas. True, his type of outlook may have been anticipated; but it was he who first realized its possibilities and gave it supreme form and systematic expression. True also, that subsequent writers may have produced greater single tales than his; but again we must comprehend that it was only he who taught them by example and precept the art which they, having the way cleared for them and given an explicit guide, were perhaps able to carry to greater lengths. Whatever his limitations, Poe did that which no one else ever did or could have done; and to him we owe the modern horror-story in its final and perfected state.

Before Poe the bulk of weird writers had worked largely in the dark; without an understanding of the psychological basis of the horror appeal, and hampered by more or less of conformity to certain empty literary conventions such as the happy ending, virtue rewarded, and in general a hollow moral didacticism, acceptance of popular standards and values, and striving of the author to obtrude his own emotions into the story and take sides with the partisans of the majority's artificial ideas. Poe, on the other hand, perceived the essential impersonality of the real artist; and knew that the function of creative fiction is merely to express and interpret events and sensations as they are, regardless of how they tend or what they prove – good or evil, attractive or repulsive, stimulating or depressing, with the author always acting as a vivid and detached chronicler rather than as a teacher, sympathizer, or vendor of opinion. He saw clearly that all phases of life and thought are equally eligible as a subject matter for the artist, and being inclined by temperament to strangeness and gloom, decided to be the interpreter of those powerful feelings and frequent happenings which attend pain rather than pleasure, decay rather than growth, terror rather than tranquillity, and which are fundamentally either adverse or indifferent to the tastes and traditional outward sentiments of mankind, and to the health, sanity, and normal expansive welfare of the species.

Poe's spectres thus acquired a convincing malignity possessed by none of their predecessors, and established a new standard of realism in the annals of literary horror. The impersonal and artistic intent, moreover, was aided by a scientific attitude not often found before; whereby Poe studied the human mind rather than the usages of Gothic fiction, and worked with an analytical knowledge of terror's true sources which doubled the force of his narratives and emancipated him from all the absurdities inherent in merely conventional shudder-coining. This example having been set, later authors were naturally forced to conform to it in order to compete at all; so that in this way a definite change began to affect the main stream of macabre writing. Poe, too, set a fashion in consummate craftsmanship; and although today some of his own work seems slightly melodramatic and unsophisticated, we can constantly trace his influence in such things as the maintenance of a single mood and achievement of a single impression in a tale, and the rigorous paring down of incidents to such as have a direct bearing on the plot and will figure prominently in the climax. Truly may it be said that Poe invented the short story in its present form. His elevation of disease, perversity, and decay to the level of artistically expressible themes was likewise infinitely far-reaching in effect; for avidly seized, sponsored, and intensified by his eminent French admirer Charles Pierre Baudelaire, it became the nucleus of the principal aesthetic movements in France, thus making Poe in a sense the father of the Decadents and the Symbolists.

Poet and critic by nature and supreme attainment, logician and philosopher by taste and mannerism, Poe was by no means immune from defects and affectations. His pretence to profound and obscure scholarship, his blundering ventures in stilted and laboured pseudo-humour, and his often vitriolic outbursts of critical prejudice must all be recognized and forgiven. Beyond and above them, and dwarfing them to insignificance, was a master's vision of the terror that stalks about and within us, and the worm that writhes and slavers in the hideously close abyss. Penetrating to every festering horror in the gaily painted mockery called existence, and in the solemn masquerade called human thought and feeling, that vision had power to project itself in blackly magical crystallisations and transmutations; till there bloomed in the sterile America of the thirties and forties such a moon-nourished garden of gorgeous poison fungi as not even the nether slopes of Saturn might boast. Verses and tales alike sustain the burthen of cosmic panic. The raven whose noisome beak pierces the heart, the ghouls that toll iron bells in pestilential steeples, the vault of

Ulalume in the black October night, the shocking spires and domes
under the sea, the 'wild, weird clime that lieth, sublime, out of Space –
out of Time' – all these things and more leer at us amidst maniacal
rattlings in the seething nightmare of the poetry. And in the prose
there yawn open for us the very jaws of the pit – inconceivable
abnormalities slyly hinted into a horrible half-knowledge by words
whose innocence we scarcely doubt till the cracked tension of the
speaker's hollow voice bids us fear their nameless implications;
daemoniac patterns and presences slumbering noxiously till waked
for one phobic instant into a shrieking revelation that cackles itself to
sudden madness or explodes in memorable and cataclysmic echoes. A
Witches' Sabbath of horror flinging off decorous robes is flashed
before us – a sight the more monstrous because of the scientific skill
with which every particular is marshalled and brought into an easy
apparent relation to the known gruesomeness of material life.

   Poe's tales, of course, fall into several classes; some of which contain
a purer essence of spiritual horror than others. The tales of logic and
ratiocination, forerunners of the modern detective story, are not to be
included at all in weird literature; whilst certain others, probably
influenced considerably by Hoffmann, possess an extravagance which
relegates them to the borderline of the grotesque. Still a third group
deal with abnormal psychology and monomania in such a way as to
express terror but not weirdness. A substantial residuum, however,
represent the literature of supernatural horror in its acutest form; and
give their author a permanent and unassailable place as deity and
fountainhead of all modern diabolical fiction. Who can forget the
terrible swollen ship poised on the billow-chasm's edge in *MS. Found
in a Bottle* – the dark intimations of her unhallowed age and monstrous
growth, her sinister crew of unseeing greybeards, and her frightful
southward rush under full sail through the ice of the Antarctic night,
sucked onward by some resistless devil-current toward a vortex of
eldritch enlightenment which must end in destruction?

   Then there is the unutterable *M. Valdemar*, kept together by
hypnotism for seven months after his death, and uttering frantic
sounds but a moment before the breaking of the spell leaves him 'a
nearly liquid mass of loathsome, of detestable putrescence.' In the
Narrative of A. Gordon Pym the voyagers reach first a strange south
polar land of murderous savages where nothing is white and where
vast rocky ravines have the form of titanic Egyptian letters spelling
terrible primal arcana of earth; and thereafter a still more mysterious
realm where everything is white, and where shrouded giants and

snowy-plumed birds guard a cryptic cataract of mist which empties from immeasurable celestial heights into a torrid milky sea. *Metzengerstein* horrifies with its malign hints of a monstrous metempsychosis – the mad nobleman who burns the stable of his hereditary foe; the colossal unknown horse that issues from the blazing building after the owner has perished therein; the vanishing bit of ancient tapestry where was shown the giant horse of the victim's ancestor in the Crusades; the madman's wild and constant riding on the great horse, and his fear and hatred of the steed; the meaningless prophecies that brood obscurely over the warring houses; and finally, the burning of the madman's palace and the death therein of the owner, borne helpless into the flames and up the vast staircase astride the beast he had ridden so strangely. Afterward the rising smoke of the ruins take the form of a gigantic horse. *The Man of the Crowd*, telling of one who roams day and night to mingle with streams of people as if afraid to be alone, has quieter effects, but implies nothing less of cosmic fear. Poe's mind was never far from terror and decay, and we see in every tale, poem, and philosophical dialogue a tense eagerness to fathom unplumbed wells of night, to pierce the veil of death, and to reign in fancy as lord of the frightful mysteries of time and space.

Certain of Poe's tales possess an almost absolute perfection of artistic form which makes them veritable beaconlights in the province of the short story. Poe could, when he wished, give to his prose a richly poetic cast; employing that archaic and Orientalised style with jewelled phrase, quasi-Biblical repetition, and recurrent burthen so successfully used by later writers like Oscar Wilde and Lord Dunsany; and in the cases where he has done this we have an effect of lyrical phantasy almost narcotic in essence – an opium pageant of dream in the language of dream, with every unnatural colour and grotesque image bodied forth in a symphony of corresponding sound. *The Masque of the Red Death*, *Silence, a Fable*, and *Shadow, a Parable*, are assuredly poems in every sense of the word save the metrical one, and owe as much of their power to aural cadence as to visual imagery. But it is in two of the less openly poetic tales, *Ligeia* and *The Fall of the House of Usher* – especially the latter – that one finds those very summits of artistry whereby Poe takes his place at the head of fictional miniaturists. Simple and straightforward in plot, both of these tales owe their supreme magic to the cunning development which appears in the selection and collocation of every least incident. *Ligeia* tells of a first wife of lofty and mysterious origin, who after death returns through a preternatural force of will to take possession of the body of a second wife; imposing even her physical appearance on the temporarily reanimated corpse of her victim at the last moment. Despite a suspicion of prolixity and topheaviness, the narrative reaches its terrific climax with relentless power. *Usher*, whose superiority in detail and proportion is very marked, hints shudderingly of obscure life in inorganic things, and displays an abnormally linked trinity of entities at the end of a long and isolated family history – a brother, his twin sister, and their incredibly ancient house all sharing a single soul and meeting one common dissolution at the same moment.

These bizarre conceptions, so awkward in unskilful hands, become under Poe's spell living and convincing terrors to haunt our nights; and all because the author understood so perfectly the very mechanics and physiology of fear and strangeness – the essential details to emphasise, the precise incongruities and conceits to select as pre-liminaries or concomitants to horror, the exact incidents and allusions to throw out innocently in advance as symbols or prefigurings of each major step toward the hideous denouement to come, the nice adjustments of cumulative force and the unerring accuracy in linkage of parts which make for faultless unity throughout and thunderous effectiveness at the climactic moment, the delicate nu-ances of scenic and landscape value to select in establishing and sustaining the desired mood and vitalising the desired illusion – principles of this kind, and dozens of obscurer ones too elusive to be described or even fully comprehended by any ordinary commen-tator. Melodrama and unsophistication there may be – we are told of one fastidious Frenchman who could not bear to read Poe except in Baudelaire's urbane and Gallically modulated translation – but all traces of such things are wholly overshadowed by a potent and inborn sense of the spectral, the morbid, and the horrible which gushed forth from every cell of the artist's creative mentality and stamped his macabre work with the ineffaceable mark of supreme genius. Poe's weird tales are *alive* in a manner that few others can ever hope to be.

Like most fantaisistes, Poe excels in incidents and broad narrative effects rather than in character drawing. His typical protagonist is generally a dark, handsome, proud, melancholy, intellectual, highly sensitive, capricious, introspective, isolated, and sometimes slightly mad gentleman of ancient family and opulent circumstances; usually deeply learned in strange lore, and darkly ambitious of penetrating to forbidden secrets of the universe. Aside from a high-sounding name, this character obviously derives little from the early Gothic novel; for he is clearly neither the wooden hero nor the diabolical villain of Radcliffian or Ludovician romance. Indirectly, however, he does possess a sort of genealogical connection; since his gloomy, ambitious and anti-social qualities savour strongly of the typical Byronic hero, who in turn is definitely an offspring of the Gothic Manfreds, Montonis, and Ambrosios. More particular qualities appear to be derived from the psychology of Poe himself, who certainly possessed much of the depression, sensitiveness, mad aspiration, loneliness, and extravagant freakishness which he attributes to his haughty and solitary victims of Fate.

8. The Weird Tradition in America

The public for whom Poe wrote, though grossly unappreciative of his art, was by no means unaccustomed to the horrors with which he dealt. America, besides inheriting the usual dark folk-lore of Europe, had an additional fund of weird associations to draw upon; so that spectral legends had already been recognised as fruitful subject-matter for literature. Charles Brockden Brown had achieved phenomenal fame with his Radcliffian romances, and Washington Irving's lighter treatment of eerie themes had quickly become classic. This additional fund proceeded, as Paul Elmer More has pointed out, from the keen spiritual and theological interests of the first colonists, plus the strange and forbidding nature of the scene into which they were plunged. The vast and gloomy virgin forests in whose perpetual twilight all terrors might well lurk; the hordes of coppery Indians whose strange, saturnine visages and violent customs hinted strongly at traces of infernal origin; the free rein given under the influence of Puritan theocracy to all manner of notions respecting man's relation to the stern and vengeful God of the Calvinists, and to the sulphurous Adversary of that God, about whom so much was thundered in the pulpits each Sunday; and the morbid introspection developed by an isolated backwoods life devoid of normal amusements and of the recreational mood, harassed by commands for theological self-examination, keyed to unnatural emotional repression, and forming above all a mere grim struggle for survival – all these things conspired to produce an environment in which the black whisperings of sinister grandams were heard far beyond the chimney corner, and in which tales of witchcraft and unbelievable secret monstrosities lingered long after the dread days of the Salem nightmare.

Poe represents the newer, more disillusioned, and more technically finished of the weird schools that rose out of this propitious milieu. Another school – the tradition of moral values, gentle restraint, and mild, leisurely phantasy tinged more or less with the whimsical – was represented by another famous, misunderstood, and lonely figure in American letters – the shy and sensitive Nathaniel Hawthorne, scion of antique Salem and great-grandson of one of the bloodiest of the old witchcraft judges. In Hawthorne we have none of the violence, the daring, the high colouring, the intense dramatic sense, the cosmic malignity, and the undivided and impersonal artistry of Poe. Here, instead, is a gentle soul cramped by the Puritanism of early New England; shadowed and wistful, and grieved at an unmoral universe which everywhere transcends the conventional patterns thought by our forefathers to represent divine and immutable law. Evil, a very real force to Hawthorne, appears on every hand as a lurking and conquering adversary; and the visible world becomes in his fancy a theatre of infinite tragedy and woe, with unseen half-existent influences hovering over it and through it, battling for supremacy and moulding the destinies of the hapless mortals who form its vain and self-deluded population. The heritage of American weirdness was his to a most intense degree, and he saw a dismal throng of vague spectres behind the common phenomena of life; but he was not disinterested enough to value impressions, sensations, and beauties of narration for their own sake. He must needs weave his phantasy into some quietly melancholy fabric of didactic or allegorical cast, in which his meekly resigned cynicism may display with naive moral appraisal the perfidy of a human race which he cannot cease to cherish and mourn despite his insight into its hypocrisy. Supernatural horror, then, is never a primary object with Hawthorne; though its impulses were so deeply woven into his personality that he cannot help suggesting it with the force of genius when he calls upon the unreal world to illustrate the pensive sermon he wishes to preach.

Hawthorne's intimations of the weird, always gentle, elusive, and restrained, may be traced throughout his work. The mood that produced them found one delightful vent in the Teutonised retelling of classic myths for children contained in *A Wonder Book* and *Tanglewood Tales*, and at other times exercised itself in casting a certain strangeness and intangible witchery or malevolence over events not meant to be actually supernatural; as in the macabre posthumous novel *Dr. Grimshawe's Secret*, which invests with a peculiar sort of repulsion a house existing to this day in Salem, and abutting on the ancient Charter Street Burying Ground. In *The Marble Faun*, whose design was sketched out in an Italian villa reputed to be haunted, a tremendous background of genuine phantasy and mystery palpitates just beyond the common reader's sight; and glimpses of fabulous blood in mortal veins are hinted at during the course of a romance which cannot help being interesting despite the persistent incubus of moral allegory, anti-Popery propaganda, and a Puritan prudery which has caused the modern writer D. H. Lawrence to express a longing to treat the author in a highly undignified manner. *Septimius Felton*, a posthumous novel whose idea was to have been elaborated and incorporated into the unfinished *Dolliver Romance*, touches on the Elixir of Life in a more or less capable fashion; whilst the notes for a never-written tale to be called *The Ancestral Footstep* show what Hawthorne would have done with an intensive treatment of an old English superstition – that of an ancient and accursed line whose members left footprints of blood as they walked – which appears incidentally in both *Septimius Felton* and *Dr. Grimshawe's Secret*.

Many of Hawthorne's shorter tales exhibit weirdness, either of atmosphere or of incident, to a remarkable degree. *Edward Randolph's Portrait*, in *Legends of the Province House*, has its diabolic moments. *The Minister's Black Veil* (founded on an actual incident) and *The Ambitious Guest* imply much more than they state, whilst *Ethan Grand* – a fragment of a longer work never completed – rises to genuine heights of cosmic fear with its vignette of the wild hill country and the blazing, desolate lime-kilns, and its delineation of the Byronic 'unpardonable sinner,' whose troubled life ends with a peal of fearful laughter in the night as he seeks rest amidst the flames of the furnace. Some of Hawthorne's notes tell of weird tales he would have written had he lived longer – an especially vivid plot being that concerning a baffling stranger who appeared now and then in public assemblies, and who was at last followed and found to come and go from a very ancient grave.

But foremost as a finished, artistic unit among all our author's weird material is the famous and exquisitely wrought novel, *The House of the Seven Gables*, in which the relentless working out of an ancestral curse is developed with astonishing power against the sinister background of a very ancient Salem house – one of those peaked Gothic affairs which formed the first regular building-up of our New England coast towns but which gave way after the seventeenth century to the more familiar gambrel-roofed or classic Georgian types now known as 'Colonial.' Of these old gabled Gothic houses scarcely a dozen are to be seen today in their original condition throughout the United States, but one well known to Hawthorne still stands in Turner Street, Salem, and is pointed out with doubtful authority as the scene and inspiration of the romance. Such an edifice, with its spectral peaks, its clustered chimneys, its overhanging second storey, its grotesque corner-brackets, and its diamond-paned lattice windows, is indeed an object well calculated to evoke sombre reflections; typifying as it does the dark Puritan age of concealed horror and witch-whispers which preceded the beauty, rationality, and spaciousness of the eighteenth century. Hawthorne saw many in his youth, and knew the black tales connected with some of them. He heard, too, many rumours of a curse upon his own line as the result of his great-grandfather's severity as a witchcraft judge in 1692.

From this setting came the immortal tale – New England's greatest contribution to weird literature – and we can feel in an instant the authenticity of the atmosphere presented to us. Stealthy horror and disease lurk within the weather-blackened, moss-crusted, and elm-shadowed walls of the archaic dwelling so vividly displayed, and we grasp the brooding malignity of the place when we read that its builder – old Colonel Pyncheon – snatched the land with peculiar ruthlessness from its original settler, Matthew Maule, whom he condemned to the gallows as a wizard in the year of the panic. Maule died cursing old Pyncheon – 'God will give him blood to drink' – and the waters of the old well on the seized land turned bitter. Maule's carpenter son consented to build the great gabled house for his father's triumphant enemy, but the old Colonel died strangely on the day of its dedication. Then followed generations of odd vicissitudes, with queer whispers about the dark powers of the Maules, and sometimes terrible ends befalling the Pyncheons.

The overshadowing malevolence of the ancient house – almost as alive as Poe's House of Usher, though in a subtler way – pervades the tale as a recurrent motif pervades an operatic tragedy; and when the main story is reached, we behold the modern Pyncheons in a pitiable state of decay. Poor old Hepzibah, the eccentric reduced gentlewoman; childlike, unfortunate Clifford, just released from undeserved imprisonment; sly and treacherous Judge Pyncheon, who is the old Colonel all over again – all these figures are tremendous symbols, and are well matched by the stunted vegetation and anaemic fowls in the garden. It was almost a pity to supply a fairly happy ending, with a union of sprightly Phoebe, cousin and last scion of the Pyncheons, to the prepossessing young man who turns out to be the last of the

Maules. This union, presumably, ends the curse. Hawthorne avoids all violence of diction or movement, and keeps his implications of terror well in the background; but occasional glimpses amply serve to sustain the mood and redeem the work from pure allegorical aridity. Incidents like the bewitching of Alice Pyncheon in the early eighteenth century, and the spectral music of her harpsichord which precedes a death in the family – the latter a variant of an immemorial type of Aryan myth – link the action directly with the supernatural; whilst the dead nocturnal vigil of old Judge Pyncheon in the ancient parlour, with his frightfully ticking watch, is stark horror of the most poignant and genuine sort. The way in which the Judge's death is first adumbrated by the motions and sniffing of a strange cat outside the window, long before the fact is suspected by the reader or by any of the characters, is a stroke of genius which Poe could not have surpassed. Later the strange cat watches intently outside that same window in the night and on the next day, for – something. It is clearly the psychopomp of primeval myth, fitted and adapted with infinite deftness to its latter-day setting.

But Hawthorne left no well-defined literary posterity. His mood and attitude belonged to the age which closed with him, and it is the spirit of Poe – who so clearly and realistically understood the natural basis of the horror-appeal and the correct mechanics of its achievement – which survived and blossomed. Among the earliest of Poe's disciples may be reckoned the brilliant young Irishman Fitz James O'Brien (1828–1862), who became naturalised as an American and perished honourably in the Civil War. It is he who gave us *What Was It?*, the first well-shaped short story of a tangible but invisible being, and the prototype of de Maupassant's *Horla*; he also who created the inimitable *Diamond Lens*, in which a young microscopist falls in love with a maiden of an infinitesimal world which he has discovered in a drop of water. O'Brien's early death undoubtedly deprived us of some masterful tales of strangeness and terror, though his genius was not, properly speaking, of the same titan quality which characterised Poe and Hawthorne.

Closer to real greatness was the eccentric and saturnine journalist Ambrose Bierce, born in 1842; who likewise entered the Civil War, but survived to write some immortal tales and to disappear in 1913 in as great a cloud of mystery as any he ever evoked from his nightmare fancy. Bierce was a satirist and pamphleteer of note, but the bulk of his artistic reputation must rest upon his grim and savage short stories; a large number of which deal with the Civil War and form the most vivid and realistic expression which that conflict has yet received in fiction. Virtually all of Bierce's tales are tales of horror; and whilst many of them treat only of the physical and psychological horrors within Nature, a substantial proportion admit the malignly supernatural and form a leading element in America's fund of weird literature. Mr. Samuel Loveman, a living poet and critic who was personally acquainted with Bierce, thus sums up the genius of the great 'shadow-maker' in the preface to some of his letters:

'In Bierce the evocation of horror becomes for the first time not so much the prescription or perversion of Poe and Maupassant, but an atmosphere definite and uncannily precise. Words, so simple that one would be prone to ascribe them to the limitations of a literary hack, take on an unholy horror, a new and unguessed transformation. In Poe one finds it a *tour de force*, in Maupassant a nervous engagement of the flagellated climax. To Bierce, simply and sincerely, diabolism held in its tormented death a legitimate and reliant means to the end. Yet a tacit confirmation with Nature is in every instance insisted upon.

'In *The Death of Halpin Frayser* flowers, verdure, and the boughs and leaves of trees are magnificently placed as an opposing foil to unnatural malignity. Not the accustomed golden world, but a world pervaded with the mystery of blue and the breathless recalcitrance of dreams is Bierce's. Yet, curiously, inhumanity is not altogether absent.'

The 'inhumanity' mentioned by Mr. Loveman finds vent in a rare strain of sardonic comedy and graveyard humour, and a kind of delight in images of cruelty and tantalising disappointment. The former quality is well illustrated by some of the subtitles in the darker narratives; such as 'One does not always eat what is on the table', describing a body laid out for a coroner's inquest, and 'A man though naked may be in rags,' referring to a frightfully mangled corpse.

Bierce's work is in general somewhat uneven. Many of the stories are obviously mechanical, and marred by a jaunty and commonplacely artificial style derived from journalistic models; but the grim malevolence stalking through all of them is unmistakable, and several stand out as permanent mountain-peaks of American weird writing. *The Death of Halpin Frayser*, called by Frederick Taber Cooper the most fiendishly ghastly tale in the literature of the Anglo-Saxon race, tells of a body skulking by night without a soul in a weird and horribly ensanguined wood, and of a man beset by ancestral memories who met death at the claws of that which had been his fervently loved mother. *The Damned Thing*, frequently copied in popular anthologies, chronicles the hideous devastations of an invisible entity that waddles and flounders on the hills and in the wheatfields by night and day. *The Suitable Surroundings* evokes with singular subtlety yet apparent simplicity a piercing sense of the terror which may reside in the written word. In the story the weird author Colston says to his friend Marsh, 'You are brave enough to read me in a street-car, but – in a deserted house – alone – in the forest – at night! Bah! I have a manuscript in my pocket that would kill you!' Marsh reads the manuscript in 'the suitable surroundings' – and it does kill him. *The Middle Toe of the Right Foot* is clumsily developed, but has a powerful climax. A man named Manton has horribly killed his two children and his wife, the latter of whom lacked the middle toe of the right foot. Ten years later he returns much altered to the neighbourhood; and, being secretly recognised, is provoked into a bowie-knife duel in the dark, to be held in the now abandoned house where his crime was committed. When the moment of the duel arrives a trick is played upon him; and he is left without an antagonist, shut in the nightblack ground floor room of the reputedly haunted edifice, with the thick dust of a decade on every hand. No knife is drawn against him, for only a thorough scare is intended; but on the next day he is found crouched in a corner with distorted face, dead of sheer fright at something he has seen. The only clue visible to the discoverers is one having terrible implications: 'In the dust of years that lay thick upon the floor – leading from the door by which they had entered, straight across the room to within a yard of Manton's crouching corpse – were three parallel lines of footprints – light but definite impressions of bare feet, the outer ones those of small children, the inner a woman's. From the point at which they ended they did not return; they pointed all one way.' And, of course, the woman's prints showed a lack of the middle toe of the right foot. *The Spook House*, told with a severely homely air of journalistic verisimilitude, conveys terrible hints of shocking mystery. In 1858 an entire family of seven persons disappears suddenly and unaccountably from a plantation house in eastern Kentucky, leaving all its possessions untouched – furniture, clothing, food supplies, horses, cattle, and slaves. About a year later two men of high standing are forced by a storm to take shelter in the deserted dwelling, and in so doing stumble into a strange subterranean room lit by an unaccountable greenish light and having an iron door which cannot be opened from within. In this room lie the decayed corpses of all the missing family; and as one of the discoverers rushes forward to embrace a body he seems to recognise, the other is so overpowered by a strange foetor that he accidentally shuts his companion in the vault and loses consciousness. Recovering his senses six weeks later, the survivor is unable to find the hidden room; and the house is burned during the Civil War. The imprisoned discoverer is never seen or heard of again.

Bierce seldom realises the atmospheric possibilities of his themes as vividly as Poe; and much of his work contains a certain touch of naiveté, prosaic angularity, or early-American provincialism which contrasts somewhat with the efforts of later horror-masters. Nevertheless the genuineness and artistry of his dark intimations are always unmistakable, so that his greatness is in no danger of eclipse. As arranged in his definitively collected works, Bierce's weird tales occur mainly in two volumes, *Can Such Things Be?* and *In the Midst of Life.* The former, indeed, is almost wholly given over to the supernatural.

Much of the best in American horror-literature has come from pens not mainly devoted to that medium. Oliver Wendell Holmes's historic *Elsie Venner* suggests with admirable restraint an unnatural ophidian element in a young woman prenatally influenced, and sustains the atmosphere with finely discriminating landscape touches. In *The Turn of the Screw* Henry James triumphs over his inevitable pomposity and prolixity sufficiently well to create a truly potent air of sinister menace; depicting the hideous influence of two dead and evil servants, Peter Quint and the governess, Miss Jessel, over a small boy and girl who had been under their care. James is perhaps too diffuse, too unctuously urbane, and too much addicted to subtleties of speech to realise fully all the wild and devastating horror in his situations; but for all that there is a rare and mounting tide of fright, culminating in the death of the little boy, which gives the novelette a permanent place in its special class.

F. Marion Crawford produced several weird tales of varying quality, now collected in a volume entitled *Wandering Ghosts. For the Blood Is the Life* touches powerfully on a case of moon-cursed vampirism near an ancient tower on the rocks of the lonely South Italian seacoast. *The Dead Smile* treats of family horrors in an old house and an ancestral vault in Ireland, and introduces the banshee with considerable force. *The Upper Berth*, however, is Crawford's weird masterpiece; and is one of the most tremendous horror-stories in all literature. In this tale of a suicide-haunted stateroom such things as the spectral saltwater dampness, the strangely open port-hole, and the nightmare struggle with the nameless object are handled with incomparable dexterity.

Very genuine, though not without the typical mannered extravagance of the eighteen-nineties, is the strain of horror in the early work of Robert W. Chambers, since renowned for products of a very different quality. *The King in Yellow*, a series of vaguely connected short stories having as a background a monstrous and suppressed book whose perusal brings fright, madness, and spectral tragedy, really achieves notable heights of cosmic fear in spite of uneven interest and a somewhat trivial and affected cultivation of the Gallic studio atmosphere made popular by Du Maurier's *Trilby*. The most powerful of its tales, perhaps, is *The Yellow Sign*, in which is introduced a silent and terrible churchyard watchman with a face like a puffy grave-worm's. A boy, describing a tussle he has had with this creature, shivers and sickens as he relates a certain detail. 'Well, it's Gawd's truth that when I 'it 'im 'e grabbed me wrists, sir, and when I twisted 'is soft, mushy fist one of his fingers come off in me 'and.' An artist, who after seeing him has shared with another a strange dream of a nocturnal hearse, is shocked by the voice with which the watchman accosts him. The fellow emits a muttering sound that fills the head 'like thick oily smoke from a fat-rendering vat or an odour of noisome decay.' What he mumbles is merely this: 'Have you found the Yellow Sign?'

A weirdly hieroglyphed onyx talisman, picked up on the street by the sharer of his dream, is shortly given the artist; and after stumbling queerly upon the hellish and forbidden book of horrors the two learn, among other hideous things which no sane mortal should know, that this talisman is indeed the nameless Yellow Sign handed down from the accursed cult of Hastur – from primordial Carcosa, whereof the volume treats, and some nightmare memory of which seeks to lurk latent and ominous at the back of all men's minds. Soon they hear the rumbling of the black-plumed hearse driven by the flabby and corpse-faced watchman. He enters the night-shrouded house in quest of the Yellow Sign, all bolts and bars rotting at his touch. And when the people rush in, drawn by a scream that no human throat could utter, they find three forms on the floor – two dead and one dying. One of the dead shapes is far gone in decay. It is the churchyard watchman, and the doctor exclaims, 'That man must have been dead for months.' It is worth observing that the author derives most of the names and allusions connected with his eldritch land of primal memory from the tales of Ambrose Bierce. Other early works of Mr. Chambers displaying the outré and macabre element are *The Maker of Moons* and *In Search of the Unknown*. One cannot help regretting that he did not further develop a vein in which he could so easily have become a recognised master.

Horror material of authentic force may be found in the work of the New England realist Mary E. Wilkins, whose volume of short tales, *The Wind in the Rosebush*, contains a number of noteworthy achievements. In *The Shadows on the Wall* we are shown with consummate skill the response of a staid New England household to uncanny tragedy; and the sourceless shadow of the poisoned brother well prepares us for the climactic moment when the shadow of the secret murderer, who has killed himself in a neighbouring city, suddenly appears beside it. Charlotte Perkins Gilman, in *The Yellow Wall Paper*, rises to a classic level in subtly delineating the madness which crawls over a woman dwelling in the hideously papered room where a madwoman was once confined.

In *The Dead Valley* the eminent architect and mediaevalist Ralph Adams Cram achieves a memorably potent degree of vague regional horror through subleties of atmosphere and description.

Still further carrying on our spectral tradition is the gifted and versatile humorist Irvin S. Cobb, whose work both early and recent contains some finely weird specimens. *Fishhead*, an early achievement, is banefully effective in its portrayal of unnatural affinities between a hybrid idiot and the strange fish of an isolated lake, which at the last avenge their biped kinsman's murder. Later work of Mr. Cobb introduces an element of possible science, as in the tale of hereditary memory where a modern man with a negroid strain utters words in African jungle speech when run down by a train under visual and aural circumstances recalling the maiming of his black ancestor by a rhinoceros a century before.

Extremely high in artistic stature is the novel *The Dark Chamber* (1927) by the late Leonard Cline. This is the tale of a man who – with the characteristic ambition of the Gothic or Byronic hero-villain – seeks to defy nature and recapture every moment of his past life through the abnormal stimulation of memory. To this end he employs endless notes, records, mnemonic objects, and pictures – and finally odours, music, and exotic drugs. At last his ambition goes beyond his personal life and reaches toward the black abysses of *hereditary* memory – even back to prehuman days amidst the steaming swamps of the carboniferous age, and to still more unimaginable deeps of primal time and entity. He calls for madder music and takes stranger drugs, and finally his great dog grows oddly afraid of him. A noxious animal stench encompasses him, and he grows vacant-faced and subhuman. In the end he takes to the woods, howling at night beneath windows. He is finally found in a thicket, mangled to death. Beside him is the mangled corpse of his dog. They have killed each other. The atmosphere of this novel is malevolently potent, much attention being paid to the central figure's sinister home and household.

A less subtle and well-balanced but nevertheless highly effective creation is Herbert S. Gorman's novel, *The Place Called Dagon*, which relates the dark history of a western Massachusetts back-water where the descendants of refugees from the Salem witchcraft still keep alive the morbid and degenerate horrors of the Black Sabbat.

Sinister House, by Leland Hall, has touches of magnificent atmosphere but is marred by a somewhat mediocre romanticism.

Very notable in their way are some of the weird conceptions of the novelist and short-story writer Edward Lucas White, most of whose themes arise from actual dreams. *The Song of the Siren* has a very persuasive strangeness, while such things as *Lukundoo* and *The Snout* arouse darker apprehensions. Mr. White imparts a very peculiar quality to his tales – an oblique sort of glamour which has its own distinctive type of convincingness.

Of younger Americans, none strikes the note of cosmic horror so well as the California poet, artist and fictionist Clark Ashton Smith, whose bizarre writing, drawings, paintings and stories are the delight of a sensitive few. Mr. Smith has for his background a universe of remote and paralysing fright – jungles of poisonous and iridescent blossoms on the moons of Saturn, evil and grotesque temples in Atlantis, Lemuria, and forgotten elder worlds, and dank morasses of spotted death-fungi in spectral countries beyond earth's rim. His longest and most ambitious poem, *The Hashish-Eater*, is in pentameter blank verse; and opens up chaotic and incredible vistas of kaleidoscopic nightmare in the spaces between the stars. In sheer daemonic strangeness and fertility of conception, Mr. Smith is perhaps unexcelled by any other writer dead or living. Who else has seen such gorgeous, luxuriant, and feverishly distorted visions of infinite spheres and multiple dimensions and lived to tell the tale? His short stories deal powerfully with other galaxies, worlds, and dimensions, as well as with strange regions and aeons on the earth. He tells of primal Hyperborea and its black amorphous god Tsathoggua; of the lost continent Zothique, and of

the fabulous, vampire-curst land of Averoigne in mediaeval France.
Some of Mr. Smith's best work can be found in the brochure entitled
The Double Shadow and Other Fantasies (1933)..

9. The Weird Tradition in the British Isles

Recent British literature, besides including the three or four greatest
fantaisistes of the present age, has been gratifyingly fertile in the
element of the weird. Rudyard Kipling has often approached it, and
has, despite the omnipresent mannerisms, handled it with indubitable
mastery in such tales as *The Phantom Rickshaw*, *The Finest Story in the
World*, *The Recrudescence of Imray*, and *The Mark of the Beast*. This latter
is of particular poignancy; the pictures of the naked leper-priest who
mewed like an otter, of the spots which appeared on the chest of the
man that priest cursed, of the growing carnivorousness of the victim
and of the fear which horses began to display toward him, and of the
eventually half-accomplished transformation of that victim into a
leopard, being things which no reader is ever likely to forget. The final
defeat of the malignant sorcery does not impair the force of the tale or
the validity of its mystery.

Lafcadio Hearn, strange, wandering, and exotic, departs still
farther from the realm of the real; and with the supreme artistry
of a sensitive poet weaves phantasies impossible to an author of the
solid roast beef type. His *Fantastics*, written in America, contains some
of the most impressive ghoulishness in all literature; whilst his
Kwaidan, written in Japan, crystallises with matchless skill and
delicacy the eerie lore and whispered legends of that richly colourful
nation. Still more of Hearn's wizardry of language is shown in some of
his translations from the French, especially from Gautier and Flaubert. His version of the latter's *Temptation of St. Anthony* is a classic of
fevered and riotous imagery clad in the magic of singing words.

Oscar Wilde may likewise be given a place amongst weird writers,
both for certain of his exquisite fairy tales, and for his vivid *Picture of
Dorian Gray*, in which a marvellous portrait for years assumes the duty
of aging and coarsening instead of its original, who meanwhile
plunges into every excess of vice and crime without the outward
loss of youth, beauty, and freshness. There is a sudden and potent
climax when Dorian Gray, at last become a murderer, seeks to
destroy the painting whose changes testify to his moral degener-
acy. He stabs it with a knife, and a hideous cry and crash are heard;

but when the servants enter they find it in all its pristine loveliness. 'Lying on the floor was a dead man, in evening dress, with a knife in his heart. He was withered, wrinkled, and loathsome of visage. It was not until they had examined the rings that they recognised who he was.'

Matthew Phipps Shiel, author of many weird, grotesque, and adventurous novels and tales, occasionally attains a high level of horrific magic. *Xelucha* is a noxiously hideous fragment, but is excelled by Mr. Shiel's undoubted masterpiece, *The House of Sounds*, floridly written in the 'yellow nineties,' and recast with more artistic restraint in the early twentieth century. This story, in final form, deserves a place among the foremost things of its kind. It tells of a creeping horror and menace trickling down the centuries on a subarctic island off the coast of Norway; where, amidst the sweep of daemon winds and the ceaseless din of hellish waves and cataracts, a vengeful dead man built a brazen tower of terror. It is vaguely like, yet infinitely unlike, Poe's *Fall of the House of Usher*. In the novel *The Purple Cloud* Mr. Shiel describes with tremendous power a curse which came out of the arctic to destroy mankind, and which for a time appears to have left but a single inhabitant on our planet. The sensations of this lone survivor as he realises his position, and roams through the corpse-littered and treasure-strewn cities of the world as their absolute master, are delivered with a skill and artistry falling little short of actual majesty. Unfortunately the second half of the book, with its conventionally romantic element, involves a distinct letdown.

Better known than Shiel is the ingenious Bram Stoker, who created many starkly horrific conceptions in a series of novels whose poor technique sadly impairs their net effect. *The Lair of the White Worm*, dealing with a gigantic primitive entity that lurks in a vault beneath an ancient castle, utterly ruins a magnificent idea by a development almost infantile. *The Jewel of Seven Stars*, touching on a strange Egyptian resurrection, is less crudely written. But best of all is the famous *Dracula*, which has become almost the standard modern exploitation of the frightful vampire myth. Count Dracula, a vampire, dwells in a horrible castle in the Carpathians, but finally migrates to England with the design of populating the country with fellow vampires. How an Englishman fares within Dracula's stronghold of terrors, and how the dead fiend's plot for domination is at last defeated, are elements which unite to form a tale now justly assigned a permanent place in English letters. *Dracula* evoked many similar novels of supernatural horror, among which the best are perhaps

The Beetle, by Richard Marsh, *Brood of the Witch-Queen*, by 'Sax Rohmer' (Arthur Sarsfield Ward), and *The Door of the Unreal*, by Gerald Biss. The latter handles quite dexterously the standard werewolf superstition. Much subtler and more artistic, and told with singular skill through the juxtaposed narratives of the several characters, is the novel *Cold Harbour*, by Francis Brett Young, in which an ancient house of strange malignancy is powerfully delineated. The mocking and well-nigh omnipotent fiend Humphrey Furnival holds echoes of the Manfred-Montoni type of early Gothic 'villain,' but is redeemed from triteness by many clever individualities. Only the slight diffuseness of explanation at the close, and the somewhat too free use of divination as a plot factor, keep this tale from approaching absolute perfection.

In the novel *Witch Wood* John Buchan depicts with tremendous force a survival of the evil Sabbat in a lonely district of Scotland. The description of the black forest with the evil stone, and of the terrible cosmic adumbrations when the horror is finally extirpated, will repay one for wading through the very gradual action and plethora of Scottish dialect. Some of Mr. Buchan's short stories are also extremely vivid in their spectral intimations; *The Green Wildebeest*, a tale of African witchcraft, *The Wind in the Portico*, with its awakening of dead Britanno-Roman horrors, and *Skule Skerry*, with its touches of sub-arctic fright, being especially remarkable.

Clemence Housman, in the brief novelette *The Werewolf*, attains a high degree of gruesome tension and achieves to some extent the atmosphere of authentic folklore. In *The Elixir of Life* Arthur Ransome attains some darkly excellent effects despite a general naiveté of plot, while H. B. Drake's *The Shadowy Thing* summons up strange and terrible vistas. George Macdonald's *Lilith* has a compelling bizarrerie all its own, the first and simpler of the two versions being perhaps the more effective.

Deserving of distinguished notice as a forceful craftsman to whom an unseen mystic world is ever a close and vital reality is the poet Walter de la Mare, whose haunting verse and exquisite prose alike bear consistent traces of a strange vision reaching deeply into veiled spheres of beauty and terrible and forbidden dimensions of being. In the novel *The Return* we see the soul of a dead man reach out of its grave of two centuries and fasten itself upon the flesh of the living, so that even the face of the victim becomes that which had long ago returned to dust. Of the shorter tales, of which several volumes exist, many are unforgettable for their command of fear's and sorcery's darkest ramifications;

notably *Seaton's Aunt*, in which there lowers a noxious background of malignant vampirism; *The Tree*, which tells of a frightful vegetable growth in the yard of a starving artist; *Out of the Deep*, wherein we are given leave to imagine what thing answered the summons of a dying wastrel in a dark lonely house when he pulled a long-feared bell-cord in the attic of his dread-haunted boyhood; *A Recluse*, which hints at what sent a chance guest flying from a house in the night; *Mr. Kempe*, which shows us a mad clerical hermit in quest of the human soul, dwelling in a frightful sea-cliff region beside an archaic abandoned chapel; and *All-Hallows*, a glimpse of daemoniac forces besieging a lonely mediaeval church and miraculously restoring the rotting masonry. De la Mare does not make fear the sole or even the dominant element of most of his tales, being apparently more interested in the subleties of character involved. Occasionally he sinks to sheer whimsical phantasy of the Barrie order. Still he is among the very few to whom unreality is a vivid, living presence; and as such he is able to put into his occasional fear-studies a keen potency which only a rare master can achieve. His poem *The Listeners* restores the Gothic shudder to modern verse.

The weird short story has fared well of late, an important contributor being the versatile E. F. Benson, whose *The Man Who Went Too Far* breathes whisperingly of a house at the edge of a dark wood, and of Pan's hoof-mark on the breast of a dead man. Mr. Benson's volume, *Visible and Invisible*, contains several stories of singular power; notably *Negotium Perambulans*, whose unfolding reveals an abnormal monster from an ancient ecclesiastical panel which performs an act of miraculous vengeance in a lonely village on the Cornish coast, and *The Horror-Horn*, through which lopes a terrible half-human survival dwelling on unvisited Alpine peaks. *The Face*, in another collection, is lethally potent, in its relentless aura of doom. H. R. Wakefield, in his collections, *They Return at Evening* and *Others Who Return*, manages now and then to achieve great heights of horror despite a vitiating air of sophistication. The most notable stories are *The Red Lodge* with its slimy aqueous evil, *He Cometh and He Passeth By*, *And He Shall Sing*, *The Cairn*, *Look Up There*, *Blind Man's Buff*, and that bit of lurking millennial horror, *The Seventeenth Hole at Duncaster*. Mention has been made of the weird work of H. G. Wells and A. Conan Doyle. The former, in *The Ghost of Fear*, reaches a very high level while all the items in *Thirty Strange Stories* have strong fantastic implications. Doyle now and then struck a powerfully spectral note, as in *The Captain of the Pole-Star*, a tale of arctic ghostliness, and *Lot No. 249*, wherein the reanimated mummy theme is used with more than ordinary skill. Hugh Walpole, of the same family as the founder of Gothic fiction, has sometimes approached the bizarre with much success, his short story *Mrs. Lunt* carrying a very poignant shudder. John Metcalfe, in the collection published as *The Smoking Leg*, attains now and then a rare pitch of potency, the tale entitled *The Bad Lands*, containing graduations of horror that strongly savour of genius. More whimsical and inclined toward the amiable and innocuous phantasy of Sir J. M. Barrie are the short tales of E. M. Forster, grouped under the title of *The Celestial Omnibus*. Of these only one, dealing with a glimpse of Pan and his aura of fright, may be said to hold the true element of cosmic horror. Mrs. H. D. Everett, though adhering to very old and conventional models, occasionally reaches singular heights of spiritual terror in her collection of short stories, *The Death Mask*. L. P. Hartley is notable for his incisive and extremely ghastly tale, *A Visitor from Down Under*. May Sinclair's *Uncanny Stories* contain more of traditional 'occultism' than of that creative treatment of fear which marks mastery in this field, and are inclined to lay more stress on human emotions and psychological delving than upon the stark phenomena of a cosmos utterly unreal. It may be well to remark here that occult believers are probably less effective than materialists in delineating the spectral and the fantastic, since to them the phantom world is so commonplace a reality that they tend to refer to it with less awe, remoteness, and impressiveness than do those who see in it an absolute and stupendous violation of the natural order.

Of rather uneven stylistic quality, but vast occasional power in its suggestion of lurking worlds and beings behind the ordinary surface of life, is the work of William Hope Hodgson, known today far less than it deserves to be. Despite a tendency toward conventionally sentimental conceptions of the universe, and of man's relation to it and to his fellows, Mr. Hodgson is perhaps second only to Algernon Blackwood in his serious treatment of unreality. Few can equal him in adumbrating the nearness of nameless forces and monstrous besieging entities through casual hints and insignificant details, or in conveying feelings of the spectral and the abnormal in connection with regions or buildings.

In *The Boats of the Glen Carrig* (1907) we are shown a variety of malign marvels and accursed unknown lands as encountered by the survivors of a sunken ship. The brooding menace in the earlier parts of the book is impossible to surpass, though a letdown in the direction of ordinary romance and adventure occurs toward the end. An inaccurate and pseudo-romantic attempt to reproduce eighteenth-century prose detracts from the general effect, but the really profound nautical erudition everywhere displayed is a compensating factor.

The House on the Borderland (1908) – perhaps the greatest of all Mr. Hodgson's works – tells of a lonely and evilly regarded house in Ireland which forms a focus for hideous otherworld forces and sustains a siege by blasphemous hybrid anomalies from a hidden abyss below. The wanderings of the Narrator's spirit through limitless light-years of cosmic space and Kalpas of eternity, and its witnessing of the solar system's final destruction, constitute something almost unique in standard literature. And everywhere there is manifest the author's power to suggest vague, ambushed horrors in natural scenery. But for a few touches of commonplace sentimentality this book would be a classic of the first water.

The Ghost Pirates (1909), regarded by Mr. Hodgson as rounding out a trilogy with the two previously mentioned works, is a powerful account of a doomed and haunted ship on its last voyage, and of the terrible sea-devils (of quasi-human aspect, and perhaps the spirits of bygone buccaneers) that besiege it and finally drag it down to an unknown fate. With its command of maritime knowledge, and its clever selection of hints and incidents suggestive of latent horrors in nature, this book at times reaches enviable peaks of power.

The Night Land (1912) is a long-extended (538 pp.) tale of the earth's infinitely remote future – billions of billions of years ahead, after the death of the sun. It is told in a rather clumsy fashion, as the dreams of a man in the seventeenth century, whose mind merges with its own future incarnation; and is seriously marred by painful verboseness, repetitiousness, artificial and nauseously sticky romantic sentimentality, and an attempt at archaic language even more grotesque and absurd than that in *Glen Carrig*.

Allowing for all its faults, it is yet one of the most potent pieces of macabre imagination ever written. The picture of a night-black, dead planet, with the remains of the human race concentrated in a stupendously vast metal pyramid and besieged by monstrous, hybrid, and altogether unknown forces of the darkness, is something that no reader can ever forget. Shapes and entities of an altogether non-human and inconceivable sort – the prowlers of the black, man-forsaken, and unexplored world outside the pyramid – are *suggested* and *partly* described with ineffable potency; while the night-land landscape with its chasms and slopes and dying volcanism takes on an almost sentient terror beneath the author's touch.

Midway in the book the central figure ventures outside the

pyramid on a quest through death-haunted realms untrod by man for millions of years – and in his slow, minutely described, day-by-day progress over unthinkable leagues of immemorial blackness there is a sense of cosmic alienage, breathless mystery, and terrified expectancy unrivalled in the whole range of literature. The last quarter of the book drags woefully, but fails to spoil the tremendous power of the whole.

Mr. Hodgson's later volume, *Carnacki, the Ghost-Finder*, consists of several longish short stories published many years before in magazines. In quality it falls conspicuously below the level of the other books. We here find a more or less conventional stock figure of the 'infallible detective' type – the progeny of M. Dupin and Sherlock Holmes, and the close kin of Algernon Blackwood's John Silence – moving through scenes and events badly marred by an atmosphere of professional 'occultism.' A few of the episodes, however, are of undeniable power, and afford glimpses of the peculiar genius characteristic of the author.

Naturally it is impossible in brief sketch to trace out all the classic modern uses of the terror element. The ingredient must of necessity enter into all work, both prose and verse, treating broadly of life; and we are therefore not surprised to find a share in such writers as the poet Browning, whose *Childe Roland to the Dark Tower Came* is instinct with hideous menace, or the novelist Joseph Conrad, who often wrote of the dark secrets within the sea, and of the daemoniac driving power of Fate as influencing the lives of lonely and maniacally resolute men. Its trail is one of infinite ramifications; but we must here confine ourselves to its appearance in a relatively unmixed state, where it determines and dominates the work of art containing it.

Somewhat separate from the main British stream is that current of weirdness in Irish literature which came to the fore in the Celtic Renaissance of the later nineteenth and early twentieth centuries. Ghost and fairy lore have always been of great prominence in Ireland, and for over a hundred years have been recorded by a line of such faithful transcribers and translators as William Carleton, T. Crofton Croker, Lady Wilde – mother of Oscar Wilde – Douglas Hyde, and W. B. Yeats. Brought to notice by the modern movement, this body of myth has been carefully collected and studied; and its salient features reproduced in the work of later figures like Yeats, J. M. Synge, 'A. E.,' Lady Gregory, Padraic Colum, James Stephens and their colleagues.

Whilst on the whole more whimsically fantastic than terrible, such folklore and its consciously artistic counterparts contain much that falls truly within the domain of cosmic horror. Tales of burials in sunken churches beneath haunted lakes, accounts of death-heralding banshees and sinister changelings, ballads of spectres and 'the unholy creatures of the Raths' – all these have their poignant and definite shivers and mark a strong and distinctive element in weird literature. Despite homely grotesqueness and absolute naiveté, there is genuine nightmare in the class of narrative represented by the yarn of Teig O'Kane, who in punishment for his wild life was ridden all night by a hideous corpse that demanded burial and drove him from churchyard to churchyard as the dead rose up loathsomely in each one and refused to accommodate the newcomer with a berth. Yeats, undoubtedly the greatest figure of the Irish revival if not the greatest of all living poets, has accomplished notable things both in original work and in the codification of old legends.

10. The Modern Masters

The best horror-tales of today, profiting by the long evolution of the type, possess a naturalness, convincingness, artistic smoothness, and skilful intensity of appeal quite beyond comparison with anything in the Gothic work of a century or more ago. Technique, craftsmanship, experience, and psychological knowledge have advanced tremendously with the passing years, so that much of the older work seems naive and artificial; redeemed, when redeemed at all, only by a genius which conquers heavy limitations. The tone of jaunty and inflated romance, full of false motivation and investing every conceivable event with a counterfeit significance and carelessly inclusive glamour, is now confined to lighter and more whimsical phases of supernatural writing. Serious weird stories are either made realistically intense by close consistency and perfect fidelity to Nature except in the one supernatural direction which the author allows himself, or else cast altogether in the realm of phantasy, with atmosphere cunningly adapted to the visualisation of a delicately exotic world of unreality beyond space and time, in which almost anything may happen if it but happen in true accord with certain types of imagination and illusion normal to the sensitive human brain. This, at least, is the dominant tendency; though of course many great contemporary writers slip occasionally into some of the flashy postures of immature romanticism or into bits of the equally empty and absurd jargon of pseudo-scientific 'occultism,' now at one of its periodic high tides.

Of living creators of cosmic fear raised to its most artistic pitch, few if any can hope to equal the versatile Arthur Machen, author of some dozen tales long and short, in which the elements of hidden horror and brooding fright attain an almost incomparable substance and realistic acuteness. Mr. Machen, a general man of letters and master of an exquisitely lyrical and expressive prose style, has perhaps put more conscious effort into his picaresque *Chronicles of Clemendy*, his refreshing essays, his vivid autobiographical volumes, his fresh and spirited translations, and above all his memorable epic of the sensitive aesthetic mind, *The Hill of Dreams*, in which the youthful hero responds to the magic of that ancient Welsh environment which is the author's own, and lives a dream-life in the Roman city of Isca Silurum, now shrunk to the relic-strewn village of Caerleon-on-Usk. But the fact remains that his powerful horror-material of the nineties and earlier nineteen-hundreds stands alone in its class, and marks a distinct epoch in the history of this literary form.

Mr. Machen, with an impressionable Celtic heritage linked to keen youthful memories of the wild domed hills, archaic forests, and cryptical Roman ruins of the Gwent countryside, has developed an imaginative life of rare beauty, intensity, and historic background. He has absorbed the mediaeval mystery of dark woods and ancient customs, and is a champion of the Middle Ages in all things – including the Catholic faith. He has yielded, likewise, to the spell of the Britanno-Roman life which once surged over his native region; and finds strange magic in the fortified camps, tessellated pavements, fragments of statues, and kindred things which tell of the day when classicism reigned and Latin was the language of the country. A young American poet, Frank Belknap Long, has well summarised this dreamer's rich endowments and wizardry of expression in the sonnet *On Reading Arthur Machen*:

> There is a glory in the autumn wood,
> The ancient lanes of England wind and climb
> Past wizard oaks and gorse and tangled thyme
> To where a fort of mighty empire stood:
> There is a glamour in the autumn sky;
> The reddened clouds are writhing in the glow
> Of some great fire, and there are glints below
> Of tawny yellow where the embers die.
> I wait, for he will show me, clear and cold,
> High-rais'd in splendour, sharp against the North,

The Roman eagles, and through mists of gold
The marching legions as they issue forth:
I wait, for I would share with him again
The ancient wisdom, and the ancient pain.

Of Mr. Machen's horror-tales the most famous is perhaps *The Great God Pan* (1894) which tells of a singular and terrible experiment and its consequences. A young woman, through surgery of the brain-cells, is made to see the vast and monstrous deity of Nature, and becomes an idiot in consequence, dying less than a year later. Years afterward a strange, ominous, and foreign-looking child named Helen Vaughan is placed to board with a family in rural Wales, and haunts the woods in unaccountable fashion. A little boy is thrown out of his mind at sight of someone or something he spies with her, and a young girl comes to a terrible end in similar fashion. All this mystery is strangely interwoven with the Roman rural deities of the place, as sculptured in antique fragments. After another lapse of years, a woman of strangely exotic beauty appears in society, drives her husband to horror and death, causes an artist to paint unthinkable paintings of Witches' Sabbaths, creates an epidemic of suicide among the men of her acquaintance, and is finally discovered to be a frequenter of the lowest dens of vice in London, where even the most callous degenerates are shocked at her enormities. Through the clever comparing of notes on the part of those who have had word of her at various stages of her career, this woman is discovered to be the girl Helen Vaughan, who is the child – by no mortal father – of the young woman on whom the brain experiment was made. She is a daughter of hideous Pan himself, and at the last is put to death amidst horrible transmutations of form involving changes of sex and a descent to the most primal manifestations of the life-principle.

But the charm of the tale is in the telling. No one could begin to describe the cumulative suspense and ultimate horror with which every paragraph abounds without following fully the precise order in which Mr. Machen unfolds his gradual hints and revelations. Melodrama is undeniably present, and coincidence is stretched to a length which appears absurd upon analysis; but in the malign witchery of the tale as a whole these trifles are forgotten, and the sensitive reader reaches the end with only an appreciative shudder and a tendency to repeat the words of one of the characters: 'It is too incredible, too monstrous; such things can never be in this quiet world . . . Why, man, if such a case were possible, our earth would be a nightmare.'

Less famous and less complex in plot than *The Great God Pan*, but definitely finer in atmosphere and general artistic value, is the curious and dimly disquieting chronicle called *The White People*, whose central portion purports to be the diary or notes of a little girl whose nurse has introduced her to some of the forbidden magic and soul-blasting traditions of the noxious witch-cult – the cult whose whispered lore was handed down long lines of peasantry throughout Western Europe, and whose members sometimes stole forth at night, one by one, to meet in black woods and lonely places for the revolting orgies of the Witches' Sabbath. Mr. Machen's narrative, a triumph of skilful selectiveness and restraint, accumulates enormous power as it flows on in a stream of innocent childish prattle, introducing allusions to strange 'nymphs,' 'Dols,' 'voolas,' 'white, green, and scarlet ceremonies,' 'Aklo letters,' 'Chian language,' 'Mao games,' and the like. The rites learned by the nurse from her witch grandmother are taught to the child by the time she is three years old, and her artless accounts of the dangerous secret revelations possess a lurking terror generously mixed with pathos. Evil charms well known to anthropologists are described with juvenile naiveté, and finally there comes a winter afternoon journey into the old Welsh hills, performed under an imaginative spell which lends to the wild scenery an added weirdness, strangeness, and suggestion of grotesque sentience. The details of this journey are given with marvellous vividness, and form to the keen critic a masterpiece of fantastic writing, with almost unlimited power in the intimation of potent hideousness and cosmic aberration. At length the child – whose age is then thirteen – comes upon a cryptic and banefully beautiful thing in the midst of a dark and inaccessible wood. In the end horror overtakes her in a manner deftly prefigured by an anecdote in the prologue, but she poisons herself in time. Like the mother of Helen Vaughan in *The Great God Pan*, she has seen that frightful deity. She is discovered dead in the dark wood beside the cryptic thing she found; and that thing – a whitely luminous statue of Roman workmanship about which dire mediaeval rumours had clustered – is affrightedly hammered into dust by the searchers.

In the episodic novel of *The Three Impostors*, a work whose merit as a whole is somewhat marred by an imitation of the jaunty Stevenson manner, occur certain tales which perhaps represent the highwater mark of Machen's skill as a terror-weaver. Here we find in its most artistic form a favourite weird conception of the author's; the notion that beneath the mounds and rocks of the wild Welsh hills dwell subterraneously that squat primitive race whose vestiges gave rise to our common folk legends of fairies, elves, and the 'little people,' and whose acts are even now responsible for certain unexplained disappearances, and occasional substitutions of strange dark 'changelings' for normal infants. This theme receives its finest treatment in the episode entitled *The Novel of the Black Seal*; where a professor, having discovered a singular identity between certain characters scrawled on Welsh limestone rocks and those existing in a prehistoric black seal from Babylon, sets out on a course of discovery which leads him to unknown and terrible things. A queer passage in the ancient geographer Solinus, a series of mysterious disappearances in the lonely reaches of Wales, a strange idiot son born to a rural mother after a fright in which her inmost faculties were shaken; all these things suggest to the professor a hideous connection and a condition revolting to any friend and respecter of the human race. He hires the idiot boy, who jabbers strangely at times in a repulsive hissing voice, and is subject to odd epileptic seizures. Once, after such a seizure in the professor's study by night, disquieting odours and evidences of unnatural presences are found; and soon after that the professor leaves a bulky document and goes into the weird hills with feverish expectancy and strange terror in his heart. He never returns, but beside a fantastic stone in the wild country are found his watch, money, and ring, done up with catgut in a parchment bearing the same terrible characters as those on the black Babylonish seal and the rock in the Welsh mountains.

The bulky document explains enough to bring up the most hideous vistas. Professor Gregg, from the massed evidence presented by the Welsh disappearances, the rock inscription, the accounts of ancient geographers, and the black seal, has decided that a frightful race of dark primal beings of immemorial antiquity and wide former diffusion still dwell beneath the hills of unfrequented Wales. Further research has unriddled the message of the black seal, and proved that the idiot boy, a son of some father more terrible than mankind, is the heir of monstrous memories and possibilities. That strange night in the study the professor invoked 'the awful transmutation of the hills' by the aid of the black seal, and aroused in the hybrid idiot the horrors of his shocking paternity. He 'saw his body swell and become distended as a bladder, while the face blackened . . .' And then the supreme effects of the invocations appeared, and Professor Gregg knew the stark frenzy of cosmic panic in its darkest form. He knew the abysmal gulfs of abnormality that he had opened, and went forth into the wild hills prepared and resigned. He would meet the unthinkable 'Little People' – and his document ends with a rational observation: 'If unhappily I do not return from my journey, there is no need to conjure up here a picture of the awfulness of my fate.'

Also in *The Three Impostors* is the *Novel of the White Powder*, which approaches the absolute culmination of loathsome fright. Francis Leicester, a young law student nervously worn out by seclusion and overwork, has a prescription filled by an old apothecary none too careful about the state of his drugs. The substance, it later turns out, is an unusual salt which time and varying temperature have accidentally changed to something very strange and terrible; nothing less, in short, than the mediaeval *vinum sabbati*, whose consumption at the horrible orgies of the Witches' Sabbath gave rise to shocking transformations and – if injudiciously used – to unutterable consequences. Innocently enough, the youth regularly imbibes the powder in a glass of water after meals; and at first seems substantially benefited. Gradually, however, his improved spirits take the form of dissipation; he is absent from home a great deal, and appears to have undergone a repellent psychological change. One day an odd livid spot appears on his right hand, and he afterward returns to his seclusion; finally keeping himself shut within his room and admitting none of the household. The doctor calls for an interview, and departs in a palsy of horror, saying that he can do no more in that house. Two weeks later the patient's sister, walking outside, sees a monstrous thing at the sickroom window; and servants report that food left at the locked door is no longer touched. Summons at the door bring only a sound of shuffling and a demand in a thick gurgling voice to be let alone. At last an awful happening is reported by a shuddering housemaid. The ceiling of the room below Leicester's is stained with a hideous black fluid, and a pool of viscid abomination has dripped to the bed beneath. Dr. Haberden, now persuaded to return to the house, breaks down the young man's door and strikes again and again with an iron bar at the blasphemous semi-living thing he finds there. It is 'a dark and putrid mass, seething with corruption and hideous rottenness, neither liquid nor solid, but melting and changing.' Burning points like eyes shine out of its midst, and before it is dispatched it tries to lift what might have been an arm. Soon afterward the physician, unable to endure the memory of what he has beheld, dies at sea while bound for a new life in America.

Mr. Machen returns to the daemoniac 'Little People' in *The Red Hand* and *The Shining Pyramid*; and in *The Terror*, a wartime story, he

treats with very potent mystery the effect of man's modern repudiation of spirituality on the beasts of the world, which are thus led to
question his supremacy and to unite for his extermination. Of utmost
delicacy, and passing from mere horror into true mysticism, is *The
Great Return*, a story of the Graal, also a product of the war period. Too
well known to need description here is the tale of *The Bowmen*; which,
taken for authentic narration, gave rise to the widespread legend of
the 'Angels of Mons' – ghosts of the old English archers of Crécy and
Agincourt who fought in 1914 beside the hard-pressed ranks of
England's glorious 'Old Contemptibles.'

Less intense than Mr. Machen in delineating the extremes of stark
fear, yet infinitely more closely wedded to the idea of an unreal world
constantly pressing upon ours is the inspired and prolific Algernon
Blackwood, amidst whose voluminous and uneven work may be
found some of the finest spectral literature of this or any age. Of
the quality of Mr. Blackwood's genius there can be no dispute; for no
one has even approached the skill, seriousness, and minute fidelity
with which he records the overtones of strangeness in ordinary things
and experiences, or the preternatural insight with which he builds up
detail by detail the complete sensations and perceptions leading from
reality into supernormal life or vision. Without notable command of
the poetic witchery of mere words, he is the one absolute and
unquestioned master of weird atmosphere; and can evoke what
amounts almost to a story from a simple fragment of humourless
psychological description. Above all others he understands how fully
some sensitive minds dwell forever on the borderland of dream, and
how relatively slight is the distinction betwixt those images formed
from actual objects and those excited by the play of the imagination.

Mr. Blackwood's lesser work is marred by several defects such as
ethical didacticism, occasional insipid whimsicality, the flatness of
benignant supernaturalism, and a too free use of the trade jargon of
modern 'occultism.' A fault of his more serious efforts is that diffuseness and long-windedness which results from an excessively elaborate
attempt, under the handicap of a somewhat bald and journalistic
style devoid of intrinsic magic, colour, and vitality, to visualise precise
sensations and nuances of uncanny suggestion. But in spite of all this,
the major products of Mr. Blackwood attain a genuinely classic level,
and evoke as does nothing else in literature an awed convinced sense
of the imminence of strange spiritual spheres or entities.

The well-nigh endless array of Mr. Blackwood's fiction includes
both novels and shorter tales, the latter sometimes independent and

sometimes arrayed in series. Foremost of all must be reckoned *The Willows*, in which the nameless presences on a desolate Danube island are horribly felt and recognised by a pair of idle voyagers. Here art and restraint in narrative reach their very highest development, and an impression of lasting poignancy is produced without a single strained passage or a single false note. Another amazingly potent though less artistically finished tale is *The Wendigo*, where we are confronted by horrible evidences of a vast forest daemon about which North Woods lumbermen whisper at evening. The manner in which certain footprints tell certain unbelievable things is really a marked triumph in craftsmanship. In *An Episode in a Lodging House* we behold frightful presences summoned out of black space by a sorcerer, and *The Listener* tells of the awful psychic residuum creeping about an old house where a leper died. In the volume titled *Incredible Adventures* occur some of the finest tales which the author has yet produced, leading the fancy to wild rites on nocturnal hills, to secret and terrible aspects lurking behind stolid scenes, and to unimaginable vaults of mystery below the sands and pyramids of Egypt; all with a serious finesse and delicacy that convince where a cruder or lighter treatment would merely amuse. Some of these accounts are hardly stories at all, but rather studies in elusive impressions and half-remembered snatches of dream. Plot is everywhere negligible, and atmosphere reigns untrammelled.

John Silence – Physician Extraordinary is a book of five related tales, through which a single character runs his triumphant course. Marred only by traces of the popular and conventional detective-story atmosphere – for Dr. Silence is one of those benevolent geniuses who employ their remarkable powers to aid worthy fellow-men in difficulty – these narratives contain some of the author's best work, and produce an illusion at once emphatic and lasting. The opening tale, *A Psychical Invasion*, relates what befell a sensitive author in a house once the scene of dark deeds, and how a legion of fiends was exorcised. *Ancient Sorceries*, perhaps the finest tale in the book, gives an almost hypnotically vivid account of an old French town where once the unholy Sabbath was kept by all the people in the form of cats. In *The Nemesis of Fire* a hideous elemental is evoked by new-spilt blood, whilst *Secret Worship* tells of a German school where Satanism held sway, and where long afterward an evil aura remained. *The Camp of the Dog* is a werewolf tale, but is weakened by moralisation and professional 'occultism.'

Too subtle, perhaps, for definite classification as horror-tales, yet possibly more truly artistic in an absolute sense, are such delicate phantasies as *Jimbo* or *The Centaur*. Mr. Blackwood achieves in these novels a close and palpitant approach to the inmost substance of dream, and works enormous havoc with the conventional barriers between reality and imagination.

Unexcelled in the sorcery of crystalline singing prose, and supreme in the creation of a gorgeous and languorous world of iridescently exotic vision, is Edward John Moreton Drax Plunkett, Eighteenth Baron Dunsany, whose tales and short plays form an almost unique element in our literature. Inventor of a new mythology and weaver of surprising folk-lore, Lord Dunsany stands dedicated to a strange world of fantastic beauty, and pledged to eternal warfare against the coarseness and ugliness of diurnal reality. His point of view is the most truly cosmic of any held in the literature of any period. As sensitive as Poe to dramatic values and the significance of isolated words and details, and far better equipped rhetorically through a simple lyric style based on the prose of the King James Bible, this author draws with tremendous effectiveness on nearly every body of myth and legend within the circle of European culture; producing a composite or eclectic cycle of phantasy in which Eastern colour, Hellenic form, Teutonic sombreness and Celtic wistfulness are so superbly blended that each sustains and supplements the rest without sacrifice or perfect congruity and homogeneity. In most cases Dunsany's lands are fabulous – 'beyond the East,' or 'at the edge of the world.' His system of original personal and place names, with roots drawn from classical, Oriental, and other sources, is a marvel of versatile inventiveness and poetic discrimination; as one may see from such specimens as 'Argimenes,' 'Bethmoora,' 'Poltarnees,' 'Camorak,' 'Iluriel,' or 'Sardathrion.'

Beauty rather than terror is the keynote of Dunsany's work. He loves the vivid green of jade and of copper domes, and the delicate flush of sunset on the ivory minarets of impossible dream-cities. Humour and irony, too, are often present to impart a gentle cynicism and modify what might otherwise possess a naive intensity. Nevertheless, as is inevitable in a master of triumphant unreality, there are occasional touches of cosmic fright which come well within the authentic tradition. Dunsany loves to hint slyly and adroitly of monstrous things and incredible dooms, as one hints in a fairy tale. In *The Book of Wonder* we read of Hlo-Hlo, the gigantic spider-idol which does not always stay at home; of what the Sphinx feared in the forest; of Slith, the thief who jumps over the edge of the world after seeing a certain light lit and knowing *who* lit it; of the anthropophagous Gibbelins, who inhabit an evil tower and guard a treasure; of the Gnoles, who live in the forest and from whom it is not well to steal; of the City of Never, and the eyes that watch in the Under Pits; and of kindred things of darkness. *A Dreamer's Tales* tells of the mystery that sent forth all men from Bethmoora in the desert; of the vast gate of Perdondaris, that was carved from a *single piece* of ivory; and of the voyage of poor old Bill, whose captain cursed the crew and paid calls on nasty-looking isles new-risen from the sea, with low thatched cottages having evil, obscure windows.

Many of Dunsany's short plays are replete with spectral fear. In *The Gods of the Mountain* seven beggars impersonate the seven green idols on a distant hill, and enjoy ease and honour in a city of worshippers until they hear that *the real idols are missing from their wonted seats*. A very ungainly sight in the dusk is reported to them – 'rock should not walk in the evening' – and at last, as they sit awaiting the arrival of a troop of dancers, they note that the approaching footsteps are heavier than those of good dancers ought to be. Then things ensue, and in the end the presumptuous blasphemers are turned to green jade statues by the very walking statues whose sanctity they outraged. But mere plot is the very least merit of this marvellously effective play. The incidents and developments are those of a supreme master, so that the whole forms one of the most important contributions of the present age not only to drama, but to literature in general. *A Night at an Inn* tells of four thieves who have stolen the emerald eye of Klesh, a monstrous Hindoo god. They lure to their room and succeed in slaying the three priestly avengers who are on their track, but in the night Klesh comes gropingly for his eye; and having gained it and departed, calls each of the despoilers out into the darkness for an unnamed punishment. In *The Laughter of the Gods* there is a doomed city at the jungle's edge, and a ghostly lutanist heard only by those about to die (cf. Alice's spectral harpsichord in Hawthorne's *House of the Seven Gables*) whilst *The Queen's Enemies* retells the anecdote of Herodotus in which a vengeful princess invites her foes to a subterranean banquet and lets in the Nile to drown them. But no amount of mere description can convey more than a fraction of Lord Dunsany's pervasive charm. His prismatic cities and unheard of rites are touched with a sureness which only mastery can engender, and we thrill with a sense of actual participation in his secret mysteries. To the truly imaginative he is a talisman and a key unlocking rich storehouses of dream and fragmentary memory; so that we may think of him not only as a poet, but as one who makes each reader a poet as well.

At the opposite pole of genius from Lord Dunsany, and gifted with an almost diabolic power of calling horror by gentle steps from the midst of prosaic daily life, is the scholarly Montague Rhodes James, Provost of Eton College, antiquary of note, and recognized authority on mediaeval manuscripts and cathedral history. Dr. James, long fond of telling spectral tales at Christmastide, has become by slow degrees a literary weird fictionist of the very first rank; and has developed a distinctive style and method likely to serve as models for an enduring line of disciples.

The art of Dr. James is by no means haphazard, and in the preface to one of his collections he has formulated three very sound rules for macabre composition. A ghost story, he believes, should have a familiar setting in the modern period, in order to approach closely the reader's sphere of experience. Its spectral phenomena, moreover, should be malevolent rather than beneficent; since *fear* is the emotion primarily to be excited. And finally, the technical patois of 'occultism' or pseudo-science ought carefully to be avoided; lest the charm of casual verisimilitude be smothered in unconvincing pedantry.

Dr. James, practising what he preaches, approaches his themes in a light and often conversational way. Creating the illusion of every-day events, he introduces his abnormal phenomena cautiously and gradually; relieved at every turn by touches of homely and prosaic detail, and sometimes spiced with a snatch or two of antiquarian scholarship. Conscious of the close relation between present weirdness and accumulated tradition, he generally provides remote historical antecedents for his incidents; thus being able to utilise very aptly his exhaustive knowledge of the past, and his ready and convincing command of archaic diction and colouring. A favourite scene for a James tale is some centuried cathedral, which the author can describe with all the familiar minuteness of a specialist in that field.

Sly humorous vignettes and bits of lifelike genre portraiture and characterisation are often to be found in Dr. James's narratives, and serve in his skilled hands to augment the general effect rather than to spoil it, as the same qualities would tend to do with a lesser craftsman. In inventing a new type of ghost, he has departed considerably from the conventional Gothic tradition; for where the older stock ghosts were pale and stately, and apprehended chiefly through the sense of sight, the average James ghost is lean, dwarfish, and hairy – a sluggish, hellish night-abomination midway betwixt beast and man – and usually *touched* before it is *seen*. Sometimes the spectre is of still more eccentric composition; a roll of flannel with spidery eyes, or an invisible entity which moulds itself in bedding and shows *a face of crumpled linen*. Dr. James has, it is clear, an intelligent and scientific knowledge of human nerves and feelings; and knows just how to apportion statement, imagery, and subtle suggestions in order to secure the best results with his readers. He is an artist in incident and arrangement rather than in atmosphere, and reaches the emotions more often through the intellect than directly. This method, of course, with its occasional absences of sharp climax, has its drawbacks as well as its advantages; and many will miss the thorough atmospheric tension which writers like Machen are careful to build up with words and scenes. But only a few of the tales are open to the charge of tameness. Generally the laconic unfolding of abnormal events in adroit order is amply sufficient to produce the desired effect of cumulative horror.

The short stories of Dr. James are contained in four small collections, entitled respectively *Ghost Stories of an Antiquary, More Ghost Stories of an Antiquary, A Thin Ghost and Others*, and *A Warning to the Curious*. There is also a delightful juvenile phantasy, *The Five Jars*, which has its spectral adumbrations. Amidst this wealth of material it is hard to select a favourite or especially typical tale, though each reader will no doubt have such preferences as his temperament may determine.

Count Magnus is assuredly one of the best, forming as it does a veritable Golconda of suspense and suggestion. Mr. Wraxall is an English traveller of the middle nineteenth century, sojourning in Sweden to secure material for a book. Becoming interested in the ancient family of De La Gardie, near the village of Råbäck, he studies its records; and finds particular fascination in the builder of the existing manor-house, one Count Magnus, of whom strange and terrible things are whispered. The Count, who flourished early in the seventeenth century, was a stern landlord, and famous for his severity toward poachers and delinquent tenants. His cruel punishments were bywords, and there were dark rumours of influences which even survived his interment in the great mausoleum he built near the church – as in the case of the two peasants who hunted on his preserves one night a century after his death. There were hideous screams in the woods, and near the tomb of Count Magnus an unnatural laugh and the clang of a great door. Next morning the priest found the two men; one a maniac, and the other dead, with the flesh of his face sucked from the bones.

Mr. Wraxall hears all these tales, and stumbles on more guarded references to a Black Pilgrimage once taken by the Count, a pilgrimage to Chorazin in Palestine, one of the cities denounced by Our Lord in the Scriptures, and in which old priests say that Antichrist is to be born. No one dares to hint just what that Black Pilgrimage was, or what strange being or thing the Count brought back as a companion. Meanwhile Mr. Wraxall is increasingly anxious to explore the mausoleum of Count Magnus, and finally secures permission to do so, in the company of a deacon. He finds several monuments and three copper sarcophagi, one of which is the Count's. Round the edge of this latter are several bands of engraved scenes, including a singular and hideous delineation of a pursuit – the pursuit of a frantic man through a forest by a squat muffled figure with a devilfish's tentacle, directed by a tall cloaked man on a neighbouring hillock. The sarcophagus has three massive steel padlocks, one of which is lying open on the floor, reminding the traveller of a metallic clash he heard the day before when passing the mausoleum and wishing idly that he might see Count Magnus.

His fascination augmented, and the key being accessible, Mr. Wraxall pays the mausoleum a second and solitary visit and finds another padlock unfastened. The next day, his last in Råbäck, he again goes alone to bid the long-dead Count farewell. Once more queerly impelled to utter a whimsical wish for a meeting with the buried nobleman, he now sees to his disquiet that only one of the padlocks remains on the great sarcophagus. Even as he looks, that last lock drops noisily to the floor, and there comes a sound as of creaking hinges. Then the monstrous lid appears very slowly to rise, and Mr. Wraxall flees in panic fear without refastening the door of the mausoleum.

During his return to England the traveller feels a curious uneasiness about his fellow-passengers on the canal-boat which he employs for the earlier stages. Cloaked figures make him nervous, and he has a sense of being watched and followed. Of twenty-eight persons whom he counts, only twenty-six appear at meals; and the missing two are always a tall cloaked man and a shorter muffled figure. Completing his water travel at Harwich, Mr. Wraxall takes frankly to flight in a closed carriage, but sees two cloaked figures at a crossroad. Finally he lodges at a small house in a village and spends the time making frantic notes. On the second morning he is found dead, and during the inquest seven jurors faint at sight of the body. The house where he stayed is never again inhabited, and upon its demolition half a century later his manuscript is discovered in a forgotten cupboard.

In *The Treasure of Abbot Thomas* a British antiquary unriddles a cipher on some Renaissance painted windows, and thereby discovers a centuried hoard of gold in a niche halfway down a well in the courtyard of a German abbey. But the crafty depositor had set a guardian over that treasure, and something in the black well twines its arms around the searcher's neck in such a manner that the quest is abandoned, and a clergyman sent for. Each night after that the discoverer feels a stealthy presence and detects a horrible odour of mould outside the door of his hotel room, till finally the clergyman makes a daylight replacement of the stone at the mouth of the treasure-vault in the well – out of which something had come in the dark to avenge the disturbing of old Abbot Thomas's gold. As he completes his work the cleric observes a curious toad-like carving on the ancient well-head, with the Latin motto '*Depositum custodi* – keep that which is committed to thee.'

Other notable James tales are *The Stalls of Barchester Cathedral*, in which a grotesque carving comes curiously to life to avenge the secret and subtle murder of an old Dean by his ambitious successor; *Oh, Whistle, and I'll Come to You*, which tells of the horror summoned by a strange metal whistle found in a mediaeval church ruin; and *An Episode of Cathedral History*, where the dismantling of a pulpit uncovers an archaic tomb whose lurking daemon spreads panic and pestilence. Dr. James, for all his light touch, evokes fright and hideousness in their most shocking form, and will certainly stand as one of the few really creative masters in his darksome province.

For those who relish speculation regarding the future, the tale of supernatural horror provides an interesting field. Combated by a mounting wave of plodding realism, cynical flippancy, and sophisticated disillusionment, it is yet encouraged by a parallel tide of growing mysticism, as developed both through the fatigued reaction of 'occultists' and religious fundamentalists against materialistic discovery and through the stimulation of wonder and fancy by such enlarged vistas and broken barriers as modern science has given us with its intra-atomic chemistry, advancing astrophysics, doctrines of relativity, and probings into biology and human thought. At the present moment the favouring forces would appear to have somewhat of an advantage; since there is unquestionably more cordiality shown toward weird writings than when, thirty years ago, the best of Arthur Machen's work fell on the stony ground of the smart and cocksure 'nineties. Ambrose Bierce, almost unknown in his own time, has now reached something like general recognition.

Startling mutations, however, are not to be looked for in either direction. In any case an approximate balance of tendencies will continue to exist; and while we may justly expect a further subtilisation of technique, we have no reason to think that the general position of the spectral in literature will be altered. It is a narrow though essential branch of human expression, and will chiefly appeal as always to a limited audience with keen special sensibilities. Whatever universal masterpiece of tomorrow may be wrought from phantasm or terror will owe its acceptance rather to a supreme workmanship than to a sympathetic theme. Yet who shall declare the dark theme a positive handicap? Radiant with beauty, the Cup of the Ptolemies was carven of onyx.

THE SIGNALMAN

Charles Dickens

[1812–1870]

'No one need wonder at the existence of a literature of cosmic fear. It has always existed, and always will exist; and no better evidence of its tenacious vigour can be cited than the impulse which now and then drives writers of totally opposite leanings to try their hands at it in isolated tales, as if to discharge from their minds certain phantasmal shapes which would otherwise haunt them . . . Dickens now rises with occasional weird bits like The Signalman, *a tale of ghastly warning conforming to a very common pattern and touched with a verisimilitude which allied it as much with the coming psychological school as with the dying Gothic school.'*

– H.P. Lovecraft

'HALLOA! BELOW THERE!'

When he heard a voice thus calling to him, he was standing at the door of his box, with a flag in his hand, furled round its short pole. One would have thought, considering the nature of the ground, that he could not have doubted from what quarter the voice came; but, instead of looking up to where I stood on the top of the steep cutting nearly over his head, he turned himself about and looked down the Line. There was something remarkable in his manner of doing so, though I could not have said, for my life, what. But, I know it was remarkable enough to attract my notice, even though his figure was foreshortened and shadowed, down in the deep trench, and mine was high above him, so steeped in the glow of an angry sunset that I had shaded my eyes with my hand before I saw him at all.

'Halloa! Below!'

From looking down the Line, he turned himself about again, and, raising his eyes, saw my figure high above him.

'Is there any path by which I can come down and speak to you?'

He looked up at me without replying, and I looked down at him without pressing him too soon with a repetition of my idle question. Just then, there came a vague vibration in the earth and air, quickly changing into a violent pulsation, and an oncoming rush that caused me to start back, as though it had force to draw me down. When such vapour as rose to my height from this rapid train had passed me and was skimming away over the landscape, I looked down again, and saw him re-furling the flag he had shown while the train went by.

I repeated my enquiry. After a pause, during which he seemed to regard me with fixed attention, he motioned with his rolled-up flag towards a point on my level, some two or three hundred yards distant. I called down to him, 'All right!' and made for that point. There, by dint of looking closely about me, I found a rough zigzag descending path notched out: which I followed.

The cutting was extremely deep, and unusually precipitate. It was made through a clammy stone that became oozier and wetter as I went down. For these reasons, I found the way long enough to give me time to recall a singular air of reluctance or compulsion with which he had pointed out the path.

When I came down low enough upon the zigzag descent, to see him again, I saw that he was standing between the rails on the way by which the train had lately passed, in an attitude as if he were waiting for me to appear. He had his left hand at his chin, and that left elbow rested on his right hand crossed over his breast. His attitude was one of such expectation and watchfulness, that I stopped a moment, wondering at it.

I resumed my downward way, and, stepping out upon the level of the railroad and drawing nearer to him, saw that he was a dark sallow man, with a dark beard and rather heavy eyebrows. His post was in as solitary and dismal a place as ever I saw. On either side, a dripping wet wall of jagged stone, excluding all view but a strip of sky; the perspective one way, only a crooked prolongation of this great dungeon; the shorter perspective in the other direction, terminating in a gloomy red light, and the gloomier entrance to a black tunnel, in whose massive architecture there was a barbarous, depressing and forbidding air. So little sunlight ever found its way to this spot, that it had an earthy, deadly smell; and so much cold wind rushed through it, that it struck chill to me, as if I had left the natural world.

Before he stirred, I was near enough to him to have touched him. Not even then removing his eyes from mine, he stepped back one step, and lifted his hand.

This was a lonesome post to occupy (I said), and it had riveted my attention when I looked down from up yonder. A visitor was a rarity, I should suppose; not an unwelcome rarity, I hoped? In me, he merely saw a man who had been shut up within narrow limits all his life, and who, being at last set free, had a newly awakened interest in these great works. To such purpose I spoke to him; but I am far from sure of the terms I used, for, besides that I am not happy in opening any conversation, there was something in the man that daunted me.

He directed a most curious look towards the red light near the tunnel's mouth, and looked all about it, as if something were missing from it, and then looked at me.

That light was part of his charge? Was it not?

He answered in a low voice: 'Don't you know it is?'

The monstrous thought came into my mind as I perused the fixed eyes and the saturnine face, that this was a spirit, not a man. I have speculated since, whether there may have been infection in his mind.

In my turn, I stepped back. But in making the action, I detected in his eyes some latent fear of me. This put the monstrous thought to flight.

'You look at me,' I said, forcing a smile, 'as if you had a dread of me.'

'I was doubtful,' he returned, 'whether I had seen you before.'

'Where?'

He pointed to the red light he had looked at.

'There?' I said.

Intently watchful of me, he replied (but without sound), 'Yes.'

'My good fellow, what should I do there? However, be that as it may, I never was there, you may swear.'

'I think I may,' he rejoined. 'Yes. I am sure I may.'

His manner cleared, like my own. He replied to my remarks with readiness, and in well chosen words. Had he much to do there? Yes; that was to say, he had enough responsibility to bear; but exactness and watchfulness were what was required of him, and of actual work – manual labour he had next to none. To change that signal, to trim those lights, and to turn this iron handle now and then, was all he had to do under that head. Regarding those many long and lonely hours of which I seemed to make so much, he could only say that the routine of his life had shaped itself into that form, and he had grown used to it. He had taught himself a language down here – if only to know it by sight, and to have formed his own crude ideas of its pronunciation, could be called learning it. He had also worked at fractions and decimals, and tried a little algebra; but he was, and had been as a boy, a poor hand at figures. Was it necessary for him when on duty, always to remain in that channel of damp air, and could he never rise into the sunshine from between those high stone walls? Why, that depended upon times and circumstances. Under some conditions there would be less upon the Line than under others, and the same held good as to certain hours of the day and night. In bright weather, he did choose occasions for getting a little above these lower shadows; but, being at all times liable to be called by his electric bell, and at such times listening for it with redoubled anxiety, the relief was less than I would suppose.

He took me into his box, where there was a fire, a desk for an official book in which he had to make certain entries, a telegraphic instrument with its dial face and needles, and the little bell of which he had spoken. On my trusting that he would excuse the remark that he had been well educated, and (I hoped I might say without offence), perhaps educated above that station, he observed that instances of slight incongruity in such-wise would rarely be found wanting among large bodies of men; that he had heard it was so in workhouses, in the police force, even in that last desperate resource, the army; and that he knew it was so, more or less, in any great railway staff. He had been, when young (if I could believe it, sitting in that hut; he scarcely could), a student of natural philosophy, and had attended lectures; but he had run wild, misused his opportunities, gone down, and never risen again. He had no complaint to offer about that. He had made his bed, and he lay upon it. It was far too late to make another.

All that I have here condensed, he said in a quiet manner, with his grave dark regards divided between me and the fire. He threw in the word 'Sir' from time to time, and especially when he referred to his youth: as though to request me to understand that he claimed to be nothing but what I found him. He was several times interrupted by the little bell, and had to read off messages, and send replies. Once, he had to stand without the door, and display a flag as a train passed, and make some verbal communication to the driver. In the discharge of his duties I observed him to be remarkably exact and vigilant, breaking off his discourse at a syllable, and remaining silent until what he had to do was done.

In a word, I should have set this man down as one of the safest of men to be employed in that capacity, but for the circumstance that while he was speaking to me he twice broke off with a fallen colour, turned his face towards the little bell when it did *not* ring, opened the door of the hut (which was kept shut to exclude the unhealthy damp), and looked out towards the red light near the mouth of the tunnel. On both those occasions, he came back to the fire with the inexplicable air upon him which I had remarked, without being able to define, when we were so far asunder.

Said I when I rose to leave him: 'You almost make me think that I have met with a contented man.'

(I am afraid I must acknowledge that I said it to lead him on.)

'I believe I used to be so,' he rejoined, in the low voice in which he had first spoken; 'but I am troubled, sir, I am troubled.'

He would have recalled the words if he could. He had said them, however, and I took them up quickly.

'With what? What is your trouble?'

'It is very difficult to impart, sir. It is very, very difficult to speak of. If ever you make me another visit, I will try to tell you.'

'But I expressly intend to make you another visit. Say, when shall it be?'

'I go off early in the morning, and I shall be on again at ten tomorrow night, sir.'

'I will come at eleven.'

He thanked me, and went out at the door with me. 'I'll show my white light, sir,' he said, in his peculiar low voice, 'till you have found the way up. When you have found it, don't call out! And when you are at the top, don't call out!'

His manner seemed to make the place strike colder to me, but I said no more than 'Very well.'

'And when you come down tomorrow night, don't call out! Let me ask you a parting question. What made you cry "Halloa! Below there!" tonight?'

'Heaven knows,' said I. 'I cried something to that effect – '

'Not to that effect, sir. Those were the very words. I know them well.'

'Admit those were the very words. I said them, no doubt, because I saw you below.'

'For no other reason?'

'What other reason could I possibly have?'

'You had no feeling that they were conveyed to you in any supernatural way?'

'No.'

He wished me goodnight, and held up his light. I walked by the side of the down Line of rails (with a very disagreeable sensation of a train coming behind me), until I found the path. It was easier to mount than to descend, and I got back to my inn without any adventure.

Punctual to my appointment, I placed my foot on the first notch of the zigzag next night, as the distant clocks were striking eleven. He was waiting for me at the bottom, with his white light on. 'I have not called out,' I said, when we came close together; 'may I speak now?' 'By all means, sir.' 'Goodnight then, and here's my hand.' 'Goodnight, sir, and here's mine.' With that, we walked side by side to his box, entered it, closed the door, and sat down by the fire.

'I have made up my mind, sir,' he began, bending forward as soon as we were seated, and speaking in a tone but a little above a whisper, 'that you shall not have to ask me twice what troubles me. I took you for someone else yesterday evening. That troubles me.'

'That mistake?'

'No. That someone else.'

'Who is it?'

'I don't know.'

'Like me?'

'I don't know. I never saw the face. The left arm is across the face, and the right arm is waved. Violently waved. This way.'

I followed his action with my eyes, and it was the action of an arm gesticulating with the utmost passion and vehemence: 'For God's sake clear the way!'

'One moonlit night,' said the man, 'I was sitting here, when I heard a voice cry "Halloa! Below there!" I stared up, looked from that door, and saw this someone else standing by the red light near the tunnel, waving as I just now showed you. The voice seemed hoarse with shouting, and it cried, "Look out! Look out!" And then again "Halloa! Below there! Look out!" I caught up my lamp, turned it on red, and ran towards the figure, calling, "What's wrong? What has happened? Where?" It stood just outside the blackness of the tunnel. I

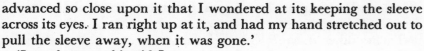

advanced so close upon it that I wondered at its keeping the sleeve across its eyes. I ran right up at it, and had my hand stretched out to pull the sleeve away, when it was gone.'

'Into the tunnel,' said I.

'No. I ran on into the tunnel, five hundred yards. I stopped and held my lamp above my head, and saw the figures of the measured distance, and saw the wet stains stealing down the walls and trickling through the arch. I ran out again, faster than I had run in (for I had a mortal abhorrence of the place upon me), and I looked all round the red light with my own red light, and I went up the iron ladder to the gallery atop of it, and I came down again, and ran back here. I telegraphed both ways, "An alarm has been given. Is anything wrong?" The answer came back, both ways: "All well." '

Resisting the slow touch of a frozen finger tracing out my spine, I showed him how that this figure must be a deception of his sense of sight, and how that figures, originating in disease of the delicate nerves that minister to the functions of the eye, were known to have often troubled patients, some of whom had become conscious of the nature of their affliction, and had even proved it by experiments upon themselves. 'As to an imaginary cry,' said I, 'do but listen for a moment to the wind in this unnatural valley while we speak so low, and to the wild harp it makes of the telegraph wires!'

That was all very well, he returned, after we had sat listening for a while, and he ought to know something of the wind and the wires, he who so often passed long winter nights there, alone and watching. But he would beg to remark that he had not finished.

I asked his pardon, and he slowly added these words, touching my arm:

'Within six hours after the appearance, the memorable accident on this Line happened, and within ten hours the dead and wounded were brought along through the tunnel over the spot where the figure had stood.'

A disagreeable shudder crept over me, but I did my best against it. It was not to be denied, I rejoined, that this was a remarkable coincidence, calculated deeply to impress his mind. But it was unquestionable that remarkable coincidences did continually occur, and they must be taken into account in dealing with such a subject. Though to be sure I must admit, I added (for I thought I saw that he was going to bring the objection to bear upon me), men of common sense did not allow much for coincidences in making the ordinary calculations of life.

He again begged to remark that he had not finished.

I again begged his pardon for being betrayed into interruptions.

'This,' he said, again laying his hand upon my arm, and glancing over his shoulder with hollow eyes, 'was just a year ago. Six or seven months passed, and I had recovered from the surprise and shock, when one morning, as the day was breaking, I, standing at that door, looked towards the red light, and saw the spectre again.' He stopped, with a fixed look at me.

'Did it cry out?'

'No. It was silent.'

'Did it wave its arm?'

'No. It leaned against the shaft of the light, with both hands before the face. Like this.'

Once more, I followed his action with my eyes. It was an action of mourning. I have seen such an attitude in stone figures on tombs.

'Did you go up to it?'

'I came in and sat down, partly to collect my thoughts, partly because it had turned me faint. When I went to the door again, daylight was above me, and the ghost was gone.'

'But nothing followed? Nothing came of this?'

He touched me on the arm with his forefinger twice or thrice, giving a ghastly nod each time:

'That very day, as a train came out of the tunnel, I noticed, at a carriage window on my side, what looked like a confusion of hands and heads, and something waved. I saw it, just in time to signal the driver, Stop! He shut off, and put his brake on, but the train drifted past here a hundred and fifty yards or more. I ran after it, and, as I went along, heard terrible screams and cries. A beautiful young lady had died instantaneously in one of the compartments, and was brought in here, and laid down on this floor between us.'

Involuntarily, I pushed my chair back, as I looked from the boards at which he pointed, to himself.

'True, sir. True. Precisely as it happened, so I tell it you.'

I could think of nothing to say, to any purpose, and my mouth was very dry. The wind and the wires took up the story with a long lamenting wail.

He resumed. 'Now, sir, mark this, and judge how my mind is troubled. The spectre came back, a week ago. Ever since, it has been there, now and again, by fits and starts.'

'At the light?'

'At the Danger-light.'

'What does it seem to do?'

He repeated, if possible with increased passion and vehemence, that former gesticulation of 'For God's sake clear the way!'

Then, he went on. 'I have no peace or rest for it. It calls to me for many minutes together, in an agonized manner, "Below there! Look out! Look out!" It stands waving to me. It rings my little bell – '

I caught at that. 'Did it ring your bell yesterday evening when I was here, and you went to the door?'

'Twice.'

'Why, see,' said I, 'how your imagination misleads you. My eyes were on the bell, and my ears were open to the bell, and if I am a living man, it did *not* ring at those times. No, nor at any other time, except when it was rung in the natural course of physical things by the station communicating with you.'

He shook his head. 'I have never made a mistake as to that, yet, sir. I have never confused the spectre's ring with the man's. The ghost's ring is a strange vibration in the bell that it derives from nothing else, and I have not asserted that the bell stirs to the eye. I don't wonder that you failed to hear it. But *I* heard it.'

'And did the spectre seem to be there, when you looked out?'

'It was there.'

'Both times?'

He repeated firmly: 'Both times.'

'Will you come to·the door with me, and look for it now?'

He bit his underlip as though he were somewhat unwilling, but arose. I opened the door, and stood on the step, while he stood in the doorway. There, was the Danger-light. There, was the dismal mouth of the tunnel. There, were the high wet stone walls of the cutting. There, were the stars above them.

'Do you see it?' I asked him, taking particular note of his face. His eyes were prominent and strained; but not very much more so, perhaps, than my own had been when I had directed them earnestly towards the same spot.

'No,' he answered. 'It is not there.'

'Agreed,' said I.

We went in again, shut the door, and resumed our seats. I was thinking how best to improve this advantage, if it might be called one, when he took up the conversation in such a matter of course way, so assuming that there could be no serious question of fact between us, that I felt myself placed in the weakest of positions.

'By this time you will fully understand, sir,' he said, 'that what troubles me so dreadfully, is the question, What does the spectre mean?'

I was not sure, I told him, that I did fully understand.

'What is its warning against?' he said, ruminating, with his eyes on the fire, and only by times turning them on me. 'What is the danger? Where is the danger? There is danger overhanging, somewhere on the Line. Some dreadful calamity will happen. It is not to be doubted this third time, after what has gone before. But surely this is a cruel haunting of *me*. What can I do?'

He pulled out his handkerchief, and wiped the drops from his heated forehead.

'If I telegraph Danger, on either side of me, or on both, I can give no reason for it,' he went on, wiping the palms of his hands. 'I should get into trouble, and do no good. They would think I was mad. This is the way it would work: Message: "Danger! Take care!" Answer: "What danger? Where?" Message: "Don't know. But for God's sake take care!" They would displace me. What else could they do?'

His pain of mind was most pitiable to see. It was the mental torture of a conscientious man, oppressed beyond endurance by an unintelligible responsibility involving life.

'When it first stood under the Danger-light,' he went on, putting his dark hair back from his head, and drawing his hands outwards across and across his temples in an extremity of feverish distress, 'why not tell me where that accident was to happen – if it must happen? Why not tell me how it could be averted – if it could have been averted? When on its second coming it hid its face, why not tell me instead: "She is going to die. Let them keep her at home"? If it came, on those two occasions, only to show me that its warnings were true, and so to prepare me for the third, why not warn me plainly now? And I, Lord help me! A mere poor signalman on this solitary station! Why not go to somebody with credit to be believed, and power to act!'

When I saw him in this state, I saw that for the poor man's sake, as well as for the public safety, what I had to do for the time was, to compose his mind. Therefore, setting aside all question of reality or unreality between us, I represented to him that whoever thoroughly discharged his duty, must do well, and that at least it was his comfort that he understood his duty, though he did not understand these confounding appearances. In this effort I succeeded far better than in the attempt to reason him out of his conviction. He became calm; the occupations incidental to his post as the night advanced, began to make larger demands on his attention; and I left him at two in the morning. I had offered to stay through the night, but he would not hear of it.

That I more than once looked back at the red light as I ascended the pathway, that I did not like the red light, and that I should have slept but poorly if my bed had been under it, I see no reason to conceal. Nor did I like the two sequences of the accident and the dead girl. I see no reason to conceal that, either.

But, what ran most in my thoughts was the consideration how ought I to act, having become the recipient of this disclosure? I had proved the man to be intelligent, vigilant, painstaking and exact; but how long might he remain so, in his state of mind? Though in a subordinate position, still he held a most important trust, and would I (for instance) like to stake my own life on the chances of his continuing to execute it with precision?

Unable to overcome a feeling that there would be something treacherous in my communicating what he had told me to his superiors in the company, without first being plain with himself and proposing a middle course to him, I ultimately resolved to offer to accompany him (otherwise keeping his secret for the present) to the wisest medical practitioner we could hear of in those parts, and to take his opinion. A change in his time of duty would come round next night, he had apprised me, and he would be off an hour or two after sunrise, and on again soon after sunset. I had appointed to return accordingly.

Next evening was a lovely evening, and I walked out early to enjoy it. The sun was not yet quite down when I traversed the field-path near the top of the deep cutting. I would extend my walk for an hour, I said to myself, half an hour on and half an hour back, and it would then be time to go to my signalman's box.

Before pursuing my stroll, I stepped to the brink, and mechanically looked down, from the point from which I had first seen him. I cannot describe the thrill that seized upon me, when, close at the mouth of the tunnel, I saw the appearance of a man, with his left sleeve across his eyes, passionately waving his right arm.

The nameless horror that oppressed me, passed in a moment, for in a moment I saw that this appearance of a man was a man indeed, and that there was a little group of other men standing at a short distance, to whom he seemed to be rehearsing the gesture he made. The Danger-light was not yet lighted. Against its shaft, a little low hut, entirely new to me, had been made of some wooden supports and tarpaulin. It looked no bigger than a bed.

With an irresistible sense that something was wrong – with a flashing self-reproachful fear that fatal mischief had come of my leaving the man there, and causing no one to be sent to overlook or correct what he did – I descended the notched path with all the speed I could make.

'What is the matter?' I asked the men.

'Signalman killed this morning, sir.'

'Not the man belonging to that box?'

'Yes, sir.'

'Not the man I know?'

'You will recognize him, sir, if you knew him,' said the man who spoke for the others, solemnly uncovering his own head and raising an end of the tarpaulin, 'for his face is quite composed.'

'O! how did this happen, how did this happen?' I asked, turning from one to another as the hut closed in again.

'He was cut down by an engine, sir. No man in England knew his work better. But somehow he was not clear of the outer rail. It was just at broad day. He had struck the light, and had the lamp in his hand. As the engine came out of the tunnel, his back was towards her, and she cut him down. That man drove her, and was showing how it happened. Show the gentleman, Tom.'

The man who wore a rough dark dress, stepped back to his former place at the mouth of the tunnel!

'Coming round the curve in the tunnel, sir,' he said, 'I saw him at the end, like as if I saw him down a perspective-glass. There was no time to check speed, and I knew him to be very careful. As he didn't seem to take heed of the whistle, I shut it off when we were running down upon him, and called to him as loud as I could call.'

'What did you say?'

'I said, Below there! Look out! Look out! For God's sake clear the way!'

I started.

'Ah! it was a dreadful time, sir. I never left off calling to him. I put this arm before my eyes, not to see, and I waved this arm to the last; but it was no use.'

Without prolonging the narrative to dwell on any one of its curious circumstances more than on any other, I may, in closing it, point out the coincidence that the warning of the engine-driver included, not only the words which the unfortunate signalman had repeated to me as haunting him, but also the words which I myself – not he – had attached, and that only in my own mind, to the gesticulation he had imitated.

THE HOUSE AND THE BRAIN

Edward Bulwer-Lytton

[1803–1873]

'*At this time a wave of interest in spiritualistic charlatanry, mediumism, Hindoo theosophy, and such matters, much like that of the present day, was flourishing; so that the number of weird tales with a "psychic" or pseudo-scientific basis became very considerable. For a number of these the prolific and popular Edward Bulwer-Lytton was responsible; and despite the large doses of turgid rhetoric and empty romanticism in his products, his success in the weaving of a certain kind of bizarre charm cannot be denied.*

'The House and the Brain, *which hints of Rosicrucianism and at a malign and deathless figure perhaps suggested by Louis XV's mysterious courtier St. Germain, yet survives as one of the best short haunted-house tales ever written.*'

– H.P. Lovecraft

A FRIEND OF MINE, who is a man of letters and a philosopher, said to me one day, as if between jest and earnest, 'Fancy! since we last met I have discovered a haunted house in the midst of London.'

'Really haunted? and by what – ghosts?'

'Well, I can't answer these questions; all I know is this: six weeks ago I and my wife were in search of a furnished apartment. Passing a quiet street, we saw on the window of one of the houses a bill, "Apartments Furnished." The situation suited us; we entered the house, liked the rooms, engaged them by the week, and left them the third day. No power on earth could have reconciled my wife to stay longer; and I don't wonder at it.'

'What did you see?'

'Excuse me; I have no desire to be ridiculed as a superstitious dreamer, nor, on the other hand, could I ask you to accept on my affirmation what you would hold to be incredible, without the evidence of your own senses. Let me only say this: it was not so much what we saw or heard (in which you might fairly suppose that we were the dupes of our own excited fancy, or the victims of imposture in others) that drove us away, as it was an undefinable terror which seized both of us whenever we passed by the door of a certain unfurnished room, in which we neither saw nor heard anything; and the strangest marvel of all was that for once in my life I agreed with my wife, silly woman though she be, and allowed after the third night that it was impossible to stay a fourth in that house.

'Accordingly, on the fourth morning I summoned the woman who kept the house and attended on us, and told her that the rooms did not quite suit us, and we would not stay out our week. She said dryly:

' "I know why; you have stayed longer than any other lodger. Few ever stayed a second night; none before you a third. But I take it that they have been very kind to you.'

' "They – who?" I asked, affecting a smile.

' "Why, they who haunt the house, whoever they are; I don't mind them; I remember them many years ago, when I lived in this house not as a servant; but I know they will be the death of me some day. I don't care – I'm old and must die soon anyhow; and then I shall be with them, and in this house still.'

'The woman spoke with so dreary a calmness that really it was a sort of awe that prevented my conversing with her further. I paid for my week, and too happy were I and my wife to get off so cheaply.'

'You excite my curiosity,' said I; 'nothing I should like better than to sleep in a haunted house. Pray give me the address of the one which you left so ignominiously.'

My friend gave me the address; and when we parted I walked straight towards the house thus indicated.

It is situated on the north side of Oxford Street, in a dull but respectable thoroughfare. I found the house shut up; no bill on the window, and no response to my knock. As I was turning away, a beer-boy, collecting pewter pots at the neighbouring areas, said to me, 'Do you want anyone at that house, sir?'

'Yes; I heard it was to be let.'

'Let! Why, the woman who kept it is dead; has been dead these three weeks; and no one can be found to stay there, though Mr. J— offered ever so much. He offered mother, who chars for him, one pound a week just to open and shut the windows, and she would not.'

'Would not! and why?'

'The house is haunted; and the old woman who kept it was found dead in her bed with her eyes wide open. They say the devil strangled her.'

'Pooh! You speak of Mr. J—. Is he the owner of the house?'

'Yes.'

'Where does he live?'

'In G— Street, No.— '

'What is he – in any business?'

'No, sir, nothing particular; a single gentleman.'

I gave the pot-boy the gratuity earned by his liberal information, and proceeded to Mr. J— in G— Street, which was close by the street that boasted the haunted house. I was lucky enough to find Mr. J— at home; an elderly man with intelligent countenance and prepossessing manners.

I communicated my name and my business frankly. I said I heard the house was considered to be haunted; that I had a strong desire to examine a house with so equivocal a reputation; that I should be greatly obliged if he would allow me to hire it, though only for a night. I was willing to pay for that privilege whatever he might be inclined to ask.

'Sir,' said Mr. J—, with great courtesy, 'the house is at your service for as short or as long a time as you please. Rent is out of the question; the obligation will be on my side, should you be able to discover the cause of the strange phenomena which at present deprive it of all value. I cannot let it, for I cannot even get a servant to keep it in order or answer the door.

'Unluckily, the house is haunted, if I may use that expression, not only by night but by day; though at night the disturbances are of a more unpleasant and sometimes of a more alarming character. The poor old woman who died in it three weeks ago was a pauper whom I took out of a workhouse; for in her childhood she had been known to some of my family, and had once been in such good circumstances that she had rented that house of my uncle. She was a woman of superior education and strong mind, and was the only person I could ever induce to remain in the house. Indeed, since her death, which was sudden, and the coroner's inquest, which gave it a notoriety in the neighbourhood, I have so despaired of finding any person to take charge of it, much more a tenant, that I would most willingly let it rent free for a year to anyone who would pay its rates and taxes.'

'How long ago did the house acquire this character?'

'That I can scarcely tell you, but many years since; the old woman I spoke of said it was haunted when she rented it, between thirty and forty years ago. The fact is that my life has been spent in the East Indies, and in the civil service of the East India Company.

'I returned to England last year, on inheriting the fortune of an uncle, among whose possessions was the house in question. I found it shut up and uninhabited. I was told that it was haunted, and no one would inhabit it. I smiled at what seemed to me so idle a story.

'I spent some money in repainting and roofing it, added to its old-fashioned furniture a few modern articles, advertised it, and obtained a lodger for a year. He was a colonel retired on half pay. He came in with his family, a son and a daughter, and four or five servants; they all left the house the next day; and although they deponed that they had all seen something different, that something was equally terrible to all. I really could not in conscience sue, or even blame, the colonel for breach of agreement.

'Then I put in the old woman I have spoken of, and she was empowered to let the house in apartments. I never had one lodger who stayed more than three days. I do not tell you their stories; to no two lodgers have exactly the same phenomena been repeated. It is better that you should judge for yourself than enter the house with an imagination influenced by previous narratives; only be prepared to see and to hear something or other, and take whatever precautions you yourself please.'

'Have you never had a curiosity yourself to pass a night in that house?'

'Yes; I passed, not a night, but three hours in broad daylight alone in that house. My curiosity is not satisfied, but it is quenched. I have no desire to renew the experiment. You cannot complain, you see, sir, that I am not sufficiently candid; and unless your interest be exceedingly eager and your nerves unusually strong, I honestly add that I advise you *not* to pass a night in that house.'

'My interest *is* exceedingly keen,' said I; 'and though only a coward will boast of his nerves in situations wholly unfamiliar to him, yet my nerves have been seasoned in such variety of danger that I have the right to rely on them, even in a haunted house.'

Mr. J— said very little more; he took the keys of the house out of his bureau, and gave them to me; and, thanking him cordially for his frankness and his urbane concession to my wish, I carried off my prize.

Impatient for the experiment, as soon as I reached home I summoned my confidential servant – a young man of gay spirits, fearless temper, and as free from superstitious prejudice as anyone I could think of.

'F—,' said I, 'you remember in Germany how disappointed we were at not finding a ghost in that old castle which was said to be haunted by a headless apparition? Well, I have heard of a house in London which, I have reason to hope, is decidedly haunted. I mean to sleep there to-night. From what I hear, there is no doubt that something will allow itself to be seen or to be heard – something perhaps excessively horrible. Do you think, if I take you with me, I may rely on your presence of mind, whatever may happen?'

'Oh, sir; pray trust me!' said he, grinning with delight.

'Very well, then, here are the keys of the house; this is the address. Go now, select for me any bedroom you please; and since the house has not been inhabited for weeks, make up a good fire, air the bed well; see, of course, that there are candles as well as fuel. Take with you my revolver and my dagger – so much for my weapons – arm yourself equally well; and if we are not a match for a dozen ghosts, we shall be but a sorry couple of Englishmen.'

I was engaged for the rest of the day on business so urgent that I had not leisure to think much on the nocturnal adventure to which I had plighted my honour. I dined alone and very late, and while dining read, as is my habit. The volume I selected was one of Macaulay's essays. I thought to myself that I would take the book with me; there was so much of healthfulness in the style, and practical life in the subjects, that it would serve as an antidote against the influences of superstitious fancy.

Accordingly, about half-past nine I put the book into my pocket and strolled leisurely towards the haunted house. I took with me a favourite dog – an exceedingly sharp, bold, and vigilant bull-terrier, a dog fond of prowling about strange ghostly corners and passages at night in search of rats, a dog of dogs for a ghost.

It was a summer night, but chilly, the sky somewhat gloomy and overcast; still there was a moon – faint and sickly, but still a moon – and if the clouds permitted, after midnight it would be brighter.

I reached the house, knocked, and my servant opened with a cheerful smile.

'All right, sir, and very comfortable.'

'Oh!' said I, rather disappointed; 'have you not seen nor heard anything remarkable?'

'Well, sir, I must own that I have heard something queer.'

'What? – what?'

'The sound of feet pattering behind me; and once or twice small noises like whispers close at my ear; nothing more.'

'You are not at all frightened?'

'I! Not a bit of it, sir!'

And the man's bold look reassured me on one point, namely, that, happen what might, he would not desert me.

We were in the hall, the street door closed, and my attention was now drawn to my dog. He had at first run in eagerly enough, but had sneaked back to the door, and was scratching and whining to get out. After I had patted him on the head and encouraged him gently, the dog seemed to reconcile himself to the situation, and followed me and F— through the house, but keeping close at my heels, instead of hurrying inquisitively in advance, which was his usual and normal habit in all strange places.

We first visited the subterranean apartments, the kitchen and other offices, and especially the cellars, in which last were two or three bottles of wine still left in a bin, covered with cobwebs, and evidently, by their appearance, undisturbed for many years. It was clear that the ghosts were not wine-bibbers.

For the rest, we discovered nothing of interest. There was a gloomy little back yard, with very high walls. The stones of this yard were very damp; and what with the damp and what with the dust and smoke-grime on the pavement, our feet left a slight impression where we passed.

And now appeared the first strange phenomenon witnessed by myself in this strange abode.

I saw, just before me, the print of a foot suddenly form itself, as it were. I stopped, caught hold of my servant, and pointed to it. In advance of that footprint as suddenly dropped another. We both saw it. I advanced quickly to the place; the footprint kept advancing before me; a small footprint – the foot of a child; the impression was too faint thoroughly to distinguish the shape, but it seemed to us both that it was the print of a naked foot.

This phenomenon ceased when we arrived at the opposite wall, nor did it repeat itself when we returned. We remounted the stairs and entered the rooms on the ground floor – a dining-parlour, a small back-parlour, and a still smaller third room that had probably been appropriated to a footman – all still as death.

We then visited the drawing-rooms, which seemed fresh and new. In the front room I seated myself in an arm-chair. F— placed on the table the candlestick with which he had lighted us. I told him to shut the door. As he turned to do so, a chair opposite to me moved from the wall quickly and noiselessly, and dropped itself about a yard from my own chair, immediately fronting it.

'Why, this is better than the turning-tables,' said I, laughing; and as I laughed, my dog put back his head and howled.

F—, coming back, had not observed the movement of the chair. He employed himself now in stilling the dog. I continued to gaze on the chair, and fancied I saw on it a pale, blue, misty outline of a human figure; but an outline so indistinct that I could only distrust my own vision. The dog was now quiet.

'Put back the chair opposite to me,' said I to F—; 'put it back to the wall.'

F— obeyed.

'Was that you, sir?' said he, turning abruptly.

'I – what?'

'Why, something struck me. I felt it sharply on the shoulder, just here.'

'No,' said I; 'but we have jugglers present, and though we may not discover their tricks, we shall catch *them* before they frighten *us*.'

We did not stay long in the drawing-rooms; in fact, they felt so damp and so chilly that I was glad to get to the fire upstairs. We locked the doors of the drawing-rooms – a precaution which, I should observe, we had taken with all the rooms we had searched below.

The bedroom my servant had selected for me was the best on the floor; a large one, with two windows fronting the street. The four-posted bedstead, which took up no inconsiderable space, was opposite to the fire, which burned clear and bright; a door in the wall to the left, between the bed and the window, communicated with the room which my servant appropriated to himself. This last was a small room with a sofa-bed, and had no communication with the landing-place; no other door but that which conducted to the bedroom I was to occupy.

On either side of my fireplace was a cupboard, without locks, flush with the wall, and covered with the same dull-brown paper. We examined these cupboards; only hooks to suspend female dresses – nothing else. We sounded the walls; evidently solid – the outer walls of the building.

Having finished the survey of these apartments, warmed myself a few moments, and lighted my cigar, I then, still accompanied by F—, went forth to complete my reconnoitre. In the landing-place there was another door; it was closed firmly.

'Sir,' said my servant in surprise, 'I unlocked this door with all the others when I first came in; it cannot have got locked from the inside, for it is a – '

Before he had finished his sentence, the door, which neither of us was then touching, opened quietly of itself. We looked at each other a single instant. The same thought seized both: some human agency might be detected here. I rushed in first, my servant followed. A small, blank, dreary room without furniture, a few empty boxes and hampers in a corner, a small window, the shutters closed – not even a fireplace – no other door but that by which we had entered, no carpet on the floor, and the floor seemed very old, uneven, wormeaten, mended here and there, as was shown by the whiter patches on the wood; but no living being, and no visible place in which a living being could have hidden.

As we stood gazing round, the door by which we had entered closed as quietly as it had before opened; we were imprisoned.

For the first time I felt a creep of undefinable horror. Not so my servant.

'Why, they don't think to trap us, sir; I could break that trumpery door with a kick of my foot.'

'Try first if it will open to your hand,' said I, shaking off the vague apprehension that had seized me, 'while I open the shutters and see what is without.'

I unbarred the shutters; the window looked on the little back yard I have before described; there was no ledge without, nothing but sheer descent. No man getting out of that window would have found any footing till he had fallen on the stones below.

F— meanwhile was vainly attempting to open the door. He now turned round to me and asked my permission to use force. And I should here state, in justice to the servant, that, far from evincing any superstitious terror, his nerve, composure, and even gaiety amid circumstances so extraordinary, compelled my admiration and made me congratulate myself on having secured a companion in every way fitted to the occasion. I willingly gave him the permission he required.

But, though he was a remarkably strong man, his force was as idle as his milder efforts; the door did not even shake to his stoutest kick.

Breathless and panting, he desisted. I then tried the door myself, equally in vain. As I ceased from the effort, again that creep of horror came over me; but this time it was more cold and stubborn, I felt as if some strange and ghastly exhalation were rising from the chinks of that rugged floor and filling the atmosphere with a venomous influence hostile to human life.

The door now very slowly and quietly opened as of its own accord. We precipitated ourselves on to the landing-place. We both saw a large, pale light – as large as the human figure, but shapeless and unsubstantial – move before us and ascend the stairs that led from the landing into the attics.

I followed the light, and my servant followed me. It entered, to the right of the landing, a small garret, of which the door stood open. I entered in the same instant. The light then collapsed into a small globule, exceedingly brilliant and vivid; rested a moment on a bed in the corner, quivered, and vanished.

We approached the bed and examined it – a half-tester, such as is commonly found in attics devoted to servants. On the drawers that stood near it we perceived an old faded silk kerchief, with the needle still left in the rent half repaired. The kerchief was covered with dust; probably it had belonged to the old woman who had last died there, and this might have been her sleeping-room.

I had sufficient curiosity to open the drawers; there were a few odds and ends of female dress, and two letters tied round with a narrow ribbon of faded yellow. I took the liberty to possess myself of the letters. We found nothing else in the room worth noticing, nor did the light reappear; but we distinctly heard, as we turned to go, a pattering footfall on the floor just before us.

We went through the other attics (in all four), the footfall still preceding us. Nothing to be seen, nothing but the footfall heard. I had the letters in my hand; just as I was descending the stairs I distinctly felt my wrist seized, and a faint, soft effort made to draw the letters from my clasp. I only held them the more tightly, and the effort ceased.

We regained the bedchamber appropriated to myself, and I then remarked that my dog had not followed us when we had left it. He was thrusting himself close to the fire and trembling. I was impatient to examine the letters; and while I read them my servant opened a little box in which he had deposited the weapons I had ordered him to bring, took them out, placed them on a table close at my bed-head,

and then occupied himself in soothing the dog, who, however, seemed
to heed him very little.

The letters were short; they were dated – the dates exactly thirty-
five years ago. They were evidently from a lover to his mistress, or a
husband to some young wife. Not only the terms of expression, but a
distinct reference to a former voyage indicated the writer to have been
a seafarer. The spelling and handwriting were those of a man
imperfectly educated; but still the language itself was forcible. In
the expressions of endearment there was a kind of rough, wild love;
but here and there were dark, unintelligible hints at some secret not of
love – some secret that seemed of crime.

'We ought to love each other,' was one of the sentences I remember,
'for how everyone else would execrate us if all was known.'

Again: 'Don't let anyone be in the same room with you at night –
you talk in your sleep.'

And again: 'What's done can't be undone; and I tell you there's
nothing against us, unless the dead should come to life.'

Here was interlined, in a better handwriting (a female's), 'They do!'

At the end of the letter latest in date the same female hand had
written these words:

'Lost at sea the 4th of June, the same day as – '

I put down the letters, and began to muse over their contents.

Fearing, however, that the train of thought into which I fell might
unsteady my nerves, I fully determined to keep my mind in a fit state
to cope with whatever of the marvellous the advancing night might
bring forth. I roused myself, laid the letters on the table, stirred up the
fire, which was still bright and cheering, and opened my volume of
Macaulay.

I read quietly enough till about half-past eleven. I then threw
myself dressed upon the bed, and told my servant he might retire to
his own room, but must keep himself awake. I bade him leave open
the doors between the two rooms. Thus alone I kept two candles
burning on the table by my bed-head. I placed my watch beside the
weapons, and calmly resumed my Macaulay. Opposite to me the fire
burned clear, and on the hearth-rug, seemingly asleep, lay the dog. In
about twenty minutes I felt an exceedingly cold air pass by my cheek,
like a sudden draught. I fancied the door to my right, communicating
with the landing-place, must have got open; but no, it was closed.

I then turned my glance to the left, and saw the flames of the
candles violently swayed as by a wind. At the same moment the watch
beside the revolver softly slid from the table – softly, softly – no visible

hand – it was gone. I sprang up, seizing the revolver with the one hand, the dagger with the other: I was not willing that my weapons should share the fate of the watch.

Thus armed, I looked round the floor: no sign of the watch. Three slow, loud, distinct knocks were now heard at the bed-head; my servant called out:

'Is that you, sir?'

'No; be on your guard.'

The dog now roused himself and sat on his haunches, his ears moving quickly backward and forward. He kept his eyes fixed on me with a look so strange that he concentred all my attention on himself. Slowly he rose, all his hair bristling, and stood perfectly rigid, and with the same wild stare.

I had no time, however, to examine the dog. Presently my servant emerged from his room; and if I ever saw horror in the human face, it was then. I should not have recognized him had we met in the streets, so altered was every lineament. He passed by me quickly, saying, in a whisper that seemed scarcely to come from his lips:

'Run! run! It is after me!'

He gained the door to the landing, pulled it open, and rushed forth. I followed him on to the landing involuntarily, calling him to stop; but, without heeding me, he bounded down the stairs, clinging to the balusters and taking several steps at a time. I heard, where I stood, the street door open, heard it again clap to.

I was left alone in the haunted house.

It was but for a moment that I remained undecided whether or not to follow my servant; pride and curiosity alike forbade so dastardly a flight. I re-entered my room, closing the door after me, and proceeded cautiously into the interior chamber. I encountered nothing to justify my servant's terror.

I again carefully examined the walls to see if there were any concealed door. I could find no trace of one – not even a seam in the dull-brown paper with which the room was hung. How then had the THING, whatever it was, which had so scared him, obtained ingress, except through my own chamber?

I returned to my room, shut and locked the door that opened upon the interior one, and stood on the hearth, expectant and prepared.

I now perceived that the dog had slunk into an angle of the wall, and was pressing close against it, as if literally striving to force his way into it. I approached the animal and spoke to it; the poor brute was evidently beside itself with terror. It showed all its teeth, the slaver dropping from its jaws, and would certainly have bitten me if I had touched it. It did not seem to recognize me. Whoever has seen at the Zoological Gardens a rabbit fascinated by a serpent, cowering in a corner, may form some idea of the anguish which the dog exhibited.

Finding all efforts to soothe the animal in vain, and fearing that his bite might be as venomous in that state as if in the madness of hydrophobia, I left him alone, placed my weapons on the table beside the fire, seated myself, and recommenced my Macaulay.

Perhaps, in order not to appear seeking credit for a courage, or rather a coolness, which the reader may conceive I exaggerate, I may be pardoned if I pause to indulge in one or two egotistical remarks.

As I hold presence of mind, or what is called courage, to be precisely proportioned to familiarity with the circumstances that lead to it, so I should say that I had been long sufficiently familiar with all experiments that appertain to the marvellous. I had witnessed many very extraordinary phenomena in various parts of the world – phenomena that would be either totally disbelieved if I stated them, or ascribed to supernatural agencies.

Now, my theory is that the supernatural is the impossible, and that what is called supernatural is only a something in the laws of nature of which we have been hitherto ignorant. Therefore, if a ghost rise before me, I have not the right to say, 'So, then, the supernatural is possible,' but rather, 'So, then, the apparition of a ghost is, contrary to received opinion, within the laws of nature, namely, not supernatural.'

Now, in all that I had hitherto witnessed, and indeed in all the wonders which the amateurs of mystery in our age record as facts, a material living agency is always required. On the Continent you will still find magicians who assert that they can raise spirits. Assume for a moment that they assert truly, still the living material form of the magician is present; he is the material agency by which, from some constitutional peculiarities, certain strange phenomena are represented to your natural senses.

Accept, again, as truthful the tales of spirit manifestation in America – musical or other sounds, writings on paper, produced by no discernible hand, articles of furniture moved without apparent human agency, or the actual sight and touch of hands, to which no bodies seem to belong – still there must be found the medium, or living being, with constitutional peculiarities capable of obtaining these signs.

In fine, in all such marvels, supposing even that there is no imposture, there must be a human being like ourselves, by whom or through whom the effects presented to human beings are produced.

It is so with the now familiar phenomena of mesmerism or electro-biology; the mind of the person operated on is affected through a material living agent.

Nor, supposing it true that a mesmerized patient can respond to the will or passes of a mesmerizer a hundred miles distant, is the response less occasioned by a material being. It may be through a material fluid, call it Electric, call it Odic, call it what you will, which has the power of traversing space and passing obstacles, that the material effect is communicated from one to the other.

Hence, all that I had hitherto witnessed, or expected to witness, in this strange house, I believed to be occasioned through some agency or medium as mortal as myself; and this idea necessarily prevented the awe with which those who regard as supernatural things that are not within the ordinary operations of nature might have been impressed by the adventures of that memorable night.

As, then, it was my conjecture that all that was presented, or would be presented, to my senses, must originate in some human being gifted by constitution with the power so to present them, and having some motive so to do, I felt an interest in my theory which, in its way, was rather philosophical than superstitious. And I can sincerely say that I was in as tranquil a temper for observation as any practical experi-mentalist could be in awaiting the effects of some rare though perhaps perilous chemical combination. Of course, the more I kept my mind detached from fancy the more the temper fitted for observation would be obtained; and I therefore riveted eye and thought on the strong daylight sense in the page of my Macaulay.

I now became aware that something interposed between the page and the light: the page was overshadowed. I looked up and saw what I shall find very difficult, perhaps impossible, to describe.

It was a darkness shaping itself out of the air in very undefined outline. I cannot say it was of a human form, and yet it had more of a resemblance to a human form, or rather shadow, than anything else. As it stood, wholly apart and distinct from the air and the light around it, its dimensions seemed gigantic; the summit nearly touched the ceiling.

While I gazed, a feeling of intense cold seized me. An iceberg before me could not more have chilled me; nor could the cold of an iceberg have been more purely physical. I feel convinced that it was not the cold caused by fear. As I continued to gaze, I thought – but this I cannot say with precision – that I distinguished two eyes looking down on me from the height. One moment I seemed to distinguish them clearly, the next they seemed gone; but two rays of a pale, blue light frequently shot through the darkness, as from the height on which I half believed, half doubted, that I had encountered the eyes.

I strove to speak; my voice utterly failed me. I could only think to myself, 'Is this fear? it is *not* fear!' I strove to rise, in vain; I felt as weighed down by an irresistible force. Indeed, my impression was that of an immense and overwhelming power opposed to my volition; that sense of utter inadequacy to cope with a force beyond man's, which one may feel *physically* in a storm at sea, in a conflagration, or when confronting some terrible wild beast, or rather, perhaps, the shark of the ocean, I felt *morally*. Opposed to my will was another will, as far superior to its strength as storm, fire, and shark are superior in material force to the force of man.

And now, as this impression grew on me, now came, at last, horror – horror to a degree that no words can convey. Still I retained pride, if not courage; and in my own mind I said, 'This is horror, but it is not fear; unless I fear, I cannot be harmed; my reason rejects this thing; it is an illusion, I do not fear.'

With a violent effort I succeeded at last in stretching out my hand towards the weapon on the table; as I did so, on the arm and shoulder I received a strange shock, and my arm fell to my side powerless. And now, to add to my horror, the light began slowly to wane from the candles; they were not, as it were, extinguished, but their flame seemed very gradually withdrawn; it was the same with the fire, the light was extracted from the fuel; in a few minutes the room was in utter darkness.

The dread that came over me to be thus in the dark with that dark thing, whose power was so intensely felt, brought a reaction of nerve. In fact, terror had reached that climax that either my senses must have deserted me, or I must have burst through the spell.

I did burst through it.

I found voice, though the voice was a shriek. I remember that I broke forth with words like these, 'I do not fear, my soul does not fear'; and at the same time I found strength to rise.

Still in that profound gloom, I rushed to one of the windows, tore aside the curtain, flung open the shutters; my first thought was, LIGHT.

And when I saw the moon, high, clear, and calm, I felt a joy that almost compensated for the previous terror. There was the moon, there was also the light from the gas-lamps in the deserted, slumberous street. I turned to look back into the room; the moon penetrated its shadow very palely and partially, but still there was light. The dark thing, whatever it might be, was gone; except that I could yet see a dim shadow, which seemed the shadow of that shade, against the opposite wall.

My eye now rested on the table, and from under the table (which was without cloth or cover, an old mahogany round table) rose a hand, visible as far as the wrist. It was a hand, seemingly, as much of flesh and blood as my own, but the hand of an aged person, lean, wrinkled, small too, a woman's hand. That hand very softly closed on the two letters that lay on the table; hand and letters both vanished. Then came the same three loud measured knocks I had heard at the bed-head before this extraordinary drama had commenced.

As these sounds slowly ceased, I felt the whole room vibrate sensibly; and at the far end rose, as from the floor, sparks or globules like bubbles of light, many-coloured – green, yellow, fire-red, azure – up and down, to and fro, hither, thither, as tiny will-o'-the-wisps the sparks moved, slow or swift, each at its own caprice. A chair (as in the drawing-room below) was now advanced from the wall without apparent agency, and placed at the opposite side of the table.

Suddenly, as forth from the chair, grew a shape, a woman's shape. It was distinct as a shape of life, ghastly as a shape of death. The face was that of youth, with a strange, mournful beauty; the throat and shoulders were bare, the rest of the form in a loose robe of cloudy white.

It began sleeking its long yellow hair, which fell over its shoulders; its eyes were not turned towards me, but to the door; it seemed listening, watching, waiting. The shadow of the shade in the background grew darker, and again I thought I beheld the eyes gleaming out from the summit of the shadow, eyes fixed upon that shape.

As if from the door, though it did not open, grew out another shape, equally distinct, equally ghastly – a man's shape, a young man's. It was in the dress of the last century, or rather in a likeness of such dress; for both the male shape and the female, though defined, were evidently unsubstantial, impalpable – simulacre, phantasms; and there was something incongruous, grotesque, yet fearful, in the contrast between the elaborate finery, the courtly precision of that old-fashioned garb, with its ruffles and lace and buckles, and the corpse-like aspect and ghost-like stillness of the flitting wearer. Just as the male shape approached the female, the dark shadow darted from the wall, all three for a moment wrapped in darkness.

When the pale light returned, the two phantoms were as if in the grasp of the shadow that towered between them, and there was a bloodstain on the breast of the female; and the phantom male was leaning on its phantom sword, and blood seemed trickling fast from the ruffles, from the lace; and the darkness of the intermediate shadow swallowed them up – they were gone. And again the bubbles of light shot, and sailed, and undulated, growing thicker and thicker and more wildly confused in their movements.

The closet door to the right of the fireplace now opened, and from the aperture came the form of a woman, aged. In her hand she held letters – the very letters over which I had seen *the* hand close; and behind her I heard a footstep. She turned round as if to listen, and then she opened the letters and seemed to read: and over her shoulder I saw a livid face, the face as of a man long drowned – bloated, bleached, sea-weed tangled in its dripping hair; and at her feet lay a form as of a corpse, and beside the corpse cowered a child, a miserable squalid child, with famine in its cheeks and fear in its eyes. As I looked in the old woman's face, the wrinkles and lines vanished, and it became a face of youth – hard-eyed, stony, but still youth; and the shadow darted forth and darkened over these phantoms, as it had darkened over the last.

Nothing now was left but the shadow, and on that my eyes were intently fixed, till again eyes grew out of the shadow – malignant, serpent eyes. And the bubbles of light again rose and fell, and in their disordered, irregular, turbulent maze mingled with the wan moon-light. And now from these globules themselves, as from the shell of an egg, monstrous things burst out; the air grew filled with them; larvæ so bloodless and so hideous that I can in no way describe them except to remind the reader of the swarming life which the solar microscope brings before his eyes in a drop of water – things transparent, supple, agile, chasing each other, devouring each other – forms like naught ever beheld by the naked eye.

As the shapes were without symmetry, so their movements were without order. In their very vagrancies there was no sport; they came round me and round, thicker and faster and swifter, swarming over my head, crawling over my right arm, which was outstretched in involuntary command against all evil beings.

Sometimes I felt myself touched, but not by them; invisible hands touched me. Once I felt the clutch as of cold, soft fingers at my throat. I was still equally conscious that if I gave way to fear I should be in bodily peril, and I concentred all my faculties in the single focus of resisting, stubborn will. And I turned my sight from the shadow, above all from those strange serpent eyes – eyes that had now become distinctly visible. For there, though in naught else around me, I was aware that there was a will, and a will of intense, creative, working evil, which might crush down my own.

The pale atmosphere in the room began now to redden as if in the air of some near conflagration. The larvae grew lurid as things that live in fire. Again the room vibrated; again were heard the three measured knocks; and again all things were swallowed up in the darkness of the dark shadow, as if out of that darkness all had come, into that darkness all returned.

As the gloom receded, the shadow was wholly gone. Slowly as it had been withdrawn, the flame grew again into the candles on the table, again into the fuel in the grate. The whole room came once more calmly, healthfully into sight.

The two doors were still closed, the door communicating with the servant's room still locked. In the corner of the wall, into which he had convulsively niched himself, lay the dog. I called to him – no movement; I approached – the animal was dead; his eyes protruded, his tongue out of his mouth, the froth gathered round his jaws. I took him in my arms; I brought him to the fire; I felt acute grief for the loss of my poor favourite, acute self-reproach; I accused myself of his death; I imagined he had died of fright. But what was my surprise on finding that his neck was actually broken – actually twisted out of the vertebræ. Had this been done in the dark? Must it not have been done by a hand human as mine? Must there not have been a human agency all the while in that room? Good cause to suspect it. I cannot tell. I cannot do more than state the fact fairly; the reader may draw his own inference.

Another surprising circumstance – my watch was restored to the table from which it had been so mysteriously withdrawn; but it had stopped at the very moment it was so withdrawn; nor, despite all the skill of the watchmaker, has it ever gone since – that is, it will go in a strange, erratic way for a few hours, and then come to a dead stop; it is worthless.

Nothing more chanced for the rest of the night; nor, indeed, had I long to wait before the dawn broke. Not till it was broad daylight did I quit the haunted house. Before I did so I revisited the little blind room in which my servant and I had been for a time imprisoned.

I had a strong impression, for which I could not account, that from that room had originated the mechanism of the phenomena, if I may use the term, which had been experienced in my chamber; and though I entered it now in the clear day, with the sun peering through the filmy window, I still felt, as I stood on its floor, the creep of the horror which I had first experienced there the night before, and which had been so aggravated by what had passed in my own chamber.

I could not, indeed, bear to stay more than half a minute within those walls. I descended the stairs, and again I heard the footfall before me; and when I opened the street door I thought I could distinguish a very low laugh. I gained my own home, expecting to find my runaway servant there. But he had not presented himself; nor did I hear more of him for three days, when I received a letter from him, dated from Liverpool, to this effect:

HONOURED SIR, – *I humbly entreat your pardon, though I can scarcely hope that you will think I deserve it, unless – which heaven forbid! – you saw what I did. I feel that it will be years before I can recover myself; and as to being fit for service, it is out of the question. I am therefore going to my brother-in-law at Melbourne. The ship sails to-morrow. Perhaps the long voyage may set me up. I do nothing now but start and tremble, and fancy it is behind me. I humbly beg you, honoured sir, to order my clothes, and whatever wages are due to me, to be sent to my mother's, at Walworth: John knows her address.*

The letter ended with additional apologies, somewhat incoherent, and explanatory details as to effects that had been under the writer's charge.

This flight may perhaps warrant a suspicion that the man wished to go to Australia, and had been somehow or other fraudulently mixed up with the events of the night. I say nothing in refutation of that conjecture; rather, I suggest it as one that would seem to many persons the most probable solution of improbable occurrences.

My own theory remained unshaken. I returned in the evening to the house, to bring away in a hack cab the things I had left there, with my poor dog's body. In this task I was not disturbed, nor did any incident worth note befall me, except that still, on ascending and descending the stairs, I heard the same footfall in advance. On leaving the house, I went to Mr. J—'s. He was at home. I returned him the keys, told him that my curiosity was sufficiently gratified, and was about to relate quickly what had passed, when he stopped me and said, though with much politeness, that he had no longer any interest in a mystery which none had ever solved.

I determined at least to tell him of the two letters I had read, as well as of the extraordinary manner in which they had disappeared; and I then inquired if he thought they had been addressed to the woman who had died in the house, and if there were anything in her early history which could possibly confirm the dark suspicions to which the letters gave rise.

Mr. J— seemed startled, and after musing a few moments, answered:

'I know but little of the woman's earlier history, except, as I before told you, that her family were known to mine. But you revive some vague reminiscences to her prejudice. I will make inquiries, and inform you of their result. Still, even if we could admit the popular superstition that a person who had been either the perpetrator or the victim of dark crimes in life could revisit, as a restless spirit, the scene in which those crimes had been committed, I should observe that the house was infested by strange sights and sounds before the old woman died. You smile; what would you say?'

'I would say this: that I am convinced, if we could get to the bottom of these mysteries, we should find a living, human agency.'

'What! you believe it is all an imposture? For what object?'

'Not an imposture, in the ordinary sense of the word. If suddenly I were to sink into a deep sleep, from which you could not awake me, but in that deep sleep could answer questions with an accuracy which I could not pretend to when awake – tell you what money you had in your pocket, nay, describe your very thoughts – it is not necessarily an imposture, any more than it is necessarily supernatural. I should be, unconsciously to myself, under a mesmeric influence, conveyed to me from a distance by a human being who had acquired power over me by previous *rapport*.'

'Granting mesmerism, so far carried, to be a fact, you are right. And you would infer from this that a mesmerizer might produce the extraordinary effects you and others have witnessed over inanimate objects – fill the air with sights and sounds?'

'Or impress our senses with the belief in them, we never having been *en rapport* with the person acting on us? No. What is commonly called mesmerism could not do this; but there may be a power akin to mesmerism and superior to it – the power that in the old days was called magic. That such a power may extend to all inanimate objects of matter, I do not say; but if so, it would not be against nature, only a rare power in nature, which might be given to constitutions with certain peculiarities, and cultivated by practice to an extraordinary degree.

'That such a power might extend over the dead – that is, over certain thoughts and memories that the dead may still retain – and compel, not that which ought properly to be called the soul, and which is far beyond human reach, but rather a phantom of what has been most earth-stained on earth, to make itself apparent to our senses

— is a very ancient though obsolete theory, upon which I will hazard no opinion. But I do not conceive the power would be supernatural.

'Let me illustrate what I mean, from an experiment which Paracelsus describes as not difficult, and which the author of the *Curiosities of Literature* cites as credible: A flower perishes; you burn it. Whatever were the elements of that flower while it lived are gone, dispersed, you know not whither; you can never discover nor re-collect them. But you can, by chemistry, out of the burnt dust of that flower, raise a spectrum of the flower, just as it seemed in life.

'It may be the same with a human being. The soul has as much escaped you as the essence or elements of the flower. Still you may make a spectrum of it. And this phantom, though in the popular superstition it is held to be the soul of the departed, must not be confounded with the true soul; it is but the eidolon of the dead form.

'Hence, like the best-attested stories of ghosts or spirits, the thing that most strikes us is the absence of what we hold to be soul — that is, of superior, emancipated intelligence. They come for little or no object; they seldom speak, if they do come; they utter no ideas above those of an ordinary person on earth. These American spirit-seers have published volumes of communications in prose and verse, which they assert to be given in the names of the most illustrious dead — Shakespeare, Bacon, heaven knows whom.

'Those communications, taking the best, are certainly not of a whit higher order than would be communications from living persons of fair talent and education; they are wondrously inferior to what Bacon, Shakespeare, and Plato said and wrote when on earth. Nor, what is more notable, do they ever contain an idea that was not on the earth before.

'Wonderful, therefore, as such phenomena may be (granting them to be truthful), I see much that philosophy may question, nothing that it is incumbent on philosophy to deny, namely, nothing super-natural. They are but ideas conveyed somehow or other (we have not yet discovered the means) from one mortal brain to another. Whether in so doing tables walk of their own accord, or fiend-like shapes appear in a magic circle, or bodiless hands rise and remove material objects, or a thing of darkness, such as presented itself to me, freeze our blood — still am I persuaded that these are but agencies conveyed, as by electric wires, to my own brain from the brain of another.

'In some constitutions there is a natural chemistry, and these may produce chemic wonders; in others a natural fluid, call it electricity, and these produce electric wonders. But they differ in this from normal science: they are alike objectless, purposeless, puerile, frivolous. They lead on to no grand results, and therefore the world does not heed, and true sages have not cultivated them. But sure I am, that of all I saw or heard, a man, human as myself, was the remote originator; and, I believe, unconsciously to himself as to the exact effects produced, for this reason: no two persons, you say, have ever told you that they experienced exactly the same thing; well, observe, no two persons ever experience exactly the same dream.

'If this were an ordinary imposture, the machinery would be arranged for results that would but little vary; if it were a supernatural agency permitted by the Almighty, it would surely be for some definite end. These phenomena belong to neither class. My persuasion is that they originate in some brain now far distant; that that brain had no distinct volition in anything that occurred; that what does occur reflects but its devious, motley, ever shifting, half-formed thoughts; in short, that it has been but the dreams of such a brain put into action and invested with a semi-substance.

'That this brain is of immense power, that it can set matter into movement, that it is malignant and destructive, I believe. Some material force must have killed my dog; it might, for aught I know, have sufficed to kill myself, had I been as subjugated by terror as the dog – had my intellect or my spirit given me no countervailing resistance in my will.'

'It killed your dog! That is fearful! Indeed, it is strange that no animal can be induced to stay in that house; not even a cat. Rats and mice are never found in it.'

'The instincts of the brute creation detect influences deadly to their existence. Man's reason has a sense less subtle, because it has a resisting power more supreme. But enough; do you comprehend my theory?'

'Yes, though imperfectly; and I accept any crotchet (pardon the word), however odd, rather than embrace at once the notion of ghosts and hobgoblins we imbibed in our nurseries. Still, to my unfortunate house the evil is the same. What on earth can I do with the house?'

'I will tell you what I would do. I am convinced from my own internal feelings that the small unfurnished room, at right angles to the door of the bedroom which I occupied, forms a starting-point or receptacle for the influences which haunt the house; and I strongly advise you to have the walls opened, the floor removed, nay, the whole room pulled down. I observe that it is detached from the body of the house, built over the small back yard, and could be removed without injury to the rest of the building.'

'And you think that if I did that – '

'You would cut off the telegraph wires. Try it. I am so persuaded that I am right that I will pay half the expense if you will allow me to direct the operations.'

'Nay, I am well able to afford the cost; for the rest, allow me to write to you.'

About ten days afterwards I received a letter from Mr. J—, telling me that he had visited the house since I had seen him; that he had found the two letters I had described replaced in the drawer from which I had taken them; that he had read them with misgivings like my own; that he had instituted a cautious inquiry about the woman to whom I rightly conjectured they had been written.

It seemed that thirty-six years ago (a year before the date of the letters) she had married, against the wish of her relatives, an American of very suspicious character; in fact, he was generally believed to have been a pirate. She herself was the daughter of very respectable tradespeople, and had served in the capacity of nursery governess before her marriage. She had a brother, a widower, who was considered wealthy, and who had one child about six years old. A month after the marriage the body of this brother was found in the Thames, near London Bridge; there seemed some marks of violence about his throat, but they were not deemed sufficient to warrant the inquest in any other verdict than that of 'found drowned.'

The American and his wife took charge of the little boy, the deceased brother having by his will left his sister the guardian of his only child, and in the event of the child's death the sister inherited. The child died about six months afterwards; it was supposed to have been neglected and ill-treated. The neighbours deposed to have heard it shriek at night.

The surgeon who had examined it after death said that it was emaciated as if from want of nourishment, and the body was covered with livid bruises. It seemed that one winter night the child had sought to escape; had crept out into the back yard, tried to scale the wall, fallen back exhausted, and had been found at morning on the stones in a dying state.

But though there was some evidence of cruelty, there was none of murder; and the aunt and her husband had sought to palliate cruelty by alleging the exceeding stubbornness and perversity of the child, who was declared to be half-witted. Be that as it may, at the orphan's death the aunt inherited her brother's fortune.

Before the first wedded year was out, the American quitted

England abruptly, and never returned to it. He obtained a cruising vessel, which was lost in the Atlantic two years afterwards. The widow was left in affluence; but reverses of various kinds had befallen her; a bank broke, an investment failed, she went into a small business and became insolvent, then she entered into service, sinking lower and lower, from housekeeper down to maid-of-all-work, never long retaining a place, though nothing peculiar against her character was ever alleged.

She was considered sober, honest, and peculiarly quiet in her ways; still nothing prospered with her. And so she had dropped into the workhouse, from which Mr. J— had taken her, to be placed in charge of the very house which she had rented as mistress in the first year of her wedded life.

Mr. J— added that he had passed an hour alone in the unfurnished room which I had urged him to destroy, and that his impressions of dread while there were so great, though he had neither heard nor seen anything, that he was eager to have the walls bared and the floors removed, as I had suggested. He had engaged persons for the work, and would commence any day I would name.

The day was accordingly fixed. I repaired to the haunted house; we went into the blind, dreary room, took up the skirting and then the floors. Under the rafters, covered with rubbish, was found a trap-door, quite large enough to admit a man. It was closely nailed down with clamps and rivets of iron. On removing these we descended into a room below, the existence of which had never been suspected.

In this room there had been a window and a flue, but they had been bricked over, evidently for many years. By the help of candles we examined this place; it still retained some mouldering furniture – three chairs, an oak settee, a table – all of the fashion of about eighty years ago.

There was a chest of drawers against the wall, in which we found, half rotted away, old-fashioned articles of a man's dress, such as might have been worn eighty or a hundred years ago, by a gentleman of some rank; costly steel buckles and buttons, like those yet worn in court-dresses, a handsome court-sword; in a waistcoat which had once been rich with gold lace, but which was now blackened and foul with damp, we found five guineas, a few silver coins, and an ivory ticket, probably for some place of entertainment long since passed away.

But our main discovery was in a kind of iron safe fixed to the wall, the lock of which it cost us much trouble to get picked.

In this safe were three shelves and two small drawers. Ranged on the shelves were several small bottles of crystal, hermetically stopped. They contained colourless volatile essences, of what nature I shall say no more than that they were not poisons; phosphor and ammonia entered into some of them. There were also some very curious glass tubes, and a small pointed rod of iron, with a large lump of rock crystal, and another of amber, also a lodestone of great power.

In one of the drawers we found a miniature portrait set in gold, and retaining the freshness of its colours most remarkably, considering the length of time it had probably been there. The portrait was that of a man who might be somewhat advanced in middle life, perhaps forty-seven or forty-eight.

It was a most peculiar face, a most impressive face. If you could fancy some mighty serpent transformed into man, preserving in the human lineaments the old serpent type, you would have a better idea of that countenance than long descriptions can convey; the width and flatness of frontal, the tapering elegance of contour, disguising the strength of the deadly jaw; the long, large, terrible eye, glittering and green as the emerald, and withal a certain ruthless calm, as if from the consciousness of an immense power.

The strange thing was this: the instant I saw the miniature I recognized a startling likeness to one of the rarest portraits in the world; the portrait of a man of rank only below that of royalty, who in his own day had made a considerable noise. History says little or nothing of him; but search the correspondence of his contemporaries, and you find reference to his wild daring, his bold profligacy, his restless spirit, his taste for the occult sciences.

While still in the meridian of life he died and was buried, so say the chronicles, in a foreign land. He died in time to escape the grasp of the law; for he was accused of crimes which would have given him to the headsman. After his death the portraits of him, which had been numerous, for he had been a munificent encourager of art, were bought up and destroyed, it was supposed by his heirs, who might have been glad could they have razed his very name from their splendid line.

He had enjoyed vast wealth; a large portion of this was believed to have been embezzled by a favourite astrologer or soothsayer; at all events, it had unaccountably vanished at the time of his death. One portrait alone of him was supposed to have escaped the general destruction; I had seen it in the house of a collector some months before. It had made on me a wonderful impression, as it does on all who behold it – a face never to be forgotten; and there was that face in the miniature that lay within my hand. True that in the miniature the man was a few years older than in the portrait I had seen, or than the original was even at the time of his death. But a few years! – why, between the date in which flourished that direful noble and the date in which the miniature was evidently painted there was an interval of more than two centuries. While I was thus gazing, silent and wondering, Mr. J— said:

'But is it possible? I have known this man.'

'How? where?' cried I.

'In India. He was high in the confidence of the Rajah of—, and well-nigh drew him into a revolt which would have lost the Rajah his dominions. The man was a Frenchman; his name De V—; clever, bold, lawless; we insisted on his dismissal and banishment. It must be the same man, no two faces like his, yet this miniature seems nearly a hundred years old.'

Mechanically I turned round the miniature to examine the back of it, and on the back was engraved a pentacle; in the middle of the pentacle a ladder, and the third step of the ladder was formed by the date 1765. Examining still more minutely, I detected a spring; this, on being pressed, opened the back of the miniature as a lid.

Within-side the lid were engraved: 'Mariana, to thee. Be faithful in life and in death to—.'

Here follows a name that I will not mention, but it was not unfamiliar to me. I had heard it spoken of by old men in my childhood as the name borne by a dazzling charlatan, who had made a great sensation in London for a year or so, and had fled the country on the charge of a double murder within his own house – that of his mistress and his rival. I said nothing of this to Mr. J—, to whom reluctantly I resigned the miniature.

We had found no difficulty in opening the first drawer within the iron safe; we found great difficulty in opening the second: it was not locked, but it resisted all efforts, till we inserted in the chinks the edge of a chisel. When we had thus drawn it forth we found a very singular apparatus, in the nicest order.

Upon a small, thin book, or rather tablet, was placed a saucer of crystal; this saucer was filled with a clear liquid; on that liquid floated a kind of compass, with a needle shifting rapidly round; but instead of the usual points of a compass, were seven strange characters, not very unlike those used by astrologers to denote the planets.

A very peculiar, but not strong nor displeasing, odour came from this drawer, which was lined with a wood that we afterwards discovered to be hazel. Whatever the cause of this odour, it produced

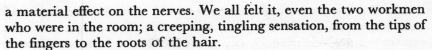

a material effect on the nerves. We all felt it, even the two workmen who were in the room; a creeping, tingling sensation, from the tips of the fingers to the roots of the hair.

Impatient to examine the tablet, I removed the saucer. As I did so, the needle of the compass went round and round with exceeding swiftness, and I felt a shock that ran through my whole frame, so that I dropped the saucer on the floor. The liquid was spilt, the saucer was broken, the compass rolled to the end of the room, and at that instant the walls shook to and fro as if a giant had swayed and rocked them.

The two workmen were so frightened that they ran up the ladder by which we had descended from the trap-door; but, seeing that nothing more happened, they were easily induced to return.

Meanwhile I had opened the tablet; it was bound in plain red leather, with a silver clasp; it contained but one sheet of thick vellum, and on that sheet were inscribed, within a double pentacle, words in old monkish Latin, which are literally to be translated thus:

On all that it can reach within these walls, sentient or inanimate, living or dead, as moves the needle, so works my will! Accursed be the house, and restless the dwellers therein.

We found no more. Mr. J— burned the tablet and its anathema. He razed to the foundation the part of the building containing the secret room, with the chamber over it. He had then the courage to inhabit the house himself for a month, and a quieter, better conditioned house could not be found in all London. Subsequently he let it to advantage, and his tenant has made no complaints.

But my story is not yet done. A few days after Mr. J— had removed into the house, I paid him a visit. We were standing by the open window and conversing. A van containing some articles of furniture which he was moving from his former house was at the door.

I had just urged on him my theory that all those phenomena regarded as supermundane had emanated from a human brain; adducing the charm, or rather curse we had found and destroyed, in support of my theory.

Mr. J— was observing in reply, 'that even if mesmerism, or whatever analogous power it might be called, could really thus work in the absence of the operator, and produce effects so extraordinary, still could those effects continue when the operator himself was dead? and if the spell had been wrought, and, indeed, the room walled up, more than seventy years ago, the probability was that the operator had long since departed this life'— Mr. J—, I say, was thus answering, when I caught hold of his arm and pointed to the street below.

A well-dressed man had crossed from the opposite side, and was accosting the carrier in charge of the van. His face, as he stood, was exactly fronting our window. It was the face of the miniature we had discovered; it was the face of the portrait of the noble three centuries ago.

'Good heavens!' cried Mr. J—, 'that is the face of De V—, and scarcely a day older than when I saw it in the Rajah's court in my youth!'

Seized by the same thought, we both hastened downstairs; I was first in the street, but the man had already gone. I caught sight of him, however, not many yards in advance, and in another moment I was by his side.

I had resolved to speak to him, but when I looked into his face I felt as if it were impossible to do so. That eye – the eye of the serpent – fixed and held me spellbound. And withal, about the man's whole person there was a dignity, an air of pride and station and superiority that would have made anyone, habituated to the usages of the world, hesitate long before venturing upon a liberty or impertinence.

And what could I say? What was it I could ask?

Thus ashamed of my first impulse, I fell a few paces back, still, however, following the stranger, undecided what else to do. Meanwhile he turned the corner of the street; a plain carriage was in waiting with a servant out of livery, dressed like a *valet de place*, at the carriage door. In another moment he had stepped into the carriage, and it drove off. I returned to the house.

Mr. J— was still at the street door. He had asked the carrier what the stranger had said to him.

'Merely asked whom that house now belonged to.'

The same evening I happened to go with a friend to a place in town called the Cosmopolitan Club, a place open to men of all countries, all opinions, all degrees. One orders one's coffee, smokes one's cigar. One is always sure to meet agreeable, sometimes remarkable persons.

I had not been two minutes in the room before I beheld at table, conversing with an acquaintance of mine, whom I will designate by the initial G—, the man, the original of the miniature. He was now without his hat, and the likeness was yet more startling, only I observed that while he was conversing there was less severity in the countenance; there was even a smile, though a very quiet and very cold one. The dignity of mien I had acknowledged in the street was also more striking; a dignity akin to that which invests some prince of the East, conveying the idea of supreme indifference and habitual, indisputable, indolent but resistless power.

G— soon after left the stranger, who then took up a scientific journal, which seemed to absorb his attention.

I drew G— aside.

'Who and what is that gentleman?'

'That? Oh, a very remarkable man indeed! I met him last year amid the caves of Petra, the Scriptural Edom. He is the best Oriental scholar I know. We joined company, had an adventure with robbers, in which he showed a coolness that saved our lives; afterwards he invited me to spend a day with him in a house he had bought at Damascus, buried among almond blossoms and roses – the most beautiful thing! He had lived there for some time, quite as an Oriental, in grand style.

'I half suspect he is a renegade, immensely rich, very odd; by the by, a great mesmerizer. I have seen him with my own eyes produce an effect on inanimate things. If you take a letter from your pocket and throw it to the other end of the room, he will order it to come to his feet, and you will see the letter wriggle itself along the floor till it has obeyed his command. 'Pon my honour 'tis true; I have seen him affect even the weather, disperse or collect clouds by means of a glass tube or wand. But he does not like talking of these matters to strangers. He has only just arrived in England; says he has not been here for a great many years; let me introduce him to you.'

'Certainly! He is English, then? What is his name?'

'Oh! a very homely one – Richards.'

'And what is his birth – his family?'

'How do I know? What does it signify? No doubt some *parvenu*; but rich, so infernally rich!'

G— drew me up to the stranger, and the introduction was effected. The manners of Mr. Richards were not those of an adventurous traveller. Travellers are in general gifted with high animal spirits; they are talkative, eager, imperious. Mr. Richards was calm and subdued in tone, with manners which were made distant by the loftiness of punctilious courtesy, the manners of a former age.

I observed that the English he spoke was not exactly of our day. I should even have said that the accent was slightly foreign. But then Mr. Richards remarked that he had been little in the habit for years of speaking in his native tongue.

The conversation fell upon the changes in the aspect of London since he had last visited our metropolis. G— then glanced off to the moral changes – literary, social, political – the great men who were removed from the stage within the last twenty years; the new great men who were coming on.

In all this Mr. Richards evinced no interest. He had evidently read none of our living authors, and seemed scarcely acquainted by name with our younger statesmen. Once, and only once, he laughed; it was when G— asked him whether he had any thoughts of getting into Parliament; and the laugh was inward, sarcastic, sinister – a sneer raised into a laugh.

After a few minutes, G— left us to talk to some other acquaintances who had just lounged into the room, and I then said, quietly:

'I have seen a miniature of you, Mr. Richards, in the house you once inhabited, and perhaps built – if not wholly, at least in part – in Oxford Street. You passed by that house this morning.'

Not till I had finished did I raise my eyes to his, and then he fixed my gaze so steadfastly that I could not withdraw it – those fascinating serpent-eyes. But involuntarily, and as if the words that translated my thoughts were dragged from me, I added, in a low whisper, 'I have been a student in the mysteries of life and nature; of those mysteries I have known the occult professors. I have the right to speak to you thus.' And I uttered a certain password.

'Well, I concede the right. What would you ask?'

'To what extent human will in certain temperaments can extend?'

'To what extent can thought extend? Think, and before you draw breath you are in China!'

'True; but my thought has no power in China.'

'Give it expression, and it may have. You may write down a thought which, sooner or later, may alter the whole condition of China. What is a law but a thought? Therefore thought is infinite. Therefore thought has power; not in proportion to its value – a bad thought may make a bad law as potent as a good thought can make a good one.'

'Yes; what you say confirms my own theory. Through invisible currents one human brain may transmit its ideas to other human brains, with the same rapidity as a thought promulgated by visible means. And as thought is imperishable, as it leaves its stamp behind it in the natural world, even when the thinker has passed out of this world, so the thought of the living may have power to rouse up and revive the thoughts of the dead, such as those thoughts *were in life*, though the thought of the living cannot reach the thoughts which the dead *now* may entertain. Is it not so?'

'I decline to answer, if in my judgment thought has the limit you

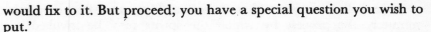

would fix to it. But proceed; you have a special question you wish to put.'

'Intense malignity in an intense will, engendered in a peculiar temperament, and aided by natural means within the reach of science, may produce effects like those ascribed of old to evil magic. It might thus haunt the walls of a human habitation with spectral revivals of all guilty thoughts and guilty deeds once conceived and done within those walls; all, in short, with which the evil will claims *rapport* and affinity – imperfect, incoherent, fragmentary snatches at the old dramas acted therein years ago.

'Thoughts thus crossing each other haphazard, as in the nightmare of a vision, growing up into phantom sights and sounds, and all serving to create horror; not because those sights and sounds are really visitations from a world without, but that they are ghastly, monstrous renewals of what have been in this world itself, set into malignant play by a malignant mortal. And it is through the material agency of that human brain that these things would acquire even a human power; would strike as with the shock of electricity, and might kill, if the thought of the person assailed did not rise superior to the dignity of the original assailer; might kill the most powerful animal, if unnerved by fear, but not injure the feeblest man, if, while his flesh crept, his mind stood out fearless.

'Thus when in old stories we read of a magician rent to pieces by the fiends he had invoked, or still more, in Eastern legends, that one magician succeeds by arts in destroying another, there may be so far truth, that a material being has clothed, from his own evil propensities, certain elements and fluids, usually quiescent or harmless, with awful shapes and terrific force; just as the lightning, that has lain hidden and innocent in the cloud, becomes by natural law suddenly visible, takes a distinct shape to the eye, and can strike destruction on the object to which it is attracted.'

'You are not without glimpses of a mighty secret,' said Mr. Richards composedly. 'According to your view, could a mortal obtain the power you speak of, he would necessarily be a malignant and evil being.'

'If the power were exercised as I have said, most malignant and most evil; though I believe in the ancient traditions that he could not injure the good. His will could only injure those with whom it has established an affinity, or over whom it forces unresisted sway. I will now imagine an example that may be within the laws of nature, yet seem wild as the fables of a bewildered monk.

'You will remember that Albertus Magnus, after describing minutely the process by which the spirits may be invoked and commanded, adds emphatically that the process will instruct and avail only to the few; that *a man must be born a magician!* – that is, born with a peculiar physical temperament, as a man is born a poet.

'Rarely are men in whose constitutions lurks this occult power of the highest order of intellect; usually in the intellect there is some twist, perversity, or disease. But on the other hand, they must possess, to an astonishing degree, the faculty to concentrate thought on a single object – the energic faculty that we call WILL. Therefore, though their intellect be not sound, it is exceedingly forcible for the attainment of what it desires. I will imagine such a person, pre-eminently gifted with this constitution and its concomitant forces. I will place him in the loftier grades of society.

'I will suppose his desires emphatically those of the sensualist; he has, therefore, a strong love of life. He is an absolute egotist; his will is concentred in himself; he has fierce passions; he knows no enduring, no holy affections, but he can covet eagerly what for the moment he desires; he can hate implacably what opposes itself to his objects; he can commit fearful crimes, yet feel small remorse; he resorts rather to curses upon others than to penitence for his misdeeds. Circumstances to which his constitution guides him, lead him to a rare knowledge of the natural secrets which may serve his egotism. He is a close observer where his passions encourage observation; he is a minute calculator, not from love of truth, but where love of self sharpens his faculties; therefore he can be a man of science.

'I suppose such a being, having by experience learned the power of his arts over others, trying what may be the power of will over his own frame, and studying all that in natural philosophy may increase that power. He loves life, he dreads death; *he wills to live on.* He cannot restore himself to youth; he cannot entirely stay the progress of death; he cannot make himself immortal in the flesh and blood. But he may arrest, for a time so long as to appear incredible if I said it, that hardening of the parts which constitutes old age.

'A year may age him no more than an hour ages another. His intense will, scientifically trained into system, operates, in short, over the wear and tear of his own frame. He lives on. That he may not seem a portent and a miracle, he *dies*, from time to time, seemingly, to certain persons. Having schemed the transfer of a wealth that suffices to his wants, he disappears from one corner of the world, and contrives that his obsequies shall be celebrated.

'He reappears at another corner of the world, where he resides undetected, and does not visit the scenes of his former career till all who could remember his features are no more. He would be profoundly miserable if he had affections; he has none but for himself. No good man would accept his longevity; and to no man, good or bad, would he or could he communicate its true secret.

'Such a man might exist; such a man as I have described I see now before me – Duke of—, in the court of—, dividing time between lust and brawl, alchemists and wizards; again, in the last century, charlatan and criminal, with name less noble, domiciled in the house at which you gazed to-day, and flying from the law you had outraged, none knew whither; traveller once more revisiting London with the same earthly passion which filled your heart when races now no more walked through yonder streets; outlaw from the school of all the nobler and diviner mysteries. Execrable image of life in death and death in life, I warn you back from the cities and homes of healthful men! back to the ruins of departed empires! back to the deserts of nature unredeemed!'

There answered me a whisper so musical, so potently musical, that it seemed to enter into my whole being and subdue me despite myself. Thus it said:

'I have sought one like you for the last hundred years. Now I have found you, we part not till I know what I desire. The vision that sees through the past and cleaves through the veil of the future is in you at this hour – never before, never to come again. The vision of no puling, fantastic girl, of no sick-bed somnambule, but of a strong man with a vigorous brain. Soar, and look forth!'

As he spoke, I felt as if I rose out of myself upon eagle wings. All the weight seemed gone from air, roofless the room, roofless the dome of space. I was not in the body – where, I knew not; but aloft over time, over earth.

Again I heard the melodious whisper:

'You say right. I have mastered great secrets by the power of will. True, by will and by science I can retard the process of years, but death comes not by age alone. Can I frustrate the accidents which bring death upon the young?'

'No; every accident is a providence. Before a providence snaps every human will.'

'Shall I die at last, ages and ages hence, by the slow though inevitable growth of time, or by the cause that I call accident?'

'By a cause you call accident.'

'Is not the end still remote?' asked the whisper, with a slight tremor.

'Regarded as my life regards time, it is still remote.'

'And shall I, before then, mix with the world of men as I did ere I learned these secrets; resume eager interest in their strife and their trouble; battle with ambition, and use the power of the sage to win the power that belongs to kings?'

'You will yet play a part on the earth that will fill earth with commotion and amaze. For wondrous designs have you, a wonder yourself, been permitted to live on through the centuries. All the secrets you have stored will then have their uses; all that now makes you a stranger amid the generations will contribute then to make you their lord. As the trees and the straws are drawn into a whirlpool, as they spin round, are sucked to the deep, and again tossed aloft by the eddies, so shall races and thrones be drawn into your vortex. Awful destroyer! but in destroying, made, against your own will, a constructor.'

'And that date, too, is far off?'

'Far off; when it comes, think your end in this world is at hand!'

'How and what is the end? Look east, west, south, and north.'

'In the north, where you never yet trod, towards the point whence your instincts have warned you, there a spectre will seize you. 'Tis Death! I see a ship; it is haunted; 'tis chased! it sails on. Baffled navies sail after that ship. It enters the region of ice. It passes a sky red with meteors. Two moons stand on high, over ice-reefs. I see the ship locked between white defiles; they are ice-rocks. I see the dead strew the decks, stark and livid, green mould on their limbs. All are dead but one man – it is you! But years, though so slowly they come, have then scathed you. There is the coming of age on your brow, and the will is relaxed in the cells of the brain. Still that will, though enfeebled, exceeds all that man knew before you; through the will you live on, gnawed with famine. And Nature no longer obeys you in that death-spreading region; the sky is a sky of iron, and the air has iron clamps, and the ice-rocks wedge in the ship. Hark how it cracks and groans! Ice will imbed it as amber imbeds a straw. And a man has gone forth, living yet, from the ship and its dead; and he has clambered up the spikes of an iceberg, and the two moons gaze down on his form. That man is yourself, and terror is on you – terror; and terror has swallowed up your will.

'And I see, swarming up the steep ice-rock, grey, grizzly things. The bears of the North have scented their quarry; they come nearer and nearer, shambling, and rolling their bulk. In that day every moment shall seem to you longer than the centuries through which you have passed. Heed this: after life, moments continued make the bliss or the hell of eternity.'

'Hush!' said the whisper. 'But the day, you assure me, is far off, very far! I go back to the almond and rose of Damascus! Sleep!'

The room swam before my eyes. I became insensible. When I recovered, I found G— holding my hand and smiling. He said, 'You, who have always declared yourself proof against mesmerism, have succumbed at last to my friend Richards.'

'Where is Mr. Richards?'

'Gone, when you passed into a trance, saying quietly to me, "Your friend will not wake for an hour." '

I asked, as collectedly as I could, where Mr. Richards lodged.

'At the Trafalgar Hotel.'

'Give me your arm,' said I to G—. 'Let us call on him; I have something to say.'

When we arrived at the hotel we were told that Mr. Richards had returned twenty minutes before, paid his bill, left directions with his servant (a Greek) to pack his effects, and proceed to Malta by the steamer that should leave Southampton the next day. Mr. Richards had merely said of his own movements that he had visits to pay in the neighbourhood of London, and it was uncertain whether he should be able to reach Southampton in time for that steamer; if not, he should follow in the next one.

The waiter asked me my name. On my informing him, he gave me a note that Mr. Richards had left for me in case I called.

The note was as follows:

I wished you to utter what was in your mind. You obeyed. I have therefore established power over you. For three months from this day you can communicate to no living man what has passed between us. You cannot even show this note to the friend by your side. During three months silence complete as to me and mine. Do you doubt my power to lay on you this command? Try to disobey me. At the end of the third month the spell is raised. For the rest, I spare you. I shall visit your grave a year and a day after it has received you.

So ends this strange story, which I ask no one to believe. I write it down exactly three months after I received the above note. I could not write it before, nor could I show to G—, in spite of his urgent request, the note which I read under the gas lamp by his side.

THE BODY SNATCHER

Robert Louis Stevenson

[1850–1894]

'*The romantic, semi-Gothic, quasi-moral tradition here represented was carried far down the nineteenth century by such authors as Joseph Sheridan LeFanu, Wilkie Collins, the late Sir H. Rider Haggard (whose* She *is really remarkably good), Sir A. Conan Doyle, H.G. Wells, and Robert Louis Stevenson – the latter of whom, despite an atrocious tendency toward jaunty mannerisms, created permanent classics with* Markheim, The Body Snatcher, *and* Dr. Jekyll and Mr. Hyde.'

– H.P. Lovecraft

EVERY NIGHT IN THE YEAR, four of us sat in the small parlor of the George at Debenham – the undertaker, and the landlord, and Fettes, and myself. Sometimes there would be more; but blow high, blow low, come rain or snow or frost, we four would be each planted in his own particular armchair. Fettes was an old drunken Scotsman, a man of education obviously, and a man of some property, since he lived in idleness. He had come to Debenham years ago, while still young, and

by a mere continuance of living had grown to be an adopted towns-
man. His blue camlet cloak was a local antiquity, like the church spire.
His place in the parlor at the George, his absence from church, his old,
crapulous, disreputable vices, were all things of course in Debenham.
He had some vague radical opinions and some fleeting infidelities,
which he would now and again set forth and emphasize with tottering
slaps upon the table. He drank rum – five glasses regularly every
evening; and for the greater portion of his nightly visit to the George
sat, with his glass in his right hand, in a state of melancholy alcoholic
saturation. We called him the doctor, for he was supposed to have
some special knowledge of medicine, and had been known, upon a
pinch, to set a fracture or reduce a dislocation; but, beyond these slight
particulars, we had no knowledge of his character and antecedents.

One dark winter night – it had struck nine some time before the
landlord joined us – there was a sick man in the George, a great
neighboring proprietor suddenly struck down with apoplexy on his
way to Parliament; and the great man's still greater London doctor
had been telegraphed to his bedside. It was the first time that such a
thing had happened in Debenham, for the railway was but newly
open, and we were all proportionately moved by the occurrence.

'He's come,' said the landlord, after he had filled and lighted his
pipe.

'He?' said I. 'Who? – not the doctor?'

'Himself,' replied our host.

'What is his name?'

'Dr. Macfarlane,' said the landlord.

Fettes was far through his third tumbler, stupidly fuddled, now
nodding over, now staring mazily around him; but at the last word he
seemed to awaken, and repeated the name 'Macfarlane' twice,
quietly enough the first time, but with sudden emotion at the second.

'Yes,' said the landlord, 'that's his name, Dr. Wolfe Macfarlane.'

Fettes became instantly sober; his eyes awoke, his voice became
clear, loud and steady, his language forcible and earnest. We were all
startled by the transformation, as if a man had risen from the dead.

'I beg your pardon,' he said; 'I am afraid I have not been paying
much attention to your talk. Who is this Wolfe Macfarlane?' And
then, when he had heard the landlord out, 'It cannot be, it cannot
be,' he added; 'and yet I would like well to see him face to face.'

'Do you know him, doctor?' asked the undertaker, with a gasp.

'God forbid!' was the reply. 'And yet the name is a strange one; it
were too much to fancy two. Tell me, landlord, is he old?'

'Well,' said the host, 'he's not a young man, to be sure, and his hair is white; but he looks younger than you.'

'He is older, though; years older. But,' with a slap upon the table, 'it's the rum you see in my face – rum and sin. This man, perhaps, may have an easy conscience and a good digestion. Conscience! Hear me speak. You would think I was some good, old, decent Christian, would you not? But no, not I; I never canted. Voltaire might have canted if he'd stood in my shoes; but the brains' – with a rattling fillip on his bald head – 'the brains were clear and active, and I saw and made no deductions.'

'If you know this doctor,' I ventured to remark, after a somewhat awful pause, 'I should gather that you do not share the landlord's good opinion.'

Fettes paid no regard to me.

'Yes,' he said, with sudden decision, 'I must see him face to face.'

There was another pause, and then a door was closed rather sharply on the first floor, and a step was heard upon the stair.

'That's the doctor,' cried the landlord. 'Look sharp, and you can catch him.'

It was but two steps from the small parlor to the door of the old George Inn; the wide oak staircase landed almost in the street; there was room for a Turkey rug and nothing more between the threshold and the last round of the descent; but this little space was every evening brilliantly lit up, not only by the light upon the stair and the great signal-lamp below the sign, but by the warm radiance of the barroom window. The George thus brightly advertised itself to passers-by in the cold street. Fettes walked steadily to the spot, and we, who were hanging behind, beheld the two men meet, as one of them had phrased it, face to face. Dr. Macfarlane was alert and vigorous. His white hair set off his pale and placid, although energetic countenance. He was richly dressed in the finest of broadcloth and the whitest of linen, with a great gold watch-chain, and studs and spectacles of the same precious material. He wore a broad folded tie, white and speckled with lilac, and he carried on his arm a comfortable driving coat of fur. There was no doubt but he became his years, breathing, as he did, of wealth and consideration; and it was a surprising contrast to see our parlor sot – bald, dirty, pimpled, and robed in his old camlet cloak – confront him at the bottom of the stairs.

'Macfarlane!' he said somewhat loudly, more like a herald than a friend.

The great doctor pulled up short on the fourth step, as though the familiarity of the address surprised and somewhat shocked his dignity.

'Toddy Macfarlane!' repeated Fettes.

The London man almost staggered. He stared for the swiftest of seconds at the man before him, glanced behind him with a sort of scare, and then in a startled whisper, 'Fettes!' he said, 'you!'

'Ay,' said the other, 'me! Did you think I was dead, too? We are not so easy shut of our acquaintance.'

'Hush, hush!' exclaimed the doctor. 'Hush, hush! this meeting is so unexpected – I can see you are unmanned. I hardly knew you, I confess, at first; but I am overjoyed – overjoyed to have this opportunity. For the present it must be how-d'ye-do and good-bye in one, for my fly is waiting, and I must not fail the train; but you shall – let me see – yes – you shall give me your address, and you can count on early news of me. We must do something for you, Fettes. I fear you are out at elbows; but we must see to that for auld lang syne, as once we sang at suppers.'

'Money!' cried Fettes; 'money from you! The money that I had from you is lying where I cast it in the rain.'

Dr. Macfarlane had talked himself into some measure of superiority and confidence, but the uncommon energy of this refusal cast him back into his first confusion.

A horrible, ugly look came and went across his almost venerable countenance, 'My dear fellow,' he said, 'be it as you please; my last thought is to offend you. I would intrude on none. I will leave you my address, however – '

'I do not wish it – I do not wish to know the roof that shelters you,' interrupted the other. 'I heard your name; I feared it might be you; I wished to know if, after all, there were a God; I know now that there is none. Begone!'

He still stood in the middle of the rug, between the stair and doorway; and the great London physician, in order to escape, would be forced to step to one side. It was plain that he hesitated before the thought of this humiliation. White as he was, there was a dangerous glitter in his spectacles; but, while he still paused uncertain, he became aware that the driver of his fly was peering in from the street at this unusual scene, and caught a glimpse at the same time of our little body from the parlor, huddled by the corner of the bar. The presence of so many witnesses decided him at once to flee. He crouched together, brushing on the wainscot, and made a dart like a serpent, striking for the door. But his tribulation was not yet entirely at an end, for even as he was passing Fettes clutched him by the arm and these words came in a whisper, and yet painfully distinct, 'Have you seen it again?'

The great rich London doctor cried out aloud with a sharp, throttling cry; he dashed his questioner across the open space, and, with his hands over his head, fled out of the door like a detected thief. Before it had occurred to one of us to make a movement the fly was already rattling toward the station. The scene was over like a dream, but the dream had left proofs and traces of its passage. Next day the servant found the fine gold spectacles broken on the threshold, and that very night we were all standing breathless by the barroom window, and Fettes at our side, sober, pale, and resolute in look.

'God protect us, Mr. Fettes!' said the landlord, coming first into possession of his customary senses. 'What in the universe is all this? These are strange things you have been saying.'

Fettes turned toward us; he looked us each in succession in the face. 'See if you can hold your tongues,' said he. 'That man Macfarlane is not safe to cross; those that have done so already have repented it too late.'

And then, without so much as finishing his third glass, far less waiting for the other two, he bade us good-bye and went forth, under the lamp of the hotel, into the black night.

We three turned to our places in the parlor, with the big red fire and four clear candles; and, as we recapitulated what had passed, the first chill of our surprise soon changed into a glow of curiosity. We sat late; it was the latest session I have known in the old George. Each man, before we parted, had his theory that he was bound to prove; and none of us had any nearer business in this world than to track out the past of our condemned companion, and surprise the secret that he shared with the great London doctor. It is no great boast, but I believe I was a better hand at worming out a story than either of my fellows at the George; and perhaps there is now no other man alive who could narrate to you the following foul and unnatural events.

In his young days Fettes studied medicine in the schools of Edinburgh. He had talent of a kind, the talent that picks up swiftly what it hears and readily retains it for its own. He worked little at home; but he was civil, attentive, and intelligent in the presence of his masters. They soon picked him out as a lad who listened closely and remembered well; nay, strange as it seemed to me when I first heard it, he was in those days well-favored, and pleased by his exterior.

There was, at that period, a certain extramural teacher of anatomy, whom I shall here designate by the letter K. His name was subsequently too well-known. The man who bore it skulked through the streets of Edinburgh in disguise, while the mob that applauded at the execution of Burke called loudly for the blood of his employer. But Mr. K— was then at the top of his vogue; he enjoyed the popularity due partly to his own talent and address, partly to the incapacity of his rival, the university professor. The students, at least, swore by his name, and Fettes believed himself, and was believed by others, to have laid the foundations of success when he had acquired the favor of this meteorically famous man. Mr. K— was a *bon vivant* as well as an accomplished teacher; he liked a sly illusion no less than a careful preparation. In both capacities Fettes enjoyed and deserved his notice, and by the second year of his attendance he held the half-regular position of second demonstrator or subassistant in his class.

In this capacity the charge of the theater and lecture room devolved in particular upon his shoulders. He had to answer for the cleanliness of the premises and the conduct of the other students, and it was a part of his duty to supply, receive and divide the various subjects. It was with a view to this last – at that time very delicate – affair that he was lodged by Mr. K— in the same wynd, and at last in the same building, with the dissecting rooms. Here, after a night of turbulent pleasures, his hand still tottering, his sight still misty and confused, he would be called out of bed in the black hours before the winter dawn by the unclean and desperate interlopers who supplied the table. He would open the door to these men, since infamous throughout the land. He would help them with their tragic burden, pay them their sordid price, and remain alone, when they were gone, with the unfriendly relics of humanity. From such a scene he would return to snatch another hour or two of slumber, to repair the abuses of the night, and refresh himself for the labors of the day.

Few lads could have been more insensible to the impressions of a life thus passed among the ensigns of morality. His mind was closed against all general considerations. He was incapable of interest in the fate and fortunes of another, the slave of his own desires and low ambitions. Cold, light and selfish in the last resort, he had that modicum of prudence, miscalled morality, which keeps a man from inconvenient drunkenness or punishable theft. He coveted, besides, a measure of consideration from his masters and his fellow pupils, and he had no desire to fail conspicuously in the external parts of life. Thus he made it his pleasure to gain some distinction in his studies, and day after day rendered unimpeachable eye-service to his employer, Mr. K—. For his day of work he indemnified himself by nights of roaring, blackguardly enjoyment; and when that balance had been struck, the organ that he called his conscience declared itself content.

The supply of subjects was a continual trouble to him as well as to his master. In that large and busy class, the raw material of the anatomists kept perpetually running out; and the business thus rendered necessary was not only unpleasant in itself, but threatened dangerous consequences to all who were concerned. It was the policy of Mr. K— to ask no questions in his dealings with the trade. 'They bring the body, and we pay the price,' he used to say, dwelling on the alliteration – '*quid pro quo*.' And, again, and somewhat profanely, 'Ask no questions,' he would tell his assistants, 'for conscience sake.' There was no understanding that the subjects were provided by the crime of murder. Had that idea been broached to him in words, he would have recoiled in horror; but the lightness of his speech upon so grave a matter was, in itself, an offense against good manners, and a temptation to the men with whom he dealt. Fettes, for instance, had often remarked to himself upon the singular freshness of the bodies. He had been struck again and again by the hangdog, abominable looks of the ruffians who came to him before the dawn; and, putting things together clearly in his private thoughts, he perhaps attributed a meaning too immoral and too categorical to the unguarded councils of his master. He understood his duty, in short, to have three branches; to take what was brought, to pay the price, and to avert the eye from any evidence of crime.

One November morning this policy of silence was put sharply to the test. He had been awake all night with a racking toothache – pacing his room like a caged beast or throwing himself in fury on his bed – and had fallen at last into that profound, uneasy slumber that so often follows on a night of pain, when he was awakened by the third or fourth angry repetition of the concerted signal. There was a thin, bright moonshine; it was bitter cold, windy and frosty; the town had not yet awakened, but an indefinable stir already preluded the noise and business of the day. The ghouls had come later than usual, and they seemed more than usually eager to be gone. Fettes, sick with sleep, lighted them upstairs. He heard their grumbling Irish voices through a dream; and as they stripped the sack from their sad merchandise he leaned dozing, with his shoulder propped against the wall; he had to shake himself to find the men their money. As he did so his eyes lighted on the dead face. He started; he took two steps nearer, with the candle raised.

'God Almighty!' he cried. 'That is Jane Galbraith!'

The men answered nothing, but they shuffled nearer the door.

'I know her, I tell you,' he continued. 'She was alive and hearty yesterday. It's impossible she can be dead; it's impossible you should have got this body fairly.'

'Sure, sir, you're mistaken entirely,' said one of the men.

But the other looked Fettes darkly in the eyes, and demanded the money on the spot.

It was impossible to misconceive the threat or to exaggerate the danger. The lad's heart failed him. He stammered some excuse, counted out the sum, and saw his hateful visitors depart. No sooner were they gone than he hastened to confirm his doubts. By a dozen unquestionable marks he identified the girl he had jested with the day before. He saw, with horror, marks upon her body that might well be taken as violence. A panic seized him, and he took refuge in his room. There he reflected at length over the discovery that he had made; considered soberly the bearing of Mr. K——'s instructions and the danger to himself of interference in so serious a business, and at last, in sore perplexity, determined to wait for the advice of his immediate superior, the class assistant.

This was a young doctor, Wolfe Macfarlane, a high favorite among the reckless students, clever, dissipated, and unscrupulous to the last degree. He had traveled and studied abroad. His manners were agreeable and a little forward. He was an authority on the stage, skillful on the ice or the links with skate or golf club; he dressed with nice audacity, and, to put the finishing touch upon his glory, he kept a gig and a strong trotting horse. With Fettes he was on terms of intimacy; indeed, their relative positions called for some community of life; and when subjects were scarce the pair would drive far into the country in Macfarlane's gig, visit and desecrate some lonely graveyard, and return before dawn with their booty to the door of the dissecting room.

On that particular morning Macfarlane arrived somewhat earlier than his wont. Fettes heard him, and met him on the stairs, told him his story, and showed him the cause of his alarm. Macfarlane examined the marks on her body.

'Yes,' he said with a nod, 'it looks fishy.'

'Well, what should I do?' asked Fettes.

'Do?' repeated the other. 'Do you want to do anything? Least said sooner mended, I should say.'

'Someone else might recognize her,' objected Fettes. 'She was as well-known at the Castle Rock.'

'We'll hope not,' said Macfarlane, 'and if anybody does – well, you didn't, don't you see, and there's an end. The fact is, this has been going on too long. Stir up the mud, and you'll get K – into the most unholy trouble; you'll be in a shocking box yourself. So will I, if you come to that. I should like to know how anyone of us would look, or what the devil we should have to say ourselves, in any Christian witness box. For me, you know, there's one thing certain – that, practically speaking, all our subjects have been murdered.'

'Macfarlane!' cried Fettes.

'Come now!' sneered the other. 'As if you hadn't suspected it yourself!'

'Suspecting is one thing – '

'And proof another. Yes, I know; and I'm as sorry as you are this should have come here,' tapping the body with his cane. 'The next best thing for me is not to recognize it; and,' he added coolly, 'I don't. You may, if you please. I don't dictate, but I think a man of the world would do as I do; and, I may add, I fancy that is what K— would look for at our hands. The question is, Why did he choose us two for his assistants? And I answer, Because he didn't want old wives.'

This was the tone of all others to affect the mind of a lad like Fettes. He agreed to imitate Macfarlane. The body of the unfortunate girl was duly dissected, and no one remarked or appeared to recognize her.

One afternoon, when his day's work was over, Fettes dropped into a popular tavern and found Macfarlane sitting with a stranger. This was a small man, very pale and dark, with coal-black eyes. The cut of his features gave a promise of intellect and refinement which was but feebly realized in his manners, for he proved, upon a nearer acquaintance, coarse, vulgar and stupid. He exercised, however, a very remarkable control over Macfarlane; issued orders like the Great Bashaw; became inflamed at the least discussion or delay, and commented rudely on the servility with which he was obeyed. This most offensive person took a fancy to Fettes on the spot, plied him with drinks, and honored him with unusual confidences on his past career. If a tenth of what he confessed were true, he was a very loathsome rogue; and the lad's vanity was tickled by the attention of so experienced a man.

'I'm a pretty bad fellow myself,' the stranger remarked, 'but Macfarlane is the boy – Toddy Macfarlane I call him. Toddy, order your friend another glass. Or it might be, Toddy, you jump up and shut the door. Toddy hates me,' he said again. 'Oh, yes, Toddy, you do!'

'Don't you call me that confounded name,' growled Macfarlane.

'Hear him! Did you ever see the lads play knife? He would like to do that all over my body,' remarked the stranger.

'We medicals have a better way than that,' said Fettes. 'When we dislike a dead friend of ours, we dissect him.'

Macfarlane looked up sharply, as though this jest were scarcely to his mind.

The afternoon passed. Gray, for that was the stranger's name, invited Fettes to join them at dinner, ordered a feast so sumptuous that the tavern was thrown into commotion, and when all was done commanded Macfarlane to settle the bill. It was late before they separated; the man Gray was incapably drunk. Macfarlane, sobered by his fury, chewed the cud of the money he had been forced to squander and the slights he had been obliged to swallow. Fettes, with various liquors singing in his head, returned home with devious footsteps and a mind entirely in abeyance. Next day Macfarlane was absent from the class, and Fettes smiled to himself as he imagined him still squiring the intolerable Gray from tavern to tavern. As soon as the hour of liberty had struck, he posted from place to place in quest of his last night's companions. He could find them, however, nowhere; so returned early to his rooms, went early to bed, and slept the sleep of the just.

At four in the morning he was awakened by the well-known signal. Descending to the door, he was filled with astonishment to find Macfarlane with his gig, and in the gig one of those long and ghastly packages with which he was so well-acquainted.

'What?' he cried. 'Have you been out alone? How did you manage?'

But Macfarlane silenced him roughly, bidding him turn to business. When they had got the body upstairs and laid it on the table, Macfarlane made at first as if he were going away. Then he paused and seemed to hesitate; and then, 'You had better look at the face,' said he, in tones of some constraint. 'You had better,' he repeated, as Fettes only stared at him in wonder.

'But where, and how, and when did you come by it?' cried the other.

'Look at the face,' was the only answer.

Fettes was staggered; strange doubts assailed him. He looked from the young doctor to the body, and then back again. At last, with a start, he did as he was bidden. He had almost expected the sight that met his eyes, and yet the shock was cruel. To see, fixed in the rigidity of death and naked on that coarse layer of sackcloth, the man whom he had left well-clad and full of meat and sin upon the threshold of a tavern, awoke, even in the thoughtless Fettes, some of the terrors of the conscience. It was a *cras tibi* which reechoed in his soul, that two whom he had known should have come to lie upon these icy tables. Yet these were only secondary thoughts. His first concern regarded Wolfe. Unprepared for a challenge so momentous, he knew not how to look his comrade in the face. He durst not meet his eye, and he had neither words nor voice at his command.

It was Macfarlane himself who made the first advance. He came up quietly behind and laid his hand gently but firmly on the other's shoulder.

'Richardson,' said he, 'may have the head.'

Now, Richardson was a student who had long been anxious for that portion of the human subject to dissect. There was no answer, and the murderer resumed: 'Talking of business, you must pay me; your accounts, you see, must tally.'

Fettes found a voice, the ghost of his own: 'Pay you!' he cried. 'Pay you for that?'

'Why, yes, of course you must. By all means and on every possible account, you must,' returned the other. 'I dare not give it for nothing, you dare not take it for nothing; it would compromise us both. This is another case like Jane Galbraith's. The more things are wrong, the more we must act as if all were right. Where does old K— keep his money?'

'There,' answered Fettes hoarsely, pointing to a cupboard in the corner.

'Give me the key, then,' said the other calmly, holding out his hand.

There was an instant's hesitation, and the die was cast. Macfarlane could not suppress a nervous twitch, the infinitesimal mark of an immense relief, as he felt the key between his fingers. He opened the cupboard, brought out pen and ink and a paper book that stood in one compartment, and separated from the funds in a drawer a sum suitable to the occasion.

'Now; look here,' he said, 'there is the payment made – first proof of your good faith: first step to your security. You have now to clinch it by a second. Enter the payment in your book, and then you for your part may defy the devil.'

The next few seconds were for Fettes an agony of thought; but in balancing his terrors it was the most immediate that triumphed. Any future difficulty seemed almost welcome if he could avoid a present quarrel with Macfarlane. He set down the candle which he had been carrying all this time, and with a steady hand entered the date, the nature and the amount of the transaction.

'And now,' said Macfarlane, 'it's only fair that you should pocket the lucre. I've had my share already. By the by, when a man of the world falls into a bit of luck, has a few extra shillings in his pocket – I'm ashamed to speak of it, but there's a rule of conduct in the case. No treating, no purchase of expensive class books, no squaring of old debts; borrow, don't lend.'

'Macfarlane,' began Fettes, still somewhat hoarsely, 'I have put my neck in a halter to oblige you.'

'To oblige me?' cried Wolfe. 'Oh, come! You did, as near as I can see the matter, what you downright had to do in self-defense. Suppose I got into trouble, where would you be? This second little matter flows clearly from the first. Mr. Gray is the continuation of Miss Galbraith. You can't begin and then stop. If you begin, you must keep on beginning; that's the truth. No rest for the wicked.'

A horrible sense of blackness and the treachery of fate seized hold upon the soul of the unhappy student.

'My God!' he cried, 'but what have I done?' And when did I begin? To be made a class assistant – in the name of reason, where's the harm in that? Service wanted the position; Service might have got it. Would *he* have been where *I* am now?'

'My dear fellow,' said Macfarlane, 'what a boy you are! What harm *has* come to you? What harm *can* come to you if you hold your tongue? Why, man, do you know what this life is? There are two squads of us – the lions and the lambs. If you're a lamb, you'll come to lie upon these tables like Gray or Jane Galbraith; if you're a lion, you'll live and drive a horse like me, like K—, like all the world with any wit or courage. You're staggered at the first. But look at K—! My dear fellow, you're clever, you have pluck. I like you, and K— likes you. You were born to lead the hunt; and I tell you, on my honor and my experience of life, three days from now you'll laugh at all these scarecrows like a high school boy at a farce.'

And with that Macfarlane took his departure and drove off up the wynd in his gig to get under cover before daylight. Fettes was thus left alone with his regrets. He saw the miserable peril in which he stood involved. He saw, with inexpressible dismay, that there was no limit to his weakness, and that, from concession to concession, he had fallen from the arbiter of Macfarlane's destiny to his paid and helpless accomplice. He would have given the world to have been a little braver at the time, but it did not occur to him that he might still be brave. The secret of Jane Galbraith and the cursed entry in the day book closed his mouth.

Hours passed; the class began to arrive; the members of the unhappy Gray were dealt out to one and to another, and received without remark. Richardson was made happy with the head; and, before the hour of freedom rang, Fettes trembled with exultation to perceive how far they had already gone toward safety.

For two days he continued to watch, with an increasing joy, the dreadful process of disguise.

On the third day Macfarlane made his appearance. He had been ill, he said; but he made up for lost time by the energy with which he directed the students. To Richardson in particular he extended the most valuable assistance and advice, and that student, encouraged by the praise of the demonstrator, burned high with ambitious hopes, and saw the medal already in his grasp.

Before the week was out Macfarlane's prophecy had been fulfilled. Fettes had outlived his terrors and had forgotten his baseness. He began to plume himself upon his courage, and had so arranged the story in his mind that he could look back on these events with an unhealthy pride. Of his accomplice he saw but little. They met, of course, in the business of the class; they received their orders together from Mr. K—. At times they had a word or two in private, and Macfarlane was from first to last particularly kind and jovial. But it was plain that he avoided any reference to their common secret; and even when Fettes whispered to him that he had cast in his lot with the lions and forsworn the lambs, he only signed to him smilingly to hold his peace.

At length an occasion arose which threw the pair once more into a closer union. Mr. K— was again short of subjects; pupils were eager, and it was a part of this teacher's pretensions to be always well-supplied. At the same time there came the news of a burial in the rustic graveyard of Glencorse. Time has little changed the place in question. It stood then, as now, upon a crossroad, out of call of human habitations, and buried fathom deep in the foliage of six cedar trees. The cries of the sheep upon the neighboring hills, the streamlets upon either hand, one loudly singing among pebbles, the other dripping furtively from pond to pond, the stir of the wind in mountainous old flowering chestnuts, and once in seven days the voice of the bell and the old tunes of the precentor, were the only sounds that disturbed the silence around the rural church. The Resurrection Man – to use a byname of the period – was not to be deterred by any of the sanctities of customary piety. It was part of his trade to despise and desecrate the scrolls and trumpets of old tombs, the paths worn by the feet of worshipers and mourners, and the offerings and the inscriptions of bereaved affection. To rustic neighborhoods where love is more than commonly tenacious, and where some bonds of blood or fellowship unite the entire society of a parish, the body snatcher, far from being repelled by natural respect, was attracted by the ease and safety of the task. To bodies that had been laid in earth, in joyful expectation of a far different awakening, there came that hasty, lamplit, terror-haunted resurrection of the spade and mattock. The coffin was forced, the cerements torn, and the melancholy relics, clad in sackcloth, after being rattled for hours on moonless byways, were at length exposed to uttermost indignities before a class of gaping boys.

Somewhat as two vultures may swoop upon a dying lamb, Fettes and Macfarlane were to be let loose upon a grave in that green and quiet resting place. The wife of a farmer, a woman who had lived for sixty years, and been known for nothing but good butter and a godly conversation, was to be rooted from her grave at midnight and carried, dead and naked, to that faraway city that she had always honored with her Sunday's best; the place beside her family was to be empty till the crack of doom; her innocent and always venerable members to be exposed to that last curiosity of the anatomist.

Late one afternoon the pair set forth, well-wrapped in cloaks and furnished with a formidable bottle. It rained without remission – a cold, dense, lashing rain. Now and again there blew a puff of wind, but these sheets of falling water kept it down. Bottle and all, it was a sad and silent drive as far as Penicuik, where they were to spend the evening. They stopped once, to hide their implements in a thick bush not far from the church-yard, and once again at the Fisher's Tryst, to have a toast before the kitchen fire and vary their nips of whisky with a glass of ale. When they reached their journey's end the gig was housed, the horse was fed and comforted, and the two young doctors in a private room sat down to the best dinner and the best wine the house afforded. The lights, the fire, the beating rain upon the window, the cold, incongruous work that lay before them, added zest to their enjoyment of the meal. With every glass their cordiality increased. Soon Macfarlane handed a little pile of gold to his companion.

'A compliment,' he said. 'Between friends these little damned accommodations ought to fly like pipelights.'

Fettes pocketed the money, and applauded the sentiment to the echo. 'You are a philosopher,' he cried. 'I was an ass till I knew you. You and K— between you, by the Lord Harry! But you'll make a man of me.'

'Of course we shall,' applauded Macfarlane. 'A man? I tell you, it required a man to back me up the other morning. There are some big, brawling, forty-year-old cowards who would have turned sick at the look of the damned thing; but not you – you kept your head. I watched you.'

'Well, and why not?' Fettes thus vaunted himself. 'It was no affair of mine. There was nothing to gain on the one side but disturbance, and on the other I could count on your gratitude, don't you see?' And he slapped his pocket till the gold pieces rang.

Macfarlane somehow felt a certain touch of alarm at these unpleasant words. He may have regretted that he had taught his young companion so successfully, but he had no time to interfere, for the other noisily continued in this boastful strain:

'The great thing is not to be afraid. No, between you and me, I don't want to hang – that's practical; but for all cant, Macfarlane, I was born with a contempt. Hell, God, devil, right, wrong, sin, crime and all the old gallery of curiosities – they may frighten boys, but men of the world, like you and me, despise them. Here's to the memory of Gray!'

It was by this time growing somewhat late. The gig, according to order, was brought round to the door with both lamps brightly shining, and the young men had to pay their bill and take the road. They announced that they were bound for Peebles, and drove in that direction till they were clear of the last houses of the town; then, extinguishing the lamps, returned upon their course, and followed a byroad toward Glencorse. There was no sound but that of their own passage, and the incessant, strident pouring of the rain. It was pitch dark; here and there a white gate or a white stone in the wall guided them for a short space across the night; but for the most part it was at a foot pace, and almost groping, that they picked their way through that resonant blackness to their solemn and isolated destination. In the sunken woods that traverse the neighborhood of the burying ground the last glimmer failed them, and it became necessary to kindle a match and reillumine one of the lanterns of the gig. Thus, under the dripping trees, and environed by huge and moving shadows, they reached the scene of their inhallowed labors.

They were both experienced in such affairs, and powerful with the spade; and they had scarce been twenty minutes at their task before they were rewarded by a dull rattle on the coffin lid. At the same moment, Macfarlane, having hurt his hand upon a stone, flung it carelessly above his head. The grave, in which they now stood almost to the shoulders, was close to the edge of the platform of the graveyard; and the gig lamp had been propped, the better to illuminate their labors, against a tree, and on the immediate verge of the steep bank descending to the stream. Chance had taken a sure aim with the stone. Then came a clang of broken glass; night fell upon them; sounds alternately dull and ringing announced the bounding of the lantern down the bank, and its occasional collision with the trees. A stone or two, which it had dislodged in its descent, rattled behind it into the profundities of the glen; and then silence, like night, resumed its sway; and they might bend their hearing to its utmost pitch, but naught was to be heard except the rain, now marching to the wind, now steadily falling over miles of open country.

They were so nearly at an end of their abhorred task that they judged it wisest to complete it in the dark. The coffin was exhumed and broken open; the body inserted in the dripping sack and carried between them to the gig; one mounted to keep it in its place, and the other, taking the horse by the mouth, groped along by wall and bush until they reached the wider road by the Fisher's Tryst. Here was a faint, diffused radiancy, which they hailed like daylight; by that they pushed the horse to a good pace and began to rattle along merrily in the direction of the town.

They had both been wetted to the skin during their operations, and now, as the gig jumped among the deep ruts, the thing that stood propped between them fell now upon one and now upon the other. At every repetition of the horrid contact each instinctively repelled it with the greater haste; and the process, natural although it was, began to tell upon the nerves of the companions. Macfarlane made some ill-favored jest about the farmer's wife, but it came hollowly from his lips, and was allowed to drop in silence. Still their unnatural burden bumped from side to side; and now the head would be laid, as if in confidence, upon their shoulders, and now the drenching sackcloth would flap icily about their faces. A creeping chill began to possess the soul of Fettes. He peered at the bundle, and it seemed somehow larger than at first. All over the countryside, and from every degree of distance, the farm dogs accompanied their passage with tragic ululations; and it grew and grew upon his mind that some unnatural miracle had been accomplished, that some nameless change had befallen the dead body, and that it was in fear of their unholy burden that the dogs were howling.

'For God's sake,' said he, making a great effort to arrive at speech, 'for God's sake, let's have a light!'

Seemingly Macfarlane was affected in the same direction; for, though he made no reply, he stopped the horse, passed the reins to his companion, got down, and proceeded to kindle the remaining lamp. They had by that time got no farther than the crossroad down to Auchenclinny. The rain still poured as though the deluge were returning, and it was no easy matter to make a light in such a world of wet and darkness. When at last the flickering blue flame had been transferred to the wick and began to expand and clarify, and shed a wide circle of misty brightness round the gig, it became possible for the two young men to see each other and the thing they had along with them. The rain had molded the rough sacking to the outlines of the body underneath, the head was distinct from the trunk, the shoulders plainly modeled; something at once spectral and human riveted their eyes upon the ghastly comrade of their drive.

For some time Macfarlane stood motionless, holding up the lamp. A nameless dread was swathed, like a wet sheet, about the body, and tightened the white skin upon the face of Fettes; a fear that was meaningless, a horror of what could not be, kept mounting to his brain; another beat of the watch, and he had spoken. But his comrade forestalled him.

'That is not a woman,' said Macfarlane, in a hushed voice.

'It was a woman when we put her in,' whispered Fettes.

'Hold that lamp,' said the other. 'I must see her face.'

And as Fettes took the lamp his companion untied the fastenings of the sack and drew down the cover from the head. The light fell very clear upon the dark, well-molded features and smooth-shaven cheeks of a too familiar countenance, often beheld in dreams of both of these young men. A wild yell rang up into the night; each leaped from his own side into the roadway: the lamp fell, broke, and was extinguished; and the horse, terrified by this unusual commotion, bounded and went off toward Edinburgh at a gallop, bearing along with it, the sole occupant of the gig, the body of the dead and long-dissected Gray.

THE SPIDER

Hanns Heinz Ewers

[1872–1943]

'*In the present generation German horror-fiction is most notably represented by Hanns Heinz Ewers, who brings to bear on his dark conceptions an effective knowledge of modern psychology. Novels like* The Sorcerer's Apprentice *and* Alrune, *and short stories like* The Spider, *contain distinctive qualities which raise them to a classic level.*'

– H.P. Lovecraft

WHEN RICHARD BRACQUEMONT, medical student, decided to move into Room No. 7 of the little Hotel Stevens at 6 rue Alfred Stevens, three people had already hanged themselves from the window-sash of the room on three successive Fridays.

The first was a Swiss travelling salesman. His body was not discovered until Saturday evening; but the physician established the fact that death must have come between five and six o'clock on Friday afternoon. The body hung suspended from a strong hook which had been driven into the window-sash, and which ordinarily

served for hanging clothes. The window was closed, and the dead
man had used the curtain cord as a rope. Since the window was
rather low, his legs dragged on the ground almost to his knees. The
suicide must consequently have exercised considerable will power in
carrying out his intention. It was further established that he was
married and the father of four children; that he unquestionably had
an adequate and steady income; and that he was of a cheerful
disposition, and well content in life. Neither a will nor anything in
writing that might give a clue to the cause of the suicide was found;
nor had he ever intimated leanings towards suicide to any of his
friends or acquaintances.

The second case was not very different. The actor Karl Krause,
who was employed at the nearby Cirque Medrano as a lightning
bicycle artiste, engaged Room No. 7 two days after the first suicide.
When he failed to appear at the performance the following Friday
evening, the manager of the theatre sent an usher to the little hotel.
The usher found the actor hanged from the window-sash in the
unlocked room, in identically the same circumstances that had
attended the suicide of the Swiss travelling salesman. This second
suicide seemed no less puzzling than the first; the actor was popular,
drew a very large salary, was only twenty-five years old, and seemed
to enjoy life to the utmost. Again, nothing was left in writing, nor were
there any other clues that might help solve the mystery. The actor was
survived by an aged mother, to whom he used to send three hundred
marks for her support promptly on the first of each month.

For Madame Dubonnet, who owned the cheap little hotel, and
whose clientele was made up almost exclusively of the actors of the
nearby vaudevilles of Montmartre, this second suicide had very
distressing consequences. Already several of her guests had moved
out, and other regular customers had failed to come back. She
appealed to the Commissioner of the IXth Ward, whom she knew
well, and he promised to do everything in his power to help her. So he
not only pushed his investigation of reasons for the suicides with
considerable zeal, but he also placed at her disposal a police officer
who took up his residence in the mysterious room.

It was the policeman Charles-Maria Chaumié who had volun-
teered his services in solving the mystery. An old 'Márousin' who had
been a marine infantryman for eleven years, this sergeant had
guarded many a lonely post in Tonkin and Annam single-handed,
and had greeted many an uninvited deputation of river pirates,
sneaking like cats through the jungle darkness, with a refreshing

shot from his rifle. Consequently he felt himself well heeled to meet the
'ghosts' of which the rue Stevens gossiped. He moved into the room on
Sunday evening and went contentedly to sleep after doing high justice
to the food and drink Madame Dubonnet set before him.

Every morning and evening Chaumié paid a brief visit to the police
station to make his reports. During the first few days his reports
confined themselves to the statement that he had not noticed even the
slightest thing out of the ordinary. On Wednesday evening, however,
he announced that he believed he had found a clue. When pressed for
details he begged to be allowed to say nothing for the present: he said
he was not certain that the thing he thought he had discovered
necessarily had any bearing on the two suicides. And he was afraid of
being ridiculed in case it should all turn out to be a mistake. On
Thursday evening he seemed to be even more uncertain, although
somewhat graver; but again he had nothing to report. On Friday
morning he seemed quite excited: half seriously and half in jest he
ventured the statement that the window of the room certainly had a
remarkable power of attraction. Nevertheless he still clung to the
theory that that fact had nothing whatever to do with the suicides,
and that he would only be laughed at if he told more. That evening he
failed to come to the police station: they found him hanged from the
hook on the window-sash.

Even in this case the circumstances, down to the minutest detail,
were again the same as they had been in the other cases: the legs
dragged on the floor, and the curtain cord had been used as a rope.
The window was closed, and the door had not been locked; death had
evidently come at about six o'clock in the afternoon. The dead man's
mouth was wide open and his tongue hung out.

As a consequence of this third suicide in Room No. 7, all the guests
left the Hotel Stevens that same day, with the exception of the
German high school teacher in Room No. 16, who took advantage
of this opportunity to have his rent reduced one-third. It was small
consolation for Madame Dubonnet to have Mary Garden, the famous
star of the Opéra Comique, drive by in her Renault a few days later
and stop to buy the red curtain cord for a price she beat down to two
hundred francs. Of course she had two reasons for buying it; in the
first place, it would bring luck; and in the second – well, it would get
into the newspaper.

If these things had happened in summer, say in July or August,
Madame Dubonnet might have got three times as much for her
curtain cord; at that time of the year the newspapers would certainly

have filled their columns with the case for weeks. But at an uneasy time of the year, with elections, disorders in the Balkans, a bank failure in New York, a visit of the English King and Queen – well, where could the newspapers find room for a mere murder case? The result was that the affair in the rue Alfred Stevens got less attention than it deserved, and such notices of it as appeared in the newspapers were concise and brief, and confined themselves practically to repetitions of the police reports, without exaggerations.

These reports furnished the only basis for what little knowledge of the affair the medical student Richard Bracquemont had. He knew nothing of one other little detail that seemed so inconsequential that neither the Commissioner nor any of the other witnesses had mentioned it to the reporters. Only afterwards, after the adventure the medical student had in the room, was this detail remembered. It was this: when the police took the body of Sergeant Charles-Maria Chaumié down from the window-sash, a large black spider crawled out of the mouth of the dead man. The porter flicked it away with his finger, crying: 'Ugh! Another such ugly beast!' In the course of the subsequent autopsy – that is, the one held later for Bracquemont – the porter told that when they had taken down the corpse of the Swiss travelling salesman, a similar spider had been seen crawling on his shoulder – But of this Richard Bracquemont knew nothing.

He did not take up his lodging in the room until two weeks after the last suicide, on a Sunday. What he experienced there he entered very conscientiously in a diary.

THE DIARY OF RICHARD BRACQUEMONT, MEDICAL STUDENT

Monday, February 28

I moved in here last night. I unpacked my two suitcases, put a few things in order, and went to bed. I slept superbly: the clock was just striking nine when a knock at the door awakened me. It was the landlady, who brought me my breakfast herself. She is evidently quite solicitous about me, judging from the eggs, the ham, and the splendid coffee she brought me. I washed and dressed, and then watched the porter make up my room. I smoked my pipe while he worked.

So, here I am. I know right well that this business is dangerous, but I know too that my fortune is made if I solve the mystery. And if Paris was once worth a mass – one could hardly buy it that cheaply nowadays – it might be worth risking my little life for it. Here is my chance, and I intend to make the most of it.

At that there were plenty of others who saw this chance. No less than twenty-seven people tried, some through the police, some through the landlady, to get the room. Three of them were women. So there were enough rivals – probably all poor devils like myself.

But I got it! Why? Oh, I was probably the only one who could offer a 'solution' to the police. A neat solution! Of course it was a bluff.

These entries are of course intended for the police, too. And it amuses me considerably to tell these gentlemen right at the outset that it was all a trick on my part. If the Commissioner is sensible he will say, 'Hm! Just because I knew he was tricking us, I had all the more confidence in him!' As far as that is concerned, I don't care what he says afterwards; now I'm here. And it seems to me a good omen to have begun my work by bluffing the police so thoroughly.

Of course I first made my application to Madame Dubonnet, but she sent me to the police station. I lounged about the station every day for a week, only to be told that my application 'was being given consideration' and to be asked always to come again next day. Most of my rivals had long since thrown up the sponge; they probably found some better way to spend their time than waiting for hour after hour in the musty police court. But it seems the Commissioner was by this time quite irritated by my perseverance. Finally he told me point blank that my coming back would be quite useless. He was very grateful to me as well as to all the other volunteers for our good intentions, but the police could not use the assistance of 'dilettante laymen'. Unless I had some carefully worked out plan of procedure . . .

So I told him that I had exactly that kind of plan. Of course I had no such thing and couldn't have explained a word of it. But I told him that I could tell him about my plan – which was good, although dangerous, and which might possibly come to the same conclusion as the investigation of the police sergeant – only in case he promised me on his word of honour that he was ready to carry it out. He thanked me for it, but regretted that he had no time for such things. But I saw that I was getting the upper hand when he asked me whether I couldn't at least give him some intimation of what I planned doing.

And I gave it to him. I told him the most glorious nonsense, of which I myself hadn't had the least notion even a second beforehand. I don't know even now how I came by this unusual inspiration so opportunely. I told him that among all the hours of the week there was one that had a secret significance. That was the hour in which Christ left His grave to go down to hell: the sixth hour of the afternoon of the last day of the Jewish week. And he might take into consideration, I went on, that it was exactly in this hour, between five and six o'clock on Friday afternoon, in which all three of the suicides had been committed. For the present I could not tell him more, but I might refer him to the Book of Revelations according to St. John.

The Commissioner put on a wise expression, as if he had understood it all, thanked me, and asked me to come back in the evening. I came back to his office promptly at the appointed time; I saw a copy of the New Testament lying in front of him on the table. In the meantime I had done just what he had: I had read the Book of Revelations through and – had not understood a word of it. Perhaps the Commissioner was more intelligent than I was; at least he told me that he understood what I was driving at in spite of my very vague hints. And that he was ready to grant my request and to aid me in every possible way.

I must admit that he has actually been of very considerable assistance. He has made arrangements with the landlady under which I am to enjoy all the comforts and facilities of the hotel free of charge. He has given me an exceptionally fine revolver and a police pipe. The policemen on duty have orders to go through the little rue Alfred Stevens as often as possible, and to come up to the room at a given signal. But the main thing is his installation of a desk telephone that connects directly with the police station. Since the station is only four minutes' walk from the hotel, I am thus enabled to have all the help I want immediately. With all this, I can't understand what there is to be afraid of . . .

Tuesday, March 1

Nothing has happened, neither yesterday nor today. Madame Dubonnet brought me a new curtain cord from another room – Heavens knows she has enough of them vacant. For that matter, she seems to take every possible opportunity to come to my room; every time she comes she brings me something. I have again had all the details of the suicides told me, but have discovered nothing new. As far as the causes of the suicides were concerned, she had her own opinions. As for the actor, she thought he had had an unhappy love affair; when he had been her guest the year before, he had been visited frequently by a young woman who had not come at all this year. She admittedly couldn't quite make out why the Swiss gentleman had decided to commit suicide, but of course one couldn't know everything. But there was no doubt that the police sergeant had committed suicide only to spite her.

I must confess these explanations of Madame Dubonnet's are rather inadequate. But I let her gabble on; at least she helps break up my boredom.

Thursday, March 3

Still nothing. The Commissioner rings me up several times a day and I tell him that everything is going splendidly. Evidently this information doesn't quite satisfy him. I have taken out my medical books and begun to work. In this way I am at least getting something out of my voluntary confinement.

Friday, March 4, 2 p.m.

I had an excellent luncheon. Madame Dubonnet brought a half bottle of champagne along with it. It was the kind of dinner you get before your execution. She already regards me as being three-fourths dead. Before she left me she wept and begged me to go with her. Apparently she is afraid I might also hang myself 'just to spite her'.

I have examined the new curtain cord in considerable detail. So I am to hang myself with that? Well, I can't say that I feel much like doing it. The cord is raw and hard, and it would make a good slipknot only with difficulty – one would have to be pretty powerfully determined to emulate the example of the other three suicides in order to make a success of the job. But now I'm sitting at the table, the telephone at my left, the revolver at my right. I certainly have no fear – but I am curious.

6 p.m.

Nothing happened – I almost write it with regret. The crucial hour came and went, and was just like all the others. Frankly I can't deny that sometimes I felt a certain urge to go to the window – oh, yes, but for other reasons! The Commissioner called me up at least ten times between five and six. He was just as impatient as I was. But Madame Dubonnet is satisfied; someone has lived for a week in No. 7 without hanging himself. Miraculous!

Monday, March 7

I am now convinced that I shall discover nothing; and I am inclined to think that the suicides of my predecessors were a matter of pure coincidence. I have asked the Commissioner to go over all the evidence in all three cases again, for I am convinced that eventually a solution of the mystery will be found. But as far as I am concerned, I intend to stay here as long as possible. I probably will not conquer Paris, but in the meantime I'm living here free and am already gaining considerably in health and weight. On top of it all I'm studying a great deal, and I notice I am rushing through in great style. And of course there is another reason that keeps me here.

Wednesday, March 9

I've progressed another step. Clarimonde –

Oh, but I haven't said a word about Clarimonde yet. Well, she is – my third reason for staying here. And it would have been for her sake that I would gladly have gone to the window in that fateful hour – but certainly not to hang myself. Clarimonde – but why do I call her that? I haven't the least idea as to what her name might be; but it seems to me as if I simply *must* call her Clarimonde. And I'd like to bet that some day I'll find out that that is really her name.

I already noticed Clarimonde the first few days I was here. She lives on the other side of this very narrow street, and her window is directly opposite mine. She sits there back of her curtains. And let me also say that she noticed me before I was aware of her, and that she visibly manifested an interest in me. No wonder – everyone on the street knows that I am here, and knows why, too. Madame Dubonnet saw to that.

I am in no way the kind of person who falls in love. My relations with women have always been very slight. When one comes to Paris from Verdun to study medicine and hardly has enough money to have a decent meal once every three days, one has other things beside love to worry about. I haven't much experience, and I probably began this affair pretty stupidly. Anyhow, it's quite satisfactory as it stands.

At first it never occurred to me to establish communications with my strange neighbour. I simply decided that since I was here to make observations, and that I probably had nothing real to investigate anyhow, I might as well observe my neighbour while I was at it. After all, one can't pore over one's books all day long. So I have come to the conclusion that, judging from appearances, Clarimonde lives all alone in her little apartment. She has three windows, but she sits only at the one directly opposite mine. She sits there and spins, spins at a little old-fashioned distaff. I once saw such a distaff at my grandmother's but even my grandmother never used it. It was merely an heirloom left her by some great-aunt or other. I didn't know that they were still in use. For that matter, Clarimonde's distaff is a very tiny, fine thing, white, and apparently made of ivory. The threads she spins must be infinitely fine. She sits behind her curtains all day long and works incessantly, stopping only when it gets dark. Of course it gets dark very early these foggy days. In this narrow street the loveliest twilight comes about five o'clock. I have never seen a light in her room.

How does she look? – Well, I really don't know. She wears her black hair in wavy curls, and is rather pale. Her nose is small and narrow, and her nostrils quiver. Her lips are pale, too, and it seems as if her little teeth might be pointed, like those of a beast of prey. Her eyelids throw long shadows; but when she opens them her large, dark eyes are full of light. Yet I seem to sense rather than know all this. It is difficult to identify anything clearly back of those curtains.

One thing further: she always wears a black, closely-buttoned dress, with large purple dots. And she always wears long black gloves, probably to protect her hands while working. It looks strange to see her narrow black fingers quickly taking and drawing the threads, seemingly almost through each other – really almost like the wriggling of an insect's legs.

Our relations with each other? Oh, they are really quite superficial. And yet it seems as if they were truly much deeper. It began by her looking over to my window, and my looking over to hers. She noticed me, and I her. And then I evidently must have pleased her, because one day when I looked at her she smiled. And of course I did, too. That went on for several days, and we smiled at each other more and more. Then I decided almost every hour that I would greet her; I don't know exactly what it is that keeps me from carrying out my decision.

I have finally done it, this afternoon. And Clarimonde returned the greeting. Of course the greeting was ever so slight, but nevertheless I distinctly saw her nod.

Thursday, March 10

Last night I sat up late over my books. I can't truthfully say that I studied a great deal: I spent my time building air castles and dreaming about Clarimonde. I slept very lightly, but very late into the morning.

When I stepped up to the window, Clarimonde was sitting at hers. I greeted her and she nodded. She smiled, and looked at me for a long time.

I wanted to work, but couldn't seem to find the necessary peace of mind. I sat at the window and stared at her. Then I suddenly noticed that she, too, folded her hands in her lap. I pulled at the cord of the white curtain and – practically at the same instant – she did the same. We both smiled and looked at one another.

I believe we must have sat like that for an hour.

Then she began spinning again.

Saturday, March 12

These days pass swiftly. I eat and drink, and sit down to work. I light my pipe and bend over my books. But I don't read a word. Of course I always make the attempt, but I know beforehand that it won't do any good. Then I go to the window. I greet Clarimonde, and she returns my greeting. We smile and gaze at one another – for hours.

Yesterday afternoon at six I felt a little uneasy. Darkness settled very early, and I felt a certain nameless fear. I sat at my desk and waited. I felt an almost unconquerable urge to go to the window – certainly not to hang myself, but to look at Clarimonde. I jumped up and stood back of the curtain. It seemed as if I had never seen her so clearly, although it was already quite dark. She was spinning, but her eyes looked across at me. I felt a strange comfort and a very subtle fear.

The telephone rang. I was furious at the silly old Commissioner for interrupting my dreams with his stupid questions.

This morning he came to visit me, along with Madame Dubonnet. She seems to be satisfied enough with my activities: she takes sufficient consolation from the fact that I have managed to *live* in Room No. 7 for two whole weeks. But the Commissioner wants results besides. I confided to him that I had made some secret observations, and that I was tracking down a very strange clue. The old fool believed all I told him. In any event I can still stay here for weeks – and that's all I care about. Not on account of Madame Dubonnet's cooking and cellar – God, how soon one becomes indifferent to that when one always has enough to eat! – only because of the window, which she hates and fears, and which I love so dearly: this window that reveals Clarimonde to me.

When I light the lamp I no longer see her. I have strained my eyes trying to see whether she goes out, but I have never seen her set foot on the street. I have a comfortable easy chair and a green lampshade whose glow warmly suffuses me. The Commissioner has sent me a large package of tobacco. I have never smoked such good tobacco.

And yet I cannot do any work. I read two or three pages, and when I have finished I realize that I haven't understood a word of their contents. My eyes grasp the significance of the letters, but my brain refuses to supply the connotations. Queer! Just as if my brain bore the legend: 'No Admittance.' Just as if it refused to admit any thought other than the one: Clarimonde . . .

Finally I push my books aside, lean far back in my chair, and dream.

Sunday, March 13

This morning I witnessed a little tragedy. I was walking up and down in the corridor while the porter made up my room. In front of the little court window there is a spider web hanging, with a fat garden spider sitting in the middle of it. Madame Dubonnet refuses to let it be swept away: spiders bring luck, and Heaven knows she has had enough bad luck in her house. Presently I saw another much smaller male spider cautiously running around the edge of the web. Tentatively he ventured down one of the precarious threads towards the middle; but the moment the female moved, he hastily withdrew. He ran around to another end of the web and tried again to approach her. Finally the powerful female spider in the centre of the web seemed to look upon his suit with favour, and stopped moving. The male spider pulled at one of the threads of the web – first lightly, then so vigorously that the whole web quivered. But the object of his attention remained immovable. Then he approached her very quickly, but carefully. The female spider received him quietly and let him embrace her delicately while she retained the utmost passivity. Motionless the two of them hung for several minutes in the centre of the large web.

Then I saw how the male spider slowly freed himself, one leg after another. It seemed as if he wanted to retreat quietly, leaving his companion alone in her dream of love. Suddenly he let her go entirely and ran out of the web as fast as he could. But at the same instant the female seemed to awaken to a wild rush of activity, and she chased rapidly after him. The weak male spider let himself down by a thread, but the female followed immediately. Both of them fell to the window-sill; and, gathering all his energies, the male spider tried to run away. But it was too late. The female spider seized him in her powerful grip, carried him back up into the net, and set him down squarely in the middle of it. And this same place that had just been a bed for passionate desire now became the scene of something quite different. The lover kicked in vain, stretched his weak legs out again and again, and tried to disentangle himself from this wild embrace. But the female would not let him go. In a few minutes she had spun him in so completely that he could not move a single member. Then she thrust her sharp pincers into his body and sucked out the young blood of her lover in deep draughts. I even saw how she finally let go of the pitiful unrecognizable little lump – legs, skin, and threads – and threw it contemptuously out of the net.

So that's what love is like among these creatures! Well, I can be glad I'm not a young spider.

Monday, March 14

I no longer so much as glance at my books. Only at the window do I pass all my days. And I keep on sitting there even after it gets dark. Then she is no longer there; but I close my eyes and see her anyhow . . .

Well, this diary has become quite different than I thought it would be. It tells about Madame Dubonnet and the Commissioner, about spiders and about Clarimonde. But not a word about the discovery I had hoped to make – Well, is it my fault?

Tuesday, March 15

Clarimonde and I have discovered a strange new game, and we play it all day long. I greet her, and immediately she returns the greeting. Then I drum with my fingers on my window-pane. She has hardly had time to see it before she begins drumming on hers. I wink at her, and she winks at me. I move my lips as if I were talking to her and she follows suit. Then I brush the hair back from my temples, and immediately her hand is at the side of her forehead. Truly child's play. And we both laugh at it. That is, she really doesn't laugh: it's only a quiet, passive smile she has, just as I suppose mine must be.

For that matter all this isn't nearly as senseless as it must seem. It isn't imitation at all: I think we would both tire of that very quickly. There must be a certain telepathy or thought transference involved in it. For Clarimonde repeats my motions in the smallest conceivable fraction of a second. She hardly has time to see what I am doing before she does the same thing. Sometimes it even seems to me that her action is simultaneous with mine. That is what entices me: always doing something new and unpremeditated. And it's astounding to see her doing the same thing at the same time. Sometimes I try to catch her. I make a great many motions in quick succession, and then repeat them again; and then I do them a third time. Finally I repeat them for the fourth time, but change their order, introduce some new motion, or leave out one of the old ones. It's like children playing

Follow the Leader. It's really remarkable that Clarimonde never makes a single mistake, although I sometimes change the motions so rapidly that she hardly has time to memorize each one.

That is how I spend my days. But I never feel for a second that I'm squandering my time on something nonsensical. On the contrary, it seems as if nothing I had ever done were more important.

Wednesday, March 16

Isn't it queer that I have never thought seriously about putting my relations with Clarimonde on a more sensible basis than that of these hour-consuming games? I thought about it last night. I could simply take my hat and coat and go down two flights of stairs, five steps across the street, and then up two other flights of stairs. On her door there is a little coat-of-arms engraved with her name: 'Clarimonde . . .' Clarimonde what? I don't know what; but the name Clarimonde is certainly there. Then I could knock, and then . . .

That far I can imagine everything perfectly, down to the last move I might make. But for the life of me I can't picture what would happen after that. The door would open – I can conceive that. But I would remain standing in front of it and looking into her room, into a darkness – a darkness so utter that not a solitary thing could be distinguished in it. She would not come – nothing would come; as a matter of fact, there would be nothing there. Only the black impenetrable darkness.

Sometimes it seems as if there could be no other Clarimonde than the one I play with at my window. I can't picture what this woman would look like if she wore a hat, or even some dress other than her black one with the large purple dots; I can't even conceive her without her gloves. If I could see her on the street, or even in some restaurant, eating, drinking, talking – well, I really have to laugh: the thing seems so utterly inconceivable.

Sometimes I ask myself whether I love her. I can't answer that question entirely, because I have never been in love. But if the feeling I bear towards Clarimonde is really – well, love – then love is certainly very, very different than I saw it among my acquaintances or learned about it in novels.

It is becoming quite difficult to define my emotions. In fact, it is becoming difficult even to think about anything at all that has no bearing on Clarimonde – or rather, on our game. For there is truly no denying it: it's really the game that preoccupies me – nothing else. And that's the thing I understand least of all.

Clarimonde – well, yes, I feel attracted to her. But mingled with the attraction there is another feeling – almost like a sense of fear. Fear? No, it isn't fear either: it is more of a temerity, a certain inarticulate alarm or apprehension before something I cannot define. And it is just this apprehension that has some strange compulsion, something curiously passionate that keeps me at a distance from her and at the same time draws me constantly nearer to her. It is as if I were going around her in a wide circle, came a little nearer at one place, withdrew again, went on, approached her again at another point and again retreated rapidly. Until finally – of that I am absolutely certain – I *must* go to her.

Clarimonde is sitting at her window and spinning. Threads – long, thin, infinitely fine threads. She seems to be making some fabric – I don't know just what it is to be. And I can't understand how she can make the network without tangling or tearing the delicate fabric. There are wonderful patterns in her work – patterns full of fabulous monsters and curious grotesques.

For that matter – but what am I writing? The fact of the matter is that I can't even see what it is she is spinning: the threads are much too fine. And yet I can't help feeling that her work must be exactly as I see it – when I close my eyes. Exactly. A huge network peopled with many creatures – fabulous monsters, and curious grotesques . . .

Thursday, March 17
I find myself in a strange state of agitation. I no longer talk to anyone; I hardly even say good morning to Madame Dubonnet or the porter. I hardly take time to eat; I only want to sit at the window and play with her. It's an exacting game. Truly it is.

And I have a premonition that tomorrow something must happen.

Friday, March 18
Yes, yes. Something must happen today . . . I tell myself – oh, yes, I talk aloud, just to hear my own voice – that it is just for *that* that I am here. But the worst of it is that I am afraid. And this fear that what has happened to my predecessors in this room may also happen to me is curiously mingled with my other fear – the fear of Clarimonde. I can hardly keep them apart.

6 p.m.
Let me put down a few words quickly, and then get into my hat and coat.

By the time five o'clock came, my strength was gone. Oh, I know now for certain that it must have something to do with this sixth hour of the next to the last day of the week . . . Now I can no longer laugh at the fraud with which I duped the Commissioner. I sat on my chair and stayed there only by exerting my will power to the utmost. But this thing drew me, almost pulled me to the window. I had to play with Clarimonde – and then again there rose that terrible fear of the window. I saw them hanging there – the Swiss travelling salesman, a large fellow with a thick neck and a grey stubble beard. And the lanky acrobat and the stocky, powerful police sergeant. I saw all three of them, one after another and then all three together, hanging from the same hook with open mouths and with tongues lolling far out. And then I saw myself among them.

Oh, this fear! I felt I was as much afraid of the window-sash and the terrible hook as I was of Clarimonde. May she forgive me for it, but that's the truth: in my ignominious fear I always confused her image with that of the three who hanged there, dragging their legs heavily on the floor.

But the truth is that I never felt for an instant any desire or inclination to hang myself: I wasn't even afraid I would do it. No – I was afraid only of the window itself – and of Clarimonde – and of something terrible, something uncertain and unpredictable that was now to come. I had the pathetic irresistible longing to get up and go to the window. And I *had* to do it . . .

Then the telephone rang. I grabbed the receiver and before I could hear a word I myself cried into the mouthpiece: 'Come! Come at once!'

It was just as if my unearthly yell had instantly chased all the shadows into the farthest cracks of the floor. I became composed immediately. I wiped the sweat from my forehead and drank a glass of water. Then I considered what I ought to tell the Commissioner when he came. Finally I went to the window, greeted Clarimonde, and smiled.

Five minutes later the Commissioner was here. I told him that I had finally struck the root of the whole affair; if he would only refrain from questioning me today, I would certainly be able to make some remarkable disclosures in the very near future. The queer part of it was that while I was lying to him I was at the same time fully convinced in my own mind that I was telling the truth. And I still feel that is the truth – against my better judgement.

He probably noticed the unusual condition of my temper, especially when I apologized for screaming into the telephone and tried to explain – and failed to find any plausible reason for my agitation. He suggested very amiably that I need not take undue consideration of him: he was always at my service – that was his duty. He would rather make a dozen useless trips over here than to let me wait for him once when I really needed him. Then he invited me to go out with him tonight, suggesting that that might help distract me – it wasn't a good thing to be alone all the time. I have accepted his invitation, although I think it will be difficult to go out: I don't like to leave this room.

Saturday, March 19

We went to the Gaieté Rochechouart, to the Cigale, and to the Lune Rousse. The Commissioner was right: it was a good thing for me to go out and breathe another atmosphere. At first I felt rather uncomfortable, as if I were doing something wrong, as if I were a deserter, running away from our flag. But by and by that feeling died; we drank a good deal, laughed, and joked.

When I went to the window this morning, I seemed to read a reproach in Clarimonde's look. But perhaps I only imagined it: how could she know that I had gone out last night? For that matter, it seemed to last for only a moment; then she smiled again.

We played all day long.

Sunday, March 20

Today I can only repeat: we played all day long.

Monday, March 21

We played all day long.

Tuesday, March 22

Yes, and today we did the same. Nothing, absolutely nothing else. Sometimes I ask myself why we do it. What is it all for? Or, what do I really want, to what can it all lead? But I never answer my own question. For it's certain that I want nothing other than just this. Come what may, that which is coming is exactly what I long for.

We have been talking to one another these last few days, of course not with any spoken word. Sometimes we moved our lips, at other times we only looked at one another. But we understood each other perfectly.

I was right: Clarimonde reproached me for running away last Friday. But I begged her forgiveness and told her I realized that it

had been very unwise and horrid of me. She forgave me and I
promised her never again to leave the window. And we kissed each
other, pressing our lips against the panes for a long, long time.

Wednesday, March 23

I know now that I love her. It must be love – I feel it tingling in
every fibre of my being. It may be that with other people love is
different. But is there anyone among a thousand millions who has a
head, an ear, a hand that is like anyone else's? Everyone is different, so
it is quite conceivable that our love is unlike that of other people. I
know that my love is very singular. But does that make it any less
beautiful? I am almost happy in this love.

If only there would not be this fear! Sometimes it falls asleep. Then
I forget it. But only for a few minutes. Then it wakes up again and will
not let me go. It seems to me like a poor little mouse fighting against a
huge and beautiful snake, trying to free itself from its overpowering
embrace. Just wait, you poor foolish little fear, soon our love will
devour you!

Thursday, March 24

I have made a discovery: I don't play with Clarimonde – *she plays
with me.*

It happened like this.

Last night, as usual, I thought about our game. I wrote down five
intricate movements with which I wanted to surprise her today. I
gave every motion a number. I practised them so as to be able to
execute them as quickly as possible, first in order, and then backwards. Then only the even numbers and then the odd, and then only
the first and last parts of each of the five motions. It was very
laborious, but it gave me great satisfaction because it brought me
nearer to Clarimonde, even though I could not see her. I practised in
this way for hours, and finally they went like clock-work.

This morning I went to the window. We greeted each other, and
the game began. Forward, backward – it was incredible to see how
quickly she understood me, and how instantaneously she repeated all
the things I did.

Then there was a knock at my door. It was the porter, bringing me
my boots. I took them; but when I was going back to the window my
glance fell on the sheet of paper on which I had recorded the order of
the movements. *And I saw that I had not executed a single one of these
movements.*

I almost reeled. I grabbed the back of the easy chair and let myself down into it. I couldn't believe it. I read the sheet again and again. But it was true: of all the motions I had made at the window, not a single one was mine.

And again I was aware of a door opening somewhere far away – her door. I was standing before it and looking in . . . nothing, nothing – only an empty darkness. Then I knew that if I went out, I would be saved; and I realized that now I *could* go. Nevertheless I did not go. That was because I was distinctly aware of one feeling: that I held the secret of the mystery. Held it tightly in both hands – Paris – I was going to conquer Paris!

For a moment Paris was stronger than Clarimonde.

Oh, I've dropped all thought of it now. Now I am aware only of my love, and in the midst of it this quiet, passionate fear.

But in that instant I felt suddenly strong. I read through the details of my first movement once more and impressed it firmly in my memory. Then I went back to the window.

And I took exact notice of what I did; *not a single motion I executed was among those I had set out to do*.

Then I decided to run my index finger along my nose. But instead I kissed the window-pane. I wanted to drum on the window-sill, but ran my hand through my hair instead. So it was true: Clarimonde did not imitate the things I did: on the contrary, I repeated the things she indicated. And I did it so quickly, with such lightning rapidity, that I followed her motions in the same second, so that even now it seems as if I were the one who exerted the will power to do these things.

So it is I – I who was so proud of the fact that I had determined her mode of thought – I was the one who was being so completely influenced. Only, her influence is so soft, so gentle that it seems as if nothing on earth could be so soothing.

I made other experiments. I put both my hands in my pockets and resolved firmly not to move them; then I looked across at her. I noticed how she lifted her hand and smiled, and gently chided me with her index finger. I refused to budge. I felt my right hand wanting to take itself out of my pocket, but I dug my fingers deep into the pocket lining. Then slowly, after several minutes, my fingers relaxed, my hand came out of the pocket, and I lifted my arm. And I chided her with my index finger and smiled. It seemed as if it were really not I that was doing all this, but some stranger whom I watched from a distance. No, no – that wasn't the way of it. I, I was the one who did it

— and some stranger was watching me. It was the stranger — that other me — who was so strong, who wanted to solve this mystery with some great discovery. But that was no longer I.

I — oh, what do I care about the discovery? I am only here to do her bidding, the bidding of my Clarimonde, whom I love with such tender fear.

Friday, March 25

I have cut the telephone wire. I can no longer stand being perpetually bothered by the silly old Commissioner, least of all when the fateful hour is at hand . . .

God, why am I writing all this? Not a word of it is true. It seems as if someone else were guiding my pen.

But I do — I do want to set down here what actually happens. It is costing me a tremendous effort. But I want to do it. If only, for the last time to do — what I really want to do.

I cut the telephone wire . . . oh . . .

Because I had to . . . There, I finally got it out! Because I had to, I had to!

We stood at the window this morning and played. Our game has changed a little since yesterday. She goes through some motions and I defend myself as long as possible. Until finally I have to surrender, powerless to do anything but her bidding. And I can scarcely tell what a wonderful sense of exaltation and joy it gives me to be conquered by her will to make this surrender.

We played. And then suddenly she got up and went back into her room. It was so dark that I couldn't see her; she seemed to disappear into the darkness. But she came back very shortly, carrying in her hands a desk telephone just like mine. Smiling, she set it down on the window-sill, took a knife, cut the wire, and carried it back again.

I defended myself for about a quarter of an hour. My fear was greater than ever, but that made my slow surrender all the more delectable. And I finally brought my telephone to the window, cut the wire, and set it back on the table.

That is how it happened.

I am sitting at the table. I have had my tea, and the porter has just taken the dishes out. I asked him what time it was — it seems my watch isn't keeping time. It's five fifteen . . . five fifteen . . .

I know that if I look up now Clarimonde will be doing something or other. Doing something or other that I will have to do too.

I look up anyhow. She is standing there and smiling. Well . . . if I could only tear my eyes away from her! . . . now she is going to the curtain. She is taking the cord off – it is red, just like the one on my window. She is tying a knot – a slipknot. She is hanging the cord up on the hook in the window-sash.

She is sitting down and smiling.

. . . No, this is no longer a thing one can call fear, this thing I am experiencing. It is a maddening, choking terror – but nevertheless I wouldn't trade it for anything in the world. It is a compulsion of an unheard-of nature and power, yet so subtly sensual in its inescapable ferocity.

Of course I could rush up to the window and do exactly what she wants me to do. But I am waiting, struggling, and defending myself. I feel this uncanny thing getting stronger every minute . . .

So, here I am, still sitting here. I ran quickly to the window and did the thing she wanted me to do: I took the curtain cord, tied a slipknot in it, and hung it from the hook . . .

And now I am not going to look up any more. I am going to stay here and look only at this sheet of paper. For I know now what she would do if I looked up again – now in the sixth hour of the next to the last day of the week. If I see her, I shall have to do her bidding . . . I shall have to . . .

I shall refuse to look at her.

But I am suddenly laughing – loudly. No, I'm not laughing – it is something laughing within me. I know why, too: it's because of this 'I will not . . .'

I don't want to, and yet I know certainly that I must. I must look at her . . . must, must do it . . . and then – the rest.

I am only waiting to stretch out the torment. Yes, that is it . . . For these breathless sufferings are my most rapturous transports. I am writing quickly, quickly, so that I can remain sitting here longer . . . in order to stretch out these seconds of torture, which carry the ecstasy of love into infinity . . .

More . . . longer . . .

Again this fear, again! I know that I shall look at her, that I shall get up, that I shall hang myself. *But it isn't that that I fear*. Oh, no – that is sweet, that is beautiful.

But there is something else . . . something else associated with it – *something that will happen afterwards*. I don't know what it will be – but it is coming, it is certainly coming, certainly . . . certainly. For the joy of my torments is so infinitely great – oh, I feel it is so great that something terrible must follow it.

Only I must not think . . .

Let me write something, anything, no matter what. Only quickly, without thinking . . .

My name – Richard Bracquemont, Richard Bracquemont, Richard – oh, I can't go any further – Richard Bracquemont – Richard Bracquemont – now – now – I must look at her . . . Richard Bracquemont – I must – no – no, more – more . . . Richard . . . Richard Bracque –

The Commissioner of the IXth Ward, after failing repeatedly to get a reply to his telephone calls, came to the Hotel Stevens at five minutes after six. In Room No. 7 he found the body of the student Richard Bracquemont hanging from the window-sash, in exactly the same position as that of his three predecessors.

Only his face had a different expression; it was distorted in a horrible fear, and his eyes, wide open, seemed to be pushing themselves out of their sockets. His lips were drawn apart, but his powerful teeth were firmly and desperately clenched.

And glued between them, bitten and crushed to pieces, there was a large black spider, with curious purple dots.

On the table lay the medical student's diary. The Commissioner read it and went immediately to the house across the street. There he discovered that the second apartment had been vacant and unoccupied for months and months . . .

THE FOOT
OF THE MUMMY

Théophile Gautier

[1811–1872]

'*It is in Théophile Gautier that we first seem to find an authentic French sense of the unreal world, and here there appears a special mystery which, though not continuously used, is recognizable at once as something alike genuine and profound. Short tales like* Avatar, The Foot of the Mummy, *and* Clarimonde *display glimpses of forbidden vistas that allure, tantalize and sometimes horrify.*'

– H.P. Lovecraft

HAVING NOTHING PARTICULAR TO DO, I had entered the shop of one of those dealers in curiosities called bric-à-brac dealers in our Parisian slang, which is utterly unintelligible in other parts of France. No doubt you have sometimes glanced at the windows of some of these shops, which have multiplied since it has become fashionable to purchase old furniture, and every stockbroker thinks he must have a medieval room. They have at one and the same time something of the junk dealer, the upholsterer, the alchemist's laboratory, and the painter's studio. In these mysterious dens, through which a prudent half-light filters, what is most genuinely old is the dirt. The cobwebs there are more authentic than the lace, and old pear tree wood is younger than mahogany imported last week from America.

The shop of my bric-à-brac dealer was a regular lumber room; every age and every country appeared to be represented in it. A red clay Etruscan lamp rested upon a cabinet by Boule, with ebony panels austerely inlaid with brass; a half-lounge of the days of Louis XV carelessly extended its fawn feet under a thick Louis XIII table, with heavy oaken spirals and carved foliage and monsters. In one corner gleamed the wavy breastplate of a damascened suit of Milan armor. Parian porcelain cupids and nymphs, Chinese grotesques, vases of céladon and craquelé, cups of Dresden and old Sèvres china, covered the shelves and filled up the corners. On the denticulated shelves of the sideboards shone resplendently great Japanese dishes with red and blue ornaments, set off by gold hatchings, side by side with enamels by Bernard Palissy, representing adders, frogs, and lizards in relief. From wardrobes that burst open escaped cascades of silk damask, overlaid with silver, waves of brocatelle, which a sunbeam covered with luminous dots; while portraits of every period in more or less dull gold frames smiled through their yellow varnish.

The dealer carefully followed me along the narrow passage left, open between the piles of furniture, keeping down the fluttering skirts of my coat, and watching my elbows, with the restless attention of an antiquarian and a usurer.

He had a curious face, that dealer; a big skull, polished like marble, with a thin aureole of white hair, brought out more strongly by the pale salmon color of his skin, giving him a sham look of patriarchal kindness, which was neutralized, however, by the sparkling of two little yellow eyes that shone in their orbs like two gold coins laid on mercury. The aquiline profile of his nose recalled the Oriental or Jewish type; his thin, slender hands, covered with veins and full of nerves standing out like the strings of a violin, and provided with nails like the claws at the end of a bat's wings, had a most unpleasant senile trembling; but when they lifted some precious object, an onyx cup, a Venetian glass, or a tray of Bohemian crystal, these trembling hands became stronger than steel pincers or lobster's claws. The old rascal had such a thoroughly rabbinical and cabalistic look that he would have burned at the stake three centuries ago merely on account of his appearance.

'Are you not going to buy anything today, sir? Here is a Malay creese, the blade of which is waved like a flame. Look at the grooves for the blood to run down; and at these teeth cut the reverse way to tear the entrails as you pull out the weapon. It is a ferocious arm, very characteristic, which would look uncommonly well on your wall. This two-handed sword is very handsome. It is by Joseph de la Hera. And this great dueling sword with openwork pearl handle is a superb piece of work.'

'No, I have enough weapons and instruments of destruction. I want a statuette, a trifle, for a paperweight, for I cannot bear those cheap bronzes sold by stationers, which are to be found on every writing table.'

The old gnome, rummaging among his possessions, spread out before me antique bronzes – or at least claimed to be antique – pieces of malachite, small Hindu or Chinese jade idols, grotesque incarnations of Brahma or Vishnu, uncommonly well fitted to the not very divine purpose of keeping down newspapers and letters.

I was hesitating between a porcelain dragon covered with warts, its mouth adorned with fangs and tentacles, and a small abominable Mexican fetish representing the god Witziliputzili, when I noticed a lovely foot, which at first I thought must be a fragment of some antique Venus. It had the lovely tawny, ruddy tints that give to Florentine bronze its warm and living tints so preferable to the verdigrised tone of ordinary bronzes, which might easily be mistaken for statues in a state of putrefaction. Satiny gleams shimmered over its round forms, polished by the loving kisses of twenty centuries; for it unquestionably was of Corinthian brass, a piece of work of the best epoch, perhaps a casting by Lysippus.

'This foot will do for me,' said I to the dealer, who looked at me with a sly, ironical glance, as he held it out to allow me to examine it more comfortably.

I was surprised at its lightness. It was not a foot of metal, but of flesh; an embalmed foot, a mummy's foot. On looking closely the grain of the skin and the almost imperceptible mark made by the bandages could be perceived. The toes were small and delicate, with perfect, pure nails, transparent as agate; the great toe, somewhat apart, after the fashion of antiquity, contrasted happily with the direction of the other toes, and gave it a free attitude, the neat aspect of a bird's foot. The sole, scarcely marked by a few faint lines, had evidently never come in contact with the ground, and had trodden only upon the finest matting of Nile reeds, and the softest carpets of panther's skins.

'Ha! ha! you want the foot of the princess Hermonthis,' said the dealer, with a horrible chuckle, as he fixed upon me his owllike glance. 'Ha! ha! – for a paperweight! That is a novel idea; that is an artist's idea. If old pharaoh had been told that his adored daughter's foot would be used as a paperweight he would have been astounded, considering that he was having a mountain of granite hollowed out in order to put inside the triple painted and gilded coffin, covered with hieroglyphs, with beautiful paintings representing the judgment of the soul,' added the queer little dealer, in a low voice, as if speaking to himself.

'How much will you sell me this fragment of a mummy for?'

'As dear as I can, for it is quite a curiosity. If I had the companion to it, I would not let you have the pair for less than five hundred francs. Pharaoh's daughters are scarce, very scarce.'

'I know it; I am aware that it is not very common; but how much do you want? To begin with, I must inform you that my whole wealth amounts to five louis. I shall buy whatever may cost five louis, but nothing more. You might search the back pockets of my vests, and my most secret drawers, you would not find another sou in them.'

'Five louis for the foot of Princess Hermonthis! That is very little, very little indeed for an authentic foot,' said the dealer, wagging his head and rolling his eyes. 'Well, take it. I will give you the wrapper into the bargain,' he added, as he rolled the foot in an old piece of damask. 'It is very beautiful genuine Indian damask; never has been dyed; it is strong and sound,' he muttered, as he rubbed with his fingers the worn tissue; the force of commercial habit making him praise an object of so little value that even he thought it might as well be given away.

He slipped the gold pieces into a sort of medieval purse hanging from his belt, repeating, 'The foot of Princess Hermonthis for a paperweight!'

Then, fixing on me his flaming eyes, he said, in a voice as strident as the mewing of a cat that has just swallowed a fishbone: 'Old pharaoh will not be very pleased; he was very fond of his daughter, the worthy man.'

'You talk about him as if you were his contemporary. Old though you are, you do not quite go back to the pyramids of Egypt,' I replied laughingly, as I passed out of the shop.

I returned home, very well satisfied with my purchase, and in order to turn it to account at once, I placed the foot of the divine Princess Hermonthis upon a bundle of papers, drafts of verses, an undecipherable mosaic of corrections, beginnings of articles, forgotten letters which I had posted in the drawer – a mistake often committed by absentminded people. The effect the foot produced was charming, eccentric, and romantic.

Greatly pleased with this embellishment of my table, I went out into the street and walked along with the gravity and the pride that become a man who has over every passerby he elbows the ineffable advantage of possessing a portion of the princess Hermonthis, daughter of the pharaoh. I considered as beneath contempt all those who did not possess, as I did, so notoriously Egyptian a paperweight, and it appeared to me that the proper business in the life of a sensible man was to have a mummy's foot on his writing table. Happily, I met some friends, who drew me out of my infatuation. I went to dinner with them, for it would have been difficult for me to dine with myself.

When I returned at night, my head filled with a light, pearly gray vapor, a faint puff of Oriental perfume tickled my olfactory nerves. The warmth of the room had warmed up the natron, bitumen, and myrrh in which the embalmers had dipped the princess's body. It was a sweet and penetrating perfume that had not wholly evaporated during the lapse of four thousand years; for Egypt dreamed of eternity: its odors have the solidity of granite and last as long.

I soon drank deep of the black cup of sleep. For an hour or two everything remained a blank, and I sank in the somber waves of forgetfulness and nothingness. Then my intellectual darkness lightened, and dreams began to flutter silently around. The eyes of my soul were opened, and I saw my room such as it actually was. I might have thought myself awake. A strange feeling convinced me that I was asleep and that something curious was about to happen.

The odor of myrrh had grown stronger, and I felt a slight headache, which I very naturally attributed to a number of glasses of champagne which we had drunk to the unknown gods and our future success. I looked round the room with a feeling of expectation that nothing justified. The furniture was in its place, the lamp burning on the table, pleasantly softened by the milky whiteness of the ground-glass globe; the water-colors shimmered under their Bohemian glass; the curtains hung languidly; everything looked serene and quiet.

But after a few moments this peaceful interior seemed to be disturbed. The woodwork cracked furtively, the log buried in the ashes suddenly shot out a jet of blue flame, and the disks of the coathooks looked like metal eyes, attentively watching, as I was, for whatever was about to happen.

By chance I glanced at the table on which I had placed the foot of the princess Hermonthis. Instead of resting quietly as became a foot embalmed for more than four thousand years, it was moving, contracting, and hopping about the papers like a frightened frog. I could have sworn it was in contact with a voltaic battery. I could quite distinctly hear the sharp sound made by its little heel, as hard as a gazelle's hoof.

I was not quite satisfied with my purchase, for I prefer sedentary paperweights, and it does not seem natural to me to see feet going about without limbs. Indeed, I began to experience something not unlike fear.

Suddenly I saw a fold of one of my curtains move, and I heard a sound like that made by a person hopping round on one foot. I must confess I turned cold and hot alternately; a strange chill ran up and down my back, and my hair stood up on my head.

The curtains opened, and I saw coming forward the strangest figure imaginable. It was that of a young girl of a very dark coffee-color, like Amani the bayadere, of perfect beauty, and recalling the purest Egyptian type. Her almond-shaped eyes were turned up at the corners, and her eyebrows were so black that they showed blue. Her nose was delicately shaped, almost Greek in its outline, and she might have been taken for a Corinthian bronze statue, but that the prominence of the cheekbones and the somewhat African size of the mouth showed plainly that she belonged to the hieroglyphic race of the banks of the Nile. Her well-shaped arms, slender like those of very young girls, were clasped by metal and glass bracelets; her hair was plaited into little tresses; and on her bosom hung an idol of green clay, which I recognized by the seven-tailed whip as Isis, the conductress of souls; on her brow shone a plate of gold, and some traces of rouge were visible on her copper-colored cheeks.

As for her costume, it was strange indeed. Imagine a loin cloth of narrow bands covered with black and red hieroglyphics, stiff with bitumen, which seemed to belong to a recently unrolled mummy.

By one of those sudden changes of thought which are so frequent in dreams, I heard the shrill, hoarse voice of the bric-à-brac dealer repeating like a monotonous refrain the remark he had made in his shop in so enigmatic a tone –

'Old pharaoh will not be very much pleased. He was very fond of his daughter, the worthy man.'

There was one curious peculiarity which did not contribute to reassure me – the apparition had but one foot. The other leg was broken off at the ankle.

She went to the table, where the mummy's foot was jumping and quivering with greater rapidity. On reaching it, she leaned upon the edge, and I saw a tear grow in her eyes. Though she said not a word, I could clearly make out her thoughts. She looked at the foot, for it was hers, with an infinitely graceful expression of coquettish sadness, while the foot ran and leaped hither and thither as if moved by steel springs.

Twice or thrice she stretched out her hand to seize it, but failed to do so.

Then there took place between the princess Hermonthis and her foot, which appeared endowed with a life of its own, a very curious dialogue, in a very ancient Coptic dialect, such as was spoken some thirty centuries ago in the mummy pits of the country of Ser. Luckily that night I happened to know Coptic perfectly well.

Princess Hermonthis said in a sweet voice that vibrated like a crystal bell –

'Well, my dear little foot, so you are still fleeing from me, though I took good care of you. I washed you with scented water in an alabaster basin; I polished your heel with pumice stone dipped in palm oil; I cut your nails with golden scissors, and polished them with hippopotamus teeth; I took care to choose for you painted and embroidered sandals with turned-up points, that made every Egyptian girl envy us. I put on your toes rings representing the sacred scarabaeus, and you supported one of the daintiest bodies that a lazy foot could wish for.'

The foot replied in a sulky tone –

'You know very well I do not belong to myself any more. I have been purchased and paid for. The old dealer knew what he was doing. He is still angry with you for refusing to marry him. It is a trick that he is playing upon you. The Arab that broke open your royal coffin in the subterranean well of the Theban Necropolis had been sent by him. He meant to prevent your going to the meeting of the people in darkness in the lower cities. Have you got five gold pieces to buy me back with?'

'Alas, I have not. My gems, my rings, my purses of gold and silver, everything has been stolen from me,' replied Princess Hermonthis, with a sigh.

'Princess,' I cried then, 'I have never unjustly kept back anyone's foot. Although you have not got the five louis which I paid for it, I return it to you most willingly. I should be uncommonly sorry to cripple so lovely a person as Princess Hermonthis.'

The beautiful Egyptian must have been surprised at the Regency manner and the troubadour tone in which I spoke this speech. She cast upon me a glance full of gratitude, and her eyes lighted up with blue flashes. She took her foot, which allowed itself to be caught this time, like a woman about to put on a shoe, and fitted it very skillfully to her leg, after which she took two or three steps through the room, as if to make certain that she was really no longer a cripple.

'How glad my father will be, for he was so troubled by the multilation I suffered. The very day I was born he had set a whole nation to work to dig me a tomb deep enough to preserve me intact until the great day when souls are to be weighed in the balances of Amenthi. Come with me to him. He will welcome you, for you have restored my foot to me.'

The proposal struck me as quite natural. I put on a dressing gown with a great flowered pattern, in which I looked most pharaohlike, hastily slipped my feet into a pair of Turkish slippers, and told Princess Hermonthis that I was ready to follow her.

Before leaving, she took from her neck the little figure in green china, and placed it upon the scattered papers that covered my table. 'It is only right,' she said, 'that I should give you something in place of your paperweight.'

She held out her hand to me. It was soft and cold as a serpent's skin. We were off.

We sped for some time as swift as an arrow through a grayish fluid air in which faintly outlined forms passed to right and left. At one time nothing was visible but sky and water. Presently obelisks began to show up; pylons and long stairs, with sphinxes ranged all the way down, stood out against the horizon. We had arrived.

The princess led me to a mountain of rose granite, in which there was a low, narrow opening which it would have been difficult to distinguish from the cracks in the stone had not a couple of stelae covered with carvings made it recognizable.

Hermonthis lighted a torch and walked on before me.

We entered corridors cut in the living rock; the walls, covered with panels of hieroglyphs and allegorical processions, must have occupied thousands of men for thousands of years. These corridors, interminably long, ended in square halls, in the center of which were dug wells. We descended these by means of cramp-irons or of spiral staircases. The wells led into other chambers from which issued other corridors, also adorned with hawks, serpents biting their tails, representations of the mystic tau, pedum, and bari – a prodigious piece of work which no living eye was to see, endless legends in granite which the dead alone had time to read during eternity.

At last we entered so vast, so enormous, so immense a hall that its limits were invisible. As far as I could see stretched rows of monstrous pillars, between which gleamed limpid stars of yellow light. These brilliant points indicated incalculable depths.

Princess Hermonthis still held my hand, and bowed graciously to the mummies of her acquaintance.

My eyes becoming accustomed to the twilight, I began to discern objects. I saw seated upon thrones the kings of subterranean races. They were tall, dry old men, wrinkled, parchment-like, black with naphtha and bitumen, wearing the golden pschent, pectorals, and neckplates covered with gems, their eyes staring like those of sphinxes, and they wore long beards, whitened with the snow of centuries. Behind them stood their embalmed peoples, in the stiff, constrained attitudes of Egyptian art, preserving forever the pose prescribed by the hieratic code; behind the peoples, the cats, ibises, and crocodiles of those days, made more mysterious still by being swathed up in bands, mewed, flapped their wings, and chuckled.

Every pharaoh was there, Cheops, Chephrenes, Psammetichus, Sesostris, Amenoteph; all the swarthy lords of pyramids and pits. On a higher throne sat King Chronos, Xixouthros, who lived in the days of the deluge, and Tubal Cain, who preceded him.

King Xixouthros's beard had grown so much that it had already circled seven times the granite table on which he leaned, dreamy and sleepy.

Farther away, through a dusty vapor, through the mist of eternities, I managed to make out the seventy-two pre-Adamite kings, with their seventy-two peoples, vanished forever.

Princess Hermonthis, having allowed me to enjoy this marvelous spectacle for a few moments, presented me to the pharaoh, her father, who nodded to me most majestically.

'I have found my foot, I have found my foot!' cried the princess, clapping her little hands together, with every mark of mad joy. 'It is this gentleman who gave it back to me.'

The races of Keme, of Nahasi, all the black, bronze, and copper-colored nations, repeated together –

'The princess Hermonthis has found her foot again.'

Xixouthros himself was interested. He raised his heavy lids, stroked his moustache, and let fall upon me his glance, laden with centuries.

'By Oms, the dog of Hades, and Tmei, daughter of the Sun and of Truth, you are a fine and worthy fellow,' said the pharaoh, extending towards me his scepter, ending in a lotus flower. 'What will you have for a reward?'

Bold as one is in dreams, in which nothing seems impossible, I asked for the hand of Hermonthis. It struck me that to get the hand in return for the foot was an antithetical reward in pretty good taste.

The pharaoh opened wide his glass eyes, amazed at my joke and my request.

'What is your country, and what is your age?'

'I am a Frenchman, and I am twenty-seven years old, venerable pharaoh.'

'Twenty-seven years! and he proposes to wed Princess Hermonthis, who is thirty centuries old,' cried out together all the thrones and all the circles of nations.

Hermonthis alone did not think my request at all improper.

'If you were only two thousand years old,' answered the old king, 'I would willingly give you the princess; but the disproportion is too great; and then, we must have for our daughters husbands that can last. You people do not know how to preserve yourselves. The last, brought here scarcely fifteen centuries ago, are now nothing but a handful of ashes. See, my own flesh is hard as basalt, my bones are like bars of steel. I shall see the last day of the world with the same body and the same face as I had when alive. My daughter Hermonthis will endure longer than a bronze statue. By that time the wind will have scattered the last grain of your dust, and Isis herself, who managed to find the pieces of Osiris, would be hard put to it to reconstruct your frame. See how vigorous I am yet, and how strong my arms are,' said he, as he shook hands with me in English fashion, so that he cut my fingers with my rings.

He squeezed my hand so hard that I awoke, and perceived my friend Alfred, pulling me by the arm, and shaking me to make me get up.

'Look here, you confounded sleeper, shall I have to take you out into the street and to set off fireworks at your ears? It is past noon. Have you forgotten that you promised to call for me to go to see Aguado's Spanish paintings?'

'Good gracious, I had forgotten all about it,' replied I, as I dressed. 'We shall go at once. I have the invitation here on my table.'

As I spoke, I stepped forward to take up the card; but judge of my astonishment when, instead of the mummy's foot which I had bought the night before, I saw the little figure of green clay put in its place by the princess Hermonthis.

THE HORLA

Guy de Maupassant

[1850–1893]

'*The horror-tales of the powerful and cynical Guy de Maupassant, written as his final madness gradually overtook him, present individualities of their own; being rather the morbid outpourings of a realistic mind in a pathological state than the healthy imaginative products of a vision naturally disposed toward phantasy and sensitive to the normal illusions of the unseen. Nevertheless they are of the keenest interest and poignancy; suggesting with marvelous force the imminence of nameless terrors, and the relentless dogging of an ill-starred individual by hideous and menacing representatives of the outer blackness. Of these stories* The Horla *is generally regarded as the masterpiece. Relating the advent to France of an individual being who lives on water and milk, sways the minds of others, and seems to be the vanguard of a horde of extra-terrestrial organisms arrived on earth to subjugate and overwhelm mankind, this tense narrative is perhaps without a peer in its particular department.*'

– H.P. Lovecraft

MAY 8. What a lovely day! I have spent all the morning lying in the grass in front of my house, under the enormous plane tree that shades the whole of it. I like this part of the country and I like to live here because I am attached to it by old associations, by those deep and delicate roots which attach a man to the soil on which his ancestors were born and died, which attach him to the ideas and usages of the place as well as to the food, to local expressions, to the peculiar twang of the peasants, to the smell of the soil, of the villages, and of the atmosphere itself.

I love my house in which I grew up. From my windows I can see the Seine which flows alongside my garden, on the other side of the high road, almost through my grounds, the great and wide Seine, which goes to Rouen and Havre, and is covered with boats passing to and fro.

On the left, down yonder, lies Rouen, that large town, with its blue roofs, under its pointed Gothic towers. These are innumerable, slender or broad, dominated by the spire of the cathedral, and full of bells which sound through the blue air on fine mornings, sending their sweet and distant iron clang even as far as my home; that song of the metal, which the breeze wafts in my direction, now stronger and now weaker, according as the wind is stronger or lighter.

What a delicious morning it was!

About eleven o'clock, a long line of boats drawn by a steam tug as big as a fly, and which scarcely puffed while emitting its thick smoke, passed my gate.

After two English schooners, whose red flag fluttered in space, there came a magnificent Brazilian three-master; she was perfectly white, and wonderfully clean and shining. I saluted her, I hardly knew why, except that the sight of the vessel gave me great pleasure.

May 12. I have had a slight feverish attack for the last few days, and I feel ill, or rather I feel low-spirited.

Whence come those mysterious influences which change our happiness into discouragement, and our self-confidence into diffidence? One might almost say that the air, the invisible air, is full of unknowable Powers whose mysterious presence we have to endure. I wake up in the best spirits, with an inclination to sing. Why? I go down to the edge of the water, and suddenly, after walking a short distance, I return home wretched, as if some misfortune were awaiting me there. Why? Is it a cold shiver which, passing over my skin, has upset my nerves and given me low spirits? Is it the form of the clouds, the colour of the sky, or the colour of the surrounding objects, which is so changeable, that has troubled my thoughts as they passed before my eyes? Who can tell? Everything that surrounds us, everything that we see, without looking at it, everything that we touch, without knowing it, everything that we handle, without feeling it, all that we meet, without clearly distinguishing it, has a rapid, surprising and inexplicable effect upon us and upon our senses, and, through them, on our ideas and on our heart itself.

How profound that mystery of the Invisible is! We cannot fathom it with our miserable senses, with our eyes which are unable to perceive what is either too small or too great, too near to us, or too far from us – neither the inhabitants of a star nor of a drop of water; nor with our ears that deceive us, for they transmit to us the vibrations of the air in sonorous notes. They are fairies who work the miracle of changing these vibrations into sound, and by that metamorphosis give birth to music, which makes the silent motion of nature musical . . . with our sense of smell which is less keen than that of a dog . . . with our sense of taste which can scarcely distinguish the age of a wine!

Oh! If we only had other organs which would work other miracles in our favour, what a number of fresh things we might discover around us!

May 16. I am ill, decidedly! I was so well last month! I am feverish, horribly feverish, or rather I am in a state of feverish enervation, which makes my mind suffer as much as my body. I have, continually, that horrible sensation of some impending danger, that apprehension of some coming misfortune, or of approaching death; that presentiment which is, no doubt, an attack of some illness which is still unknown, which germinates in the flesh and in the blood.

May 17. I have just come from consulting my physician, for I could no longer get any sleep. He said my pulse was rapid, my eyes dilated, my nerves highly strung, but there were no alarming symptoms. I must take a course of shower baths and of bromide of potassium.

May 25. No change! My condition is really very peculiar. As the evening comes on, an incomprehensible feeling of disquietude seizes me, just as if night concealed some threatening disaster. I dine hurriedly, and then try to read, but I do not understand the words, and can scarcely distinguish the letters. Then I walk up and down my drawing-room, oppressed by a feeling of confused and irresistible fear, the fear of sleep and fear of my bed.

About ten o'clock I go up to my room. As soon as I enter it I double-lock and bolt the door; I am afraid – of what? Up to the present time I have been afraid of nothing . . . I open my cupboards, and look under my bed; I listen – to what? How strange it is that a simple feeling of discomfort, impeded or heightened circulation, perhaps the irritation of a nerve filament, a slight congestion, a small disturbance in the imperfect delicate functioning of our living machinery, may turn the most light-hearted of men into a melancholy one, and make a coward of the bravest? Then I go to bed, and wait for sleep as a man might wait for the executioner. I wait for its coming with dread, and my heart beats and my legs tremble, while my whole body shivers beneath the warmth of the bedclothes, until all at once I fall asleep, as though one should plunge into a pool of stagnant water in order to drown. I do not feel it coming on as I did formerly, this perfidious sleep which is close to me and watching me, which is going to seize me by the head, to close my eyes and annihilate me.

I sleep – a long time – two or three hours perhaps – then a dream – no – a nightmare lays hold on me. I feel that I am in bed and asleep . . . I feel it and I know it . . . and I feel also that somebody is coming close to me, is looking at me, touching me, is getting on to my bed, is kneeling on my chest, is taking my neck between his hands and squeezing it . . . squeezing it with all his might in order to strangle me.

I struggle, bound by that terrible sense of powerlessness which paralyses us in our dreams; I try to cry out – but I cannot; I want to move – I cannot do so; I try, with the most violent efforts and breathing hard, to turn over and throw off this being who is crushing and suffocating me – I cannot!

And then, suddenly, I wake up, trembling and bathed in perspiration; I light a candle and find that I am alone, and after that crisis, which occurs every night, I at length fall asleep and slumber tranquilly till morning.

June 2. My condition has grown worse. What is the matter with me? The bromide does me no good, and the shower baths have no effect. Sometimes, in order to tire myself thoroughly, though I am fatigued enough already, I go for a walk in the forest of Roumare. I used to think at first that the fresh light and soft air, impregnated with the odour of herbs and leaves, would instill new blood into my veins and impart fresh energy to my heart. I turned into a broad hunting road, and then turned towards La Bouille, through a narrow path, between two rows of exceedingly tall trees, which placed a thick green, almost black, roof between the sky and me.

A sudden shiver ran through me, not a cold shiver, but a strange shiver of agony, and I hastened my steps, uneasy at being alone in the forest, afraid, stupidly and without reason, of the profound solitude.

Suddenly it seemed to me as if I were being followed, as if somebody were walking at my heels, close, quite close to me, near enough to touch me.

I turned round suddenly, but I was alone. I saw nothing behind me except the straight, broad path, empty and bordered by high trees, horribly empty; before me it also extended until it was lost in the distance, and looked just the same – terrible.

I closed my eyes. Why? And then I began to turn round on one heel very quickly, just like a top. I nearly fell down, and opened my eyes; the trees were dancing round me and the earth heaved; I was obliged to sit down. Then, ah! I no longer remembered how I had come! What a strange idea! What a strange, strange idea! I did not in the least know. I started off to the right, and got back into the avenue which had led me into the middle of the forest.

June 3. I have had a terrible night. I shall go away for a few weeks, for no doubt a journey will set me up again.

July 2. I have come back, quite cured, and have had a most delightful trip into the bargain. I have been to Mont Saint-Michel, which I had not seen before.

What a sight, when one arrives as I did, at Avranches towards the end of the day! The town stands on a hill, and I was taken into the public garden at the extremity of the town. I uttered a cry of astonishment. An extraordinarily large bay lay extended before me, as far as my eyes could reach, between two hills which were lost to sight in the mist; and in the middle of this immense yellow bay, under a clear, golden sky, a peculiar hill rose up, sombre and pointed in the midst of the sand. The sun had just disappeared, and under the still flaming sky appeared the outline of that fantastic rock which bears on its summit a fantastic monument.

At daybreak I went out to it. The tide was low, as it had been the night before, and I saw that wonderful abbey rise up before me as I approached it. After several hours' walking, I reached the enormous mass of rocks which supports the little town, dominated by the great church. Having climbed the steep and narrow street, I entered the most wonderful Gothic building that has ever been built to God on earth, as large as a town, full of low rooms which seem buried beneath vaulted roofs, and lofty galleries supported by delicate columns.

I entered this gigantic granite gem, which is as light as a bit of lace, covered with towers, with slender belfries with spiral staircases, which raise their strange heads that bristle with chimeras, with devils, with fantastic animals, with monstrous flowers, to the blue sky by day, and to the black sky by night, and are connected by finely carved arches.

When I had reached the summit I said to the monk who accompanied me: 'Father, how happy you must be here!' And he replied: 'It is very windy here, monsieur'; and so we began to talk while watching the rising tide, which ran over the sand and covered it as with a steel cuirass.

And then the monk told me stories, all the old stories belonging to the place, legends, nothing but legends.

One of them struck me forcibly. The country people, those belonging to the Mount, declare that at night one can hear voices talking on the sands, and that one then hears two goats bleating, one with a strong, the other with a weak voice. Incredulous people declare that it is nothing but the cry of the sea birds, which occasionally resembles bleatings, and occasionally, human lamentations; but belated fishermen swear that they have met an old shepherd wandering between tides on the sands around the little town. His head is completely concealed by his cloak and he is followed by a billy goat with a man's face, and a nanny goat with a woman's face, both having long, white hair, and talking incessantly and quarrelling in an unknown tongue. Then suddenly they cease and begin to bleat with all their might.

'Do you believe it?' I asked the monk. 'I scarcely know,' he replied, and I continued: 'If there are other beings besides ourselves on this earth, how comes it that we have not known it long since, or why have *you* not seen them? How is it that *I* have not seen them?' He replied: 'Do we see the hundred-thousandth part of what exists? Look here; there is the wind, which is the strongest force in nature, which knocks down men, and blows down buildings, uproots trees, raises the sea into mountains of water, destroys cliffs and casts great ships on the rocks; the wind which kills, which whistles, which sighs, which roars – have you ever seen it, and can you see it? It exists for all that, however.'

I was silent before this simple reasoning. That man was a philosopher, or perhaps a fool; I could not say which exactly, so I held my tongue. What he had said had often been in my own thoughts.

July 3. I have slept badly; certainly there is some feverish influence here, for my coachman is suffering in the same way as I am. When I went back home yesterday, I noticed his singular paleness, and I asked him: 'What is the matter with you, Jean?' 'The matter is that I never get any rest, and my nights devour my days. Since your departure, monsieur, there has been a spell over me.'

However, the other servants are all well, but I am very much afraid of having another attack myself.

July 4. I am decidedly ill again; for my old nightmares have returned. Last night I felt somebody leaning on me and sucking my life from between my lips. Yes, he was sucking it out of my throat, like a leech. Then he got up, satiated, and I woke up, so exhausted, crushed and weak that I could not move. If this continues for a few days, I shall certainly go away again.

July 5. Have I lost my reason? What happened last night is so strange that my head wanders when I think of it!

I had locked my door, as I do now every evening, and then, being thirsty, I drank half a glass of water, and accidentally noticed that the water-bottle was full up to the cut-glass stopper.

Then I went to bed and fell into one of my terrible sleeps, from which I was aroused in about two hours by a still more frightful shock.

Picture to yourself a sleeping man who is being murdered and who wakes up with a knife in his lung, and whose breath rattles, who is covered with blood, and who can no longer breathe and is about to die, and does not understand – there you have it.

Having recovered my senses, I was thirsty again, so I lit a candle and went to the table on which stood my water bottle. I lifted it up and tilted it over my glass, but nothing came out. It was empty! It was completely empty! At first I could not understand it at all, and then suddenly I was seized by such a terrible feeling that I had to sit down, or rather I fell into a chair! Then I sprang up suddenly to look about me; then I sat down again, overcome by astonishment and fear, in front of the transparent glass bottle! I looked at it with fixed eyes, trying to conjecture, and my hands trembled! Somebody had drunk the water, but who? I? I, without any doubt. It could surely only be I. In that case I was a somnambulist; I lived, without knowing it, that mysterious double life which makes us doubt whether there are not two beings in us, or whether a strange, unknowable and invisible being does not at such moments, when our soul is in a state of torpor, animate our captive body, which obeys this other being, as it obeys us, and more than it obeys ourselves.

Oh! Who will understand my horrible agony? Who will understand the emotion of a man who is sound in mind, wide awake, full of common sense, who looks in horror through the glass of a water bottle for a little water that disappeared while he was asleep? I remained thus until it was daylight, without venturing to go to bed again.

July 6. I am going mad. Again all the contents of my water bottle have been drunk during the night – or rather, I have drunk it!

But is it I? Is it I? Who could it be? Who? Oh, God! Am I going mad? Who will save me?

July 10. I have just been through some surprising ordeals. Decidedly I am mad! And yet! . . .

On 6th July, before going to bed, I put some wine, milk, water, bread and strawberries on my table. Somebody drank – I drank – all the water and a little of the milk, but neither the wine, bread, nor the strawberries were touched.

On the seventh of July I renewed the same experiment, with the same results, and on 8th July, I left out the water and the milk, and nothing was touched.

Lastly, on 9th July I put only water and milk on my table, taking care to wrap up the bottles in white muslin and to tie down the stoppers. Then I rubbed my lips, my beard and my hands with pencil lead, and went to bed.

Irresistible sleep seized me, which was soon followed by a terrible awakening. I had not moved, and there was no mark of lead on the sheets. I rushed to the table. The muslin round the bottles remained intact; I undid the string, trembling with fear. All the water had been drunk, and so had the milk! Ah! Great God! . . .

I must start for Paris immediately.

July 12. Paris. I must have lost my head during the last few days! I must be the plaything of my enervated imagination, unless I am really a somnambulist, or perhaps I have been under the power of one of those hitherto unexplained influences which are called suggestions. In any case, my mental state bordered on madness, and twenty-four hours of Paris sufficed to restore my equilibrium.

Yesterday, after doing some business and paying some visits which instilled fresh and invigorating air into my soul, I wound up the evening at the *Théâtre-Français*. A play by Alexandre Dumas the younger was being acted, and his active and powerful imagination completed my cure. Certainly solitude is dangerous for active minds. We require around us men who can think and talk. When we are alone for a long time, we people space with phantoms.

I returned along the boulevards to my hotel in excellent spirits. Amid the jostling of the crowd I thought, not without irony, of my terrors and surmises of the previous week, because I had believed – yes, I had believed – that an invisible being lived beneath my roof. How weak our brains are, and how quickly they are terrified and led into error by a small incomprehensible fact.

Instead of saying simply: 'I do not understand because I do not know the cause,' we immediately imagine terrible mysteries and supernatural powers.

July 14. Fête of the Republic. I walked through the streets, amused as a child at the firecrackers and flags. Still it is very foolish to be merry on a fixed date, by Government decree. The populace is an imbecile flock of sheep, now stupidly patient, and now in ferocious revolt. Say to it: 'Amuse yourself,' and it amuses itself. Say to it: 'Go and fight with your neighbour,' and it goes and fights. Say to it: 'Vote for the Emperor,' and it votes for the Emperor, and then say to it: 'Vote for the Republic,' and it votes for the Republic.

Those who direct it are also stupid; only, instead of obeying men, they obey principles which can only be stupid, sterile, and false, for the very reason that they are principles, that is to say, ideas which are considered as certain and unchangeable in this world where one is certain of nothing, since light is an illusion and noise is an illusion.

July 16. I saw some things yesterday that troubled me very much.

I was dining at the house of my cousin, Madame Sablé, whose husband is colonel of the 76th Chasseurs at Limoges. There were two young women there, one of whom had married a medical man, Dr. Parent, who devotes much attention to nervous diseases and to the remarkable manifestations taking place at this moment under the influence of hypnotism and suggestion.

He related to us at some length the wonderful results obtained by English scientists and by the doctors of the Nancy school; and the facts which he adduced appeared to me so strange that I declared that I was altogether incredulous.

'We are,' he declared, 'on the point of discovering one of the most important secrets of nature; I mean to say, one of its most important secrets on this earth, for there are certainly others of a different kind of importance up in the stars, yonder. Ever since man has thought, ever since he has been able to express and write down his thoughts, he has felt himself close to a mystery which is impenetrable to his gross and imperfect senses, and he endeavours to supplement through his intellect the inefficiency of his senses. As long as that intellect remained in its elementary stage, these apparitions of invisible spirits assumed forms that were commonplace, though terrifying. Thence sprang the popular belief in the supernatural, the legends of wandering spirits, of fairies, of gnomes, ghosts, I might even say the legend of God; for our conceptions of the workman-creator, from whatever religion they may have come down to us, are certainly the most mediocre, the most stupid and the most incredible inventions that ever sprang from the terrified brain of any human beings. Nothing is truer than what Voltaire says: "God made man in His own image, but man has certainly paid Him back in his own coin."

'However, for rather more than a century men seem to have had a presentiment of something new. Mesmer and some others have put us on an unexpected track, and, especially within the last two or three years, we have arrived at really surprising results.'

My cousin, who is also very incredulous, smiled, and Dr. Parent said to her: 'Would you like me to try and send you to sleep, madame?' 'Yes, certainly.'

She sat down in an easy chair, and he began to look at her fixedly, so as to fascinate her. I suddenly felt myself growing uncomfortable, my heart beating rapidly and a choking sensation in my throat. I saw Madame Sablé's eyes becoming heavy, her mouth twitching and her bosom heaving, and at the end of ten minutes she was asleep.

'Go behind her,' the doctor said to me, and I took a seat behind her. He put a visiting card into her hands, and said to her: 'This is a looking-glass; what do you see in it?' And she replied: 'I see my cousin.' 'What is he doing?' 'He is twisting his moustache.' 'And now?' 'He is taking a photograph out of his pocket.' 'Whose photograph is it?' 'His own.'

That was true, and the photograph had been given me that same evening at the hotel.

'What is his attitude in this portrait?' 'He is standing up with his hat in his hand.'

She saw, therefore, on that card, on that piece of white pasteboard, as if she had seen it in a mirror.

The young women were frightened, and exclaimed: 'That is enough! Quite, quite enough!'

But the doctor said to Madame Sablé authoritatively: 'You will rise at eight o'clock to-morrow morning; then you will go and call on your cousin at his hotel and ask him to lend you five thousand francs which your husband demands of you, and which he will ask for when he sets out on his coming journey.'

Then he woke her up.

On returning to my hotel, I thought over this curious séance, and I was assailed by doubts, not as to my cousin's absolute and undoubted good faith, for I had known her as well as if she were my own sister ever since she was a child, but as to a possible trick on the doctor's part. Had he not, perhaps, kept a glass hidden in his hand, which he showed to the young woman in her sleep, at the same time as he did the card? Professional conjurors do things that are just as singular.

So I went home and to bed, and this morning, at about half-past eight, I was awakened by my valet, who said to me: 'Madame Sablé has asked to see you immediately, monsieur.' I dressed hastily and went to her.

She sat down in some agitation, with her eyes on the floor, and without raising her veil she said to me: 'My dear cousin, I am going to ask a great favour of you.' 'What is it, cousin?' 'I do not like to tell you, and yet I must. I am in absolute need of five thousand francs.' 'What, you?' 'Yes, I, or rather my husband, who has asked me to procure them for him.'

I was so thunderstruck that I stammered out my answers. I asked myself whether she had not really been making fun of me with Dr. Parent, if it was not merely a very well-acted farce which had been rehearsed beforehand. On looking at her attentively, however, all my doubts disappeared. She was trembling with grief, so painful was this step to her, and I was convinced that her throat was full of sobs.

I knew that she was very rich and I continued: 'What! Has not your husband five thousand francs at his disposal? Come, think. Are you sure that he commissioned you to ask me for them?'

She hesitated for a few seconds, as if she were making a great effort to search her memory, and then she replied: 'Yes . . . yes, I am quite sure of it.' 'He has written to you?'

She hesitated again and reflected, and I guessed the torture of her thoughts. She did not know. She only knew that she was to borrow five thousand francs of me for her husband. So she told a lie. 'Yes, he has written to me.' 'When, pray? You did not mention it to me yesterday.' 'I received his letter this morning.' 'Can you show it me?' 'No . . . no . . . no . . . it contains private matters . . . things too personal to ourselves . . . I burned it.' 'So your husband runs into debt?'

She hesitated again, and then murmured: 'I do not know.' Thereupon I said bluntly: 'I have not five thousand francs at my disposal at this moment, my dear cousin.'

She uttered a kind of cry as if she were in pain and said: 'Oh! oh! I beseech you, I beseech you to get them for me . . .'

She got excited and clasped her hands as if she were praying to me! I heard her voice change its tone; she wept and stammered, harassed and dominated by the irresistible order that she had received.

'Oh! oh! I beg you to . . . if you knew what I am suffering . . . I want them to-day.'

I had pity on her: 'You shall have them by and by, I swear to you.' 'Oh! thank you! thank you! How kind you are.'

I continued: 'Do you remember what took place at your house last night?' 'Yes.' 'Do you remember that Dr. Parent sent you to sleep?' 'Yes.' 'Oh! Very well, then; he ordered you to come to me this morning to borrow five thousand francs, and at this moment you are obeying that suggestion.'

She considered for a few moments, and then replied: 'But as it is my husband who wants them – '

For a whole hour I tried to convince her, but could not succeed, and when she had gone I went to the doctor. He was just going out, and he listened to me with a smile, and said: 'Do you believe now?' 'Yes, I cannot help it.' 'Let us go to your cousin's.'

She was already half asleep on a reclining chair, overcome with fatigue. The doctor felt her pulse, looked at her for some time with one hand raised towards her eyes, which she closed by degrees under the irresistible power of this magnetic influence, and when she was asleep, he said:

'Your husband does not require the five thousand francs any longer! You must, therefore, forget that you asked your cousin to lend them to you, and, if he speaks to you about it, you will not understand him.'

Then he woke her up, and I took out a pocketbook and said: 'Here is what you asked me for this morning, my dear cousin.' But she was so surprised that I did not venture to persist; nevertheless, I tried to recall the circumstance to her, but she denied it vigorously, thought I was making fun of her, and, in the end, very nearly lost her temper.

There! I have just come back, and I have not been able to eat any lunch, for this experiment has altogether upset me.

July 19. Many people to whom I told the adventure laughed at me. I no longer know what to think. The wise man says: 'It may be!'

July 21. I dined at Bougival, and then I spent the evening at a boatman's ball. Decidedly everything depends on place and surroundings. It would be the height of folly to believe in the supernatural on the Ile de la Grenouillière . . . but on the top of Mont Saint-Michel? . . . and in India? We are terribly influenced by our surroundings. I shall return home next week.

July 30. I came back to my own house yesterday. Everything is going on well.

August 2. Nothing new; it is splendid weather, and I spent my days in watching the Seine flowing past.

August 4. Quarrels among my servants. They declare that the glasses are broken in the cupboards at night. The footman accuses the cook, who accuses the seamstress, who accuses the other two. Who is the culprit? It is a clever person who can tell.

August 6. This time I am not mad. I have seen . . . I have seen . . . I have seen! . . . I can doubt no longer . . . I have seen it! . . .

I was walking at two o'clock among my rose trees, in the full sunlight . . . in the walk bordered by autumn roses which are beginning to fall. As I stopped to look at a Géant de Bataille, which had three splendid blossoms, I distinctly saw the stalk of one of the roses near me bend, as if an invisible hand had bent it, and then break, as if that hand had picked it! Then the flower raised itself, following the curve which a hand would have described in carrying it towards a mouth, and it remained suspended in the transparent air, all alone and motionless, a terrible red spot, three yards from my eyes. In desperation I rushed at it to take it! I found nothing; it had disappeared. Then I was seized with furious rage against myself, for a reasonable and serious man should not have such hallucinations.

But was it an hallucination? I turned round to look for the stalk, and I found it at once, on the bush, freshly broken, between two other roses which remained on the branch. I returned home then, my mind greatly disturbed; for I am certain now, as certain as I am of the alternation of day and night, that there exists close to me an invisible being that lives on milk and water, that can touch objects, take them and change their places; that is, consequently, endowed with a material nature, although it is imperceptible to our senses, and that lives as I do, under my roof.

August 7. I slept tranquilly. He drank the water out of my decanter, but did not disturb my sleep.

I wonder if I am mad. As I was walking just now in the sun by the riverside, doubts as to my sanity arose in me; not vague doubts such as I have had hitherto, but definite, absolute doubts. I have seen mad people, and I have known some who have been quite intelligent, lucid, even clear-sighted at every concern of life, except on one point. They spoke clearly, readily, profoundly on everything, when suddenly their mind struck upon the shoals of their madness and broke to pieces there, and scattered and foundered in that furious and terrible sea, full of rolling waves, fogs and squalls, which is called *madness*.

I certainly should think that I was mad, absolutely mad, if I were not conscious, did not perfectly know my condition, did not fathom it by analysing it with the most complete lucidity. I should, in fact, be only a rational man who was labouring under an hallucination. Some unknown disturbance must have arisen in my brain, one of those disturbances which physiologists of the present day try to note and to verify; and that disturbance must have caused a deep gap in my mind and in the sequence and logic of my ideas. Similar phenomena occur in dreams which lead us among the most unlikely phantasmagoria, without causing us any surprise, because our verifying apparatus and our organ of control are asleep, while our imaginative faculty is awake and active. Is it not possible that one of the imperceptible notes of the cerebral keyboard has been paralysed in me? Some men lose the recollection of proper names, of verbs, or of numbers, or merely of dates, in consequence of an accident. The localization of all the variations of thought has been established nowadays; why, then, should it be surprising if my faculty of controlling the unreality of certain hallucinations were dormant in me for the time being?

I thought of all this as I walked by the side of the water. The sun shone brightly on the river and made earth delightful, while it filled me with a love for life, for the swallows, whose agility always delights my eye, for the plants by the riverside, the rustle of whose leaves is a pleasure to my ears.

By degrees, however, an inexplicable feeling of discomfort seized me. It seemed as if some unknown force were numbing and stopping me, were preventing me from going farther, and were calling me back. I felt that painful wish to return which oppresses you when you have left a beloved invalid at home, and when you are seized with a presentiment that he is worse.

I, therefore, returned in spite of myself, feeling certain that I should find some bad news awaiting me, a letter or a telegram. There was nothing, however, and I was more surprised and uneasy than if I had had another fantastic vision.

August 8. I spent a terrible evening yesterday. He does not show himself any more, but I feel that he is near me, watching me, looking at me, penetrating me, dominating me, and more redoubtable when he hides himself thus than if he were to manifest his constant and invisible presence by supernatural phenomena. However, I slept.

August 9. Nothing, but I am afraid.

August 10. Nothing; what will happen to-morrow?

August 11. Still nothing; I cannot stop at home with this fear hanging over me and these thoughts in my mind; I shall go away.

August 12. Ten o'clock at night. All day long I have been trying to get away, and have not been able. I wished to accomplish this simple and easy act of freedom – to go out – to get into my carriage in order to go to Rouen – and I have not been able to do it. What is the reason?

August 13. When we are attacked by certain maladies, all the springs of our physical being appear to be broken, all our energies destroyed, all our muscles relaxed; our bones, too, have become as soft as flesh, and our blood as liquid as water. I am experiencing these sensations in my moral being in a strange and distressing manner. I have no longer any strength, any courage, any self-control, not even any power to set my own will in motion. I have no power left to will anything; but someone does it for me and I obey.

August 14. I am lost! Somebody possesses my soul and dominates it. Somebody orders all my acts, all my movements, all my thoughts. I am no longer anything in myself, nothing except an enslaved and terrified spectator of all the things I do. I wish to go out; I cannot. He does not wish to, and so I remain, trembling and distracted, in the armchair in which he keeps me sitting. I merely wish to get up and to rouse myself; I cannot! I am riveted to my chair, and my chair adheres to the ground in such a manner that no power could move us.

Then, suddenly, I must, I must go to the bottom of my garden to pick some strawberries and eat them, and I go there. I pick the strawberries and eat them! Oh, my God! My God! Is there a God? If there be one, deliver me! Save me! Succour me! Pardon! Pity! Mercy! Save me! Oh, what sufferings! What torture! What horror!

August 15. This is certainly the way in which my poor cousin was possessed and controlled when she came to borrow five thousand francs of me. She was under the power of a strange will which had entered into her, like another soul, like another parasitic and dominating soul. Is the world coming to an end?

But who is he, this invisible being that rules me? This unknowable being, this rover of a supernatural race?

Invisible beings exist, then! How is it, then, that since the beginning of the world they have never manifested themselves precisely as they do to me? I have never read of anything that resembles what goes on in my house. Oh, if I could only leave it, if I could only go away, escape, and never return! I should be saved, but I cannot.

August 16. I managed to escape to-day for two hours, like a prisoner who finds the door of his dungeon accidentally open. I suddenly felt that I was free and that he was far away, and so I gave orders to harness the horses as quickly as possible, and I drove to Rouen. Oh, how delightful to be able to say to a man who obeys you: 'Go to Rouen!'

I made him pull up before the library, and I begged them to lend me Dr. Herrmann Herestauss' treatise on the unknown inhabitants of the ancient and modern world.

Then, as I was getting into my carriage, I intended to say: 'To the railway station!' but instead of this I shouted – I did not say, but I shouted – in such a loud voice that all the passers-by turned round: 'Home!' and I fell back on the cushion of my carriage, overcome by mental agony. He had found me again and regained possession of me.

August 17. Oh, what a night! What a night! And yet it seems to me that I ought to rejoice. I read until one o'clock in the morning! Herestauss, doctor of philosophy and theogony, wrote the history of the manifestation of all those invisible beings which hover around man, or of whom he dreams. He describes their origin, their domain, their power; but none of them resembles the one which haunts me. One might say that man, ever since he began to think, has had a foreboding fear of a new being, stronger than himself, his successor in this world, and that, feeling his presence, and not being able to foresee the nature of that master, he has, in his terror, created the whole race of occult beings, of vague phantoms born of fear.

Having, therefore, read until one o'clock in the morning, I went and sat down at the open window, in order to cool my forehead and my thoughts, in the calm night air. It was very pleasant and warm! How I should have enjoyed such a night formerly!

There was no moon, but the stars darted out their rays in the dark heavens. Who inhabits those worlds? What forms, what living beings, what animals are there yonder? What do the thinkers in those distant worlds know more than we do? What can they do more than we can? What do they see which we do not know? Will not one of them, some day or other, traversing space, appear on our earth to conquer it, just as the Norsemen formerly crossed the sea in order to subjugate nations more feeble than themselves?

We are so weak, so defenceless, so ignorant, so small, we who live on this particle of mud which revolves in a drop of water.

I fell asleep, dreaming thus in the cool night air, and when I had slept for about three-quarters of an hour, I opened my eyes without moving, awakened by I know not what confused and strange sensation. At first I saw nothing, and then suddenly it appeared to me as if a page of a book which had remained open on my table turned over of its own accord. Not a breath of air had come in at my window, and I was surprised, and waited. In about four minutes, I saw, I saw, yes, I saw with my own eyes, another page lift itself up and fall down on the others, as if a finger had turned it over. My armchair was empty, appeared empty, but I knew that he was there, he, and sitting in my place, and that he was reading. With a furious bound, the bound of an enraged wild beast that springs at its tamer, I crossed my room to seize him, to strangle him, to kill him! But before I could reach it, the chair fell over as if somebody had run away from me – my table rocked, my lamp fell and went out, and my window closed as if some thief had been surprised and had fled out into the night, shutting it behind him.

So he had run away; he had been afraid; he, afraid of me!

But – but – to-morrow – or later – some day or other – I should be able to hold him in my clutches and crush him against the ground! Do not dogs occasionally bite and strangle their masters?

August 18. I have been thinking the whole day long. Oh, yes, I will obey him, follow his impulses, fulfil all his wishes, show myself humble, submissive, a coward. He is the stronger; but the hour will come –

August 19. I know – I know – I know all! I have just read the following in the *Revue du Monde Scientifique*: 'A curious piece of news comes to us from Rio de Janeiro. Madness, an epidemic of madness, which may be compared to that contagious madness which attacked the people of Europe in the Middle Ages, is at this moment raging in the Province of San-Paolo. The terrified inhabitants are leaving their houses, saying that they are pursued, possessed, dominated like human cattle by invisible, though tangible, beings, a species of vampires, which feed on their life while they are asleep, and which, besides, drink water and milk without appearing to touch any other nourishment.

'Professor Don Pedro Henriques, accompanied by several medical savants, has gone to the Province of San-Paolo, in order to study the origin and the manifestations of this surprising madness on the spot, and to propose such measures to the Emperor as may appear to him to be most fitted to restore the mad population to reason.'

Ah! Ah! I remember now that fine Brazilian three-master which passed in front of my windows as she was going up the Seine, on the 8th day of last May! I thought she looked so pretty, so white and bright! That Being was on board of her, coming from there, where its race originated. And it saw me! It saw my house which was also white, and it sprang from the ship on to the land. Oh, merciful heaven!

Now I know, I can divine. The reign of man is over, and he has come. He who was feared by primitive man; whom disquieted priests exorcised; whom sorcerers evoked on dark nights, without having seen him appear, to whom the imagination of the transient masters of the world lent all the monstrous or graceful forms of gnomes, spirits, genii, fairies, and familiar spirits. After the coarse conceptions of primitive fear, more clear-sighted men foresaw it more clearly. Mesmer divined it, and ten years ago physicians accurately discovered the nature of his power, even before he exercised it himself. They played with this new weapon of the Lord, the sway of a mysterious will over the human soul, which had become a slave. They called it magnetism, hypnotism, suggestion – what do I know? I have seen them amusing themselves like rash children with this horrible power! Woe to us! Woe to man! He has come, the – the – what does he call himself – the – I fancy that he is shouting out his name to me and I do not hear him – the – yes – he is shouting it out – I am listening – I cannot – he repeats it – the – Horla – I hear – the Horla – it is he – the Horla – he has come!

Ah! the vulture has eaten the pigeon; the wolf has eaten the lamb; the lion has devoured the sharp-horned buffalo; man has killed the lion with an arrow, with a sword, with gunpowder; but the Horla will make of man what we have made of the horse and of the ox; his chattel, his slave, and his food, by the mere power of his will. Woe to us!

But, nevertheless, the animal sometimes revolts and kills the man who has subjugated it. I should also like – I shall be able to – but I must know him, touch him, see him! Scientists say that animals' eyes, being different from ours, do not distinguish objects as ours do. And my eye cannot distinguish this newcomer who is oppressing me.

Why? Oh, now I remember the words of the monk at Mont Saint-Michel: 'Can we see the hundred-thousandth part of what exists? See here; there is the wind, which is the strongest force in nature, which knocks men down, and wrecks buildings, uproots trees, raises the sea into mountains of water, destroys cliffs and casts great ships on the breakers; the wind which kills, which whistles, which sighs, which roars – have you ever seen it, and can you see it? It exists for all that, however!'

And I went on thinking: my eyes are so weak, so imperfect, that they do not even distinguish hard bodies, if they are as transparent as glass! If a glass without tinfoil behind it were to bar my way, I should run into it, just as a bird which has flown into a room breaks its head against the window-panes. A thousand things, moreover, deceive man and lead him astray. Why should it then be surprising that he cannot perceive an unknown body through which the light passes?

A new being! Why not? It was assuredly bound to come! Why should we be the last? We do not distinguish it any more than all the others created before us! The reason is, that its nature is more perfect, its body finer and more finished than ours, that ours is so weak, so awkwardly constructed, encumbered with organs that are always tired, always on the strain like machinery that is too complicated, which lives like a plant and like a beast, nourishing itself with difficulty on air, herbs, and flesh, an animal machine which is a prey to maladies, to malformations, to decay; broken-winded, badly regulated, simple and eccentric, ingeniously badly made, at once a coarse and a delicate piece of workmanship, the rough sketch of a being that might become intelligent and grand.

We are only a few, so few in this world, from the oyster up to man. Why should there not be one more, once that period is passed which separates the successive apparitions from all the different species?

Why not one more? Why not, also, other trees with immense, splendid flowers, perfuming whole regions? Why not other elements besides fire, air, earth, and water? There are four, only four, those nursing fathers of various beings! What a pity! Why are there not forty, four hundred, four thousand? How poor everything is, how mean and wretched! grudgingly produced, roughly constructed, clumsily made! Ah, the elephant and the hippopotamus, what grace! And the camel, what elegance!

But the butterfly, you will say, a flying flower! I dream of one that should be as large as a hundred worlds, with wings whose shape, beauty, colour, and motion I cannot even express. But I see it – it flutters from star to star, refreshing them and perfuming them with the light and harmonious breath of its flight! And the people up there look at it as it passes in an ecstasy of delight!

What is the matter with me? It is he, the Horla, who haunts me, and who makes me think of these foolish things! He is within me, he is becoming my soul; I shall kill him!

August 29. I shall kill him. I have seen him! Yesterday I sat down at my table and pretended to write very assiduously. I knew quite well that he would come prowling round me, quite close to me, so close that I might perhaps be able to touch him, to seize him. And then – then I should have the strength of desperation; I should have my hands, my knees, my chest, my forehead, my teeth to strangle him, to crush him, to bite him, to tear him to pieces. And I watched for him with all my over-excited senses.

I had lighted my two lamps and the eight wax candles on my mantelpiece, as if with this light I could discover him.

My bedstead, my old oak post bedstead, stood opposite to me; on my right was the fireplace; on my left, the door which was carefully closed, after I had left it open for some time in order to attract him; behind me was a very high wardrobe with a looking-glass in it, before which I stood to shave and dress every day, and in which I was in the habit of glancing at myself from head to foot every time I passed it.

I pretended to be writing in order to deceive him, for he also was watching me, and suddenly I felt – I was certain that he was reading over my shoulder, that he was there, touching my ear.

I got up, my hands extended, and turned round so quickly that I almost fell. Eh! well? It was as bright as at midday, but I did not see my reflection in the mirror! It was empty, clear, profound, full of light! But my figure was not reflected in it – and I, I was opposite to it! I saw the large, clear glass from top to bottom, and I looked at it with unsteady eyes; and I did not dare to advance; I did not venture to make a movement, feeling that he was there, but that he would escape me again, he whose imperceptible body had absorbed my reflection.

How frightened I was! And then, suddenly, I began to see myself in a mist in the depths of the looking-glass, in a mist as it were a sheet of water; and it seemed to me as if this water were flowing clearer every moment. It was like the end of an eclipse. Whatever it was that hid me did not appear to possess any clearly defined outlines, but a sort of opaque transparency which gradually grew clearer.

At last I was able to distinguish myself completely, as I do every day when I look at myself.

I had seen it! And the horror of it remained with me, and makes me shudder even now.

August 30. How could I kill it, as I could not get hold of it? Poison? But it would see me mix it with the water; and then, would our poisons have any effect on its impalpable body? No – no – no doubt about the matter – Then – then? –

August 31. I sent for a blacksmith from Rouen, and ordered iron shutters for my room, such as some private hotels in Paris have on the ground floor, for fear of burglars, and he is going to make me an iron door as well. I have made myself out a coward, but I do not care about that!

September 10. Rouen, Hotel Continental. It is done – it is done – but is he dead? My mind is thoroughly upset by what I have seen.

Well, then, yesterday, the locksmith having put on the iron shutters and door, I left everything open until midnight, although it was getting cold.

Suddenly I felt that he was there, and joy, mad joy, took possession of me. I got up softly, and walked up and down for some time, so that he might not suspect anything; then I took off my boots and put on my slippers carelessly; then I fastened the iron shutters, and, going back to the door, quickly double-locked it with a padlock, putting the key into my pocket.

Suddenly I noticed that he was moving restlessly round me, that in his turn he was frightened and was ordering me to let him out. I nearly yielded; I did not, however, but, putting my back to the door, I half opened it, just enough to allow me to go out backward, and as I am very tall my head touched the casing. I was sure that he had not been able to escape, and I shut him up quite alone, quite alone. What happiness! I had him fast. Then I ran downstairs; in the drawing-room, which was under my bedroom, I took the two lamps and I poured all the oil on the carpet, the furniture, everywhere; then I set fire to it and made my escape, after having carefully double-locked the door.

I went and hid myself at the bottom of the garden, in a clump of laurel bushes. How long it seemed! How long it seemed! Everything was dark, silent, motionless, not a breath of air and not a star, but heavy banks of clouds which one could not see, but which weighed, oh, so heavily on my soul.

I looked at my house and waited. How long it was! I already began to think that the fire had gone out of its own accord, or that he had extinguished it, when one of the lower windows gave way under the violence of the flames, and a long, soft, caressing sheet of red flame mounted up the white wall, and enveloped it as far as the roof. The light fell on the trees, the branches, and the leaves, and a shiver of fear pervaded them also! The birds awoke, a dog began to howl, and it seemed to me as if the day were breaking! Almost immediately two other windows flew into fragments, and I saw that the whole of the lower part of my house was nothing but a terrible furnace. But a cry, a horrible, shrill, heartrending cry, a woman's cry, sounded through the night, and two garret windows were opened! I had forgotten the servants! I saw their terror-stricken faces, and their arms waving frantically.

Then, overwhelmed with horror, I set off to run to the village, shouting: 'Help! help! fire! fire!' I met some people who were already coming to the scene, and I returned with them.

By this time the house was nothing but a horrible and magnificent funeral pile, a monstrous funeral pile which lit up the whole country, a funeral pile where men were burning, and where he was burning also, He, He, my prisoner, that new Being, the new master, the Horla!

Suddenly the whole roof fell in between the walls, and a volcano of flames darted up to the sky. Through all the windows which opened on that furnace, I saw the flames darting, and I thought that he was there, in that kiln, dead.

Dead? Perhaps. – His body? Was not his body, which was transparent, indestructible by such means as would kill ours?

If he were not dead? – Perhaps time alone has power over that Invisible and Redoubtable Being. Why this transparent, unrecognizable body, this body belonging to a spirit, if it also has to fear ills, infirmities and premature destruction?

Premature destruction? All human terror springs from that! After man, the Horla. After him who can die every day, at any hour, at any moment, by any accident, comes the one who will die only at his own proper hour, day, and minute, because he has touched the limits of his existence!

No – no – without any doubt – he is not dead – Then – then – I suppose I must kill *myself!* . . .

THE FALL OF THE HOUSE OF USHER

Edgar Allan Poe

[1809–1849]

'Certain of Poe's tales possess an almost absolute perfection of artistic form which makes them veritable beacon-lights in the province of the short story. Poe could, when he wished, give to his prose a richly poetic cast; employing the archaic and Orientalised style with jewelled phrase, quasi-Biblical repetition, and recurrent burthen so successfully used by later writers like Oscar Wilde and Lord Dunsany . . . But it is in two of the less openly poetic tales, Ligeia *and* The Fall of the House of Usher *– especially the latter – that one finds those very summits of artistry whereby Poe takes his place at the head of fictional miniaturists. Simple and straightforward of plot; both of these tales owe their supreme magic to the cunning development which appears in the selection and collocation of every least incident . . .* Usher, *whose superiority in detail and proportion is very marked, hints shudderingly of obscure life in inorganic things, and displays an abnormally linked trinity of entities at the end of a long and isolated family history – a brother, his twin sister, and their incredibly ancient*

house all sharing a single soul and meeting one common dissolution at the same moment.

'*These bizarre conceptions, so awkward in unskilful hands, become under Poe's spell living and convincing terrors to haunt our nights.*'

– H.P. Lovecraft

> Son coeur est un luth suspendu;
> Sitôt qu'on le touche il résonne.
>
> DE BERANGER

DURING THE WHOLE OF A dull, dark, and soundless day in the autumn of the year, when the clouds hung oppressively low in the heavens, I had been passing alone, on horseback, through a singularly dreary tract of country, and at length found myself, as the shades of the evening drew on, within view of the melancholy House of Usher. I know not how it was – but, with the first glimpse of the building, a sense of insufferable gloom pervaded my spirit. I say insufferable; for the feeling was unrelieved by any of that half-pleasurable, because poetic, sentiment with which the mind usually receives even the sternest natural images of the desolate or terrible. I looked upon the scene before me – upon the mere house, and the simple landscape features of the domain – upon the bleak walls – upon the vacant eye-like windows – upon a few rank sedges – and upon a few white trunks of decayed trees – with an utter depression of soul which I can compare to no earthly sensation more properly than to the after-dream of the reveller upon opium – the bitter lapse into every-day life – the hideous dropping off of the veil. There was an iciness, a sinking, a sickening of the heart – an unredeemed dreariness of thought which no goading of the imagination could torture into aught of the sublime. What was it – I paused to think – what was it that so unnerved me in the contemplation of the House of Usher?

It was a mystery all insoluble; nor could I grapple with the shadowy fancies that crowded upon me as I pondered. I was forced to fall back upon the unsatisfactory conclusion, that while, beyond doubt, there *are* combinations of very simple natural objects which have the power of thus affecting us, still the analysis of this power lies among considerations beyond our depth. It was possible, I reflected, that a mere different arrangement of the particulars of the scene, of the details of the picture, would be sufficient to modify, or perhaps to annihilate its capacity for sorrowful impression; and, acting upon this idea, I reined my horse to the precipitous brink of a black and lurid tarn that lay in unruffled lustre by the dwelling, and gazed down – but with a shudder even more thrilling than before – upon the remodelled and inverted images of the gray sedge, and the ghastly tree-stems, and the vacant and eye-like windows.

Nevertheless, in this mansion of gloom I now proposed to myself a sojourn of some weeks. Its proprietor, Roderick Usher, had been one of my boon companions in boyhood; but many years had elapsed since our last meeting. A letter, however, had lately reached me in a distant part of the country – a letter from him – which, in its wildly importunate nature, had admitted of no other than a personal reply. The MS. gave evidence of nervous agitation. The writer spoke of acute bodily illness – of a mental disorder which oppressed him – and of an earnest desire to see me, as his best and indeed his only personal friend, with a view of attempting, by the cheerfulness of my society, some alleviation of his malady. It was the manner in which all this, and much more, was said – it was the apparent *heart* that went with his request – which allowed me no room for hesitation; and I accordingly obeyed forthwith what I still considered a very singular summons.

Although, as boys, we had been even intimate associates, yet I really knew little of my friend. His reserve had been always excessive and habitual. I was aware, however, that his very ancient family had been noted, time out of mind, for a peculiar sensibility of temperament, displaying itself, through long ages, in many works of exalted art, and manifested, of late, in repeated deeds of munificent yet unobtrusive charity, as well as in a passionate devotion to the intricacies, perhaps even more than to the orthodox and easily recognizable beauties, of musical science. I had learned, too, the very remarkable fact, that the stem of the Usher race, all time-honored as it was, had put forth, at no period, any enduring branch; in other words, that the entire family lay in the direct line of descent, and had always, with very trifling and very temporary variation, so lain. It was this deficiency, I considered, while running over in thought the perfect keeping of the character of the premises with the accredited character of the people, and while speculating upon the possible influence which the one, in the long lapse of centuries, might have exercised upon the other – it was this deficiency, perhaps, of collateral issue, and the consequent undeviating transmission, from sire to son, of the patrimony with the name, which had, at length, so ·identified the two as to merge the original title of the estate in the quaint and equivocal appellation of the 'House of Usher' – an appellation which seemed to include, in the minds of the peasantry who used it, both the family and the family mansion.

I have said that the sole effect of my somewhat childish experiment – that of looking down within the tarn – had been to deepen the first singular impression. There can be no doubt that the consciousness of the rapid increase of my superstition – for why should I not so term it? – served mainly to accelerate the increase itself. Such, I have long known, is the paradoxical law of all sentiments having terror as a basis. And it might have been for this reason only, that, when I again uplifted my eyes to the house itself, from its image in the pool, there grew in my mind a strange fancy – a fancy so ridiculous, indeed, that I but mention it to show the vivid force of the sensations which oppressed me. I had so worked upon my imagination as really to believe that about the whole mansion and domain there hung an atmosphere peculiar to themselves and their immediate vicinity – an atmosphere which had no affinity with the air of heaven, but which had reeked up from the decayed trees, and the gray wall, and the silent tarn – a pestilent and mystic vapor, dull, sluggish, faintly discernible, and leaden-hued.

Shaking off from my spirit what *must* have been a dream, I scanned more narrowly the real aspect of the building. Its principal feature seemed to be that of an excessive antiquity. The discoloration of ages had been great. Minute fungi overspread the whole exterior, hanging in a fine tangled web-work from the eaves. Yet all this was apart from any extraordinary dilapidation. No portion of the masonry had fallen; and there appeared to be a wild inconsistency between its still perfect adaptation of parts, and the crumbling condition of the individual stones. In this there was much that reminded me of the specious totality of old wood-work which has rotted for long years in some neglected vault, with no disturbance from the breath of the external air. Beyond this indication of extensive decay, however, the fabric gave little token of instability. Perhaps the eye of a scrutinizing observer might have discovered a barely perceptible fissure, which, extending from the roof of the building in front, made its way down the wall in a zigzag direction, until it became lost in the sullen waters of the tarn.

Noticing these things, I rode over a short causeway to the house. A servant in waiting took my horse, and I entered the Gothic archway of the hall. A valet, of stealthy step, thence conducted me, in silence, through many dark and intricate passages in my progress to the *studio*

of his master. Much that I encountered on the way contributed, I know not how, to heighten the vague sentiments of which I have already spoken. While the objects around me – while the carvings of the ceilings, the sombre tapestries of the walls, the ebon blackness of the floors, and the phantasmagoric armorial trophies which rattled as I strode, were but matters to which, or to such as which, I had been accustomed from my infancy – while I hesitated not to acknowledge how familiar was all this – I still wondered to find how unfamiliar were the fancies which ordinary images were stirring up. On one of the staircases, I met the physician of the family. His countenance, I thought, wore a mingled expression of low cunning and perplexity. He accosted me with trepidation and passed on. The valet now threw open a door and ushered me into the presence of his master.

The room in which I found myself was very large and lofty. The windows were long, narrow, and pointed, and at so vast a distance from the black oaken floor as to be altogether inaccessible from within. Feeble gleams of encrimsoned light made their way through the trellised panes, and served to render sufficiently distinct the more prominent objects around; the eye, however, struggled in vain to reach the remoter angles of the chamber, or the recesses of the vaulted and fretted ceiling. Dark draperies hung upon the walls. The general furniture was profuse, comfortless, antique, and tattered. Many books and musical instruments lay scattered about, but failed to give any vitality to the scene. I felt that I breathed an atmosphere of sorrow. An air of stern, deep, and irredeemable gloom hung over and pervaded all.

Upon my entrance, Usher arose from a sofa on which he had been lying at full length, and greeted me with a vivacious warmth which had much in it, I at first thought, of an overdone cordiality – of the constrained effort of the *ennuyé* man of the world. A glance, however, at his countenance convinced me of his perfect sincerity. We sat down; and for some moments, while he spoke not, I gazed upon him with a feeling half of pity, half of awe. Surely, man had never before so terribly altered, in so brief a period, as had Roderick Usher! It was with difficulty that I could bring myself to admit the identity of the wan being before me with the companion of my early boyhood. Yet the character of his face had been at all times remarkable. A cadaverousness of complexion; an eye large, liquid, and luminous beyond comparison; lips somewhat thin and very pallid, but of a surpassingly beautiful curve; a nose of a delicate Hebrew model, but with a breadth of nostril unusual in similar formations; a finely molded chin, speaking, in its want of prominence, of a want of moral energy; hair of a more than web-like softness and tenuity; – these features, with an inordinate expansion above the regions of the temple, made up altogether a countenance not easily to be forgotten. And now in the mere exaggeration of the prevailing character of these features, and of the expression they were wont to convey, lay so much of change that I doubted to whom I spoke. The now ghastly pallor of the skin, and the now miraculous lustre of the eye, above all things startled and even awed me. The silken hair, too, had been suffered to grow all unheeded, and as, in its wild gossamer texture, it floated rather than fell about the face, I could not, even with effort, connect its Arabesque expression with any idea of simple humanity.

In the manner of my friend I was at once struck with an incoherence – an inconsistency; and I soon found this to arise from a series of feeble and futile struggles to overcome an habitual trepidancy – an excessive nervous agitation. For something of this nature I had indeed been prepared, no less by his letter, than by reminiscences of certain boyish traits, and by conclusions deduced from his peculiar physical conformation and temperament. His action was alternately vivacious and sullen. His voice varied rapidly from a tremulous indecision (when the animal spirits seemed utterly in abeyance) to that species of energetic concision – that abrupt, weighty, unhurried, and hollow-sounding enunciation – that leaden, self-balanced, and perfectly modulated guttural utterance, which may be observed in the lost drunkard, or the irreclaimable eater of opium, during the periods of his most intense excitement.

It was thus that he spoke of the object of my visit, of his earnest desire to see me, and of the solace he expected me to afford him. He entered, at some length, into what he conceived to be the nature of his malady. It was, he said, a constitutional and a family evil, and one for which he despaired to find a remedy – a mere nervous affection, he immediately added, which would undoubtedly soon pass off. It displayed itself in a host of unnatural sensations. Some of these, as he detailed them, interested and bewildered me; although, perhaps, the terms and the general manner of their narration had their weight. He suffered much from a morbid acuteness of the senses; the most insipid food was alone endurable; he could wear only garments of certain texture; the odors of all flowers were oppressive; his eyes were tortured by even a faint light; and there were but peculiar sounds, and these from stringed instruments, which did not inspire him with horror.

To an anomalous species of terror I found him a bounden slave. 'I shall perish,' said he, 'I *must* perish in this deplorable folly. Thus, thus, and not otherwise, shall I be lost. I dread the events of the future not in themselves, but in their results. I shudder at the thought of any, even the most trivial, incident, which may operate upon this intolerable agitation of soul. I have, indeed, no abhorrence of danger, except in its absolute effect – in terror. In this unnerved, in this pitiable, condition I feel that the period will sooner or later arrive when I must abandon life and reason together, in some struggle with the grim phantasm, FEAR.'

I learned, moreover, at intervals, and through broken and equivocal hints, another singular feature of his mental condition. He was enchained by certain superstitious impressions in regard to the dwelling which he tenanted, and whence, for many years, he had never ventured forth – in regard to an influence whose suppositious force was conveyed in terms too shadowy here to be re-stated – an influence which some peculiarities in the mere form and substance of his family mansion had, by dint of long sufferance, he said, obtained over his spirit – an effect which the *physique* of the gray walls and turrets, and of the dim tarn into which they all looked down, had, at length, brought about upon the *morale* of his existence.

He admitted, however, although with hesitation, that much of the peculiar gloom which thus afflicted him could be traced to a more natural and far more palpable origin – to the severe and long-continued illness – indeed to the evidently approaching dissolution – of a tenderly beloved sister, his sole companion for long years, his last and only relative on earth. 'Her decease,' he said, with a bitterness which I can never forget, 'would leave him (him, the hopeless and the frail) the last of the ancient race of the Ushers.' While he spoke, the lady Madeline (for so was she called) passed through a remote portion of the apartment, and, without having noticed my presence, disappeared. I regarded her with an utter astonishment not unmingled with dread; and yet I found it impossible to account for such feelings. A sensation of stupor oppressed me as my eyes followed her retreating steps. When a door, at length, closed upon her, my glance sought instinctively and eagerly the countenance of the brother; but he had buried his face in his hands, and I could only perceive that a far more than ordinary wanness had overspread the emaciated fingers through which trickled many passionate tears.

The disease of the lady Madeline had long baffled the skill of her physicians. A settled apathy, a gradual wasting away of the person, and frequent although transient affections of a partially cataleptical character were the unusual diagnosis. Hitherto she had steadily borne up against the pressure of her malady, and had not betaken herself finally to bed; but on the closing in of the evening of my arrival at the house, she succumbed (as her brother told me at night with inexpressible agitation) to the prostrating power of the destroyer; and I learned that the glimpse I had obtained of her person would thus probably be the last I should obtain – that the lady, at least while living, would be seen by me no more.

For several days ensuing, her name was unmentioned by either Usher or myself; and during this period I was busied in earnest endeavors to alleviate the melancholy of my friend. We painted and read together, or I listened, as if in a dream, to the wild improvisations of his speaking guitar. And thus, as a closer and still closer intimacy admitted me more unreservedly into the recesses of his spirit, the more bitterly did I perceive the futility of all attempt at cheering a mind from which darkness, as if an inherent positive quality, poured forth upon all objects of the moral and physical universe in one unceasing radiation of gloom.

I shall ever bear about me a memory of the many solemn hours I thus spent alone with the master of the House of Usher. Yet I should fail in any attempt to convey an idea of the exact character of the studies, or of the occupations, in which he involved me, or led me the way. An excited and highly distempered ideality threw a sulfurous lustre over all. His long improvised dirges will ring forever in my ears. Among other things, I hold painfully in mind a certain singular perversion and amplification of the wild air of the last waltz of Von Weber. From the paintings over which his elaborate fancy brooded, and which grew, touch by touch, into vaguenesses at which I shuddered the more thrillingly, because I shuddered knowing not why – from these paintings (vivid as their images now are before me) I would in vain endeavor to educe more than a small portion which should lie within the compass of merely written words. By the utter simplicity, by the nakedness of his designs, he arrested and overawed attention. If ever mortal painted an idea, that mortal was Roderick Usher. For me at least, in the circumstances then surrounding me, there arose out of the pure abstractions which the hypochondriac contrived to throw upon his canvas, an intensity of intolerable awe, no shadow of which felt I ever yet in the contemplation of the certainly glowing yet too concrete reveries of Fuseli.

One of the phantasmagoric conceptions of my friend, partaking not so rigidly of the spirit of abstraction, may be shadowed forth, although feebly, in words. A small picture presented the interior of an immensely long and rectangular vault or tunnel, with low walls, smooth, white, and without interruption or device. Certain accessory points of the design served well to convey the idea that this excavation lay at an exceeding depth below the surface of the earth. No outlet was observed in any portion of its vast extent, and no torch or other artificial source of light was discernible; yet a flood of intense rays rolled throughout, and bathed the whole in a ghastly and inappropriate splendor.

I have just spoken of that morbid condition of the auditory nerve which rendered all music intolerable to the sufferer, with the exception of certain effects of stringed instruments. It was, perhaps, the narrow limits to which he thus confined himself upon the guitar which gave birth, in great measure, to the fantastic character of his performances. But the fervid *facility* of his *impromptus* could not be so accounted for. They must have been, and were, in the notes, as well as in the words of his wild fantasias (for he not unfrequently accompanied himself with rhymed verbal improvisations), the result of that intense mental collectedness and concentration to which I have previously alluded as observable only in particular moments of the highest artificial excitement. The words of one of these rhapsodies I have easily remembered. I was, perhaps, the more forcibly impressed with it as he gave it, because, in the under or mystic current of its meaning, I fancied that I perceived, and for the first time, a full consciousness on the part of Usher of the tottering of his lofty reason upon her throne. The verses, which were entitled 'The Haunted Palace,' ran very nearly, if not accurately, thus: –

I.

In the greenest of our valleys,
    By good angels tenanted,
Once a fair and stately palace –
    Radiant palace – reared its head.
In the monarch Thought's dominion –
    It stood there!
Never seraph spread a pinion
    Over fabric half so fair.

II.

Banners yellow, glorious, golden,
  On its roof did float and flow
(This – all this – was in the olden
  Time long ago);
And every gentle air that dallied,
  In that sweet day,
Along the ramparts plumed and pallid,
A wingèd odor went away.

III.

Wanderers in that happy valley
  Through two luminous windows saw
Spirits moving musically
  To a lute's well-tunèd law;
Round about a throne, where sitting
  (Porphyrogene!)
In state his glory well befitting,
  The ruler of the realm was seen.

IV.

And all with pearl and ruby glowing
  Was the fair palace door,
Through which came flowing, flowing, flowing
  And sparkling evermore,
A troop of Echoes whose sweet duty
  Was but to sing,
In voices of surpassing beauty,
  The wit and wisdom of their king.

V.

But evil things, in robes of sorrow,
  Assailed the monarch's high estate;
(Ah, let us mourn, for never morrow
  Shall dawn upon him, desolate!)
And, round about his home, the glory
  That blushed and bloomed
Is but a dim-remembered story
  Of the old time entombed.

VI.
And travellers now within that valley,
    Through the red-litten windows see
Vast forms that move fantastically
    To a discordant melody;
While, like a rapid ghastly river,
    Through the pale door;
A hideous throng rush out forever,
    And laugh – but smile no more.

I well remember that suggestions arising from this ballad led us into
a train of thought wherein there became manifest an opinion of
Usher's which I mention not so much on account of its novelty (for
other men have thought thus), as on account of the pertinacity with
which he maintained it. This opinion, in its general form, was that of
the sentience of all vegetable things. But, in his disordered fancy, the
idea had assumed a more daring character, and trespassed, under
certain conditions, upon the kingdom of inorganization. I lack words
to express the full extent, or the earnest *abandon* of his persuasion. The
belief, however, was connected (as I have previously hinted) with the
gray stones of the home of his forefathers. The conditions of the
sentience had been here, he imagined, fulfilled in the method of
collocation of these stones – in the order of their arrangement, as well
as in that of the many *fungi* which overspread them, and of the
decayed trees which stood around – above all, in the long undisturbed
endurance of this arrangement, and in its reduplication in the still
waters of the tarn. Its evidence – the evidence of the sentience – was to
be seen, he said (and I here started as he spoke), in the gradual yet
certain condensation of an atmosphere of their own about the waters
and the walls. The result was discoverable, he added, in that silent yet
importunate and terrible influence which for centuries had molded
the destinies of his family, and which made *him* what I now saw him –
what he was. Such opinions need no comment, and I will make none.
    Our books – the books which, for years, had formed no small
portion of the mental existence of the invalid – were, as might be
supposed, in strict keeping with this character of phantasm. We pored
together over such works as the 'Ververt et Chartreuse' of Gresset; the
'Belphegor' of Machiavelli; the 'Heaven and Hell' of Swedenborg; the
'Subterranean Voyage of Nicholas Klimn' of Holberg; the 'Chiro-
mancy' of Robert Flud, of Jean D'Indaginé, and of De la Chambre;
the 'Journey into the Blue Distance' of Tieck; and the 'City of the

Sun' of Campanella. One favorite volume was a small octavo edition
of the 'Directorium Inquisitorium,' by the Dominican Eymeric de
Gironne; and there were passages in Pomponius Mela, about the old
African Satyrs and Egipans, over which Usher would sit dreaming for
hours. His chief delight, however, was found in the perusal of an
exceedingly rare and curious book in quarto Gothic – the manual of a
forgotten church – the *Vigiliæ Mortuorum secundum Chorum Ecclesiæ
Maguntinæ*.

I could not help thinking of the wild ritual of this work, and of its
probable influence upon the hypochondriac, when, one evening,
having informed me abruptly that the lady Madeline was no
more, he stated his intention of preserving her corpse for a fortnight
(previously to its final interment), in one of the numerous vaults
within the main walls of the building. The worldly reason, however,
assigned for this singular proceeding, was one which I did not feel at
liberty to dispute. The brother had been led to his resolution (so he
told me) by consideration of the unusual character of the malady of
the deceased, of certain obtrusive and eager inquiries on the part of
her medical men, and of the remote and exposed situation of the
burial-ground of the family. I will not deny that when I called to
mind the sinister countenance of the person whom I met upon the
staircase, on the day of my arrival at the house, I had no desire to
oppose what I regarded as at best but a harmless, and by no means an
unnatural, precaution.

At the request of Usher, I personally aided him in the arrangements for the temporary entombment. The body having been
encoffined, we two alone bore it to its rest. The vault in which we
placed it (and which had been so long unopened that our torches, half
smothered in its oppressive atmosphere, gave us little opportunity for
investigation) was small, damp, and entirely without means of
admission for light; lying, at great depth, immediately beneath that
portion of the building in which was my own sleeping apartment. It
had been used, apparently, in remote feudal times, for the worst
purposes of a donjon-keep, and, in later days, as a place of deposit for
powder, or some other highly combustible substance, as a portion of
its floor, and the whole interior of a long archway through which we
reached it, were carefully sheathed with copper. The door, of massive
iron, had been, also, similarly protected. Its immense weight caused
an unusually sharp, grating sound, as it moved upon its hinges.

Having deposited our mournful burden upon tressels within this
region of horror, we partially turned aside the yet unscrewed lid of the

coffin, and looked upon the face of the tenant. A striking similitude between the brother and sister now first arrested my attention; and Usher, divining, perhaps, my thoughts, murmured out some few words from which I learned that the deceased and himself had been twins, and that sympathies of a scarcely intelligible nature had always existed between them. Our glances, however, rested not long upon the dead – for we could not regard her unawed. The disease which had thus entombed the lady in the maturity of youth, had left, as usual in all maladies of a strictly cataleptical character, the mockery of a faint blush upon the bosom and the face, and that suspiciously lingering smile upon the lip which is so terrible in death. We replaced and screwed down the lid, and, having secured the door of iron, made our way, with toil, into the scarcely less gloomy apartments of the upper portion of the house.

And now, some days of bitter grief having elapsed, an observable change came over the features of the mental disorder of my friend. His ordinary manner had vanished. His ordinary occupations were neglected or forgotten. He roamed from chamber to chamber with hurried, unequal, and objectless step. The pallor of his countenance had assumed, if possible, a more ghastly hue – but the luminousness of his eye had utterly gone out. The once occasional huskiness of his tone was heard no more; and a tremulous quaver, as if of extreme terror, habitually characterized his utterance. There were times, indeed, when I thought his unceasingly agitated mind was laboring with some oppressive secret, to divulge which he struggled for the necessary courage. At times, again, I was obliged to resolve all into the mere inexplicable vagaries of madness, for I beheld him gazing upon vacancy for long hours, in an attitude of the profoundest attention, as if listening to some imaginary sound. It was no wonder that his condition terrified – that it infected me. I felt creeping upon me, by slow yet certain degrees, the wild influences of his own fantastic yet impressive superstitions.

It was, especially, upon retiring to bed late in the night of the seventh or eighth day after the placing of the lady Madeline within the donjon, that I experienced the full power of such feelings. Sleep came not near my couch – while the hours waned and waned away. I struggled to reason off the nervousness which had dominion over me. I endeavored to believe that much, if not all of what I felt, was due to the bewildering influence of the gloomy furniture of the room – of the dark and tattered draperies, which, tortured into motion by the breath of a rising tempest, swayed fitfully to and fro upon the walls, and rustled uneasily about the decorations of the bed. But my efforts were fruitless. An irrepressible tremor gradually pervaded my frame; and, at length, there sat upon my very heart an incubus of utterly causeless alarm. Shaking this off with a gasp and a struggle, I uplifted myself upon the pillows, and, peering earnestly within the intense darkness of the chamber, hearkened – I know not why, except that an instinctive spirit prompted me – to certain low and indefinite sounds which came, through the pauses of the storm, at long intervals, I knew not whence. Overpowered by an intense sentiment of horror, unaccountable yet unendurable, I threw on my clothes with haste (for I felt that I should sleep no more during the night), and endeavored to arouse myself from the pitiable condition into which I had fallen, by pacing rapidly to and fro through the apartment.

I had taken but few turns in this manner, when a light step on an adjoining staircase arrested my attention. I presently recognized it as that of Usher. In an instant afterward he rapped, with a gentle touch, at my door, and entered, bearing a lamp. His countenance was, as usual, cadaverously wan – but, moreover, there was a species of mad hilarity in his eyes – an evidently restrained *hysteria* in his whole demeanor. His air appalled me – but anything was preferable to the solitude which I had so long endured, and I even welcomed his presence as a relief.

'And you have not seen it?' he said abruptly, after having stared about him for some moments in silence – 'you have not then seen it? – but, stay! you shall.' Thus speaking, and having carefully shaded his lamp, he hurried to one of the casements, and threw it freely open to the storm.

The impetuous fury of the entering gust nearly lifted us from our feet. It was, indeed, a tempestuous yet sternly beautiful night, and one wildly singular in its terror and its beauty. A whirlwind had apparently collected its force in our vicinity; for there were frequent and violent alterations in the direction of the wind; and the exceeding density of the clouds (which hung so low as to press upon the turrets of the house) did not prevent our perceiving the life-like velocity with which they flew careering from all points against each other, without passing away into the distance. I say that even their exceeding density did not prevent our perceiving this – yet we had no glimpse of the moon or stars, nor was there any flashing forth of the lightning. But the under surfaces of the huge masses of agitated vapor, as well as all terrestrial objects immediately around us, were glowing in the unnatural light of a faintly luminous and distinctly visible gaseous exhalation which hung about and enshrouded the mansion.

'You must not – you shall not behold this!' said I, shuddering, to Usher, as I led him, with a gentle violence, from the window to a seat. 'These appearances, which bewilder you, are merely electrical phenomena not uncommon – or it may be that they have their ghastly origin in the rank miasma of the tarn. Let us close this casement; – the air is chilling and dangerous to your frame. Here is one of your favorite romances. I will read, and you shall listen; – and so we will pass away this terrible night together.'

The antique volume which I had taken up was the 'Mad Trist' of Sir Launcelot Canning; but I had called it a favorite of Usher's more in sad jest than in earnest; for, in truth, there is little in its uncouth and unimaginative prolixity which could have had interest for the lofty and spiritual ideality of my friend. It was, however, the only book immediately at hand; and I indulged a vague hope that the excitement which now agitated the hypochondriac, might find relief (for the history of mental disorder is full of similar anomalies) even in the extremeness of the folly which I should read. Could I have judged, indeed, by the wild overstrained air of vivacity with which he hearkened, or apparently hearkened, to the words of the tale, I might well have congratulated myself upon the success of my design.

I had arrived at that well-known portion of the story where Ethelred, the hero of the Trist, having sought in vain for peaceable admission into the dwelling of the hermit, proceeds to make good an entrance by force. Here, it will be remembered, the words of the narrative run thus:

'And Ethelred, who was by nature of a doughty heart, and who was now mighty withal, on account of the powerfulness of the wine which he had drunken, waited no longer to hold parley with the hermit, who, in sooth, was of an obstinate and maliceful turn, but, feeling the rain upon his shoulders, and fearing the rising of the tempest, uplifted his mace outright, and, with blows, made quickly room in the plankings of the door for his gauntleted hand; and now pulling therewith sturdily, he so cracked, and ripped, and tore all asunder, that the noise of the dry and hollow-sounding wood alarumed and reverberated throughout the forest.'

At the termination of this sentence I started and, for a moment, paused; for it appeared to me (although I at once concluded that my excited fancy had deceived me) – it appeared to me that, from some very remote portion of the mansion, there came, indistinctly to my ears, what might have been, in its exact similarity of character, the echo (but a stifled and dull one certainly) of the very cracking and ripping sound which Sir Launcelot had so particularly described. It was, beyond doubt, the coincidence alone which had arrested my attention; for, amid the rattling of the sashes of the basements, and the ordinary commingled noises of the still increasing storm, the sound, in itself, had nothing, surely, which should have interested or disturbed me. I continued the story:

'But the good champion Ethelred, now entering within the door, was sore enraged and amazed to perceive no signal of the maliceful hermit; but, in the stead thereof, a dragon of a scaly and prodigious demeanor, and of a fiery tongue, which sate in guard before a palace of gold, with a floor of silver; and upon the wall there hung a shield of shining brass with this legend enwritten –

Who entereth herein, a conqueror hath bin;
Who slayeth the dragon, the shield he shall win.

And Ethelred uplifted his mace, and struck upon the head of the dragon, which fell before him, and gave up his pesty breath, with a shriek so horrid and harsh, and withal so piercing, that Ethelred had fain to close his ears with his hands against the dreadful noise of it, the like whereof was never before heard.'

Here again I paused abruptly, and now with a feeling of wild amazement – for there could be no doubt whatever that, in this instance, I did actually hear (although from what direction it proceeded I found it impossible to say) a low and apparently distant, but harsh, protracted, and most unusual screaming or grating sound – the exact counterpart of what my fancy had already conjured up for the dragon's unnatural shriek as described by the romancer.

Oppressed, as I certainly was, upon the occurrence of this second and most extraordinary coincidence, by a thousand conflicting sensations, in which wonder and extreme terror were predominant, I still retained sufficient presence of mind to avoid exciting, by any observation, the sensitive nervousness of my companion. I was by no means certain that he had noticed the sounds in question; although, assuredly, a strange alteration had, during the last few minutes, taken place in his demeanor. From a position fronting my own, he had gradually brought round his chair, so as to sit with his face to the door of the chamber; and thus I could but partially perceive his features, although I saw that his lips trembled as if he were murmuring inaudibly. His head had dropped upon his breast – yet I knew that he was not asleep, from the wide and rigid opening of the eye as I caught a glance of it in profile. The motion of his body, too, was at variance with this idea – for he rocked from side to side with a gentle yet constant and uniform sway. Having rapidly taken notice of all this, I resumed the narrative of Sir Launcelot, which thus proceeded:

'And now, the champion, having escaped from the terrible fury of the dragon, bethinking himself of the brazen shield, and of the breaking up of the enchantment which was upon it, removed the carcass from out of the way before him, and approached valorously over the silver pavement of the castle to where the shield was upon the wall; which in sooth tarried not for his full coming, but fell down at his feet upon the silver floor, with a mighty great and terrible ringing sound.'

No sooner had these syllables passed my lips, than – as if a shield of brass had indeed, at the moment, fallen heavily upon a floor of silver – I became aware of a distinct, hollow, metallic, and clangorous, yet apparently muffled, reverberation. Completely unnerved, I leaped to my feet; but the measured rocking movement of Usher was undisturbed. I rushed to the chair in which he sat. His eyes were bent fixedly before him, and throughout his whole countenance there reigned a stony rigidity. But, as I placed my hand upon his shoulder, there came a strong shudder over his whole person; a sickly smile quivered about his lips; and I saw that he spoke in a low, hurried, and gibbering murmur, as if unconscious of my presence. Bending closely over him, I at length drank in the hideous import of his words.

'Now hear it? – yes, I hear it, and *have* heard it. Long – long – long – many minutes, many hours, many days, have I heard it – yet I dared not – oh, pity me, miserable wretch that I am! – I dared not – I *dared* not speak! *We have put her living in the tomb!* Said I not that my senses were acute? I *now* tell you that I heard her first feeble movements in the hollow coffin. I heard them – many, many days ago – yet I dared not – *I dared not speak!* And now – to-night – Ethelred – ha! ha! – the breaking of the hermit's door, and the death-cry of the dragon, and the clangor of the shield – say, rather, the rending of her coffin, and the grating of the iron hinges of her prison, and her struggles within the coppered archway of the vault? Oh! whither shall I fly? Will she not be here anon? Is she not hurrying to upbraid me for my haste? Have I not heard her footstep on the stair? Do I not distinguish that heavy and horrible beating of her heart? Madman!' – here he sprang furiously to his feet, and shrieked out his syllables, as if in the effort he were giving up his soul – '*Madman! I tell you that she now stands without the door!*'

As if in the superhuman energy of his utterance there had been found the potency of a spell, the huge antique panels to which the speaker pointed threw slowly back, upon the instant, their ponderous and ebony jaws. It was the work of the rushing gust – but then without those doors there *did* stand the lofty and enshrouded figure of the lady Madeline of Usher. There was blood upon her white robes, and the evidence of some bitter struggle upon every portion of her emaciated frame. For a moment she remained trembling and reeling to and fro upon the threshold – then, with a low moaning cry, fell heavily inward upon the person of her brother, and in her violent and now final death-agonies, bore him to the floor a corpse, and a victim to the terrors he had anticipated.

From that chamber, and from that mansion, I fled aghast. The storm was still abroad in all its wrath as I found myself crossing the old causeway. Suddenly there shot along the path a wild light, and I turned to see whence a gleam so unusual could have issued; for the vast house and its shadows were alone behind me. The radiance was that of the full, setting, and blood-red moon, which now shone vividly through that once barely discernible fissure, of which I have before spoken as extending from the roof of the building, in a zigzag direction, to the base. While I gazed, this fissure rapidly widened – there came a fierce breath of the whirlwind – the entire orb of the satellite burst at once upon my sight – my brain reeled as I saw the mighty walls rushing asunder – there was a long tumultuous shouting sound like the voice of a thousand waters – and the deep and dank tarn at my feet closed sullenly and silently over the fragments of the '*House of Usher.*'

THE DAMNED THING

Ambrose Bierce

[1842–c1913]

'*Closer to real greatness was the eccentric and saturnine journalist Ambrose Bierce, born in 1842; who entered the Civil War, but survived to write some immortal tales and to disappear in 1913 in as great a cloud of mystery as any he ever evoked from his nightmare fancy . . .*

'*Bierce's work is in general somewhat uneven. Many of the stories are obviously mechanical, and marred by a jaunty and commonplacely artificial style derived from journalistic models; but the grim malevolence stalking through all of them is unmistakable, and several stand out as permanent mountain-peaks of American weird writing . . . The Damned Thing, frequently copied in popular anthologies, chronicles the hideous devastations of an invisible entity that waddles and flounders on the hills and in the wheatfields by night and day.*'

– H.P. Lovecraft

I

ONE DOES NOT ALWAYS EAT
WHAT IS ON THE TABLE

BY THE LIGHT of a tallow candle which had been placed on one end of a rough table a man was reading something written in a book. It was an old account book, greatly worn; and the writing was not, apparently, very legible, for the man sometimes held the page close to the flame of the candle to get a stronger light on it. The shadow of the book would then throw into obscurity a half of the room, darkening a number of faces and figures; for besides the reader, eight other men were present. Seven of them sat against the rough log walls, silent, motionless, and the room being small, not very far from the table. By extending an arm any one of them could have touched the eighth man, who lay on the table, face upward, partly covered by a sheet, his arms at his sides. He was dead.

The man with the book was not reading aloud; and no one spoke; all seemed to be waiting for something to occur; the dead man only was without expectation. From the blank darkness outside came in, through the aperture that served for a window, all the ever unfamiliar noises of night in the wilderness – the long nameless note of a distant coyote; the stilly pulsing thrill of tireless insects in trees; strange cries of night birds so different from those of the birds of day; the drone of great blundering beetles, and all that mysterious chorus of small sounds that seem always to have been but heard when they have suddenly ceased, as if conscious of an indiscretion. But nothing of all this was noted in that company; its members were not overmuch addicted to idle interest in matters of no practical importance; that was obvious in every line of their rugged faces – obvious even in the dim light of the single candle. They were evidently men of the vicinity – farmers and woodsmen.

The person reading was a trifle different; one would have said of him that he was of the world, worldly, albeit there was that in his attire which attested a certain fellowship with the organisms of his environment. His coat would hardly have passed in San Francisco; his foot-gear was not of urban origin, and the hat that lay by him on the floor (he was the only one uncovered) was such that if one had considered it as an article of mere personal adornment he would have missed its meaning. In countenance the man was rather prepossessing, with just a hint of sternness; though that he may have assumed or cultivated, as appropriate to one in authority. For he was a coroner. It was by virtue of his office that he had possession of the book in which he was reading; it had been found among the dead man's effects – in his cabin, where the inquest was now taking place.

When the coroner had finished reading he put the book into his breast pocket. At that moment the door was pushed open and a young man entered. He, clearly, was not of mountain birth and breeding: he was clad as those who dwell in cities. His clothing was dusty, however, as from travel. He had, in fact, been riding hard to attend the inquest.

The coroner nodded; no one else greeted him.

'We have waited for you,' said the coroner. 'It is necessary to have done with this business to-night.'

The young man smiled. 'I am sorry to have kept you,' he said. 'I went away, not to evade your summons, but to post to my newspaper an account of what I suppose I am called back to relate.'

The coroner smiled.

'The account that you posted to your newspaper,' he said, 'differs, probably, from that which you will give here under oath.'

'But you say it is incredible.'

'That is nothing to you, sir, if I also swear that it is true.'

The coroner was silent for a time, his eyes upon the floor. The men about the sides of the cabin talked in whispers, but seldom withdrew their gaze from the face of the corpse. Presently the coroner lifted his eyes and said: 'We will resume the inquest.'

The men removed their hats. The witness was sworn.

'What is your name?' the coroner asked.

'William Harker.'

'Age?'

'Twenty-seven.'

'You knew the deceased, Hugh Morgan?'

'Yes.'

'You were with him when he died?'

'Near him.'

'How did that happen – your presence, I mean?'

'I was visiting at this place to shoot and fish. A part of my purpose, however, was to study him and his odd, solitary way of life. He seemed a good model for a character in fiction. I sometimes write stories.'

'I sometimes read them.'

'Thank you.'

'Stories in general – not yours.'

Some of the jurors laughed. Against a sombre background humor shows high lights. Soldiers in the intervals of battle laugh easily, and a jest in the death chambers conquers by surprise.

'Relate the circumstances of this man's death,' said the coroner. 'You may use any notes or memoranda that you please.'

The witness understood. Pulling a manuscript from his breast pocket he held it near the candle and turning the leaves until he found the passage that he wanted began to read.

II

WHAT MAY HAPPEN IN A FIELD OF WILD OATS

'. . . The sun had hardly risen when we left the house. We were looking for quail, each with a shotgun, but we had only one dog. Morgan said that our best ground was beyond a certain ridge that he pointed out, and we crossed it by a trail through the *chaparral*. On the other side was comparatively level ground, thickly covered with wild oats. As we emerged from the *chaparral* Morgan was but a few yards in advance. Suddenly we heard, at a little distance to our right and partly in front, a noise as of some animal thrashing about in the bushes which we could see were violently agitated.

' "We've started a deer," I said. "I wish we had brought a rifle."

'Morgan, who had stopped and was intently watching the agitated *chaparral*, said nothing, but had cocked both barrels of his gun and was holding it in readiness to aim. I thought him a trifle excited, which surprised me, for he had a reputation for exceptional coolness, even in moments of sudden and imminent peril.

' "O, come," I said. "You are not going to fill up a deer with quail-shot, are you?"

'Still he did not reply; but catching a sight of his face as he turned it slightly toward me I was struck by the intensity of his look. Then I understood that we had serious business in hand and my first conjecture was that we had "jumped" a grizzly. I advanced to Morgan's side, cocking my piece as I moved.

'The bushes were now quiet and the sounds had ceased, but Morgan was as attentive to the place as before.

' "What is it? What the devil is it?" I asked.

' "That Damned Thing!" he replied, without turning his head. His voice was husky and unnatural. He trembled visibly.

'I was about to speak further, when I observed the wild oats near the place of the disturbance moving in the most inexplicable way. I can hardly describe it. It seemed as if stirred by a streak of wind, which not only bent it, but pressed it down – crushed it so that it did not rise; and this movement was slowly prolonging itself directly toward us.

'Nothing that I had ever seen affected me so strangely as this unfamiliar and unaccountable phenomenon, yet I am unable to recall any sense of fear. I remember – and tell it here because, singularly enough, I recollected it then – that once in looking carelessly out of an open window I momentarily mistook a small tree close at hand for one of a group of larger trees at a little distance away. It looked the same size as the others, but being more distinctly and sharply defined in mass and detail seemed out of harmony with them. It was a mere falsification of the law of aërial perspective, but it startled, almost terrified me. We so rely upon the orderly operation of familiar natural laws that any seeming suspension of them is noted as a menace to our safety, a warning of unthinkable calamity. So now the apparently causeless movement of the herbage and the slow, undeviating approach of the line of disturbance were distinctly disquieting. My companion appeared actually frightened, and I could hardly credit my senses when I saw him suddenly throw his gun to his shoulder and fire both barrels at the agitated grain! Before the smoke of the discharge had cleared away I heard a loud savage cry – a scream like that of a wild animal – and flinging his gun upon the ground Morgan sprang away and ran swiftly from the spot. At the same instant I was thrown violently to the ground by the impact of something unseen in the smoke – some soft, heavy substance that seemed thrown against me with great force.

'Before I could get upon my feet and recover my gun, which seemed to have been struck from my hands, I heard Morgan crying out as if in mortal agony, and mingling with his cries were such hoarse, savage sounds as one hears from fighting dogs. Inexpressibly terrified, I struggled to my feet and looked in the direction of Morgan's retreat; and may Heaven in mercy spare me from another sight like that! At a distance of less than thirty yards was my friend, down upon one knee, his head thrown back at a frightful angle, hatless, his long hair in disorder and his whole body in violent movement from side to side, backward and forward. His right arm was lifted and seemed to lack the hand – at least, I could see none. The other arm was invisible. At times, as my memory now reports this extraordinary scene, I could discern but a part of his body; it was as if he had been partly blotted out – I cannot otherwise express it – then a shifting of his position would bring it all into view again.

'All this must have occurred within a few seconds, yet in that time Morgan assumed all the postures of a determined wrestler vanquished by superior weight and strength. I saw nothing but him, and him not always distinctly. During the entire incident his shouts and curses were heard, as if through an enveloping uproar of such sounds of rage and fury as I had never heard from the throat of man or brute!

'For a moment only I stood irresolute, then throwing down my gun I ran forward to my friend's assistance. I had a vague belief that he was suffering from a fit, or some form of convulsion. Before I could reach his side he was down and quiet. All sounds had ceased, but with a feeling of such terror as even these awful events had not inspired I now saw again the mysterious movements of the wild oats, prolonging itself from the trampled area about the prostrate man towards the edge of a wood. It was only when it had reached the wood that I was able to withdraw my eyes and look at my companion. He was dead.'

III

A MAN THOUGH NAKED MAY BE IN RAGS

The coroner rose from his seat and stood beside the dead man. Lifting an edge of the sheet he pulled it away, exposing the entire body, althogether naked and showing in the candle-light a claylike yellow. It had, however, broad maculations of bluish black, obviously caused by extravasated blood from contusions. The chest and sides looked as if they had been beaten with a bludgeon. There were dreadful lacerations; the skin was torn in strips and shreds.

The coroner moved round to the end of the table and undid a silk handkerchief which had been passed under the chin and knotted on the top of the head. When the handkerchief was drawn away it exposed what had been the throat. Some of the jurors who had risen to get a better view repented their curiosity and turned away their faces. Witness Harker went to the open window and leaned out across the sill, faint and sick. Dropping the handkerchief upon the dead man's neck the coroner stepped to an angle of the room and from a pile of clothing produced one garment after another, each of which he held up a moment for inspection. All were torn, and stiff with blood. The jurors did not make a closer inspection. They seemed rather uninterested. They had, in truth, seen all this before; the only thing that was new to them being Harker's testimony.

'Gentlemen,' the coroner said, 'we have no more evidence, I think. Your duty has been already explained to you; if there is nothing you wish to ask you may go outside and consider your verdict.'

The foreman rose – a tall, bearded man of sixty, coarsely clad.

'I should like to ask one question, Mr. Coroner,' he said. 'What asylum did this yer last witness escape from?'

'Mr. Harker,' said the coroner, gravely and tranquilly, 'from what asylum did you last escape?'

Harker flushed crimson again, but said nothing, and the seven jurors rose and solemnly filed out of the cabin.

'If you have done insulting me, sir,' said Harker, as soon as he and the officer were left alone with the dead man, 'I suppose I am at liberty to go?'

'Yes.'

Harker started to leave, but paused, with his hand on the door latch. The habit of his profession was strong in him – stronger than his sense of personal dignity. He turned about and said:

'The book that you have there – I recognize it as Morgan's diary. You seemed greatly interested in it; you read in it while I was testifying. May I see it? The public would like – '

'The book will cut no figure in this matter,' replied the official; slipping it into his coat pocket; 'and the entries in it were made before the writer's death.'

As Harker passed out of the house the jury reëntered and stood about the table, on which the now covered corpse showed under the sheet with sharp definition. The foreman seated himself near the candle, produced from his breast pocket a pencil and scrap of paper and wrote rather laboriously the following verdict, which with various degrees of effort all signed:

'We, the jury, do find that the remains come to their death at the hands of a mountain lion, but some of us thinks, all the same, they had fits.'

IV

AN EXPLANATION FROM THE TOMB

In the diary of the late Hugh Morgan are certain interesting entries having, possibly, a scientific value as suggestions. At the inquest upon his body the book was not put in evidence; possibly the coroner thought it not worth while to confuse the jury. The date of the first of the entries mentioned cannot be ascertained; the upper part of the leaf is torn away; the part of the entry remaining follows:

' . . . would run in a half-circle, keeping his head turned always toward the centre, and again he would stand still, barking furiously. At last he ran away into the brush as fast as he could go. I thought at first that he had gone mad, but on returning to the house found no other alteration in his manner than what was obviously due to fear of punishment.

'Can a dog see with his nose? Do odors impress some cerebral centre with images of the thing that emitted them? . . .

'*Sept. 2.* – Looking at the stars last night as they rose above the crest of the ridge east of the house, I observed them successively disappear – from left to right. Each was eclipsed but an instant, and only a few at the same time, but along the entire length of the ridge all that were within a degree or two of the crest were blotted out. It was as if something had passed along between me and them; but I could not see it, and the stars were not thick enough to define its outline. Ugh! I don't like this.'

Several weeks' entries are missing, three leaves being torn from the book.

'*Sept. 27.* – It has been about here again – I find evidences of its presence every day. I watched again all last night in the same cover, gun in hand, double-charged with buckshot. In the morning the fresh footprints were there, as before. Yet I would have sworn that I did not sleep – indeed, I hardly sleep at all. It is terrible, insupportable! If these amazing experiences are real I shall go mad; if they are fanciful I am mad already.

'*Oct. 3.* – I shall not go – it shall not drive me away. No, this is *my* house, *my* land. God hates a coward . . .

'*Oct. 5.* – I can stand it no longer; I have invited Harker to pass a few weeks with me – he has a level head. I can judge from his manner if he thinks me mad.

'*Oct. 7.* – I have the solution of the mystery; it came to me last night – suddenly, as by revelation. How simple – how terribly simple!

'There are sounds that we cannot hear. At either end of the scale are notes that stir no chord of that imperfect instrument, the human ear. They are too high or too grave. I have observed a flock of blackbirds occupying an entire tree-top – the tops of several trees – and all in full song. Suddenly – in a moment – at absolutely the same instant – all spring into the air and fly away. How? They could not all see one another – whole tree-tops intervened. At no point could a leader have been visible to all. There must have been a signal of warning or command, high and shrill above the din, but by me unheard. I have observed, too, the same simultaneous flight when all were silent, among not only blackbirds, but other birds – quail, for example, widely separated by bushes – even on opposite sides of a hill.

'It is known to seamen that a school of whales basking or sporting on the surface of the ocean, miles apart, with the convexity of the earth between, will sometimes dive at the same instant – all gone out of sight in a moment. The signal has been sounded – too grave for the ear of the sailor at the masthead and his comrades on the deck – who nevertheless feel its vibrations in the ship as the stones of a cathedral are stirred by the bass of the organ.

'As with sounds, so with colors. At each end of the solar spectrum the chemist can detect the presence of what are known as 'actinic' rays. They represent colors – integral colors in the composition of light – which we are unable to discern. The human eye is an imperfect instrument; its range is but a few octaves of the real 'chromatic scale.' I am not mad; there are colors that we cannot see.

'And, God help me! the Damned Thing is of such a color!'

THE UPPER BERTH

F. Marion Crawford

[1854–1909]

'*F. Marion Crawford produced several weird tales of varying quality, now collected in a volume entitled* Wandering Ghosts. For the Blood is the Life *touches powerfully on a case of moon-cursed vampirism near an ancient tower on the rocks of the lonely South Italian seacoast. The* Dead Smile *treats of family horrors in an old house and an ancestral vault in Ireland, and introduces the banshee with considerable force.* The Upper Berth, *however, is Crawford's weird masterpiece; and is one of the most tremendous horror-stories in all literature. In this tale of a suicide-haunted stateroom such things as the spectral salt-water dampness, the strangely open porthole, and the nightmare struggle with the nameless object are handled with incomparable dexterity.*'

– H.P. Lovecraft

I AM AN OLD SAILOR, said Brisbane, and as I have to cross the Atlantic pretty often, I have my favourites. Most men have their favourites. I have seen a man wait in a Broadway bar for three-quarters of an hour for a particular car which he liked. I believe the bar keeper made at least one-third of his living by that man's preference. I have a habit of waiting for certain ships when I am obliged to cross that duck pond. It may be a prejudice, but I was never cheated out of a good passage but once in my life. I remember it very well; it was a warm morning in June, and the Customs House officials, who were hanging about waiting for a steamer already on her way up from the Quarantine, presented a peculiarly haze and thoughtful appearance. I had not much luggage – I never have. I mingled with the crowd of passengers, porters, and officious individuals in blue coats and brass buttons, who seemed to spring up like mushrooms from the deck of a moored steamer to obtrude their unnecessary services upon the independent passenger. I have often noticed with a certain interest the spontaneous evolution of these fellows. They are not there when you arrive; five minutes after the pilot has called 'Go ahead!' they, or at least their blue coats and brass buttons, have disappeared from deck and gangway as completely as though they had been consigned to that locker which tradition unanimously ascribes to Davy Jones. But, at the moment of starting, they are there, clean shaved, blue coated, and ravenous for fees. I hastened on board. The *Kamtschatka* was one of my favourite ships. I say was, because she emphatically no longer is. I cannot conceive of any inducement which could entice me to take another voyage in her. Yes, I know what you are going to say. She is uncommonly clean in the run aft, she has enough bluffing off in the bows to keep her dry, and the lower berths are most of them double. She has a lot of advantages, but I won't cross in her again. Excuse the digression. I got on board. I hailed a steward, whose red nose and redder whiskers were equally familiar to me.

'One hundred and five, lower berth,' said I, in the business-like tone peculiar to men who think no more of crossing the Atlantic than taking a whisky cocktail at down-town Delmonico's.

The steward took my portmanteau, greatcoat, and rug. I shall never forget the expression of his face. Not that he turned pale. It is maintained by the most eminent divines that even miracles cannot change the course of nature. I have no hesitation in saying that he did not turn pale; but, from his expression, I judged that he was either about to shed tears, to sneeze, or to drop my portmanteau. As the latter contained two bottles of particularly fine old sherry presented to me for my voyage by my old friend Snigginson van Pickyns, I felt extremely nervous. But the steward did none of these things.

'Well, I'm d—d!' he said in a low voice, and led the way.

I suppose my Hermes, as he led me to the lower regions, had had a
little grog, but I said nothing, and followed him. 105 was on the port
side, well aft. There was nothing remarkable about the state-room.
The lower berth, like most of those upon the *Kamtschatka*, was double.
There was plenty of room; there was the usual washing apparatus,
calculated to convey an idea of luxury to the mind of a North
American Indian; there was the usual inefficient racks of brown
wood, in which it is more easy to hang a large-sized umbrella than
the common tooth-brush of commerce. Upon the uninviting mat-
tresses were carefully folded together those blankets which a great
modern humorist has aptly compared to cold buckwheat cakes. The
question of towels was left entirely to the imagination. The glass
decanters were filled with a transparent liquid faintly tinged with
brown, but from which an odour less faint, but not more pleasing,
ascended to the nostrils, like a far off sea-sick reminiscence of oily
machinery. Sand-coloured curtains half closed the upper berth. The
hazy June daylight shed a faint illumination upon the desolate little
scene. Ugh! How I hated that state-room!

The steward deposited my traps and looked at me, as though he
wanted to get away – probably in search of more passengers and more
fees. It is always a good plan to start in favour with those function-
aries, and I accordingly gave him certain coins there and then.

'I'll try and make yer comfortable all I can,' he remarked, as he put
the coins in his pocket. Nevertheless, there was a doubtful intonation
in his voice which surprised me. Possibly his scale of fees had gone up,
and he was not satisfied; but on the whole I was inclined to think that,
as he himself would have expressed it, he was 'the better for a glass'. I
was wrong, however, and did the man injustice.

Nothing especially worthy of mention occurred during that day. We
left the pier punctually, and it was very pleasant to be fairly under
way, for the weather was warm and sultry, and the motion of the
steamer produced a refreshing breeze. Everybody knows what the
first day at sea is like. People pace the decks and stare at each other,
and occasionally meet acquaintances whom they did not know to be
on board. There is the usual uncertainty as to whether the food will be
good, bad, or indifferent, until the first two meals have put the matter
beyond a doubt; there is the usual uncertainty about the weather,
until the ship is fairly off Fire Island. The tables are crowded at first,
and then suddenly thinned. Pale-faced people spring from their seats
and precipitate themselves towards the door, and each old sailor

breathes more freely as his sea-sick neighbour rushes from his side, leaving him plenty of elbow-room and an unlimited command over the mustard.

One passage across the Atlantic is very much like another, and we who cross very often do not make the voyage for the sake of novelty. Whales and icebergs are indeed always objects of interest, but, after all, one whale is very much like another whale, and one rarely sees an iceberg at close quarters. To the majority of us the most delightful moment of the day on board an ocean steamer is when we have taken our last turn on deck, have smoked our last cigar, and having succeeded in tiring ourselves, feel at liberty to turn in with a clear conscience. On that first night of the voyage I felt particularly lazy, and went to bed in 105 rather earlier than I usually do. As I turned in, I was amazed to see that I was to have a companion. A portmanteau, very like my own, lay in the opposite corner, and in the upper berth had been deposited a neatly folded rug, with a stick and umbrella. I had hoped to be alone, and I was disappointed; but I wondered who my room-mate was to be, and I determined to have a look at him.

Before I had been long in bed he entered. He was, as far as I could see, a very tall man, very thin, very pale, with sandy hair and whiskers and colourless grey eyes. He had about him, I thought, an air of rather dubious fashion; the sort of man you might see in Wall Street, without being able precisely to say what he was doing there – the sort of man who frequents the Café Anglais, who always seems to be alone and who drinks champagne; you might meet him on a racecourse, but he would never appear to be doing anything there either. A little over-dressed – a little odd. There are three or four of his kind on every ocean steamer. I made up my mind that I did not care to make his acquaintance, and I went to sleep saying to myself that I would study his habits in order to avoid him. If he rose early, I would rise late; if he went to bed late, I would go to bed early. I did not care to know him. If you once know people of that kind they are always turning up. Poor fellow! I need not have taken the trouble to come to so many decisions about him, for I never saw him again after that first night in 105.

I was sleeping soundly when I was suddenly waked by a loud noise. To judge from the sound, my room-mate must have sprung with a single leap from the upper berth to the floor. I heard him fumbling with the latch and bolt of the door, which opened almost immediately, and then I heard his footsteps as he ran at full speed down the passage, leaving the door open behind him. The ship was rolling a little, and I expected to hear him stumble or fall, but he ran as though he were running for his life. The door swung on its hinges with the motion of the vessel, and the sound annoyed me. I got up and shut it, and groped my way back to my berth in the darkness. I went to sleep again; but I had no idea how long I slept.

When I awoke it was still quite dark, but I felt a disagreeable sensation of cold, and it seemed to me that the air was damp. You know the peculiar smell of a cabin which has been wet with sea-water. I covered myself up as well as I could and dozed off again, framing complaints to be made the next day, and selecting the most powerful epithets in the language. I could hear my room-mate turn over in the upper berth. He had probably returned while I was asleep. Once I thought I heard him groan, and I argued that he was sea-sick. That is particularly unpleasant when one is below. Nevertheless, I dozed off and slept till early daylight.

The ship was rolling heavily, much more than on the previous evening, and the grey light which came in through the porthole changed in tint with every movement according as the angle of the vessel's side turned the glass seawards or skywards. It was very cold – unaccountably so for the month of June. I turned my head and looked at the porthole, and I saw to my surprise that it was wide open and hooked back. I believe I swore audibly. Then I got up and shut it. As I turned back I glanced at the upper berth. The curtains were drawn close together; my companion had probably felt cold as well as I. It struck me that I had slept enough. The state-room was uncomfortable, though, strange to say, I could not smell the dampness which had annoyed me in the night. My room-mate was still asleep – excellent opportunity for avoiding him, so I dressed at once and went on deck. The day was warm and cloudy, with an oily smell on the water. It was seven o'clock as I came out – much later than I had imagined. I came across the doctor, who was taking his first sniff of the morning air. He was a young man from the west of Ireland – a tremendous fellow, with black hair and blue eyes, already inclined to be stout; he had a happy-go-lucky, healthy look about him which was rather attractive.

'Fine morning,' I remarked, by way of introduction.

'Well,' said he, eyeing me with an air of ready interest, 'it's a fine morning and it's not a fine morning. I don't think it's much of a morning.'

'Well, no – it is not so very fine,' said I.

'It's just what I call fuggly weather,' replied the doctor.

'It was very cold last night, I thought,' I remarked. 'However, when

I looked about I found that the porthole was wide open. I had not
noticed it when I went to bed. And the state-room was damp, too.'

'Damp!' said he. 'Whereabouts are you?'

'One hundred and five – '

To my surprise the doctor started visibly, and stared at me.

'What is the matter?' I asked.

'Oh – nothing,' he answered; 'only everybody has complained of
that state-room for the last three trips.'

'I shall complain, too,' I said. 'It has certainly not been properly
aired. It is a shame!'

'I don't believe it can be helped,' answered the doctor. 'I believe
there is something – well, it is not my business to frighten passengers.'

'You need not be afraid of frightening me,' I replied. 'I can stand
any amount of damp. If I should get a bad cold I will come to you.'

I offered the doctor a cigar, which he took and examined very
critically.

'It is not so much the damp,' he remarked. 'However, I dare say
you will get on very well. Have you a room-mate?'

'Yes; a deuce of a fellow, who bolts out in the middle of the night,
and leaves the door open.'

Again the doctor glanced curiously at me. Then he lit the cigar and
looked grave.

'Did he come back?' he asked presently.

'Yes. I was asleep, but I waked up and heard him moving. Then I
felt cold and went to sleep again. This morning I found the porthole
open.'

'Look here,' said the doctor quietly, 'I don't care much for this ship.
I don't care a rap for her reputation. I tell you what I will do. I have a
good-sized place up here. I will share it with you, though I don't
know you from Adam.'

I was very much surprised at the proposition. I could not imagine
why he should take such a sudden interest in my welfare. However,
his manner as he spoke of the ship was peculiar.

'You are very good, Doctor,' I said. 'But, really, I believe even now
the cabin could be aired, or cleaned out, or something. Why do you
not care for the ship?'

'We are not superstitious in our profession, sir,' replied the doctor,
'but the sea makes people so. I don't want to prejudice you, and I
don't want to frighten you, but if you will take my advice you will
move in here. I would as soon see you overboard,' he added earnestly,
'as know that you or any other man was to sleep in 105.'

'Good gracious! Why?' I asked.

'Just because on the three last trips the people who have slept there actually have gone overboard,' he answered gravely.

The intelligence was startling and exceedingly unpleasant, I confess. I looked hard at the doctor to see whether he was making game of me, but he looked perfectly serious. I thanked him warmly for his offer, but told him I intended to be the exception to the rule by which everybody who slept in that particular state-room went overboard. He did not say much, but looked grave as ever, and hinted that, before we got across, I should probably reconsider his proposal. In the course of time we went to breakfast, at which only an inconsiderable number of passengers assembled. I noticed that one or two of the officers who breakfasted with us looked grave. After breakfast I went into my state-room in order to get a book. The curtains of the upper berth were still closely drawn. Not a word was to be heard. My room-mate was probably still asleep.

As I came out I heard the steward whose business it was to look after me. He whispered that the captain wanted to see me, and then scuttled away down the passage as if very anxious to avoid any questions. I went towards the captain's cabin, and found him waiting for me.

'Sir,' said he, 'I want to ask a favour of you.'

I answered that I would do anything to oblige him.

'Your room-mate has disappeared,' he said. 'He is known to have turned in early last night. Did you notice anything extraordinary in his manner?'

The question, coming as it did, in exact confirmation of the fears the doctor had expressed half an hour earlier, staggered me.

'You don't mean to say he has gone overboard?' I asked.

'I fear he has,' answered the captain.

'This is the most extraordinary thing – ' I began.

'Why?' he asked.

'He is the fourth, then,' I explained. In answer to another question from the captain, I explained, without mentioning the doctor, that I had heard the story concerning 105. He seemed very much annoyed at hearing that I knew of it. I told him what had occurred in the night.

'What you say,' he replied, 'coincides almost exactly with what was told to me by the room-mates of two of the other three. They bolt out of bed and run down the passage. Two of them were seen to go overboard by the watch; we stopped and lowered boats, but they were not found. Nobody, however, saw or heard the man who was lost last night – if he is really lost. The steward, who is a superstitious fellow, perhaps, and expected something to go wrong, went to look for him this morning, and found his berth empty, but his clothes lying about, just as he had left them. The steward was the only man on board who knew him by sight, and he has been searching everywhere for him. He has disappeared! Now sir, I want to beg you not to mention the circumstance to any of the passengers; I don't want the ship to get a bad name, and nothing hangs about an ocean-goer like stories of suicides. You shall have your choice of any one of the officers' cabins you like, including my own, for the rest of the passage. Is that a fair bargain?'

'Very,' said I; 'and I am much obliged to you. But since I am alone, and have the state-room to myself, I would rather not move. If the steward will take out that unfortunate man's things, I would as lief stay where I am. I will not say anything about the matter, and I think I can promise you that I will not follow my room-mate.'

The captain tried to dissuade me from my intention, but I preferred having a state-room alone to being the chum of any officer on board. I do not know whether I acted foolishly, but if I had taken his advice I should have had nothing more to tell. There would have remained the disagreeable coincidence of several suicides occurring among men who had slept in the same cabin, but that would have been all.

That was not the end of the matter, however, by any means. I obstinately made up my mind that I would not be disturbed by such tales, and I even went so far as to argue the question with the captain. There was nothing wrong about the state-room, I said. It was rather damp. The porthole had been left open last night. My room-mate might have been ill when he came on board, and he might have become delirious after he went to bed. He might even now be hiding somewhere on board, and might be found later. The place ought to be aired and the fastening of the port looked to. If the captain would give me leave, I would see that what I thought necessary was done immediately.

'Of course you have a right to stay where you are if you please,' he replied, rather petulantly, 'but I wish you would turn out and let me lock the place up, and be done with it.'

I did not see it in the same light, and left the captain, after promising to be silent concerning the disappearance of my companion. The latter had had no acquaintances on board, and was not missed in the course of the day. Towards evening I met the doctor again, and he asked me whether I had changed my mind. I told him I had not.

'Then you will before long,' he said, very gravely.

We played whist in the evening, and I went to bed late. I will confess now that I felt a disagreeable sensation when I entered my state-room. I could not help thinking of the tall man I had seen on the previous night, who was now dead, drowned, tossing about in the long swell, two or three hundred miles astern. His face rose very distinctly before me as I undressed, and I even went so far as to draw back the curtains of the upper berth, as though to persuade myself that he was actually gone. I also bolted the door of the state-room. Suddenly I became aware that the porthole was open, and fastened back. This was more than I could stand. I hastily drew on my dressing-gown and went in search of Robert, the steward of my passage. I was very angry, I remember, and when I found him I dragged him roughly to the door of 105, and pushed him towards the open porthole.

'What the deuce do you mean, you scoundrel, by leaving that port open every night? Don't you know it is against the regulations? Don't you know that if the ship heeled and the water began to come in, ten men could not shut it? I will report you to the captain, you black-guard, for endangering the ship!'

I was exceedingly wroth. The man trembled and turned pale, and then began to shut the round glass plate with the heavy brass fittings.

'Why don't you answer me?' I said roughly.

'If you please, sir,' faltered Robert, 'there's nobody on board as can keep this 'ere port shut at night. You can try it yourself, sir, I ain't a-going to stop hany longer on board o' this vessel, sir; I ain't, indeed. But if I was you, sir, I'd just clear out and go and sleep with the surgeon, or something, I would. Look 'ere, sir, is that fastened what you may call securely, or not, sir? Try it, sir; see if it will move a hinch.'

I tried the port, and found it perfectly tight.

'Well, sir,' continued Robert triumphantly, 'I wager my reputation as an A1 steward that in 'arf an hour it will be open again; fastened back, too, sir, that's the horful thing – fastened back!'

I examined the great screw and the looped nut that ran on it.

'If I find it open in the night, Robert, I will give you a sovereign. It is not possible. You may go.'

'Soverin' did you say, sir? Very good, sir. Thank ye, sir. Goodnight, sir. Pleasant reepose, sir, and all manner of hinchantin' dreams, sir.'

Robert scuttled away, delighted at being released. Of course, I thought he was trying to account for his negligence by a silly story, intended to frighten me, and I disbelieved him. The consequence was that he got his sovereign, and I spent a very peculiarly unpleasant night.

I went to bed, and five minutes after I had rolled myself up in my blankets the inexorable Robert extinguished the light that burned steadily behind the ground-glass pane near the door. I lay quite still in the dark trying to go to sleep, but I soon found that impossible. It had been some satisfaction to be angry with the steward, and the diversion had banished that unpleasant sensation I had at first experienced when I thought of the drowned man who had been my chum; but I was no longer sleepy, and I lay awake for some time, occasionally glancing at the porthole, which I could just see from where I lay, and which, in the darkness, looked like a faintly luminous soup-plate suspended in blackness. I believe I must have lain there for an hour, and, as I remember, I was just dozing into sleep when I was roused by a draught of cold air, and by distinctly feeling the spray of the sea blown upon my face. I started to my feet, and not having allowed in the dark for the motion of the ship, I was instantly thrown violently across the state-room upon the couch which was placed beneath the porthole. I recovered myself immediately, however, and climbed upon my knees. The porthole was again wide open and fastened back!

Now these things are facts. I was wide awake when I got up, and I should certainly have been waked by the fall had I still been dozing. Moreover, I bruised my elbows and knees badly, and the bruises were there on the following morning to testify to the fact, if I myself had doubted it. The porthole was wide open and fastened back – a thing so unaccountable that I remember very well feeling astonishment rather than fear when I discovered it. I at once closed the plate again, and screwed down the loop-nut with all my strength. It was very dark in the state-room. I reflected that the port had certainly been opened within an hour after Robert had at first shut it in my presence, and I determined to watch it, and see whether it would open again. Those brass fittings are very heavy and by no means easy to move. I could not believe that the clump had been turned by the shaking of the screw. I stood peering out through the thick glass at the alternate white and grey streaks of the sea that foamed beneath the ship's side. I must have remained there a quarter of an hour.

Suddenly, as I stood, I distinctly heard something moving behind me in one of the berths, and a moment afterwards, just as I turned instinctively to look – though I could, of course, see nothing in the darkness – I heard a very faint groan. I sprang across the state-room, and tore the curtains of the upper berth aside, thrusting in my hands to discover if there were anyone there. There was someone.

I remember that the sensation as I put my hands forward was as though I were plunging them into the air of a damp cellar, and from behind the curtains came a gust of wind that smelled horribly of stagnant sea-water. I laid hold of something that had the shape of a man's arm, but was smooth, and wet, and icy cold. But suddenly, as I pulled, the creature sprang violently forward against me, a clammy, oozy mass, as it seemed to me, heavy and wet, yet endowed with a sort of supernatural strength. I reeled across the state-room, and in an instant the door opened and the thing rushed out. I had not had time to be frightened, and quickly recovered myself, I sprang through the door and gave chase at the top of my speed, but I was too late. Ten yards before me I could see – I am sure I saw it – a dark shadow moving in the dimly lighted passage, quickly as the shadow of a fast horse thrown before a dogcart by the lamp on a dark night. But in a moment it had disappeared, and I found myself holding on to the polished rail that ran along the bulkhead where the passage turned towards the companion. My hair stood on end, and the cold perspiration rolled down my face. I am not ashamed of it in the least: I was very badly frightened.

Still I doubted my senses, and pulled myself together. It was absurd, I thought. The Welsh rarebit I had eaten had disagreed with me. I had been in a nightmare. I made my way back to my state-room, and entered it with an effort. The whole place smelled of stagnant sea-water, as it had when I had waked on the previous evening. It required my utmost strength to go in, and grope among my things for a box of wax lights. As I lighted a railway reading lantern which I always carry in case I want to read after the lamps are out, I perceived that the porthole was again open, and a sort of creeping horror began to take possession of me which I never felt before, nor wish to feel again. But I got a light and proceeded to examine the upper berth, expecting to find it drenched with sea-water.

But I was disappointed. The bed had been slept in, and the smell of the sea was strong; but the bedding was as dry as a bone. I fancied that Robert had not had the courage to make the bed after the accident of the previous night – it had all been a hideous dream. I drew the curtains back as far as I could and examined the place very carefully. It was perfectly dry. But the porthole was open again. With a sort of dull bewilderment of horror I closed it and screwed it down, and thrusting my heavy stick through the brass loop, wrenched it with all my might, till the thick metal began to bend under the pressure. Then I hooked my reading lantern into the red velvet at the head of the couch, and sat down to recover my senses if I could. I sat there all night, unable to think of rest – hardly able to think at all. But the porthole remained closed, and I did not believe it would now open again without the application of a considerable force.

The morning dawned at last, and I dressed myself slowly, thinking over all that had happened in the night. It was a beautiful day and I went on deck, glad to get out into the early, pure sunshine, and to smell the breeze from the blue water, so different from the noisome, stagnant odour of my state-room. Instinctively I turned aft, towards the surgeon's cabin. There he stood, with a pipe in his mouth, taking his morning airing precisely as on the preceding day.

'Good morning,' said he quietly, but looking at me with evident curiosity.

'Doctor, you were quite right,' said I. 'There is something wrong about that place.'

'I thought you would change your mind,' he answered, rather triumphantly. 'You have had a bad night, eh? Shall I make you a pick-me-up? I have a capital recipe.'

'No, thanks,' I cried. 'But I would like to tell you what happened.'

I then tried to explain, as clearly as possible, precisely what had occurred, not omitting to state that I had been scared as I had never been scared in my whole life before. I dwelt particularly on the phenomenon of the porthole, which was a fact to which I could testify, even if the rest had been an illusion. I had closed it twice in the night, and the second time I had actually bent the brass in wrenching it with my stick. I believe I insisted a good deal on this point.

'You seem to think I am likely to doubt your story,' said the doctor, smiling at the detailed account of the state of the porthole. 'I do not doubt it in the least. I renew my invitation to you. Bring your traps here and take half my cabin.'

'Come and take half of mine for one night,' I said. 'Help me to get to the bottom of this thing.'

'You will get to the bottom of something else if you try,' answered the doctor.

'What?' I asked.

'The bottom of the sea. I am going to leave this ship. It is not canny.'

'Then you will not help to find out – '

'Not I,' said the doctor quickly. 'It is my business to keep my wits about me – not to go fiddling about with ghosts and things.'

'Do you really believe it is a ghost?' I enquired, rather contemptuously. But as I spoke I remembered very well the horrible sensation of the supernatural which had got possession of me during the night. The doctor turned sharply on me.

'Have you any reasonable explanation of these things to offer?' he asked. 'No; you have not. Well, you say you will find an explanation. I say that you won't, sir, simply because there is not any.'

'But, my dear sir,' I retorted, 'do you, a man of science, mean to tell me that such things cannot be explained?'

'I do,' he answered stoutly. 'And, if they could, I would not be concerned in the explanation.'

I did not care to spend another night alone in the state-room, and yet I was obstinately determined to get at the root of the disturbances. I do not believe there are many men who would have slept there alone, after passing two such nights. But I made up my mind to try it, if I could not get anyone to share a watch with me. The doctor was evidently not inclined for such an experiment. He said he was a surgeon, and that in case any accident occurred on board he must always be in readiness. He could not afford to have his nerves unsettled. Perhaps he was quite right, but I am inclined to think that his precaution was prompted by his inclination. On enquiry, he informed me that there was no one on board who would be likely to join me in my investigations, and after a little more conversation I left him. A little later I met the captain, and told my story. I said that, if no one would spend the night with me, I would ask leave to have the light burning all night, and would try it alone.

'Look here,' said he, 'I will tell you what I will do. I will share your watch myself, and we will see what happens. It is my belief that we can find out between us. There may be some fellow skulking on board who steals a passage by frightening the passengers. It is just possible that there may be something queer in the carpentering of that berth.'

I suggested taking the ship's carpenter below and examining the place; but I was overjoyed at the captain's offer to spend the night with me. He accordingly sent for the workman and ordered him to do anything I required. We went below at once. I had all the bedding cleared out of the upper berth, and we examined the place thoroughly to see if there was a board loose anywhere, or a panel which could be opened or pushed aside. We tried the planks everywhere, tapped the flooring, unscrewed the fittings of the lower berth and took it to pieces – in short, there was not a square inch of the state-room which was not searched and tested. Everything was in perfect order, and we put everything back in its place. As we were finishing our work, Robert came to the door and looked in.

'Well, sir – find anything, sir?' he asked, with a ghastly grin.

'You were right about the porthole, Robert,' I said, and gave him the promised sovereign. The carpenter did his work silently and skilfully, following my directions. When he had done he spoke.

'I'm a plain man, sir,' he said. 'But it's my belief you had better just turn out your things, and let me run a dozen four-inch screws through the door of this cabin. There's no good ever came o' this cabin yet, sir, and that's all about it. There's been four lives lost out o' here to my own remembrance, and that in four trips. Better give it up, sir – better give it up!'

'I will try it for one night more,' I said.

'Better give it up, sir – better give it up! It's a precious bad job,' repeated the workman, putting his tools in his bag and leaving the cabin.

But my spirits had risen considerably at the prospects of having the captain's company, and I made up my mind not to be prevented from going to the end of the strange business. I abstained from Welsh rarebits and grog that evening, and did not even join in the customary game of whist. I wanted to be quite sure of my nerves, and my vanity made me anxious to make a good figure in the captain's eyes.

The captain was one of those spendidly tough and cheerful specimens of seafaring humanity whose combined courage, hardihood, and calmness in difficulty leads them naturally into high positions of trust. He was not the man to be led away by an idle tale, and the mere fact that he was willing to join me in the investigation was proof that he thought there was something seriously wrong, which could not be accounted for on ordinary theories, nor laughed down as a common superstition. To some extent, too, his reputation was at stake, as well as the reputation of the ship. It is no light thing to lose passengers overboard, and he knew it.

About ten o'clock that evening, as I was smoking a last cigar, he came up to me, and drew me aside from the beat of the other passengers who were patrolling the deck in the warm darkness.

'This is a serious matter, Mr. Brisbane,' he said. 'We must make up our minds either way – to be disappointed or to have a pretty rough time of it. You see I cannot afford to laugh at the affair, and I will ask you to sign your name to a statement of whatever occurs. If nothing happens tonight we will try it again tomorrow and next day. Are you ready?'

So we went below, and entered the state-room. As we went in I could see Robert the steward, who stood a little farther down the passage, watching us, with his usual grin, as though certain that something dreadful was about to happen. The captain closed the door behind us and bolted it.

'Supposing we put your portmanteau before the door,' he suggested. 'One of us can sit on it. Nothing can get out then. Is the port screwed down?'

I found it as I had left it in the morning. Indeed, without using a lever, as I had done, no one could have opened it. I drew back the curtains of the upper berth so that I could see well into it. By the captain's advice I lighted my reading lantern, and placed it so that it shone upon the white sheets above. He insisted upon sitting on the portmanteau, declaring that he wished to be able to swear that he had sat before the door.

Then he requested me to search the state-room thoroughly, an operation very soon accomplished, as it consisted merely in looking beneath the lower berth and under the couch below the porthole. The spaces were quite empty.

'It is impossible for any human being to get in,' I said, 'or for any human being to open the port.'

'Very good,' said the captain calmly. 'If we see anything now, it must be either imagination or something supernatural.'

I sat down on the edge of the lower berth.

'The first time it happened,' said the captain, crossing his legs and leaning back against the door, 'was in March. The passenger who slept here, in the upper berth, turned out to have been a lunatic – at all events, he was known to have been a little touched, and he had taken his passage without the knowledge of his friends. He rushed out in the middle of the night, and threw himself overboard, before the officer who had the watch could stop him. We stopped and lowered a boat; it was a quiet night, just before that heavy weather came on; but we could not find him. Of course his suicide was afterwards accounted for on the grounds of his insanity.'

'I suppose that often happens?' I remarked rather absently.

'Not often – no,' said the captain; 'never before in my experience, though I have heard of it happening on board other ships. Well, as I was saying, that occurred in March. On the very next trip – What are you looking at?' he asked, stopping suddenly in his narration.

I believe I gave no answer. My eyes were riveted upon the porthole. It seemed to me that the brass loop-nut was beginning to turn very slowly upon the screw – so slowly, however, that I was not sure it moved at all. I watched it intently, fixing its position in my mind and trying to ascertain whether it changed. Seeing where I was looking, the captain looked, too.

'It moves!' he exclaimed, in a tone of conviction. 'No, it does not,' he added, after a minute.

'If it were the jarring of the screw,' said I, 'it would have opened during the day; but I found it this evening jammed tight as I left it this morning.'

I rose and tried the nut. It was certainly loosened, for by an effort I could move it with my hands.

'The queer thing,' said the captain, 'is that the second man who was lost is supposed to have got through that very port. We had a terrible time over it. It was in the middle of the night, and the weather was very heavy; there was an alarm that one of the ports was open and the sea running in. I came below and found everything flooded, the water pouring in every time she rolled, and the whole port swimming from the top bolts – not the porthole in the middle. Well, we managed to shut it, but the water did some damage. Ever since that the place smells of seawater from time to time. We supposed the passenger had thrown himself out, though the Lord only knows how he did it. The steward kept telling me that he cannot keep anything shut here. Upon my word – I can smell it now, cannot you?' he enquired, sniffing the air suspiciously.

'Yes – distinctly,' I said, and I shuddered as that same odour of stagnant sea-water grew stronger in the cabin. 'Now, to smell like this, the place must be damp,' I continued, 'and yet when I examined it with the carpenter this morning everything was perfectly dry. It is most extraordinary – hallo!'

My reading lantern, which had been placed in the upper berth, was suddenly extinguished. There was still a good deal of light from the pane of ground glass near the door, behind which loomed the regulation lamp. The ship rolled heavily, and the curtain of the upper berth swung far out into the state-room and back again. I rose quickly from my seat on the edge of the bed, and the captain at the same moment started to his feet with a loud cry of surprise. I had turned with the intention of taking down the lantern to examine it, when I heard his exclamation, and immediately afterwards his call for help. I sprang towards him. He was wrestling with all his might with the brass loop of the port. It seemed to turn against his hands in spite of all his efforts. I caught up my cane, a heavy oak stick I always used to carry, and thrust it through the ring and bore on it with all my strength. But the strong wood snapped suddenly and I fell upon the couch. When I rose again the port was wide open, and the captain was standing with his back against the door, pale to the lips.

'There is something in that berth!' he cried, in a strange voice, his eyes almost starting from his head. 'Hold the door, while I look – it shall not escape us, whatever it is!'

But instead of taking his place, I sprang upon the lower bed, and seized something which lay in the upper berth.

It was something ghastly, horrible beyond words, and it moved in my grip. It was like the body of a man long drowned, and yet it moved, and had the strength of ten men living; but I gripped it with all my might – the slippery, oozy, horrible thing – the dead white eyes seemed to stare at me out of the dusk; the putrid odour of rank sea-water was about it, and its shiny hair hung in foul wet curls over its dead face. I wrestled with the dead thing; it thrust upon me and forced me back and nearly broke my arms; it wound its corpse's arms about my neck, the living death, and overpowered me, so that I, at last, cried aloud and fell, and left my hold.

As I fell the thing sprang across me, and seemed to throw itself upon the captain. When I last saw him on his feet his face was white and his lips set. It seemed to me that he struck a violent blow at the dead being, and then he, too, fell forward upon his face, with an inarticulate cry of horror.

The thing paused an instant, seeming to hover over his prostrate body, and I could have screamed again for very fright, but I had no voice left. The thing vanished suddenly, and it seemed to my disturbed senses that it made its exit through the open port, though how that was possible, considering the smallness of the aperture, is more than anyone can tell. I lay a long time upon the floor, and the captain lay beside me. At last I partially recovered my senses and moved, and instantly knew that my arm was broken – the small bone of the left forearm near the wrist.

I got upon my feet somehow, and with my remaining hand I tried to raise the captain. He groaned and moved, and at last came to himself. He was not hurt, but he seemed badly stunned.

Well, do you want to hear any more? There is nothing more. That is the end of my story. The carpenter carried out his scheme of running half a dozen four-inch screws through the door of 105; and if ever you take a passage in the *Kamtschatka*, you may ask for a berth in that state-room. You will be told that it is engaged – yes – it is engaged by that dead thing.

I finished the trip in the surgeon's cabin. He doctored my broken arm, and advised me not to 'fiddle about with ghosts and things' any more. The captain was very silent, and never sailed again in that ship, though it is still running. And I will not sail in her either. It was a very disagreeable experience, and I was very badly frightened, which is a thing I do not like. That is all. That is how I saw a ghost – if it was a ghost. It was dead, anyhow.

THE YELLOW SIGN

Robert W. Chambers

[1865–1933]

'*Very genuine, though not without the typical mannered extravagance of the 1890s, is the strain of horror in the early work of Robert W. Chambers, since renowned for products of a very different quality.* The King in Yellow, *a series of vaguely connected short stories having as a background a monstrous and suppressed book whose perusal brings fright, madness, and spectral tragedy, really achieves notable heights of cosmic fear in spite of uneven interest and a somewhat trivial and affected cultivation of the Gallic studio atmosphere made popular by Du Maurier's* Trilby. *The most powerful of its tales, perhaps, is* The Yellow Sign, *in which is introduced a silent and terrible churchyard watchman with a face like a puffy grave-worm's.*'

– H.P. Lovecraft

I

'Let the red dawn surmise
What we shall do,
When this blue starlight dies
And all is through.'

THERE ARE SO MANY THINGS which are impossible to explain! Why should certain chords in music make me think of the brown and golden tints of autumn foliage? Why should the Mass of Sainte Cécile send my thoughts wandering among caverns whose walls blaze with ragged masses of virgin silver? What was it in the roar and turmoil of Broadway at six o'clock that flashed before my eyes the picture of a still Breton forest where sunlight filtered through spring foliage and Silvia bent, half curiously, half tenderly, over a small green lizard, murmuring: 'To think that this also is a little ward of God!'

When I first saw the watchman his back was toward me. I looked at him indifferently until he went into the church. I paid no more attention to him than I had to any other man who lounged through Washington Square that morning, and when I shut my window and turned back into my studio I had forgotten him. Late in the afternoon, the day being warm, I raised the window again and leaned out to get a sniff of air. A man was standing in the courtyard of the church, and I noticed him again with as little interest as I had that morning. I looked across the square to where the fountain was playing and then, with my mind filled with vague impressions of trees, asphalt drives, and the moving groups of nursemaids and holiday-makers, I started to walk back to my easel. As I turned, my listless glance included the man below in the churchyard. His face was toward me now, and with a perfectly involuntary movement I bent to see it. At the same moment he raised his head and looked at me. Instantly I thought of a coffin-worm. Whatever it was about the man that repelled me I did not know, but the impression of a plump white grave-worm was so intense and nauseating that I must have shown it in my expression, for he turned his puffy face away with a movement which made me think of a disturbed grub in a chestnut.

I went back to my easel and motioned the model to resume her pose. After working awhile I was satisfied that I was spoiling what I had done as rapidly as possible, and I took up a palette knife and scraped the color out again. The flesh tones were sallow and unhealthy, and I did not understand how I could have painted such sickly color into a study which before that had glowed with healthy tones.

I looked at Tessie. She had not changed, and the clear flush of health dyed her neck and cheeks as I frowned.

'Is it something I've done?' she said.

'No, – I've made a mess of this arm, and for the life of me I can't see how I came to paint such mud as that into the canvas,' I replied.

'Don't I pose well?' she insisted.

'Of course, perfectly?'

'Then it's not my fault?'

'No, it's my own.'

'I'm very sorry,' she said.

I told her she could rest while I applied rag and turpentine to the plague spot on my canvas, and she went off to smoke a cigarette and look over the illustrations in the *Courier Français*.

I did not know whether it was something in the turpentine or a defect in the canvas, but the more I scrubbed the more that gangrene seemed to spread. I worked like a beaver to get it out, and yet the disease appeared to creep from limb to limb of the study before me. Alarmed I strove to arrest it, but now the color on the breast changed and the whole figure seemed to absorb the infection as a sponge soaks up water. Vigorously I plied palette knife, turpentine, and scraper, thinking all the time what a séance I should hold with Duval who had sold me the canvas; but soon I noticed that it was not the canvas which was defective nor yet the colors of Edward. 'It must be the turpentine,' I thought angrily, 'or else my eyes have become so blurred and confused by the afternoon light that I can't see straight.' I called Tessie, the model. She came and leaned over my chair blowing rings of smoke into the air.

'What *have* you been doing to it?' she exclaimed.

'Nothing,' I growled, 'it must be this turpentine!'

'What a horrible color it is now,' she continued. 'Do you think my flesh resembles green cheese?'

'No, I don't,' I said angrily. 'Did you ever know me to paint like that before?'

'No, indeed!'

'Well, then!'

'It must be the turpentine, or something,' she admitted.

She slipped on a Japanese robe and walked to the window. I

scraped and rubbed until I was tired and finally picked up my brushes
and hurled them through the canvas with a forcible expression, the
tone alone of which reached Tessie's ears.

Nevertheless she promptly began: 'That's it! Swear and act silly
and ruin your brushes! You have been three weeks on that study, and
now look! What's the good of ripping the canvas? What creatures
artists are!'

I felt about as much ashamed as I usually did after such an
outbreak, and I turned the ruined canvas to the wall. Tessie helped
me clean my brushes, and then danced away to dress. From the screen
she regaled me with bits of advice concerning whole or partial loss of
temper, until, thinking, perhaps, I had been tormented sufficiently,
she came out to implore me to button her waist where she could not
reach it on the shoulder.

'Everything went wrong from the time you came back from the
window and talked about that horrid-looking man you saw in the
churchyard,' she announced.

'Yes, he probably bewitched the picture,' I said yawning. I looked
at my watch.

'It's after six, I know,' said Tessie, adjusting her hat before the
mirror.

'Yes,' I replied, 'I didn't mean to keep you so long.' I leaned out of
the window but recoiled with disgust, for the young man with the
pasty face stood below in the churchyard. Tessie saw my gesture of
disapproval and leaned from the window.

'Is that the man you don't like?' she whispered.

I nodded.

'I can't see his face, but he does look fat and soft. Someway or
other,' she continued, turning to look at me, 'he reminds me of a
dream, – an awful dream I once had. Or,' she mused, looking down at
her shapely shoes, 'was it a dream after all?'

'How should I know?' I smiled.

Tessie smiled in reply.

'You were in it,' she said, 'so perhaps you might know something
about it.

'Tessie! Tessie!' I protested, 'don't you dare flatter by saying that
you dream about me!'

'But I did,' she insisted; 'shall I tell you about it?'

Tessie leaned back on the open window-sill and began very
seriously.

'One night last winter I was lying in bed thinking about nothing at all in particular. I had been posing for you and I was tired out, yet it seemed impossible for me to sleep. I heard the bells in the city ring, ten, eleven, and midnight. I must have fallen asleep about midnight because I don't remember hearing the bells after that. It seemed to me that I had scarcely closed my eyes when I dreamed that something impelled me to go to the window. I rose, and raising the sash leaned out. Twenty-fifth Street was deserted as far as I could see. I began to be afraid; everything outside seemed so – so black and uncomfortable. Then the sound of wheels in the distance came to my ears, and it seemed to me as though that was what I must wait for. Very slowly the wheels approached, and, finally, I could make out a vehicle moving along the street. It came nearer and nearer, and when it passed beneath my window I saw it was a hearse. Then, as I trembled with fear, the driver turned and looked straight at me. When I awoke I was standing by the open window shivering with cold, but the black-plumed hearse and the driver were gone. I dreamed this dream again in March last, and again awoke beside the open window. Last night the dream came again. You remember how it was raining; when I awoke, standing at the open window, my night-dress was soaked.'

'But where did I come into the dream?' I asked.

'You – you were in the coffin; but you were not dead.'

'In the coffin?'

'Yes.'

'How did you know? Could you see me?'

'No; I only knew you were there.'

'Had you been eating Welsh rarebits, or lobster salad?' I began laughing, but the girl interrupted me with a frightened cry.

'Hello! What's up?' I said, as she shrank into the embrasure by the window.

'The – the man below in the churchyard; – he drove the hearse.'

'Nonsense,' I said, but Tessie's eyes were wide with terror. I went to the window and looked out. The man was gone. 'Come, Tessie,' I urged, 'don't be foolish. You have posed too long; you are nervous.'

'Do you think I could forget that face?' she murmured. 'Three times I saw the hearse pass below my window, and every time the driver turned and looked up at me. Oh, his face was so white and – and soft? It looked dead – it looked as if it had been dead a long time.'

I induced the girl to sit down and swallow a glass of Marsala. Then I sat down beside her, and tried to give some advice.

'Look here, Tessie,' I said, 'you go to the country for a week or two, and you'll have no more dreams about hearses. You pose all day, and when night comes your nerves are upset. You can't keep this up. Then again, instead of going to bed when your day's work is done, you run off to picnics at Sulzer's Park, or go to the Eldorado or Coney Island, and when you come down here next morning you are fagged out. There was no real hearse. That was a soft-shell crab dream.'

She smiled faintly.

'What about the man in the churchyard?'

'Oh, he's only an ordinary unhealthy, everyday creature.'

'As true as my name is Tessie Reardon, I swear to you, Mr. Scott, that the face of the man below in the churchyard is the face of the man who drove the hearse!'

'What of it?' I said. 'It's an honest trade.'

'Then you think I *did* see the hearse?'

'Oh,' I said diplomatically, 'if you really did, it might not be unlikely that the man below drove it. There is nothing in that.'

Tessie rose, unrolled her scented handkerchief and taking a bit of gum from a knot in the hem, placed it in her mouth. Then drawing on her gloves she offered me her hand, with a frank, 'Good-night, Mr. Scott,' and walked out.

II

The next morning, Thomas, the bellboy, brought me the *Herald* and a bit of news. The church next door had been sold. I thanked Heaven for it, not that it being a Catholic I had any repugnance for the congregation next door, but because my nerves were shattered by a blatant exhorter, whose every word echoed through the aisle of the church as if it had been my own rooms, and who insisted on his r's with a nasal persistence which revolted my every instinct. Then, too, there was a fiend in human shape, an organist, who reeled off some of the grand old hymns with an interpretation of his own, and I longed for the blood of a creature who could play the doxology with an amendment of minor chords which one hears only in a quartet of very young undergraduates. I believe the minister was a good man, but when he bellowed: 'And the Lorrrd said unto Moses, the Lorrrd is a man of war; the Lorrrd is his name. My wrath shall wax hot and I will kill you with the sworrrd!' I wondered how many centuries of purgatory it would take to atone for such a sin.

'Who bought the property?' I asked Thomas.

'Nobody that I knows, sir. They do say the gent wot owns this 'ere 'Amilton flats was lookin' at it. 'E might be a bildin' more studios.

I walked to the window. The young man with the unhealthy face stood by the churchyard gate, and at the mere sight of him the same overwhelming repugnance took possession of me.

'By the way, Thomas,' I said, 'who is that fellow down there?'

Thomas sniffed. 'That there worm, sir? 'E's night-watchman of the church, sir. 'E maikes me tired-a-sittin' out all night on them steps and lookin' at you insultin' like. I'd a punched 'is 'ed, sir – beg pardon, sir – '

'Go on, Thomas.'

'One night a comin' 'ome with 'Arry, the other English boy, I sees 'im a sittin' there on them steps. We 'ad Molly and Jen with us, sir, the two girls on the tray service, an 'e looks so insultin' at us that I up and sez: "Wat you looking hat, you fat slug?" – beg pardon, sir, but that's 'ow I sez, sir. Then 'e don't say nothin' and I sez: "Come out and I'll punch that puddin' 'ed." Then I hopens the gate and goes in, but 'e don't say nothin', only looks insultin' like. Then I 'its 'im one, but, ugh! 'is 'ed was that cold and mushy it ud sicken you to touch 'im.'

'What did he do then?' I asked, curiously.

''Im? Nawthin'.'

'And you, Thomas?'

The young fellow flushed with embarrassment and smiled uneasily.

'Mr. Scott, sir, I ain't no coward an' I can't make it out at all why I run. I was in the 5th Lawncers, sir, bugler at Tel-el-Kebir, an' was shot by the wells.'

'You don't mean to say you ran away?'

'Yes, sir; I run.'

'Why?'

'That's just what I want to know, sir. I grabbed Molly an' run, an' the rest was as frightened as I.'

'But what were they frightened at?'

Thomas refused to answer for a while, but now my curiosity was aroused about the repulsive young man below and I pressed him. Three years' sojourn in America had not only modified Thomas' cockney dialect but had given him the American's fear of ridicule.

'You won't believe me, Mr. Scott, sir?'

'Yes, I will.'

'You will lawf at me, sir?'

'Nonsense!'

He hesitated. 'Well, sir, it's Gawd's truth that when I 'it 'im 'e grabbed me wrists, sir, and when I twisted 'is soft, mushy fist one of 'is fingers come off in me 'and.'

The utter loathing and horror of Thomas' face must have been reflected in my own for he added:

'It's orful, an' now when I see 'im I just go away. 'E maikes me hill.'

When Thomas had gone I went to the window. The man stood beside the church-railing with both hands on the gate, but I hastily retreated to my easel again, sickened and horrified, for I saw that the middle finger of his right hand was missing.

At nine o'clock Tessie appeared and vanished behind the screen with a merry 'good morning, Mr. Scott.' When she had reappeared and taken her pose upon the model-stand I started a new canvas much to her delight. She remained silent as long as I was on the drawing, but as soon as the scrape of the charcoal ceased and I took up my fixative she began to chatter.

'Oh, I had such a lovely time last night. We went to Tony Pastor's.'

'Who are "we"?' I demanded.

'Oh, Maggie, you know, Mr. Whyte's model, and Pinkie McCormack – we call her Pinkie because she's got that beautiful red hair you artists like so much – and Lizzie Burke.'

I sent a shower of spray from the fixative over the canvas, and said: 'Well, go on.'

'We saw Kelly and Baby Barnes the skirt-dancer and – and all the rest. I made a mash.'

'Then you have gone back on me, Tessie?'

She laughed and shook her head.

'He's Lizzie Burke's brother, Ed. He's a perfect gen'l'man.'

I felt constrained to give her some parental advice concerning mashing, which she took with a bright smile.

'Oh, I can take care of a strange mash,' she said, examining her chewing gum, 'but Ed is different. Lizzie is my best friend.'

Then she related how Ed had come back from the stocking mill in Lowell, Massachusetts, to find her and Lizzie grown up, and what an accomplished young man he was, and how he thought nothing of squandering half a dollar for ice-cream and oysters to celebrate his entry as clerk into the woollen department of Macy's. Before she finished I began to paint, and she resumed the pose, smiling and chattering like a sparrow. By noon I had the study fairly well rubbed in and Tessie came to look at it.

'That's better,' she said.

I thought so too, and ate my lunch with a satisfied feeling that all was going well. Tessie spread her lunch on a drawing table opposite me and we drank our claret from the same bottle and lighted our cigarettes from the same match. I was very much attached to Tessie. I had watched her shoot up into a slender but exquisitely formed woman from a frail, awkward child. She had posed for me during the last three years, and among all my models she was my favorite. It would have troubled me very much indeed had she become 'tough' or 'fly,' as the phrase goes, but I never noticed any deterioration of her manner, and felt at heart that she was all right. She and I never discussed morals at all, and I had no intention of doing so, partly because I had none myself, and partly because I knew she would do what she liked in spite of me. Still I did hope she would steer clear of complications, because I wished her well, and then also I had a selfish desire to retain the best model I had. I knew that mashing, as she termed it, had no significance with girls like Tessie, and that such things in America did not resemble in the least the same things in Paris. Yet having lived with my eyes open, I also knew that somebody would take Tessie away some day, in one manner or another, and though I professed to myself that marriage was nonsense, I sincerely hoped that, in this case, there would be a priest at the end of the vista. I am a Catholic. When I listen to high mass, when I sign myself, I feel that everything, including myself, is more cheerful, and when I confess, it does me good. A man who lives as much alone as I do, must confess to somebody. Then, again, Sylvia was Catholic, and it was reason enough for me. But I was speaking of Tessie, which is very different. Tessie also was Catholic and much more devout than I, so, taking it all in all, I had little fear for my pretty model until she should fall in love. But *then* I knew that fate alone would decide her future for her, and I prayed inwardly that fate would keep her away from men like me and throw into her path nothing but Ed Burkes and Jimmy McCormicks, bless her sweet face!

Tessie sat blowing rings of smoke up to the ceiling and tinkling the ice in her tumbler.

'Do you know that I also had a dream last night?' I observed.

'Not about that man,' she laughed.

'Exactly. A dream similar to yours, only much worse.'

It was foolish and thoughtless of me to say this, but you know how little tact the average painter has.

'I must have fallen asleep about 10 o'clock,' I continued, 'and after a while I dreamt that I awoke. So plainly did I hear the midnight bells, the wind in the tree-branches, and the whistle of steamers from the bay, that even now I can scarcely believe I was not awake. I seemed to be lying in a box which had a glass cover. Dimly I saw the street lamps as I passed, for I must tell you, Tessie, the box in which I reclined appeared to lie in a cushioned wagon which jolted me over a stony pavement. After a while I became impatient and tried to move but the box was too narrow. My hands were crossed on my breast so I could not raise them to help myself. I listened and then tried to call. My voice was gone. I could hear the trample of the horses attached to the wagon and even the breathing of the driver. Then another sound broke upon my ears like the raising of a window sash. I managed to turn my head a little, and found I could look, not only through the glass cover of my box, but also through the glass panes in the side of the covered vehicle. I saw houses, empty and silent, with neither light nor life about any of them excepting one. In that house a window was open on the first floor and a figure all in white stood looking down into the street. It was you.'

Tessie had turned her face away from me and leaned on the table with her elbow.

'I could see your face,' I resumed, 'and it seemed to me to be very sorrowful. Then we passed on and turned into a narrow black lane. Presently the horses stopped. I waited and waited, closing my eyes with fear and impatience, but all was silent as the grave. After what seemed to me hours, I began to feel uncomfortable. A sense that somebody was close to me made me unclose my eyes. Then I saw the white face of the hearse-driver looking at me through the coffin-lid – '

A sob from Tessie interrupted me. She was trembling like a leaf. I saw I had made an ass of myself and attempted to repair the damage.

'Why, Tess,' I said, 'I only told you this to show you what influence your story might have on another person's dreams. You don't suppose I really lay in a coffin, do you? What are you trembling for? Don't you see that your dream and my unreasonable dislike for that inoffensive watchman of the church simply set my brain working as soon as I fell asleep?'

She laid her head between her arms and sobbed as if her heart would break. What a precious triple donkey I had made of myself! But I was about to break my record. I went over and put my arm about her.

'Tessie dear, forgive me,' I said; 'I had no business to frighten you with such nonsense. You are too sensible a girl, too good a Catholic to believe in dreams.'

Her hand tightened on mine and her head fell back upon my shoulder, but she still trembled and I petted her and comforted her.

'Come, Tess, open your eyes and smile.'

Her eyes opened with a slow languid movement and met mine, but their expression was so queer that I hastened to reassure her again.

'It's all humbug, Tessie, you surely are not afraid that any harm will come to you because of that.'

'No,' she said, but her scarlet lips quivered.

'Then what's the matter? Are you afraid?'

'Yes. Not for myself.'

'For me, then?' I demanded gayly.

'For you,' she murmured in a voice almost inaudible, 'I – I care for you.'

At first I started to laugh but when I understood her, a shock passed through me and I sat like one turned to stone. This was the crowning bit of idiocy I had committed. During the moment which elapsed between her reply and my answer I thought of a thousand responses to that innocent confession. I could pass it by with a laugh, I could misunderstand her and reassure her as to my health, I could simply point out that it was impossible she could love me. But my reply was quicker than my thoughts, and I might think and think now when it was too late, for I had kissed her on the mouth.

That evening I took my usual walk in Washington Park, pondering over the occurrences of the day. I was thoroughly committed. There was no back out now, and I stared the future straight in the face. I was not good, not even scrupulous, but I had no idea of deceiving either myself or Tessie. The one passion of my life lay buried in the sunlit forests of Brittany. Was it buried forever? Hope cried 'No!' For three years I had been listening to the voice of Hope, and for three years I had waited for a footstep on my threshold. Had Sylvia forgotten? 'No!' cried Hope.

I said that I was not good. That is true, but still I was not exactly a comic opera villain. I had led an easy-going reckless life, taking what invited me of pleasure, deploring and sometimes bitterly regretting consequences. In one thing alone, except my painting, was I serious, and that was something which lay hidden if not lost in the Breton forests.

It was too late now for me to regret what had occurred during the day. Whatever it had been, pity, a sudden tenderness for sorrow, or the more brutal instinct of gratified vanity, it was all the same now, and unless I wished to bruise an innocent heart my path lay marked before me. The fire and strength, the depth of passion of a love which I had never even suspected, with all my

imagined experience in the world, left me no alternative but to
respond or send her away. Whether because I am so cowardly
about giving pain to others, or whether it was that I have little of
the gloomy Puritan in me, I do not know, but I shrank from
disclaiming responsibility for that thoughtless kiss, and in fact had
no time to do so before the gates of her heart opened and the flood
poured forth. Others who habitually do their duty and find a sullen
satisfaction in making themselves and everybody else unhappy,
might have withstood it. I did not. I dared not. After the storm
had abated I did tell her that she might better have loved Ed
Burke and worn a plain gold ring, but she would not hear of it, and
I thought perhaps that as long as she had decided to love somebody she could not marry, it had better be me. I, at least could
treat her with an intelligent affection, and whenever she became
tired of her infatuation she could go none the worse for it. For I
was decided on that point although I knew how hard it would be. I
remembered the usual termination of Platonic liaisons and thought
how disgusted I had been whenever I heard of one. I knew I was
undertaking a great deal for so unscrupulous a man as I was, and I
dreaded the future, but never for one moment did I doubt that she
was safe with me. Had it been anybody but Tessie I should not
have bothered my head about scruples. For it did not occur to me
to sacrifice Tessie as I would have sacrificed a woman of the world.
I looked the future squarely in the face and saw the several
probable endings to the affair. She would either tire of the whole
thing, or become so unhappy that I should have either to marry
her or go away. If I married her we would be unhappy. I with a
wife unsuited to me, and she with a husband unsuitable for any
woman. For my past life could scarcely entitle me to marry. If I
went away she might either fall ill, recover, and marry some Eddie
Burke, or she might recklessly or deliberately go and do something
foolish. On the other hand if she tired of me, then her whole life
would be before her with beautiful vistas of Eddie Burkes and
marriage rings and twins and Harlem flats and Heaven knows
what. As I strolled along through the trees by the Washington
Arch, I decided that she should find a substantial friend in me
anyway and the future could take care of itself. Then I went into
the house and put on my evening dress for the little faintly
perfumed note on my dresser said, 'Have a cab at the stage door
at eleven,' and the note was signed 'Edith Carmichel, Metropolitan
Theatre.'

I took supper that night, or rather we took supper, Miss Carmichel and I, at Solari's and the dawn was just beginning to gild the cross on the Memorial Church as I entered Washington Square after leaving Edith at the Brunswick. There was not a soul in the park as I passed among the trees and took the walk which leads from the Garibaldi statue to the Hamilton Apartment House, but as I passed the churchyard I saw a figure sitting on the stone steps. In spite of myself a chill crept over me at the sight of the white puffy face, and I hastened to pass. Then he said something which might have been addressed to me or might merely have been a mutter to himself, but a sudden furious anger flamed up within me that such a creature should address me. For an instant I felt like wheeling about and smashing my stick over his head, but I walked on, and entering the Hamilton went to my apartment. For some time I tossed about the bed trying to get the sound of his voice out of my ears, but could not. It filled my head, that muttering sound, like thick oily smoke from a fat-rendering vat or an odor of noisome decay. And as I lay and tossed about, the voice in my ears seemed more distinct, and I began to understand the words he had muttered. They came to me slowly as if I had forgotten them, and at last I could make some sense out of the sounds. It was this:

'Have you found the Yellow Sign?'

'Have you found the Yellow Sign?'

'Have you found the Yellow Sign?'

I was furious. What did he mean by that? Then with a curse upon him and his I rolled over and went to sleep, but when I awoke later I looked pale and haggard, for I had dreamed the dream of the night before and it troubled me more than I cared to think.

I dressed and went down into my studio. Tessie sat by the window, but as I came in she rose and put both arms around my neck for an innocent kiss. She looked so sweet and dainty that I kissed her again and then sat down before the easel.

'Hello! Where's the study I began yesterday?' I asked.

Tessie looked conscious, but did not answer. I began to hunt among the piles of canvases, saying, 'Hurry up, Tess, and get ready; we must take advantage of the morning light.'

When at last I gave up the search among the other canvases and turned to look around the room for the missing study I noticed Tessie standing by the screen with her clothes still on.

'What's the matter,' I asked, 'don't you feel well?'

'Yes.'

'Then hurry.'

'Do you want me to pose as – as I have always posed?'

Then I understood. Here was a new complication. I had lost, of course, the best nude model I had ever seen. I looked at Tessie. Her face was scarlet. Alas! Alas! We had eaten of the tree of knowledge, and Eden and native innocence were dreams of the past – I mean for her.

I suppose she noticed the disappointment on my face, for she said: 'I will pose if you wish. The study is behind the screen here where I put it.'

'No,' I said, 'we will begin something new;' and I went into my wardrobe and picked out a Moorish costume which fairly blazed with tinsel. It was a genuine costume, and Tessie retired to the screen with it enchanted. When she came forth again I was astonished. Her long black hair was bound above her forehead with a circlet of turquoises, and the ends curled about her glittering girdle. Her feet were encased in the embroidered pointed slippers and the skirt of her costume, curiously wrought with arabesques in silver, fell to her angles. The deep metallic blue vest embroidered with silver and the short Mauresque jacket spangled and sewn with turquoises became her wonderfully. She came up to me and held up her face smiling. I slipped my hand into my pocket and drawing out a gold chain with a cross attached, dropped it over her head.

'It's yours, Tessie.'

'Mine?' she faltered.

'Yours. Now go and pose.' Then with a radiant smile she ran behind the screen and presently re-appeared with a little box on which was written my name.

'I had intended to give it to you when I went home tonight,' she said, 'but I can't wait now.'

I opened the box. On the pink cotton inside lay a clasp of black onyx, on which was inlaid a curious symbol or letter in gold. It was neither Arabic nor Chinese, nor as I found afterwards did it belong to any human script.

'It's all I had to give you for a keepsake,' she said, timidly.

I was annoyed, but I told her how much I should prize it, and promised to wear it always. She fastened it on my coat beneath the lapel.

'How foolish, Tess, to go and buy me such a beautiful thing as this,' I said.

'I did not buy it,' she laughed.

'Where did you get it?'

Then she told me how she had found it one day while coming from the Aquarium in the Battery, how she had advertised it and watched the papers, but at last gave up all hopes of finding the owner.

'That was last winter,' she said, 'the very day I had the first horrid dream about the hearse.'

I remembered my dream of the previous night but said nothing, and presently my charcoal was flying over a new canvas, and Tessie stood motionless on the model stand.

III

The day following was a disastrous one for me. While moving a framed canvas from one easel to another my foot slipped on the polished floor and I fell heavily on both wrists. They were so badly sprained that it was useless to attempt to hold a brush, and I was obliged to wander about the studio, glaring at unfinished drawings and sketches until despair seized me and I sat down to smoke and twiddle my thumbs with rage. The rain blew against the windows and rattled on the roof of the church, driving me into a nervous fit with its interminable patter. Tessie sat sewing by the window, and every now and then raised her head and looked at me with such innocent compassion that I began to feel ashamed of my irritation and looked about for something to occupy me. I had read all the papers and all the books in the library, but for the sake of something to do I went to the bookcases and shoved them open with my elbow. I knew every volume by its color and examined them all, passing slowly around the library and whistling to keep up my spirits. I was turning to go into the dining-room when my eye fell upon a book bound in serpent skin, standing in a corner of the top shelf of the last bookcase. I did not remember it and from the floor could not decipher the pale lettering on the back, so I went to the smoking-room and called Tessie. She came in from the studio and climbed up to reach the book.

'What is it?' I asked.

'The King in Yellow.'

I was dumfounded. Who had placed it there? How came it in my rooms? I had long ago decided that I should never open that book, and nothing on earth could have persuaded me to buy it. Fearful lest curiosity might tempt me to open it, I had never even looked at it in book-stores. If I ever had had any curiosity to read it, the awful tragedy of young Castaigne, whom I knew, prevented me from exploring its wicked pages. I had always refused to listen to any description of it, and indeed, nobody ever ventured to discuss the second part aloud, so I had absolutely no knowledge of what those leaves might reveal. I stared at the poisonous mottled binding as I would at a snake.

'Don't touch it, Tessie,' I said; 'come down.'

Of course my admonition was enough to arouse her curiosity, and before I could prevent it she took the book and, laughing, danced off into the studio with it. I called to her but she slipped away with a tormenting smile at my helpless hands, and I followed her with some impatience.

'Tessie!' I cried, entering the library, 'listen, I am serious. Put that book away. I do not wish you to open it!' The library was empty. I went into both drawing-rooms, then into the bedrooms, laundry, kitchen, and finally returned to the library and began a systematic search. She had hidden herself so well that it was half an hour later when I discovered her crouching white and silent by the latticed window in the store-room above. At the first glance I saw she had been punished for her foolishness. 'The King in Yellow' lay at her feet, but the book was open at the second part. I looked at Tessie and saw it was too late. She had opened 'The King in Yellow.' Then I took her by the hand and led her into the studio. She seemed dazed, and when I told her to lie down on the sofa she obeyed me without a word. After a while she closed her eyes and her breathing became regular and deep but I could not determine whether or not she slept. For a long while I sat silently beside her, but she neither stirred nor spoke, and at last I rose and entering the unused store-room took the book in my least injured hand. It seemed heavy as lead, but I carried it into the studio again, and sitting down on the rug beside the sofa, opened it and read it through from beginning to end.

When, faint with the excess of my emotions, I dropped the volume and leaned wearily back against the sofa, Tessie opened her eyes and looked at me.

We had been speaking for some time in a dull monotonous strain before I realized that we were discussing 'The King in Yellow.' Oh the sin of writing such words; – words which are clear as crystal, limpid and musical as bubbling springs, words which sparkle and glow like the poisoned diamonds of the Medicis! Oh the wickedness, the hopeless damnation of a soul who could fascinate and paralyze human creatures with such words, – words understood by the

ignorant and wise alike, words which are more precious than jewels, more soothing than music, more awful than death!

We talked on, unmindful of the gathering shadows, and she was begging me to throw away the clasp of black onyx quaintly inlaid with what we now knew to be the Yellow Sign. I never shall know why I refused, though even at this hour, here in my bedroom as I write this confession, I should be glad to know *what* it was that prevented me from tearing the Yellow Sign from my breast and casting it into the fire. I am sure I wished to do so, and yet Tessie pleaded with me in vain. Night fell and hours dragged on, but still we murmured to each other of the King and the Pallid Mask, and midnight sounded from the misty spires in the fog-wrapped city. We spoke of Hastur and of Cassilda, while outside the fog rolled against the blank window-panes as the cloud waves roll and break on the shores of Hali.

The house was very silent now and not a sound came up from the misty streets. Tessie lay among the cushions, her face a gray blot in the gloom, but her hands were clasped in mine and I knew that she knew and read my thoughts as I read hers, for we had understood the mystery of the Hyades and the Phantom of Truth was laid. Then as we answered each other, swiftly, silently, thought on thought, the shadows stirred in the gloom about us, and far in the distant streets we heard a sound. Nearer and nearer it came, the dull crunching of wheels, nearer and yet nearer, and now, outside before the door it ceased, and I dragged myself to the window and saw a black-plumed hearse. The gate below opened and shut, and I crept shaking to my door and bolted it, but I knew no bolts, no locks, could keep that creature out who was coming for the Yellow Sign. And now I heard him moving very softly along the hall. Now he was at the door, and the bolts rotted at his touch. Now he had entered. With eyes starting from my head I peered into the darkness, but when he came into the room I did not see him. It was only when I felt him envelop me in his cold soft grasp that I cried out and struggled with deadly fury, but my hands were useless and he tore the onyx clasp from my coat and struck me full in the face. Then, as I fell, I heard Tessie's soft cry and her spirit fled: and even while falling I longed to follow her, for I knew that the King in Yellow had opened his tattered mantle and there was only God to cry to now.

I could tell more, but I cannot see what help it will be to the world. As for me I am past human help or hope. As I lie here, writing, careless even whether or not I die before I finish, I can see the doctor gathering up his powders and phials with a vague gesture to the good priest beside me, which I understand.

They will be very curious to know the tragedy – they of the outside world who write books and print millions of newspapers, but I shall write no more, and the father confessor will seal my last words with the seal of sanctity when his holy office is done. They of the outside world may send their creatures into wrecked homes and death-smitten firesides, and their newspapers will batten on blood and tears, but with me their spies must halt before the confessional. They know that Tessie is dead and that I am dying. They know how the people in the house, aroused by an infernal scream, rushed into my room and found one living and two dead, but they do not know what I shall tell them now; they do not know that the doctor said as he pointed to a horrible decomposed heap on the floor – the livid corpse of the watchman from the church: 'I have no theory, no explanation. That man must have been dead for months!'

I think I am dying. I wish the priest would –

THE SHADOWS ON THE WALL

Mary E. Wilkins-Freeman

[1852–1930]

'Horror material of authentic force may be found in the work of the New England realist Mary E. Wilkins, whose volume of short tales, The Wind in the Rosebush, *contains a number of noteworthy achievements. In* The Shadows on the Wall *we are shown with consummate skill the response of a staid New England household to uncanny tragedy.'*

– H.P. Lovecraft

'HENRY HAD WORDS WITH EDWARD in the study the night before Edward died,' said Caroline Glynn.

She was elderly, tall, and harshly thin, with a hard colourlessness of face. She spoke not with acrimony, but with grave severity. Rebecca Ann Glynn, younger, stouter and rosy of face between her crinkling puffs of gray hair, gasped, by way of assent. She sat in a wide flounce of black silk in the corner of the sofa, and rolled terrified eyes from her

sister Caroline to her sister Mrs. Stephen Brigham, who had been
Emma Glynn, the one beauty of the family. She was beautiful still,
with a large, splendid, full-blown beauty; she filled a great rocking-
chair with her superb bulk of femininity, and swayed gently back and
forth, her black silks whispering and her black frills fluttering. Even
the shock of death (for her brother Edward lay dead in the house)
could not disturb her outward serenity of demeanour. She was
grieved over the loss of her brother: he had been the youngest,
and she had been fond of him, but never had Emma Brigham lost
sight of her own importance amidst the waters of tribulation. She was
always awake to the consciousness of her own stability in the midst of
vicissitudes and the splendour of her permanent bearing.

But even her expression of masterly placidity changed before her
sister Caroline's announcement and her sister Rebecca Ann's gasp of
terror and distress in response.

'I think Henry might have controlled his temper, when poor
Edward was so near his end,' said she with an asperity which
disturbed slightly the roseate curves of her beautiful mouth.

'Of course he did not *know*,' murmured Rebecca Ann in a faint tone
strangely out of keeping with her appearance.

One involuntarily looked again to be sure that such a feeble pipe
came from that full-swelling chest.

'Of course he did not know it,' said Caroline quickly. She turned on
her sister with a strange sharp look of suspicion. 'How could he have
known it?' said she. Then she shrank as if from the other's possible
answer. 'Of course you and I both know he could not,' said she
conclusively, but her pale face was paler than it had been before.

Rebecca gasped again. The married sister, Mrs. Emma Brigham,
was now sitting up straight in her chair; she had ceased rocking, and
was eyeing them both intently with a sudden accentuation of family
likeness in her face. Given one common intensity of emotion and
similar lines showed forth, and the three sisters of one race were
evident.

'What do you mean?' said she impartially to them both. Then she,
too, seemed to shrink before a possible answer. She even laughed an
evasive sort of laugh. 'I guess you don't mean anything,' said she, but
her face wore still the expression of shrinking horror.

'Nobody means anything,' said Caroline firmly. She rose and
crossed the room toward the door with grim decisiveness.

'Where are you going?' asked Mrs. Brigham.

'I have something to see to,' replied Caroline, and the others at once knew by her tone that she had some solemn and sad duty to perform in the chamber of death.

'Oh,' said Mrs. Brigham.

After the door had closed behind Caroline, she turned to Rebecca. 'Did Henry have many words with him?' she asked.

'They were talking very loud,' replied Rebecca evasively, yet with an answering gleam of ready response to the other's curiosity in the quick lift of her soft blue eyes.

Mrs. Brigham looked at her. She had not resumed rocking. She still sat up straight with a slight knitting of intensity on her fair forehead, between the pretty rippling curves of her auburn hair.

'Did you – hear anything?' she asked in a low voice with a glance toward the door.

'I was just across the hall in the south parlour, and that door was open and this door ajar,' replied Rebecca with a slight flush.

'Then you must have – '

'I couldn't help it.'

'Everything?'

'Most of it.'

'What was it?'

'The old story.'

'I suppose Henry was mad, as he always was, because Edward was living on here for nothing, when he had wasted all the money father left him.'

Rebecca nodded with a fearful glance at the door.

When Emma spoke again her voice was still more hushed. 'I know how he felt,' said she. 'He had always been so prudent himself, and worked hard at his profession, and there Edward had never done anything but spend, and it must have looked to him as if Edward was living at his expense, but he wasn't.'

'No, he wasn't.'

'It was the way father left the property – that all the children should have a home here – and he left money enough to buy the food and all if we had all come home.'

'Yes.'

'And Edward had a right here according to the terms of father's will, and Henry ought to have remembered it.'

'Yes, he ought.'

'Did he say hard things?'

'Pretty hard from what I heard.'

'What?'

'I heard him tell Edward that he had no business here at all, and he thought he had better go away.'

'What did Edward say?'

'That he would stay here as long as he lived and afterward, too, if he was a mind to, and he would like to see Henry get him out; and then – '

'What?'

'Then he laughed.'

'What did Henry say?'

'I didn't hear him say anything, but – '

'But what?'

'I saw him when he came out of this room.'

'He looked mad?'

'You've seen him when he looked so.'

Emma nodded; the expression of horror on her face had deepened.

'Do you remember that time he killed the cat because she had scratched him?'

'Yes. Don't!'

Then Caroline reentered the room. She went up to the stove in which a wood fire was burning – it was a cold, gloomy day of fall – and she warmed her hands, which were reddened from recent washing in cold water.

Mrs. Brigham looked at her and hesitated. She glanced at the door, which was still ajar, as it did not easily shut, being still swollen with the damp weather of the summer. She rose and pushed it together with a sharp thud which jarred the house. Rebecca started painfully with a half exclamation. Caroline looked at her disapprovingly.

'It is time you controlled your nerves, Rebecca,' said she.

'I can't help it,' replied Rebecca with almost a wail. 'I am nervous. There's enough to make me so, the Lord knows.'

'What do you mean by that?' asked Caroline with her old air of sharp suspicion, and something between challenge and dread of its being met.

Rebecca shrank.

'Nothing,' said she.

'Then I wouldn't keep speaking in such a fashion.'

Emma, returning from the closed door, said imperiously that it ought to be fixed, it shut so hard.

'It will shrink enough after we have had the fire a few days,' replied Caroline. 'If anything is done to it, it will be too small; there will be a crack at the sill.'

'I think Henry ought to be ashamed of himself for talking as he did to Edward,' said Mrs. Brigham abruptly, but in an almost inaudible voice.

'Hush!' said Caroline, with a glance of actual fear at the closed door.

'Nobody can hear with the door shut.'

'He must have heard it shut, and – '

'Well, I can say what I want to before he comes down, and I am not afraid of him.'

'I don't know who is afraid of him! What reason is there for anybody to be afraid of Henry?' demanded Caroline.

Mrs. Brigham trembled before her sister's look. Rebecca gasped again. 'There isn't any reason, of course. Why should there be?'

'I wouldn't speak so, then. Somebody might overhear you and think it was queer. Miranda Joy is in the south parlour sewing, you know.'

'I thought she went upstairs to stitch on the machine.'

'She did, but she has come down again.'

'Well, she can't hear.'

'I say again I think Henry ought to be ashamed of himself. I shouldn't think he'd ever get over it, having words with poor Edward the very night before he died. Edward was enough sight better disposition than Henry, with all his faults. I always thought a great deal of poor Edward, myself.'

Mrs. Brigham passed a large fluff of handkerchief across her eyes; Rebecca sobbed outright.

'Rebecca,' said Caroline admonishingly, keeping her mouth stiff and swallowing determinately.

'I never heard him speak a cross word, unless he spoke cross to Henry that last night. I don't know, but he did from what Rebecca overheard,' said Emma.

'Not so much cross as sort of soft, and sweet, and aggravating,' sniffled Rebecca.

'He never raised his voice,' said Caroline; 'but he had his way.'

'He had a right to in this case.'

'Yes, he did.'

'He had as much of a right here as Henry,' sobbed Rebecca, 'and now he's gone, and he will never be in this home that poor father left him and the rest of us again.'

'What do you really think ailed Edward?' asked Emma in hardly more than a whisper. She did not look at her sister.

Caroline sat down in a nearby armchair, and clutched the arms convulsively until her thin knuckles whitened.

'I told you,' said she.

Rebecca held her handkerchief over her mouth, and looked at them above it with terrified, streaming eyes.

'I know you said that he had terrible pains in his stomach, and had spasms, but what do you think made him have them?'

'Henry called it gastric trouble. You know Edward has always had dyspepsia.'

Mrs. Brigham hesitated a moment. 'Was there any talk of an – examination?' said she.

Then Caroline turned on her fiercely.

'No,' said she in a terrible voice. 'No.'

The three sisters' souls seemed to meet on one common ground of terrified understanding through their eyes. The old-fashioned latch of the door was heard to rattle, and a push from without made the door shake ineffectually. 'It's Henry,' Rebecca sighed rather than whispered. Mrs. Brigham settled herself after a noiseless rush across the floor into her rocking-chair again, and was swaying back and forth with her head comfortably leaning back, when the door at last yielded and Henry Glynn entered. He cast a covertly sharp, comprehensive glance at Mrs. Brigham with her elaborate calm; at Rebecca quietly huddled in the corner of the sofa with her handkerchief to her face and only one small reddened ear as attentive as a dog's uncovered and revealing her alertness for his presence; at Caroline sitting with a strained composure in her armchair by the stove. She met his eyes quite firmly with a look of inscrutable fear, and defiance of the fear and of him.

Henry Glynn looked more like this sister than the others. Both had the same hard delicacy of form and feature, both were tall and almost emaciated, both had a sparse growth of gray blond hair far back from high intellectual foreheads, both had an almost noble aquilinity of feature. They confronted each other with the pitiless immovability of two statues in whose marble lineaments emotions were fixed for all eternity.

Then Henry Glynn smiled and the smile transformed his face. He looked suddenly years younger, and an almost boyish recklessness and irresolution appeared in his face. He flung himself into a chair with a gesture which was bewildering from its incongruity with his general appearance. He leaned his head back, flung one leg over the other, and looked laughingly at Mrs. Brigham.

'I declare, Emma, you grow younger every year,' he said.

She flushed a little, and her placid mouth widened at the corners. She was susceptible to praise.

'Our thoughts today ought to belong to the one of us who will never grow older,' said Caroline in a hard voice.

Henry looked at her, still smiling. 'Of course, we none of us forget that,' said he, in a deep, gentle voice, 'but we have to speak to the living, Caroline, and I have not seen Emma for a long time, and the living are as dear as the dead.'

'Not to me,' said Caroline.

She rose, and went abruptly out of the room again. Rebecca also rose and hurried after her, sobbing loudly.

Henry looked slowly after them.

'Caroline is completely unstrung,' said he.

Mrs. Brigham rocked. A confidence in him inspired by his manner was stealing over her. Out of that confidence she spoke quite easily and naturally.

'His death was very sudden,' said she.

Henry's eyelids quivered slightly but his gaze was unswerving.

'Yes,' said he; 'it was very sudden. He was sick only a few hours.'

'What did you call it?'

'Gastric.'

'You did not think of an examination?'

'There was no need. I am perfectly certain as to the cause of his death.'

Suddenly Mrs. Brigham felt a creep as of some live horror over her very soul. Her flesh prickled with cold, before an inflection of his voice. She rose, tottering on weak knees.

'Where are you going?' asked Henry in a strange, breathless voice.

Mrs. Brigham said something incoherent about some sewing which she had to do, some black for the funeral, and was out of the room. She went up to the front chamber which she occupied. Caroline was there. She went close to her and took her hands, and the two sisters looked at each other.

'Don't speak, don't, I won't have it!' said Caroline finally in an awful whisper.

'I won't,' replied Emma.

That afternoon the three sisters were in the study, the large front room on the ground floor across the hall from the south parlour, when the dusk deepened.

Mrs. Brigham was hemming some black material. She sat close to the west window for the waning light. At last she laid her work on her lap.

'It's no use, I cannot see to sew another stitch until we have a light,' said she.

Caroline, who was writing some letters at the table, turned to Rebecca, in her usual place on the sofa.

'Rebecca, you had better get a lamp,' she said.

Rebecca started up; even in the dusk her face showed her agitation.

'It doesn't seem to me that we need a lamp quite yet,' she said in a piteous, pleading voice like a child's.

'Yes, we do,' returned Mrs. Brigham peremptorily. 'We must have a light. I must finish this tonight or I can't go to the funeral, and I can't see to sew another stitch.'

'Caroline can see to write letters, and she is farther from the window than you are,' said Rebecca.

'Are you trying to save kerosene or are you lazy, Rebecca Glynn?' cried Mrs. Brigham. 'I can go and get the light myself, but I have this work in my lap.'

Caroline's pen stopped scratching.

'Rebecca, we must have the light,' said she.

'Had we better have it in here?' asked Rebecca weakly.

'Of course! Why not?' cried Caroline sternly.

'I am sure I don't want to take my sewing into the other room, when it is all cleaned up for tomorrow,' said Mrs. Brigham.

'Why, I never heard such a to-do about lighting a lamp.'

Rebecca rose and left the room. Presently she entered with a lamp – a large one with a white porcelain shade. She set it on a table, an old-fashioned card-table which was placed against the opposite wall from the window. That wall was clear of bookcases and books, which were only on three sides of the room. That opposite wall was taken up with three doors, the one small space being occupied by the table. Above the table on the old-fashioned paper, of a white satin gloss, traversed by an indeterminate green scroll, hung quite high a small gilt and black-framed ivory miniature taken in her girlhood of the mother of the family. When the lamp was set on the table beneath it, the tiny pretty face painted on the ivory seemed to gleam out with a look of intelligence.

'What have you put that lamp over there for?' asked Mrs. Brigham, with more of impatience than her voice usually revealed. 'Why didn't you set it in the hall and have done with it? Neither Caroline nor I can see if it is on that table.'

'I thought perhaps you would move,' replied Rebecca hoarsely.

'If I do move, we can't both sit at that table. Caroline has her paper all spread around. Why don't you set the lamp on the study table in the middle of the room, then we can both see?'

Rebecca hesitated. Her face was very pale. She looked with an appeal that was fairly agonizing at her sister Caroline.

'Why don't you put the lamp on this table, as she says?' asked Caroline, almost fiercely. 'Why do you act so, Rebecca?'

'I should think you *would* ask her that,' said Mrs. Brigham. 'She doesn't act like herself at all.'

Rebecca took the lamp and set it on the table in the middle of the room without another word. Then she turned her back upon it quickly and seated herself on the sofa, and placed a hand over her eyes as if to shade them, and remained so.

'Does the light hurt your eyes, and is that the reason why you didn't want the lamp?' asked Mrs. Brigham kindly.

'I always like to sit in the dark,' replied Rebecca chokingly. Then she snatched her handkerchief hastily from her pocket and began to weep. Caroline continued to write, Mrs. Brigham to sew.

Suddenly Mrs. Brigham as she sewed glanced at the opposite wall. The glance became a steady stare. She looked intently, her work suspended in her hands. Then she looked away again and took a few more stitches, then she looked again, and again turned to her task. At last she laid her work in her lap and stared concentratedly. She looked from the wall around the room, taking note of the various objects; she looked at the wall long and intently. Then she turned to her sisters.

'What *is* that?' said she.

'What?' asked Caroline harshly; her pen scratched loudly across the paper.

Rebecca gave one of her convulsive gasps.

'That strange shadow on the wall,' replied Mrs. Brigham.

Rebecca sat with her face hidden: Caroline dipped her pen in the inkstand.

'Why don't you turn around and look?' asked Mrs. Brigham in a wondering and somewhat aggrieved way.

'I am in a hurry to finish this letter, if Mrs. Wilson Ebbit is going to get word in time to come to the funeral,' replied Caroline shortly.

Mrs. Brigham rose, her work slipping to the floor, and she began walking around the room, moving various articles of furniture, with her eyes on the shadow.

Then suddenly she shrieked out:

'Look at this awful shadow! What is it? Caroline, look, look! Rebecca, look! *What is it?*'

All Mrs. Brigham's triumphant placidity was gone. Her handsome face was livid with horror. She stood stiffly pointing at the shadow.

'Look!' said she, pointing her finger at it. 'Look! What is it?'

Then Rebecca burst out in a wild wail after a shuddering glance at the wall:

'Oh, Caroline, there it is again! There it is again!'

'Caroline Glynn, you look!' said Mrs. Brigham. 'Look! What is that dreadful shadow?'

Caroline rose, turned, and stood confronting the wall.

'How should I know?' she said.

'It has been there every night since he died,' cried Rebecca.

'Every night?'

'Yes. He died Thursday and this is Saturday; that makes three nights,' said Caroline rigidly. She stood as if holding herself calm with a vice of concentrated will.

'It – it looks like – like –' stammered Mrs. Brigham in a tone of intense horror.

'I know what it looks like well enough,' said Caroline. 'I've got eyes in my head.'

'It looks like Edward,' burst out Rebecca in a sort of frenzy of fear. 'Only – '

'Yes, it does,' assented Mrs. Brigham, whose horror-stricken tone matched her sister's, 'only – Oh, it is awful! What is it, Caroline?'

'I ask you again, how should I know?' replied Caroline. 'I see it there like you. How should I know any more than you?'

'It *must* be something in the room,' said Mrs. Brigham, staring wildly around.

'We moved everything in the room the first night it came,' said Rebecca; 'it is not anything in the room.'

Caroline turned upon her with a sort of fury. 'Of course it is something in the room,' said she. 'How you act! What do you mean by talking so? Of course it is something in the room.'

'Of course, it is,' agreed Mrs. Brigham, looking at Caroline suspiciously. 'Of course it must be. It is only a coincidence. It just happens so. Perhaps it is that fold of the window curtain that makes it. It must be something in the room.'

'It is not anything in the room,' repeated Rebecca with obstinate horror.

The door opened suddenly and Henry Glynn entered. He began to speak, then his eyes followed the direction of the others'. He stood stock still staring at the shadow on the wall. It was life size and stretched across the white parallelogram of a door, half across the wall space on which the picture hung.

'What is that?' he demanded in a strange voice.

'It must be due to something in the room,' Mrs. Brigham said faintly.

'It is not due to anything in the room,' said Rebecca again with the shrill insistency of terror.

'How you act, Rebecca Glynn,' said Caroline.

Henry Glynn stood and stared a moment longer. His face showed a gamut of emotions – horror, conviction, then furious incredulity. Suddenly he began hastening hither and thither about the room. He moved the furniture with fierce jerks, turning ever to see the effect upon the shadow on the wall. Not a line of its terrible outlines wavered.

'It must be something in the room!' he declared in a voice which seemed to snap like a lash.

His face changed. The inmost secrecy of his nature seemed evident until one almost lost sight of his lineaments. Rebecca stood close to her sofa, regarding him with woeful, fascinated eyes. Mrs. Brigham clutched Caroline's hand. They both stood in a corner out of his way. For a few moments he raged about the room like a caged wild animal. He moved every piece of furniture; when the moving of a piece did not affect the shadow, he flung it to the floor, the sisters watching.

Then suddenly he desisted. He laughed and began straightening the furniture which he had flung down.

'What an absurdity,' he said easily. 'Such a to-do about a shadow.'

'That's so,' assented Mrs. Brigham, in a scared voice which she tried to make natural. As she spoke she lifted a chair near her.

'I think you have broken the chair that Edward was so fond of,' said Caroline.

Terror and wrath were struggling for expression on her face. Her mouth was set, her eyes shrinking. Henry lifted the chair with a show of anxiety.

'Just as good as ever,' he said pleasantly. He laughed again, looking at his sisters. 'Did I scare you?' he said. 'I should think you might be used to me by this time. You know my way of wanting to leap to the bottom of a mystery, and that shadow does look – queer, like – and I thought if there was any way of accounting for it I would like to without any delay.'

'You don't seem to have succeeded,' remarked Caroline dryly, with a slight glance at the wall.

Henry's eyes followed hers and he quivered perceptibly.

'Oh, there is no accounting for shadows,' he said, and he laughed again. 'A man is a fool to try to account for shadows.'

Then the supper bell rang, and they all left the room, but Henry kept his back to the wall, as did, indeed, the others.

Mrs. Brigham pressed close to Caroline as she crossed the hall. 'He looked like a demon!' she breathed in her ear.

Henry led the way with an alert motion like a boy; Rebecca brought up the rear; she could scarcely walk, her knees trembled so.

'I can't sit in that room again this evening,' she whispered to Caroline after supper.

'Very well, we will sit in the south room,' replied Caroline. 'I think we will sit in the south parlour,' she said aloud; 'it isn't as damp as the study, and I have a cold.'

So they all sat in the south room with their sewing. Henry read the newspaper, his chair drawn close to the lamp on the table. About nine o'clock he rose abruptly and crossed the hall to the study. The three sisters looked at one another. Mrs. Brigham rose, folded her rustling skirts compactly around her, and began tiptoeing toward the door.

'What are you going to do?' inquired Rebecca agitatedly.

'I am going to see what he is about,' replied Mrs. Brigham cautiously.

She pointed as she spoke to the study door across the hall; it was ajar. Henry had striven to pull it together behind him, but it had somehow swollen beyond the limit with curious speed. It was still ajar and a streak of light showed from top to bottom. The hall lamp was not lit.

'You had better stay where you are,' said Caroline with guarded sharpness.

'I am going to see,' repeated Mrs. Brigham firmly.

Then she folded her skirts so tightly that her bulk with its swelling curves was revealed in a black silk sheath, and she went with a slow toddle across the hall to the study door. She stood there, her eye at the crack.

In the south room Rebecca stopped sewing and sat watching with dilated eyes. Caroline sewed steadily. What Mrs. Brigham, standing at the crack in the study door, saw was this:

Henry Glynn, evidently reasoning that the source of the strange shadow must be between the table on which the lamp stood and the wall, was making systematic passes and thrusts all over and through the intervening space with an old sword which had belonged to his father. Not an inch was left unpierced. He seemed to have divided the space into mathematical sections. He brandished the sword with a sort of cold fury and calculation; the blade gave out flashes of light, the shadow remained unmoved. Mrs. Brigham, watching, felt herself cold with horror.

Finally Henry ceased and stood with the sword in hand and raised as if to strike, surveying the shadow on the wall threateningly. Mrs. Brigham toddled back across the hall and shut the south room door behind her before she related what she had seen.

'He looked like a demon!' she said again. 'Have you got any of that old wine in the house, Caroline? I don't feel as if I could stand much more.'

Indeed, she looked overcome. Her handsome placid face was worn and strained and pale.

'Yes, there's plenty,' said Caroline; 'you can have some when you go to bed.'

'I think we had all better take some,' said Mrs. Brigham. 'Oh, my God, Caroline, what – '

'Don't ask and don't speak,' said Caroline.

'No, I am not going to,' replied Mrs. Brigham; 'but – '

Rebecca moaned aloud.

'What are you doing that for?' asked Caroline harshly.

'Poor Edward,' returned Rebecca.

'That is all you have to groan for,' said Caroline. 'There is nothing else.'

'I am going to bed,' said Mrs. Brigham. 'I shan't be able to be at the funeral if I don't.'

Soon the three sisters went to their chambers and the south parlour was deserted. Caroline called to Henry in the study to put out the light before he came upstairs. They had been gone about an hour when he came into the room bringing the lamp which had stood in the study. He set it on the table and waited a few minutes, pacing up and down. His face was terrible, his fair complexion showed livid; his blue eyes seemed dark blanks of awful reflections.

Then he took the lamp up and returned to the library. He set the lamp on the centre table, and the shadow sprang out on the wall. Again he studied the furniture and moved it about, but deliberately, with none of his former frenzy. Nothing affected the shadow. Then he returned to the south room with the lamp and again waited. Again he returned to the study and placed the lamp on the table, and the shadow sprang out upon the wall. It was midnight before he went upstairs. Mrs. Brigham and the other sisters, who could not sleep, heard him.

The next day was the funeral. That evening the family sat in the south room. Some relatives were with them. Nobody entered the study until Henry carried a lamp in there after the others had retired for the night. He saw again the shadow on the wall leap to an awful life before the light.

The next morning at breakfast Henry Glynn announced that he had to go to the city for three days. The sisters looked at him with surprise. He very seldom left home, and just now his practice had been neglected on account of Edward's death. He was a physician.

'How can you leave your patients now?' asked Mrs. Brigham wonderingly.

'I don't know how to, but there is no other way,' replied Henry easily. 'I have had a telegram from Doctor Mitford.'

'Consultation?' inquired Mrs. Brigham.

'I have business,' replied Henry.

Doctor Mitford was an old classmate of his who lived in a neighbouring city and who occasionally called upon him in the case of a consultation.

After he had gone Mrs. Brigham said to Caroline that after all Henry had not said that he was going to consult with Doctor Mitford, and she thought it very strange.

'Everything is very strange,' said Rebecca with a shudder.

'What do you mean?' inquired Caroline sharply.

'Nothing,' replied Rebecca.

Nobody entered the library that day, nor the next, nor the next. The third day Henry was expected home, but he did not arrive and the last train from the city had come.

'I call it pretty queer work,' said Mrs. Brigham. 'The idea of a doctor leaving his patients for three days anyhow, at such a time as this, and I know he has some very sick ones; he said so. And the idea of a consultation lasting three days! There is no sense in it, and *now* he has not come. I don't understand it, for my part.'

'I don't either,' said Rebecca.

They were all in the south parlour. There was no light in the study opposite, and the door was ajar.

Presently Mrs. Brigham rose – she could not have told why; something seemed to impel her, some will outside her own. She went out of the room, again wrapping her rustling skirts around that she might pass noiselessly, and began pushing at the swollen door of the study.

'She has not got any lamp,' said Rebecca in a shaking voice.

Caroline, who was writing letters, rose again, took a lamp (there were two in the room) and followed her sister. Rebecca had risen, but she stood trembling, not venturing to follow.

The doorbell rang, but the others did not hear it; it was on the south door on the other side of the house from the study. Rebecca, after hesitating until the bell rang the second time, went to the door; she remembered that the servant was out.

Caroline and her sister Emma entered the study. Caroline set the lamp on the table. They looked at the wall. 'Oh, my God,' gasped Mrs. Brigham, 'there are – there are *two* – shadows.' The sisters stood clutching each other, staring at the awful things on the wall. Then Rebecca came in, staggering with a telegram in her hand. 'Here is – a telegram,' she gasped. 'Henry is – dead.'

THE DEAD VALLEY

Ralph Adams Cram

[1863–1942]

'*In* The Dead Valley *the eminent architect and mediaevalist Ralph Adams Cram achieves a memorably potent degree of vague regional horror through subtleties of atmosphere and description.*'

– H.P. Lovecraft

I HAVE A FRIEND, Olof Ehrensvärd, a Swede by birth, who yet, by reason of a strange and melancholy mischance of his early boyhood, has thrown his lot with that of the New World. It is a curious story of a headstrong boy and a proud and relentless family: the details do not matter here, but they are sufficient to weave a web of romance around the tall yellow-bearded man with sad eyes and the voice that gives itself perfectly to plaintive little Swedish songs remembered out of child-hood. In the winter evenings we play chess together, he and I, and after some close, fierce battle has been fought to a finish – usually with my own defeat – we fill our pipes again, and Ehrensvärd tells me stories of the far, half-remembered days in the fatherland, before he went to sea:

stories that grow very strange and incredible as the night deepens and
the fire falls together, but stories that, nevertheless, I fully believe.

One of them made a strong impression on me, so I set it down here,
only regretting that I cannot reproduce the curiously perfect English
and the delicate accent which to me increased the fascination of the
tale. Yet, as best I can remember it, here it is.

'I never told you how Nils and I went over the hills to Hallsberg, and
how we found the Dead Valley, did I? Well, this is the way it happened.
I must have been about twelve years old, and Nils Sjöberg, whose
father's estate joined ours, was a few months younger. We were
inseparable just at that time, and whatever we did, we did together.

'Once a week it was market day in Engelholm, and Nils and I went
always there to see the strange sights that the market gathered from
all the surrounding country. One day we quite lost our hearts, for an
old man from across the Elfborg had brought a little dog to sell, that
seemed to us the most beautiful dog in all the world. He was a round,
woolly puppy, so funny that Nils and I sat down on the ground and
laughed at him, until he came and played with us in so jolly a way
that we felt that there was only one really desirable thing in life, and
that was the little dog of the old man from across the hills. But alas!
we had not half money enough wherewith to buy him, so we were
forced to beg the old man not to sell him before the next market day,
promising that we would bring the money for him there. He gave us
his word, and we ran home very fast and implored our mothers to
give us money for the little dog.

'We got the money, but we could not wait for the next market day.
Suppose the puppy should be sold! The thought frightened us so that
we begged and implored that we might be allowed to go over the hills
to Hallsberg where the old man lived, and get the little dog ourselves,
and at last they told us we might go. By starting early in the morning
we should reach Hallsberg by three o'clock, and it was arranged that
we should stay there that night with Nils's aunt, and, leaving by noon
the next day, be home again by sunset.

'Soon after sunrise we were on our way, after having received
minute instructions as to just what we should do in all possible and
impossible circumstances, and finally a repeated injunction that we
should start for home at the same hour the next day, so that we might
get back safely before nightfall.

'For us, it was magnificent sport, and we started off with our rifles,
full of the sense of our very great importance: yet the journey was
simple enough, along a good road, across the big hills we knew so well,

for Nils and I had shot over half the territory this side of the dividing ridge of the Elfborg. Back of Engelholm lay a long valley, from which rose the low mountains, and we had to cross this, and then follow the road along the side of the hills for three or four miles, before a narrow path branched off to the left, leading up through the pass.

'Nothing occurred of interest on the way over, and we reached Hallsberg in due season, found to our inexpressible joy that the little dog was not sold, secured him, and so went to the house of Nils's aunt to spend the night.

'Why we did not leave early on the following day, I can't quite remember; at all events, I know we stopped at a shooting range just outside of the town, where most attractive pasteboard pigs were sliding slowly through painted foliage, serving so as beautiful marks. The result was that we did not get fairly started for home until afternoon, and as we found ourselves at last pushing up the side of the mountain with the sun dangerously near their summits, I think we were a little scared at the prospect of the examination and possible punishment that awaited us when we got home at midnight.

'Therefore we hurried as fast as possible up the mountain side, while the blue dusk closed in about us, and the light died in the purple sky. At first we had talked hilariously, and the little dog had leaped ahead of us with the utmost joy. Latterly, however, a curious oppression came on us; we did not speak or even whistle, while the dog fell behind, following us with hesitation in every muscle.

'We had passed through the foothills and the low spurs of the mountains, and were almost at the top of the main range, when life seemed to go out of everything, leaving the world dead, so suddenly silent the forest became, so stagnant the air. Instinctively we halted to listen.

'Perfect silence, – the crushing silence of the deep forests at night; and more, for always, even in the most impenetrable fastnesses of the wooded mountains, is the multitudinous murmur of little lives, awakened by the darkness, exaggerated and intensified by the stillness of the air and the great dark: but here and now the silence seemed unbroken even by the turn of a leaf, the movement of a twig, the note of night bird or insect. I could hear the blood beat through my veins; and the crushing of the grass under our feet as we advanced with hesitating steps sounded like the falling of trees.

'And the air was stagnant, – dead. The atmosphere seemed to lie upon the body like the weight of sea on a diver who has ventured too far into its awful depths. What we usually call silence seems so only in relation to the din of ordinary experience. This was silence in the absolute, and it crushed the mind while it intensified the senses, bringing down the awful weight of inextinguishable fear.

'I know that Nils and I stared towards each other in abject terror, listening to our quick, heavy breathing, that sounded to our acute senses like the fitful rush of waters. And the poor little dog we were leading justified our terror. The black oppression seemed to crush him even as it did us. He lay close on the ground, moaning feebly, and dragging himself painfully and slowly closer to Nils's feet. I think this exhibition of utter animal fear was the last touch, and must inevitably have blasted our reason – mine anyway; but just then, as we stood quaking on the bounds of madness, came a sound, so awful, so ghastly, so horrible, that it seemed to rouse us from the dead spell that was on us.

'In the depth of the silence came a cry, beginning as a low, sorrowful moan, rising to a tremendous shriek, culminating in a yell that seemed to tear the night in sunder and rend the world as by a cataclysm. So fearful was it that I could not believe it had actual existence: it passed previous experience, the powers of belief, and for a moment I thought it had the result of my own animal terror, an hallucination born of tottering reason.

'A glance at Nils dispelled this thought in a flash. In the pale light of the high stars he was the embodiment of all possible human fear, quaking with an ague, his jaw fallen, his tongue out, his eyes protruding like those of a hanged man. Without a word we fled, the panic of fear giving us strength, and together, the little dog caught close in Nils's arms, we sped down the side of the cursed mountains, – anywhere, goal was of no account: we had but one impulse – to get away from that place.

'So under the black trees and the far white stars that flashed through the still leaves overhead, we leaped down the mountain side, regardless of path or landmark, straight through the tangled underbrush, across mountain streams, through fens and copses, anywhere, so only that our course was downward.

'How long we ran thus, I have no idea, but by and by the forest fell behind, and we found ourselves among the foothills, and fell exhausted on the dry short grass, panting like tired dogs.

'It was lighter here in the open, and presently we looked around to see where we were, and how we were to strike out in order to find the path that would lead us home. We looked in vain for a familiar sign. Behind us rose the great wall of black forest on the flank of the mountain: before us lay the undulating mounds of low foothills, unbroken by trees or rocks, and beyond, only the fall of black sky bright with multitudinous stars that turned its velvet depth to a luminous gray.

'As I remember, we did not speak to each other once: the terror was too heavy on us for that, but by and by we rose simultaneously and started out across the hills.

'Still the same silence, the same dead, motionless air – air that was at once sultry and chilling: a heavy heat struck through with an icy chill that felt almost like the burning of frozen steel. Still carrying the helpless dog, Nils pressed on through the hills, and I followed close behind. At last, in front of us, rose a slope of moor touching the white stars. We climbed it wearily, reached the top, and found ourselves gazing down into a great, smooth valley, filled half way to the brim with – what?

'As far as the eye could see stretched a level plain of ashy white, faintly phosphorescent, a sea of velvet fog that lay like motionless water, or rather like a floor of alabaster, so dense did it appear, so seemingly capable of sustaining weight. If it were possible, I think that sea of dead white mist struck even greater terror into my soul than the heavy silence or the deadly cry – so ominous was it, so utterly unreal, so phantasmal, so impossible, as it lay there like a dead ocean under the steady stars. Yet through that mist *we must go!* there seemed no other way home, and, shattered with abject fear, mad with the one desire to get back, we started down the slope to where the sea of milky mist ceased, sharp and distinct around the stems of the rough grass.

'I put one foot into the ghostly fog. A chill as of death struck through me, stopping my heart, and I threw myself backward on the slope. At that instant came again the shriek, close, close, right in our ears, in ourselves, and far out across that damnable sea I saw the cold fog lift like a water-spout and toss itself high in writhing convolutions towards the sky. The stars began to grow dim as thick vapor swept across them, and in the growing dark I saw a great, watery moon lift itself slowly above the palpitating sea, vast and vague in the gathering mist.

'This was enough: we turned and fled along the margin of the white sea that throbbed now with fitful motion below us, rising, rising, slowly and steadily, driving us higher and higher up the side of the foothills.

'It was a race for life; that we know. How we kept it up I cannot understand, but we did, and at last we saw the white sea fall behind us as we staggered up the end of the valley, and then down into a region that we knew, and so into the old path. The last thing I remember was hearing a strange voice, that of Nils, but horribly changed, stammer brokenly, 'The dog is dead!' and then the whole world turned around twice, slowly and resistlessly, and consciousness went out with a crash.

'It was some three weeks later, as I remember, that I awoke in my own room, and found my mother sitting beside the bed. I could not think very well at first, but as I slowly grew strong again, vague flashes of recollection began to come to me, and little by little the whole sequence of events of that awful night in the Dead Valley came back. All that I could gain from what was told me was that three weeks before I had been found in my own bed, raging sick, and that my illness grew fast into brain fever. I tried to speak of the dread things that had happened to me, but I saw at once that no one looked on them save as the hauntings of a dying frenzy, and so I closed my mouth and kept my own counsel.

'I must see Nils, however, and so I asked for him. My mother told me that he also had been ill with a strange fever, but that he was now quite well again. Presently they brought him in, and when we were alone I began to speak to him of the night on the mountain. I shall never forget the shock that struck me down on my pillow when the boy denied everything: denied having gone with me, ever having heard the cry, having seen the valley, or feeling the deadly chill of the ghostly fog. Nothing would shake his determined ignorance, and in spite of myself I was forced to admit that his denials came from no policy of concealment, but from blank oblivion.

'My weakened brain was in a turmoil. Was it all but the floating phantasm of delirium? Or had the horror of the real thing blotted Nils's mind into blankness so far as the events of the night in the Dead Valley were concerned? The latter explanation seemed the only one, else how explain the sudden illness which in a night had struck us both down? I said nothing more, either to Nils or to my own people, but waited, with a growing determination that, once well again, I would find that valley if it really existed.

'It was some weeks before I was really well enough to go, but finally, late in September, I chose a bright, warm, still day, the last smile of the dying summer, and started early in the morning along the path that led to Hallsberg. I was sure I knew where the trail struck off to the right, down which we had come from the valley of dead water, for a great tree grew by the Hallsberg path at the point where, with a sense of salvation, we had found the home road. Presently I saw it to the right, a little distance ahead.

'I think the bright sunlight and the clear air had worked as a tonic to me, for by the time I came to the foot of the great pine, I had quite lost faith in the verity of the vision that haunted me, believing at last that it was indeed but the nightmare of madness. Nevertheless, I

turned sharply to the right, at the base of the tree, into a narrow path
that led through a dense thicket. As I did so I tripped over something.
A swarm of flies sung into the air around me, and looking down I saw
the matted fleece, with the poor little bones thrusting through, of the
dog we had bought in Hallsberg.

'Then my courage went out with a puff, and I knew that it all was
true, and that now I was frightened. Pride and the desire for
adventure urged me on, however, and I pressed into the close thicket
that barred my way. The path was hardly visible: merely the worn
road of some small beasts, for, though it showed in the crisp grass, the
bushes above grew thick and hardly penetrable. The land rose slowly,
and rising grew clearer, until at last I came out on a great slope of hill,
unbroken by trees or shrubs, very like my memory of that rise of land
we had topped in order that we might find the dead valley and the icy
fog. I looked at the sun; it was bright and clear, and all around insects
were humming in the autumn air, and birds were darting to and fro.
Surely there was no danger, not until nightfall at least; so I began to
whistle, and with a rush mounted the last crest of brown hill.

'There lay the Dead Valley! A great oval basin, almost as smooth
and regular as though made by man. On all sides the grass crept over
the brink of the encircling hills, dusty green on the crests, then fading
into ashy brown, and so to a deadly white, this last color forming a
thin ring, running in a long line around the slope. And then? Nothing.
Bare, brown, hard earth, glittering with grains of alkali, but otherwise
dead and barren. Not a tuft of grass, not a stick of brushwood, not
even a stone, but only the vast expanse of beaten clay.

'In the midst of the basin, perhaps a mile and a half away, the level
expanse was broken by a great dead tree, rising leafless and gaunt into
the air. Without a moment's hesitation I started down into the valley
and made for this goal. Every particle of fear seemed to have left me,
and even the valley itself did not look so very terrifying. At all events,
I was driven by an overwhelming curiosity, and there seemed to be
but one thing in the world to do, – to get to that Tree! As I trudged
along over the hard earth, I noticed that the multitudinous voices of
birds and insects had died away. No bee or butterfly hovered through
the air, no insects leaped or crept over the dull earth. The very air
itself was stagnant.

'As I drew near the skeleton tree, I noticed the glint of sunlight on a
kind of white mound around its roots, and I wondered curiously. It
was not until I had come close that I saw its nature.

'All around the roots and barkless trunk was heaped a wilderness of little bones. Tiny skulls of rodents and of birds, thousands of them, rising about the dead tree and streaming off for several yards in all directions, until the dreadful pile ended in isolated skulls and scattered skeletons. Here and there a larger bone appeared, – the thigh of a sheep, the hoofs of a horse, and to one side, grinning slowly, a human skull.

'I stood quite still, staring with all my eyes, when suddenly the dense silence was broken by a faint, forlorn cry high over my head. I looked up and saw a great falcon turning and sailing downward just over the tree. In a moment more she fell motionless on the bleaching bones.

'Horror struck me, and I rushed for home, my brain whirling, a strange numbness growing in me. I ran steadily, on and on. At last I glanced up. Where was the rise of hill? I looked around wildly. Close before me was the dead tree with its pile of bones. I had circled it round and round, and the valley wall was still a mile and a half away.

'I stood dazed and frozen. The sun was sinking, red and dull, towards the line of hills. In the east the dark was growing fast. Was there still time? *Time!* It was not *that* I wanted, it was *will!* My feet seemed clogged as in a nightmare. I could hardly drag them over the barren earth. And then I felt the slow chill creeping through me. I looked down. Out of the earth a thin mist was rising, collecting in little pools that grew ever larger until they joined here and there, their currents swirling slowly like thin blue smoke. The western hills halved the copper sun. When it was dark I should hear that shriek again, and then I should die. I knew that, and with every remaining atom of will I staggered towards the red west through the writhing mist that crept clammily around my ankles, retarding my steps.

'And as I fought my way off from the Tree, the horror grew, until at last I thought I was going to die. The silence pursued me like dumb ghosts, the still air held my breath, the hellish fog caught at my feet like cold hands.

'But I won! though not a moment too soon. As I crawled on my hands and knees up the brown slope, I heard, far away and high in the air, the cry that already had almost bereft me of reason. It was faint and vague, but unmistakable in its horrible intensity. I glanced behind. The fog was dense and pallid, heaving undulously up the brown slope. The sky was gold under the setting sun, but below was the ashy gray of death. I stood for a moment on the brink of this sea of hell, and then leaped down the slope. The sunset opened before me, the night closed behind, and as I crawled home weak and tired, darkness shut down on the Dead Valley.'

FISHHEAD

Irvin S. Cobb

[1876–1944]

'*Still further carrying on our spectral tradition is the gifted and versatile humorist Irvin S. Cobb, whose work both early and recent contains some finely weird specimens. Fishhead, an early achievement, is banefully effective in its portrayal of unnatural affinities between a hybrid idiot and the strange fish of an isolated lake, which at the last avenge their biped kinsman's murder.*'

– H.P. Lovecraft

IT GOES PAST THE POWERS of my pen to try to describe Reelfoot Lake for you so that you, reading this, will get the picture of it in your mind as I have it in mine.

For Reelfoot Lake is like no other lake that I know anything about. It is an after-thought of Creation.

The rest of this continent was made and had dried in the sun for thousands of years – millions of years, for all I know – before Reelfoot came to be. It's the newest big thing in nature on this hemisphere, probably, for it was formed by the great earthquake of 1811.

That earthquake of 1811 surely altered the face of the earth on the then far frontier of this country.

It changed the course of rivers, it converted hills into what are now the sunk lands of three states, and it turned the solid ground to jelly and made it roll in waves like the sea.

And in the midst of the retching of the land and the vomiting of the waters it depressed to varying depths a section of the earth crust sixty miles long, taking it down – trees, hills, hollows, and all; and a crack broke through to the Mississippi River so that for three days the river ran up stream, filling the hole.

The result was the largest lake south of the Ohio, lying mostly in Tennessee, but extending up across what is now the Kentucky line, and taking its name from a fancied resemblance in its outline to the splay, reeled foot of a cornfield negro. Niggerwool Swamp, not so far away, may have got its name from the same man who christened Reelfoot; at least so it sounds.

Reelfoot is, and has always been, a lake of mystery.

In places it is bottomless. Other places the skeletons of the cypress-trees that went down when the earth sank, still stand upright so that if the sun shines from the right quarter, and the water is less muddy than common, a man, peering face downward into its depths, sees, or thinks he sees, down below him the bare top-limbs upstretching like drowned men's fingers, all coated with the mud of years and bandaged with pennons of the green lake slime.

In still other places the lake is shallow for long stretches, no deeper than breast high to a man, but dangerous because of the weed growths and the sunken drifts which entangle a swimmer's limbs. Its banks are mainly mud, its waters are muddied, too, being a rich coffee color in the spring and a copperish yellow in the summer, and the trees along its shore are mud colored clear up their lower limbs after the spring floods, when the dried sediment covers their trunks with a thick, scrofulous-looking coat.

There are stretches of unbroken woodland around it, and slashes where the cypress knees rise countlessly like headstones and footstones for the dead snags that rot in the soft ooze.

There are deadenings with the lowland corn growing high and rank below and the bleached, fire-blackened girdled trees rising above, barren of leaf and limb.

There are long, dismal flats where in the spring the clotted frogspawn cling like patches of white mucus among the weed-stalks, and at night the turtles crawl out to lay clutches of perfectly round, white eggs with tough, rubbery shells in the sand.

There are bayous leading off to nowhere, and sloughs that wind aimlessly, like great, blind worms, to finally join the big river that rolls its semi-liquid torrents a few miles to the westward.

So Reelfoot lies there, flat in the bottoms, freezing lightly in the winter, steaming torridly in the summer, swollen in the spring when the woods have turned a vivid green and the buffalo-gnats by the million and the billion fill the flooded hollows with their pestilential buzzing and in the fall ringed about gloriously with all the colors which the first frost brings – gold of hickory, yellow-russet of sycamore, red of dogwood and ash, and purple-black of sweet-gum.

But the Reelfoot country has its uses. It is the best game and fish country, natural or artificial, that is left in the South today.

In their appointed seasons the duck and the geese flock in, and even semi-tropical birds, like the brown pelican and the Florida snake-bird, have been known to come there to nest.

Pigs, gone back to wildness, range the ridges, each razor-backed drove captained by a gaunt, savage, slab-sided old boar. By night the bullfrogs, inconceivably big and tremendously vocal, bellow under the banks.

It is a wonderful place for fish – bass and crappie, and perch, and the snouted buffalo fish.

How these edible sorts live to spawn, and how their spawn in turn live to spawn again is a marvel, seeing how many of the big fish-eating cannibal-fish there are in Reelfoot.

Here, bigger than anywhere else, you find the garfish, all bones and appetite and horny plates, with a snout like an alligator, the nearest link, naturalists say, between the animal life of today and the animal life of the Reptilian Period.

The shovel-nose cat, really a deformed kind of fresh-water sturgeon, with a great fan-shaped membranous plate jutting out from his nose like a bowsprit, jumps all day in the quiet places with mighty splashing sounds, as though a horse had fallen into the water.

On every stranded log the huge snapping turtles lie on sunny days in groups of four and six, baking their shells black in the sun, with their little snaky heads raised watchfully, ready to slip noiselessly off at the first sound of oars grating in the row-locks. But the biggest of them all are the catfish!

These are monstrous creatures, these catfish of Reelfoot – scaleless, slick things, with corpsy, dead eyes and poisonous fins, like javelins, and huge whiskers dangling from the sides of their cavernous heads.

Six and seven feet long they grow to be, and weigh 200 pounds or more, and they have mouths wide enough to take in a man's foot or a man's fist, and strong enough to break any hook save the strongest, and greedy enough to eat anything, living or dead or putrid, that the horny jaws can master.

Oh, but they are wicked things, and they tell wicked tales of them down there. They call them man-eaters, and compare them, in certain of their habits, to sharks.

Fishhead was of a piece with this setting.

He fitted into it as an acorn fits its cup. All his life he had lived on Reelfoot, always in the one place, at the mouth of a certain slough.

He had been born there, of a negro father and a half-breed Indian mother, both of them now dead, and the story was that before his birth his mother was frightened by one of the big fish, so that the child came into the world hideously marked.

Anyhow, Fishhead was a human monstrosity, the veritable embodiment of nightmare!

He had the body of a man – a short, stocky, sinewy body – but his face was as near to being the face of a great fish as any face could be and yet retain some trace of human aspect.

His skull sloped back so abruptly that he could hardly be said to have a forehead at all; his chin slanted off right into nothing. His eyes were small and round with shallow, glazed, pale-yellow pupils, and they were set wide apart in his head, and they were unwinking and staring, like a fish's eyes.

His nose was no more than a pair of tiny slits in the middle of the yellow mask. His mouth was the worst of all. It was the awful mouth of a catfish, lipless and almost inconceivably wide, stretching from side to side.

Also when Fishhead became a man grown his likeness to a fish increased, for the hair upon his face grew out into two tightly kinked slender pendants that drooped down either side of the mouth like the beards of a fish!

If he had any other name than Fishhead, none excepting he knew it. As Fishhead he was known, and as Fishhead he answered. Because he knew the waters and the woods of Reelfoot better than any other man there, he was valued as a guide by the city men who came every year to hunt or fish; but there were few such jobs that Fishhead would take.

Mainly he kept to himself, tending his corn patch, netting the lake, trapping a little, and in season pot hunting for the city markets. His

neighbors, ague-bitten whites and malaria-proof negroes alike, left
him to himself.

Indeed, for the most part they had a superstitious fear of him. So he
lived alone, with no kith nor kin, nor even a friend, shunning his kind
and shunned by them.

His cabin stood just below the State line, where Mud Slough runs
into the lake. It was a shack of logs, the only human habitation for
four miles up or down.

Behind it the thick timber came shouldering right up to the edge of
Fishhead's small truck patch, enclosing it in thick shade except when
the sun stood just overhead.

He cooked his food in a primitive fashion, outdoors, over a hole in
the soggy earth or upon the rusted red ruin of an old cookstove, and
he drank the saffron water of the lake out of a dipper made of a gourd,
faring and fending for himself, a master hand at skiff and net,
competent with duck gun and fishspear, yet a creature of affliction
and loneliness, part savage, almost amphibious, set apart from his
fellows, silent and suspicious.

In front of his cabin jutted out a long fallen cottonwood trunk, lying
half in and half out of the water, its top side burnt by the sun and worn
by the friction of Fishhead's bare feet until it showed countless patterns
of tiny scrolled lines, its underside black and rotted, and lapped at
unceasingly by little waves like tiny licking tongues.

Its farther end reached deep water. And it was a part of Fishhead,
for no matter how far his fishing and trapping might take him in the
daytime, sunset would find him back there, his boat drawn up on the
bank, and he on the other end of this log.

From a distance men had seen him there many times, sometimes
squatted motionless as the big turtles that would crawl upon its
dipping tip in his absence, sometimes erect and motionless like a
creek crane, his misshapen yellow form outlined against the yellow
sun, the yellow water, the yellow banks – all of them yellow
together.

If the Reelfooters shunned Fishhead by day they feared him by
night and avoided him as a plague, dreading even the chance of a
casual meeting. For there were ugly stories about Fishhead – stories
which all the negroes and some of the whites believed.

They said that a cry which had been heard just before dusk and just
after, skittering across the darkened waters, was his calling cry to the
big cats, and at his bidding they came trooping in, and that in their
company he swam in the lake on moonlight nights, sporting with

them, diving with them, even feeding with them on what manner of unclean things they fed.

The cry had been heard many times, that much was certain, and it was certain also that the big fish were noticeably thick at the mouth of Fishhead's slough. No native Reelfooter, white or black, would willingly wet a leg or an arm there.

Here Fishhead had lived, and here he was going to die. The Baxters were going to kill him, and this day in late summer was to be the time of the killing.

The two Baxters – Jake and Joel – were coming in their dugout to do it!

This murder had been a long time in the making. The Baxters had to brew their hate over a slow fire for months before it reached the pitch of action.

They were poor whites, poor in everything, repute, and wordly goods, and standing – a pair of fever-ridden squatters who lived on whiskey and tobacco when they could get it, and on fish and cornbread when they couldn't.

The feud itself was of months' standing.

Meeting Fishhead one day in the spring on the spindly scaffolding of the skiff landing at Walnut Log, and being themselves far overtaken in liquor and vainglorious with a bogus alcoholic substitute for courage, the brothers had accused him, wantonly and without proof, of running their trout-line and stripping it of the hooked catch – an unforgivable sin among the water dwellers and the shanty boaters of the South.

Seeing that he bore this accusation in silence, only eyeing them steadfastly, they had been emboldened then to slap his face, where-upon he turned and gave them both the beating of their lives – bloodying their noses and bruising their lips with hard blows against their front teeth, and finally leaving them, mauled and prone, in the dirt.

Moreover, in the onlookers a sense of the everlasting fitness of things had triumphed over race prejudice and allowed them – two freeborn, sovereign whites – to be licked by a nigger! Therefore they were going to get the nigger!

The whole thing had been planned out amply. They were going to kill him on his log at sundown. There would be no witnesses to see it, no retribution to follow after it. The very ease of the undertaking made them forget even their inborn fear of the place of Fishhead's habitation.

For more than an hour they had been coming from their shack across a deeply indented arm of the lake.

Their dugout, fashioned by fire and adz and draw-knife from the bole of a gum-tree, moved through the water as noiselessly as a swimming mallard, leaving behind it a long, wavy trail on the stilled waters.

Jake, the better oarsman, sat flat in the stern of the round-bottomed craft, paddling with quick, splashless strokes. Joel, the better shot, was squatted forward. There was a heavy, rusted duck gun between his knees.

Though their spying upon the victim had made them certain sure he would not be about the shore for hours, a doubled sense of caution led them to hug closely the weedy banks. They slid along the shore like shadows, moving so swiftly and in such silence that the watchful mudturtles barely turned their snaky heads as they passed.

So, a full hour before the time, they came slipping around the mouth of the slough and made for a natural ambuscade which the mixed-breed had left within a stone's jerk of his cabin to his own undoing.

Where the slough's flow joined deeper water a partly uprooted tree was stretched, prone from shore, at the top still thick and green with leaves that drew nourishment from the earth in which the half uncovered roots yet held, and twined about with an exuberance of trumpet vines and wild fox-grapes. All about was a huddle of drift – last year's corn-stalks, shreddy strips of bark, chunks of rotted weed, all the riffle and dunnage of a quiet eddy.

Straight into this green clump glided the dugout and swung, broadside on, against the protecting trunk of the tree, hidden from the inner side by the intervening curtains of rank growth, just as the Baxters had intended it should be hidden, when days before in their scouting they marked this masked place of waiting and included it, then and there, in the scope of their plans.

There had been no hitch or mishap. No one had been abroad in the late afternoon to mark their movements – and in a little while Fishhead ought to be due. Jake's woodman's eye followed the downward swing of the sun speculatively.

The shadows, thrown shoreward, lengthened and slithered on the small ripples. The small noises of the day died out; the small noises of the coming night began to multiply.

The green-bodied flies went away and big mosquitoes, with speckled gray legs, came to take the places of the flies.

The sleepy lake sucked at the mud banks with small mouthing sounds, as though it found the taste of the raw mud agreeable. A monster crawfish, big as a chicken lobster, crawled out of the top of his dried mud chimney and perched himself there, an armored sentinel on the watchtower.

Bull bats began to flitter back and forth, above the tops of the trees. A pudgy muskrat, swimming with head up, was moved to sidle off briskly as he met a cotton-mouth moccasin snake, so fat and swollen with summer poison that it looked almost like a legless lizard as it moved along the surface of the water in a series of slow torpid *s's*. Directly above the head of either of the waiting assassins a compact little swarm of midges hung, holding to a sort of kite-shaped formation.

A little more time passed and Fishhead came out of the woods at the back, walking swiftly, with a sack over his shoulder.

For a few seconds his deformities showed in the clearing, then the black inside of the cabin swallowed him up.

By now the sun was almost down. Only the red nub of it showed above the timber line across the lake, and the shadows lay inland a long way. Out beyond, the big cats were stirring, and the great smacking sounds as their twisting bodies leaped clear and fell back in the water, came shoreward in a chorus.

But the two brothers, in their green covert, gave heed to nothing except the one thing upon which their hearts were set and their nerves tensed. Joel gently shoved his gun barrels across the log, cuddling the stock to his shoulder and slipping two fingers caressingly back and forth upon the triggers. Jake held the narrow dugout steady by a grip upon a fox-grape tendril.

A little wait and then the finish came!

Fishhead emerged from the cabin door and came down the narrow footpath to the water and out upon the water on his log.

He was barefooted and bareheaded, his cotton shirt open down the front to show his yellow neck and breast, his dungaree trousers held about his waist by a twisted tow string.

His broad splay feet, with the prehensile toes outspread, gripped the polished curve of the log as he moved along its swaying, dipping surface until he came to its outer end, and stood there erect, his chest filling, his chinless face lifted up, and something of mastership and dominion in his poise.

And then – his eye caught what another's eyes might have missed – the round, twin ends of the gun barrels, the fixed gleam of Joel's eyes, aimed at him through the green tracery!

In that swift passage of time, too swift almost to be measured by seconds, realization flashed all through him, and he threw his head

still higher and opened wide his shapeless trap of a mouth, and out across the lake he sent skittering and rolling his cry.

And in his cry was the laugh of a loon, and the croaking bellow of a frog, and the bay of a hound, all the compounded night noises of the lake. And in it, too, was a farewell, and a defiance, and an appeal!

The heavy roar of the duck gun came!

At twenty yards the double charge tore the throat out of him. He came down, face forward, upon the log and clung there, his trunk twisting distortedly, his legs twitching and kicking like the legs of a speared frog; his shoulders hunching and lifting spasmodically as the life ran out of him all in one swift coursing flow.

His head canted up between the heaving shoulders, his eyes looked full on the staring face of his murderer, and then the blood came out of his mouth, and Fishhead, in death still as much fish as man, slid flopping, head first, off the end of the log, and sank, face downward slowly, his limbs all extended out.

One after another a string of big bubbles came up to burst in the middle of a widening reddish stain on the coffee-colored water.

The brothers watched this, held by the horror of the thing they had done, and the cranky dugout, having been tipped far over by the recoil of the gun, took water steadily across its gunwale; and now there was a sudden stroke from below upon its careening bottom and it went over and they were in the lake.

But shore was only twenty feet away, the trunk of the uprooted tree only five. Joel, still holding fast to his shot gun, made for the log, gaining it with one stroke. He threw his free arm over it and clung there, treading water, as he shook his eyes free.

Something gripped him – some great, sinewy, unseen thing gripped him fast by the thigh, crushing down on his flesh!

He uttered no cry, but his eyes popped out, and his mouth set in a square shape of agony, and his fingers gripped into the bark of the tree like grapples. He was pulled down and down, by steady jerks, not rapidly but steadily, so steadily, and as he went his fingernails tore four little white strips in the tree-bark. His mouth went under, next his popping eyes, then his erect hair, and finally his clawing, clutching hand, and that was the end of him.

Jake's fate was harder still, for he lived longer – long enough to see Joel's finish. He saw it through the water that ran down his face, and with a great surge of his whole body, he literally flung himself across the log and jerked his legs up high into the air to save them. He flung himself too far, though, for his face and chest hit the water on the far side.

And out of this water rose the head of a great fish, with the lake slime of years on its flat, black head, its whiskers bristling, its corpsy eyes alight. Its horny jaws closed and clamped in the front of Jake's flannel shirt. His hand struck out wildly and was speared on a poisoned fin, and, unlike Joel, he went from sight with a great yell, and a whirling and churning of the water that made the corn stalks circle on the edges of a small whirlpool.

But the whirlpool soon thinned away into widening rings of ripples, and the corn stalks quit circling and became still again, and only the multiplying night noises sounded about the mouth of the slough.

The bodies of all three came ashore on the same day near the same place. Except for the gaping gunshot wound where the neck met the chest, Fishhead's body was unmarked.

But the bodies of the two Baxters were so marred and mauled that the Reelfooters buried them together on the bank without ever knowing which might be Jake's and which might be Joel's.

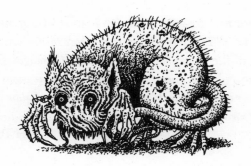

LUKUNDOO

Edward Lucas White

[1866–1934]

'Very notable in their way are some of the weird conceptions of the novelist and short-story writer Edward Lucas White, most of whose themes arise from actual dreams. The Song of the Siren *has a very persuasive strangeness, while such things as* Lukundoo *and* The Snout *arouse darker apprehensions. Mr. White imparts a very peculiar quality to his tales — an oblique sort of glamour which has its own distinctive type of convincingness.'*

– H.P. Lovecraft

'IT STANDS TO REASON,' said Twombly, 'that a man must accept the evidence of his own eyes, and when eyes and ears agree, there can be no doubt. He has to believe what he has both seen and heard.'

'Not always,' put in Singleton, softly.

Every man turned towards Singleton. Twombly was standing on the hearthrug, his back to the grate, his legs spread out, with his habitual air of dominating the room. Singleton, as usual, was as much as possible effaced in a corner. But when Singleton spoke he said something. We faced him in that flattering spontaneity of expectant silence which invites utterance.

'I was thinking,' he said, after an interval, 'of something I both saw and heard in Africa.'

Now, if there was one thing we had found impossible, it had been to elicit from Singleton anything definite about his African experiences. As with the Alpinist in the story, who could tell only that he went up and came down, the sum of Singleton's revelations had been that he went there and came away. His words now riveted our attention at once. Twombly faded from the hearthrug, but not one of us could ever recall having seen him go. The room readjusted itself, focused on Singleton, and there was some hasty and furtive lighting of fresh cigars. Singleton lit one also, but it went out immediately, and he never relit it.

I

We were in the Great Forest, exploring for pigmies. Van Rieten had a theory that the dwarfs found by Stanley and others were a mere cross-breed between ordinary negroes and the real pigmies. He hoped to discover a race of men three feet tall at most, or shorter. We had found no trace of any such beings.

Natives were few, game scarce; food, except game, there was none; and the deepest, dankest, drippingest forest all about. We were the only novelty in the country, no native we met had even seen a white man before, most had never heard of white men. All of a sudden, late one afternoon, there came into our camp an Englishman, and pretty well used up he was, too. We had heard no rumour of him; he had not only heard of us but had made an amazing five-day march to reach us. His guide and two bearers were nearly as done up as he. Even though he was in tatters and had five days' beard on, you could see he was naturally dapper and neat and the sort of man to shave daily. He was small, but wiry. His face was the sort of British face from which emotion has been so carefully banished that a foreigner is apt to think the wearer of the face incapable of any sort of feeling; the kind of face which, if it has any expression at all, expresses principally the resolution to go through the world decorously, without intruding upon or annoying anyone.

His name was Etcham. He introduced himself modestly, and ate with us so deliberately that we should never have suspected, if our bearers had not had it from his bearers, that he had had but three meals in the five days, and those small. After we had lit up he told us why he had come.

'My chief is ve'y seedy,' he said between puffs. 'He is bound to go out if he keeps this way. I thought perhaps . . .'

He spoke quietly in a soft, even tone, but I could see little beads of sweat oozing out on his upper lip under his stubby moustache, and there was a tingle of repressed emotion in his tone, a veiled eagerness in his eye, a palpitating inward solicitude in his demeanour that moved me at once. Van Rieten had no sentiment in him; if he was moved he did not show it. But he listened. I was surprised at that. He was just the man to refuse at once. But he listened to Etcham's halting, difficult hints. He even asked questions.

'Who is your chief?'

'Stone,' Etcham lisped.

That electrified both of us.

'Ralph Stone?' we ejaculated together.

Etcham nodded.

For some minutes Van Rieten and I were silent. Van Rieten had never seen him, but I had been a classmate of Stone's, and Van Rieten and I had discussed him over many a camp fire. We had heard of him two years before, south of Luebo in the Balunda country, which had been ringing with his theatrical strife against a Balunda witch-doctor, ending in the sorcerer's complete discomfiture and the abasement of his tribe before Stone. They had even broken the fetish-man's whistle and given Stone the pieces. It had been like the triumph of Elijah over the prophets of Baal, only more real to the Balunda.

We had thought of Stone as far off, if still in Africa at all, and here he turned up ahead of us and probably forestalling our quest.

II

Etcham's naming of Stone brought back to us all his tantalizing story, his fascinating parents, their tragic death; the brilliance of his college days; the dazzle of his millions; the promise of his young manhood; his wide notoriety, so nearly real fame; his romantic elopement with the meteoric authoress whose sudden cascade of fiction had made her so great a name so young, whose beauty and charm were so much heralded; the frightful scandal of the breach-of-promise suit that followed; his bride's devotion through it all; their sudden quarrel after it was all over; their divorce; the too much advertised announcement of his approaching marriage to the plaintiff in the breach-of-promise suit; his precipitate remarriage to his divorced bride; their second quarrel and second divorce; his departure from his native land; his advent in the dark continent. The sense of all this rushed over me and I believe Van Rieten felt it, too, as he sat silent.

Then he asked:

'Where is Werner?'

'Dead,' said Etcham. 'He died before I joined Stone.'

'You were not with Stone above Luebo?'

'No,' said Etcham, 'I joined him at Stanley Falls.'

'Who is with him?' Van Rieten asked.

'Only his Zanzibar servants and the bearers,' Etcham replied.

'What sort of bearers?' Van Rieten demanded.

'Mang-Battu men,' Etcham responded simply.

Now that impressed both Van Rieten and myself greatly. It bore out Stone's reputation as a notable leader of men. For up to that time no one had been able to use Mang-Battu as bearers outside of their own country, or to hold them for long or difficult expeditions.

'Were you long among the Mang-Battu?' was Van Rieten's next question.

'Some weeks,' said Etcham. 'Stone was interested in them and made up a fair-sized vocabulary of their words and phrases. He had a theory that they are an offshoot of the Balunda and he found much confirmation in their customs.' ·

'What do you live on?' Van Rieten inquired.

'Game, mostly,' Etcham lisped.

'How long has Stone been laid up?' Van Rieten next asked.

'More than a month,' Etcham answered.

'And you have been hunting for the camp?' Van Rieten exclaimed.

Etcham's face, burnt and flayed as it was, showed a flush.

'I missed some easy shots,' he admitted ruefully. 'I've not felt ve'y fit myself.'

'What's the matter with your chief?' Van Rieten inquired.

'Something like carbuncles,' Etcham replied.

'He ought to get over a carbuncle or two,' Van Rieten declared.

'They are not carbuncles,' Etcham explained. 'Nor one or two. He has had dozens, sometimes five at once. If they had been carbuncles he would have been dead long ago. But in some ways they are not so bad, though in others they are worse.'

'How do you mean?' Van Rieten queried.

'Well,' Etcham hesitated, 'they do not seem to inflame so deep nor so wide as carbuncles, nor to be so painful, nor to cause so much fever.

But then they seem to be part of a disease that affects his mind. He let me help him dress the first, but the others he has hidden most carefully, from me and from the men. He keeps his tent when they puff up, and will not let me change the dressings or be with him at all.'

'Have you plenty of dressings?' Van Rieten asked.

'We have some,' said Etcham doubtfully. 'But he won't use them; he washes out the dressings and uses them over and over.'

'How is he treating the swellings?' Van Rieten inquired.

'He slices them off clear down to flesh level, with his razor.'

'What?' Van Rieten shouted.

Etcham made no answer but looked him steadily in the eyes.

'I beg pardon,' Van Rieten hastened to say. 'You startled me. They can't be carbuncles. He'd have been dead long ago.'

'I thought I had said they are not carbuncles,' Etcham lisped.

'But the man must be crazy!' Van Rieten exclaimed.

'Just so,' said Etcham. 'He is beyond my advice or control.'

'How many has he treated that way?' Van Rieten demanded.

'Two, to my knowledge,' Etcham said.

'Two?' Van Rieten queried.

Etcham flushed again.

'I saw him,' he confessed, 'through a crack in the hut. I felt impelled to keep a watch on him, as if he was not responsible.'

'I should think not,' Van Rieten agreed. 'And you saw him do that twice?'

'I conjecture,' said Etcham, 'that he did the like with all the rest.'

'How many has he had?' Van Rieten asked.

'Dozens,' Etcham lisped.

'Does he eat?' Van Rieten inquired.

'Like a wolf,' said Etcham. 'More than any two bearers.'

'Can he walk?' Van Rieten asked.

'He crawls a bit, groaning,' said Etcham simply.

'Little fever, you say,' Van Rieten ruminated.

'Enough and too much,' Etcham declared.

'Has he been delirious?' Van Rieten asked.

'Only twice,' Etcham replied; 'once when the first swelling broke, and once later. He would not let anyone come near him then. But we could hear him talking, talking steadily, and it scared the natives.'

'Was he talking their patter in delirium?' Van Rieten demanded.

'No,' said Etcham, 'but he was talking some similar lingo. Hamed Burghash said he was talking Balunda. I know too little Balunda. I do not learn languages readily. Stone learned more Mang-Battu in a week than I could have learned in a year. But I seemed to hear words like Mang-Battu words. Anyhow, the Mang-Battu bearers were scared.'

'Scared?' Van Rieten repeated, questioningly.

'So were the Zanzibar men, even Hamed Burghash, and so was I,' said Etcham, 'only for a different reason. He talked in two voices.'

'In two voices,' Van Rieten reflected.

'Yes,' said Etcham, more excitedly than he had yet spoken. 'In two voices, like a conversation. One was his own, one a small, thin, bleaty voice like nothing I ever heard. I seemed to make out, among the sounds the deep voice made, something like Mang-Battu words I knew, as *nedru*, *metababa*, and *nedo*, their terms for 'head,' 'shoulder,' 'thigh,' and perhaps *kudra* and *nekere* ('speak' and 'whistle'); and among the noises of the shrill voice *matomipa*, *angunzi*, and *kamomami* ('kill,' 'death,' and 'hate'). Hamed Burghash said he also heard those words. He knew Mang-Battu far better than I.'

'What did the bearers say?' Van Rieten asked.

'They said, "*Lukundoo, Lukundoo!*" ' Etcham replied. 'I did not know that word; Hamed Burghash said it was Mang-Battu for "leopard." '

'It's Mang-Battu for "witchcraft," ' said Van Rieten.

'I don't wonder they thought so,' said Etcham. 'It was enough to make one believe in sorcery to listen to those two voices.'

'One voice answering the other?' Van Rieten asked perfunctorily.

Etcham's face went grey under his tan.

'Sometimes both at once,' he answered huskily.

'Both at once!' Van Rieten ejaculated.

'It sounded that way to the men, too,' said Etcham. 'And that was not all.'

He stopped and looked helplessly at us for a moment.

'Could a man talk and whistle at the same time?' he asked.

'How do you mean?' Van Rieten queried.

'We could hear Stone talking away, his big, deep-chested baritone rumbling along, and through it all we could hear a high, shrill whistle, the oddest, wheezy sound. You know, no matter how shrilly a grown man may whistle, the note has a different quality from the whistle of a boy or a woman or a little girl. They sound more treble, somehow. Well, if you can imagine the smallest girl who could whistle keeping it up tunelessly right along, that whistle was like that, only even more piercing, and it sounded right through Stone's bass tones.'

'And you didn't go to him?' Van Rieten cried.

'He is not given to threats,' Etcham disclaimed. 'But he had threatened, not volubly, nor like a sick man, but quietly and firmly, that if any man of us (he lumped me in with the men) came near him while he was in his trouble, that man should die. And it was not so much his words as his manner. It was like a monarch commanding respected privacy for a deathbed. One simply could not transgress.'

'I see,' said Van Rieten shortly.

'He's ve'y seedy,' Etcham repeated helplessly. 'I thought perhaps. . .'

His absorbing affection for Stone, his real love for him, shone out through his envelope of conventional training. Worship of Stone was plainly his master passion.

Like many competent men, Van Rieten had a streak of hard selfishness in him. It came to the surface then. He said we carried our lives in our hands from day to day just as genuinely as Stone; that he did not forget the ties of blood and calling between any two explorers, but that there was no sense in imperilling one party for a very problematical benefit to a man probably beyond any help; that it was enough of a task to hunt for one party; that if two were united, providing food would be more than doubly difficult; that the risk of starvation was too great. Deflecting our march seven full days' journey (he complimented Etcham on his marching powers) might ruin our expedition entirely.

III

Van Rieten had logic on his side and he had a way with him. Etcham sat there apologetic and deferential, like a fourth-form schoolboy before a headmaster. Van Rieten wound up.

'I am after pigmies, at the risk of my life. After pigmies I go.'

'Perhaps, then, these will interest you,' said Etcham, very quietly.

He took two objects out of the side-pocket of his blouse, and handed them to Van Rieten. They were round, bigger than big plums, and smaller than small peaches, about the right size to enclose in an average hand. They were black, and at first I did not see what they were.

'Pigmies!' Van Rieten exclaimed. 'Pigmies, indeed! Why, they wouldn't be two feet high! Do you mean to claim that these are adult heads?'

'I claim nothing,' Etcham answered evenly. 'You can see for yourself.'

Van Rieten passed one of the heads to me. The sun was just setting and I examined it closely. A dried head it was, perfectly preserved, and the flesh as hard as Argentine jerked beef. A bit of a vertebra stuck out where the muscles of the vanished neck had shrivelled into folds. The puny chin was sharp on a projecting jaw, the minute teeth white and even between the retracted lips, the tiny nose was flat, the little forehead retreating, there were inconsiderable clumps of stunted wool on the Lilliputian cranium. There was nothing babyish, childish or youthful about the head; rather it was mature to senility.

'Where did these come from?' Van Rieten inquired.

'I do not know,' Etcham replied precisely. 'I found them among Stone's effects while rummaging for medicines or drugs or anything that could help me to help him. I do not know where he got them. But I'll swear he did not have them when we entered this district.'

'Are you sure?' Van Rieten queried, his eyes big and fixed on Etcham's.

'Ve'y sure,' lisped Etcham.

'But how could he have come by them without your knowledge?' Van Rieten demurred.

'Sometimes we were apart ten days at a time hunting,' said Etcham. 'Stone is not a talking man. He gave me no account of his doings, and Hamed Burghash keeps a still tongue and a tight hold on the men.'

'You have examined these heads?' Van Rieten asked.

'Minutely,' said Etcham.

Van Rieten took out his notebook. He was a methodical chap. He tore out a leaf, folded it and divided it equally into three pieces. He gave one to me and one to Etcham.

'Just for a test of my impressions,' he said, 'I want each of us to write separately just what he is most reminded of by these heads. Then I want to compare the writings.'

I handed Etcham a pencil and he wrote. Then he handed the pencil back to me and I wrote.

'Read the three,' said Van Rieten, handing me his piece.

Van Rieten had written:

'An old Balunda witch-doctor.'

Etcham had written:

'An old Mang-Battu fetish-man.'

I had written:

'An old Katongo magician.'

'There!' Van Rieten exclaimed. 'Look at that! There is nothing Wagabi or Batwa or Wambuttu or Wabotu about these heads. Nor anything pigmy either.'

'I thought as much,' said Etcham.

'And you say he did not have them before?'

'To a certainty he did not,' Etcham asserted.

'It is worth following up,' said Van Rieten. 'I'll go with you. And first of all, I'll do my best to save Stone.'

He put out his hand and Etcham clasped it silently. He was grateful all over.

IV

Nothing but Etcham's fever of solicitude could have taken him in five days over the track. It took him eight days to retrace with full knowledge of it and our party to help. We could not have done it in seven, and Etcham urged us on, in a repressed fury of anxiety, no mere fever of duty to his chief, but a real ardour of devotion, a glow of personal adoration for Stone which blazed under his dry conventional exterior and showed in spite of him.

We found Stone well cared for. Etcham had seen to a good high thorn *zareeba* round the camp, the huts were well built and thatched, and Stone's was as good as their resources would permit. Hamed Burghash was not named after two Seyyids for nothing. He had in him the making of a sultan. He had kept the Mang-Battu together, not a man had slipped off, and he had kept them in order. Also he was a deft nurse and a faithful servant.

The two other Zanzibaris had done some creditable hunting. Though all were hungry, the camp was far from starvation.

Stone was on a canvas cot and there was a sort of collapsible camp-stool-table, like a Turkish tabouret, by the cot. It had a water-bottle and some vials on it and Stone's watch, also his razor in its case.

Stone was clean and not emaciated, but he was far gone; not unconscious, but in a daze; past commanding or resisting anyone. He did not seem to see us enter or to know we were there. I should have recognized him anywhere. His boyish dash and grace had vanished utterly, of course. But his head was even more leonine; his hair was still abundant, yellow and wavy; the close, crisped blond beard he had grown during his illness did not alter him. He was big and big-chested yet. His eyes were dull and he mumbled and babbled mere meaningless syllables, not words.

Etcham helped Van Rieten to uncover him and look him over. He was in good muscle for a man so long bedridden. There were no scars on him except about his knees, shoulders and chest. On each

knee and above it he had a full score of roundish cicatrices, and a
dozen or more on each shoulder, all in front. Two or three were
open wounds and four or five barely healed. He had no fresh
swellings, except two, one on each side, on his pectoral muscles,
the one on the left being higher up and farther out than the other.
They did not look like boils or carbuncles, but as if something blunt
and hard were being pushed up through the fairly healthy flesh and
skin, not much inflamed.

'I should not lance those,' said Van Rieten, and Etcham assented.

They made Stone as comfortable as they could, and just before
sunset we looked in at him again. He was lying on his back, and his
chest showed big and massive yet, but he lay as if in a stupor. We left
Etcham with him and went into the next hut, which Etcham had
resigned to us. The jungle noises were no different there than
anywhere else for months past, and I was soon fast asleep.

V

Some time in the pitch dark I found myself awake and listening. I
could hear two voices, one Stone's, the other sibilant and wheezy. I
knew Stone's voice after all the years that had passed since I heard it
last. The other was like nothing I remembered. It had less volume
than the wail of a new-born baby, yet there was an insistent carrying
power to it, like the shrilling of an insect. As I listened I heard Van
Rieten breathing near me in the dark; then he heard me and realized
that I was listening too. Like Etcham I knew little Balunda, but I
could make out a word or two. The voices alternated, with intervals of
silence between.

Then suddenly both sounded at once and fast. Stone's baritone
basso, full as if he were in perfect health, and that incredibly
stridulous falsetto, both jabbering at once like the voices of two
people quarrelling and trying to talk each other down.

'I can't stand this,' said Van Rieten. 'Let's have a look at him.'

He had one of those cylindrical electric night-candles. He fumbled
about for it, touched the button and beckoned me to come with him.
Outside the hut he motioned me to stand still, and instinctively
turned off the light, as if seeing made listening difficult.

Except for a faint glow from the embers of the bearers' fire we were
in complete darkness, little starlight struggled through the trees, the
river made but a faint murmur. We could hear the two voices
together and then suddenly the creaking voice changed into a

razor-edged, slicing whistle, indescribably cutting, continuing right through Stone's grumbling torrent of croaking words.

'Good God!' exclaimed Van Rieten.

Abruptly he turned on the light.

We found Etcham utterly asleep, exhausted by his long anxiety and the exertions of his phenomenal march, and relaxed completely now that the load was in a sense shifted from his shoulders to Van Rieten's. Even the light on his face did not wake him.

The whistle had ceased and the two voices now sounded together. Both came from Stone's cot, where the concentrated white ray showed him lying just as we had left him, except that he had tossed his arms above his head and had torn the coverings and bandages from his chest.

The swelling on the right breast had broken. Van Rieten aimed the centre line of the light at it and we saw it plainly. From his flesh, grown out of it, there protruded a head, such a head as the dried specimens Etcham had shown us, as if it were a miniature of the head of a Balunda fetish-man. It was black, shining black as the blackest African skin; it rolled the whites of its wicked, wee eyes and showed its microscopic teeth between lips repulsively negroid in their red fullness, even in so diminutive a face. It had crisp, fuzzy wool on its minikin skull, it turned malignantly from side to side and chittered incessantly in that inconceivable falsetto. Stone babbled brokenly against its patter.

Van Rieten turned from Stone and waked Etcham, with some difficulty. When he was awake and saw it all, Etcham stared and said not one word.

'You saw him slice off two swellings?' Van Rieten asked.

Etcham nodded, chokingly.

'Did he bleed much?' Van Rieten demanded.

'Ve'y little,' Etcham replied.

'You hold his arms,' said Van Rieten to Etcham.

He took up Stone's razor and handed me the light. Stone showed no sign of seeing the light or of knowing we were there. But the little head mewled and screeched at us.

Van Rieten's hand was steady, and the sweep of the razor even and true. Stone bled amazingly little and Van Rieten dressed the wound as if it had been a bruise or scrape.

Stone had stopped talking the instant the excrescent head was severed. Van Rieten did all that could be done for Stone and then fairly grabbed the light from me. Snatching up a gun he scanned the ground by the cot and brought the butt down once and twice, viciously.

We went back to our hut, but I doubt if I slept.

VI

Next day, near noon, in broad daylight, we heard the two voices from Stone's hut. We found Etcham dropped asleep by his charge. The swelling on the left had broken, and just such another head was there miauling and spluttering. Etcham woke up and the three of us stood there and glared. Stone interjected hoarse vocables into the tinkling gurgle of the portent's utterance.

Van Rieten stepped forward, took up Stone's razor and knelt down by the cot. The atomy of a head squealed a wheezy snarl at him.

Then suddenly Stone spoke English.

'Who are you with my razor?'

Van Rieten started back and stood up.

Stone's eyes were clear now and bright, they roved about the hut.

'The end,' he said; 'I recognize the end. I seem to see Etcham, as if in life. But Singleton! Ah, Singleton! Ghosts of my boyhood come to watch me pass! And you, strange spectre with the black beard and my razor! Aroint ye all!'

'I'm no ghost, Stone,' I managed to say. 'I'm alive. So are Etcham and Van Rieten. We are here to help you.'

'Van Rieten!' he exclaimed. 'My work passes on to a better man. Luck go with you, Van Rieten.'

Van Rieten went nearer to him.

'Just hold still a moment, old man,' he said soothingly. 'It will be only one twinge.'

'I've held still for many such twinges,' Stone answered quite distinctly. 'Let me be. Let me die in my own way. The hydra was nothing to this. You can cut off ten, a hundred, a thousand heads, but the curse you cannot cut off, or take off. What's soaked into the bone won't come out of the flesh, any more than what's bred there. Don't hack me any more. Promise!'

His voice had all the old commanding tone of his boyhood and it swayed Van Rieten as it always had swayed everybody.

'I promise,' said Van Rieten.

Almost as he said the word Stone's eyes filmed again.

Then we three sat about Stone and watched that hideous, gibbering prodigy grow up out of Stone's flesh, till two horrid, spindling little black arms disengaged themselves. The infinitesimal nails were perfect to the barely perceptible moon at the quick, the pink spot on the palm was horridly natural. These arms gesticulated and the right plucked towards Stone's blond beard.

'I can't stand this,' Van Rieten exclaimed and took up the razor again.

Instantly Stone's eyes opened, hard and glittering.

'Van Rieten break his word?' he enunciated slowly. 'Never!'

'But we must help you,' Van Rieten gasped.

'I am past all help and all hurting,' said Stone. 'This is my hour. This curse is not put on me; it grew out of me, like this horror here. Even now I go.'

His eyes closed and we stood helpless, the adherent figure spouting shrill sentences.

In a moment Stone spoke again.

'You speak all tongues?' he asked quickly.

And the mergent minikin replied in sudden English:

'Yea, verily, all that you speak,' putting out its microscopic tongue, writhing its lips and wagging its head from side to side. We could see the thready ribs on its exiguous flanks heave as if the thing breathed.

'Has she forgiven me?' Stone asked in a muffled strangle.

'Not while the moss hangs from the cypresses,' the head squeaked. 'Not while the stars shine on Lake Pontchartrain will she forgive.'

And then Stone, all with one motion, wrenched himself over on his side. The next instant he was dead.

When Singleton's voice ceased the room was hushed for a space. We could hear each other breathing. Twombly, the tactless, broke the silence.

'I presume,' he said, 'you cut off the little minikin and brought it home in alcohol.'

Singleton turned on him a stern countenance.

'We buried Stone,' he said, 'unmutilated as he died.'

'But,' said the unconscionable Twombly, 'the whole thing is incredible.'

Singleton stiffened.

'I did not expect you to believe it,' he said; 'I began by saying that although I heard and saw it, when I look back on it I cannot credit it myself.'

THE DOUBLE SHADOW

Clark Ashton Smith

[1893–1961]

'*Of younger Americans, none strikes the note of cosmic horror so well as the California poet, artist and fictionist Clark Ashton Smith, whose bizarre writing, drawings, paintings and stories are the delight of a sensitive few. Mr. Smith has for his background a universe of remote and paralysing fright – jungles of poisonous and iridescent blossoms on the moons of Saturn, evil and grotesque temples in Atlantis, Lemuria, and forgotten elder worlds, and dank morasses of spotted death-fungi in spectral countries beyond earth's rim . . . Mr. Smith is perhaps unexcelled by any other writer dead or living. Who else has seen such gorgeous, luxuriant, and feverishly distorted visions of infinite spheres and multiple dimensions and lived to tell the tale? His short stories deal powerfully with other galaxies, worlds, and dimensions, as well as with strange regions and aeons on the earth. He tells of primal Hyperborea and its black amorphous god Tsathoggua; of the lost continent Zothique, and of the fabulous, vampire-curst land of Averoigne in mediaeval France. Some of Mr. Smith's best work can be found in the brochure entitled* The Double Shadow and Other Fantasies *(1933)*.

– H.P. Lovecraft

My name is Pharpetron, among those who have known me in Poseidonis: but even I, the last and most forward pupil of the wise Avyctes, know not the name of that which I am fated to become ere tomorrow, therefore, by the ebbing silver lamps, in my master's marble house above the loud sea, I write this tale with a hasty hand, scrawling an ink of wizard virtue on the gray, priceless, antique parchment of dragons. And having written, I shall enclose the pages in a sealed cylinder of orichalchum, and shall cast the cylinder from a high window into the sea, lest that which I am doomed to become should haply destroy the writing. And it may be that mariners from Lephara, passing to Umb and Pneor in their tall triremes, will find the cylinder; or fishers will draw it from the wave in their seines; and having read my story, men will learn the truth and take warning; and no man's feet, henceforward, will approach the pale and demon-haunted house of Avyctes.

For six years I have dwelt apart with the aged master, forgetting youth and its wonted desires in the study of arcanic things. We have delved more deeply than all others before us in an interdicted lore; we have called up the dwellers in sealed crypts, in fearful abysses beyond space. Few are the sons of mankind who have cared to seek us out among the bare, wind-worn crags; and many, but nameless, are the visitants who have come to us from further bourns of place and time.

Stern and white as a tomb is the mansion wherein we dwell. Far below, on black, naked reefs, the northern sea climbs and roars indomitably, or ebbs with a ceaseless murmur as of armies of baffled demons; and the house is filled evermore, like a hollow-sounding sepulcher, with the drear echo of its tumultuous voices; and the winds wail in dismal wrath around the high towers but shake them not. On the seaward side the mansion rises sheerly from the straight-falling cliff; but on the other sides there are narrow terraces, grown with dwarfish, crooked cedars that bow always beneath the gales. Giant marble monsters guard the landward portals; and huge marble women ward the strait porticos above the surf; and mighty statues and mummies stand everywhere in the chambers and along the halls. But, saving these, and the entities we have summoned, there is none to companion us; and liches and shadows have been the servitors of our daily needs.

Not without terror (since man is but mortal) did I, the neophyte, behold at first the abhorrent and tremendous faces of them that obeyed Avyctes. I shuddered at the black writhing of submundane things from the maney-volumed smoke of the braziers; I cried in horror at the gray foulnesses, colossal, without form, that crowded malignly about the drawn circle of seven colors, threatening unspeakable trespass on us that stood at the center. Not without revulsion did I drink wine that was poured by cadavers, and eat bread that was purveyed by phantoms. But use and custom dulled the strangeness, destroyed the fear; and in time I believed implicitly that Avyctes was the lord of all incantations and exorcisms, with infallible power to dismiss the beings he evoked.

Well had it been for Avyctes – and for me – if the master had contented himself with the lore preserved from Atlantis and Thule, or brought over from Mu. Surely this should have been enough: for in the ivory-sheeted books of Thule there were blood-writ runes that would call the demons of the fifth and seventh planets if spoken aloud at the hour of their ascent; and the sorcerers of Mu had left record of a process whereby the doors of far-future time could be unlocked; and our fathers, the Atlanteans, had known the road between the atoms and the path into far stars. But Avyctes thirsted for a darker knowledge, a deeper empery. . . . And into his hands, in the third year of my novitiate, there came the mirror-bright tablet of the lost serpent people.

At certain hours, when the tide had fallen from the steep rocks, we were wont to descend by cavern-hidden stairs to a cliff-walled crescent beach behind the promontory on which stood Avyctes' house. There, on the dun, wet sands, beyond the foamy tongues of the surf, would lie the worn and curious driftage of alien shores and trove the hurricanes had cast up from unsounded deeps. And there we had found the purple and sanguine volutes of great shells, and rude lumps of ambergris, and white flowers of perpetually blooming coral; and once, the barbaric idol of green brass that had been the figurehead of a galley from far hyperborean isles . . .

There had been a great storm, such as must have riven the sea to its last profound; but the tempest had gone by with morning, and the heavens were cloudless on that fatal day; and the demon winds were hushed among the black crags and chasms; and the sea lisped with a low whisper, like the rustle of gowns of samite trailed by fleeing maidens on the sand. And just beyond the ebbing wave, in a tangle of russet seaweed, we descried a thing that glittered with blinding sun-like brilliance.

And running forward, I plucked it from the wrack before the wave's return, and bore it to Avyctes.

The tablet was wrought of some nameless metal, like never-rusting iron, but heavier. It had the form of a triangle and was broader at the widest than a man's heart. On one side it was wholly blank, like a mirror. On the other side many rows of small crooked ciphers were incised deeply in the metal, as if by the action of some mordant acid; and these ciphers were not the hieroglyphs or alphabetic characters of any language known to the master or to me.

Of the tablet's age and origin we could form no conjecture; and our erudition was wholly baffled. For many days thereafter we studied the writing and held argument that came to no issue. And night by night, in a high chamber closed against the perennial winds, we pondered over the dazzling triangle by the tall straight flames of silver lamps. For Avyctes deemed that knowledge of rare value, some secret of an alien or elder magic, was held by the clueless crooked ciphers. Then, since all our scholarship was in vain, the master sought another divination, and had recourse to wizardry and necromancy. But at first, among all the devils and phantoms that answered our interrogation, none could tell us aught concerning the tablet. And any other than Avyctes would have despaired in the end . . . and well would it have been if he had despaired, and had sought no longer to decipher the writing.

The months and years went by with a slow thundering of seas on the dark rocks, and a headlong clamor of winds around the white towers. Still we continued our delving and evocations; and farther, always farther we went into the lampless realms of space and spirit; learning, perchance, to unlock the hithermost of the manifold infinities. And at whiles Avyctes would resume his pondering of the seafound tablet, or would question some visitant regarding its interpretation.

At length, by the use of a chance formula, in idle experiment, he summoned up the dim, tenuous ghost of a sorcerer from prehistoric years; and the ghost, in a thin whisper of uncouth, forgotten speech, informed us that the letters on the tablet were those of a language of the serpent-men, whose primal continent had sunk eons before the lifting of Hyperborea from the ooze. But the ghost could tell us naught of their significance; for, even in his time, the serpent-people had become a dubious legend; and their deep, antehuman lore and sorcery were things irretrievable by man.

Now, in all the books of conjuration owned by Avyctes, there was no spell whereby we could call the lost serpent-men from their fabulous epoch. But there was an old Lemurian formula, recondite and uncertain, by which the shadow of a dead man could be sent into years posterior to those of his own lifetime, and could be recalled after an interim by the wizard. And the shade, being wholly insubstantial, would suffer no harm from the temporal transition, and would remember, for the information of the wizard, that which he had been instructed to learn during the journey.

So, having called again the ghost of the prehistoric sorcerer, whose name was Ybith, Avyctes made a singular use of several very ancient gums and combustible fragments of fossil wood; and he and I, reciting the responses of the formula, sent the thin spirit of Ybith into the far ages of the serpent-men.

And after a time which the master deemed sufficient, we performed the curious rites of incantation that would recall Ybith. And the rites were successful; and Ybith stood before us again, like a blown vapor that is nigh to vanishing. And in words faint as the last echo of perishing memories, the specter told us the key to the meaning of the letters, which he had learned in the prehuman past. And after this, we questioned Ybith no more but suffered him to return unto slumber and oblivion.

Then, knowing the import of the tiny, twisted ciphers, we read the tablet's writing and made thereof a transliteration, though not without labor and difficulty, since the very phonetics of the serpent tongue, and the symbols and ideas, were somewhat alien to those of mankind. And when we had mastered the inscription, we found that it contained the formula for a certain evocation which, no doubt, had been used by the serpent sorcerers. But the object of the evocation was not named; nor was there any clue to the nature or identity of that which would come in answer to the rites. And, moreover, there was no corresponding rite of exorcism nor spell of dismissal.

Great was Avyctes' jubilation, deeming that we had learned a lore beyond the memory or prevision of man. And though I sought to dissuade him, he resolved to employ the evocation, arguing that our discovery was no chance thing but was fatefully predestined from the beginning. And he seemed to think lightly of the menace that might be brought upon us by the conjuration of things whose nativity and attributes were wholly obscure. 'For,' said Avyctes, 'I have called up, in all the years of my sorcery, no god or devil, no demon or lich or shadow which I could not control and dismiss at will. And I am loath to believe that any spirit or power beyond the subversion of my spells could have been summoned by a race of serpents, whatever their skill in necromancy and demonism.'

So, seeing that he was obstinate, and acknowledging him for my master in all ways, I agreed to aid Avyctes in the experiment, though not without misgivings. And then we gathered together, in the chamber of conjuration, at the specified hour and configuration of the stars, the equivalents of sundry rare materials that the tablet had instructed us to use in the ritual.

Of much that we did, and of certain agents that we employed, it were better not to tell; nor shall I record the shrill, sibilant words, difficult for beings not born of serpents to articulate, whose intonation formed a signal part of the ceremony. Toward the last, we drew a triangle on the marble floor with the fresh blood of birds; and Avyctes stood at one angle, and I at another; and the gaunt umber mummy of an Atlantean warrior, whose name had been Oigos, was stationed at the third angle. And standing thus, Avyctes and I held tapers of corpse-tallow in our hands, till the tapers had burned down between our fingers as into a socket. And in the outstretched palms of the mummy of Oigos, as if in shallow thuribles, talc and asbestos burned, ignited by a strange fire whereof we knew the secret. At one side we had traced on the floor an infrangible ellipse, made by an endless linked repetition of the twelve unspeakable Signs of Oumor, to which we could retire if the visitant should prove inimical or rebellious. We waited while the pole-circling stars went over, as had been prescribed. Then, when the tapers had gone out between our seared fingers, and the talc and asbestos were wholly consumed in the mummy's eaten palms, Avyctes uttered a single word whose sense was obscure to us; and Oigos, being animated by sorcery and subject to our will, repeated the word after a given interval, in tones that were hollow as a tomb-born echo; and I, in my turn, also repeated it.

Now, in the chamber of evocation, before beginning the ritual, we had opened a small window giving upon the sea, and had likewise left open a high door on the hall to landward, lest that which came in answer to us should require a spatial mode of entrance. And during the ceremony, the sea became still and there was no wind, and it seemed that all things were hushed in expectation of the nameless visitor. But after all was done, and the last word had been repeated by Oigos and me, we stood and waited vainly for a visible sign or other manifestation. The lamps burned stilly; and no shadows fell, other than were cast by ourselves and Oigos and by the great marble women along the walls. And in the magic mirrors we had placed cunningly, to reflect those that were otherwise unseen, we beheld no breath or trace of any image.

At this, after a given interim, Avyctes was sorely disappointed, deeming that the evocation had failed of its purpose; and I, having the same thought, was secretly relieved. We questioned the mummy of Oigos, to learn if he had perceived in the room, with such senses as are peculiar to the dead, the sure token or doubtful proof of a presence undescried by us the living. And the mummy gave a necromantic answer, saying that there was nothing.

'Verily,' said Avyctes, 'it were useless to wait longer. For surely in some way we have misunderstood the purport of the writing, or have failed to duplicate the matters used in the evocation, or the correct intonement of the words. Or it may be that in the lapse of so many eons, the thing that was formerly wont to respond has long ceased to exist, or has altered in its attributes, so that the spell is now void and valueless.'

To this I assented readily, hoping that the matter was at an end. And afterward we resumed our habitual studies, but made no mention to each other of the strange tablet or the vain formula.

Even as before, our days went on; and the sea climbed and roared in white fury on the cliffs; and the winds wailed by in their unseen, sullen wrath, bowing the dark cedars as witches are bowed by the breath of Taaran, god of Evil. Almost, in the marvel of new tests and cantraips, I forgot the ineffectual conjuration; and I deemed that Avyctes had forgotten it.

All things were as of yore, to our sorcerous perception; and there was naught to trouble us in our wisdom and power and serenity, which we deemed secure above the sovereignty of kings. Reading the horoscopic stars, we found no future ill in their aspect; nor was any shadow of bale foreshown to us through geomancy, or such other modes of divination as we employed. And our familiars, though grisly and dreadful to mortal gaze, were wholly obedient to us the masters.

Then, on a clear summer afternoon, we walked, as was often our custom, on the marble terrace behind the house. In robes of ocean-purple, we paced among the windy trees with their blown crooked shadows; and there, following us, I saw the blue shadow of Avyctes and my own shadow on the marble; and between them, an adumbration that was not wrought by any of the cedars. And I was greatly startled, but spoke not of the matter to Avyctes, and observed the unknown shadow with covert care.

I saw that it followed closely the master's shadow, keeping ever the same distance. And it fluttered not in the wind, but moved with a flowing as of some heavy, thick and purulent liquid; and its color was not blue nor purple nor black, nor any other hue to which man's eyes are habituated, but a hue as of some darker putrescence than that of death: and its form was altogether monstrous, seeming to move as if cast by one that trod erect, but having the squat head and long, undulant body of things that should creep rather than walk.

Avyctes heeded not the shadow, and still I feared to speak, though I thought it an ill thing for the master to be companioned thus. And I moved closer to him, in order to detect by touch or other perception the invisible presence that had cast the adumbration. But the air was void to sunward of the shadow; and I found nothing opposite the sun nor in any oblique direction, though I searched closely, knowing that certain beings cast their shadows in such wise.

After a while, at the customary hour, we returned by the coiling stairs and monster-flanked portals into the house. And I saw that the strange adumbration moved ever behind the shadow of Avyctes, falling horrible and unbroken on the steps and passing clearly separate and distinct amid the long umbrage of the towering monsters. And in the dim halls beyond the sun, where shadows should not have been, I beheld with terror the loathly, distorted blot, having a pestilential hue without name, that followed Avyctes as if in lieu of his own extinguished shadow. And all that day, everywhere that we went, at the table served by specters, or in the mummy-warded room of volumes and books, the thing pursued Avyctes, clinging to him even as leprosy to the leper. And still the master had perceived it not; and still I forbore to warn him, hoping that the visitant would withdraw in its own time, going obscurely as it had come.

But at midnight, when we sat together by the silver lamps, pondering the blood-writ runes of Hyperborea, I saw that the shadow had drawn closer to the shadow of Avyctes, towering behind his chair on the wall. And the thing was a streaming ooze of charnel pollution, a foulness beyond the black leprosies of hell; and I could bear it no more; and I cried out in my fear and loathing, and informed the master of its presence.

Beholding now the shadow, Avyctes considered it closely; and there was neither fear nor awe nor abhorrence in the deep-graven wrinkles of his visage. And he said to me at last: 'This thing is a mystery beyond my lore: but never, in all the practise of my art, has any shadow come to me unbidden. And since all others of our evocations have found answer ere this, I must deem that the shadow is a very entity, or the shade or sign of an entity, that has come in belated response to the formula of the serpent-sorcerers, which we thought powerless and void. And I think it well that we should now repair to the chamber of conjuration, and interrogate the shadow in such manner as we may.'

We went forthwith into the chamber of conjuration, and made such preparations as were both needful and possible. And when we were prepared to question it, the unknown shadow had drawn closer still to the shadow of Avyctes, so that the clear space between the two was no wider than the thickness of a necromancer's rod.

Now, in all feasible ways, we interrogated the shadow, speaking through our own lips and the lips of mummies and statues. But there was no answer; and calling certain of the devils and phantoms that were our familiars, we made question through the mouths of these, but without result. And all the while, our mirrors were void of any presence that might have cast the shadow; and they that had been our spokesmen could detect nothing in the room. And there was no spell, it seemed, that had power upon the visitant. So Avyctes became troubled; and drawing on the floor with blood and ashes the ellipse of Oumor, wherein no demon nor spirit may intrude, he retired to its center. But still, within the ellipse, like a flowing taint of liquid corruption, the shadow followed his shadow; and the space between the two was no wider than the thickness of a wizard's pen.

On the face of Avyctes, horror had graved new wrinkles; and his brow was beaded with a deathly sweat. For he knew, even as I, that this was a thing beyond all laws, and foreboding naught but untold disaster and evil. And he cried to me in a shaken voice, and said:

'I have no knowledge of this thing nor its intention toward me, and no power to stay its progress. Go forth and leave me now: for I would not that any man should witness the defeat of my sorcery and the doom that may follow thereupon. Also, it were well to depart while there is yet time, lest you too should become the quarry of the shadow . . .'

Though terror had fastened upon my inmost soul, I was loath to leave Avyctes. But I had sworn to obey his will at all times and in every respect; and moreover I knew myself doubly powerless against the adumbration, since Avyctes himself was impotent.

So, bidding him farewell, I went forth with trembling limbs from the haunted chamber; and peering back from the threshold, I saw that the alien umbrage, creeping like a noisome blotch on the floor, had touched the shadow of Avyctes. And at that moment the master shrieked aloud like one in nightmare; and his face was no longer the face of Avyctes but was convulsed and contorted like that of some helpless madman who wrestles with an unseen incubus. And I looked no more, but fled along the dim outer hall and through the portals giving upon the terrace.

A red moon, ominous and gibbous, had declined above the crags; and the shadows of the cedars were elongated in the moon; and they wavered in the gale like the blown cloaks of enchanters. And stooping against the gale, I fled across the terrace toward the outer stairs that led to a steep path in the waste of rocks and chasms lying behind Avyctes' house. I neared the terrace-edge, running with the speed of fear; but I could not reach the topmost outer stair: for at every step the marble flowed beneath me, fleeing like a pale horizon before the seeker. And though I raced and panted without pause, I could draw no nearer to the terrace-edge.

At length I desisted, seeing that an unknown spell had altered the very space around the house of Avyctes, so that none could escape therefrom. So, resigning myself to whatever might befall, I returned toward the house. And climbing the white stairs in the low, level beams of the crag-caught moon, I saw a figure that awaited me in the portals. And I knew by the trailing robe of sea-purple, but by no other token, that the figure was Avyctes. For the face was no longer in its entirety the face of man, but was become a loathly fluid amalgam of human features with a thing not to be identified on earth. The transfiguration was ghastlier than death or decay; and the face was already hued with the nameless, corrupt and purulent color of the strange shadow; and its outlines had assumed a partial likeness to the squat profile of the shadow. The hands of the figure were not those of any terrene being; and the shape beneath the robe had lengthened with a nauseous undulant pliancy; and the face and fingers seemed to drip in the moonlight with a deliquescent corruption. And the pursuing umbrage, like a thickly flowing blight, had corroded and distorted the very shadow of Avyctes, which was now double in a manner not to be narrated here.

Fain would I have cried or spoken aloud: but horror had dried up the font of speech. And the thing that had been Avyctes beckoned me in silence, uttering no word from its living and putrescent lips. And with eyes that were no longer eyes but an oozing abomination, it peered steadily upon me. And it clutched my shoulder closely with the soft leprosy of its fingers, and led me half swooning with revulsion along the hall, and into that room where the mummy of Oigos, who had assisted us in the threefold incantation of the serpent-men, was stationed with several of his fellows.

By the lamps which illumed the chamber, burning with pale, still, perpetual flames, I saw that the mummies stood erect along the wall in their exanimate repose, each in his wonted place, with his tall shadow beside him. But the great, gaunt shadow of Oigos on the wall was companioned by an adumbration similar in all respects to the evil thing that had followed the master and was now incorporate with him. I remembered that Oigos had performed his share of the ritual, and had repeated an unknown stated word in turn after Avyctes; and so I knew that the horror had come to Oigos in turn and would wreak itself upon the dead even as upon the living. For the foul, anonymous thing that we had called in our presumption could manifest itself to mortal ken in no other way than this. We had drawn it from fathomless deeps of time and space, using ignorantly a dire formula; and the thing had come at its own chosen hour, to stamp itself in abomination uttermost on the evocators.

Since then, the night had ebbed away, and a second day has gone by like a sluggish ooze of horror . . . I have seen the complete identification of the shadow with the flesh and the shadow of Avyctes . . . and also I have seen the slow encroachment of that other umbrage, mingling itself with the lank shadow and the sere, bituminous body of Oigos, and turning them to a similitude of the thing which Avyctes has become. And I have heard the mummy cry out like a living man in great pain and fear, as with the throes of a second dissolution, at the impingement of the shadow. And long since it has grown silent, like the other horror, and I know not its thoughts or its intent . . . And verily I know not if the thing that has come to us be one or several; nor if its avatar will rest complete with the three that summoned it forth into time, or be extended to others.

But these things, and much else, I shall soon know: for now, in turn, there is a shadow that follows mine, drawing ever closer. The air congeals and curdles with unknown fear; and they that were our familiars have fled from the mansion; and the great marble women seem to tremble visibly where they stand along the walls. But the horror that was Avyctes, and the second horror that was Oigos, have left me not, and neither do they tremble. With eyes that are not eyes, they seem to brood and watch, waiting till I too shall become as they. And their stillness is more terrible than if they had rended me limb from limb. And there are strange voices in the wind, and alien roarings upon the sea; and the walls quiver like a thin veil in the black breath of remote abysses.

So, knowing that the time is brief, I have shut myself in the room of volumes and books and have written this account. And I have taken the bright triangular tablet, whose solution was our undoing, and have cast it from the window into the sea, hoping that none will find it after us. And now I must make an end, and enclose this writing in the sealed cylinder of orichalchum, and fling it forth to drift upon the sea-wave. For the space between my shadow and the shadow of the horror is straitened momently . . . and the space is no wider than the thickness of a wizard's pen.

THE MARK OF THE BEAST

Rudyard Kipling

[1865–1936]

'*Recent British literature, besides including the three or four greatest fantaisistes of the present age, has been gratifyingly fertile in the element of the weird. Rudyard Kipling has often approached it, and has, despite the omnipresent mannerisms, handled it with indubitable mastery in such tales as* The Phantom Rickshaw, The Finest Story in the World, The Recrudescence of Imray, *and* The Mark of the Beast. *This latter is of particular poignancy; the pictures of the naked leper-priest who mewed like an otter, of the spots which appeared on the chest of the man that priest cursed, of the growing carnivorousness of the victim and of the fear which horses began to display toward him, and of the eventually half-accomplished transformation of that victim into a leopard, being things which no reader is ever likely to forget.*'

– H.P. Lovecraft

Your Gods and my Gods – do you or I know which are the stronger?

Native Proverb

EAST OF SUEZ, SOME HOLD, the direct control of providence ceases; man being there handed over to the power of the gods and devils of Asia, and the Church of England providence only exercising an occasional and modified supervision in the case of Englishmen.

This theory accounts for some of the more unnecessary horrors of life in India: it may be stretched to explain my story.

My friend Strickland of the police who knows as much of natives of India as is good for any man, can bear witness to the facts of the case. Dumiose, our doctor, also saw what Strickland and I saw. The inference which he drew from the evidence was entirely incorrect. He is dead now; he died in a rather dubious manner, which has been elsewhere described.

When Fleete came to India he owned a little money and some land in the Himalayas, near a place called Dharmsala. Both properties had been left him by an uncle, and he came out to finance them. He was a big, heavy, genial and inoffensive man. His knowledge of natives was, of course, limited, and he complained of the difficulties of the language.

He rode in from his place in the hills to spend New Year in the station, and he stayed with Strickland. On New Year's Eve there was a big dinner at the club, and the night was excusably wet. When men foregather from the uttermost ends of the Empire, they have a right to be riotous. The Frontier had sent down a contingent of 'Catch-'em-Alive-O's' who had not seen twenty white faces for a year, and were used to riding fifteen miles to dinner at the next fort at the risk of a Khyberee bullet where their drink should lie. They profited by their new security, for they tried to play pool with a curled up hedgehog found in the garden, and one of them carried the marker round the room in his teeth. Half a dozen planters had come in from the south and were talking 'horse' to the biggest liar in Asia, who was trying to cap all their stories at once. Everybody was there, and there was a general closing up of ranks and taking stock of our losses in dead or disabled that had fallen during the past year. It was a very wet night, and I remember that we sang 'Auld Lang Syne' with our feet in the Polo Championship Cup, and our heads among the stars, and swore that we were all dear friends. Then some of us went away and annexed Burma, and some tried to open up the Soudan and were opened up by Fuzzies in that cruel scrub outside Suakim, and some found stars and medals, and some were married, which was bad, and some did other things which were worse, and the others of us stayed in our chains and strove to make money on insufficient experiences.

Fleete began the night with sherry and bitters, drank champagne steadily up to dessert, then raw, rasping Capri with all the strength of whisky, took Benedictine with his coffee, four or five whiskys and sodas to improve his pool strokes, beer and bones at half past two, winding up with old brandy. Consequently, when he came out, at half past three in the morning, into fourteen degrees of frost, he was very angry with his horse for coughing, and tried to leapfrog into the saddle. The horse broke away and went to his stables; so Strickland and I formed a guard of dishonour to take Fleete home.

Our road lay through the bazaar, close to a little temple of Hanuman, the monkey-god, who is a leading divinity worthy of respect. All gods have good points, just as have all priests. Personally I attach much importance to Hanuman, and am kind to his people – the great grey apes of the hills. One never knows when one may want a friend.

There was a light in the temple, and as we passed we could hear voices of men chanting hymns. In a native temple the priests rise at all hours of the night to do honour to their god. Before we could stop him, Fleete dashed up the steps, patted two priests on the back, and was gravely grinding the ashes of his cigar butt into the forehead of the red stone image of Hanuman. Strickland tried to drag him out, but he sat down and said solemnly:

'Shee that? Mark of the B-beasht! *I* made it. Ishn't it fine?'

In half a minute the temple was alive and noisy, and Strickland, who knew what came of polluting gods, said that things might occur. He, by virtue of his official position, long residence in the country, and weakness for going among the natives, was known to the priests, and he felt unhappy. Fleete sat on the ground and refused to move. He said that 'good old Hanuman' made a very soft pillow.

Then, without any warning, a silver man came out of a recess behind the image of the god. He was perfectly naked in that bitter, bitter cold, and his body shone like frosted silver, for he was what the Bible calls 'a leper as white as snow'. Also he had no face, because he was a leper of some years' standing, and his disease was heavy upon him. We two stooped to haul Fleete up, and the temple was filling and filling with folk who seemed to spring from the earth, when the silver man ran in under our arms, making a noise exactly like the mewing of an otter, caught Fleete round the body and dropped his head on Fleete's breast before we could wrench him away. Then he retired to a corner and sat mewing while the crowd blocked all the doors.

The priests were very angry until the silver man touched Fleete. That nuzzling seemed to sober them.

At the end of a few minutes' silence one of the priests came to Strickland and said, in perfect English, 'Take your friend away. He has done with Hanuman, but Hanuman has not done with him.' The crowd gave room and we carried Fleete into the road.

Strickland was very angry. He said that we might all three have been knifed, and that Fleete should thank his stars that he had escaped without injury.

Fleete thanked no one. He said that he wanted to go to bed. He was gorgeously drunk.

We moved on, Strickland silent and wrathful, until Fleete was taken with violent shivering fits and sweating. He said that the smells of the bazaar were overpowering, and he wondered why slaughter-houses were permitted so near English residences. 'Can't you smell the blood?' said Fleete.

We put him to bed at last, just as the dawn was breaking, and Strickland invited me to have another whisky and soda. While we were drinking he talked of the trouble at the temple, and admitted that it baffled him completely. Strickland hates being mystified by natives, because his business in life is to overmatch them with their own weapons. He has not yet succeeded in doing this, but in fifteen or twenty years he will have made some small progress.

'They should have mauled us,' he said, 'instead of mewing at us. I wonder what they meant. I don't like it one little bit.'

I said that the managing committee of the temple would in all probability bring a criminal action against us for insulting their religion. There was a section of the Indian Penal Code which exactly met Fleete's offence. Strickland said he only hoped and prayed that they would do this. Before I left I looked into Fleete's room, and saw him lying on his right side, scratching his left breast. Then I went to bed, cold, depressed, and unhappy, at seven o'clock in the morning.

At one o'clock I rode over to Strickland's house to enquire after Fleete's head. I imagined it would be a sore one. Fleete was break-fasting and seemed unwell. His temper was gone, for he was abusing the cook for not supplying him with an underdone chop. A man who can eat raw meat after a wet night is a curiosity. I told Fleete this, and he laughed.

'You breed queer mosquitoes in these parts,' he said. 'I've been bitten to pieces, but only in one place.'

'Let's have a look at the bite,' said Strickland. 'It may have gone down since this morning.'

While the chops were being cooked, Fleete opened his shirt and showed us, just over his left breast, a mark, the perfect double of the black rosettes – the five or six irregular blotches arranged in a circle – on a leopard's hide. Strickland looked and said, 'It was only pink this morning. It's gone black now.'

Fleete ran to a glass.

'By Jove!' he said, 'this is nasty. What is it?'

We could not answer. Here the chops came in, all red and juicy, and Fleete bolted three in a most offensive manner. He ate on his right grinders only, and threw his head over his right shoulder as he snapped the meat. When he had finished, it struck him that he had been behaving strangely, for he said apologetically, 'I don't think I ever felt so hungry in my life. I've bolted like an ostrich.'

After breakfast Strickland said to me, 'Don't go. Stay here, and stay for the night.'

Seeing that my house was not three miles from Strickland's, this request was absurd. But Strickland insisted, and was going to say something when Fleete interrupted by declaring in a shamefaced way that he felt hungry again. Strickland sent a man to my house to fetch over my bedding and a horse, and we three went down to Strickland's stables to pass the hours until it was time to go out for a ride. The man who has a weakness for horses never wearies of inspecting them; and when two men are killing time in this way they gather knowledge and lies, the one from the other.

There were five horses in the stables, and I shall never forget the scene as we tried to look them over. They seemed to have gone mad. They reared and screamed and nearly tore up their pickets; they sweated and shivered and lathered and were distraught with fear. Strickland's horses used to know him as well as his dogs; which made the matter more curious. We left the stables for fear of the brutes throwing themselves in their panic. Then Strickland turned back and called me. The horses were still frightened, but they let us 'gentle' and make much of them, and put their heads in our bosoms.

'They aren't afraid of *us*,' said Strickland. 'D'you know, I'd give three months' pay if Outrage here could talk.'

But Outrage was dumb, and could only cuddle up to his master and blow out his nostrils, as is the custom of horses when they wish to explain things but can't. Fleete came up when we were in the stalls, and as soon as the horses saw him their fright broke out afresh. It was all we could do to escape from the place unkicked. Strickland said, 'They don't seem to love you, Fleete.'

'Nonsense,' said Fleete; 'my mare will follow me like a dog.' He went to her; she was in a loose box; but as he slipped the bars she plunged, knocked him down, and broke away into the garden. I laughed, but Strickland was not amused. He took his moustache in both fists, and pulled at it till it nearly came out. Fleete, instead of going off to chase his property, yawned, saying that he felt sleepy. He went to the house to lie down, which was a foolish way of spending New Year's Day.

Strickland sat with me in the stables and asked if I had noticed anything peculiar in Fleete's manner. I said that he ate his food like a beast; but that this might have been the result of living alone in the hills out of the reach of society as refined and elevating as ours, for instance. Strickland was not amused. I do not think that he listened to me, for his next sentence referred to the mark on Fleete's breast, and I said that it might have been caused by blister flies, or that it was possibly a birthmark newly born and now visible for the first time. We both agreed that it was unpleasant to look at, and Strickland found occasion to say that I was a fool.

'I can't tell you what I think now,' said he, 'because you would call me a madman; but you must stay with me for the next few days, if you can. I want you to watch Fleete, but don't tell me what you think till I have made up my mind.'

'But I am dining out tonight,' I said.

'So am I,' said Strickland, 'and so is Fleete. At least if he doesn't change his mind.'

We walked about the garden smoking, but saying nothing – because we were friends, and talking spoils good tobacco – till our pipes were out. Then we went to wake up Fleete. He was wide awake and fidgeting about his room.

'I say, I want some more chops,' he said. 'Can I get them?'

We laughed and said, 'Go and change. The ponies will be round in a minute.'

'All right,' said Fleete. 'I'll go when I get the chops – underdone ones, mind.'

He seemed to be quite in earnest. It was four o'clock, and we had breakfast at one; still, for a long time, he demanded those underdone chops. Then he changed into riding clothes and went out onto the verandah. His pony – the mare had not been caught – would not let him come near. All three horses were unmanageable – mad with fear – and finally Fleete said that he would stay at home and get something to eat. Strickland and I rode out wondering. As we passed the temple of Hanuman, the silver man came out and mewed at us.

'He is not one of the regular priests of the temple,' said Strickland. 'I think I should peculiarly like to lay my hands on him.'

There was no spring in our gallop on the race course that evening. The horses were stale, and moved as though they had been ridden out.

'The fright after breakfast has been too much for them,' said Strickland.

That was the only remark he made through the remainder of the ride. Once or twice I think he swore to himself; but that did not count.

We came back in the dark at seven o'clock, and saw that there were no lights in the bungalow. 'Careless ruffians my servants are!' said Strickland.

My horse reared at something on the carriage-drive and Fleete stood up under its nose.

'What are you doing, grovelling about the garden?' said Strickland.

But both horses bolted and nearly threw us. We dismounted by the stables and returned to Fleete, who was on his hands and knees under the orange-bushes.

'What the devil's wrong with you?' said Strickland.

'Nothing, nothing in the world,' said Fleete, speaking very quickly and thickly. 'I've been gardening – botanizing, you know. The smell of the earth is delightful. I think I'm going for a walk – long walk – all night.'

Then I saw that there was something excessively out of order somewhere, and I said to Strickland, 'I am not dining out.'

'Bless you!' said Strickland. 'Here, Fleete, get up. You'll catch fever there. Come in to dinner and let's have the lamps lit. We'll all dine at home.'

Fleete stood up unwillingly, and said, 'No lamps – no lamps. It's much nicer here. Let's dine outside and have some more chops – lots of 'em and underdone – bloody ones with gristle.'

Now a December evening in Northern India is bitterly cold, and Fleete's suggestion was that of a maniac.

'Come in,' said Strickland sternly. 'Come in at once.'

Fleete came, and when the lamps were brought, we saw that he was literally plastered with dirt from head to foot. He must have been rolling in the garden. He shrank from the light and went to his room. His eyes were horrible to look at. There was a green light behind them, not in them, if you understand, and the man's lower lip hung down.

Strickland said, 'There is going to be trouble – big trouble – tonight. Don't you change your riding things.'

We waited and waited for Fleete's reappearance, and ordered dinner in the meantime. We could hear him moving about his own room, but there was no light there. Presently from the room came the long-drawn howl of a wolf.

People write and talk lightly of blood running cold and hair standing up and things of that kind. Both sensations are too horrible to be trifled with. My heart stopped as though a knife had been driven through it, and Strickland turned as white as the table-cloth.

The howl was repeated and was-answered by another howl far across the fields.

That set the gilded roof on the horror. Strickland dashed into Fleete's room. I followed, and we saw Fleete getting out of the window. He made beast noises in the back of his throat. He could not answer us when we shouted at him. He spat.

I don't quite remember what followed, but I think that Strickland must have stunned him with the long boot-jack or else I should never have been able to sit on his chest. Fleete could not speak, he could only snarl, and his snarls were those of a wolf, not of a man. The human spirit must have been giving way all day and have died out with the twilight. We were dealing with a beast that had once been Fleete.

The affair was beyond any human and rational experience. I tried to say 'Hydrophobia', but the word wouldn't come, because I knew I was lying.

We bound this beast with leather thongs of the punkah-rope, and tied its thumbs and big toes together, and gagged it with a shoe horn, which makes a very efficient gag if you know how to arrange it. Then we carried it into the dining-room and sent a man to Dumoise, the doctor, telling him to come over at once. After we had despatched the messenger and were drawing breath, Strickland said, 'It's no good. This isn't any doctor's work.' I, also, knew that he spoke the truth.

The beast's head was free, and it threw it about from side to side. Anyone entering the room would have believed that we were curing a wolf's pelt. That was the most loathsome accessory of all.

Strickland sat with his chin in the heel of his fist, watching the beast as it wriggled on the ground, but saying nothing. The shirt had been torn open in the scuffle and showed the black rosette mark on the left breast. It stood out like a blister.

In the silence of the watching we heard something without, mewing like a she-otter. We both rose to our feet, and, I answer for myself, not Strickland, felt sick – actually and physically sick. We told each other, as did the men in 'Pingafore', that it was the cat.

Dumoise arrived, and I never saw a little man so unprofessionally shocked. He said that it was a heartrending case of hydrophobia and that nothing could be done. At least any palliative measures would only prolong the agony. The beast was foaming at the mouth. Fleete, as we told Dumoise, had been bitten by dogs once or twice. Any man who keeps half a dozen terriers must expect a nip now and again. Dumoise could offer no help. He could only certify that Fleete was dying of hydrophobia. The beast was then howling, for it had managed to spit out the shoe horn. Dumoise said that he would be ready to certify to the cause of death, and that the end was certain. He was a good little man, and he offered to remain with us; but Strickland refused the kindness. He did not wish to poison Dumoise's New Year. He would only ask him not to give the real cause of Fleete's death to the public.

So Dumoise left, deeply agitated; and as soon as the noise of the cartwheels had died away, Strickland told me, in a whisper, his suspicions. They were so wildly improbable that he dared not say them aloud; and I, who entertained all Strickland's beliefs, was so ashamed of owning to them that I pretended to disbelieve.

'Even if the silver man had bewitched Fleete for polluting the image of Hanuman, the punishment could not have fallen so quickly.'

As I was whispering this the cry outside the house rose again, and the beast fell into a fresh paroxysm of struggling till we were afraid that the thongs that held it would give way.

'Watch!' said Strickland. 'If this happens six times I shall take the law into my own hands. I order you to help me.'

He went into his room and came out in a few minutes with the barrels of an old shotgun, a piece of fishing-line, some thick cord, and his heavy wooden bedstead. I reported that the convulsions had followed the cry by two seconds in each case, and the beast seemed perceptibly weaker.

Strickland muttered, 'But he can't take away the life! He can't take away the life!'

I said, though I knew that I was arguing against myself, 'It may be a cat. It must be a cat. If the silver man is responsible, why does he dare to come here?'

Strickland arranged the wood on the hearth, put the gun-barrels into the glow of the fire, spread the twine on the table, and broke a walking-stick in two. There was one yard of fishing-line, gut, lapped with wire, such as is used for *mahseer*-fishing, and he tied the two ends together in a loop.

Then he said, 'How can we catch him? He must be taken alive and unhurt.'

I said that we must trust in Providence, and go out softly with polo-sticks into the shrubbery at the front of the house. The man or animal that made the cry was evidently moving round the house as regularly as a night-watchman. We could wait in the bushes till he came by, and knock him over.

Strickland accepted this suggestion, and we slipped out from a bathroom window onto the front verandah and then across the carriage-drive into the bushes.

In the moonlight we could see the leper coming round the corner of the house. He was perfectly naked, and from time to time he mewed and stopped to dance with his shadow. It was an unattractive sight, and thinking of poor Fleete, brought to such degradation by so foul a creature, I put away all my doubts and resolved to help Strickland from the heated gun-barrels to the loop of twine – from the loins to the head and back again – with all tortures that might be needful.

The leper halted in the front porch for a moment and we jumped out on him with the sticks. He was wonderfully strong, and we were afraid that he might escape or be fatally injured before we caught him. We had an idea that lepers were frail creatures, but this proved to be incorrect. Strickland knocked his legs from under him, and I put my foot on his neck. He mewed hideously, and even through my riding-boots I could feel that his flesh was not the flesh of a clean man.

He struck at us with his hand and feet stumps. We looped the lash of a dog-whip round him, under the armpits, and dragged him backwards into the hall and so into the dining-room where the beast lay. There we tied him with trunk-straps. He made no attempt to escape, but mewed.

When we confronted him with the beast the scene was beyond description. The beast doubled backwards into a bow, as though he had been poisoned with strychnine, and moaned in the most pitiable fashion. Several other things happened also, but they cannot be put down here.

'I think I was right,' said Strickland. 'Now we will ask him to cure this case.'

But the leper only mewed. Strickland wrapped a towel round his hand and took the gun-barrels out of the fire. I put the half of the broken walking-stick through the loop of fishing-line and buckled the leper comfortably to Strickland's bedstead. I understood then how men and women and little children can endure to see a witch burnt alive; for the beast was moaning on the floor, and though the silver man had no face, you could see horrible feelings passing through the slab that took its place, exactly as waves of heat play across red-hot iron gun-barrels for instance.

Strickland shaded his eyes with his hands for a moment, and we got to work. This part is not to be printed.

The dawn was beginning to break when the leper spoke. His mewings had not been satisfactory up to that point. The beast had fainted from exhaustion, and the house was very still. We unstrapped the leper and told him to take away the evil spirit. He crawled to the beast and laid his hand upon the left breast. That was all. Then he fell face down and whined, drawing in his breath as he did so.

We watched the face of the beast, and saw the soul of Fleete coming back into the eyes. Then a sweat broke out on the forehead, and the eyes – they were human eyes – closed. We waited for an hour, but Fleete still slept. We carried him to his room and bade the leper go, giving him the bedstead, and the sheet on the bedstead to cover his nakedness, the gloves and the towels with which we had touched him, and the whip that had been hooked round his body. He put the sheet about him and went out into the early morning without speaking or mewing.

Strickland wiped his face and sat down. A night-gong, far away in the city, made seven o'clock.

'Exactly four-and-twenty hours!' said Strickland. 'And I've done enough to ensure my dismissal from the service, besides permanent quarters in a lunatic asylum. Do you believe that we are awake?'

The red-hot gun-barrel had fallen on the floor and was singeing the carpet. The smell was entirely real.

That morning at eleven we two together went to wake up Fleete. We looked and saw that the black leopard-rosette on his chest had disappeared. He was very drowsy and tired, but as soon as he saw us, he said, 'Oh! Confound you fellows. Happy New Year to you. Never mix your liquors. I'm nearly dead.'

'Thanks for your kindness, but you're over time,' said Strickland. 'Today is the morning of the second. You've slept the clock round with a vengeance.'

The door opened, and little Dumoise put his head in. He had come on foot, and fancied that we were laying out Fleete.

'I've brought a nurse,' said Dumoise. 'I suppose that she can come in for . . . what is necessary.'

'By all means,' said Fleete cheerily, sitting up in bed. 'Bring on your nurses.'

Dumoise was dumb. Strickland led him out and explained that there must have been a mistake in the diagnosis. Dumoise remained dumb and left the house hastily. He considered that his professional reputation had been injured, and was inclined to make a personal matter of the recovery. Strickland went out too. When he came back, he said that he had been to call on the temple of Hanuman to offer redress for the pollution of the god, and had been solemnly assured that no white man had ever touched the idol, and that he was an incarnation of all the virtues labouring under a delusion. 'What do you think?' said Strickland.

I said. 'There are more things . . .'

But Strickland hates that quotation. He says that I have worn it threadbare.

One other curious thing happened which frightened me as much as anything in all the night's work. When Fleete was dressed he came into the dining-room and sniffed. He had a quaint trick of moving his nose when he sniffed. 'Horrid doggy smell, here,' said he. 'You should really keep those terriers of yours in better order. Try sulphur, Strick.'

But Strickland did not answer. He caught hold of the back of a chair, and, without warning, went into an amazing fit of hysterics. It is terrible to see a strong man overtaken with hysteria. Then it struck me that we had fought for Fleete's soul with the silver man in that room, and that we had disgraced ourselves as Englishmen for ever, and I laughed and gasped and gurgled just as shamefully as Strickland, while Fleete thought that we had both gone mad. We never told him what we had done.

Some years later, when Strickland had married and was a church-going member of society for his wife's sake, we reviewed the incident dispassionately, and Strickland suggested that I should put it before the public.

I cannot myself see that this step is likely to clear up the mystery; because, in the first place, no one will believe a rather unpleasant story, and, in the second, it is well known to every right-minded man that the gods of the heathen are stone and brass, and any attempt to deal with them otherwise is justly condemned.

NEGOTIUM PERAMBULANS

E. F. Benson

[1867–1940]

'*The weird short story has fared well of late, an important contributor being the versatile E.F. Benson . . . Mr. Benson's volume,* Visible and Invisible, *contains several stories of singular power; notably* Negotium Perambulans, *whose unfolding reveals an abnormal monster from an ancient ecclesiastical panel which performs an act of miraculous vengeance in a lonely village on the Cornish coast.*'

– H.P. Lovecraft

THE CASUAL TOURIST IN West Cornwall may just possibly have noticed, as he bowled along over the bare high plateau between Penzance and the Land's End, a dilapidated signpost pointing down a steep lane and bearing on its battered finger the faded inscription 'Polearn 2 miles,' but probably very few have had the curiosity to traverse those two miles in order to see a place to which their guide-books award so cursory a notice. It is described there, in a couple of unattractive lines, as a small fishing village with a church of no particular interest except for certain carved and painted wooden panels (originally belonging to an earlier edifice), which form an altar-rail. But the church at St. Creed (the tourist is reminded) has a similar decoration far superior in point of preservation and interest, and thus even the ecclesiastically disposed are not lured to Polearn. So meagre a bait is scarce worth swallowing, and a glance at the very steep lane which in dry weather presents a carpet of sharp-pointed stones, and after rain a muddy water-course, will almost certainly decide him not to expose his motor or his bicycle to risks like these in so sparsely populated a district. Hardly a house has met his eye since he left Penzance, and the possible trundling of a punctured bicycle for half a dozen weary miles seems a high price to pay for the sight of a few painted panels.

Polearn, therefore, even in the high noon of the tourist season, is little liable to invasion, and for the rest of the year I do not suppose that a couple of folk a day traverse those two miles (long ones at that) of steep and stony gradient. I am not forgetting the postman in this exiguous estimate, for the days are few when, leaving his pony and cart at the top of the hill, he goes as far as the village, since but a few hundred yards down the lane there stands a large white box, like a sea-trunk, by the side of the road, with a slit for letters and a locked door. Should he have in his wallet a registered letter or be the bearer of a parcel too large for insertion in the square lids of the sea-trunk, he must needs trudge down the hill and deliver the troublesome missive, leaving it in person on the owner, and receiving some small reward of coin or refreshment for his kindness. But such occasions are rare, and his general routine is to take out of the box such letters as may have been deposited there, and insert in their place such letters as he has brought. These will be called for, perhaps that day or perhaps the next, by an emissary from the Polearn post-office. As for the fishermen of the place, who, in their export trade, constitute the chief link of movement between Polearn and the outside world, they would not dream of taking their catch up the steep lane and so, with six miles farther of travel, to the market at Penzance. The sea route is shorter and easier, and they deliver their wares to the pier-head. Thus, though the sole industry of Polearn is sea-fishing, you will get no fish there unless you have bespoken your requirements to one of the fishermen. Back come the trawlers as empty as a haunted house, while their spoils are in the fish-train that is speeding to London.

Such isolation of a little community, continued, as it has been, for centuries, produces isolation in the individual as well, and nowhere will you find greater independence of character than among the people of Polearn. But they are linked together, so it has always seemed to me, by some mysterious comprehension: it is as if they had all been initiated into some ancient rite, inspired and framed by forces visible and invisible. The winter storms that batter the coast, the vernal spell of the spring, the hot, still summers, the season of rains and autumnal decay, have made a spell which, line by line, has been communicated to them, concerning the powers, evil and good, that rule the world, and manifest themselves in ways benignant or terrible . . .

I came to Polearn first at the age of ten, a small boy, weak and sickly, and threatened with pulmonary trouble. My father's business kept him in London, while for me abundance of fresh air and a mild climate were considered essential conditions if I was to grow to manhood. His sister had married the vicar of Polearn, Richard Bolitho, himself native to the place, and so it came about that I spent three years, as a paying guest, with my relations. Richard Bolitho owned a fine house in the place, which he inhabited in preference to the vicarage, which he let to a young artist, John Evans, on whom the spell of Polearn had fallen, for from year's beginning to year's end he never left it. There was a solid roofed shelter, open on one side to the air, built for me in the garden, and here I lived and slept, passing scarcely one hour of the twenty-four behind walls and windows. I was out on the bay with the fisher-folk, or wandering along the gorse-clad cliffs that climbed steeply to right and left of the deep combe where the village lay, or pottering about on the pier-head, or bird's-nesting in the bushes with boys of the village. Except on Sunday and for the few daily hours of my lessons, I might do what I pleased so long as I remained in the open air. About the lessons there was nothing formidable; my uncle conducted me through flowering bypaths among the thickets of arithmetic, and made pleasant excursions into the elements of Latin grammar, and above all, he made me daily give him an account, in clear and grammatical sentences, of what had been occupying my mind or my movements. Should I select to tell him about a walk along the cliffs, my speech must be orderly, not vague, slip-shod notes of what I had observed. In this way, too, he trained my observation, for he would bid me tell him what flowers were in bloom, and what birds hovered fishing over the sea or were building in the bushes. For that I owe him a perennial gratitude, for to observe and to express my thoughts in the clear spoken word became my life's profession.

But far more formidable than my weekday tasks was the prescribed routine for Sundays. Some dark embers compounded of Calvinism and mysticism smouldered in my uncle's soul, and made it a day of terror. His sermon in the morning scorched us with a foretaste of the eternal fires reserved for unrepentant sinners, and he was hardly less terrifying at the children's service in the afternoon. Well do I remember his exposition of the doctrine of guardian angels. A child, he said, might think himself secure in such angelic care, but let him beware of committing any of those numerous offences which would cause his guardian to turn his face from him, for as sure as there were angels to protect us, there were also evil and awful presences which were ready to pounce; and on them he dwelt with peculiar gusto. Well, too, do I remember in the morning sermon his commentary on the carved panels of the altar-rails to which I have already alluded. There was the angel of the Annunciation there, and the angel of the Resurrection, but not less was there the witch of Endor, and, on the fourth panel, a scene that concerned me most of all. This fourth panel (he came down from his pulpit to trace its time-worn features) represented the lych-gate of the church-yard at Polearn itself, and indeed the resemblance when thus pointed out was remarkable. In the entry stood the figure of a robed priest holding up a cross, with which he faced a terrible creature like a gigantic slug, that reared itself up in front of him. That, so ran my uncle's interpretation, was some evil agency, such as he had spoken about to us children, of almost infinite malignity and power, which could alone be combated by firm faith and a pure heart. Below ran the legend '*Negotium perambulans in tenebris*' from the ninety-first Psalm. We should find it translated there, 'the pestilence that walketh in darkness,' which but feebly rendered the Latin. It was more deadly to the soul than any pestilence that can only kill the body: it was the Thing, the Creature, the Business that trafficked in the outer Darkness, a minister of God's wrath on the unrighteous . . .

I could see, as he spoke, the looks which the congregation exchanged with each other, and knew that his words were evoking a surmise, a remembrance. Nods and whispers passed between them, they understood to what he alluded, and with the inquisitiveness of boyhood I could not rest till I had wormed the story out of my friends among the fisher-boys, as, next morning, we sat basking and naked in the sun after our bathe. One knew one bit of it, one another, but it pieced together into a truly alarming legend. In bald outline it was as follows:

A church far more ancient than that in which my uncle terrified us every Sunday had once stood not three hundred yards away, on the shelf of level ground below the quarry from which its stones were hewn. The owner of the land had pulled this down, and erected for himself a house on the same site out of these materials, keeping, in a very ecstasy of wickedness, the altar, and on this he dined and played dice afterwards. But as he grew old some black melancholy seized him, and he would have lights burning there all night, for he had deadly fear of the darkness. On one winter evening there sprang up such a gale as was never before known, which broke in the windows of the room where he had supped, and extinguished the lamps. Yells of terror brought in his servants, who found him lying on the floor with the blood streaming from his throat. As they entered some huge black shadow seemed to move away from him, crawled across the floor and up the wall and out of the broken window.

'There he lay a-dying,' said the last of my informants, 'and him that had been a great burly man was withered to a bag o' skin, for the critter had drained all the blood from him. His last breath was a scream, and he hollered out the same words as passon read off the screen.'

'*Negotium perambulans in tenebris*,' I suggested eagerly.

'Thereabouts. Latin anyhow.'

'And after that?' I asked.

'Nobody would go near the place, and the old house rotted and fell in ruins till three years ago, when along comes Mr. Dooliss from Penzance, and built the half of it up again. But he don't care much about such critters, nor about Latin neither. He takes his bottle of whisky a day and gets drunk's a lord in the evening. Eh, I'm gwine home to my dinner.'

Whatever the authenticity of the legend, I had certainly heard the truth about Mr. Dooliss from Penzance, who from that day became an object of keen curiosity on my part, the more so because the quarry-house adjoined my uncle's garden. The Thing that walked in the dark failed to stir my imagination, and already I was so used to sleeping alone in my shelter that the night had no terrors for me. But it would be intensely exciting to wake at some timeless hour and hear Mr. Dooliss yelling, and conjecture that the Thing had got him.

But by degrees the whole story faded from my mind, overscored by the more vivid interest of the day, and, for the last two years of my out-door life in the vicarage garden, I seldom thought about

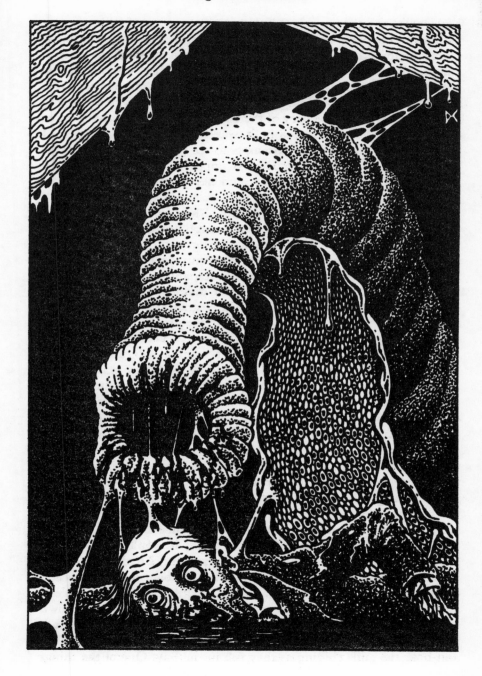

E. F. Benson

Mr. Dooliss and the possible fate that might await him for his temerity
in living in the place where that Thing of darkness had done business.
Occasionally I saw him over the garden fence, a great yellow lump of
a man, with slow and staggering gait, but never did I set eyes on him
outside his gate, either in the village street or down on the beach. He
interfered with none, and no one interfered with him. If he wanted to
run the risk of being the prey of the legendary nocturnal monster, or
quietly drink himself to death, it was his affair. My uncle, so I
gathered, had made several attempts to see him when first he came
to live at Polearn, but Mr. Dooliss appeared to have no use for
parsons, said he was not at home, and never returned the call.

After three years of sun, wind and rain, I had completely outgrown
my early symptoms and had become a tough, strapping youngster of
thirteen. I was sent to Eton and Cambridge, and in due course ate
my dinners and became a barrister. In twenty years from that time I
was earning a yearly income of five figures, and had already laid by
in some securities a sum that brought me dividends which would, for
one of my simple tastes and frugal habits, supply me with all the
material comforts I needed on this side of the grave. The great prizes
of my profession were already within my reach, but I had no
ambition beckoning me on, nor did I want a wife and children,
being, I must suppose, a natural celibate. In fact there was only one
ambition which through these busy years had held the lure of blue
and far-off hills to me, and that was to get back to Polearn, and live
once more isolated from the world with the sea and the gorse-clad
hills for play-fellows, and the secrets that lurked there for explora-
tion. The spell of it had been woven about my heart, and I can truly
say that there had hardly passed a day in all those years in which the
thought of it and the desire for it had been wholly absent from my
mind. Though I had been in frequent communication with my uncle
there during his lifetime, and, after his death, with his widow who
still lived there, I had never been back to it since I embarked on my
profession, for I knew that if I went there, it would be a wrench
beyond my power to tear myself away again. But I had made up my
mind that when once I had provided for my own independence, I
would go back there not to leave it again. And yet I did leave it
again, and now nothing in the world would induce me to turn down
the lane from the road that leads from Penzance to the Land's End,
and see the sides of the combe rise steep above the roofs of the village
and hear the gulls chiding as they fish in the bay. One of the things

invisible, of the dark powers, leaped into light, and I saw it with my eyes.

The house where I had spent those three years of boyhood had been left for life to my aunt, and when I made known to her my intention of coming back to Polearn, she suggested that, till I found a suitable house or found her proposal unsuitable, I should come to live with her.

'The house is too big for a lone old woman,' she wrote, 'and I have often thought of quitting and taking a little cottage sufficient for me and my requirements. But come and share it, my dear, and if you find me troublesome, you or I can go. You may want solitude – most people in Polearn do – and will leave me. Or else I will leave you: one of the main reasons of my stopping here all these years was a feeling that I must not let the old house starve. Houses starve, you know, if they are not lived in. They die a lingering death; the spirit in them grows weaker and weaker, and at last fades out of them. Isn't this nonsense to your London notions? . . .'

Naturally I accepted with warmth this tentative arrangement, and on an evening in June found myself at the head of the lane leading down to Polearn, and once more I descended into the steep valley between the hills. Time had stood still apparently for the combe, the dilapidated signpost (or its successor) pointed a rickety finger down the lane, and a few hundred yards farther on was the white box for the exchange of letters. Point after remembered point met my eye, and what I saw was not shrunk, as is often the case with the revisited scenes of childhood, into a smaller scale. There stood the post-office, and there the church and close beside the vicarage, and beyond, the tall shrubberies which separated the house for which I was bound from the road, and beyond that again the grey roofs of the quarry-house, damp and shining with the moist evening wind from the sea. All was exactly as I remembered it, and, above all that sense of exclusion and isolation. Somewhere above the tree-tops climbed the lane which joined the main road to Penzance, but all that had become immeasurably distant. The years that had passed since I last turned in at the well-known gate faded like a frosty breath, and vanished in this warm, soft air. There were law-courts somewhere in memory's dull book which, if I cared to turn the pages, would tell me that I had made a name and a great income there. But the dull book was closed now, for I was back in Polearn, and the spell was woven around me again.

And if Polearn was unchanged, so too was Aunt Hester, who met me at the door. Dainty and china-white she had always been, and the years had not aged but only refined her. As we sat and talked after dinner she spoke of all that had happened in Polearn in that score of years, and yet somehow the changes of which she spoke seemed but to confirm the immutability of it all. As the recollection of names came back to me, I asked her about the quarry-house and Mr. Dooliss, and her face gloomed a little as with the shadow of a cloud on a spring day.

'Yes, Mr. Dooliss,' she said, 'poor Mr. Dooliss, how well I remember him, though it must be ten years and more since he died. I never wrote to you about it, for it was all very dreadful, my dear, and I did not want to darken your memories of Polearn. Your uncle always thought that something of the sort might happen if he went on in his wicked, drunken ways, and worse than that, and though nobody knew exactly what took place, it was the sort of thing that might have been anticipated.'

'But what more or less happened, Aunt Hester?' I asked.

'Well, of course, I can't tell you everything, for no one knew it. But he was a very sinful man, and the scandal about him at Newlyn was shocking. And then he lived, too, in the quarry-house . . . I wonder if by any chance you remember a sermon of your uncle's when he got out of the pulpit and explained that panel in the altar-rails, the one, I mean, with the horrible creature rearing itself up outside the lych-gate?'

'Yes, I remember it perfectly,' said I.

'Ah. It made an impression on you, I suppose, and so it did on all who heard him, and that impression got stamped and branded on us all when the catastrophe occurred. Somehow Mr. Dooliss got to hear about your uncle's sermon, and in some drunken fit he broke into the church and smashed the panel to atoms. He seems to have thought that there was some magic in it, and that if he destroyed that he would get rid of the terrible fate that was threatening him. For I must tell you that before he committed that dreadful sacrilege he had been a haunted man: he hated and feared darkness, for he thought that the creature on the panel was on his track, but that as long as he kept lights burning it could not touch him. But the panel, to his disordered mind, was the root of his terror, and so, as I said, he broke into the church and attempted – you will see why I said "attempted" – to destroy it. It certainly was found in splinters next morning, when your uncle went into church for matins, and knowing Mr. Dooliss's fear of the panel, he went across to the quarry-house afterwards and taxed him with its destruction. The man never denied it; he boasted of what he had done. There he sat, though it was early morning, drinking his whisky.

' "I've settled your Thing for you," he said, "and your sermon too. A fig for such superstitions."

'Your uncle left him without answering his blasphemy, meaning to go straight into Penzance and give information to the police about this outrage to the church, but on his way back from the quarry-house he went into the church again, in order to be able to give details about the damage, and there in the screen was the panel, untouched and uninjured. And yet he had himself seen it smashed, and Mr. Dooliss had confessed that the destruction of it was his work. But there it was, and whether the power of God had mended it or some other power, who knows?'

This was Polearn indeed, and it was the spirit of Polearn that made me accept all Aunt Hester was telling me as attested fact. It had happened like that. She went on in her quiet voice.

'Your uncle recognised that some power beyond police was at work, and he did not go to Penzance or give information about the outrage, for the evidence of it had vanished.'

A sudden wave of scepticism swept over me.

'There must have been some mistake,' I said. 'It hadn't been broken . . .'

She smiled.

'Yes, my dear, but you have been in London so long,' she said. 'Let me, anyhow, tell you the rest of my story. That night, for some reason, I could not sleep. It was very hot and airless; I dare say you will think that the sultry conditions accounted for my wakefulness. Once and again, as I went to the window to see if I could not admit more air, I could see from it the quarry-house, and I noticed the first time that I left my bed that it was blazing with lights. But the second time I saw that it was all in darkness, and as I wondered at that, I heard a terrible scream, and the moment afterwards the steps of someone coming at full speed down the road outside the gate. He yelled as he ran; "Light, light!" he called out. "Give me light, or it will catch me!" It was very terrible to hear that, and I went to rouse my husband, who was sleeping in the dressing-room across the passage. He wasted no time, but by now the whole village was aroused by the screams, and when he got down to the pier he found that all was over. The tide was low, and on the rocks at its foot was lying the body of Mr. Dooliss. He must have cut some artery when he fell on those sharp edges of

stone, for he had bled to death, they thought, and though he was a big
burly man, his corpse was but skin and bones. Yet there was no pool of
blood round him, such as you would have expected. Just skin and
bones as if every drop of blood in his body had been sucked out of
him!'

She leaned forward.

'You and I, my dear, know what happened,' she said, 'or at least
can guess. God has His instruments of vengeance on those who bring
wickedness into places that have been holy. Dark and mysterious are
His ways.'

Now what I should have thought of such a story if it had been told
me in London I can easily imagine. There was such an obvious
explanation: the man in question had been a drunkard, what wonder
if the demons of delirium pursued him? But here in Polearn it was
different.

'And who is in the quarry-house now?' I asked. 'Years ago the
fisher-boys told me the story of the man who first built it and of his
horrible end. And now again it has happened. Surely no one has
ventured to inhabit it once more?'

I saw in her face, even before I asked this question, that somebody
had done so.

'Yes, it is lived in again,' said she, 'for there is no end to blindness
. . . I don't know if you remember him. He was tenant of the vicarage
many years ago.'

'John Evans,' said I.

'Yes. Such a nice fellow he was too. Your uncle was pleased to get so
good a tenant. And now – '

She rose.

'Aunt Hester, you shouldn't leave your sentences unfinished,' I
said.

She shook her head.

'My dear, that sentence will finish itself,' she said. 'But what a time
of night! I must go to bed, and you too, or they will think we have to
keep lights burning here through the dark hours.'

Before getting into bed I drew my curtains wide and opened all the
windows to the warm tide of the sea air that flowed softly in. Looking
out into the garden I could see in the moonlight the roof of the shelter,
in which for three years I had lived, gleaming with dew. That, as
much as anything, brought back the old days to which I had now
returned, and they seemed of one piece with the present, as if no gap
of more than twenty years sundered them. The two flowed into one

like globules of mercury uniting into a softly shining globe of mysterious lights and reflections. Then, raising my eyes a little, I saw against the black hill-side the windows of the quarry-house still alight.

Morning, as is so often the case, brought no shattering of my illusion. As I began to regain consciousness, I fancied that I was a boy again waking up in the shelter of the garden, and though, as I grew more widely awake, I smiled at the impression, that on which it was based I found to be indeed true. It was sufficient now as then to be here, to wander again on the cliffs, and hear the popping of the ripened seed-pods on the gorse-bushes; to stray along the shore to the bathing-cove, to float and drift and swim in the warm tide, and bask on the sand, and watch the gulls fishing, to lounge on the pier-head with the fisher-folk, to see in their eyes and hear in their quiet speech the evidence of secret things not so much known to them as part of their instincts and their very being. There were powers and presences about me; the white poplars that stood by the stream that babbled down the valley knew of them, and showed a glimpse of their knowledge sometimes, like the gleam of their white under leaves; the very cobbles that paved the street were soaked in it . . . All that I wanted was to lie there and grow soaked in it too; unconsciously, as a boy, I had done that, but now the process must be conscious. I must know what stir of forces, fruitful and mysterious, seethed along the hill-side at noon, and sparkled at night on the sea. They could be known, they could even be controlled by those who were masters of the spell, but never could they be spoken of, for they were dwellers in the innermost, grafted into the eternal life of the world. There were dark secrets as well as these clear, kindly powers, and to these no doubt belonged the *negotium perambulans in tenebris* which, though of deadly malignity, might be regarded not only as evil, but as the avenger of sacrilegious and impious deeds . . . All this was part of the spell of Polearn, of which the seeds had long lain dormant in me. But now they were sprouting, and who knew what strange flower would unfold in their stems?

It was not long before I came across John Evans. One morning, as I lay on the beach, there came shambling across the sand a man stout and middle-aged with the face of Silenus. He paused as he drew near and regarded me from narrow eyes.

'Why, you're the little chap that used to live in the parson's garden,' he said. 'Don't you recognise me?'

I saw who it was when he spoke: his voice, I think, instructed me, and recognising it, I could see the features of the strong, alert young man in this gross caricature.

'Yes, you're John Evans,' I said. 'You used to be very kind to me: you used to draw pictures for me.'

'So I did, and I'll draw you some more. Been bathing? That's a risky performance. You never know what lives in the sea, nor what lives on the land for that matter. Not that I heed them. I stick to work and whisky. God. I've learned to paint since I saw you, and drink too for that matter. I live in the quarry-house, you know, and it's a powerful thirsty place. Come and have a look at my things if you're passing. Staying with your aunt, are you? I could do a wonderful portrait of her. Interesting face; she knows a lot. People who live at Polearn get to know a lot, though I don't take much stock in that sort of knowledge myself.'

I do not know when I have been at once so repelled and interested. Behind the mere grossness of his face there lurked something which while it appalled, yet fascinated me. His thick lisping speech had the same quality. And his paintings, what would they be like? . . .

'I was just going home,' I said. 'I'll gladly come in, if you'll allow me.'

He took me through the untended and overgrown garden into the house which I had never yet entered. A great grey cat was sunning itself in the window, and an old woman was laying lunch in a corner of the cool hall into which the door opened. It was built of stone, and the carved mouldings let into the walls, the fragments of gargoyles and sculptured images, bore testimony of the truth of its having been built out of the demolished church. In one corner was an oblong and carved wooden table littered with a painter's apparatus and stacks of canvases leaned against the walls.

He jerked his thumb towards a head of an angel that was built into the mantelpiece and giggled.

'Quite a sanctified air,' he said, 'so we tone it down for the purposes of ordinary life by a different sort of art. Have a drink? No? Well, turn over some of my pictures while I put myself to rights.'

He was justified in his own estimate of his skill: he could paint (and apparently he could paint anything), but never have I seen pictures so inexplicably hellish. There were exquisite studies of trees, and you knew something lurked in the flickering shadows. There was a drawing of his cat sunning itself in the window, even as I had just now seen it, and yet it was no cat but some beast of awful malignity. There was a boy stretched naked on the sands, not human, but some evil thing which had come out of the sea. Above all there were pictures of his garden overgrown and jungle-like, and you knew that in the bushes were presences ready to spring out on you . . .

'Well, do you like my style?' he said as he came up, glass in hand. (The tumbler of spirits that he held had not been diluted.) 'I try to paint the essence of what I see, not the mere husk and skin of it, but its nature, where it comes from and what gave it birth. There's much in common between a cat and a fuchsia-bush if you look at them closely enough. Everything came out of the slime of the pit, and it's all going back there. I should like to do a picture of you some day. I'd hold the mirror up to Nature, as the old lunatic said.'

After this first meeting I saw him occasionally throughout the months of that wonderful summer. Often he kept to his house and to his painting for days together, and then perhaps some evening I would find him lounging on the pier, always alone, and every time we met thus the repulsion and interest grew, for every time he seemed to have gone further along a path of secret knowledge toward some evil shrine where complete initiation awaited him . . . And then suddenly the end came.

I had met him thus one evening on the cliffs while the October sunset still burned in the sky, but over it with amazing rapidity there spread from the west a great blackness of cloud such as I have never seen for denseness. The light was sucked from the sky, the dusk fell in ever thicker layers. He suddenly became conscious of this.

'I must get back as quick as I can,' he said. 'It will be dark in a few minutes, and my servant is out. The lamps will not be lit.'

He stepped out with extraordinary briskness for one who shambled and could scarcely lift his feet, and soon broke out into a stumbling run. In the gathering darkness I could see that his face was moist with the dew of some unspoken terror.

'You must come with me,' he panted, 'for so we shall get the lights burning the sooner. I cannot do without light.'

I had to exert myself to the full to keep up with him, for terror winged him, and even so I fell behind, so that when I came to the garden gate, he was already half-way up the path to the house. I saw him enter, leaving the door wide, and found him fumbling with matches. But his hand so trembled that he could not transfer the light to the wick of the lamp.

'But what's the hurry about?' I asked.

Suddenly his eyes focused themselves on the open door behind me, and he jumped from his seat beside the table which had once been the altar of God, with a gasp and a scream.

'No, no!' he cried. 'Keep it off! . . .'

I turned and saw what he had seen. The Thing had entered and now was swiftly sliding across the floor towards him, like some gigantic caterpillar. A stale phosphorescent light came from it, for though the dusk had grown to blackness outside, I could see it quite distinctly in the awful light of its own presence. From it too there came an odour of corruption and decay, as from slime that has long lain below water. It seemed to have no head, but on the front of it was an orifice of puckered skin which opened and shut and slavered at the edges. It was hairless, and slug-like in shape and in texture. As it advanced its forepart reared itself from the ground, like a snake about to strike, and it fastened on him . . .

At that sight, and with the yells of his agony in my ears, the panic which had struck me relaxed into a hopeless courage, and with palsied, impotent hands I tried to lay hold of the Thing. But I could not: though something material was there, it was impossible to grasp it; my hands sunk in it as in thick mud. It was like wrestling with a nightmare.

I think that but a few seconds elapsed before all was over. The screams of the wretched man sank to moans and mutterings as the Thing fell on him: he panted once or twice and was still. For a moment longer there came gurglings and sucking noises, and then it slid out even as it had entered. I lit the lamp which he had fumbled with, and there on the floor he lay, no more than a rind of skin in loose folds over projecting bones.

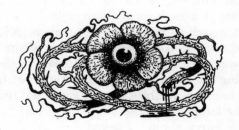

MRS. LUNT

Hugh Walpole

[1884–1941]

'*Hugh Walpole, of the same family as the founder of Gothic fiction, has sometimes approached the bizarre with much success, his short story* Mrs. Lunt *carrying a very poignant shudder.*'

– H.P. Lovecraft

'DO YOU BELIEVE IN GHOSTS?' I asked Runciman. I had to ask him this very platitudinous question more because he was so difficult a man to spend an hour with rather than for any other reason. You know his books, perhaps, or more probably you don't know them – *The Running Man*, *The Elm Tree*, and *Crystal and Candlelight*. He is one of those little men who are constant enough in this age of immense overproduction of books, men who publish every autumn their novel, who arouse by that publication in certain critics eager appreciation and praise, who have a small and faithful public, whose circulation is very small indeed, who, when you meet them, have little to say, are often shy and nervous, pessimistic and remote from daily life. Such men do fine

work, are made but little of in their own day, and perhaps fifty years
after their death are rediscovered by some digging critic and become
a sort of cult with a new generation.

I asked Runciman that question because, for some unknown
reason, I had invited him to dinner at my flat, and was now faced
with a long evening filled with that most tiresome of all conversations,
talk that dies every two minutes and has to be revived with terrific
exertions. Being myself a critic, and having on many occasions praised
Runciman's work, he was the more nervous and shy with me; had I
abused it, he would perhaps have had plenty to say – he was that kind
of man. But my question was a lucky one: it roused him instantly, his
long, bony body became full of a new energy, his eyes stared into a
rich and exciting reminiscence, he spoke without pause, and I took
care not to interrupt him. He certainly told me one of the most
astounding stories I have ever heard. Whether it was true or not I
cannot, of course, say: these ghost stories are nearly always at second
or third hand. I had, at any rate, the good fortune to secure mine from
the source. Moreover, Runciman was not a liar: he was too serious for
that. He himself admitted that he was not sure, at this distance of
time, as to whether the thing had gained as the years passed.
However, here it is as he told it.

'It was some fifteen years ago,' he said. 'I went down to Cornwall to
stay with Robert Lunt. Do you remember his name? No, I suppose
you do not. He wrote several novels; some of those half-and-half
things that are not quite novels, not quite poems, rather mystical and
picturesque, and are the very devil to do well. De la Mare's *Return* is a
good example of the kind of thing. I had reviewed somewhere his last
book, and reviewed it favourably, and received from him a really
touching letter showing that the man was thirsting for praise, and
also, I fancied, for company. He lived in Cornwall somewhere on the
sea coast, and his wife had died some two years before; he said he was
quite alone there, and would I come and spend Christmas with him;
he hoped I would not think this impertinent; he expected that I would
be engaged already, but he could not resist the chance. Well, I wasn't
engaged; far from it. If Lunt was lonely, so was I; if Lunt was a failure,
so was I; I was touched, as I have said, by his letter, and I accepted his
invitation. As I went down in the train to Penzance I wondered what
kind of a man he would be. I had never seen any photographs of him;
he was not the sort of author whose picture the newspapers publish.
He must be, I fancied, about my own age – perhaps rather older. I
know when we're lonely how some of us are for ever imagining that a

friend will somewhere turn up, that ideal friend who will understand
all one's feelings, who will give one affection without being sentimental, who will take an interest in one's affairs without being
impertinent – yes, the sort of friend one never finds.

'I fancy that I became quite romantic about Lunt before I reached
Penzance. We would talk, he and I, about all those literary questions
that seemed to me at that time so absorbing; we would, perhaps, often
stay together and even travel abroad on those little journeys that are
so swiftly melancholy when one is alone, so delightful when one has a
perfect companion. I imagined him as sparse and delicate and
refined, with a sort of wistfulness and rather childish play of fancy.
We had both, so far, failed in our careers, but perhaps together we
would do great things.

'When I arrived at Penzance it was almost dark, and the snow,
threatened all day by an overhanging sky, had begun gently and
timorously to fall. He had told me in his letter that a fly would be at the
station to take me to his house; and there I found it – a funny old
weather-beaten carriage with a funny old weather-beaten driver. At
this distance of time my imagination may have created many things,
but I fancy that from the moment I was shut into that carriage some
dim suggestion of fear and apprehension attacked me. I fancy that I
had some absurd impulse to get out of the thing and take the night train
back to London again – an action that would have been very unlike
me, as I had always a sort of obstinate determination to carry through
anything that I had begun. In any case, I was uncomfortable in that
carriage; it had, I remember, a nasty, musty smell of damp straw and
stale eggs, and it seemed to confine me so closely as though it were
determined that, once I was in, I should never get out again. Then, it
was bitterly cold; I was colder during that drive than I have ever been
before or since. It was that penetrating cold that seems to pierce your
very brain, so that I could not think with any clearness, but only wish
again and again that I hadn't come. Of course, I could see nothing –
only feel the jolt over the uneven road – and once and again we seemed
to fight our way through dark paths, because I could feel the overhanging branches of the trees knock against the cab with mysterious
taps, as though they were trying to give me some urgent message.

'Well, I mustn't make more of it than the facts allow, and I mustn't
see into it all the significance of the events that followed. I only know
that as the drive proceeded I became more and more miserable:
miserable with the cold of my body, the misgivings of my imagination, the general loneliness of my case.

'At last we stopped. The old scarecrow got slowly off his box, with many heavings and sighings, came to the cab door, and, with great difficulty and irritating slowness, opened it. I got out of it, and found that the snow was now falling very heavily indeed, and that the path was lightened with its soft, mysterious glow. Before me was a humped and ungainly shadow: the house that was to receive me. I could make nothing of it in that darkness, but only stood there shivering while the old man pulled at the doorbell with a sort of frantic energy as though he were anxious to be rid of the whole job as quickly as possible and return to his own place. At last, after what seemed an endless time, the door opened, and an old man, who might have been own brother to the driver, poked out his head. The two old men talked together, and at last my bag was shouldered and I was permitted to come in out of the piercing cold.

'Now this, I know, is not imagination. I have never at any period of my life hated at first sight so vigorously any dwelling-place into which I have entered as I did that house. There was nothing especially disagreeable about my first vision of the hall. It was a large, dark place, lit by two dim lamps, cold and cheerless; but I got no particular impression of it because at once I was conducted out of it, led along a passage, and then introduced into a room which was, I saw at once, as warm and comfortable as the hall had been dark and dismal. I was, in fact, so eagerly pleased at the large and leaping fire that I moved towards it at once, not noting, at the first moment, the presence of my host; and when I did see him I could not believe that it was he. I have told you the kind of man that I had expected; but, instead of the sparse, sensitive artist, I found facing me a large burly man, over six foot, I should fancy, as broad-shouldered as he was tall, giving evidence of great muscular strength, the lower part of his face hidden by a black, pointed beard.

'But if I was astonished at the sight of him, I was double amazed when he spoke. His voice was thin and piping, like that of some old woman, and the little nervous gestures that he made with his hands were even more feminine than his voice. But I had to allow, perhaps, for excitement, for excited he was; he came up to me, took my hand in both of his, and held it as though he would never let it go. In the evening, when we sat over our port, he apologized for this. "I was so glad to see you," he said; "I couldn't believe that really you would come; you are the first visitor of my own kind that I have had here for ever so long. I was ashamed indeed of asking you, but I had to snatch at the chance – it means so much to me."

'His eagerness, in fact, had something disturbing about it; something pathetic, too. He simply couldn't do too much for me: he led me through funny crumbling old passages, the boards creaking under us at every step, up some dark stairs, the walls hung, so far as I could see in the dim light, with faded yellow photographs of places, and showed me into my room with a deprecating agitated gesture as though he expected me at the first sight of it to turn and run. I didn't like it any more than I liked the rest of the house; but that was not my host's fault. He had done everything he possibly could for me: there was a large fire flaming in the open fireplace, there was a hot bottle, as he explained to me, in the big four-poster bed, and the old man who had opened the door to me was already taking my clothes out of my bag and putting them away. Lunt's nervousness was almost sentimental. He put both his hands on my shoulders and said, looking at me pleadingly: "If only you knew what it is for me to have you here, the talks we'll have. Well, well, I must leave you. You'll come down and join me, won't you, as soon as you can?"

'It was then, when I was left alone in my room, that I had my second impulse to flee. Four candles in tall old silver candlesticks were burning brightly, and these, with the blazing fire, gave plenty of light; and yet the room was in some way dim, as though a faint smoke pervaded it, and I remember that I went to one of the old lattice windows and threw it open for a moment as though I felt stifled. Two things quickly made me close it. One was the intense cold which, with a fluttering scamper of snow, blew into the room; the other was the quite deafening roar of the sea, which seemed to fling itself at my very face as though it wanted to knock me down. I quickly shut the window, turned round, and saw an old woman standing just inside the door. Now every story of this kind depends for its interest on its verisimilitude. Of course, to make my tale convincing I should be able to prove to you that I saw that old woman; but I can't. I can only urge upon you my rather dreary reputation of probity. You know that I'm a teetotaller, and always have been, and, most important evidence of all, I was not expecting to see an old woman; and yet I hadn't the least doubt in the world but that it was an old woman I saw. You may talk about shadows, clothes hanging on the back of the door, and the rest of it. I don't know. I've no theories about this story, I'm not a spiritualist. I don't know that I believe in anything especially, except the beauty of beautiful things. We'll put it, if you like, that I fancied that I saw an old woman, and my fancy was so strong that I can give you to this day a pretty detailed account of her appearance. She wore a black silk dress and on her breast was a large, ugly, gold brooch; she had black hair, brushed back from her forehead and parted down the middle; she wore a collar of some white stuff round her throat; her face was one of the wickedest, most malignant, and furtive that I have ever seen – very white in colour. She was shrivelled enough now, but might once have been rather beautiful. She stood there quietly, her hands at her side. I thought that she was some kind of housekeeper. "I have everything I want, thank you," I said. "What a splendid fire!" I turned for a moment towards it, and when I looked back she was gone. I thought nothing of this, of course, but drew up an old chair covered with green faded tapestry, and thought that I would read a little from some book that I had brought down with me before I went to join my host. The fact was that I was not very intent upon joining him before I must. I didn't like him, I had already made up my mind that I would find some excuse to return to London as soon as possible. I can't tell you why I didn't like him, except that I was myself very reserved and had, like many Englishmen, a great distrust of demonstrations, especially from another man. I hadn't cared for the way in which he had put his hands on my shoulders, and I felt perhaps that I wouldn't be able to live up to all his eager excitement about me.

'I sat in my chair and took up my book, but I had not been reading for more than two minutes before I was conscious of a most unpleasant smell. Now, there are all sorts of smells – healthy and otherwise – but I think the nastiest is that chilly odour that comes from bad sanitation and stuffy rooms combined; you meet it sometimes at little country inns and decrepit town lodgings. This smell was so definite that I could almost locate it; it came from near the door. I got up, approached the door, and at once it was as though I were drawing near to somebody who, if you'll forgive the impoliteness, was not accustomed to taking too many baths. I drew back just as I might had an actual person been there. Then, quite suddenly, the smell was gone, the room was fresh, and I saw, to my surprise, that one of the windows had opened and that snow was again blowing in. I closed it and went downstairs.

'The evening that followed was odd enough. My host was not in himself an unlikeable man; he did his very utmost to please me. He had a fine culture and a wide knowledge of books and things. He became quite cheerful as the evening went on; gave me a good dinner in a funny little old dining-room hung with some admirable mezzotints. The old serving man looked after us – a funny old man, with a long white beard like a goat – and, oddly enough, it was from him that I first recaught my earlier apprehension. He had just put the dessert on the table, had arranged my plate in front of me, when I saw him give a start and look towards the door. My attention was attracted to this because his hand, as it touched the plate, suddenly trembled. My eyes followed, but I could see nothing. That he was frightened of something was perfectly clear, and then (it may, of course, very easily have been fancy) I thought that I detected once more that strange unwholesome smell.

'I forgot this again when we were both seated in front of a splendid fire in the library. Lunt had a very fine collection of books, and it was delightful to him, as it is to every book collector, to have somebody with him who could really appreciate them. We stood looking at one book after another and talking eagerly about some of the minor early English novelists who were my especial hobby – Bage, Godwin, Henry Mackenzie, Mrs. Shelley, Mat Lewis, and others – when once again he affected me most unpleasantly by putting his arm round my shoulders. I have all my life disliked intensely to be touched by certain people. I suppose we all feel like this. It is one of those inexplicable things; and I disliked this so much that I abruptly drew away.

'Instantly he was changed into a man of furious and ungovernable rage; I thought that he was going to strike me. He stood there quivering all over, the words pouring out of his mouth incoherently, as though he were mad and did not know what he was saying. He accused me of insulting him, of abusing his hospitality, of throwing his kindness back into his face, and of a thousand other ridiculous things; and I can't tell you how strange it was to hear all this coming out in that shrill, piping voice as though it were from an agitated woman, and yet to see with one's eyes that big, muscular frame, those immense shoulders, and that dark bearded face.

'I said nothing. I am, physically, a coward. I dislike, above anything else in the world, any sort of quarrel. At last I brought out, 'I am very sorry. I didn't mean anything. Please forgive me,' and then hurriedly turned to leave the room. At once he changed again; now he was almost in tears. He implored me not to go; said it was his wretched temper, but that he was so miserable and unhappy, and had for so long now been alone and desolate that he hardly knew what he was doing. He begged me to give him another chance, and if I would only listen to his story, I would perhaps be more patient with him.

'At once, so oddly is man constituted, I changed in my feelings towards him. I was very sorry for him. I saw that he was a man on the edge of his nerves, and that he really did need some help and sympathy, and would be quite distracted if he could not get it. I put my hand on his shoulder to quieten him and to show him that I bore no malice, and I felt that his great body was quivering from head to foot. We sat down again, and in an odd, rambling manner he told me his story. It amounted to very little, and the gist of it was that, rather to have some sort of companionship than from any impulse of passion, he had married some fifteen years before the daughter of a neighbouring clergyman. They had had no very happy life together, and at the last, he told me quite frankly, he had hated her. She had been mean, overbearing, and narrow-minded; it had been, he confessed, nothing but a relief to him when, just a year ago, she had suddenly died from heart failure. He had thought, then, that things would go better with him, but they had not; nothing had gone right with him since. He hadn't been able to work, many of his friends had ceased to come to see him, he had found it even difficult to get servants to stay with him, he was desperately lonely, he slept badly – that was why his temper was so terribly on edge. He had no one in the house with him save the old man, who was, fortunately, an excellent cook, and a boy – the old man's grandson. 'Oh, I thought,' I said, 'that that excellent meal tonight was cooked by your housekeeper.' 'My housekeeper?' he answered. 'There's no woman in the house.' 'Oh, but one came to my room,' I replied, 'this evening – an old ladylike looking person in a black silk dress.' 'You were mistaken,' he answered in the oddest voice, as though he were exerting all the strength that he possessed to keep himself quiet and controlled. 'I am sure that I saw her,' I answered. 'There couldn't be any mistake.' And I described her to him. 'You were mistaken,' he repeated again. 'Don't you see that you must have been when I tell you there is no woman in the house?' I reassured him quickly lest there should be another outbreak of rage. Then there followed the oddest kind of appeal. Urgently, as though his very life depended upon it, he begged me to stay with him for a few days. He implied, although he said nothing definitely, that he was in great trouble, that if only I would stay for a few days all would be well, that if ever in all my life I had had a chance of doing a kind action I had one now, that he couldn't expect me to stop in so dreary a place, but that he would never forget it if I did. He spoke in a voice of such urgent distress that I reassured him as I might a child, promising that I would stay and shaking hands with him on it as though it were a kind of solemn oath between us.

'I am sure that you would wish me to give you this incident as it occurred, and if the final catastrophe seems to come, as it were, accidentally, I can only say to you that that was how it happened. It is since the event that I have tried to put two and two together, and that they don't altogether make four is the fault that mine shares, I suppose, with every true ghost story.

'But the truth is that after that very strange episode between us I had a very good night. I slept the sleep of all justice, cosy and warm, in my four-poster, with the murmur of the sea beyond the windows to rock my slumbers. Next morning, too, was bright and cheerful, the sun sparkling down on the snow, and the snow sparkling back to the sun as though they were glad to see one another. I had a very pleasant morning looking at Lunt's books, talking to him, and writing one or two letters. I must say that, after all, I liked the man. His appeal to me on the night before had touched me. So few people, you see, had ever appealed to me about anything. His nervousness was there and the constant sense of apprehension, yet he seemed to be putting the best face on it, doing his utmost to set me at my ease in order to induce me to stay, I suppose, and to give him a little of that company that he so terribly needed. I dare say if I had not been so busy about the books I would not have been so happy. There was a strange eerie silence about that house if one ever stopped to listen; and once, I remember, sitting at the old bureau writing a letter, I raised my head and looked up, and caught Lunt watching as though he wondered whether I had heard or noticed anything. And so I listened too, and it seemed to me as though someone were on the other side of the library door with their hand raised to knock; a quaint notion, with nothing to support it, but I could have sworn that if I had gone to the door and opened it suddenly someone would have been there.

'However, I was cheerful enough, and after lunch quite happy. Lunt asked me if I would like a walk, and I said I would; and we started out in the sunshine over the crunching snow towards the sea. I don't remember of what we talked; we seemed to be now quite at our ease with one another. We crossed the fields to a certain point, looked down at the sea – smooth now, like silk – and turned back. I remember that I was so cheerful that I seemed suddenly to take a happy view of all my prospects. I began to confide in Lunt, telling him of my little plans, of my hopes for the book that I was then writing, and even began rather timidly to suggest to him that perhaps we should do something together; that what we both needed was a friend of common taste with ourselves. I know that I was talking on, that we had crossed a little village street, and were turning up the path towards the dark avenue of trees that led to his house, when suddenly the change came.

'What I first noticed was that he was not listening to me; his gaze was fixed beyond me, into the very heart of the black clump of trees that fringed the silver landscape. I looked too, and my heart bounded. There was, standing just in front of the trees, as though she were waiting for us, the old woman whom I had seen in my room the night before. I stopped. "Why, there she is!" I said. "That's the old woman of whom I was speaking – the old woman who came to my room." He caught my shoulder with his hand. "There's nothing there," he said. "Don't you see that that's a shadow? What's the matter with you? Can't you see that there's nothing?" I stepped forward, and there was nothing, and I wouldn't, to this day, be able to tell you whether it was hallucination or not. I can only say that, from that moment, the afternoon appeared to become dark. As we entered into the avenue of trees, silently, and hurrying as though someone were behind us, the dusk seemed to have fallen so that I could scarcely see my way. We reached the house breathless. He hastened into his study as though I were not with him, but I followed and, closing the door behind me, said, with all the force that I had at command: "Now, what is this? What is it that's troubling you? You must tell me! How can I help you if you don't?" And he replied, in so strange a voice that it was as though he had gone out of his mind: "I tell you there's nothing! Can't you believe me when I tell you there's nothing at all? I'm quite all right . . . Oh, my God! – my God! . . . don't leave me! . . . This is the very day – the very night she said . . . But I did nothing, I tell you – I did nothing – it's only her beastly malice . . ." He broke off. He still held my arm with his hand. He made strange movements, wiping his forehead as though it were damp with sweat, almost pleading with me; then suddenly angry again, then beseeching once more, as though I had refused him the one thing he wanted.

'I saw that he was truly not far from madness, and I began myself to have a sudden terror of this damp, dark house, this great, trembling man, and something more that was worse than they. But I pitied him. How could you or any man have helped it? I made him sit down in the armchair beside the fire, which had now dwindled to a few glimmering red coals. I let him hold me close to him with his arm and clutch my hand with his, and I repeated, as quietly as I might: "But tell me; don't be afraid, whatever it is you have done. Tell me what danger it is you fear, and then we can face it together." "Fear! Fear!"

he repeated; and then, with a mighty effort which I could not but admire, he summoned all his control. "I'm off my head," he said, "with loneliness and depression. My wife died a year ago on this very night. We hated one another. I couldn't be sorry when she died, and she knew it. When that last heart attack came on, between her gasps she told me that she would return, and I've always dreaded this night. That's partly why I asked you to come, to have anyone here, anybody, and you've been very kind – more kind than I had any right to expect. You must think me insane going on like this, but see me through tonight and we'll have splendid times together. Don't desert me now – now, of all times!" I promised that I would not. I soothed him as best I could. We sat there, for I know not how long, through the gathering dark; we neither of us moved, the fire died out, and the room was lit with a strange dim glow that came from the snowy landscape beyond the uncurtained windows. Ridiculous, perhaps, as I look back at it. We sat there, I in a chair close to his, hand in hand, like a couple of lovers; but, in real truth, two men terrified, fearful of what was coming, and unable to do anything to meet it.

'I think that that was perhaps the strangest part of it; a sort of paralysis that crept over me. What would you or anyone else have done – summoned the old man, gone down to the village inn, fetched the local doctor? I could do nothing, but see the snowshine move like trembling water about the furniture and hear, through the urgent silence, the faint hoot of an owl from the trees in the wood.

'Oddly enough, I can remember nothing, try as I may, between that strange vigil and the moment when I myself, wakened out of a brief sleep, sat up in bed to see Lunt standing inside my room holding a candle. He was wearing a night-shirt, and looked huge in the candlelight, his black beard falling intensely dark on the white stuff of his shirt. He came very quietly towards my bed, the candle throwing flickering shadows about the room. When he spoke it was in a voice low and subdued, almost a whisper. "Would you come," he asked, "only for half an hour – just for half an hour?" he repeated, staring at me as though he didn't know me. "I'm unhappy without somebody – very unhappy." Then he looked over his shoulder, held the candle high above his head, and stared piercingly at every part of the room. I could see that something had happened to him, that he had taken another step into the country of Fear – a step that had withdrawn him from me and from every other human being.

He whispered: "When you come, tread softly; I don't want anyone to hear us." I did what I could. I got out of bed, put on my dressing-gown and slippers, and tried to persuade him to stay with me. The fire was almost dead, but I told him that we would build it up again, and that we would sit there and wait for the morning; but no, he repeated again and again: "It's better in my own room; we're safer there." "Safe from what?" I asked him, making him look at me. "Lunt, wake up! You're as though you were asleep. There's nothing to fear. We've nobody but ourselves. Stay here and let us talk, and have done with this nonsense." But he wouldn't answer; only drew me forward down the dark passage, and then turned into his room, beckoning me to follow. He got into bed and sat hunched up there, his hands holding his knees, staring at the door, and every once and again shivering with a little tremor. The only light in the room was that from the candle, now burning low, and the only sound was the purring whisper of the sea.

'It seemed to make little difference to him that I was there. He did not look at me, but only at the door, and when I spoke to him he did not answer me nor seem to hear what I had said. I sat down beside the bed and, in order to break the silence, talked on about anything, about nothing, and was dropping off, I think, into a confused doze, when I heard his voice breaking across mine. Very clearly and distinctly he said: "If I killed her, she deserved it; she was never a good wife to me, not from the first; she shouldn't have irritated me as she did – she knew what my temper was. She had a worse one than mine, though. She can't touch me; I'm as strong as she is." And it was then, as clearly as I can now remember, that his voice suddenly sank into a sort of gentle whisper, as though he were almost glad that his fears had been confirmed. He whispered: "She's there!" I cannot possibly describe to you how that whisper seemed to let fear loose like water through my body. I could see nothing – the candle was flaming high in the last moments of its life – I could see nothing; but Lunt suddenly screamed, with a shrill cry like a tortured animal in agony: "Keep her off – keep her away from me, keep her off – keep her off!" He caught me, his hands digging into my shoulders; then, with an awful effect of constricted muscles, as though rigor had caught and held him, his arms slowly fell away, he slipped back on to the bed as though someone were pushing him, his hands fell against the sheet, his whole body jerked with a convulsive effort, and then he rolled over. I saw nothing; only, quite distinctly, in my nostrils was that same fetid odour that I had known on the preceding evening. I rushed to the door, opened it, shouted down the long passage again and again, and soon the old man came running. I sent him for the doctor, and then could not return to the room, but stood there listening, hearing nothing save the whisper of the sea, the loud ticking of the hall clock. I flung open the window at the end of the passage; the sea rushed in with its precipitant roar; some bells chimed the hour. Then at last, beating into myself more courage, I turned back towards the room . . .'

'Well?' I asked as Runciman paused. 'He was dead, of course?'

'Dead, the doctor afterwards said, of heart failure.'

'Well?' I asked again.

'That's all.' Runciman paused. 'I don't know whether you can even call it a ghost story. My idea of the old woman may have been all hallucination. I don't even know whether his wife was like that when she was alive. She may have been large and fat. Lunt died of an evil conscience.'

'Yes,' I said.

'The only thing,' Runciman added at last, after a long pause, 'is that on Lunt's body there were marks – on his neck especially, some on his chest – as of fingers pressing in, scratches and dull blue marks. He may, in his terror, have caught at his own throat . . .'

'Yes,' I said again.

'Anyway' – Runciman shivered – 'I don't like Cornwall – beastly country. Queer things happen there – something in the air . . .'

'So I've heard,' I answered. 'And now have a drink. We both will.'

THE HOG

William Hope Hodgson

[1877–1918]

'*Of rather uneven stylistic quality, but vast occasional power in its suggestion of lurking worlds and beings behind the ordinary surface of life, is the work of William Hope Hodgson, known today far less than it deserves to be. Despite a tendency toward conventionally sentimental conceptions of the universe, and of man's relation to it and to his fellows, Mr. Hodgson is perhaps second only to Algernon Blackwood in his serious treatment of unreality. Few can equal him in adumbrating the nearness of nameless forces and monstrous besieging entities through casual hints and insignificant details, or in conveying feelings of the spectral and the abnormal in connection with regions or buildings . . .*

'*Mr. Hodgson's later volume,* Carnacki, the Ghost-Finder, *consists of several longish short stories published many years before in magazines. In quality it falls conspicuously below the level of the other books. We here find a more or less conventional stock figure of the "infallible detective" type – the progeny of M. Dupin and Sherlock Holmes, and the close kin of Algernon Blackwood's John Silence – moving through scenes and events badly marred by an atmosphere of professional "occultism". A few of the episodes, however, are of undeniable power, and afford glimpses of the peculiar genius characteristic of the author.'*

– H.P. Lovecraft

'I SAW SOMETHING WAS RISING up through the middle of the 'defence'. It rose with a steady movement. I saw it pale and huge through the whirling funnel of cloud – a monstrous pallid snout rising out of that unknowable abyss. It rose higher and higher. Through a thinning of the cloud curtain I saw one small eye . . . I shall never see a pig's eye again without feeling something of what I felt then. A pig's eye with a sort of vile understanding shining at the back of it . . .'

I

We had finished dinner and Carnacki had drawn his big chair up to the fire, and started his pipe.

Jessop, Arkright, Taylor and I had each of us taken up our favourite positions, and waited for Carnacki to begin.

'What I'm going to tell you about happened in the next room,' he said, after drawing at his pipe for a while. 'It has been a terrible experience. Doctor Witton first brought the case to my notice. We'd been chatting over a pipe at the Club one night about an article in the *Lancet*, and Witton mentioned having just such a similar case in a man called Bains. I was interested at once. It was one of those cases of a gap or flaw in a man's protection barrier, I call it. A failure to be what I might term efficiently insulated – spiritually – from the outer monstrosities.

'From what I knew of Witton, I knew he'd be no use. You all know Witton. A decent sort, hard-headed, practical, stand-no-kind-of-nonsense sort of man, all right at his own job when that job's a fractured leg or a broken collarbone; but he'd never have made anything of the Bains case.'

For a space Carnacki puffed meditatively at his pipe, and we waited for him to go on with his tale.

'I told Witton to send Bains to me,' he resumed, 'and the following Saturday he came up. A little sensitive man. I liked him as soon as I set eyes on him. After a bit, I got him to explain what was troubling him, and questioned him about what Doctor Witton had called his "dreams."

' "They're more than dreams," he said, "they're so real that they're actual experiences to me. They're simply horrible. And yet there's nothing very definite in them to tell you about. They generally come just as I am going off to sleep. I'm hardly over before suddenly I seem to have got down into some deep, vague place with some inexplicable and frightful horror all about me. I can never understand what it is, for I never see anything, only I always get a sudden knowledge like a warning that I have got down into some terrible place – a sort of hell-place I might call it, where I've no business ever to have wandered; and the warning is always insistent – even imperative – that I must get out, get out, or some enormous horror will come at me."

' "Can't you pull yourself back?" I asked him. "Can't you wake up?" '

' "No," he told me. "That's just what I can't do, try as I will. I can't stop going along this labyrinth-of-hell as I call it to myself, towards some dreadful unknown Horror. The warning is repeated, ever so strongly – almost as if the *live* me of my waking moments was awake and aware. Something seems to warn me to wake up, that whatever I do I *must* wake, wake, and then my consciousness comes suddenly alive and I know that my body is there in the bed, but my essence or spirit is still down there in that hell, wherever it is, in a danger that is both unknown and inexpressible; but so overwhelming that my whole spirit seems sick with terror.

' "I keep saying to myself all the time that I must wake up," he continued, "but it is as if my spirit is still down there, and as if my consciousness knows that some tremendous invisible Power is fighting against me. I know that if I do not wake then, I shall never wake up again, but go down deeper and deeper into some stupendous horror of soul destruction. So then I fight. My body lies in the bed there, and *pulls*. And the power down there in that labyrinth exerts itself too so that a feeling of despair, greater than any I have ever known on this earth, comes on me. I *know* that if I give way and cease to fight, and do *not* wake, then I shall pass out – out to that monstrous Horror which seems to be silently calling my soul to destruction.

' "Then I make a final stupendous effort," he continued, "and my brain seems to fill my body like the ghost of my soul. I can even open my eyes and see with my brain, or consciousness, out of my own eyes. I can see the bedclothes, and I know just how I am lying in the bed; yet the real me is down in that hell in terrible danger. Can you get me?" he asked.

' "Perfectly," I replied.

' "Well, you know," he went on, "I fight and fight. Down there in that great pit my very soul seems to shrink back from the call of some brooding horror that impels it silently a little further, always a little further round a visible corner, which if I once pass I know I shall never return again to this world. Desperately I fight; brain and consciousness fighting together to help it. The agony is so great that I could scream were it not that I am rigid and frozen in the bed with fear.

' "Then, just when my strength seems almost gone, soul and body win, and blend slowly. And I lie there worn out with this terrible extraordinary fight. I have still a sense of a dreadful horror all about me, as if out of that horrible place some brooding monstrosity had followed me up, and hangs still and silent and invisible over me, threatening me there in my bed. Do I make it clear to you?" he asked. "It's like some monstrous Presence."

' "Yes," I said. "I follow you."

'The man's forehead was actually covered with sweat, so keenly did he live again through the horrors he had experienced.

'After a while he continued:

' "Now comes the most curious part of the dream or whatever it is," he said. "There's always a sound I hear as I lie there exhausted in the bed. It comes while the bedroom is still full of the sort of atmosphere of monstrosity that seems to come up with me when I get out of that place. I hear the sound coming up out of that enormous depth, and it is always the noise of pigs – pigs grunting, you know. It's just simply dreadful. The dream is always the same. Sometimes I've had it every single night for a week, until I fight not to go to sleep; but, of course, I have to sleep sometimes. I think that's how a person might go mad, don't you?" he finished.

'I nodded, and looked at his sensitive face. Poor beggar! He had been through it, and no mistake.

' "Tell me some more," I said. "The grunting – what does it sound like exactly?"

' "It's just like pigs grunting," he told me again. "Only much more awful. There are grunts, and squeals and pig-howls, like you hear when their food is being brought to them at a pig farm. You know those large pig farms where they keep hundreds of pigs. All the grunts, squeals and howls blend into one brutal chaos of sound – only it isn't a chaos. It all blends in a queer horrible way. I've heard it. A sort of swinish clamouring melody that grunts and roars and shrieks in chunks of grunting sounds, all tied together with squealings and shot through with pig howls. I've sometimes thought there was a

definite beat in it; for every now and again there comes a gargantuan
GRUNT, breaking through the million pig-voiced roaring – a
stupendous GRUNT that comes in with a beat. Can you understand
me? It seems to shake everything . . . It's like a spiritual earthquake.
The howling, squealing, grunting, rolling clamour of swinish noise
coming up out of that place, and then the monstrous GRUNT rising
up through it all, an ever-recurring beat out of the depth – the voice of
the swine-mother of monstrosity beating up from below through that
chorus of mad swine-hunger . . . It's no use! I can't explain it. No one
ever could. It's just terrible! And I'm afraid you're saying to yourself
that I'm in a bad way; that I want a change or a tonic; that I must
buck up or I'll land myself in a madhouse. If only you could
understand! Doctor Witton seemed to half understand, I thought;
but I know he's only sent me to you as a sort of last hope. He thinks
I'm booked for the asylum. I could tell it."

    ' "Nonsense!" I said. "Don't talk such rubbish. You're as sane as I
am. Your ability to think clearly what you want to tell me, and then
to transmit it to me so well that you compel my mental retina to see
something of what you have seen, stands sponsor for your mental
balance.

    ' "I am going to investigate your case, and if it is what I suspect,
one of those rare instances of a 'flaw' or 'gap' in your protective
barrier (what I might call your spiritual insulation from the Outer
Monstrosities) I've no doubt we can end the trouble. But we've got to
go properly into the matter first, and there will certainly be danger in
doing so."

    ' "I'll risk it," replied Bains. "I can't go on like this any longer."

    ' "Very well," I told him. "Go out now, and come back at five
o'clock. I shall be ready for you then. And don't worry about your
sanity. You're all right, and we'll soon make things safe for you again.
Just keep cheerful and don't brood about it." '

II

'I put in the whole afternoon preparing my experimenting room,
across the landing there, for his case. When he returned at five o'clock
I was ready for him and took him straight into the room.

    'It gets dark now about six-thirty, as you know, and I had just nice
time before it grew dusk to finish my arrangements. I prefer always to
be ready before the dark comes.

'Bains touched my elbow as we walked into the room.

' "There's something I ought to have told you," he said, looking rather sheepish. "I've somehow felt a bit ashamed of it."

' "Out with it," I replied.

'He hesitated a moment, then it came out with a jerk.

' "I told you about the grunting of the pigs," he said. "Well, I grunt too. I know it's horrible. When I lie there in bed and hear those sounds after I've come up, I just grunt back as if in reply. I can't stop myself. I just do it. Something makes me. I never told Doctor Witton that. I couldn't. I'm sure now you think me mad," he concluded.

'He looked into my face, anxious and queerly ashamed.

' "It's only the natural sequence of the abnormal events, and I'm glad you told me," I said, slapping him on the back. "It follows logically on what you had already told me. I have had two cases that in some way resembled yours."

' "What happened?" he asked me. "Did they get better?"

' "One of them is alive and well today, Mr. Bains," I replied. "The other man lost his nerve, and fortunately for all concerned, he is dead."

'I shut the door and locked it as I spoke, and Bains stared round, rather alarmed, I fancy, at my apparatus.

' "What are you going to do?" he asked. "Will it be a dangerous experiment?"

' "Dangerous enough," I answered, "if you fail to follow my instructions absolutely in everything. We both run the risk of never leaving this room alive. Have I your word that I can depend on you to obey me whatever happens?"

'He stared round the room and then back at me.

' "Yes," he replied. And, you know, I felt he would prove the right kind of stuff when the moment came.

'I began now to get things finally in train for the night's work. I told Bains to take off his coat and his boots. Then I dressed him entirely from head to foot in a single thick rubber combination-overall, with rubber gloves, and a helmet with ear-flaps of the same material attached.

'I dressed myself in a similar suit. Then I began on the next stage of the night's preparations.

'First I must tell you that the room measures thirty-nine feet by thirty-seven, and has a plain board floor over which is fitted a heavy, half-inch rubber covering.

'I had cleared the floor entirely, all but the exact centre where I had placed a glass-legged, upholstered table, a pile of vacuum tubes and batteries, and three pieces of special apparatus which my experiment required.

' "Now Bains," I called, "come and stand over here by this table. Don't move about. I've got to erect a protective 'barrier' round us, and on no account must either of us cross over it by even so much as a hand or foot, once it is built."

'We went over to the middle of the room, and he stood by the glass-legged table while I began to fit the vacuum tubing together round us.

'I intended to use the new spectrum "defence" which I have been perfecting lately. This, I must tell you, consists of seven glass vacuum circles with the red on the outside, and the colour circles lying inside it, in the order of orange, yellow, green, blue, indigo and violet.

'The room was still fairly light, but a slight quantity of dusk seemed to be already in the atmosphere, and I worked quickly.

'Suddenly, as I fitted the glass tubes together I was aware of some vague sense of nerve-strain, and glancing round at Bains who was standing there by the table I noticed him staring fixedly before him. He looked absolutely drowned in uncomfortable memories.

' "For goodness' sake stop thinking of those horrors," I called out to him. "I shall want you to think hard enough about them later; but in this specially constructed room it is better not to dwell on things of that kind till the barriers are up. Keep your mind on anything normal or superficial – the theatre will do – think about that last piece you saw at the Gaiety. I'll talk to you in a moment."

'Twenty minutes later the "barrier" was completed all round us, and I connected up the batteries. The room by this time was greying with the coming dusk, and the seven differently coloured circles shone out with extraordinary effect, sending out a cold glare.

' "By Jove!" cried Bains, "that's very wonderful – very wonderful!"

'My other apparatus which I now began to arrange consisted of a specially made camera, a modified form of phonograph with ear-pieces instead of a horn, and a glass disk composed of many fathoms of glass vacuum tubes arranged in a special way. It had two wires leading to an electrode constructed to fit round the head.

'By the time I had looked over and fixed up these three things, night had practically come, and the darkened room shone most strangely in the curious upward glare of the seven vacuum tubes.

' "Now, Bains," I said, "I want you to lie on this table. Now put your hands down by your sides and lie quiet and think. You've just got two things to do," I told him. "One is to lie there and concentrate your thoughts on the details of the dream you are always having, and the other is not to move off this table whatever you see or hear, or whatever happens, unless I tell you. You understand, don't you?"

' "Yes," he answered, "I think you may rely on me not to make a fool of myself. I feel curiously safe with you somehow."

' "I'm glad of that," I replied. "But I don't want you to minimise the possible danger too much. There may be horrible danger. Now, just let me fix this band on your head," I added, as I adjusted the electrode. I gave him a few more instructions, telling him to concentrate his thoughts particularly upon the noises he heard just as he was waking, and I warned him again not to let himself fall asleep. "Don't talk," I said, "and don't take any notice of me. If you find I disturb your concentration keep your eyes closed."

'He lay back and I walked over to the glass disk arranging the camera in front of it on its stand in such a way that the lens was opposite the centre of the disk.

'I had scarcely done this when a ripple of greenish light ran across the vacuum tubes of the disk. This vanished, and for maybe a minute there was complete darkness. Then the green light rippled once more across it – rippled and swung round, and began to dance in varying shades from a deep heavy green to a rank ugly shade; back and forward, back and forward.

'Every half second or so there shot across the varying greens a flicker of yellow, an ugly, heavy repulsive yellow, and then abruptly there came sweeping across the disk a great beat of muddy red. This died as quickly as it came and gave place to the changing greens shot through by the unpleasant and ugly yellow hues. About every seventh second the disk was submerged, and the other colours momentarily blotted out by the great beat of heavy, muddy red which swept over everything.

' "He's concentrating on those sounds," I said to myself, and I felt queerly excited as I hurried on with my operations. I threw a word over my shoulder to Bains.

' "Don't get scared, whatever happens," I said. "You're all right!"

'I proceeded now to operate my camera. It had a long roll of specially prepared paper ribbon in place of a film or plates. By turning the handle the roll passed through the machine exposing the ribbon.

'It took about five minutes to finish the roll, and during all that time the green lights predominated; but the dull heavy beat of muddy red never ceased to flow across the vacuum tubes of the disk at every seventh second. It was like a recurrent beat in some unheard and somehow displeasing melody.

'Lifting the exposed spool of paper ribbon out of the camera I laid it horizontally in the two "rests" that I had arranged for it on my modified gramophone. Where the paper had been acted upon by the varying coloured lights which had appeared on the disk, the prepared surface had risen in curious, irregular little waves.

'I unrolled about a foot of the ribbon and attached the loose end to an empty spool-roller (on the opposite side of the machine) which I had geared to the driving clockwork mechanism of the gramophone. Then I took the diaphragm and lowered it gently into place above the ribbon. Instead of the usual needle the diaphragm was fitted with a beautifully made metal-filament brush, about an inch broad, which just covered the whole breadth of the ribbon. This fine and fragile brush rested lightly on the prepared surface of the paper, and when I started the machine the ribbon began to pass under the brush, and as it passed, the delicate metal-filament "bristles" followed every minute inequality of those tiny, irregular wave-like excrescences on the surface.

'I put the ear-pieces to my ears, and instantly I knew that I had succeeded in actually recording what Bains had heard in his sleep. In fact, I was even then hearing "mentally" by means of his effort of memory. I was listening to what appeared to be the faint, far-off squealing and grunting of countless swine. It was extraordinary, and at the same time exquisitely horrible and vile. It frightened me, with a sense of my having come suddenly and unexpectedly too near to something foul and most abominably dangerous.

'So strong and imperative was this feeling that I twitched the ear-pieces out of my ears, and sat a while staring round the room trying to steady my sensations back to normality.

'The room looked strange and vague in the dull glow of light from the circles, and I had a feeling that a taint of monstrosity was all about me in the air. I remembered what Bains had told me of the feeling he'd always had after coming up out of "that place" – as if some horrible atmosphere had followed him up and filled his bedroom. I understood him perfectly now – so much so that I had mentally used almost his exact phrase in explaining to myself what I felt.

'Turning round to speak to him I saw there was something curious about the centre of the "defence."

'Now, before I tell you fellows any more I must explain that there are certain, what I call "focussing", qualities about this new "defence" I've been trying.

'The Sigsand manuscript puts it something like this: "Avoid diversities of colour; nor stand ye within the barrier of the colour lights; for in colour hath Satan a delight. Nor can he abide in the Deep if ye adventure against him armed with red purple. So be warned. Neither forget that in blue, which is God's colour in the Heavens, ye have safety."

'You see, from that statement in the Sigsand manuscript I got my first notion for this new "defence" of mine. I have aimed to make it a "defence" and yet have "focussing" or "drawing" qualities such as the Sigsand hints at. I have experimented enormously, and I've proved that reds and purples – the two extreme colours of the spectrum – are fairly dangerous; so much so that I suspect they actually "draw" or "focus" the outside forces. Any action or "meddling" on the part of the experimentalist is tremendously enhanced in its effect if the action is taken within barriers composed of these colours, in certain proportions and tints.

'In the same way blue is distinctly a "general defence." Yellow appears to be neutral, and green a wonderful protection within limits. Orange, as far as I can tell, is slightly attractive and indigo is dangerous by itself in a limited way, but in certain combinations with the other colours it becomes a very powerful "defence". I've not yet discovered a tenth of the possibilities of these circles of mine. It's a kind of colour organ upon which I seem to play a tune of colour combinations that can be either safe or infernal in its effects. You know I have a keyboard with a separate switch to each of the colour circles.

'Well, you fellows will understand now what I felt when I saw the curious appearance of the floor in the middle of the "defence." It looked exactly as if a circular shadow lay, not just on the floor, but a few inches above it. The shadow seemed to deepen and blacken at the centre even while I watched it. It appeared to be spreading from the centre outwardly, and all the time it grew darker.

'I was watchful, and not a little puzzled; for the combination of lights that I had switched on approximated a moderately safe "general defence." Understand, I had no intention of making a focus until I had learnt more. In fact, I meant that first investigation not to go beyond a tentative inquiry into the kind of thing I had got to deal with.

'I knelt down quickly and felt the floor with the palm of my hand, but it was quite normal to the feel, and that reassured me that there was no Saaitii mischief abroad; for that is a form of danger which can involve, and make use of, the very material of the "defence" itself. It can materialise out of everything except fire.

'As I knelt there I realised all at once that the legs of the table on which Bains lay were partly hidden in the ever blackening shadow, and my hands seemed to grow vague as I felt at the floor.

'I got up and stood away a couple of feet so as to see the phenomenon from a little distance. It struck me then that there was something different about the table itself. It seemed unaccountably lower.

' "It's the shadow hiding the legs," I thought to myself. "This promises to be interesting; but I'd better not let things go too far."

'I called out to Bains to stop thinking so hard. "Stop concentrating for a bit," I said; but he never answered, and it occurred to me suddenly that the table appeared to be still lower.

' "Bains," I shouted, "stop thinking a moment." Then in a flash I realised it. "Wake up, man! Wake up!" I cried.

'He had fallen over asleep – the very last thing he should have done; for it increased the danger twofold. No wonder I had been getting such good results! The poor beggar was worn out with his sleepless nights. He neither moved nor spoke as I strode across to him.

' "Wake up!" I shouted again, shaking him by the shoulder.

'My voice echoed uncomfortably round the big empty room; and Bains lay like a dead man.

'As I shook him again I noticed that I appeared to be standing up to my knees in the circular shadow. It looked like the mouth of a pit. My legs, from the knees downwards, were vague. The floor under my feet felt solid and firm when I stamped on it; but all the same I had a feeling that things were going a bit too far, so striding across to the switchboard I switched on the "full defence."

'Stepping back quickly to the table I had a horrible and sickening shock. The table had sunk quite unmistakably. Its top was within a couple of feet of the floor, and the legs had that fore-shortened appearance that one sees when a stick is thrust into water. They looked vague and shadowy in the peculiar circle of dark shadows which had such an extraordinary resemblance to the black mouth of a pit. I could see only the top of the table plainly with Bains lying motionless on it; and the whole thing was going down, as I stared, into that black circle.'

III

'There was not a moment to lose, and like a flash I caught Bains round his neck and body and lifted him clean up into my arms off the table. And as I lifted him he grunted like a great swine in my ear.

'The sound sent a thrill of horrible funk through me. It was just as though I held a hog in my arms instead of a human. I nearly dropped him. Then I held his face to the light and stared down at him. His eyes were half opened, and he was looking at me apparently as if he saw me perfectly.

'Then he grunted again. I could feel his small body quiver with the sound.

'I called out to him. "Bains," I said, "can you hear me?"

'His eyes still gazed at me; and then, as we looked at each other, he grunted like a swine again.

'I let go one hand, and hit him across the cheek, a stinging slap.

' "Wake up, Bains!" I shouted. "Wake up!" But I might have hit a corpse. He just stared up at me. And, suddenly I bent lower and looked into his eyes more closely. I never saw such a fixed, intelligent, mad horror as I saw there. It knocked out all my sudden disgust. Can you understand?

'I glanced round quickly at the table. It stood there at its normal height; and, indeed, it was in every way normal. The curious shadow that had somehow suggested to me the black mouth of the pit had vanished. I felt relieved; for it seemed to me that I had entirely broken up any possibility of a partial "focus" by means of the full "defence" which I had switched on.

'I laid Bains on the floor, and stood up to look round and consider what was best to do. I dared not step outside of the barriers, until any "dangerous tensions" there might be in the room had been dissipated. Nor was it wise, even inside the full "defence," to have him sleeping the kind of sleep he was in; not without certain preparations having been made first, which I had not made.

'I can tell you, I felt beastly anxious. I glanced down at Bains, and had a sudden fresh shock; for the peculiar circular shadow was forming all round him again, where he lay on the floor. His hands and face showed curiously vague, and distorted, as they might have looked through a few inches of faintly stained water. But his eyes were somehow clear to see. They were staring up, mute and terrible, at me, through that horrible darkening shadow.

'I stopped, and with one quick lift, tore him up off the floor into my arms, and for the third time he grunted like a swine, there in my arms. It was damnable.

'I stood up, in the barrier, holding Bains, and looked about the room again; then back at the floor. The shadow was still thick round about my feet, and I stepped quickly across to the other side of the table. I stared at the shadow, and saw that it had vanished; then I glanced down again at my feet, and had another shock; for the shadow was showing faintly again, all round where I stood.

'I moved a pace, and watched the shadow become invisible; and then, once more, like a slow stain, it began to grow about my feet.

'I moved again, a pace, and stared round the room, meditating a break for the door. And then, in that instant, I saw that this would be certainly impossible; for there was something indefinite in the atmosphere of the room – something that moved, circling slowly about the barrier.

'I glanced down at my feet, and saw that the shadow had grown thick about them. I stepped a pace to the right, and as it disappeared, I stared again round the big room – and somehow it seemed tremendously big and unfamiliar. I wonder whether you can understand.

'As I stared I saw again the indefinite something that floated in the air of the room. I watched it steadily for maybe a minute. It went twice completely round the barrier in that time. And, suddenly, I saw it more distinctly. It looked like a small puff of black smoke.

'And then I had something else to think about; for all at once I was aware of an extraordinary feeling of vertigo, and in the same moment, a sense of sinking – I was sinking bodily. I literally sickened as I glanced down, for I saw in that moment that I had gone down, almost up to my thighs into what appeared to be actually the shadowy, but quite unmistakable, mouth of a pit. Do you understand? I was sinking down into this thing, with Bains in my arms.

'A feeling of furious anger came over me, and I swung my right boot forward with a fierce kick. I kicked nothing tangible, for I went clean through the side of the shadowy thing, and fetched up against the table, with a crash. I had come through something that made all my skin creep and tingle – an invisible, vague something which resembled an electric tension. I felt that if it had been stronger, I might not have been able to charge through as I had. I wonder if I make it clear to you?

'I whirled round, but the beastly thing had gone; yet even as I stood there by the table, the slow greying of a circular shadow began to form again about my feet.

'I stepped to the other side of the table, and leaned against it for a moment; for I was shaking from head to foot with a feeling of extraordinary horror upon me, that was in some way, different from any kind of horror I have ever felt. It was as if I had in that one moment been near something no human has any right to be near, for his soul's sake. And abruptly, I wondered whether I had not felt just one brief touch of the horror that the rigid Bains was even then enduring as I held him in my arms.

'Outside of the barrier there were now several of the curious little clouds. Each one looked exactly like a little puff of black smoke. They increased as I watched them, which I did for several minutes; but all the time as I watched, I kept moving from one part to another of the "defence", so as to prevent the shadow forming round my feet again.

'Presently, I found that my constant changing of position had resolved into a slow monotonous walk round and round, inside the "defence"; and all the time I had to carry the unnaturally rigid body of poor Bains.

'It began to tire me; for though he was small, his rigidity made him dreadfully awkward and tiring to hold, as you can understand; yet I could not think what else to do; for I had stopped shaking him, or trying to wake him, for the simple reason that he was as wide awake as I was mentally; though but physically inanimate, through one of those partial spiritual disassociations which he had tried to explain to me.

'Now I had previously switched out the red, orange, yellow and green circles, and had on the full defence of the blue end of the spectrum – I knew that one of the repelling vibrations of each of the three colours: blue, indigo and violet were beating out protectingly into space; yet they were proving insufficient, and I was in the position of having either to take some desperate action to stimulate Bains to an even greater effort of will than I judged him to be making, or else to risk experimenting with fresh combinations of the defensive colours.

'You see, as things were at that moment, the danger was increasing steadily; for plainly, from the appearance of the air of the room outside the barrier, there were some mighty dangerous tensions generating. While inside the danger was also increasing; the steady recurrence of the shadow proving that the "defence" was insufficient.

'In short, I feared that Bains in his peculiar condition was literally a "doorway" into the "defence"; and unless I could wake him or find out the correct combinations of circles necessary to set up stronger repelling vibrations against that particular danger, there were very ugly possibilities ahead. I felt I had been incredibly rash not to have foreseen the possibility of Bains falling asleep under the hypnotic effect of deliberately paralleling the associations of sleep.

'Unless I could increase the repulsion of the barriers or wake him there was every likelihood of having to choose between a rush for the door – which the condition of the atmosphere outside the barrier showed to be practically impossible – or of throwing him outside the barrier, which, of course, was equally not possible.

'All this time I was walking round and round inside the barrier, when suddenly I saw a new development of the danger which threatened us. Right in the centre of the "defence" the shadow had formed into an intensely black circle, about a foot wide.

'This increased as I looked at it. It was horrible to see it grow. It crept out in an ever widening circle till it was quite a yard across.

'Quickly I put Bains on the floor. A tremendous attempt was evidently going to be made by some outside force to enter the "defence", and it was up to me to make a final effort to help Bains to "wake up." I took out my lancet, and pushed up his left coat sleeve.

'What I was going to do was a terrible risk, I knew, for there is no doubt that in some extraordinary fashion blood attracts.

'The Sigsand mentions it particularly in one passage which runs something like this: "In blood there is the Voice which calleth through all space. Ye Monsters in ye Deep hear, and hearing, they lust. Likewise hath it a greater power to reclaim backward ye soul that doth wander foolish adrift from ye body in which it doth have natural abiding. But woe unto him that doth spill ye blood in ye deadly hour; for there will be surely Monsters that shall hear ye Blood Cry."

'That risk I had to run. I knew that the blood would call to the outer forces; but equally I knew that it should call even more loudly to that portion of Bains' "Essence" that was adrift from him, down in those depths.

'Before lancing him, I glanced at the shadow. It had spread out until the nearest edge was not more than two feet away from Bains' right shoulder; and the edge was creeping nearer, like the blackening edge of burning paper, even while I stared. The whole thing had a less shadowy, less ghostly appearance than at any time before. And it looked simply and literally like the black mouth of a pit.

' "Now, Bains," I said, "pull yourself together, man. Wake up!"
And at the same time as I spoke to him, I used my lancet quickly but
superficially.

'I watched the little red spot of blood well up, then trickle round his
wrist and fall to the floor of the "defence". And in the moment that it
fell the thing that I had feared happened. There was a sound like a
low peal of thunder in the room, and curious deadly-looking flashes of
light rippled here and there along the floor outside the barrier.

'Once more I called to him, trying to speak firmly and steadily as I
saw that the horrible shadowy circle had spread across every inch of
the floor space of the centre of the "defence", making it appear as if
both Bains and I were suspended above an unutterable black void –
the black void that stared up at me out of the throat of that shadowy
pit. And yet, all the time I could feel the floor solid under my knees as
I knelt beside Bains holding his wrist.

' "Bains!" I called once more, trying not to shout madly at him.
"Bains, wake up! Wake up, man! Wake up!"

'But he never moved, only stared up at me with eyes of quiet horror
that seemed to be looking at me out of some dreadful eternity.'

IV

'By this time the shadow had blackened all around us, and I felt that
strangely terrible vertigo coming over me again. Jumping to my feet I
caught up Bains in my arms and stepped over the first of the
protective circles – the violet, and stood between it and the indigo
circle, holding Bains as close to me as possible so as to prevent any
portion of his helpless body from protruding outside the indigo and
blue circles.

'From the black shadowy mouth which now filled the whole of the
centre of the "defence" there came a faint sound – not near but
seeming to come up at me out of unknown abysses. Very, very faint
and lost it sounded, but I recognised it as unmistakably the infinitely
remote murmur of countless swine.

'And that same moment Bains, as if answering the sound, grunted
like a swine in my arms.

'There I stood between the glass vacuum tubes of the circles, gazing
dizzily into that black shadowy pit-mouth, which seemed to drop
sheer into hell from below my left elbow.

'Things had gone so utterly beyond all that I had thought of, and it had all somehow come about so gradually and yet so suddenly, that I was really a bit below my natural self. I felt mentally paralysed, and could think of nothing except that not twenty feet away was the door and the outer natural world; and here was I face to face with some unthought-of danger, and all adrift, what to do to avoid it.

'You fellows will understand this better when I tell you that the bluish glare from the three circles showed me that there were now hundreds and hundreds of those small smoke-like puffs of black cloud circling round and round outside the barrier in an unvarying, unending procession.

'And all the time I was holding the rigid body of Bains in my arms, trying not to give way to the loathing that got me each time he grunted. Every twenty or thirty seconds he grunted, as if in answer to the sounds which were almost too faint for my normal hearing. I can tell you, it was like holding something worse than a corpse in my arms, standing there balanced between physical death on the one side and soul destruction on the other.

'Abruptly, from out of the deep that lay so close that my elbow and shoulder overhung it, there came again a faint, marvellously faint murmur of swine, so utterly far away that the sound was as remote as a lost echo.

'Bains answered it with a pig-like squeal that set every fibre in me protesting in sheer human revolt, and I sweated coldly from head to foot. Pulling myself together I tried to pierce down into the mouth of the great shadow when, for the second time, a low peel of thunder sounded in the room, and every joint in my body seemed to jolt and burn.

'In turning to look down the pit I had allowed one of Bains' heels to protrude for a moment slightly beyond the blue circle, and a fraction of the "tension" outside the barrier had evidently discharged through Bains and me. Had I been standing directly inside the "defence" instead of being "insulated" from it by the violet circle, then no doubt things might have been much more serious. As it was, I had, psychically, that dreadful *soiled* feeling which the healthy human always experiences when he comes too closely in contact with certain Outer Monstrosities. Do you fellows remember how I had just the same feeling when the Hand came too near me in the "Gateway" case?

'The physical effects were sufficiently interesting to mention; for Bains' left boot had been ripped open, and the leg of his trousers was charred to the knee, while all around the leg were numbers of bluish marks in the form of irregular spirals.

'I stood there holding Bains, and shaking from head to foot. My head ached and each joint had a queer numbish feeling; but my physical pains were nothing compared with my mental distress. I felt that we were *done*! I had no room to turn or move for the space between the violet circle which was the innermost, and the blue circle which was the outermost of those in use was thirty-one inches, including the one inch of the indigo circle. So you see I was forced to stand there like an image, fearing each moment lest I should get another shock, and quite unable to think what to do.

'I daresay five minutes passed in this fashion. Bains had not grunted once since the "tension" caught him, and for this I was just simply thankful; though at first I must confess I had feared for a moment that he was dead.

'No further sounds had come up out of the black mouth to my left, and I grew steady enough again to begin to look about me, and think a bit. I leant again so as to look directly down into the shadowy pit. The edge of the circular mouth was now quite defined, and had a curious solid look, as if it were formed out of some substance like black glass.

'Below the edge, I could trace the appearance of solidity for a considerable distance, though in a vague sort of way. The centre of this extraordinary phenomenon was simple and unmitigated blackness – an utter velvety blackness that seemed to soak the very light out of the room down into it. I could see nothing else, and if anything else came out of it except a complete silence, it was the atmosphere of frightening suggestion that was affecting me more and more every minute.

'I turned away slowly and carefully, so as not to run any risks of allowing either Bains or myself to expose any part of us over the blue circle. Then I saw that things outside of the blue circle had developed considerably; for the odd, black puffs of smoke-like cloud had increased enormously and blent into a great, gloomy, circular wall of tufted cloud, going round and round and round eternally, and hiding the rest of the room entirely from me.

'Perhaps a minute passed, while I stared at this thing; and then, you know, the room was shaken slightly. This shaking lasted for three or four seconds, and then passed; but it came again in about half a minute, and was repeated from time to time. There was a queer oscillating quality in the shaking, that made me think suddenly of that *Jarvee* Haunting case. You remember it?

'There came again the shaking, and a ripple of deadly light seemed to play round the outside of the barrier; and then, abruptly, the room was full of a strange roaring – a brutish enormous yelling, grunting storm of swine-sounds.

'They fell away into a complete silence, and the rigid Bains grunted twice in my arms, as if answering. Then the storm of swine noise came again, beating up in a gigantic riot of brute sound that roared through the room, piping, squealing, grunting, and howling. And as it sank with a steady declination, there came a single gargantuan grunt out of some dreadful throat of monstrousness, and in one beat, the crashing chorus of unknown millions of swine came thundering and raging through the room again.

'There was more in that sound than mere chaos – there was a mighty devilish rhythm in it. Suddenly, it swept down again into a multitudinous swinish whispering and minor gruntings of unthinkable millions; and then with a rolling deafening bellow of sound came the single vast grunt. And, as if lifted upon it the swine roar of the millions of the beasts beat up through the room again; and at every seventh second, as I knew well enough without the need of the watch on my wrist, came the single storm beat of the great grunt out of the throat of unknowable monstrosity – and in my arms, Bains, the human, grunted in time to the swine melody – a rigid grunting monster there in my two arms.

'I tell you from head to foot I shook and sweated. I believe I prayed; but if I did I don't know what I prayed. I have never before felt or endured just what I felt, standing there in that thirty-one-inch space, with that grunting thing in my arms, and the hell melody beating up out of the great Deeps; and to my right, "tensions" that would have torn me into a bundle of blazing tattered flesh, if I had jumped out over the barriers.

'And then, with an effect like a clap of unexpected thunder, the vast storm of sound ceased; and the room was full of silence and an unimaginable horror.

'This silence continued. I want to say something which may sound a bit silly; but the silence seemed to *trickle* round the room. I don't know why I felt it like that; but my words give you just what I seemed to feel, as I stood there holding the softly grunting body of Bains.

'The circular, gloomy wall of dense black cloud enclosed the barrier as completely as ever, and moved round and round and round, with a slow, "eternal" movement And at the back of that black wall of circling cloud, a dead silence went trickling round the room, out of my sight. Do you understand at all? . . .

'It seemed to me to show very clearly the state of almost insane mental and psychic tension I was enduring . . . The way in which my brain insisted that the silence was *trickling* round the room, interests me enormously; for I was either in a state approximating a phase of madness, or else I was, psychically, tuned to some abnormal pitch of awareness and sensitiveness in which silence had ceased to be an abstract quality, and had become to me a definite concrete element, much as (to use a stupidly crude illustration), the invisible moisture of the atmosphere becomes a visible and concrete element when it becomes deposited as water. I wonder whether this thought attracts you as it does me?

'And then, you know, a slow awareness grew in me of some further horror to come. This sensation or knowledge or whatever it should be named, was so strong that I had a sudden feeling of suffocation . . . I felt that I could bear no more; and that if anything else happened, I should just pull out my revolver and shoot Bains through the head, and then myself, and so end the whole dreadful business.

'This feeling, however, soon passed; and I felt stronger and more ready to face things again. Also, I had the first, though still indefinite, idea of a way in which to make things a bit safer; but I was too dazed to see how to "shape" to help myself efficiently.

'And then a low, far-off whining stole up into the room, and I knew that the danger was coming. I leant slowly to my left, taking care not to let Bains' feet stick over the blue circle, and stared down into the blackness of the pit that dropped sheer into some Unknown, from under my left elbow.

'The whining died; but far down in the blackness, there was something – just a remote luminous spot. I stood in a grim silence for maybe ten long minutes, and looked down at the thing. It was increasing in size all the time, and had become much plainer to see; yet it was still lost in the far, tremendous Deep.

'Then, as I stood and looked, the low whining sound crept up to me again, and Bains, who had lain like a log in my arms all the time, answered it with a long, animal-like whine, that was somehow newly abominable.

'A very curious thing happened then; for all around the edge of the pit, that looked so peculiarly like black glass, there came a sudden, luminous glowing. It came and went oddly, smouldering queerly round and round the edge in an opposite direction to the circling of the wall of black, tufted cloud on the outside of the barrier.

'This peculiar glowing finally disappeared, and, abruptly, out of the tremendous Deep, I was conscious of a dreadful quality or "atmosphere" of monstrousness that was coming up out of the pit. If I said there had been a sudden *waft* of it, this would very well describe the actuality of it; but the spiritual sickness of distress that it caused me to feel, I am simply stumped to explain to you. It was something that made me feel I should be soiled to the very core of me, if I did not beat it off from me with my will.

'I leant sharply away from the pit towards the outer of the burning circles. I meant to see that no part of my body should overhang the pit whilst that disgusting power was beating up out of the unknown depths.

'And thus it was, facing so rigidly away from the centre of the "defence", I saw presently a fresh thing; for there was something, many things, I began to think, on the other side of the gloomy wall that moved everlastingly around the outside of the barrier.

'The first thing I noticed was a queer disturbance of the ever circling cloud-wall. This disturbance was within eighteen inches of the floor, and directly before me. There was a curious, "puddling" action in the misty wall; as if something were meddling with it. The area of this peculiar little disturbance could not have been more than a foot across, and it did not remain opposite to me; but was taken round by the circling of the wall.

'When it came past me again, I noticed that it was bulging slightly inwards towards me; and as it moved away from me once more, I saw another similar disturbance, and then a third and a fourth, all in different parts of the slowly whirling black wall; and all of them were no more than about eighteen inches from the floor.

'When the first one came opposite me again, I saw that the slight bulge had grown into a very distinct protuberance towards me.

'All around the moving wall, there had now come these curious swellings. They continued to reach inwards, and to elongate; and all the time they kept in a constant movement.

'Suddenly, one of them broke, or opened, at the apex, and there protruded through, for an instant, the tip of a pallid, but unmistakable *snout*. It was gone at once, but I had seen the thing distinctly; and within a minute, I saw another one poke suddenly through the wall, to my right, and withdraw as quickly. I could not look at the base of the strange, black, moving circle about the barrier without seeing a swinish snout peep through momentarily, in this place or that.

'I stared at these things in a very peculiar state of mind. There was so great a weight of the abnormal about me, before and behind and every way, that to a certain extent it bred in me a sort of antidote to fear. Can you understand? It produced in me a temporary dazedness in which things and the horror of things became less real. I stared at them, as a child stares out from a fast train at a quickly passing night-landscape, oddly hit by the furnaces of unknown industries. I *want* you to try to understand.

'In my arms Bains lay quiet and rigid; and my arms and back ached until I was one dull ache in all my body; but I was only partly conscious of this when I roused momentarily from my psychic to my physical awareness, to shift him to another position, less intolerable temporarily to my tired arms and back.

'There was suddenly a fresh thing – a low but enormous, solitary grunt came rolling, vast and brutal into the room. It made the still body of Bains quiver against me, and he grunted thrice in return, with the voice of a young pig.

'High up in the moving wall of the barrier, I saw a fluffing out of the black tufted clouds; and a pig's hoof and leg, as far as the knuckle, came through and pawed a moment. This was about nine or ten feet above the floor. As it gradually disappeared I heard a low grunting from the other side of the veil of clouds which broke out suddenly into a diafaeon of brute-sound, grunting, squealing and swine-howling; all formed into a sound that was the essential melody of the brute – a grunting, squealing howling roar that rose, roar by roar, howl by howl and squeal by squeal to a crescendo of horrors – the bestial growths, longings, zests and acts of some grotto of hell . . . It is no use, I can't give it to you. I get dumb with the failure of my command over speech to tell you what that grunting, howling, roaring melody conveyed to me. It had in it something so inexplicably *below* the horizons of the soul in its monstrousness and fearfulness that the ordinary simple fear of death itself, with all its attendant agonies and terrors and sorrows, seemed like a thought of something peaceful and infinitely holy compared with the fear of those unknown elements in that dreadful roaring melody. And the sound was with me *inside* the room – *there right in the room with me.* Yet I seemed not to be aware of confining walls, but of echoing spaces of gargantuan corridors! Curious! I had in my mind those two words – gargantuan corridors.

As the rolling chaos of swine melody beat itself away on every side, there came booming through it a single grunt, the single recurring grunt of the HOG; for I knew now that I was actually and without any doubt hearing the beat of monstrosity, the HOG.

'In the Sigsand the thing is described something like this: "Ye

Hogge which ye Almighty alone hath power upon. If in sleep or in ye hour of danger ye hear the voice of ye Hogge, cease ye to meddle. For ye Hogge doth be of ye outer Monstrous Ones, nor shall any human come nigh him nor continue meddling when ye hear his voice for in ye earlier life upon the world did the Hogge have power, and shall again in ye end. And in that ye Hogge had once a power upon ye earth, so doth he crave sore to come again. And dreadful shall be ye harm to ye soul if ye continue to meddle, and to let ye beast come nigh. And I say unto all, if ye have brought this dire danger upon ye, have memory of ye cross, for of all sign hath ye Hogge a horror."

'There's a lot more, but I can't remember it all and that is about the substance of it.

'There was I holding Bains who was all the time howling that dreadful grunt out with the voice of a swine. I wonder I didn't go mad. It was, I believe, the antidote of dazedness produced by the strain which helped me through each moment.

'A minute later, or perhaps five minutes, I had a sudden new sensation, like a warning cutting through my dulled feelings. I turned my head; but there was nothing behind me, and bending over to my left I seemed to be looking down into that black depth which fell away sheer under my left elbow. At that moment the roaring bellow of swine-noise ceased and I seemed to be staring down into miles of black aether at something that hung there – a pallid face floating far down and remote – a great swine face.

'And as I gazed I saw it grow bigger. A seemingly motionless, pallid swine-face rising upward out of the depth. And suddenly I realised that I was actually looking at the Hog.'

V

'For perhaps a full minute I stared down through the darkness at that thing swimming like some far-off, dead-white planet in the stupendous void. And then I simply woke up bang, as you might say, to the possession of my faculties. For just a certain over-degree of strain had brought about the dumbly helpful anaesthesia of dazedness, so this sudden overwhelming supreme fact of horror produced, in turn, its reaction from inertness to action. I passed in one moment from listlessness to a fierce efficiency.

'I knew that I had, through some accident, penetrated beyond all previous "bounds", and that I stood where no human soul had any right to be, and that in but a few of the puny minutes of earth's time I might be dead.

'Whether Bains had passed beyond the "lines of retraction" or not, I could not tell. I put him down carefully but quickly on his side, between the inner circles – that is, the violet circle and the indigo circle – where he lay grunting slowly. Feeling that the dreadful moment had come I drew out my automatic. It seemed best to make sure of our end before that thing in the depth came any nearer; for once Bains in his present condition came within what I might term the "inductive forces" of the monster, he would cease to be human. There would happen, as in that case of Aster who stayed outside the pentacles in the Black Veil Case, what can only be described as a pathological, spiritual change – literally in other words, soul destruction.

'And then something seemed to be telling me not to shoot. This sounds perhaps a bit superstitious; but I meant to kill Bains in that moment, and what stopped me was a distinct message from the outside.

'I tell you, it sent a great thrill of hope through me, for I knew that the forces which govern the spinning of the outer circle were intervening. But the very fact of the intervention proved to me afresh the enormous spiritual peril into which we had stumbled; for that inscrutable Protective Force only intervenes between the human *soul* and the Outer Monstrosities.

'The moment I received that message I stood up like a flash and turned towards the pit, stepping over the violet circle slap into the mouth of darkness. I had to take the risk in order to get at the switch board which lay on the glass shelf under the table top in the centre. I could not shake free from the horror of the idea that I might fall down through that awful blackness. The floor felt solid enough under me; but I seemed to be walking on nothing above a black void, like an inverted starless night, with the face of the approaching Hog rising up from far down under my feet – a silent, incredible thing out of the abyss – a pallid, floating swine-face, framed in enormous blackness.

'Two quick, nervous strides took me to the table standing there in the centre with its glass legs apparently resting on nothing. I grabbed out the switch board, sliding out the vulcanite plate which carried the switch-control of the blue circle. The battery which fed this circle was the right-hand one of the row of seven, and each battery was marked with the letter of its circle painted on it, so that in an emergency I could select any particular battery in a moment.

'As I snatched up the B switch I had a grim enough warning of the unknown dangers that I was risking in that short journey of two steps; for that dreadful sense of vertigo returned suddenly and for one horrible moment I saw everything through a blurred medium as if I were trying to look through water.

'Below me, far away down between my feet I could see the Hog which, in some peculiar way, looked different – clearer and much nearer, and enormous. I felt it had got nearer to me all in a moment. And suddenly I had the impression I was descending bodily.

'I had a sense of a tremendous force being used to push me over the side of that pit, but with every shred of will power I had in me, I hurled myself into the smoky appearance that hid everything and reached the violet circle where Bains lay in front of me.

'Here I crouched down on my heels, and with my two arms out before me I slipped the nails of each forefinger under the vulcanite base of the blue circle, which I lifted very gently so that when the base was far enough from the floor I could push the tips of my fingers underneath. I took care to keep from reaching farther under than the inner edge of the glowing tube which rested on the two-inch-broad foundation of vulcanite.

'Very slowly I stood upright, lifting the side of the blue circle with me. My feet were between the indigo and the violet circles, and only the blue circle between me and sudden death; for if it had snapped with the unusual strain I was putting upon it by lifting it like that, I knew that I should in all probability go west pretty quickly.

'So you fellows can imagine what I felt like. I was conscious of a disagreeable faint prickling that was strongest in the tips of my fingers and wrists, and the blue circle seemed to vibrate strangely as if minute particles of something were impinging upon it in countless millions. Along the shining glass tubes for a couple of feet on each side of my hands a queer haze of tiny sparks boiled and whirled in the form of an extraordinary halo.

'Stepping forward over the indigo circle I pushed the blue circle out against the slowly moving wall of black cloud causing a ripple of tiny pale flashes to curl in over the circle. These flashes ran along the vacuum tube until they came to the place where the blue circle crossed the indigo, and there they flicked off into space with sharp cracks of sound.

'As I advanced slowly and carefully with the blue circle a most extraordinary thing happened, for the moving wall of cloud gave from it in a great belly of shadow, and appeared to thin away from before it. Lowering my edge of the circle to the floor I stepped over Bains and right into the mouth of the pit, lifting the other side of the circle over the table. It creaked as if it were about to break in half as I lifted it, but eventually it came over safely.

'When I looked again into the depth of that shadow I saw below me the dreadful pallid head of the Hog floating in a circle of night. It struck me that it glowed very slightly – just a vague luminosity. And quite near – comparatively. No one could have judged distances in that black void.

'Picking up the edge of the blue circle again as I had done before, I took it out further till it was half clear of the indigo circle. Then I picked up Bains and carried him to that portion of the floor guarded by the part of the blue circle which was clear of the "defence". Then I lifted the circle and started to move it forward as quickly as I dared, shivering each time the joints squeaked as the whole fabric of it groaned with the strain I was putting upon it. And all the time the moving wall of tufted clouds gave from the edge of the blue circle, bellying away from it in a marvellous fashion as if blown by an unheard wind.

'From time to time little flashes of light had begun to flick in over the blue circle, and I began to wonder whether it would be able to hold out the "tension" until I had dragged it clear of the defence.

'Once it was clear I hoped the abnormal stress would cease from about us, and concentrate chiefly around the "defence" again, and the attractions of the negative "tension."

'Just then I heard a sharp tap behind me, and the blue circle jarred somewhat, having now ridden completely over the violet and indigo circles, and dropped clear on to the floor. The same instant there came a low rolling noise as of thunder, and a curious roaring. The black circling wall had thinned away from around us and the room showed clearly once more, yet nothing was to be seen except that now and then a peculiar bluish flicker of light would ripple across the floor.

'Turning to look at the "defence" I noticed it was surrounded by the circling wall of black cloud, and looked strangely extraordinary seen from the outside. It resembled a slightly swaying squat funnel of whirling black mist reaching from the floor to the ceiling, and through it I could see glowing, sometimes vague and sometimes plain, the indigo and violet circles. And then as I watched, the whole room seemed suddenly filled with an awful presence which pressed upon me with a weight of horror that was the very essence of spiritual deathliness.

'Kneeling there in the blue circle by Bains, my initiative faculties stupefied and temporarily paralysed, I could form no further plan of escape, and indeed I seemed to care for nothing at the moment. I felt I had already escaped from immediate destruction and I was strung up to an amazing pitch of indifference to any minor horrors.

'Bains all this while had been quietly lying on his side. I rolled him over and looked closely at his eyes, taking care on account of his condition not to gaze *into* them; for if he had passed beyond the "line of retraction" he would be dangerous. I mean, if the "wandering" part of his essence had been assimilated by the Hog, then Bains would be spiritually accessible and might be even then no more than the outer form of the man, charged with radiation of the monstrous ego of the Hog, and therefore capable of what I might term for want of a more exact phrase, a psychically *infective* force; such force being more readily transmitted through the eyes than any other way, and capable of producing a brain storm of an extremely dangerous character.

'I found Bains, however, with both eyes with an extraordinary distressed interned quality; not the eyeballs, remember, but a reflex action transmitted from the "mental eye" to the physical eye, and giving to the physical eye an expression of thought instead of sight. I wonder whether I make this clear to you?

'Abruptly, from every part of the room there broke out the noise of those hoofs again, making the place echo with the sound as if a thousand swine had started suddenly from an absolute immobility into a mad charge. The whole riot of animal sound seemed to heave itself in one wave towards the oddly swaying and circling funnel of black cloud which rose from floor to ceiling around the violet and indigo circles.

'As the sounds ceased I saw something was rising up through the middle of the "defence". It rose with a slow steady movement. I saw it pale and huge through the swaying, whirling funnel of cloud – a monstrous pallid snout rising out of that unknowable abyss . . . It rose higher like a huge pale mound. Through a thinning of the cloud curtain I saw one small eye . . . I shall never see a pig's eye again without feeling something of what I felt then. A pig's eye with a sort of hell-light of vile understanding shining at the back of it.'

VI

'And then suddenly a dreadful terror came over me, for I saw the beginning of the end that I had been dreading all along – I saw through the slow whirl of the cloud curtains that the violet circle had begun to leave the floor. It was being taken up on the spread of the vast snout.

'Straining my eyes to see through the swaying funnel of clouds I saw that the violet circle had melted and was running down the pale sides of the snout in streams of violet-coloured fire. And as it melted there came a change in the atmosphere of the room. The black funnel shone with a dull gloomy red, and a heavy red glow filled the room.

'The change was such as one might experience if one had been looking through a protective glass at some light and the glass had been suddenly removed. But there was a further change that I realised directly through my feelings. It was as if the horrible presence in the room had come closer to my own soul. I wonder if I am making it at all clear to you. Before, it had oppressed me somewhat as a death on a very gloomy and dreary day beats down upon one's spirit. But now there was a savage menace, and the actual feeling of a foul thing *close up against me*. It was horrible, simply horrible.

'And then Bains moved. For the first time since he went to sleep the rigidity went out of him, and rolling suddenly over on to his stomach he fumbled up in a curious animal-like fashion, on to his hands and feet. Then he charged straight across the blue circle towards the thing in the 'defence'.

'With a shriek I jumped to pull him back; but it was not my voice that stopped him. It was the blue circle. It made him give back from it as though some invisible hand had jerked him backwards. He threw up his head like a hog, squealing with the voice of a swine, and started off round the inside of the blue circle. Round and round it he went, twice attempting to bolt across it to the horror in that swaying funnel of cloud. Each time he was thrown back, and each time he squealed like a great swine, the sounds echoing round the room in a horrible fashion as though they came from somewhere a long way off.

'By this time I was fairly sure that Bains had indeed passed the "line of retraction", and the knowledge brought a fresh and more hopeless horror and pity to me, and a grimmer fear for myself. I knew that if it were so, it was not Bains I had with me in the circle but a monster, and that for my own last chance of safety I should have to get him outside of the circle.

'He had ceased his tireless running round and round, and now lay on his side grunting continually and softly in a dismal kind of way. As the slowly whirling clouds thinned a little I saw again that pallid face with some clearness. It was still rising, but slowly, very slowly, and again a hope grew in me that it might be checked by the 'defence'. Quite plainly I saw that the horror was looking at Bains, and at that moment I saved my own life and soul by looking down. There, close to me on the floor was the thing that looked like Bains, its hands stretched out to grip my ankles. Another second, and I should have been tripped *outwards*. Do you realise what that would have meant?

'It was no time to hesitate. I simply jumped and came down crash with my knees on top of Bains. He lay quiet enough after a short struggle; but I took off my braces and lashed his hands up behind him. And I shivered with the very touch of him, as though I was touching something monstrous.

'By the time I had finished I noticed that the reddish glow in the room had deepened quite considerably, and the whole room was darker. The destruction of the violet circle had reduced the light perceptibly; but the darkness that I am speaking of was something more than that. It seemed as if something now had come into the atmosphere of the room – a sort of gloom, and in spite of the shining of the blue circle and the indigo circle inside the funnel of cloud, there was now more red light than anything else.

'Opposite me the huge, cloud-shrouded monster in the indigo circle appeared to be motionless. I could see its outline vaguely all the time, and only when the cloud funnel thinned could I see it plainly – a vast, snouted mound, faintly and whitely luminous, one gargantuan side turned towards me, and near the base of the slope a minute slit out of which shone one whitish eye.

'Presently through the thin gloomy red vapour I saw something that killed the hope in me, and gave me a horrible despair; for the indigo circle, the final barrier of the defence, was being slowly lifted into the air – the Hog had begun to rise higher. I could see its dreadful snout rising upwards out of the cloud. Slowly, very slowly, the snout rose up, and the indigo circle went up with it.

'In the dead stillness of that room I got a strange sense that all eternity was tense and utterly still as if certain powers knew of this horror I had brought into the world . . . And then I had an awareness of something coming . . . something from far, far away. It was as if some hidden unknown part of my brain knew it. Can you understand? There was somewhere in the heights of space a light that was coming near. I seemed to *hear* it coming. I could just see the body of Bains on the floor, huddled and shapeless and inert. Within the swaying veil of cloud the monster showed as a vast pale, faintly

luminous mound, hugely snouted – an infernal hillock of monstrosity, pallid and deadly amid the redness that hung in the atmosphere of the room.

'Something told me that it was making a final effort against the help that was coming, I saw the indigo circle was now some inches from the floor, and every moment I expected to see it flash into streams of indigo fire running down the pale slopes of the snout. I could see the circle beginning to move upward at a perceptible speed. The monster was triumphing.

'Out in some realm of space a low continuous thunder sounded. The thing in the great heights was coming fast, but it could never come in time. The thunder grew from a low, far mutter into a deep steady rolling of sound . . . It grew louder and louder, and as it grew I saw the indigo circle, now shining through the red gloom of the room, was a whole foot off the floor. I thought I saw a faint splutter of indigo light . . . The final circle of the barrier was beginning to melt.

'That instant the thunder of the thing in flight which my brain heard so plainly, rose into a crashing, a world-shaking bellow of speed, making the room rock and vibrate to an immensity of sound. A strange flash of blue flame ripped open the funnel of cloud momentarily from top to base, and I saw for one brief instant the pallid monstrosity of the Hog, stark and pale and dreadful.

'Then the sides of the funnel joined again hiding the thing from me as the funnel became submerged quickly into a dome of silent blue light – God's own colour! All at once it seemed the cloud had gone, and from floor to ceiling of the room, in awful majesty, like a living Presence, there appeared that dome of blue fire banded with three rings of green light at equal distances. There was no sound or movement, not even a flicker, nor could I see anything in the light; for looking into it was like looking into the cold blue of the skies. But I felt sure that there had come to our aid one of those inscrutable forces which govern the spinning of the outer circle, for the dome of blue light, banded with three green bands of silent fire, was the outward or visible sign of an enormous force, undoubtedly of a defensive nature.

'Through ten minutes of absolute silence I stood there in the blue circle watching the phenomenon. Minute by minute I saw the heavy repellent red driven out of the room as the place lightened quite noticeably. And as it lightened, the body of Bains began to resolve out of a shapeless length of shadow, detail by detail, until I could see the braces with which I had lashed his wrists together.

'And as I looked at him his body moved slightly, and in a weak but perfectly sane voice he said:

' "I've had it again! My God! I've had it again!" '

VII

'I knelt down quickly by his side and loosened the braces from his wrists, helping him to turn over and sit up. He gripped my arm a little crazily with both hands.

' "I went to sleep after all," he said. "And I've been down there again. My God! It nearly had me. I was down in that awful place and it seemed to be just round a great corner, and I was stopped from coming back. I seemed to have been fighting for ages and ages. I felt I was going mad. Mad! I've been nearly down into a hell. I could hear you calling down to me from some awful height. I could hear your voice echoing along yellow passages. They *were* yellow. I know they were. And I tried to come and I couldn't."

' "Did you see me?" I asked him when he stopped, gasping.

' "No," he answered, leaning his head against my shoulder. "I tell you it nearly got me that time. I shall never dare go to sleep again as long as I live. Why didn't you wake me?"

' "I did," I told him. "I had you in my arms most of the time. You kept looking up into my eyes as if you knew I was there."

' "I know," he said. "I remember now; but you seemed to be up at the top of a frightful hole, miles and miles up from me, and those horrors were grunting and squealing and howling, and trying to catch me and keep me down there. But I couldn't see anything – only the yellow walls of those passages. And all the time there was something round the corner."

' "Anyway, you're safe enough now," I told him. "And I'll guarantee you shall be safe in the future."

'The room had grown dark save for the light from the blue circle. The dome had disappeared, the whirling funnel of black cloud had gone, the Hog had gone, and the light had died out of the indigo circle. And the atmosphere of the room was safe and normal again as I proved by moving the switch, which was near me, so as to lessen the defensive power of the blue circle and enable me to "feel" the outside tension. Then I turned to Bains.

' "Come along," I said. "We'll go and get something to eat, and have a rest."

'But Bains was already sleeping like a tired child, his head pillowed on his hand. "Poor little devil!" I said as I picked him up in my arms. "Poor little devil!"

'I walked across to the main switchboard and threw over the current so as to throw the "V" protective pulse out of the four walls and the door; then I carried Bains out into the sweet wholesome normality of everything. It seemed wonderful, coming out of that chamber of horrors, and it seemed wonderful still to see my bedroom door opposite, wide open, with the bed looking so soft and white as usual – so ordinary and human. Can you chaps understand?

'I carried Bains into the room and put him on the couch; and then it was I realised how much I'd been up against, for when I was getting myself a drink I dropped the bottle and had to get another.

'After I had made Bains drink a glass I laid him on the bed. "Now," I said, "look into my eyes fixedly. Do you hear me? You are going off to sleep safely and soundly, and if anything troubles you, obey me and *wake up*. Now, sleep – sleep – sleep!"

'I swept my hands down over his eyes half a dozen times, and he fell over like a child. I knew that if the danger came again he would obey my will and wake up. I intend to cure him, partly by hypnotic suggestion, partly by a certain electrical treatment which I am getting Doctor Witton to give him.

'That night I slept on the couch, and when I went to look at Bains in the morning I found him still sleeping, so leaving him there I went into the test room to examine results. I found them very surprising.

'Inside the room I had a queer feeling, as you can imagine. It was extraordinary to stand there in that curious bluish light from the "treated" windows, and see the blue circle lying, still glowing, where I had left it; and further on, the "defence", lying circle within circle, all "out", and in the centre the glass-legged table standing where a few hours before it had been submerged in the horrible monstrosity of the Hog. I tell you, it all seemed like a wild and horrible dream as I stood there and looked. I have carried out some curious tests in there before now, as you know, but I've never come nearer to a catastrophe.

'I left the door open so as not to feel shut in, and then I walked over to the "defence". I was intensely curious to see what had happened physically under the action of such a force as the Hog. I found unmistakable signs that proved the thing had been indeed a Saaitii manifestation, for there had been no psychic or physical illusion about the melting of the violet circle. There remained nothing of it except a ring of patches of melted glass. The gutta base had been fused entirely, but the floor and everything was intact. You see, the Saaitii forms can often attack and destroy, or even make use of, the very defensive material used against them.

'Stepping over the outer circle and looking closely at the indigo circle I saw that it was melted clean through in several places. Another fraction of time and the Hog would have been free to expand as an invisible mist of horror and destruction into the atmosphere of the world. And then, in that very moment of time, salvation had come. I wonder if you can get my feelings as I stood there staring down at the destroyed barrier.'

Carnacki began to knock out his pipe which is always a sign that he has ended his tale, and is ready to answer any questions we may want to ask.

Taylor was first in. 'Why didn't you use the Electric Pentacle as well as your new spectrum circles?' he asked.

'Because,' replied Carnacki, 'the pentacle is simply "defensive" and I wished to have the power to make a "focus" during the early part of the experiment, and then, at the critical moment, to change the combination of the colours so as to have a "defence" against the results of the "focus". You follow me.

'You see,' he went on, seeing we hadn't grasped his meaning, 'there can be no "focus" within a pentacle. It is just of a "defensive" nature. Even if I had switched the current out of the electric pentacle I should still have had to contend with the peculiar and undoubtedly "defensive" power that its form seems to exert, and this would have been sufficient to "blur" the focus.

'In this new research work I'm doing, I'm bound to use a "focus" and so the pentacle is barred. But I'm not sure it matters. I'm convinced this new spectrum "defence" of mine will prove absolutely invulnerable when I've learnt how to use it; but it will take me some time. This last case has taught me something new. I had never thought of combining green with blue; but the three bands of green in the blue of that dome has set me thinking. If only I knew the right combinations! It's the combinations I've got to learn. You'll understand better the importance of these combinations when I remind you that green by itself is, in a very limited way, more deadly than red itself – and red is the danger colour of all.'

'Tell us, Carnacki,' I said, 'what is the Hog? Can you? I mean what kind of monstrosity is it? Did you *really* see it, or was it all some horrible, dangerous kind of dream? How do you know it was one of the outer monsters? And what is the difference between that sort of danger and the sort of thing you saw in the Gateway of the Monster case? And what . . .?'

'Steady!' laughed Carnacki. 'One at a time! I'll answer all your questions; but I don't think I'll take them quite in your order. For instance, speaking about actually seeing the Hog, I might say that, speaking generally, things seen of a "ghostly" nature are not seen with the eyes; they are seen with the mental eye which has this psychic quality, not always developed to a useable state, in addition to its "normal" duty of revealing to the brain what our physical eyes record.

'You will understand that when we see "ghostly" things it is often the "mental" eye performing simultaneously the duty of revealing to the brain what the physical eye sees as well as what it sees itself. The two sights blending their functions in such a fashion gives us the impression that we are actually seeing through our physical eyes the whole of the "sight" that is being revealed to the brain.

'In this way we get an impression of seeing with our physical eyes both the material and the immaterial parts of an "abnormal" scene; for each part being received and revealed to the brain by machinery suitable to the particular purpose appears to have equal value of reality – that is, it appears to be equally material. Do you follow me?'

We nodded our assent, and Carnacki continued:

'In the same way, were anything to threaten our psychic body we should have the impression, generally speaking, that it was our physical body that had been threatened, because our psychic sensations and impressions would be super-imposed upon our physical, in the same way that our psychic and our physical sight are super-imposed.

'Our sensations would blend in such a way that it would be impossible to differentiate between what we felt physically and what we felt psychically. To explain better what I mean. A man may seem to himself, in a "ghostly" adventure, to fall *actually*. That is, to be falling in a physical sense; but all the while it may be his psychic entity, or being – call it what you will – that is falling. But to his brain there is presented the sensation of falling all together. Do you get me?

'At the same time, please remember that the danger is none the less because it is his psychic body that falls. I am referring to the sensation I had of falling during the time of stepping across the mouth of that pit. My physical body could walk over it easily and feel the floor solid under me; but my psychic body was in very real danger of falling. Indeed, I may be said to have literally *carried* my psychic body over, held within me by the pull of my life-force. You see, to my psychic body the pit was as real and as actual as a coal pit would have been to my physical body. It was merely the pull of my life-force which prevented my psychic body from falling *out* of me, rather like a plummet, down through the everlasting depths in obedience to the giant pull of the monster.

'As you will remember, the pull of the Hog was too great for my life-force to withstand, and, psychically, I began to fall. Immediately on my brain was recorded a sensation identical with that which would have been recorded on it had my actual physical body been falling. It was a mad risk I took, but as you know, I had to take it to get to the switch and the battery. When I had that physical sense of falling and seemed to see the black misty sides of the pit all around me, it was my mental eye recording upon the brain what it was seeing. My psychic body had actually begun to fall and was really below the edge of the pit but still in contact with me. In other words my physical magnetic and psychic "haloes" were still mingled. My physical body was still standing firmly upon the floor of the room, but if I had not each time by effort or will forced my physical body across to the side, my psychic body would have fallen completely out of "contact" with me, and gone like some ghostly meteorite, obedient to the pull of the Hog.

'The curious sensation I had of forcing myself through an obstructing medium was not a physical sensation at all, as we understand that word, but rather the psychic sensation of forcing my entity to re-cross the "gap" that had already formed between my falling psychic body now below the edge of the pit and my physical body standing on the floor of the room. And that "gap" was full of a force that strove to prevent my body and soul from rejoining. It was a terrible experience. Do you remember how I could still see with my brain through the eyes of my psychic body, though it had already fallen some distance out of me? That is an extraordinary thing to remember.

'However, to get ahead, all "ghostly" phenomena are extremely diffuse in a normal state. They become actively physically dangerous in all cases where they are concentrated. The best off-hand illustration I can think of is the all-familiar electricity – a force which, by the way, we are too prone to imagine we understand because we've named and harnessed it, to use a popular phrase. But we don't understand it at all! It is still a complete fundamental mystery. Well, electricity when diffused is an "imagined and unpictured something", but when concentrated it is sudden death. Have you got me in that?

'Take, for instance, that explanation, as a very, very crude sort of illustration of what the Hog is. The Hog is one of those million-mile-long clouds of "nebulosity" lying in the Outer Circle. It is because of this that I term those clouds of force the Outer Monsters.

'What they are exactly is a tremendous question to answer. I sometimes wonder whether Dodgson there realises just how impossible it is to answer some of his questions,' and Carnacki laughed.

'But to make a brief attempt at it. There is around this planet, and presumably others, of course, circles of what I might call "emanations". This is an extremely light gas, or shall I say aether. Poor aether, it's been hard worked in its time!

'Go back one moment to your school-days, and bear in mind that at one time the earth was just a sphere of extremely hot gases. These gases condensed in the form of materials and other "solid" matters; but there are some that are not yet solidified – air, for instance. Well, we have an earth-sphere of solid matter on which to stamp as solidly as we like; and round about that sphere there lies a ring of gases the constituents of which enter largely into all life, as we understand life – that is, air.

'But this is not the only circle of gas which is floating round us. There are, as I have been forced to conclude, larger and more attenuated "gas" belts lying, zone on zone, far up and around us. These compose what I have called the inner circles. They are surrounded in turn by a circle or belt of what I have called, for want of a better word, "emanations".

'This circle which I have named the Outer Circle cannot lie less than a hundred thousand miles off the earth, and has a thickness which I have presumed to be anything between five and ten million miles. I believe, but I cannot prove, that it does not spin with the earth but in the opposite direction, for which a plausible cause might be found in the study of the theory upon which a certain electrical machine is constructed.

'I have reason to believe that the spinning of this, the Outer Circle, is disturbed from time to time through causes which are quite unknown to me, but which I believe are based in physical phenomena. Now, the Outer Circle is the psychic circle, yet it is also physical. To illustrate what I mean I must again instance electricity, and say that just as electricity discovered itself to us as something quite different from any of our previous conceptions of matter, so is the Psychic or Outer Circle different from any of our previous conceptions of matter. Yet it is none the less physical in its origin, and in the sense that electricity is physical, the Outer or

Psychic Circle is physical in its constituents. Speaking pictorially it is, physically, to the Inner Circle what the Inner Circle is to the upper strata of the air, and what the air – as we know that intimate gas – is to the waters and the waters to the solid world. You get my line of suggestion?'

We all nodded, and Carnacki resumed.

'Well, now let me apply all this to what I am leading up to. I suggest that these million-mile-long clouds of monstrosity which float in the Psychic or Outer Circle, are bred of the elements of that circle. They are tremendous psychic forces, bred out of its elements just as an octopus or shark is bred out of the sea, or a tiger or any other physical force is bred out of the elements of its earth-and-air surroundings.

'To go further, a physical man is composed entirely from the constituents of earth and air, by which terms I include sunlight and water and "condiments"! In other words without earth and air he could not *BE*! Or to put it another way, earth and air breed within themselves the materials of the body and the brain, and therefore, presumably, the machine of intelligence.

'Now apply this line of thought to the Psychic or Outer Circle which though so attenuated that I may crudely presume it to be approximate to our conception of aether, yet contains all the elements for the production of certain phases of force and intelligence. But these elements are in a form as little like matter as the emanations of scent are like the scent itself. Equally, the force-and-intelligence-producing capacity of the Outer Circle no more approximates to the life-and-intelligence-producing capacity of the earth and air than the results of the Outer Circle constituents resemble the results of earth and air. I wonder whether I make it clear.

'And so it seems to me we have the conception of a huge psychic world, bred out of the physical, lying far outside of this world and completely encompassing it, except for the doorways about which I hope to tell you some other evening. This enormous psychic world of the Outer Circle "breeds" if I may use the term, its own psychic forces and intelligences, monstrous and otherwise, just as this world produces its own physical forces and intelligences – beings, animals, insects, etc., monstrous and otherwise.

'The monstrosities of the Outer Circle are malignant towards all that we consider most desirable, just in the same way a shark or a tiger may be considered malignant, in a physical way, to all that we consider desirable. They are predatory – as all positive force is predatory. They have desires regarding us which are incredibly more dreadful to our minds when comprehended than an intelligent sheep would consider our desires towards its own carcass. They plunder and destroy to satisfy lusts and hungers exactly as other forms of existence plunder and destroy to satisfy their lusts and hungers. And the desire of these monsters is chiefly, if not always, for the psychic entity of the human.

'But that's as much as I can tell you tonight. Some evening I want to tell you about the tremendous mystery of the Psychic Doorways. In the meantime, have I made things a bit clearer to you, Dodgson?'

'Yes, and no,' I answered. 'You've been a brick to make the attempt, but there are still about ten thousand other things I want to know.'

Carnacki stood up. 'Out you go!' he said using the recognised formula in friendly fashion. 'Out you go! I want a sleep.'

And shaking him by the hand we strolled out on to the quiet Embankment.

THE GREAT GOD PAN

Arthur Machen

[1863–1947]

'*Of living creators of cosmic fear raised to its most artistic pitch, few if any can hope to equal the versatile Arthur Machen, author of some dozen tales long and short, in which the elements of hidden horror and brooding fright attain an almost incomparable substance and realistic acuteness . . .*

'*Of Mr. Machen's horror-tales the most famous is perhaps* The Great God Pan *(1894) which tells of a singular and terrible experiment and its consequences . . . But the charm of the tale is in the telling. No one could begin to describe the cumulative suspense and ultimate horror with which every paragraph abounds without following fully the precise order in which Mr. Machen unfolds his gradual hints and revelations. Melodrama is undeniably present, and coincidence is stretched to a length which appears absurd upon analysis; but in the malign witchery of the tale as a whole these trifles are forgotten, and the sensitive reader reaches the end with only an appreciative shudder and a tendency to repeat the words of one of the characters: "It is too incredible, too monstrous; such things can never be in this quiet world . . . Why, man, if such a case were possible, our earth would be a nightmare." '*

– H.P. Lovecraft

I

THE EXPERIMENT

'I AM glad you came, Clarke; very glad indeed. I was not sure you could spare the time.'

'I was able to make arrangements for a few days; things are not very lively just now. But have you no misgivings, Raymond? Is it absolutely safe?'

The two men were slowly pacing the terrace in front of Dr. Raymond's house. The sun still hung above the western mountain line, but it shone with a dull red glow that cast no shadows, and all the air was quiet; a sweet breath came from the great wood on the hillside above, and with it, at intervals, the soft murmuring call of the wild doves. Below, in the long, lovely valley, the river wound in and out between the lonely hills, and, as the sun hovered and vanished into the west, a faint mist, pure white, began to rise from the banks. Dr. Raymond turned sharply to his friend.

'Safe? Of course it is. In itself the operation is a perfectly simple one; any surgeon could do it.'

'And there is no danger at any other stage?'

'None; absolutely no physical danger whatever, I give you my word. You are always timid, Clarke, always; but you know my history. I have devoted myself to transcendental medicine for the last twenty years. I have heard myself called quack and charlatan and impostor, but all the while I knew I was on the right path. Five years ago I reached the goal, and since then every day has been a preparation for what we shall do to-night.'

'I should like to believe it is all true.' Clarke knit his brows, and looked doubtfully at Dr. Raymond. 'Are you perfectly sure, Raymond, that your theory is not a phantasmagoria – a splendid vision, certainly, but a mere vision after all?'

Dr. Raymond stopped in his walk and turned sharply. He was a middle-aged man, gaunt and thin, of a pale yellow complexion, but as he answered Clarke and faced him, there was a flush on his cheek.

'Look about you, Clarke. You see the mountain, and hill following after hill, as wave on wave, you see the woods and orchards, the fields of ripe corn, and the meadows reaching to the reed-beds by the river. You see me standing here beside you, and hear my voice; but I tell you that all these things – yes, from that star that has just shone out in the sky to the solid ground beneath our feet – I say that all these are but dreams and shadows: the shadows that hide the real world from our eyes. There *is* a real world, but it is beyond this glamour and this vision, beyond these "chases in Arras, dreams in a career," beyond them all as beyond a veil. I do not know whether any human being has ever lifted that veil; but I do know, Clarke, that you and I shall see it lifted this very night from before another's eyes. You may think all this strange nonsense; it may be strange, but it is true, and the ancients knew what lifting the veil means. They called it seeing the god Pan.'

Clarke shivered; the white mist gathering over the river was chilly.

'It is wonderful indeed,' he said. 'We are standing on the brink of a strange world, Raymond, if what you say is true. I suppose the knife is absolutely necessary?'

'Yes; a slight lesion in the grey matter, that is all; a trifling rearrangement of certain cells, a microscopical alteration that would escape the attention of ninety-nine brain specialists out of a hundred. I don't want to bother you with "shop," Clarke; I might give you a mass of technical detail which would sound very imposing, and would leave you as enlightened as you are now. But I suppose you have read, casually, in out-of-the-way corners of your paper, that immense strides have been made recently in the physiology of the brain. I saw a paragraph the other day about Digby's theory, and Browne Faber's discoveries. Theories and discoveries! Where they are standing now, I stood fifteen years ago, and I need not tell you that I have not been standing still for the last fifteen years. It will be enough if I say that five years ago I made the discovery to which I alluded when I said that then I reached the goal. After years of labour, after years of toiling and groping in the dark, after days and nights of disappointment and sometimes of despair, in which I used now and then to tremble and grow cold with the thought that perhaps there were others seeking for what I sought, at last, after so long, a pang of sudden joy thrilled my soul, and I knew the long journey was at an end. By what seemed then and still seems a chance, the suggestion of a moment's idle thought followed up upon familiar lines and paths that I had tracked a hundred times already, the great truth burst upon me, and I saw, mapped out in lines of light, a whole world, a sphere unknown; continents and islands, and great oceans in which no ship has sailed (to my belief) since a Man first lifted up his eyes and beheld the sun, and the stars of heaven, and the quiet earth beneath. You will think all this high-flown language, Clarke, but it is hard to be literal. And yet, I do not know whether what I am hinting at cannot be set forth in plain and homely terms. For instance, this world of ours is pretty well girded now with the telegraph wires and cables; thought, with something less than the speed of thought, flashes from sunrise to sunset, from north to south, across the floods and the desert places. Suppose that an electrician of to-day were suddenly to perceive that he and his friends have merely been playing with pebbles and mistaking them for the foundations of the world; suppose that such a man saw uttermost space lie open before the current, and words of men flash forth to the sun and beyond the sun into the systems beyond, and the voices of articulate-speaking men echo in the waste void that bounds our thought. As analogies go, that is a pretty good analogy of what I have done; you can understand now a little of what I felt as I stood here one evening; it was a summer evening, and the valley looked much as it does now; I stood here, and saw before me the unutterable, the unthinkable gulf that yawns profound between two worlds, the world of matter and the world of spirit; I saw the great empty deep stretch dim before me, and in that instant a bridge of light leapt from the earth to the unknown shore, and the abyss was spanned. You may look in Browne Faber's book, if you like, and you will find that to the present day men of science are unable to account for the presence, or to specify the functions of a certain group of nerve cells in the brain. That group is, as it were, land to let, a mere waste place for fanciful theories. I am not in the position of Browne Faber and the specialists, I am perfectly instructed as to the possible functions of those nerve centres in the scheme of things. With a touch I can bring them into play, with a touch, I say, I can set free the current, with a touch I can complete the communication between this world of sense and – we shall be able to finish the sentence later on. Yes, the knife is necessary; but think what that knife will effect. It will level utterly the solid wall of sense, and probably, for the first time since man was made, a spirit will gaze on a spirit world. Clarke, Mary will see the god Pan!'

'But you remember what you wrote to me? I thought it would be requisite that she – '

He whispered the rest into the doctor's ear.

'Not at all, not at all. That is nonsense, I assure you. Indeed, it is better as it is; I am quite certain of that.'

'Consider the matter well, Raymond. It's a great responsibility. Something might go wrong; you would be a miserable man for the rest of your days.'

'No, I think not, even if the worst happened. As you know, I rescued Mary from the gutter, and from almost certain starvation, when she was a child; I think her life is mine, to use as I see fit. Come, it is getting late; we had better go in.'

Dr. Raymond led the way into the house, through the hall, and down a long dark passage. He took a key from his pocket and opened a heavy door, and motioned Clarke into his laboratory. It had once been a billiard room, and was lighted by a glass dome in the centre of the ceiling, whence there still shone a sad grey light on the figure of the doctor as he lit a lamp with a heavy shade and placed it on a table in the middle of the room.

Clarke looked about him. Scarcely a foot of wall remained bare; there were shelves all around laden with bottles and phials of all shapes and colours, and at one end stood a little Chippendale bookcase. Raymond pointed to this.

'You see that parchment Oswald Crollius? He was one of the first to show me the way, though I don't think he ever found it himself. That is a strange saying of his: "In every grain of wheat there lies hidden the soul of a star." '

There was not much of furniture in the laboratory. The table in the centre, a stone slab with a drain in one corner, the two arm-chairs on which Raymond and Clarke were sitting; that was all, except an odd-looking chair at the farthest end of the room. Clarke looked at it, and raised his eyebrows.

'Yes, that is the chair,' said Raymond. 'We may as well place it in position.' He got up and wheeled the chair to the light, and began raising and lowering it, letting down the seat, setting the back at various angles, and adjusting the foot-rest. It looked comfortable enough, and Clarke passed his hand over the soft green velvet, as the doctor manipulated the levers.

'Now, Clarke, make yourself quite comfortable. I have a couple of hours' work before me; I was obliged to leave certain matters to the last.'

Raymond went to the stone slab, and Clarke watched him drearily as he bent over a row of phials and lit the flame under the crucible. The doctor had a small hand-lamp, shaded as the larger one, on a ledge above his apparatus, and Clarke, who sat in the shadows, looked down the great dreary room, wondering at the bizarre effects of brilliant light and undefined darkness contrasting with one another. Soon he became conscious of an odd odour, at first the merest suggestion of odour, in the room; and as it grew more decided, he felt surprised that he was not reminded of the chemist's shop or the surgery. Clarke found himself idly endeavouring to analyse the sensation, and, half conscious, he began to think of a day, fifteen years ago, that he had spent in roaming through the woods and meadows near his old home. It was a burning day at the beginning of August, the heat had dimmed the outlines of all things and all distances with a faint mist, and people who observed the thermometer spoke of an abnormal register, of a temperature that was almost tropical. Strangely that wonderful hot day of the 'fifties rose up in Clarke's imagination; the sense of dazzling, all-pervading sunlight seemed to blot out the shadows and the lights of the laboratory, and he felt again the heated air beating in gusts about his face, saw the shimmer rising from the turf, and heard the myriad murmur of the summer.

'I hope the smell doesn't annoy you, Clarke; there's nothing unwholesome about it. It may make you a bit sleepy, that's all.'

Clarke heard the words quite distinctly, and knew that Raymond was speaking to him, but for the life of him he could not rouse himself from this lethargy. He could only think of the lonely walk he had taken fifteen years ago; it was his last look at the fields and woods he had known since he was a child, and now it all stood out in brilliant light, as a picture, before him. Above all, there came to his nostrils the scent of summer, the smell of flowers mingled, and the odour of the woods, of cool shaded places, deep in the green depths, drawn forth by the sun's heat; and the scent of the good earth, lying, as it were, with arms stretched forth, and smiling lips, overpowered all. His fancies made him wander, as he had wandered long ago, from the fields into the wood, tracking a little path between the shining undergrowth of beech trees; and the trickle of water dropping from the limestone rock sounded as a clear melody in the dream. Thoughts began to go astray and to mingle with other recollections; the beech alley was transformed to a path beneath ilex trees, and here and there a vine climbed from bough to bough, and sent up waving tendrils and drooped with purple grapes, and the sparse grey-green leaves of a wild olive tree stood out against the dark shadows of the ilex. Clarke, in the deep folds of dream, was conscious that the path from his father's house had led him into an undiscovered country, and he was wondering at the strangeness of it all, when suddenly, in place of the hum and murmur of the summer, an infinite silence seemed to fall on all things, and the wood was hushed, and for a moment of time he stood face to face there with a presence, that was neither man nor beast, neither the living nor the dead, but all things mingled, the form

of all things but devoid of all form. And in that moment the sacrament
of body and soul was dissolved, and a voice seemed to cry, 'Let us go
hence,' and then the darkness of darkness beyond the stars, the
darkness of everlasting.

When Clarke woke up with a start he saw Raymond pouring a few
drops of some oily fluid into a green phial, which he stoppered tightly.

'You have been dozing,' he said; 'the journey must have tired you
out. It is done now. I am going to fetch Mary; I shall be back in ten
minutes.'

Clarke lay back in his chair and wondered. It seemed as if he had
but passed from one dream into another. He half expected to see the
walls of the laboratory melt and disappear, and to awake in London,
shuddering at his own sleeping fancies. But at last the door opened,
and the doctor returned, and behind him came a girl of about
seventeen, dressed all in white. She was so beautiful that Clarke
did not wonder at what the doctor had written to him. She was
blushing now over face and neck and arms, but Raymond seemed
unmoved.

'Mary,' he said, 'the time has come. You are quite free. Are you
willing to trust yourself to me entirely?'

'Yes, dear.'

'You hear that, Clarke? You are my witness. Here is the chair,
Mary. It is quite easy. Just sit in it and lean back. Are you ready?'

'Yes, dear, quite ready. Give me a kiss before you begin.'

The doctor stooped and kissed her mouth, kindly enough. 'Now
shut your eyes,' he said. The girl closed her eyelids, as if she were tired,
and longed for sleep, and Raymond held the green phial to her
nostrils. Her face grew white, whiter than her dress; she struggled
faintly, and then with the feeling of submission strong within her,
crossed her arms upon her breast as a little child about to say her
prayers. The bright light of the lamp beat full upon her, and Clarke
watched changes fleeting over that face as the changes of the hills
when the summer clouds float across the sun. And then she lay all
white and still, and the doctor turned up one of her eyelids. She was
quite unconscious. Raymond pressed hard on one of the levers and
the chair instantly sank back. Clarke saw him cutting away a circle,
like a tonsure, from her hair, and the lamp was moved nearer.
Raymond took a small glittering instrument from a little case, and
Clarke turned away shuddering. When he looked again, the doctor
was binding up the wound he had made.

'She will awake in five minutes.' Raymond was still perfectly cool.

'There is nothing more to be done; we can only wait.'

The minutes passed slowly; they could hear a slow, heavy ticking. There was an old clock in the passage. Clarke felt sick and faint; his knees shook beneath him, he could hardly stand.

Suddenly, as they watched, they heard a long-drawn sigh, and suddenly did the colour that had vanished return to the girl's cheeks, and suddenly her eyes opened. Clarke quailed before them. They shone with an awful light, looking far away, and a great wonder fell upon her face, and her hands stretched out as if to touch what was invisible; but in an instant the wonder faded, and gave place to the most awful terror. The muscles of her face were hideously convulsed, she shook from head to foot; the soul seemed struggling and shuddering within the house of flesh. It was a horrible sight, and Clarke rushed forward, as she fell shrieking to the floor.

Three days later Raymond took Clarke to Mary's bedside. She was lying wide-awake, rolling her head from side to side, and grinning vacantly.

'Yes,' said the doctor, still quite cool, 'it is a great pity; she is a hopeless idiot. However, it could not be helped; and, after all, she has seen the Great God Pan.'

II

MR. CLARKE'S MEMOIRS

Mr. Clarke, the gentleman chosen by Dr. Raymond to witness the strange experiment of the god Pan, was a person in whose character caution and curiosity were oddly mingled; in his sober moments he thought of the unusual and the eccentric with undisguised aversion, and yet, deep in his heart, there was a wide-eyed inquisitiveness with respect to all the more recondite and esoteric elements in the nature of men. The latter tendency had prevailed when he accepted Raymond's invitation, for though his considered judgment had always repudiated the doctor's theories as the wildest nonsense, yet he secretly hugged a belief in fantasy, and would have rejoiced to see that belief confirmed. The horrors that he witnessed in the dreary laboratory were to a certain extent salutary; he was conscious of being involved in an affair not altogether reputable, and for many years afterwards he clung bravely to the commonplace, and rejected all occasions of occult investigation. Indeed, on some homoeopathic principle, he for some time attended the séances of distinguished mediums, hoping that the clumsy tricks of these gentlemen would make him altogether disgusted with mysticism of every kind, but the remedy, though caustic, was not efficacious. Clarke knew that he still pined for the unseen, and little by little, the old passion began to reassert itself, as the face of Mary, shuddering and convulsed with an unknowable terror, faded slowly from his memory. Occupied all day in pursuits both serious and lucrative, the temptation to relax in the evening was too great, especially in the winter months, when the fire cast a warm glow over his snug bachelor apartment, and a bottle of some choice claret stood ready by his elbow. His dinner digested, he would make a brief pretence of reading the evening paper, but the mere catalogue of news soon palled upon him, and Clarke would find himself casting glances of warm desire in the direction of an old Japanese bureau, which stood at a pleasant distance from the hearth. Like a boy before a jam closet, for a few minutes he would hover indecisive, but lust always prevailed, and Clarke ended by drawing up his chair, lighting a candle, and sitting down before the bureau. Its pigeon-holes and drawers teemed with documents on the most morbid subjects, and in the well reposed a large manuscript volume, in which he had painfully entered the gems of his collection. Clarke had a fine contempt for published literature; the most ghostly story ceased to interest him if it happened to be printed; his sole pleasure was in the reading, compiling, and rearranging of what he called his 'Memoirs to prove the Existence of the Devil,' and engaged in this pursuit the evening seemed to fly and the night appeared too short.

On one particular evening, an ugly December night, black with fog, and raw with frost, Clarke hurried over his dinner, and scarcely deigned to observe his customary ritual of taking up the paper and laying it down again. He paced two or three times up and down the room, and opened the bureau, stood still a moment, and sat down. He leant back, absorbed in one of those dreams to which he was subject, and at length drew out his book, and opened it at the last entry. There were three or four pages densely covered with Clarke's round, set penmanship, and at the beginning he had written in a somewhat larger hand:

Singular Narrative told me by my Friend, Dr. Phillips. He assures me that all the facts related therein are strictly and wholly True, but refuses to give either the Surnames of the Persons concerned, or the Place where these Extraordinary Events occurred.

Mr. Clarke began to read over the account for the tenth time, glancing now and then at the pencil notes he had made when it was told him by his friend. It was one of his humours to pride himself on a certain literary ability; he thought well of his style, and took pains in arranging the circumstances in dramatic order. He read the following story:

The persons concerned in this statement are Helen V., who, if she is still alive, must now be a woman of twenty-three, Rachel M., since deceased, who was a year younger than the above, and Trevor W., an imbecile, aged eighteen. These persons were at the period of the story inhabitants of a village on the borders of Wales, a place of some importance in the time of the Roman occupation, but now a scattered hamlet, of not more than five hundred souls. It is situated on rising ground, about six miles from the sea, and is sheltered by a large and picturesque forest.

Some eleven years ago, Helen V. came to the village under rather peculiar circumstances. It is understood that she, being an orphan, was adopted in her infancy by a distant relative, who brought her up in his own house till she was twelve years old. Thinking, however, that it would be better for the child to have playmates of her own age, he advertised in several local papers for a good home in a comfortable farmhouse for a girl of twelve, and this advertisement was answered by Mr. R., a well-to-do farmer in the above-mentioned village. His references proving satisfactory, the gentleman sent his adopted daughter to Mr. R., with a letter in which he stipulated that the girl should have a room to herself, and stated that her guardians need be at no trouble in the matter of education, as she was already sufficiently educated for the position in life which she would occupy. In fact, Mr. R. was given to understand that the girl was to be allowed to find her own occupations, and to spend her time almost as she liked. Mr. R. duly met her at the nearest station, a town some seven miles away from his house, and seems to have remarked nothing extraordinary about the child, except that she was reticent as to her former life and her adopted father. She was, however, of a very different type from the inhabitants of the village; her skin was a pale, clear olive, and her features were strongly marked, and of a somewhat foreign character. She appears to have settled down easily enough into farmhouse life, and became a favourite with the children, who sometimes went with her on her rambles in the forest, for this was her amusement. Mr. R. states that he has known her to go out by herself directly after their early breakfast, and not return till after dusk, and that, feeling uneasy at a young girl being out alone for so many hours, he communicated with her adopted father, who replied in a brief note that Helen must do as she chose. In the winter, when the forest paths were impassable, she spent most of her time in her bedroom, where she slept alone, according to the instructions of her relative. It was on one of these expeditions to the forest that the first of the singular incidents with which this girl is connected occurred, the date being about a year after her arrival at the village. The preceding winter had been remarkably severe, the snow drifting to a great depth, and the frost continuing for an unexampled period, and the summer following was as noteworthy for its extreme heat. On one of the very hottest days in this summer, Helen V. left the farmhouse for one of her long rambles in the forest, taking with her, as usual, some bread and meat for lunch. She was seen by some men in the fields making for the old Roman Road, a green causeway which traverses the highest part of the wood, and they were astonished to observe that the girl had taken off her hat, though the heat of the sun was already almost tropical. As it happened, a labourer, Joseph W. by name, was working in the forest near the Roman Road, and at twelve o'clock his little son, Trevor, brought the man his dinner of bread and cheese. After the meal, the boy, who was about seven years old at the time, left his father at work, and, as he said, went to look for flowers in the wood, and the man, who could hear him shouting with delight over his discoveries, felt no uneasiness. Suddenly, however, he was horrified at hearing the most dreadful screams, evidently the result of great terror, proceeding from the direction in which his son had gone, and he hastily threw down his tools and ran to see what had happened. Tracing his path by the sound, he met the little boy, who was running headlong and was evidently terribly frightened, and on questioning him the man at last elicited that after picking a posy of flowers he felt tired, and lay down on the grass and fell asleep. He was suddenly awakened, as he stated, by a peculiar noise, a sort of singing he called it, and on peeping through the branches he saw Helen V. playing on the grass with a 'strange naked man,' whom he seemed unable to describe more fully. He said he felt dreadfully frightened, and ran away crying for his father. Joseph W. proceeded in the direction indicated by his son, and found Helen V. sitting on the grass in the middle of a glade or open space left by charcoal burners. He angrily charged her with frightening his little boy, but she entirely denied the accusation and laughed at the child's story of a 'strange man,' to which he himself did not attach much credence. Joseph W. came to the conclusion that the boy had woke up with a sudden fright, as children sometimes do, but Trevor persisted in his story, and continued in such evident distress that at last his father took him home, hoping that his mother would be able to soothe him. For many weeks, however, the boy gave his parents much anxiety; he became nervous and strange in his manner, refusing to leave the cottage by himself, and constantly alarming the household by waking in the night with cries of 'The man in the wood! father! father!'

In course of time, however, the impression seemed to have worn off, and about three months later he accompanied his father to the house of a gentleman in the neighbourhood, for whom Joseph W. occasionally did work. The man was shown into the study, and the little boy was left sitting in the hall, and a few minutes later, while the gentleman was giving W. his instructions, they were both horrified by a piercing shriek and the sound of a fall, and rushing out they found the child lying senseless on the floor, his face contorted with terror. The doctor was immediately summoned, and after some examination he pronounced the child to be suffering from a kind of fit, apparently produced by a sudden shock. The boy was taken to one of the bedrooms, and after some time recovered consciousness, but only to pass into a condition described by the medical man as one of violent hysteria. The doctor exhibited a strong sedative, and in the course of two hours pronounced him fit to walk home, but in passing through the hall the paroxysms of fright returned and with additional violence. The father perceived that the child was pointing at some object, and heard the old cry, 'The man in the wood,' and looking in the direction indicated saw a stone head of grotesque appearance, which had been built into the wall above one of the doors. It seems that the owner of the house had recently made alterations in his premises, and on digging the foundation for some offices, the men had found a curious head, evidently of the Roman period, which had been placed in the hall in the manner described. The head is pronounced by the most experienced archæologists of the district to be that of a faun or satyr.*

From whatever cause arising, this second shock seemed too severe for the boy Trevor, and at the present date he suffers from a weakness of intellect, which gives but little promise of amending. The matter caused a good deal of sensation at the time, and the girl Helen was closely questioned by Mr. R., but to no purpose, she steadfastly denying that she had frightened or in any way molested Trevor.

The second event with which this girl's name is connected took

---

* Dr. Phillips tells me that he has seen the head in question, and assures me that he has never received such a vivid presentiment of intense evil.

place about six years ago, and is of a still more extraordinary character.

At the beginning of the summer of 1882 Helen contracted a friendship of a peculiarly intimate character with Rachel M., the daughter of a prosperous farmer in the neighbourhood. This girl, who was a year younger than Helen, was considered by most people to be the prettier of the two, though Helen's features had to a great extent softened as she became older. The two girls, who were together on every available opportunity, presented a singular contrast, the one with her clear, olive skin and almost Italian appearance, and the other of the proverbial red and white of our rural districts. It must be stated that the payments made to Mr. R. for the maintenance of Helen were known in the village for their excessive liberality, and the impression was general that she would one day inherit a large sum of money from her relative. The parents of Rachel were therefore not averse from their daughter's friendship with the girl, and even encouraged the intimacy, though they now bitterly regret having done so. Helen still retained her extraordinary fondness for the forest, and on several occasions Rachel accompanied her, the two friends setting out early in the morning, and remaining in the wood till dusk. Once or twice after these excursions Mrs. M. thought her daughter's manner rather peculiar; she seemed languid and dreamy, and as it has been expressed, 'different from herself,' but these peculiarities seem to have been thought too trifling for remark. One evening, however, after Rachel had come home, her mother heard a noise which sounded like suppressed weeping in the girl's room, and on going in found her lying, half undressed, upon the bed, evidently in the greatest distress. As soon as she saw her mother, she exclaimed, 'Ah, mother, mother, why did you let me go to the forest with Helen?' Mrs. M. was astonished at so strange a question, and proceeded to make inquiries. Rachel told her a wild story. She said –

Clarke closed the book with a snap, and turned his chair towards the fire. When his friend sat one evening in that very chair, and told his story, Clarke had interrupted him at a point a little subsequent to this, had cut short his words in a paroxysm of horror. 'My God!' he had exclaimed, 'think, think what you are saying. It is too incredible, too monstrous; such things can never be in this quiet world, where men and women live and die, and struggle, and conquer, or maybe fail, and fall down under sorrow, and grieve and suffer strange fortunes for many a year; but not this, Phillips, not such things as this. There must be some explanation, some way out of the terror. Why, man, if such a case were possible, our earth would be a nightmare.'

But Phillips had told his story to the end, concluding:

'Her flight remains a mystery to this day; she vanished in broad sunlight; they saw her walking in a meadow, and a few moments later she was not there.'

Clarke tried to conceive the thing again, as he sat by the fire, and again his mind shuddered and shrank back, appalled before the sight of such awful, unspeakable elements enthroned as it were, and triumphant in human flesh. Before him stretched the long dim vista of the green causeway in the forest, as his friend had described it; he saw the swaying leaves and the quivering shadows on the grass, he saw the sunlight and the flowers, and far away, far in the long distance, the two figures moved towards him. One was Rachel, but the other?

Clarke had tried his best to disbelieve it all, but at the end of the account, as he had written it in his book, he had placed the inscription:

ET DIABOLUS INCARNATUS EST. ET HOMO FACTUS EST.

III

THE CITY OF RESURRECTIONS

'Herbert! Good God! Is it possible?'

'Yes, my name's Herbert. I think I know your face too, but I don't remember your name. My memory is very queer.'

'Don't you recollect Villiers of Wadham?'

'So it is, so it is. I beg your pardon, Villiers, I didn't think I was begging of an old college friend. Good-night.'

'My dear fellow, this haste is unnecessary. My rooms are close by, but we won't go there just yet. Suppose we walk up Shaftesbury Avenue a little way? But how in heaven's name have you come to this pass, Herbert?'

'It's a long story, Villiers, and a strange one too, but you can hear it if you like.'

'Come on, then. Take my arm, you don't seem very strong.'

The ill-assorted pair moved slowly up Rupert Street; the one in dirty, evil-looking rags, and the other attired in the regulation uniform of a man about town, trim, glossy, and eminently well-to-do. Villiers had emerged from his restaurant after an excellent dinner of many courses, assisted by an ingratiating little flask of Chianti, and, in that frame of mind which was with him almost chronic, had delayed a moment by the door, peering round in the dimly lighted street in search of those mysterious incidents and persons with which the streets of London teem in every quarter and at every hour. Villiers prided himself as a practised explorer of such obscure mazes and byways of London life, and in this unprofitable pursuit he displayed an assiduity which was worthy of more serious employment. Thus he stood beside the lamppost surveying the passers-by with undisguised curiosity, and, with that gravity known only to the systematic diner, had just enunciated in his mind the formula: 'London has been called the city of encounters; it is more than that, it is the city of Resurrections,' when these reflections were suddenly interrupted by a piteous whine at his elbow, and a deplorable appeal for alms. He looked around in some irritation, and with a sudden shock found himself confronted with the embodied proof of his somewhat stilted fancies. There, close beside him, his face altered and disfigured by poverty and disgrace, his body barely covered by greasy ill-fitting rags, stood his old friend Charles Herbert, who had matriculated on the same day as himself, with whom he had been merry and wise for twelve revolving terms. Different occupations and varying interests had interrupted the friendship, and it was six years since Villiers had seen Herbert; and now he looked upon this wreck of a man with grief and dismay, mingled with a certain inquisitiveness as to what dreary chain of circumstances had dragged him down to such a doleful pass. Villiers felt together with compassion all the relish of the amateur in mysteries, and congratulated himself on his leisurely speculations outside the restaurant.

They walked on in silence for some time, and more than one passer-by stared in astonishment at the unaccustomed spectacle of a well-dressed man with an unmistakable beggar hanging on to his arm, and, observing this, Villiers led the way to an obscure street in Soho. Here he repeated his question.

'How on earth has it happened, Herbert? I always understood you would succeed to an excellent position in Dorsetshire. Did your father disinherit you? Surely not?'

'No, Villiers; I came into all the property at my poor father's death; he died a year after I left Oxford. He was a very good father to me, and I mourned his death sincerely enough. But you know what young men are; a few months later I came up to town and went a good deal into society. Of course I had excellent introductions, and I managed to enjoy myself very much in a harmless sort of way. I played a little, certainly, but never for heavy stakes, and the few bets I made on races brought me in money – only a few pounds, you know, but enough to pay for cigars and such petty pleasures. It was in my second season that the tide turned. Of course you have heard of my marriage?'

'No, I never heard anything about it.'

'Yes, I married, Villiers. I met a girl, a girl of the most wonderful and most strange beauty, at the house of some people I knew. I cannot tell you her age; I never knew it, but, so far as I can guess, I should think she must have been about nineteen when I made her acquaintance. My friends had come to know her at Florence; she told them she was an orphan, the child of an English father and an Italian mother, and she charmed them as she charmed me. The first time I saw her was at an evening party. I was standing by the door talking to a friend, when suddenly above the hum and babble of conversation I heard a voice which seemed to thrill to my heart. She was singing an Italian song. I was introduced to her that evening and in three months I married Helen. Villiers, that woman, if I can call her woman, corrupted my soul. The night of the wedding I found myself sitting in her bedroom in the hotel, listening to her talk. She was sitting up in bed, and I listened to her as she spoke in her beautiful voice, spoke of things which even now I would not dare whisper in blackest night, though I stood in the midst of a wilderness. You, Villiers, you may think you know life, and London, and what goes on day and night in this dreadful city; for all I can say you may have heard the talk of the vilest, but I tell you you can have no conception of what I know, not in your most fantastic, hideous dreams can you have imaged forth the faintest shadow of what I have heard – and seen. Yes, seen. I have seen the incredible, such horrors that even I myself sometimes stop in the middle of the street, and ask whether it is possible for a man to behold such things and live. In a year, Villiers, I was a ruined man, in body and soul – in body and soul.'

'But your property, Herbert? You had land in Dorset.'

'I sold it all; the fields and woods, the dear old house – everything.'

'And the money?'

'She took it all from me.'

'And she left you?'

'Yes; she disappeared one night. I don't know where she went, but I am sure if I saw her again it would kill me. The rest of my story is of no interest; sordid misery, that is all. You may think, Villiers, that I have exaggerated and talked for effect; but I have not told you half. I could tell you certain things which would convince you, but you would never know a happy day again. You would pass the rest of your life, as I pass mine, a haunted man, a man who has seen hell.'

Villiers took the unfortunate man to his rooms, and gave him a meal. Herbert could eat little, and scarcely touched the glass of wine set before him. He sat moody and silent by the fire, and seemed relieved when Villiers sent him away with a small present of money.

'By the way, Herbert,' said Villiers, as they parted at the door, 'what was your wife's name? You said Helen, I think? Helen what?'

'The name she passed under when I met her was Helen Vaughan, but what her real name was I can't say. I don't think she had a name. No, no, not in that sense. Only human beings have names, Villiers; I can't say any more. Good-bye; yes, I will not fail to call if I see any way in which you can help me. Good-night.'

The man went out into the bitter night, and Villiers returned to his fireside. There was something about Herbert which shocked him inexpressibly; not his poor rags nor the marks which poverty had set upon his face, but rather an indefinite terror which hung about him like a mist. He had acknowledged that he himself was not devoid of blame; the woman, he had avowed, had corrupted him body and soul, and Villiers felt that this man, once his friend, had been an actor in scenes evil beyond the power of words. His story needed no confirmation: he himself was the embodied proof of it. Villiers mused curiously over the story he had heard, and wondered whether he had heard both the first and the last of it.

'No,' he thought, 'certainly not the last, probably only the beginning. A case like this is like a nest of Chinese boxes; you open one after another and find a quainter workmanship in every box. Most likely poor Herbert is merely one of the outside boxes; there are stranger ones to follow.'

Villiers could not take his mind away from Herbert and his story, which seemed to grow wilder as the night wore on. The fire began to burn low, and the chilly air of the morning crept into the room; Villiers got up with a glance over his shoulder, and shivering slightly, went to bed.

A few days later he saw at his club a gentleman of his acquaintance, named Austin, who was famous for his intimate knowledge of London life, both in its tenebrous and luminous phases. Villiers, still full of his encounter in Soho and its consequences, thought Austin might possibly be able to shed some light on Herbert's history, and so after some casual talk he suddenly put the question:

'Do you happen to know anything of a man named Herbert – Charles Herbert?'

Austin turned round sharply and stared at Villiers with some astonishment.

'Charles Herbert? Weren't you in town three years ago? No; then you have not heard of the Paul Street case? It caused a good deal of sensation at the time.'

'What was the case?'

'Well, a gentleman, a man of very good position, was found dead, stark dead, in the area of a certain house in Paul Street, off Tottenham Court Road. Of course the police did not make the discovery; if you happen to be sitting up all night and have a light in your window, the constable will ring the bell, but if you happen to be lying dead in somebody's area, you will be left alone. In this instance, as in many others, the alarm was raised by some kind of vagabond; I don't mean a common tramp, or a public-house loafer, but a gentleman, whose business or pleasure, or both, made him a spectator of the London streets at five o'clock in the morning. This individual was, as he said, 'going home,' it did not appear whence or whither, and had occasion to pass through Paul Street between four and five a.m. Something or other caught his eye at Number 20; he said, absurdly enough, that the house had the most unpleasant physiognomy he had ever observed, but, at any rate, he glanced down the area, and was a good deal astonished to see a man lying on the stones, his limbs all huddled together, and his face turned up. Our gentleman thought his face looked peculiarly ghastly, and so set off at a run in search of the nearest policeman. The constable was at first inclined to treat the matter lightly, suspecting common drunkenness; however, he came, and after looking at the man's face, changed his tone, quickly enough. The early bird, who had picked up this fine worm, was sent off for a doctor, and the policeman rang and knocked at the door till a slatternly servant girl came down looking more than half asleep. The constable pointed out the contents of the area to the maid, who screamed loudly enough to wake up the street, but she knew nothing of the man; had never seen him at the house, and so forth. Meanwhile the original discoverer had come back with a medical man, and the next thing was to get into the area. The gate was open, so the whole quartet stumped down the steps. The doctor hardly needed a moment's examination; he said the poor fellow had been dead for several hours, and it was then the case began to get interesting. The dead man had not been robbed, and in one of his pockets were papers identifying him as – well, as a man of good family and means, a favourite in society, and nobody's enemy, so far as could be known. I don't give his name, Villiers, because it has nothing to do with the story, and because it's no good raking up these affairs about the dead when there are no relations living. The next curious point was that the medical men couldn't agree as to how he met his death. There were some slight bruises on his shoulders, but they were so slight that it looked as if he had been pushed roughly out of the kitchen door, and not thrown over the railings from the street or even dragged down the steps. But there were positively no other marks of violence about him, certainly none that would account for his death; and when they came to the autopsy there wasn't a trace of poison of any kind. Of course the police wanted to know all about the people at Number 20, and here again, so I have heard from private sources, one or two other very curious points came out. It appears that the occupants of the house were a Mr. and Mrs. Charles Herbert; he was said to be a landed proprietor, though it struck most people that Paul Street was not exactly the place to look for county gentry. As for Mrs. Herbert, nobody seemed to know who or what she was, and, between ourselves, I fancy the divers after her history found themselves in rather strange waters. Of course they both denied knowing anything about the deceased, and in default of any evidence against them they were discharged. But some very odd things came out about them. Though it was between five and six in the morning when the dead man was removed, a large crowd had collected, and several of the neighbours ran to see what was going on. They were pretty free with their comments, by all accounts, and from these it appeared that Number 20 was in very bad odour in Paul Street. The detectives tried to trace down these rumours to some solid foundation of fact, but could not get hold of anything. People shook their heads and raised their eyebrows and thought the Herberts rather 'queer,' 'would rather not be seen going into their house,' and so on, but there was nothing tangible. The authorities were morally certain that the man met his death in some way or another in the house and was thrown out by the kitchen door, but they couldn't prove it, and the absence of any indications of violence or poisoning left them helpless. An odd case, wasn't it? But curiously enough, there's something more that I haven't told you. I happened to know one of the doctors who was consulted as to the cause of death, and some time after the inquest I met him, and asked him about it. 'Do you really mean to tell me,' I said, 'that you were baffled by the case, that you actually don't know what the man died of?' 'Pardon me,' he replied, 'I know perfectly well what caused death. Blank died of fright, of sheer, awful terror; I never saw features so hideously contorted in the entire course of my practice, and I have seen the faces of a whole host of dead.' The doctor was usually a cool customer enough, and a certain vehemence in his manner struck me, but I couldn't get anything more out of him. I suppose the Treasury didn't see their way to prosecuting the Herberts for frightening a man to death; at any rate, nothing was done, and the case dropped out of men's minds. Do you happen to know anything of Herbert?'

'Well,' replied Villiers, 'he was an old college friend of mine.'

'You don't say so? Have you ever seen his wife?'

'No, I haven't. I have lost sight of Herbert for many years.'

'It's queer, isn't it, parting with a man at the college gate or at Paddington, seeing nothing of him for years, and then finding him pop up his head in such an odd place. But I should like to have seen Mrs. Herbert; people said extraordinary things about her.'

'What sort of things?'

'Well, I hardly know how to tell you. Everyone who saw her at the police court said she was at once the most beautiful woman and the most repulsive they had ever set eyes on. I have spoken to a man who saw her, and I assure you he positively shuddered as he tried to describe the woman, but he couldn't tell why. She seems to have been a sort of enigma; and I expect if that one dead man could have told tales, he would have told some uncommonly queer ones. And there you are again in another puzzle; what could a respectable country gentleman like Mr. Blank (we'll call him that if you don't mind) want in such a very queer house as Number 20? It's altogether a very odd case, isn't it?'

'It is indeed, Austin; an extraordinary case. I didn't think, when I asked you about my old friend, I should strike on such strange metal. Well, I must be off; good-day.'

Villiers went away, thinking of his own conceit of the Chinese boxes; here was quaint workmanship indeed.

IV

THE DISCOVERY IN PAUL STREET

A few months after Villiers' meeting with Herbert, Mr. Clarke was sitting, as usual, by his after-dinner hearth, resolutely guarding his fancies from wandering in the direction of the bureau. For more than a week he had succeeded in keeping away from the 'Memoirs,' and he cherished hopes of a complete self-reformation; but, in spite of his endeavours, he could not hush the wonder and the strange curiosity that that last case he had written down had excited within him. He had put the case, or rather the outline of it, conjecturally to a scientific friend, who shook his head, and thought Clarke getting queer, and on this particular evening Clarke was making an effort to rationalize the story, when a sudden knock at his door roused him from his meditations.

'Mr. Villiers to see you, sir.'

'Dear me, Villiers, it is very kind of you to look me up; I have not seen you for many months; I should think nearly a year. Come in, come in. And how are you, Villiers? Want any advice about investments?'

'No, thanks, I fancy everything I have in that way is pretty safe. No, Clarke, I have really come to consult you about a rather curious matter that has been brought under my notice of late. I am afraid you will think it all rather absurd when I tell my tale. I sometimes think so myself, and that's just why I made up my mind to come to you, as I know you're a practical man.'

Mr. Villiers was ignorant of the 'Memoirs to prove the Existence of the Devil.'

'Well, Villiers, I shall be happy to give you my advice, to the best of my ability. What is the nature of the case?'

'It's an extraordinary thing altogether. You know my ways; I always keep my eyes open in the streets, and in my time I have chanced upon some queer customers, and queer cases too, but this, I think, beats all. I was coming out of a restaurant one nasty winter night about three months ago; I had had a capital dinner and a good bottle of Chianti, and I stood for a moment on the pavement, thinking what a mystery there is about London streets and the companies that pass along them. A bottle of red wine encourages these fancies, Clarke, and I dare say I should have thought a page of small type, but I was cut short by a beggar who had come behind me, and was making the usual appeals. Of course I looked round, and this beggar turned out to be what was left of an old friend of mine, a man named Herbert. I asked him how he had come to such a wretched pass, and he told me. We walked up and down one of those long dark Soho streets, and there I listened to his story. He said he had married a beautiful girl, some years younger than himself, and, as he put it, she had corrupted him body and soul. He wouldn't go into details; he said he dare not, that what he had seen and heard haunted him by night and day, and when I looked in his face I knew he was speaking the truth. There was something about the man that made me shiver. I don't know why, but it was there. I gave him a little money and sent him away, and I assure you that when he was gone I gasped for breath. His presence seemed to chill one's blood.'

'Isn't all this just a little fanciful, Villiers? I suppose the poor fellow had made an imprudent marriage, and, in plain English, gone to the bad.'

'Well, listen to this.' Villiers told Clarke the story he had heard from Austin.

'You see,' he concluded, 'there can be but little doubt that this Mr. Blank, whoever he was, died of sheer terror; he saw something so awful, so terrible, that it cut short his life. And what he saw, he most certainly saw in that house, which, somehow or other, had got a bad name in the neighbourhood. I had the curiosity to go and look at the place for myself. It's a saddening kind of street; the houses are old enough to be mean and dreary, but not old enough to be quaint. As far as I could see, most of them are let in lodgings, furnished and unfurnished, and almost every door has three bells to it. Here and there the ground floors have been made into shops of the commonest kind; it's a dismal street in every way. I found Number 20 was to let, and I went to the agent's and got the key. Of course I should have heard nothing of the Herberts in that quarter, but I asked the man, fair and square, how long they had left the house, and whether there had been other tenants in the meanwhile. He looked at me queerly for a minute, and told me the Herberts had left immediately after the unpleasant- ness, as he called it, and since then the house had been empty.'

Mr. Villiers paused for a moment.

'I have always been rather fond of going over empty houses; there's a sort of fascination about the desolate empty rooms, with the nails sticking in the walls, and the dust thick upon the window sills. But I didn't enjoy going over Number 20 Paul Street. I had hardly put my foot inside the passage before I noticed a queer, heavy feeling about the air of the house. Of course all empty houses are stuffy, and so forth, but this was something quite different; I can't describe it to you, but it seemed to stop the breath. I went into the front room and the back room, and the kitchen downstairs; they were all dirty and dusty enough, as you would expect, but there was something strange about them all. I couldn't define it to you, I only know I felt queer. It was one of the rooms on the first floor, though, that was the worst. It was a largish room, and once on a time the paper must have been cheerful enough, but when I saw it, paint, paper, and everything were most doleful. But the room was full of horror; I felt my teeth grinding as I put my hand on the door, and when I went in, I thought I should have fallen fainting to the floor. However, I pulled myself together, and stood against the end wall, wondering what on earth there could be about the room to make my limbs tremble, and my heart beat as if I were at the hour of death. In one corner there was a pile of newspapers littered about on the floor, and I began looking at them; they were papers of three or four years ago, some of them half torn, and some crumpled as if they had been used for packing. I turned the whole pile over, and amongst them I found a curious drawing; I will show it you presently. But I couldn't stay in the room; I felt it was overpowering me. I was thankful to come out, safe and sound, into the open air. People stared at me as I walked along the street, and one man said I was drunk. I was staggering about from one side of the pavement to the other, and it was as much as I could do to take the key back to the agent and get home. I was in bed for a week, suffering from what my doctor called nervous shock and exhaustion. One of those days I was reading the evening paper, and happened to notice a paragraph headed: 'Starved to Death.' It was the usual style of thing; a model lodging-house in Marylebone, a door locked for several days, and a dead man in his chair when they broke in. 'The deceased,' said the paragraph, 'was known as Charles Herbert, and is believed to have been once a prosperous country gentleman. His name was familiar to the public three years ago in connection with the mysterious death in Paul Street, Tottenham Court Road, the deceased being the tenant of the house Number 20, in the area of which a gentleman of good position was found dead under circumstances not devoid of suspicion.' A tragic ending, wasn't it? But after all, if what he told me were true, which I am sure it was, the man's life was all a tragedy, and a tragedy of a stranger sort than they put on the boards.'

'And that is the story, is it?' said Clarke musingly.

'Yes, that is the story.'

'Well, really, Villiers, I scarcely know what to say about it. There are, no doubt, circumstances in the case which seem peculiar, the finding of the dead man in the area of Herbert's house, for instance, and the extraordinary opinion of the physician as to the cause of death; but, after all, it is conceivable that the facts may be explained in a straightforward manner. As to your own sensations, when you went to see the house, I would suggest that they were due to a vivid imagination; you must have been brooding, in a semi-conscious way, over what you had heard. I don't exactly see what more can be said or done in the matter; you evidently think there is a mystery of some kind, but Herbert is dead; where, then, do you propose to look?'

'I propose to look for the woman; the woman whom he married. *She* is the mystery.'

The two men sat silent by the fireside; Clarke secretly congratulating himself on having successfully kept up the character of advocate of the commonplace, and Villiers wrapt in his gloomy fancies.

'I think I will have a cigarette,' he said at last, and put his hand in his pocket to feel for his cigarette case.

'Ah!' he said, starting slightly, 'I forgot I had something to show you. You remember my saying that I had found a rather curious sketch amongst the pile of old newspapers at the house in Paul Street? Here it is.'

Villiers drew out a small thin parcel from his pocket. It was covered with brown paper, and secured with string, and the knots were troublesome. In spite of himself Clarke felt inquisitive; he bent forward on his chair as Villiers painfully undid the string, and unfolded the outer covering. Inside was a second wrapping of tissue, and Villiers took it off and handed the small piece of paper to Clarke without a word.

There was dead silence in the room for five minutes or more; the two men sat so still that they could hear the ticking of the tall old-fashioned clock that stood outside in the hall, and in the mind of one of them the slow monotony of sound woke up a far, far memory. He was looking intently at the small pen-and-ink sketch of a woman's head; it had evidently been drawn with great care, and by a true artist, for the woman's soul looked out of the eyes, and the lips were parted with a strange smile. Clarke gazed still at the face; it brought to his memory one summer evening long ago; he saw again the long lovely valley, the river winding between the hills, the meadows and the cornfields, the dull red sun, and the cold white mist rising from the water. He heard a voice speaking to him across the waves of many years, and saying, 'Clarke, Mary will see the God Pan!' and then he was standing in the grim room beside the doctor, listening to the heavy ticking of the clock, waiting and watching, watching the figure lying on the green chair beneath the lamplight. Mary rose up, and he looked into her eyes, and his heart grew cold within him.

'Who is this woman?' he said at last. His voice was dry and hoarse.

'That is the woman whom Herbert married.'

Clarke looked again at the sketch; it was not Mary after all. There certainly was Mary's face, but there was something else, something he had not seen on Mary's features when the white-clad girl entered the laboratory with the doctor, nor at her terrible awakening, nor when she lay grinning on the bed. Whatever it was, the glance that came from those eyes, the smile on the full lips, or the expression of the whole face, Clarke shuddered before it in his inmost soul, and thought, unconsciously, of Dr. Phillips's words, 'the most vivid presentiment of evil I have ever seen.' He turned the paper over mechanically in his hand and glanced at the back.

'Good God! Clarke, what is the matter? You are as white as death.'

Villiers had started wildly from his chair, as Clarke fell back with a groan, and let the paper drop from his hands.

'I don't feel very well, Villiers, I am subject to these attacks. Pour me out a little wine; thanks, that will do. I shall feel better in a few minutes.'

Villiers picked up the fallen sketch and turned it over as Clarke had done.

'You saw that?' he said. 'That's how I identified it as being a portrait of Herbert's wife, or I should say his widow. How do you feel now?'

'Better, thanks, it was only a passing faintness. I don't think I quite catch your meaning. What did you say enabled you to identify the picture?'

'This word – "Helen" – written on the back. Didn't I tell you her name was Helen? Yes; Helen Vaughan.'

Clarke groaned; there could be no shadow of doubt.

'Now, don't you agree with me,' said Villiers, 'that in the story I have told you to-night, and in the part this woman plays in it, there are some very strange points?'

'Yes, Villiers,' Clarke muttered, 'it is a strange story indeed; a strange story indeed. You must give me time to think it over; I may be able to help you or I may not. Must you be going now? Well, good-night, Villiers, good-night. Come and see me in the course of a week.'

V

THE LETTER OF ADVICE

'Do you know, Austin,' said Villiers, as the two friends were pacing sedately along Piccadilly one pleasant morning in May, 'do you know

I am convinced that what you told me about Paul Street and the Herberts is a mere episode in an extraordinary history? I may as well confess to you that when I asked you about Herbert a few months ago I had just seen him.'

'You had seen him? Where?'

'He begged of me in the street one night. He was in the most pitiable plight, but I recognized the man, and I got him to tell me his history, or at least the outline of it. In brief, it amounted to this – he had been ruined by his wife.'

'In what manner?'

'He would not tell me; he would only say that she had destroyed him, body and soul. The man is dead now.'

'And what has become of his wife?'

'Ah, that's what I should like to know, and I mean to find her sooner or later. I know a man named Clarke, a dry fellow, in fact a man of business, but shrewd enough. You understand my meaning; not shrewd in the mere business sense of the word, but a man who really knows something about men and life. Well, I laid the case before him, and he was evidently impressed. He said it needed consideration, and asked me to come again in the course of a week. A few days later I received this extraordinary letter.'

Austin took the envelope, drew out the letter, and read it curiously. It ran as follows: –

'MY DEAR VILLIERS, – I have thought over the matter on which you consulted me the other night, and my advice to you is this. Throw the portrait into the fire, blot out the story from your mind. Never give it another thought, Villiers, or you will be sorry. You will think, no doubt, that I am in possession of some secret information, and to a certain extent that is the case. But I only know a little; I am like a traveller who has peered over an abyss, and has drawn back in terror. What I know is strange enough and horrible enough, but beyond my knowledge there are depths and horrors more frightful still, more incredible than any tale told of winter nights about the fire. I have resolved, and nothing shall shake that resolve, to explore no whit farther, and if you value your happiness you will make the same determination.

'Come and see me by all means; but we will talk on more cheerful topics than this.'

Austin folded the letter methodically, and returned it to Villiers.

'It is certainly an extraordinary letter,' he said; 'what does he mean by the portrait?'

'Ah! I forgot to tell you I have been to Paul Street and have made a discovery.'

Villiers told his story as he had told it to Clarke, and Austin listened in silence. He seemed puzzled.

'How very curious that you should experience such an unpleasant sensation in that room!' he said at length. 'I hardly gather that it was a mere matter of the imagination; a feeling of repulsion, in short.'

'No, it was more physical than mental. It was as if I were inhaling at every breath some deadly fume, which seemed to penetrate to every nerve and bone and sinew of my body. I felt racked from head to foot, my eyes began to grow dim; it was like the entrance of death.'

'Yes, yes, very strange, certainly. You see, your friend confesses that there is some very black story connected with this woman. Did you notice any particular emotion in him when you were telling your tale?'

'Yes, I did. He became very faint, but he assured me that it was a mere passing attack to which he was subject.'

'Did you believe him?'

'I did at the time, but I don't now. He heard what I had to say with a good deal of indifference, till I showed him the portrait. It was then he was seized with the attack of which I spoke. He looked ghastly, I assure you.'

'Then he must have seen the woman before. But there might be another explanation; it might have been the name, and not the face, which was familiar to him. What do you think?'

'I couldn't say. To the best of my belief it was after turning the portrait in his hands that he nearly dropped from his chair. The name, you know, was written on the back.'

'Quite so. After all, it is impossible to come to any resolution in a case like this. I hate melodrama, and nothing strikes me as more commonplace and tedious than the ordinary ghost story of commerce; but really, Villiers, it looks as if there were something very queer at the bottom of all this.'

The two men had, without noticing it, turned up Ashley Street, leading northward from Piccadilly. It was a long street, and rather a gloomy one, but here and there a brighter taste had illuminated the dark houses with flowers, and gay curtains, and a cheerful paint on the doors. Villiers glanced up as Austin stopped speaking, and looked at one of these houses; geraniums, red and white, drooped from every sill, and daffodil-coloured curtains were draped back from each window.

'It looks cheerful, doesn't it?' he said.

'Yes, and the inside is still more cheery. One of the pleasantest houses of the season, so I have heard. I haven't been there myself, but I've met several men who have, and they tell me it's uncommonly jovial.'

'Whose house is it?'

'A Mrs. Beaumont's.'

'And who is sne?'

'I couldn't tell you. I have heard she comes from South America, but, after all, who she is of little consequence. She is a very wealthy woman, there's no doubt of that, and some of the best people have taken her up. I hear she has some wonderful claret, really marvellous wine, which must have cost a fabulous sum. Lord Argentine was telling me about it; he was there last Sunday evening. He assures me he has never tasted such a winé, and Argentine, as you know, is an expert. By the way, that reminds me, she must be an oddish sort of woman, this Mrs. Beaumont. Argentine asked her how old the wine was, and what do you think she said? 'About a thousand years, I believe.' Lord Argentine thought she was chaffing him, you know, but when he laughed she said she was speaking quite seriously, and offered to show him the jar. Of course, he couldn't say anything more after that; but it seems rather antiquated for a beverage, doesn't it? Why, here we are at my rooms. Come in, won't you?'

'Thanks, I think I will. I haven't seen the curiosity shop for some time.'

It was a room furnished richly, yet oddly, where every chair and bookcase and table, and every rug and jar and ornament seemed to be a thing apart, preserving each its own individuality.

'Anything fresh lately?' said Villiers after a while.

'No; I think not; you saw those queer jugs, didn't you? I thought so. I don't think I have come across anything for the last few weeks.'

Austin glanced round the room from cupboard to cupboard, from shelf to shelf, in search of some new oddity. His eyes fell at last on an old chest, pleasantly and quaintly carved, which stood in a dark corner of the room.

'Ah,' he said, 'I was forgetting, I have got something to show you.' Austin unlocked the chest, drew out a thick quarto volume, laid it on the table, and resumed the cigar he had put down.

'Did you know Arthur Meyrick the painter, Villiers?'

'A little; I met him two or three times at the house of a friend of mine. What has become of him? I haven't heard his name mentioned for some time.'

'He's dead.'

'You don't say so! Quite young, wasn't he?'

'Yes; only thirty when he died.'

'What did he die of?'

'I don't know. He was an intimate friend of mine, and a thoroughly good fellow. He used to come here and talk to me for hours, and he was one of the best talkers I have met. He could even talk about painting, and that's more than can be said of most painters. About eighteen months ago he was feeling rather overworked, and partly at my suggestion he went off on a sort of roving expedition, with no very definite end or aim about it. I believe New York was to be his first port, but I never heard from him. Three months ago I got this book, with a very civil letter from an English doctor practising at Buenos Aires, stating that he had attended the late Mr. Meyrick during his illness, and that the deceased had expressed an earnest wish that the enclosed packet should be sent to me after his death. That was all.'

'And haven't you written for further particulars?'

'I have been thinking of doing so. You would advise me to write to the doctor?'

'Certainly. And what about the book?'

'It was sealed up when I got it. I don't think the doctor had seen it.'

'It is something very rare? Meyrick was a collector, perhaps?'

'No, I think not, hardly a collector. Now, what do you think of those Ainu jugs?'

'They are peculiar, but I like them. But aren't you going to show me poor Meyrick's legacy?'

'Yes, yes, to be sure. The fact is, it's rather a peculiar sort of thing, and I haven't shown it to anyone. I wouldn't say anything about it if I were you. There it is.'

Villiers took the book, and opened it at haphazard.

'It isn't a printed volume then?' he said.

'No, It is a collection of drawings in black and white by my poor friend Meyrick.'

Villiers turned to the first page, it was blank; the second bore a brief inscription, which he read:

Silet per diem universus, nec sine horrore secretus est; lucet nocturnis ignibus, chorus Ægipanum undique personatur: audiuntur et cantus tibiarum, et tinnitus cymbalorum per oram maritiman.

On the third page was a design which made Villiers start and look up at Austin; he was gazing abstractedly out of the window. Villiers turned page after page, absorbed, in spite of himself, in the frightful

Walpurgis Night of evil, strange monstrous evil, that the dead artist had set forth in hard black and white. The figures of Fauns and Satyrs and Ægipans danced before his eyes, the darkness of the thicket, the dance on the mountain-top, the scenes by lonely shores, in green vineyards, by rocks and desert places, passed before him: a world before which the human soul seemed to shrink back and shudder. Villiers whirled over the remaining pages; he had seen enough, but the picture on the last leaf caught his eye, as he almost closed the book.

'Austin!'

'Well, what is it?'

'Do you know who that is?'

It was a woman's face, alone on the white page.

'Know who it is? No, of course not.'

'I do.'

'Who is it?'

'It is Mrs. Herbert.'

'Are you sure?'

'I am perfectly certain of it. Poor Meyrick! He is one more chapter in her history.'

'But what do you think of the designs?'

'They are frightful. Lock the book up again, Austin. If I were you I would burn it; it must be a terrible companion even though it be in a chest.'

'Yes, they are singular drawings. But I wonder what connection there could be between Meyrick and Mrs. Herbert, or what link between her and these designs?'

'Ah, who can say? It is possible that the matter may end here, and we shall never know, but in my own opinion this Helen Vaughan, or Mrs. Herbert, is only the beginning. She will come back to London, Austin; depend upon it, she will come back, and we shall hear more about her then. I don't think it will be very pleasant news.'

VI

THE SUICIDES

Lord Argentine was a great favourite in London Society. At twenty he had been a poor man, decked with the surname of an illustrious family, but forced to earn a livelihood as best he could, and the most speculative of moneylenders would not have entrusted him with fifty pounds on the chance of his ever changing his name for a title, and his poverty for a great fortune. His father had been near enough to the fountain of good things to secure one of the family livings, but the son, even if he had taken orders, would scarcely have obtained so much as this, and moreover felt no vocation for the ecclesiastical estate. Thus he fronted the world with no better armour than the bachelor's gown and the wits of a younger son's grandson, with which equipment he contrived in some way to make a very tolerable fight of it. At twenty-five Mr. Charles Aubernoun saw himself still a man of struggles and of warfare with the world, but out of the seven who stood between him and the high places of his family three only remained. These three, however, were 'good lives,' but yet not proof against the Zulu assegais and typhoid fever, and so one morning Aubernoun woke up and found himself Lord Argentine, a man of thirty who had faced the difficulties of existence, and had conquered. The situation amused him immensely, and he resolved that riches should be as pleasant to him as poverty had always been. Argentine, after some little consideration, came to the conclusion that dining, regarded as a fine art, was perhaps the most amusing pursuit open to fallen humanity, and thus his dinners became famous in London, and an invitation to his table a thing covetously desired. After ten years of lordship and dinners, Argentine still declined to be jaded, still persisted in enjoying life, and by a kind of infection had become recognized as the cause of joy in others, in short, as the best of company. His sudden and tragical death therefore caused a wide and deep sensation. People could scarce believe it, even though the newspaper was before their eyes, and the cry of 'Mysterious Death of a Nobleman' came ringing up from the street. But there stood the brief paragraph: 'Lord Argentine was found dead this morning by his valet under distressing circumstances. It is stated that there can be no doubt that his lordship committed suicide, though no motive can be assigned for the act. The deceased nobleman was widely known in society, and much liked for his genial manner and sumptuous hospitality. He is succeeded by,' etc., etc.

By slow degrees the details came to light, but the case still remained a mystery. The chief witness at the inquest was the dead nobleman's valet, who said that the night before his death Lord Argentine had dined with a lady of good position, whose name was suppressed in the newspaper reports. At about eleven o'clock Lord Argentine had returned, and informed his man that he should not require his services till the next morning. A little later the valet had occasion to cross the hall and was somewhat astonished to see his master quietly letting himself out at the front door. He had taken off his evening clothes, and was dressed in a Norfolk coat and knickerbockers, and wore a low brown hat. The valet had no reason to suppose that Lord Argentine had seen him, and though his master rarely kept late hours, thought little of the occurrence till the next morning, when he knocked at the bedroom door at a quarter to nine as usual. He received no answer, and, after knocking two or three times, entered the room, and saw Lord Argentine's body leaning forward at an angle from the bottom of the bed. He found that his master had tied a cord securely to one of the short bedposts, and, after making a running noose and slipping it round his neck, the unfortunate man must have resolutely fallen forward, to die by slow strangulation. He was dressed in the light suit in which the valet had seen him go out, and the doctor who was summoned pronounced that life had been extinct for more than four hours. All papers, letters, and so forth seemed in perfect order, and nothing was discovered which pointed in the most remote way to any scandal either great or small. Here the evidence ended; nothing more could be discovered. Several persons had been present at the dinner party at which Lord Argentine had assisted, and to all these he seemed in his usual genial spirits. The valet, indeed, said he thought his master appeared a little excited when he came home, but he confessed that the alteration in his manner was very slight, hardly noticeable, indeed. It seemed hopeless to seek for any clue, and the suggestion that Lord Argentine had been suddenly attacked by acute suicidal mania was generally accepted.

It was otherwise, however, when within three weeks, three more gentlemen, one of them a nobleman, and the two others men of good position and ample means, perished miserably in almost precisely the same manner. Lord Swanleigh was found one morning in his dressing-room, hanging from a peg affixed to the wall, and Mr. Collier-Stuart and Mr. Herries had chosen to die as Lord Argentine. There was no explanation in either case; a few bald facts; a living man in the evening, and a dead body with a black swollen face in the morning. The police had been forced to confess themselves powerless to arrest or to explain the sordid murders of Whitechapel; but before the horrible suicides of Piccadilly and Mayfair they were dumbfounded, for not even the mere ferocity which did duty as an explanation of the crimes of the East End could be of service in the West. Each of these men who had resolved to die a tortured, shameful death was rich, prosperous, and to all appearances in love with the world, and not the acutest research could ferret out any shadow of a lurking motive in either case. There was a horror in the air, and men looked at one another's faces when they met, each wondering whether the other was to be the victim of the fifth nameless tragedy. Journalists sought in vain in their scrapbooks for materials whereof to concoct reminiscent articles; and the morning paper was unfolded in many a house with a feeling of awe; no man knew when or where the blow would next light.

A short while after the last of these terrible events, Austin came to see Mr. Villiers. He was curious to know whether Villiers had succeeded in discovering any fresh traces of Mrs. Herbert, either through Clarke or by other sources, and he asked the question soon after he had sat down.

'No,' said Villiers, 'I wrote to Clarke, but he remains obdurate, and I have tried other channels, but without any result. I can't find out what became of Helen Vaughan after she left Paul Street, but I think she must have gone abroad. But to tell the truth, Austin, I haven't paid very much attention to the matter for the last few weeks; I knew poor Herries intimately, and his terrible death has been a great shock to me, a great shock.'

'I can well believe it,' answered Austin gravely; 'you know Argentine was a friend of mine. If I remember rightly, we were speaking of him that day you came to my rooms.'

'Yes; it was in connection with that house in Ashley Street, Mrs. Beaumont's house. You said something about Argentine's dining there.'

'Quite so. Of course you know it was there Argentine dined the night before – before his death.'

'No, I haven't heard that.'

'Oh, yes; the name was kept out of the papers to spare Mrs. Beaumont. Argentine was a great favourite of hers, and it is said she was in a terrible state for some time after.'

A curious look came over Villiers's face; he seemed undecided whether to speak or not. Austin began again.

'I never experienced such a feeling of horror as when I read the account of Argentine's death. I didn't understand it at the time, and I don't now. I knew him well, and it completely passes my understanding for what possible cause he – or any of the others for the matter of that – could have resolved in cold blood to die in such an awful manner. You know how men babble away each other's characters in London, you may be sure any buried scandal or hidden skeleton would have been brought to light in such a case as this; but nothing of the sort has taken place. As for the theory of mania, that is very well, of course, for the coroner's jury, but everybody knows that it's all nonsense. Suicidal mania is not smallpox.'

Austin relapsed into gloomy silence. Villiers sat silent also, watching his friend. The expression of indecision still fleeted across his face; he seemed as if weighing his thoughts in the balance, and the considerations he was revolving left him still silent. Austin tried to shake off the remembrance of tragedies as hopeless and perplexed as the labyrinth of Dædalus, and began to talk in an indifferent voice of the more pleasant incidents and adventures of the season.

'That Mrs. Beaumont,' he said, 'of whom we were speaking, is a great success; she has taken London almost by storm. I met her the other night at Fulham's; she is really a remarkable woman.'

'You have met Mrs. Beaumont?'

'Yes; she had quite a court around her. She would be called very handsome, I suppose, and yet there is something about her face which I didn't like. The features are exquisite, but the expression is strange. And all the time I was looking at her, and afterwards, when I was going home, I had a curious feeling that that very expression was in some way or other familiar to me.'

'You must have seen her in the Row.'

'No, I am sure I never set eyes on the woman before; it is that which makes it puzzling. And to the best of my belief I have never seen anybody like her; what I felt was a kind of dim, far-off memory, vague but persistent. The only sensation I can compare it to is that odd feeling one sometimes has in a dream, when fantastic cities and wondrous lands and phantom personages appear familiar and accustomed.'

Villiers nodded and glanced aimlessly round the room, possibly in search of something on which to turn the conversation. His eyes fell on an old chest somewhat like that in which the artist's strange legacy lay hid beneath a Gothic scutcheon.

'Have you written to the doctor about poor Meyrick?' he asked.

'Yes; I wrote asking for full particulars as to his illness and death. I don't expect to have an answer for another three weeks or a month. I thought I might as well inquire whether Meyrick knew an English-woman named Herbert, and if so, whether the doctor could give me any information about her. But it's very possible that Meyrick fell in with her at New York, or Mexico, or San Francisco; I have no idea as to the extent or direction of his travels.'

'Yes, and it's very possible that the woman may have more than one name.'

'Exactly. I wish I had thought of asking you to lend me the portrait of her which you possess. I might have enclosed it in my letter to Dr. Matthews.'

'So you might; that never occurred to me. We might send it now. Hark! what are those boys calling?'

While the two men had been talking together a confused noise of shouting had been gradually growing louder. The noise rose from the eastward and swelled down Piccadilly, drawing nearer and nearer, a very torrent of sound; surging up streets usually quiet, and making every window a frame for a face, curious or excited. The cries and voices came echoing up the silent street where Villiers lived, growing more distinct as they advanced, and, as Villiers spoke, an answer rang up from the pavement:

'The West End Horrors; Another Awful Suicide; Full Details!'

Austin rushed down the stairs and bought a paper and read out the paragraph to Villiers as the uproar in the street rose and fell. The window was open and the air seemed full of noise and terror.

'Another gentleman has fallen a victim to the terrible epidemic of suicide which for the last month has prevailed in the West End. Mr. Sidney Crashaw, of Stoke House, Fulham, and King's Pomeroy, Devon, was found, after a prolonged search, hanging from the branch of a tree in his garden at one o'clock to-day. The deceased gentleman dined last night at the Carlton Club and seemed in his usual health and spirits. He left the Club at about ten o'clock, and was seen walking leisurely up St. James's Street a little later. Subsequent to this his movements cannot be traced. On the discovery of the body medical aid was at once summoned, but life had evidently been long extinct. So far as is known, Mr. Crashaw had no trouble or anxiety of any kind. This painful suicide, it will be remembered, is the fifth of the kind in the last month. The authorities at Scotland Yard are unable to suggest any explanation of these terrible occurrences.'

Austin put down the paper in mute horror.

'I shall leave London to-morrow,' he said; 'it is a city of nightmares. How awful this is, Villiers!'

Mr. Villiers was sitting by the window quietly looking out into the street. He had listened to the newspaper report attentively, and the hint of indecision was no longer on his face.

'Wait a moment, Austin,' he replied, 'I have made up my mind to mention a little matter that occurred last night. It is stated, I think, that Crashaw was last seen alive in St. James's Street shortly after ten?'

'Yes, I think so. I will look again. Yes, you are quite right.'

'Quite so. Well, I am in a position to contradict that statement at all events. Crashaw was seen after that; considerably later indeed.'

'How do you know?'

'Because I happened to see Crashaw myself at about two o'clock this morning.'

'You saw Crashaw? You, Villiers?'

'Yes, I saw him quite distinctly; indeed, there were but a few feet between us.'

'Where, in Heaven's name, did you see him?'

'Not far from here. I saw him in Ashley Street. He was just leaving a house.'

'Did you notice what house it was?'

'Yes. It was Mrs. Beaumont's.'

'Villiers! Think what you are saying; there must be some mistake. How could Crashaw be in Mrs. Beaumont's house at two o'clock in the morning? Surely, surely, you must have been dreaming, Villiers, you were always rather fanciful.'

'No; I was wide awake enough. Even if I had been dreaming as you say, what I saw would have roused me effectually.'

'What you saw? What did you see? Was there anything strange about Crashaw? But I can't believe it; it is impossible.'

'Well, if you like I will tell you what I saw, or if you please, what I think I saw, and you can judge for yourself.'

'Very good, Villiers.'

The noise and clamour of the street had died away, though now and then the sound of shouting still came from the distance, and the dull, leaden silence seemed like the quiet after an earthquake or a storm. Villiers turned from the window and began speaking.

'I was at a house near Regent's Park last night, and when I came away the fancy took me to walk home instead of taking a hansom. It was a clear, pleasant night enough, and after a few minutes I had the streets pretty much to myself. It's a curious thing, Austin, to be alone in London at night, the gas lamps stretching away in perspective, and the dead silence, and then perhaps the rush and clatter of a hansom on the stones, and the fire starting up under the horse's hoofs. I walked along pretty briskly, for I was feeling a little tired of being out in the night, and as the clocks were striking two I turned down Ashley Street, which, you know, is on my way. It was quieter than ever there, and the lamps were fewer; altogether, it looked as dark and gloomy as a forest in winter. I had done about half the length of the street when I heard a door closed very softly, and naturally I looked up to see who was abroad like myself at such an hour. As it happens, there is a street lamp close to the house in question, and I saw a man standing on the step. He had just shut the door and his face was towards me, and I recognized Crashaw directly. I never knew him to speak to, but I had often seen him, and I am positive that I was not mistaken in my man. I looked into his face for a moment, and then – I will confess the truth – I set off at a good run, and kept it up till I was within my own door.'

'Why?'

'Why? Because it made my blood run cold to see that man's face. I could never have supposed that such an infernal medley of passions could have glared out of any human eyes; I almost fainted as I looked. I knew I had looked into the eyes of a lost soul, Austin; the man's outward form remained, but all hell was within it. Furious lust, and hate that was like fire, and the loss of all hope, and horror that seemed to shriek aloud to the night, though his teeth were shut; and the utter blackness of despair. I am sure he did not see me; he saw nothing that you or I can see, but he saw what I hope we never shall. I do not know when he died; I suppose in an hour, or perhaps two, but when I passed down Ashley Street and heard the closing door, that man no longer belonged to this world; it was a devil's face I looked upon.'

There was an interval of silence in the room when Villiers ceased speaking. The light was failing, and all the tumult of an hour ago was quite hushed. Austin had bent his head at the close of the story, and his hand covered his eyes.

'What can it mean? he said at length.

'Who knows, Austin, who knows? It's a black business, but I think we had better keep it to ourselves, for the present at any rate. I will see if I cannot learn something about that house through private channels of information, and if I do light upon anything I will let you know.'

VII

THE ENCOUNTER IN SOHO

Three weeks later Austin received a note from Villiers, asking him to call either that afternoon or the next. He chose the nearer date, and found Villiers sitting as usual by the window, apparently lost in meditation on the drowsy traffic of the street. There was a bamboo table by his side, a fantastic thing, enriched with gilding and queer painted scenes, and on it lay a little pile of papers arranged and docketed as neatly as anything in Mr. Clarke's office.

'Well, Villiers, have you made any discoveries in the last three weeks?'

'I think so; I have here one or two memoranda which struck me as singular, and there is a statement to which I shall call your attention.'

'And these documents relate to Mrs. Beaumont? It was really Crashaw whom you saw that night standing on the doorstep of the house in Ashley Street?'

'As to that matter my belief remains unchanged, but neither my inquiries nor their results have any special relation to Crashaw. But my investigations have had a strange issue. I have found out who Mrs. Beaumont is!'

'Who she is? In what way do you mean?'

'I mean that you and I know her better under another name.'

'What name is that?'

'Herbert.'

'Herbert!' Austin repeated the word, dazed with astonishment.

'Yes, Mrs. Herbert of Paul Street, Helen Vaughan of earlier adventures unknown to me. You had reason to recognize the expression of her face; when you go home, look at the face in Meyrick's book of horrors, and you will know the sources of your recollection.'

'And you have proof of this?'

'Yes, the best of proof; I have seen Mrs. Beaumont, or shall we say Mrs. Herbert?'

'Where did you see her?'

'Hardly in a place where you would expect to see a lady who lives in Ashley Street, Piccadilly. I saw her entering a house in one of the meanest and most disreputable streets in Soho. In fact, I had made an appointment, though not with her, and she was precise both to time and place.'

'All this seems very wonderful, but I cannot call it incredible. You must remember, Villiers, that I have seen this woman, in the ordinary adventure of London society, talking and laughing, and sipping her coffee in a commonplace drawing-room with commonplace people. But you know what you are saying.'

'I do; I have not allowed myself to be led by surmises or fancies. It was with no thought of finding Helen Vaughan that I searched for Mrs. Beaumont in the dark waters of the life of London, but such has been the issue.'

'You must have been in strange places, Villiers.'

'Yes, I have been in very strange places. It would have been useless, you know, to go to Ashley Street, and ask Mrs. Beaumont to give me a short sketch of her previous history. No; assuming, as I had to assume, that her record was not of the cleanest, it would be pretty certain that at some previous time she must have moved in circles not quite so refined as her present ones. If you see mud on the top of a stream, you may be sure that it was once at the bottom. I went to the bottom. I have always been fond of diving into Queer Street for my amusement, and I found my knowledge of that locality and its inhabitants very useful. It is, perhaps, needless to say that my friends had never heard the name of Beaumont, and as I had never seen the lady, and was quite unable to describe her, I had to set to work in an indirect way. The people there know me; I have been able to do some of them a service now and again, so they made no difficulty about giving their information; they were aware I had no communication direct or indirect with Scotland Yard. I had to cast out a good many lines, though, before I got what I wanted, and when I landed the fish I did not for a moment suppose it was my fish. But I listened to what I was told out of a constitutional liking for useless information, and I found myself in possession of a very curious story, though, as I imagined, not the story I was looking for. It was to this effect. Some five or six years ago, a woman named Raymond suddenly made her appearance in the neighbourhood to which I am referring. She was described to me as being quite young, probably not more than seventeen or eighteen, very handsome, and looking as if she came from the country. I should be wrong in saying that she found her level in going to this particular quarter, or associating with these people, for from what I was told, I should think the worst den in London far too good for her. The person from whom I got my information – as you may suppose, no great Puritan – shuddered and grew sick in telling me of the nameless infamies which were laid to her charge. After living there for a year, or perhaps a little more, she disappeared as suddenly as she came, and they saw nothing of her till about the time of the Paul Street case. At first she came to her old haunts only occasionally, then more frequently, and finally took up her abode there as before, and remained for six or eight months. It's of no use my going into details as to the life that woman led; if you want particulars you can look at Meyrick's legacy. Those designs were not drawn from his imagination. She again disappeared, and the people of the place saw nothing of her till a few months ago. My informant told me that she had taken some rooms in a house which he pointed out, and these rooms she was in the habit of visiting two or three times a week and always at ten in the morning. I was led to expect that one of these visits would be paid on a certain day about a week ago, and I accordingly managed to be on the look-out in company with my cicerone at a quarter to ten, and the hour and the lady came with equal punctuality. My friend and I were standing under an archway, a little way back from the street, but she saw us, and gave me a glance that I shall be long in forgetting. That look was quite enough for me; I knew Miss Raymond to be Mrs. Herbert; as for Mrs. Beaumont she had quite gone out of my head. She went into the house, and I watched it till four o'clock, when she came out, and then I followed her. It was a long chase, and I had to be very careful to keep a long way in the background, and yet not lose sight of the woman. She took me down to the Strand, and then to Westminster, and then up St. James's Street, and along Piccadilly. I felt queerish when I saw her turn up Ashley Street; the thought that Mrs. Herbert was Mrs. Beaumont came into my mind, but it seemed too improbable to be true. I waited at the corner, keeping my eye on her all the time, and I took particular care to note the house at which she stopped. It was the house with the gay curtains, the house of flowers, the house out of which Crashaw came the night he hanged himself in his garden. I was just going away with my discovery, when I saw an empty carriage come round and draw up in front of the house, and I came to the conclusion that Mrs. Herbert was going out for a drive, and I was right. I took a hansom and followed the carriage into the Park. There, as it happened, I met a man I know, and we stood talking together a little distance from the carriageway, to which I had my back. We had not been there for ten minutes when my friend took off his hat, and I glanced round and saw the lady I had been following all day. 'Who is that?' I said, and his answer was, 'Mrs. Beaumont; lives in Ashley Street.' Of course there could be no doubt after that. I don't know whether she saw me, but I don't think she did. I went home at once, and, on consideration, I thought that I had a sufficiently good case with which to go to Clarke.'

'Why to Clarke?'

'Because I am sure that Clarke is in possession of facts about this woman, facts of which I know nothing.'

'Well, what then?'

Mr. Villiers leaned back in his chair and looked reflectively at Austin for a moment before he answered:

'My idea was that Clarke and I should call on Mrs. Beaumont.'

'You would never go into such a house as that? No, no, Villiers, you cannot do it. Besides, consider; what result . . .'

'I will tell you soon. But I was going to say that my information does not end here; it has been completed in an extraordinary manner.

'Look at this neat little packet of manuscript; it is paginated, you see, and I have indulged in the civil coquetry of a ribbon of red tape. It has almost a legal air, hasn't it? Run your eye over it, Austin. It is an account of the entertainment Mrs. Beaumont provided for her choicer guests. The man who wrote this escaped with his life, but I do not think he will live many years. The doctors tell him he must have sustained some severe shock to the nerves.'

Austin took the manuscript, but never read it. Opening the neat pages at haphazard his eye was caught by a word and a phrase that followed it; and, sick at heart, with white lips and a cold sweat pouring like water from his temples, he flung the paper down.

'Take it away, Villiers, never speak of this again. Are you made of stone, man? Why, the dread and horror of death itself, the thoughts of the man who stands in the keen morning air on the black platform, bound, the bell tolling in his ears, and waits for the harsh rattle of the bolt, are as nothing compared to this. I will not read it; I should never sleep again.'

'Very good. I can fancy what you saw. Yes; it is horrible enough; but after all, it is an old story, an old mystery played in our day, and in dim London streets instead of amidst the vineyards and the olive gardens. We know what happened to those who chanced to meet the Great God Pan, and those who are wise know that all symbols are symbols of something, not of nothing. It was, indeed, an exquisite symbol beneath which men long ago veiled their knowledge of the most awful, most secret forces which lie at the heart of all things; forces before which the souls of men must wither and die and blacken, as their bodies blacken under the electric current. Such forces cannot be named, cannot be spoken, cannot be imagined, except under a veil and a symbol, a symbol to the most of us appearing a quaint, poetic fancy – to some, a foolish tale. But you and I, at all events, have known something of the terror that may dwell in the secret place of life, manifested under human flesh; that which is without form taking to itself a form. Oh, Austin, how can it be? How is it that the very sunlight does not turn to blackness before this thing, the hard earth melt and boil beneath such a burden?'

Villiers was pacing up and down the room, and the beads of sweat stood out on his forehead. Austin sat silent for a while, but Villiers saw him make a sign upon his breast.

'I say again, Villiers, you will surely never enter such a house as that? You would never pass out alive.'

'Yes, Austin, I shall go out alive – I, and Clarke with me.'

'What do you mean? You cannot, you would not dare . . .'

'Wait a moment. The air was very pleasant and fresh this morning; there was a breeze blowing, even through this dull street, and I thought I would take a walk. Piccadilly stretched before me a clear, bright vista, and the sun flashed on the carriages and on the quivering leaves in the park. It was a joyous morning, and men and women looked at the sky and smiled as they went about their work or their pleasure, and the wind blew as blithely as upon the meadows and the scented gorse. But somehow or other I got out of the bustle and the gaiety, and found myself walking slowly along a quiet, dull street, where there seemed to be no sunshine and no air, and where the few foot-passengers loitered as they walked, and hung indecisively about corners and archways. I walked along, hardly knowing where I was going or what I did there, but feeling impelled, as one sometimes is, to explore still further, with a vague idea of reaching some unknown goal. Thus I forged up the street, noting the small traffic of the milk-shop, and wondering at the incongruous medley of penny pipes, black tobacco, sweets, newspapers, and comic songs which here and there jostled one another in the short compass of a single window. I think it was a cold shudder that suddenly passed through me that first told me that I had found what I wanted. I looked up from the pavement and stopped before a dusty shop, above which the lettering had faded, where the red bricks of two hundred years ago had grimed to black; where the windows had gathered to themselves the fog and the dirt of winters innumerable. I saw what I required; but I think it was five minutes before I had steadied myself and could walk in and ask for it in a cool voice and with a calm face. I think there must even then have been a tremor in my words, for the old man who came out from his back parlour, and fumbled slowly amongst his goods, looked oddly at me as he tied the parcel. I paid what he asked, and stood leaning by the counter, with a strange reluctance to take up my goods and go. I asked about the business, and learnt that trade was bad and the profits cut down sadly; but then the street was not what it was before traffic had been diverted, but that was done forty years ago, 'just before my father died,' he said. I got away at last, and walked along sharply; it was a dismal street indeed, and I was glad to return to the bustle and the noise. Would you like to see my purchase?'

Austin said nothing, but nodded his head slightly; he still looked white and sick. Villiers pulled out a drawer in the bamboo table, and showed Austin a long coil of cord, hard and new; and at one end was a running noose.

'It is the best hempen cord,' said Villiers, 'just as it used to be made for the old trade, the man told me. Not an inch of jute from end to end.'

Austin set his teeth hard, and stared at Villiers, growing whiter as he looked.

'You would not do it,' he murmured at last. 'You would not have blood on your hands. My God!' he exclaimed, with sudden vehemence, 'you cannot mean this, Villiers, that you will make yourself a hangman?'

'No. I shall offer a choice, and leave Helen Vaughan alone with this cord in a locked room for fifteen minutes. If when we go in it is not done, I shall call the nearest policeman. That is all.'

'I must go now. I cannot stay here any longer; I cannot bear this. Good-night.'

'Good-night, Austin.'

The door shut, but in a moment it was opened again, and Austin stood, white and ghastly, in the entrance.

'I was forgetting,' he said, 'that I too have something to tell. I have received a letter from Dr. Matthews of Buenos Aires. He says that he attended Meyrick for three weeks before his death.'

'And does he say what carried him off in the prime of life? It was not fever?'

'No, it was not fever. According to the doctor, it was an utter collapse of the whole system, probably caused by some severe shock. But he states that the patient would tell him nothing, and that he was consequently at some disadvantage in treating the case.'

'Is there anything more?'

"Yes. Dr. Matthews ends his letter by saying: "I think this is all the information I can give you about your poor friend. He had not been long in Buenos Aires, and knew scarcely anyone, with the exception of a person who did not bear the best of characters, and has since left – a Mrs. Vaughan." '

VIII

THE FRAGMENTS

[Amongst the papers of the well-known physician, Dr. Robert Matheson, of Ashley Street, Piccadilly, who died suddenly, of apoplectic seizure, at the beginning of 1892, a leaf of manuscript paper was found, covered with pencil jottings. These notes were in

Latin, much abbreviated, and had evidently been made in great haste. The Ms was only deciphered with great difficulty, and some words have up to the present time evaded all the efforts of the expert employed. The date, 'XXV Jul. 1888,' is written on the right-hand corner of the MS. The following is a translation of Dr. Matheson's manuscript.]

'Whether science would benefit by these brief notes if they could be published, I do not know, but rather doubt. But certainly I shall never take the responsibility of publishing or divulging one word of what is here written, not only on account of my oath freely given to those two persons who were present, but also because the details are too abominable. It is probable that, upon mature consideration, and after weighing the good and evil, I shall one day destroy this paper, or at least leave it under seal to my friend D., trusting in his discretion, to use it or to burn it, as he may think fit.

'As was befitting, I did all that my knowledge suggested to make sure that I was suffering under no delusion. At first astounded, I could hardly think, but in a minute's time I was sure that my pulse was steady and regular, and that I was in my real and true senses. I then fixed my eyes quietly on what was before me.

'Though horror and revolting nausea rose up within me, and an odour of corruption choked my breath, I remained firm. I was then privileged or accursed, I dare not say which, to see that which was on the bed, lying there black like ink, transformed before my eyes. The skin, and the flesh, and the muscles, and the bones and the firm structure of the human body that I had thought to be unchangeable, and permanent as adamant, began to melt and dissolve.

'I knew that the body may be separated into its elements by external agencies, but I should have refused to believe what I saw. For here there was some internal force, of which I knew nothing, that caused dissolution and change.

'Here too was all the work by which man had been made, repeated before my eyes. I saw the form waver from sex to sex, dividing itself from itself, and then again reunited. Then I saw the body descend to the beasts whence it ascended, and that which was on the heights go down to the depths, even to the abyss of all being. The principle of life, which makes organism, always remained, while the outward form changed.

'The light within the room had turned to blackness, not the darkness of night, in which objects are seen dimly, for I could see clearly and without difficulty. But it was the negation of light; objects were presented to my eyes, if I may say so, without any medium, in such a manner that if there had been a prism in the room I should have seen no colours represented in it.

'I watched, and at last I saw nothing but a substance as jelly. Then the ladder was ascended again . . . [*here the MS. is illegible*] . . . for one instant I saw a Form, shaped in dimness before me, which I will not further describe. But the symbol of this form may be seen in ancient sculptures, and in paintings which survived beneath the lava, too foul to be spoken of . . . as a horrible and unspeakable shape, neither man nor beast, was changed into human form, there came finally death.

'I who saw all this, not without great horror and loathing of soul, here write my name, declaring all that I have set on this paper to be true.

'ROBERT MATHESON, Med. Dr.'

. . . Such, Raymond, is the story of what I know and what I have seen. The burden of it was too heavy for me to bear alone, and yet I could tell it to none but you. Villiers, who was with me at the last, knows nothing of that awful secret of the wood – of how what we both saw die, lay upon the smooth, sweet turf amidst the summer flowers, half in sun and half in shadow – and holding the girl Rachel's hand, called and summoned those companions, and shaped in solid form, upon the earth we tread on, the horror which we can but hint at, which we can only name under a figure. I would not tell Villiers of this, nor of that resemblance, which struck me as with a blow upon my heart, when I saw the portrait, which filled the cup of terror at the end. What this can mean I dare not guess. I know that what I saw perish was not Mary, and yet in the last agony Mary's eyes looked into mine. Whether there be anyone who can show the last link in this chain of awful mystery, I do not know, but if there be any one who can do this, you, Raymond, are the man. And if you know the secret, it rests with you to tell it or not, as you please.

I am writing this letter to you immediately on my getting back to town. I have been in the country for the last few days; perhaps you may be able to guess in what part. While the horror and wonder of London was at its height – for 'Mrs. Beaumont,' as I have told you, was well known in society – I wrote to my friend Dr. Phillips, giving some brief outline, or rather hint, of what had happened, and asking him to tell me the name of the village where the events he had related to me occurred. He gave me the name, as he said, with the less

hesitation, because Rachel's father and mother were dead, and the
rest of the family had gone to a relative in the State of Washington six
months before. The parents, he said, had undoubtedly died of grief
and horror caused by the terrible death of their daughter, and by
what had gone before that death. On the evening of the day on which
I received Phillips's letter I was at Caermaen, and standing beneath
the mouldering Roman walls, white with the winters of seventeen
hundred years, I looked over the meadow where once had stood the
older temple of the 'God of the Deeps,' and saw a house gleaming in
the sunlight. It was the house where Helen had lived. I stayed at
Caermaen for several days. The people of the place, I found, knew
little and had guessed less. Those whom I spoke to on the matter
seemed surprised that an antiquarian (as I professed myself to be)
should trouble about a village tragedy, of which they gave a very
commonplace version, and, as you may imagine, I told nothing of
what I knew. Most of my time was spent in the great wood that rises
just above the village and climbs the hillside, and goes down to the
river in the valley; such another long lovely valley, Raymond, as that
on which we looked one summer night, walking to and fro before your
house. For many an hour I strayed through the maze of the forest,
turning now to right and now to left, pacing slowly down long alleys
of undergrowth, shadowy and chill, even under the midday sun, and
halting beneath great oaks; lying on the short turf of a clearing where
the faint sweet scent of wild roses came to me on the wind and mixed
with the heavy perfume of the elder, whose mingled odour is like the
odour of the room of the dead, a vapour of incense and corruption. I
stood at the edges of the wood, gazing at all the pomp and procession
of the foxgloves towering amidst the bracken and shining red in the
broad sunshine, and beyond them into deep thickets of close undergrowth where springs boil up from the rock and nourish the water
weeds, dank and evil. But in all my wanderings I avoided one part of
the wood; it was not till yesterday that I climbed to the summit of the
hill, and stood upon the ancient Roman road that threads the highest
ridge of the wood. Here they had walked, Helen and Rachel, along
this quiet causeway, upon the pavement of green turf, shut in on
either side by high banks of red earth and tall hedges of shining beech,
and here I followed in their steps, looking out, now and again,
through partings in the boughs, and seeing on one side the sweep
of the wood stretching far to right and left, and sinking into the broad
level, and beyond, the yellow sea, and the land over the sea. On the
other side was the valley and the river, and hill following hill as wave

on wave, and wood and meadow, and cornfield, and white houses
gleaming, and a great wall of mountain, and far blue peaks in the
north. And so at last I came to the place. The track went up a gentle
slope, and widened out into an open space with a wall of thick
undergrowth around it, and then, narrowing again, passed on into
the distance and the faint blue mist of summer heat. And into this
pleasant summer glade Rachel passed a girl, and left it, who shall say
what? I did not stay long there.

In a small town near Caermaen there is a museum, containing for
the most part Roman remains which have been found in the
neighbourhood at various times. On the day after my arrival at
Caermaen I walked over to the town in question, and took the
opportunity of inspecting this museum. After I had seen most of
the sculptured stones, the coffins, rings, coins, and fragments of
tessellated pavement which the place contains, I was shown a small
square pillar of white stone, which had been recently discovered in the
wood of which I have been speaking, and, as I found on inquiry, in
that open space where the Roman road broadens out. On one side of
the pillar was an inscription, of which I took a note. Some of the
letters have been defaced, but I do not think there can be any doubt
as to those which I supply. The inscription is as follows:

DEVOMNODENT*i*
FLA*v*IVSSENILISPOSSV*it*
PROPTERNVP*tias*
*quas*VIDITSVBVMB*ra*

'To the great god Nodens (the god of the Great Deep or Abyss)
Flavius Senilis has erected this pillar on account of the marriage
which he saw beneath the shade.'

The custodian of the museum informed me that local antiquaries
were much puzzled, not by the inscription, or by any difficulty in
translating it, but as to the circumstance or rite to which allusion is
made.

. . . And now, my dear Clarke, as to what you tell me about Helen
Vaughan, whom you say you saw die under circumstances of the
utmost and almost incredible horror. I was interested in your
account, but a good deal, nay all, of what you told me I knew
already. I can understand the strange likeness you remarked both in
the portrait and in the actual face; you have seen Helen's mother. You

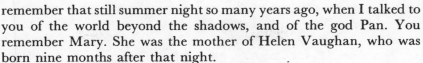

remember that still summer night so many years ago, when I talked to you of the world beyond the shadows, and of the god Pan. You remember Mary. She was the mother of Helen Vaughan, who was born nine months after that night.

Mary never recovered her reason. She lay, as you saw her, all the while upon her bed; and a few days after the child was born she died. I fancy that just at the last she knew me; I was standing by the bed, and the old look came into her eyes for a second, and then she shuddered and groaned and died. It was an ill work I did that night when you were present; I broke open the door of the house of life, without knowing or caring what might pass forth or enter in. I recollect your telling me at the time, sharply enough, and rightly enough too, in one sense, that I had ruined the reason of a human being by a foolish experiment, based on an absurd theory. You did well to blame me, but my theory was not all absurdity. What I said Mary would see, she saw, but I forgot that no human eyes could look on such a vision with impunity. And I forgot, as I have just said, that when the house of life is thus thrown open, there may enter in that for which we have no name, and human flesh may become the veil of a horror one dare not express. I played with energies which I did not understand, and you have seen the ending of it. Helen Vaughan did well to bind the cord about her neck and die, though the death was horrible. The blackened face, the hideous form upon the bed, changing and melting before your eyes from woman to man, from man to beast, and from beast to worse than beast, all the strange horror that you witnessed, surprises me but little. What you say the doctor whom you sent for saw and shuddered at, I noticed long ago; I knew what I had done the moment the child was born, and when it was scarcely five years old I surprised it, not once or twice but several times, with a playmate, you may guess of what kind. It was for me a constant, an incarnate horror, and after a few years I felt I could bear it no longer, and I sent Helen Vaughan away. You know now what frightened the boy in the wood. The rest of the strange story, and all else that you tell me, as discovered by your friend, I have contrived to learn from time to time, almost to the last chapter. And now Helen is with her companions . . .

COUNT MAGNUS

M. R. James

[1862–1936]

'*Gifted with an almost diabolic power of calling horror by gentle steps from the midst of prosaic daily life, is the scholarly Montague Rhodes James, Provost of Eton College, antiquary of note, and recognized authority on mediaeval manuscripts and cathedral history. Dr. James, long fond of telling spectral tales at Christmastide, has become by slow degrees a literary weird fictionist of the very first rank; and has developed a distinctive style and method likely to serve as models for an enduring line of disciples . . .*

'*The short stories of Dr. James are contained in four small collections, entitled respectively* Ghost Stories of an Antiquary, More Ghost stories of an Antiquary, A Thin Ghost and Others, *and* A Warning to the Curious. *There is also a delightful juvenile phantasy,* The Five Jars, *which has its spectral adumbrations. Amidst this wealth of material it is hard to select a favourite or especially typical tale, though each reader will no doubt have such preferences as his temperament may determine.*

'Count Magnus *is assuredly one of the best, forming as it does a veritable Golconda of suspense and suggestion.'*

– H.P. Lovecraft

BY WHAT MEANS THE PAPERS out of which I have made a connected story came into my hands is the last point which the reader will learn from these pages. But it is necessary to prefix to my extracts from them a statement of the form in which I possess them.

They consist, then, partly of a series of collections for a book of travels, such a volume as was a common product of the forties and fifties. Horace Marryat's *Journal of a Residence in Jutland and the Danish Isles* is a fair specimen of the class to which I allude. These books usually treated of some unfamiliar district on the Continent. They were illustrated with woodcuts or steel plates. They gave details of hotel accommodation, and of means of communication, such as we now expect to find in any well-regulated guide-book, and they dealt largely in reported conversations with intelligent foreigners, racy innkeepers and garrulous peasants. In a word, they were chatty.

Begun with the idea of furnishing material for such a book, my papers as they progressed assumed the character of a record of one single personal experience, and this record was continued up to the very eve, almost, of its termination.

The writer was a Mr. Wraxall. For my knowledge of him I have to depend entirely on the evidence his writings afford, and from these I deduce that he was a man past middle age, possessed of some private means, and very much alone in the world. He had, it seems, no settled abode in England, but was a denizen of hotels and boarding-houses. It is probable that he entertained the idea of settling down at some future time which never came; and I think it also likely that the Pantechnicon fire in the early seventies must have destroyed a great deal that would have thrown light on his antecedents, for he refers once or twice to property of his that was warehoused at that establishment.

It is further apparent that Mr. Wraxall had published a book, and that it treated of a holiday he had once taken in Brittany. More than this I cannot say about his work, because a diligent search in bibliographical works has convinced me that it must have appeared either anonymously or under a pseudonym.

As to his character, it is not difficult to form some superficial opinion. He must have been an intelligent and cultivated man. It seems that he was near being a Fellow of his college at Oxford – Brasenose, as I judge from the Calendar. His besetting fault was pretty clearly that of over-inquisitiveness, possibly a good fault in a traveller, certainly a fault for which this traveller paid dearly enough in the end.

On what proved to be his last expedition, he was plotting another book. Scandinavia, a region not widely known to Englishmen forty years ago, had struck him as an interesting field. He must have lighted on some old books of Swedish history or memoirs, and the idea had struck him that there was room for a book descriptive of travel in Sweden, interspersed with episodes from the history of some of the great Swedish families. He procured letters of introduction, therefore, to some persons of quality in Sweden, and set out thither in the early summer of 1863.

Of his travels in the North there is no need to speak, nor of his residence of some weeks in Stockholm. I need only mention that some *savant* resident there put him on the track of an important collection of family papers belonging to the proprietors of an ancient manor-house in Vestergothland, and obtained for him permission to examine them.

The manor-house, or *herrgård*, in question is to be called Råbäck (pronounced something like Roebeck), though that is not its name. It is one of the best buildings of its kind in all the country, and the picture of it in Dahlenberg's *Suecia antiqua et moderna*, engraved in 1694, shows it very much as the tourist may see it to-day. It was built soon after 1600, and is, roughly speaking, very much like an English house of that period in respect of material – red-brick with stone facings – and style. The man who built it was a scion of the great house of De la Gardie, and his descendants possess it still. De la Gardie is the name by which I will designate them when mention of them becomes necessary.

They received Mr. Wraxall with great kindness and courtesy, and pressed him to stay in the house as long as his researches lasted. But, preferring to be independent, and mistrusting his powers of conversing in Swedish, he settled himself at the village inn, which turned out quite sufficiently comfortable, at any rate during the summer months. This arrangement would entail a short walk daily to and from the manor-house of something under a mile. The house itself stood in a park, and was protected – we should say grown up – with large old timber. Near it you found the walled garden, and then entered a close wood fringing one of the small lakes with which the whole country is pitted. Then came the wall of the demesne, and you climbed a steep knoll – a knob of rock lightly covered with soil – and on the top of this stood the church, fenced in with tall dark trees. It was a curious building to English eyes. The nave and aisles were low, and filled with pews and galleries. In the western gallery stood the handsome old organ, gaily painted, and with silver pipes. The ceiling was flat, and had been adorned by a seventeenth-century artist with a strange and hideous 'Last Judgment,' full of lurid flames, falling cities, burning ships, crying souls, and brown and smiling demons. Handsome brass coronæ hung from the roof; the pulpit was like a doll's-house, covered with little painted wooden cherubs and saints; a stand with three hour-glasses was hinged to the preacher's desk. Such sights as these may be seen in many a church in Sweden now, but what distinguished this one was an addition to the original building. At the eastern end of the north aisle the builder of the manor-house had erected a mausoleum for himself and his family. It was a largish eight-sided building, lighted by a series of oval windows, and it had a domed roof, topped by a kind of pumpkin-shaped object rising into a spire, a form in which Swedish architects greatly delighted. The roof was of copper externally, and was painted black, while the walls, in common with those of the church, were staringly white. To this mausoleum there was no access from the church. It had a portal and steps of its own on the northern side.

Past the churchyard the path to the village goes, and not more than three or four minutes bring you to the inn door.

On the first day of his stay at Råbäck Mr. Wraxall found the church door open, and made those notes of the interior which I have epitomized. Into the mausoleum, however, he could not make his way. He could by looking through the keyhole just descry that there were fine marble effigies and sarcophagi of copper, and a wealth of armorial ornament, which made him very anxious to spend some time in investigation.

The papers he had come to examine at the manor-house proved to be of just the kind he wanted for his book. There were family correspondence, journals, and account-books of the earliest owners of the estate, very carefully kept and clearly written, full of amusing and picturesque detail. The first De la Gardie appeared in them as a strong and capable man. Shortly after the building of the mansion there had been a period of distress in the district, and the peasants had risen and attacked several châteaux and done some damage. The owner of Råbäck took a leading part in suppressing the trouble, and

there was reference to executions of ringleaders and severe punishments inflicted with no sparing hand.

The portrait of this Magnus de la Gardie was one of the best in the
house, and Mr. Wraxall studied it with no little interest after his day's
work. He gives no detailed description of it, but I gather that the face
impressed him rather by its power than by its beauty or goodness; in fact,
he writes that Count Magnus was an almost phenomenally ugly man.

On this day Mr. Wraxall took his supper with the family, and
walked back in the late but still bright evening.

'I must remember,' he writes, 'to ask the sexton if he can let me into
the mausoleum at the church. He evidently has access to it himself, for
I saw him to-night standing on the steps, and, as I thought, locking or
unlocking the door.'

I find that early on the following day Mr. Wraxall had some
conversation with his landlord. His setting it down at such length as
he does surprised me at first; but I soon realized that the papers I was
reading were, at least in their beginning, the materials for the book he
was meditating, and that it was to have been one of those quasi-
journalistic productions which admit of the introduction of an
admixture of conversational matter.

His object, he says, was to find out whether any traditions of Count
Magnus de la Gardie lingered on in the scenes of that gentleman's
activity, and whether the popular estimate of him were favourable or
not. He found that the Count was decidedly not a favourite. If his
tenants came late to their work on the days which they owed to him as
Lord of the Manor, they were set on the wooden horse, or flogged and
branded in the manor-house yard. One or two cases there were of
men who had occupied lands which encroached on the lord's domain,
and whose houses had been mysteriously burnt on a winter's night,
with the whole family inside. But what seemed to dwell on the
innkeeper's mind most – for he returned to the subject more than
once – was that the Count had been on the Black Pilgrimage, and had
brought something or someone back with him.

You will naturally inquire, as Mr. Wraxall did, what the Black
Pilgrimage may have been. But your curiosity on the point must
remain unsatisfied for the time being, just as his did. The landlord was
evidently unwilling to give a full answer, or indeed any answer, on the
point, and, being called out for a moment, trotted off with obvious
alacrity, only putting his head in at the door a few minutes afterwards
to say that he was called away to Skara, and should not be back till
evening.

So Mr. Wraxall had to go unsatisfied to his day's work at the manor-house. The papers on which he was just then engaged soon put his thoughts into another channel, for he had to occupy himself with glancing over the correspondence between Sophia Albertina in Stockholm and her married cousin Ulrica Leonora at Råbäck in the years 1705–1710. The letters were of exceptional interest from the light they threw upon the culture of that period in Sweden, as anyone can testify who has read the full edition of them in the publications of the Swedish Historical Manuscripts Commission.

In the afternoon he had done with these, and after returning the boxes in which they were kept to their places on the shelf, he proceeded, very naturally, to take down some of the volumes nearest to them, in order to determine which of them had best be his principal subject of investigation next day. The shelf he had hit upon was occupied mostly by a collection of account-books in the writing of the first Count Magnus. But one among them was not an account-book, but a book of alchemical and other tracts in another sixteenth-century hand. Not being very familiar with alchemical literature, Mr. Wraxall spends much space which he might have spared in setting out the names and beginnings of the various treatises: The book of the Phoenix, book of the Thirty Words, book of the Toad, book of Miriam, Turba philosophorum, and so forth; and then he announces with a good deal of circumstance his delight at finding, on a leaf originally left blank near the middle of the book, some writing of Count Magnus himself headed 'Liber nigræ peregrinationis.' It is true that only a few lines were written, but there was quite enough to show that the landlord had that morning been referring to a belief at least as old as the time of Count Magnus, and probably shared by him. This is the English of what was written:

'If any man desires to obtain a long life, if he would obtain a faithful messenger and see the blood of his enemies, it is necessary that he should first go into the city of Chorazin, and there salute the prince . . .' Here there was an erasure of one word, not very thoroughly done, so that Mr. Wraxall felt pretty sure that he was right in reading it as *aëris* ('of the air'). But there was no more of the text copied, only a line in Latin: 'Quære reliqua hujus materiei inter secretiora' (see the rest of this matter among the more private things).

It could not be denied that this threw a rather lurid light upon the tastes and beliefs of the Count; but to Mr. Wraxall, separated from him by nearly three centuries, the thought that he might have added to his general forcefulness alchemy, and to alchemy something like

magic, only made him a more picturesque figure; and when, after a
rather prolonged contemplation of his picture in the hall, Mr. Wraxall
set out on his homeward way, his mind was full of the thought of
Count Magnus. He had no eyes for his surroundings, no perception of
the evening scents of the woods or the evening light on the lake; and
when all of a sudden he pulled up short, he was astonished to find
himself already at the gate of the churchyard, and within a few
minutes of his dinner. His eyes fell on the mausoleum.

'Ah,' he said, 'Count Magnus, there you are. I should dearly like to
see you.'

'Like many solitary men,' he writes, 'I have a habit of talking to
myself aloud; and, unlike some of the Greek and Latin particles, I do
not expect an answer. Certainly, and perhaps fortunately in this case,
there was neither voice nor any that regarded: only the woman who, I
suppose, was cleaning up the church, dropped some metallic object
on the floor, whose clang startled me. Count Magnus, I think, sleeps
sound enough.'

That same evening the landlord of the inn, who had heard
Mr. Wraxall say that he wished to see the clerk or deacon (as he
would be called in Sweden) of the parish, introduced him to that
official in the inn parlour. A visit to the De la Gardie tomb-house was
soon arranged for the next day, and a little general conversation
ensued.

Mr. Wraxall, remembering that one function of Scandinavian
deacons is to teach candidates for Confirmation, thought he would
refresh his own memory on a Biblical point.

'Can you tell me,' he said, 'anything about Chorazin?'

The deacon seemed startled, but readily reminded him how that
village had once been denounced.

'To be sure,' said Mr. Wraxall; 'it is, I suppose, quite a ruin now?'

'So I expect,' replied the deacon. 'I have heard some of our old
priests say that Antichrist is to be born there; and there are tales – '

'Ah! what tales are those?' Mr. Wraxall put in.

'Tales, I was going to say, which I have forgotten,' said the deacon;
and soon after that he said good night.

The landlord was now alone, and at Mr. Wraxall's mercy; and that
inquirer was not inclined to spare him.

'Herr Nielsen,' he said, 'I have found out something about the
Black Pilgrimage. You may as well tell me what you know. What did
the Count bring back with him?'

Swedes are habitually slow, perhaps, in answering, or perhaps the landlord was an exception. I am not sure; but Mr. Wraxall notes that the landlord spent at least one minute in looking at him before he said anything at all. Then he came close up to his guest, and with a good deal of effort he spoke:

'Mr. Wraxall, I can tell you this one little tale, and no more – not any more. You must not ask anything when I have done. In my grandfather's time – that is, ninety-two years ago – there were two men who said: "The Count is dead; we do not care for him. We will go to-night and have a free hunt in his wood" – the long wood on the hill that you have seen behind Råbäck. Well, those that heard them say this, they said: "No, do not go; we are sure you will meet with persons walking who should not be walking. They should be resting, not walking." These men laughed. There were no forest-men to keep the wood, because no one wished to hunt there. The family were not here at the house. These men could do what they wished.

'Very well, they go to the wood that night. My grandfather was sitting here in this room. It was the summer, and a light night. With the window open, he could see out to the wood, and hear.

'So he sat there, and two or three men with him, and they listened. At first they hear nothing at all; then they hear someone – you know how far away it is – they hear someone scream, just as if the most inside part of his soul was twisted out of him. All of them in the room caught hold of each other, and they sat so for three-quarters of an hour. Then they hear someone else, only about three hundred ells off. They hear him laugh out loud: it was not one of those two men that laughed, and, indeed, they have all of them said that it was not any man at all. After that they hear a great door shut.

'Then, when it was just light with the sun, they all went to the priest. They said to him:

' "Father, put on your gown and your ruff, and come to bury these men, Anders Bjornsen and Hans Thorbjorn."

'You understand that they were sure these men were dead. So they went to the wood – my grandfather never forgot this. He said they were all like so many dead men themselves. The priest, too, he was in a white fear. He said when they came to him:

' "I heard one cry in the night, and I heard one laugh afterwards. If I cannot forget that, I shall not be able to sleep again."

'So they went to the wood, and they found these men on the edge of the wood. Hans Thorbjorn was standing with his back against a tree, and all the time he was pushing with his hands – pushing something away from him which was not there. So he was not dead. And they led him away, and took him to the house at Nykjoping, and he died before the winter; but he went on pushing with his hands. Also Anders Bjornsen was there; but he was dead. And I tell you this about Anders Bjornsen, that he was once a beautiful man, but now his face was not there, because the flesh of it was sucked away off the bones. You understand that? My grandfather did not forget that. And they laid him on the bier which they brought, and they put a cloth over his head, and the priest walked before; and they began to sing the psalm for the dead as well as they could. So, as they were singing the end of the first verse, one fell down, who was carrying the head of the bier, and the others looked back, and they saw that the cloth had fallen off, and the eyes of Anders Bjornsen were looking up, because there was nothing to close over them. And this they could not bear. Therefore the priest laid the cloth upon him, and sent for a spade, and they buried him in that place.'

The next day Mr. Wraxall records that the deacon called for him soon after his breakfast, and took him to the church and mausoleum. He noticed that the key of the latter was hung on a nail just by the pulpit, and it occurred to him that, as the church door seemed to be left unlocked as a rule, it would not be difficult for him to pay a second and more private visit to the monuments if there proved to be more of interest among them than could be digested at first. The building, when he entered it, he found not unimposing. The monuments, mostly large erections of the seventeenth and eighteenth centuries, were dignified if luxuriant, and the epitaphs and heraldry were copious. The central space of the domed room was occupied by three copper sarcophagi, covered with finely-engraved ornament. Two of them had, as is commonly the case in Denmark and Sweden, a large metal crucifix on the lid. The third, that of Count Magnus, as it appeared, had, instead of that, a full-length effigy engraved upon it, and round the edge were several bands of similar ornament representing various scenes. One was a battle, with cannon belching out smoke, and walled towns, and troops of pikemen. Another showed an execution. In a third, among trees, was a man running at full speed, with flying hair and outstretched hands. After him followed a strange form; it would be hard to say whether the artist had intended it for a man, and was unable to give the requisite similitude, or whether it was intentionally made as monstrous as it looked. In view of the skill with which the rest of the drawing was done, Mr. Wraxall felt inclined to adopt the latter idea. The figure was unduly short, and was for the most part muffled in a hooded garment which swept the ground. The only part of the form which projected from that shelter was not shaped like any hand or arm. Mr. Wraxall compares it to the tentacle of a devil-fish, and continues: 'On seeing this, I said to myself, "This, then, which is evidently an allegorical representation of some kind – a fiend pursuing a hunted soul – may be the origin of the story of Count Magnus and his mysterious companion. Let us see how the huntsman is pictured: doubtless it will be a demon blowing his horn." ' But, as it turned out, there was no such sensational figure, only the semblance of a cloaked man on a hillock, who stood leaning on a stick, and watching the hunt with an interest which the engraver had tried to express in his attitude.

Mr. Wraxall noted the finely-worked and massive steel padlocks – three in number – which secured the sarcophagus. One of them, he saw, was detached, and lay on the pavement. And then, unwilling to delay the deacon longer or to waste his own working-time, he made his way onward to the manor-house.

'It is curious,' he notes, 'how on retracing a familiar path one's thoughts engross one to the absolute exclusion of surrounding objects. To-night, for the second time, I had entirely failed to notice where I was going (I had planned a private visit to the tomb-house to copy the epitaphs), when I suddenly, as it were, awoke to consciousness, and found myself (as before) turning in at the churchyard gate, and, I believe, singing or chanting some such words as, "Are you awake, Count Magnus? Are you asleep, Count Magnus?" and then something more which I have failed to recollect. It seemed to me that I must have been behaving in this nonsensical way for some time.'

He found the key of the mausoleum where he had expected to find it, and copied the greater part of what he wanted; in fact, he stayed until the light began to fail him.

'I must have been wrong,' he writes, 'in saying that one of the padlocks of my Count's sarcophagus was unfastened; I see to-night that two are loose. I picked both up, and laid them carefully on the window-ledge, after trying unsuccessfully to close them. The remaining one is still firm, and, though I take it to be a spring lock, I cannot guess how it is opened. Had I succeeded in undoing it, I am almost afraid I should have taken the liberty of opening the sarcophagus. It is strange, the interest I feel in the personality of this, I fear, somewhat ferocious and grim old noble.'

The day following was, as it turned out, the last of Mr. Wraxall's stay at Råbäck. He received letters connected with certain investments which made it desirable that he should return to England; his work among the papers was practically done, and travelling was slow.

He decided, therefore, to make his farewells, put some finishing touches to his notes, and be off.

These finishing touches and farewells, as it turned out, took more time than he had expected. The hospitable family insisted on his staying to dine with them – they dined at three – and it was verging on half-past six before he was outside the iron gates of Råbäck. He dwelt on every step of his walk by the lake, determined to saturate himself, now that he trod it for the last time, in the sentiment of the place and hour. And when he reached the summit of the churchyard knoll, he lingered for many minutes, gazing at the limitless prospect of woods near and distant, all dark beneath a sky of liquid green. When at last he turned to go, the thought struck him that surely he must bid farewell to Count Magnus as well as the rest of the De la Gardies. The church was but twenty yards away, and he knew where the key of the mausoleum hung. It was not long before he was standing over the great copper coffin, and, as usual, talking to himself aloud. 'You may have been a bit of a rascal in your time, Magnus,' he was saying, 'but for all that I should like to see you, or, rather – '

'Just at that instant,' he says, 'I felt a blow on my foot. Hastily enough I drew it back, and something fell on the pavement with a clash. It was the third, the last of the three padlocks which had fastened the sarcophagus. I stooped to pick it up, and – Heaven is my witness that I am writing only the bare truth – before I had raised myself there was a sound of metal hinges creaking, and I distinctly saw the lid shifting upwards. I may have behaved like a coward, but I could not for my life stay for one moment. I was outside that dreadful building in less time than I can write – almost as quickly as I could have said – the words; and what frightens me yet more, I could not turn the key in the lock. As I sit here in my room noting these facts, I ask myself (it was not twenty minutes ago) whether that noise of creaking metal continued, and I cannot tell whether it did or not. I only know that there was something more than I have written that alarmed me, but whether it was sound or sight I am not able to remember. What is this that I have done?'

Poor Mr. Wraxall! He set out on his journey to England on the next day, as he had planned, and he reached England in safety; and yet, as I gather from his changed hand and inconsequent jottings, a broken man. One of several small notebooks that have come to me with his papers gives, not a key to, but a kind of inkling of, his experiences.

Much of his journey was made by canal-boat, and I find not less than
six painful attempts to enumerate and describe his fellow-passengers.
The entries are of this kind:

'24. Pastor of village in Skåne. Usual black coat and soft black
hat.

'25. Commercial traveller from Stockholm going to Trollhättan.
Black cloak, brown hat.

'26. Man in long black cloak, broad-leafed hat, very old-
fashioned.'

This entry is lined out, and a note added: 'Perhaps identical with
No. 13. Have not yet seen his face.' On referring to No. 13, I find that
he is a Roman priest in a cassock.

The net result of the reckoning is always the same. Twenty-eight
people appear in the enumeration, one being always a man in a long
black cloak and broad hat, and the other a 'short figure in dark cloak
and hood.' On the other hand, it is always noted that only twenty-six
passengers appear at meals, and that the man in the cloak is perhaps
absent, and the short figure is certainly absent.

On reaching England, it appears that Mr. Wraxall landed at
Harwich, and that he resolved at once to put himself out of the
reach of some person or persons whom he never specifies, but whom
he had evidently come to regard as his pursuers. Accordingly he took
a vehicle – it was a closed fly – not trusting the railway, and drove
across country to the village of Belchamp St. Paul. It was about nine
o'clock on a moonlight August night when he neared the place. He
was sitting forward, and looking out of the window at the fields and
thickets – there was little else to be seen – racing past him. Suddenly
he came to a cross-road. At the corner two figures were standing
motionless; both were in dark cloaks; the taller one wore a hat, the
shorter a hood. He had no time to see their faces, nor did they make
any motion that he could discern. Yet the horse shied violently and
broke into a gallop, and Mr. Wraxall sank back into his seat in
something like desperation. He had seen them before.

Arrived at Belchamp St. Paul, he was fortunate enough to find a
decent furnished lodging, and for the next twenty-four hours he lived,
comparatively speaking, in peace. His last notes were written on this
day. They are too disjointed and ejaculatory to be given here in full,
but the substance of them is clear enough. He is expecting a visit from

his pursuers – how or when he knows not – and his constant cry is 'What has he done?' and 'Is there no hope?' Doctors, he knows, would call him mad, policemen would laugh at him. The parson is away. What can he do but lock his door and cry to God?

People still remembered last year at Belchamp St. Paul how a strange gentleman came one evening in August years back; and how the next morning but one he was found dead, and there was an inquest; and the jury that viewed the body fainted, seven of 'em did, and none of 'em wouldn't speak to what they see, and the verdict was visitation of God; and how the people as kep' the 'ouse moved out that same week, and went away from that part. But they do not, I think, know that any glimmer of light has ever been thrown, or could be thrown, on the mystery. It so happened that last year the little house came into my hands as part of a legacy. It had stood empty since 1863, and there seemed no prospect of letting it; so I had it pulled down, and the papers of which I have given you an abstract were found in a forgotten cupboard under the window in the best bedroom.

AFTERWORD

Lovecraft and the 'Literature of Cosmic Fear'

HOWARD PHILIPS LOVECRAFT (1890–1937) is probably the most important and influential author of supernatural fiction in the twentieth century. He has become acknowledged as a master of the modern horror story and a mainstream American writer second only to Edgar Allan Poe.

Born of mentally unstable parents, he was a life-long resident of Providence, Rhode Island, where he remained a studious antiquarian and virtual recluse until his untimely death. Poor health as a child resulted in him reading voraciously, and the stories of Poe, Lord Dunsany and Arthur Machen, amongst others, inspired his own writing career.

Although never prolific, during his lifetime Lovecraft's fiction, poems and essays received popular acclaim in the amateur presses and through such pulp magazines as *Weird Tales* and *Astounding Stories*. However, more often than not, he was forced to eke-out a meagre existence revising other author's work.

Two years after he died in poverty and relative obscurity, a pair of Lovecraft's literary disciples, August Derleth and Donald Wandrei, established their own imprint, Arkham House (named after Lovecraft's fictitious New England town), to publish a posthumous collection of their mentor's best short stories, entitled *The Outsider and Others*. Eventually Arkham brought most of Lovecraft's work – fiction, essays, verse, and voluminous correspondence – back into print, since when it has continued to sell millions of copies throughout the world and been translated into every major language.

Many of the author's best tales are set in the fear-haunted towns of an imaginary area of Massachusetts or in the cosmic vistas that exist beyond space and time. A number of these loosely-connected stories, involving the Great Old Ones (a banished alien race which once ruled the Earth and strive to return) have subsequently become identified as 'The Cthulhu Mythos'.

Over the decades since his death, Lovecraft's relatively small body of work has influenced countless imitators and formed the basis of a world-wide industry of books, games and movies based on his concepts.

In November 1925, during a brief residence in New York, Lovecraft was asked by his friend and fellow member of the United Amateur Press Association, W. Paul Cook, to write a study of supernatural fiction for Cook's magazine, *The Recluse*. The 30,000-word essay, written in late 1925 or early 1926, was published in the first and only issue (alongside poetry by Clark Ashton Smith and Frank Belknap Long, and fiction by H. Warner Munn and Donald Wandrei), which appeared in the middle of 1927.

Supernatural Horror in Literature is widely regarded as one of the most scholarly and extensive studies of horror fiction and its practitioners ever written. In an attempt to define the horror story, Lovecraft states that 'a certain atmosphere of breathless and unexplainable dread of outer, unknown forces must be present', and the essay contains an obvious bias towards what he terms the 'literature of cosmic fear' (a thematic concept that formed the central core of much of his own fiction). However, the author's erudite and poignant commentary remains an exemplary introduction to the weird fiction genre and provides some unique insights into Lovecraft's own tastes in horror.

Following its publication in *The Recluse*, Lovecraft almost immediately began making notes to update his essay, and a slightly revised version was serialised in Charles D. Hornig's *The Fantasy Fan*, one of the more successful early science-fiction fanzines. It appeared over seventeen instalments between October 1933 and February 1935, but was left incomplete when the magazine was discontinued.

The author apparently put the essay aside when *The Fantasy Fan* ceased publication, and although he intended to work on it again at a later date, it was left unfinished at the time of his death. It was this final – but not completely revised – version of *Supernatural Horror in Literature* which Derleth and Wandrei included in *The Outsider and Others*, and it is the version reprinted in the present volume.

In the mid-1940s, the premier American critic Edmund Wilson (who was no fan of Lovecraft's fiction) wrote: 'Lovecraft himself, however, is a little more interesting than his stories . . . his long essay on the fiction of supernatural horror is a really able piece of work. He shows his lack of sound literary taste in his enthusiasm for Machen and Dunsany, whom he more or less acknowledged as models, but he had read comprehensively in this field – he was strong on the Gothic novelists – and writes about it with much intelligence.'

From the recommendations made by Lovecraft in his ground-breaking essay, we have selected twenty-one classic tales of the macabre, by some of the field's greatest exponents, which reflect in their themes and imagery many counterparts found in Lovecraft's own fiction.

For example, the dream-quest in Gautier's *The Foot of the Mummy*, the cursed tome of Chambers' *The Yellow Sign*, the blasted terrain in Cram's *The Dead Valley*, the piscine hybrid of Cobb's *Fishhead*, the cosmic vistas revealed in Hodgson's *The Hog* (although the story was published after Lovecraft's death), and the tentacled familiar of James' *Count Magnus* all have conceptual resonances in H.P. Lovecraft's own distinctive literature of cosmic fear – to which the modern horror reader is unreservedly referred.

– The Editors,
London, England